ROVING JACK,

THE PIRATE HUN·TER.

A Romance

OF

THE ROAD AND THE OCEAN.

~~~~~~~~~~~~~~~~~~~

ILLUSTRATED WITH NUMEROUS ENGRAVINGS.

~~~~~~~~~~~~~~~~~~~

LONDON :

BOYS OF ENGLAND OFFICE 173, FLEET STREET, LONDON, E.C.

———

MDCCCLXXXII.

Two Numbers every Week for One Penny.

ROVING JACK,

THE

PIRATE HUNTER.

"QUICK AS LIGHTNING JACK DASHED AT THE MONSTER."

Nos. 1 & 2.
NOTICE.—GIVEN AWAY an Engraving entitled "The Escape on the Road,"
Also a Beautiful Coloured Picture.

BOOK I.

THE PHANTOM OF FOAMY REEF.

CHAPTER I.

THE EAGLE'S EYRIE.

"JACK, you make me shudder. If that bough should break!"

The fair-haired, pleasant-faced boy who uttered these words in a breathless tone, was clinging like a monkey to a rugged spar of mossy, slippery rock that jutted from the windy brow of a towering cliff, over the dreadful brink of which he had just scrambled.

The companion whom he addressed, another monkey of a lad, was swaying on the leafless branch of a storm-scathed tree.

Poised in mid-air on his frail perch, which bent under his weight like a fishing-rod, he gazed down with a dauntless glance upon the white and stony sea-beech, spread out at least five hundred feet below, from whence the eternal roar of the bursting breakers soared faintly upwards to his giddy height.

Jack laughed in gleeful excitement.

"Don't you feel frightened, my chum!" asked his young comrade.

"Yes," returned Jack, naively, "just a bit qualmish, Hal. But the sensation's queer and pleasant; I rather like it. Says my heart, 'You'll tumble, old chap.' Says my head, 'It's your own fault if you do.' My hands, ye see, they keep quiet and hold tight. It's jolly!"

Jack spread wide his arms, and see-sawed up and down in vacancy, the awful abyss yawning beneath him.

"Come back, it's no go, Jack; we can't get at the bird, her eyrie is perched on that narrow ledge, where there isn't footing for a lizard to crawl on. Give it up, or you'll break your precious neck."

"But I'm not going to break my precious word, if I can help it. The pirate devil has murdered Violet's pet lamb, and I promised her I'd make a spread eagle of him, and it shall go hard but I'll do it, Hal. Hark, I can hear the nestlings squealing for prey, and yonder comes the old bird, with a fish in her beak."

"It's a white-tailed sea-eagle! Jack, Jack! do come away. If she attacks you she'll buffet you off your perch, and you'll be smashed into a jelly on the rocks below!"

Hal crawled down the face of the precipitous cliff, and held out his hand imploringly.

"Catch hold, Jack; I'll fasten on this rock-bine. Put your foot on my shoulder."

"Yes, I will, thank ye. For luck's sake, hold on—both hands; and when you feel my foot go, don't be scared, that's all."

Hal threw himself on his face, and fixed a convulsive grip upon the tendrils of the creeping plant.

"She's coming! she's coming!" cried Jack. "What a pair of wings! Their shadow flits down the white cliff, and makes me giddy. Hold on!"

Hal's foot slipped!

His heart leaped!

He madly clutched the rock-bine, and planted his knee on the sharp ridges of the stone.

He shut his eyelids tight, compressed his lips, and tried by force of will to deafen himself to every sound—to annihilate his senses, that he might quell his insufferable pangs of awe and terror.

He felt a light pressure on his shoulder.

Away!

A wild, piercing scream!

"*Jack has gone down—is smashed to atoms!*"

Such was the agonising thought which ripped through Hal's brain like a seething flash of lightning.

He dared not stir.

He was paralysed—blinded with deadly fear!

Another wild scream!

He turned his head.

It was the eagle!

But where was Jack?

Perched like a chamois on the narrow ledge below, his right arm groping in the fissure in which the eagle had built her nest.

Meanwhile the splendid mother-bird was spiring upwards in diminishing circles, and at length poised herself motionless upon her arched, wide-sweeping wings as if preparing to make a swoop upon the rash invader of her rocky fastness.

She had dropped the fish, and the sounding shores rang with her fierce screams of fury.

Aghast with dismay, Hal kept his eyes glued upon his reckless comrade, who seemed forgetful of everything but the perilous task he had imposed upon himself.

"Ahoy, there, Hal!" shouted Jack. "Tie your 'kerchief to a bit of string, and throw it down."

"No, no; for God's sake, come away!" cried his comrade, wildly.

"Oh! you're a duffer! The thing's hair done. Look sharp, toss it down!"

"I won't! I won't!"

"Don't then, stupid. Only I shall have to bring the little feathered imps in my hand, and if you won't help me, thank ye for nothing."

Hal tore the handkerchief from his pocket, fastened it to a string, and threw it down.

For an instant Jack loosened his hold of the rock, and deftly caught the fluttering 'kerchief.

Hal shuddered, and turned sick and giddy.

The next moment, he saw something glittering in Jack's mouth.

It was the bright blade of an open clasp knife which the rash boy gripped in his strong, snowy teeth.

Squeak! squall! flutter! and the little living balls of down rolled into the handkerchief.

Jack tied them up in a bundle.

"Now haul away, my hearty."

Hal obeyed.

But two or three of the fledglings slipped out of the handkerchief, and went tumbling through the air down the side of the peak.

"Now, then, butter-fingers!" cried Jack, peevishly, "I wanted to save 'em."

"Look-out, Jack!—the eagle!—the eagle!" shrieked Hal.

Sweep! with the rush of a whirlwind, the huge and magnificent bird of prey descends upon Jack's shoulders.

The mighty wings dash and winnow with astounding noise; the sharp, strong beak dashes down upon the curl-clustered forehead of the heroic boy.

Jack reels.

Still, however, he clutches the rock with his left hand, while with his right he strikes wildly over his shoulder with the flashing blade.

Hal clings to the rock, his gaze fascinated by the fearful scene.

The thrashing, flapping pennons, the swiftly plied beak, the flashing of the knife, the dreadful, unequal struggle so long protracted, the screaming of the eagle, the audible panting of the struggling boy—DOWN !—*down* !

Over and over, rolling, waning smaller and smaller, straight down the almost perpendicular surface of the cliff, Jack and his feathered foe go battling together.

They reach a projecting boulder of the rock.

They bound over, and disappear.

Hal sickens, and almost relinquishes his grip upon the rock-bine.

He creeps up to the top of the cliff.

He raises himself on his trembling legs, and peers fearfully down.

The projection of the cliff conceals a considerable span of the beach immediately below the beetling precipice.

Neither Jack nor the eagle are visible.

Hal listens with breathless intentness.

The muffled, sullen, ceaseless roar of the surf, the shrill distant quail of the shags and sea-gulls dipping their swerving white wings on the foamy crests of the surging green billows, the throb-throb-throbbing of his own excited heart—else all—ominous silence.

Hal makes an attempt to shout his comrade's name ; but his breath freezes on his quivering lips, and his voice faints in his swelling throat.

For a moment he stands as if petrified, then recovering himself, he dashes wildly off to a rugged pathway, which, some distance from the spot, winds its rugged dangerous way down to the shingly strand.

At last he reaches the beach, and crashing over the brawling shingle, he hurries madly to the point where he thinks Jack must have fallen.

He can scarcely believe the evidence of his senses.

There lies the eagle, her huge pointed wings outspread, her dark brown, finely-shaded plumage ruffled, beads of blood on her strong, hooked beak, the knife buried to the haft in her breast, dead.

As for Jack, there sits he, his bloody brow swathed with his neck-cloth, coolly engaged in fixing the long, white-tipped tail feathers of his vanquished foe in his cap as trophies of his victory.

CHAPTER II.

OUR HERO'S EARLY HISTORY.

HAL threw himself down beside his companion, without making any remark, in fact he was so wonder-struck, and so exhausted with the intense excitement through which he had passed during the course of the last few moments, that he could not summon speech.

Jack was flushed, his arched lips were parted and his breath came short and thick from his panting breast ; but he controlled his bodily infirmities, and sat with a calm clear light shining in his merry brown eyes ; his fine, boyish, perfect features beaming with a grin of triumph.

"Did you manage to bring off any of the eaglets ?" asked Jack.

"Yes, two ; the others fell out of the handkerchief. Look ! here they are ! Cheep ! cheep ! Ugly little monsters, shall I wring their necks ?"

"No ; don't Hal. Perhaps we might rear one or both of them. I should like a tame eagle ; that would be something like a pet."

"What a noble bird the old one was !" said Hal, lifting the royal creature in his hands. "What a size she is ! What a beak she has ! What a stretch of wing ! Is it an osprey ?"

"No ; it's the white-tailed sea-eagle. They are very rare. Who would imagine, now, that these hideous little puff-balls, with their weak, sprawling yellow claws, and tender beaks, would ever grow to such a size and strength ; but, there, it's the same all through nature. Fancy Timour the Tartar, or Billy the Conqueror, or any other of those fire-eating, murdering, ravaging destroyers, sitting on their nurse's knees, teeny-tiny, flabby babbies squalling for pap."

"And imperial Cæsar getting spanked and put in the corner for being naughty."

"Oh ! crikey ! But talking of 'spanking' reminds me of what a swishing I shall nab from our old Dominie for getting my head broke !" and Jack burst into a long merry laugh. "Oh, poor mother !"

"What do you mean by 'poor mother ?'"

"Why, Hal, my mother seems to think that there's no cure for a wounded head but a swinged starn. Don't you remember when our school had such a game on board the sheer hulk that lies astrand off the Sandy Point, when we played at 'cutting out by the board,' and I was captain of the man-o'-war ?"

"Oh ! yes, wasn't that a glorious lark ! You blew up the ship rather than strike your flag."

"And singed off my eye-brows, and set my hair on fire. Mother laid a complaint against me at school next morning, and I was horsed and swished without pity. I didn't grumble ; it sarved me right, ye know. I wish, I do wish, Hal, that I weren't such a mischief-loving, danger-hunting scape-grace. My wild tricks vex poor mother sadly."

"Indeed, Jack, you should be more careful. It beats cock-fighting ! You seem to have no sense of fear or danger ; you risk your life a dozen times a day."

"No, I don't. I know what I'm about. Where's the fun of swimming in shallow water, or walking on level ground ? Any fool can do that ; besides, when I'm a man—fancy being a man, Hal—I should like to be daring and adventurous. If I'm but a chick now, I should like to grow up—an eagle !"

"To get your throat cut like this poor bird ! Jack, you must always remember that your mother is a widow, that you are her only and her darling son, and Violet, your foster-sister, you should think of her. What would become of them both, if you flung away your life in some foolhardy venture ?"

"When I don't think of them I am a heartless young villain !" cried Jack, with fervour ; "I am a heedless, worthless fool, for what is the good of me ? I can do nothing but swim and run and climb——"

"And kill eagles."

"Yet I am fond of my books ; I love to prose over old histories, learn strange languages, and puzzle out hard sums. And I like the old Dominie, too, though he's rather too fond of what he calls the 'good old rule laid down by Solomon,' and the taste of the birch is more pungent than pleasant. But when the sea breeze wafts in at the open window, and the surf leaps up in the glittering sunshine, I must be off, nothing can bind me ! I play the wag, and get into scrapes ; am rated and swished by the old Dominie, and, what's worse than all, little Violet looks at me with her grave blue eyes, shakes her bright, golden ringlets, and tells me that she is ashamed of herself for loving such a wild, bad boy. Oh, blow it all, Hal ! I must be more steady. But, I say, I wonder if papa eagle will be sailing back to his desolate home? I should like to have a turn with him; might as well knotch the brace. I'll see if I can clamber up to the eyrie."

"So much for your fine promises! Oh, Jack! Jack! come away, do." And Hal took his comrade's arm, and drew him, laughing, from the spot.

"But tell me, now," said Hal, as they walked along, "how on earth you escaped breaking your neck when you rolled down the cliff; I made sure of finding you in a state of smash."

"Why, ye see, my chum, the cliff is not so stiff but that I could manage to make an occasional grab at the stones and rock weeds as I and my fluttering foe rolled downwards together, so as to break my fall, and when I bounced over yon big boulder, where I suppose you lost sight of me, I dropped flop on that high mound of soft sand. The eagle had got her talons fixed in my jacket—you see how it's torn—and was doing her best to strike my eyes out with her beak; she could not release herself, and I caught her by the leg with one hand, and with the other I drove in my knife, right under her wing; she walloped over on her side, as dead as a pickled herring. But let me tell ye, Hal, that rough tumble gave me an awful shaking, and the whacking I shall get will be quite superfluous, for I'm bruised already from head to foot like Pat just home from Donnybrook Fair."

"And where away now, Jack?"

"To meet our Violet, and the girls, her companions, and some of our school-mates, on the green before the signal house."

"By the bye, Jack, did your mother ever find out who were Violet's parents?"

"Never; as you know, Hal, she was saved from the wreck of the Indiaman that struck on the Black Rock."

"The 'Oriana,' wasn't that her name?"

"Aye; little Violet was the only soul saved. Except her, all hands perished; old Clem Cleats, the fisherman, found her lashed to a drifting spar, and he brought her ashore in his boat, which was nearly swamped in the breakers. I've heard him tell the tale many a time."

"And why did your mother call her Violet?"

"The name was worked in hair within a little gold locket found about the child's neck."

The boys proceeded for some time in silence.

Jack seemed lost in thought.

"What a curse it is to be so poor," he exclaimed, suddenly; "there is so much to be done, and promotion comes so slowly. Oh, that my father had lived!"

"What was your father, Jack? I never knew much about his history."

"And I can tell you but little," returned Jack, with a sigh. "My father was Captain Warbold, of his Majesty's navy, the youngest son of a gentleman of noble family. He gave great offence to his high and mighty sire by marrying my mother."

"Why, Jack, she must have been a very beautiful girl."

"She is still beautiful; my dear mother was poor and humbly born, the daughter of a channel pilot of Truro, in Cornwall. The starchy old nob, my grandfather, was so enraged with my father for giving his hand to one in her position of life that he would never countenance the pair. Soon after I was born poor father fell in a hot action with the Dutch, and grandfather sent mother down here into Devon to the 'Owlet's Roost,' a ruined old tower belonging to the family, and he allows her a small annuity."

"Have you ever seen him, Jack?"

"Never, and have no wish to see him," returned our hero, fiercely; "he has treated my parents with cruel harshness; if I saw him I should tell him my mind, in spite of his star, and epaulettes, and gold scraper."

"He's a port admiral, and immensely rich, is he not?"

"Yes, so I have heard," returned Jack, carelessly; "not from mother, though; she never mentions his name, and, I am sure, would not accept a penny of his bounty but for my graceless sake."

"My father rents his farm of old Admiral Warbold," said Hal. "Have you any uncles, aunts, or cousins alive?"

"None," replied Jack; "they are all dead and all died childless."

"By all that's lucky, Jack! why you must be heir to all the old curmudgeon's wealth!"

"I don't want the dirty trash!" cried Jack, fiercely; "I would rather inherit one tenth part of my father's noble qualities than the whole of this caste-proud tyrant's possessions."

"I'll wager, Jack, that you'll come in for both."

"Stopper all, my chum; don't dress me in borrowed robes; I look for nothing but what I can win by my own hard labour. Enough of this, let's talk of something else."

Thus discoursing, the boys sauntered along the silvery shining sands, from time to time glancing across the green and blue arc of the ocean, with its foamy margin creeping close upon their steps, and its hazy sky-line flecked here and there with distant sails glinting red in the slant rays of the declining sun.

Jack paused in his walk, and looked to windward.

"We shall have a squall," he said. "See, Hal, those streaks of sulphury cloud driving up from the sou'-west, and the wind comes in cat's-paws, and veers all round the compass, and there's a sullen red glow in the west; the fondling murmur of these smooth waves is but treachery; they'll be barking like hungry wolves before midnight."

As he spoke he leaped upon a rugged, green, and slimy rock, round which the rising tide dashed in a surf as white and frothy as seething yeast.

Let us avail ourselves of this favourable opportunity to sketch the portrait of our noble Boy Hero.

He stands erect and motionless as a statue, his dark, glossy, clustering curls lifted by the chill and fitful flaw, the eagle feathers fixed in the blood-stained 'kerchief, which binds his scarred but dauntless brow, fiercely fluttering, his fine hazel eyes glowing with a brave but gentle light, his thin nostrils distended, a grave but happy smile playing lightly on his fresh curling lip.

The huge dead bird of prey dangles from his careless hand, and his torn jacket, hanging loosely from his shoulder, flows idly flapping in the freshening breeze, which, blowing aside his loosened shirt, displays his marble-white but firm, square chest; his lower limbs are beautifully moulded, and his attitude is a perfect study of unconscious grace.

"Do you like the sea, Jack?" asked Hal, with a quiet smile.

"The sea!" cried our hero, with a low, musical laugh. "What boy, what *true* boy, breathing, does not love the mighty, changeful, free, and glorious ocean? Here one's soul has elbow room. Indeed, I mean to be a sailor, Hal! I mean to roam the pathless wastes of the wide, wide main, from the frozen zones to the burning tropics. I mean to be a *genuine* hero! No paltry, base, gilt-bedizened land-lubber highwayman; no mutineer nor buccaneer, but an honest rover! It shall be mine to rescue the castaway, chase the slaver, do battle with the bloody pirate, to spend my life in one bold career of wild but worthy adventures! I mean to vindicate the title you and all my young comrades have given me, for am I not, all the world over, ROVING JACK?"

CHAPTER III.

BARABBAS.

KEENLY blows the freshening gale, heavier dash and huger swell the thundering tidal waves as Roving Jack and his trusty friend mount the slippery stairs of the rugged jetty.

"Avast, my chum; look yonder at that fellow!" said our hero, suddenly checking his companion.

"What fellow? The seaman leaning against that windlass? He looks an ugly customer. Do ye know him?"

"Yes; his name's Barabbas."

"A very appropriate one for such a hang-dog-looking wretch. Did ever a human being wear such a fiendish countenance? Thief and murderer seem stamped upon his face."

"I have reason to suspect him to be both," replied our hero. "Come, let's pass him quickly; I want to have no talk with him."

"But how came he by such an undesirable name?"

"His father was hanged for highway robbery, his mother was whipped at the cart-tail through all the market towns in the county, and was afterwards transported; he was born in prison, and, I suppose, the gaolers gave him his pretty name. Come, let's step past him quickly; I don't want him to recognise me."

But the jetty was narrow, and it was impossible for the boys to pass the evil-looking fellow, who had excited their unfavourable remarks without being seen by him.

A more hideous-looking ruffian it is scarcely possible to picture; his face was broad, sallow, and of the Asiatic type; his thick, black, beetling brows met in the centre of his low, brutal forehead, and from beneath their shaggy penthouse a pair of little, blasting eyes, glittered with snake-like venom and ferocity; his large, hard mouth was deformed by an irregular row of yellow tusk-like fangs, one of which protruded over his nether lip; he was further disfigured by a broken nose and a ghastly scar, which seamed his left cheek; his hair was of reddish black, as coarse and shaggy as a bison's mane; his body was broad-built and ungainly, his arms long and wiry like those of a gorilla, and his legs bandied; he was dwarfish in stature but evidently a man of immense muscular power.

He wore a loose pea-jacket, a woollen guernsey, a leathern kilt, high boots, and a scarlet night-cap, a murderous-looking pistol, and a long, slim, sheathless knife were thrust through his heavy belt. He was smoking a short pipe, and stood leaning awkwardly with his long arms lightly folded across his wide breast.

The boys passed him with downcast eyes and hastening steps.

He started, unlocked his long arms, and as they fell by his sides his broad fists were seen to drop below his knees.

Strange devices were punctured on the back of his hands with some bluish pigment, and on the third finger of his left hand he wore a large brilliant ring, seen at a glance to be of fabulous value.

"Ahoy, there! ahoy, my little cheeries."

But the boys returned no answer.

"Ahoy, there, Roving Jack!" cried Barabbas, with a gruff laugh. "Won't ye heave to, my little cheery? Have ye forgot your old messmate? Never! Why, strike my toplights! when you were but a teething brat, didn't I use to carry ye out into the surf, and larn you to swim like a young dolphin? And who was it that made ye name every part of a wessel from hull to trucks, till ye got to be as knowing as the oldest sea-dog in the sarvice, and above all, who twisted ye the rattling yarns about Old Mob and Mull'd Sack, the high tobymen, and Captain Kid that hoisted the black flag, and sailed 'on the grand account?'

"'My name is Captain Kidd,
As I sailed, as I sailed;
I had the Bible in my hand,
And I buried it in the sand,
As I sailed!'

"Ho! ho! I won't believe ye'll sheer off without so much as a flying salute to your old chum! Roving Jack was born to be Jack the Rover. A jolly free trader or a bold buccaneer, and has he turned out a milk-sop?—a snivelling Johnny Goodchild, the parson's pet? No! no!"

"Mark me, Barabbas," said Jack, drawing himself up, and fixing a steady glance upon the coarse and hideous face of the ruffian, "I don't want ye to think me ungrateful for any favours you have done me when I was a child; but as for the fine yarns you spun about a pack of thieves and cutthroats, when I was a 'teething brat' as you say, whatever I thought of them then, I've cut my wisdom teeth since, and am now well aware that your heroes were showy, sham, paltry, ruffianly humbugs, and that there was no more of the real grit in them than there is in the cowardly skunks that fired the false beacon on the Foamy Reef, and lured that noble brigantine, the West Indiaman, 'Malabar,' on to dreadful destruction. Do ye call that a manly affair?"

"You dog!"

"You wolf! There, I don't want to quarrel with you, Barabbas; but do you think I've forgotten the awful night when I stole away from home to lend a hand to the really manly fellows who strove to save the lives of the poor sufferers betrayed by you and your treacherous, filthy gang of inhuman devils?"

"How?—what?—have a care!"

"I will have a care—to shun you as I would shun a fiend or a vampire. Perhaps you don't know who struck you down with the broken oar that night when, your hands wet and crimson with blood, you were rifling the pockets of the poor seaman, whom you murdered? I'll tell ye who it was then—it was I, Roving Jack!"

The ruffian stared aghast at the noble boy, astounded at his calm audacity.

He tried to rave out an oath; but his astonishment at the coolness and determination with which our hero spoke rendered him breathless; however, he gripped his long knife, and hissed like a roused adder.

"I give you warning, Master Barabbas," the boy continued, in the same measured tones, "that if you come athwart hawse with me I'll play the devil with ye."

The villain glared upon him for a moment, as if designing to spring upon him with the upraised knife.

Then he lowered his arm, and broke into a chuckling laugh.

"Cockalorum! crow away my game chick. Smash my eyes, if it wouldn't tickle a ship's chaplain to hear such a bantam's clarion. Ha! ha! but Jack, now, you tough little sapling of true oak, I admire your pluck, and I don't want to see ye fling away your chance for life in the miserable sarvice of the furrin-bred, miserly, whiggamore hunks of a Dutch boor, that has filched old England's crown, nor yet to have ye 'live at home at ease' as a land-lubber swab of a snip or a snob. Harkye, Jack, there's a fortune to be made by such brave sparks as you. Heaps of gold galore, sacks of Spanish doubloons, cargoes of silks and satinets, and piled velvets. Say the word, and you shall cruise with me in the Spanish main, and woo fortune under the blood-red flag of a jolly rover! Why, now, I can recollect the time when you swore that as soon as you became a man you would be a PIRATE!"

"But since then I've changed my mind," returned Jack, coolly. "When I become a man I mean to be a PIRATE-HUNTER!"

"Pah! you whelp; you'd best not growl till yer teeth grow stronger."

"They are strong enough already to defend me from such a wolf as you."

"Do ye dare me!"

"To do your worst."

"By the rolling thunder you don't know who ye brave!" roared the villain, dashing at Jack with the gleaming knife.

Our hero stepped nimbly backwards.

He was holding the eagle by the neck.

He swung round his arm and brought the body of the bird with stunning force upon the ruffian's skull.

Barabbas dropped like a stone, and flying from his hand, the knife went clattering along the slimy stones of the narrow pier-head.

The man was on his knees in an instant, but Jack was at his throat in the nick of time.

Flash! Bang!

A pistol exploded close by Jack's ear.

With a "ping," the bullet sped past his head, tearing away one of his glossy curls.

Then ensued a desperate struggle.

The ruffian clutched Jack's throat, but the boy was as lithe as an eel, and weaving his leg round the ruffian's sturdy calf he threw him heavily on the brink of the pier.

But Barabbas had not relinquished his grip on the boy's throat.

He dragged him down.

"Help, Hal! Rescue!" cried Jack, in a bold tone. "Keep his hand off the pistol-butt."

Hal flung himself down by the side of the kicking, struggling ruffian and seized him tightly by the wrist.

"Now we have him!" growled Jack. "Heave, Hal, heave! Let's pitch him into the sea."

The two boys raised the villain, and with a strong push hurled him over the brink of the pier sloush into the bouncing waves.

"Hurrah!" cried Jack, gleefully.

But his exultation was rather premature, for Barabbas came scrambling up the sea-wall, and had already got his knee upon the brink.

But quite equal to the occasion, Jack snatched up the pistol and dealt the pirate such a fearful blow on the head with the stock, that tossing up his arms, he fell prone backwards plash into the water, and sinking disappeared.

"You've killed him, Jack!" gasped Hal.

"So much the better!" cried our hero, fiercely. "I ought to be rewarded for it. Do you think I feel remorse for slaying such a shark as that? Not I. But the devil takes care of his own; see, he's afloat again."

And this was true, for though his brow was terribly gashed, Barabbas rose to the surface, and was swimming strongly back to the pier.

Jack levelled the pistol at him.

"Clear away, you pirate!" shouted Jack, "or I'll let the daylight into your black hull! Brush, you villain!"

The fellow seemed to think Jack was in earnest, for throwing up his arm and shaking his brawny fist at the boys, he raved forth a torrent of the most horrible threats and awful imprecations, and then turned towards the shore, their triumphant shout ringing in his tingling ears, and the surly breakers dashing over his head as if eager to engulph him.

CHAPTER IV.

THE LION BROKE LOOSE.

DISTANT a few hundred yards from the beach was a small plot of ground, covered with short, crisp herbage. From one side of this little lawn rose the tall flagstaff of a signal-house; on the other side was an old boat shed, beyond which stretched on a rough bit of furzy common, whereon were clustered a number of tents and wains belonging to the caravan of a travelling menagerie.

On leaving the pier, our boy hero and his friend had to pass across the patch of common in order to reach the green on which their playmates were disporting themselves.

Roving Jack, who seemed to have quite forgotten his late encounter with the ruffianly pirate, Barabbas, cast his restless eyes about him with interest and curiosity.

Coming near one of the vans, he crept up its steps and peered in through a crack in the door.

A low but tremendous growling resounded from within, and a rapid and continuous thump, thumping, as of some ferocious and captive brute, lashing with his heavy tail the wooden walls of his den. The deep growl changed into shrill, wild, and plaintive howlings, and then burst forth into an awful thunderous roar.

"Come here, Hal!" cried our hero, with boy-like zest and excitement. "Here's a male lion! What a monster! Did ever ye see such a grand brute? It seems a shame to pen up his savage majesty in this paltry gipsy cart. They may say what they will about the barbarity of such sport, but I should like to have seen the gladiators in the arena of old Rome, doing battle with a terrific fellow like this. If I were a little older and in good fettle, and armed with a strong pike or a sharp axe, I wouldn't mind a bout with him myself."

"Rest contented with your eagle, Jack."

"Oh, shades of Samson! wouldn't I like to kill a lion, though!" laughed our hero, tripping lightly down the steps.

"Come along," cried Hal, "let's get on to the green and have one game of romps before nightfall."

A group of shouting boys and laughing girls were chasing about the sunlit sward, while some half-dozen old, weather-beaten coastguards and fishermen, sat on rough benches before the signal-house, smoking long pipes, and watching the gambols of the young folks, or quietly conversing together.

As our hero walked on to the green, with the eagle dangling from his shoulder and the feather fluttering on his brow, the crowd of boys and girls ceased from their play, and came bounding towards him with a shout of welcome.

"Roving Jack! hurrah!"

One of the first to greet our hero was a charming girl of twelve or thirteen; her long, silky tresses of soft and sunny hair floated wantonly on the evening wind:

her fine, large blue eyes sparkled with mirth and enjoyment; her dimply, cherry lips were curved in such a witching smile as might have tempted the sternest ascetic with its sweetness; while on her pure smooth cheek the excitement and exercise of play had deepened the clear rose-blush into a rich glow of warm crimson.

"Oh, Jack, you tiresome boy! Where have you been?" cried the girl, in a pleasant tone. "You promised to come early. We have had such rare good fun. And what is this? An eagle, I declare!"

"Fair princess," said Jack, gracefully bending on his knee, "your own true knight, who is ever ready to go through earth, air, fire or water in your service, has, in accordance with his vow, sought out your audacious and monstrous foe, the ruthless destroyer of your innocent favourite; he has fought and conquered, and returned to lay the trophy of his victory at your feet, and to claim the reward of his devotion."

Jack's foster sister threw her arms about his neck, and kissed him affectionately.

"You dear little stupid," cried she, laughing; "but you don't mean to say you killed the monster yourself?"

"But he did though, Violet," rejoined Hal, "at the risk of his own life."

"What's that, an eagle?" asked a tall, stout lad, boisterously pushing his way through the admiring crowd. "But what a little one! You just hearken here; I once killed one forty times bigger than that; I found his eyrie on the top of a crag, I don't know how many thousand feet high. Just as I was seizing the nestlings, down swooped the old eagle, and carried me off through the air in his talons——"

"Carried you?"

"Yes; I was only a small boy at the time, not more than five or six, you see. It was a pretty scrape; I'd no sort o' weapon with me, and there I was, up in the clouds, some miles above the sea."

"Now, Ben Bouncer, none o' your crams," said Hal.

"Let him alone," rejoined Jack, with a grin.

"Well, as I was saying, being some twenty miles above the clouds, and having not so much as a pocket knife with me, I cast about to find some means of getting off the horns—or rather, I should say, out of the claws—of my dilemma; I'd a bit of top-string in my pocket, and I made a running noose with it, and slipped it over the beast of a bird's neck, and drew it tight."

"As you do the long bow now."

"What do ye say about the long bow? Well, I'll tell you what I once did with my bow and arrows."

"Stick to the eagle, Ben."

"So I did, like a leech, and I pulled the string till I throttled him, then he let me go, but I put my arms round his body, and kept his wings stretched out, and we went whirling down and down and down till I lighted on the main truck of a man-o'-war. I soon scrambled on deck, and, hang me, if the skipper didn't want to press me to join the crew; but I jumped overboard, and, being in the mid-channel, had half a mind to swim to France, but, not liking the frog-soup, and reflecting what a loss I should be to my country, I swam back to my native shores."

"That will do, Ben."

"But what about the bow and arrows, Ben?"

"Oh, I'll tell ye. Well, you know I've been to France, crossed the water many a time in the fishermen's yawls. But where was I?"

"In France."

"Of course. Well, you know that wretched country is infested with wolves?"

"Heard so."

"Yes, Hal, there are hundreds and thousands of 'em. Well, one day I went shooting with my bow and arrows in the woods when I met one of them, a great grisly brute as big as old Clem Cleat's jackass. As soon as I saw him coming—shall I tell ye what I did?"

"Aye, heave a-head."

"Well, Jack, I'll show you what I did. I—— OH!"

Ben Bouncer broke off suddenly, and, uttering a terrific yell, took to his heels and bounded off like a hunted deer.

"Just what I expected you'd do," laughed Jack.

But his mirth was instantly changed to alarm when a horrible roar and a burst of thrilling shrieks caused him to look behind him.

The lion of the menagerie had broken from his den, and came trotting towards them, his immense shaggy mane streaming in the breeze and his tremendous head upraised.

Jack's playmates scattered in all directions, stumbling over each other in their precipitous flight, and filling the air with screams of terror.

For one moment poor Jack stood transfixed with deadly fear. The huge and dreadful beast came bounding along directly towards him.

With a piercing cry Violet darted away; but as she crossed the lion's path, her foot slipped on the dewy sward, and she fell prone.

The next instant, his majestic countenance displaying the utmost ferocity of purpose, the lion clapped his mighty paw upon the tender bosom of the prostrate girl, uttering a tremendous roar, never to be forgotten by our hero.

The lion had already opened his immense jaws to seize on his prey, when, as Jack cast a rapid, wild, despairing glance around him, in search of some offensive weapon, his eyes fell upon the blue, glinting blade of a woodman's axe lying on the grass within a few yards of him.

Quick as lightning, Jack snatched it up, and dashed at the monster, who, uttering a low fierce growl, was about to transfix the poor girl's right arm with his murderous fangs.

Diverted from his helpless victim by Jack's bold attack, the brute crouched in order to spring upon his daring assailant.

Maddened by desperation, his brain awhirl with excitement, nerved by frenzy to superhuman strength and courage, Jack slashed right and left through the red mist which had gathered before his burning eyes.

Slash! smash! crash!

The axe is shivered to pieces.

Jack is drenched with gore, and drops senseless.

Armed with red-hot iron bars, a number of keepers from the caravan fly to his assistance.

Their aid is needless now; Violet, though sunk in a deep swoon, is unhurt, while the young lion-slayer lies insensible, covered with blood, his clothes torn to shreds in the very grip of the huge but lifeless monster.

CHAPTER V.
THE OWLET'S ROOST.

THE Owlet's Roost was a grey old tower perched like a pillar on the windy brow of a tall cliff that beetled over the sea.

It had been built as a place of seclusion from the world, by one of Captain Warbold's ancestors, an eccentric character, of whom strange and dark tales were told at the fire-sides of the neighbouring villages.

It was a venerable but dilapidated building, the greater part of it untenanted and unfurnished, while the inhabited portion of it consisted only of a few gloomy, picturesque chambers, the appointments of which were of the quaintest, most antique description.

Altogether the half-ruined tower seemed a fitting birth-place for one destined to a life of such strange and romantic adventures as our hero, Roving Jack.

One night, about a week after the events detailed in the last chapter, our brave young lion-slayer was reclining upon a couch before a cheerful fire, for autumn was waning, and the evenings were growing chill, while his foster sister, Violet, seated on a low stool in the chimney corner, had been reading aloud, from a large worm-eaten old volume, some wild legend of ancient superstition, and as she concluded the marrow-freezing record, raised her soft blue eyes, and with paling cheek and parted lips glanced nervously round the grim old chamber and shuddered with awe.

"Is that story true?" she asked, simply. "Do you believe in Vanderdecken and the 'Spirit of the Cape,' the handsome, giant angel with the fiery horns?"

"Yes, Violet. The phantom ship is often seen in Table Bay," returned our hero, smiling.

"The Flying Dutchman?"

"Why you see, dear, in hot, foggy climates, the forms of sailing ships are often reflected on the horizon leagues away, and so the tars get scared at the shadows of their own vessels."

"But the angel of Cape Horn?" asked the girl, with an admiring glance at the young philosopher.

"Well, I am told that sometimes huge masses of sulphury cloud rest on the summit of that tremendous peak, and shoot forth electric flashes, and it is there the superstitious sailors believe they see the guardian genius of the cape of storms, perched aloft on the fatal headland."

"But then, dear Jack, you know the reef off our own shore is haunted. Lots of people have seen the rocks aflare with a weird blue light, and many of the fishermen swear that they have beheld the Phantom Rover himself."

"Dare say they have," said Jack, dryly. "For my part, I believe him to be the skipper of that rakish-built suspicious-looking schooner that has been hovering about the coast these three weeks."

"But what can he be doing on that bare rock at midnight?"

"That's just what I want to find out, Violet," was Jack's quiet reply. "There are a lot of strange, hang-dog rascals prowling about the cliffs and the beach. I had a brush with one of them myself—but hark!—how the wind blusters!"

Jack and Violet sat silent, listening to the dreary sobbing and wailing of the rising gale rushing round the old tower, and the plashing of the rain-storm that suddenly burst against the diamond-paned windows.

Jack's mother now entered the room.

She was a gentle-looking woman, of great beauty, not more than four or five-and-thirty years of age.

"A wild night," she said, drawing the curtains close. "May He who holds the seas in the hollow of his hand shield all poor souls now tossing on the angry waves! Oh, my dear boy!" she continued, seating herself at the head of the couch on which our hero was lying, "I am sorry we live so near the coast. I trust you will never be a seaman"

"But, mother, you must remember I'm Roving Jack," returned her son, with a pleasant laugh. "It would never do if none could be found to dare the dangers of the deep—and then—my father was a sailor."

"But I am a widow, Jack, and you are my only child," returned the mother, passing her hand through his clustering curls, and fondly kissing his fair, brave brow. "How could I bear to lose my 'widow-comfort,' the only stay that binds me to the bleak world?"

"Heaven would guard me, mother, for your sake," returned our hero. "Some one must breast the old deep wave for the good of his fellow-men—why not I? I can't bear the thought of living a mere homespun landsman, sticking ashore like a limpet to the rocks. My father was a gallant sea-captain and you are the daughter of a seaman, who, they tell me, was accounted the best and bravest pilot in these parts. I don't care much for soldiering; land-fighting seems mere dull butchering; but to contend with the raging elements—to sweep the lawless, inhuman pirates from the high seas—there's something in that!"

Jack's mother drew a deep sigh.

"I hope, my dear boy, that the day when we must part is far distant."

Their conversation was interrupted by a sudden, deep-toned roll of thunder.

A bright electric flash for an instant glared through the room, and was followed by a grand and sonorous thunder-crash.

"Phew! how the lightning whizzes," said Jack.

There was a pause of deep silence.

Suddenly Jack leaped up and held up his hand.

"Hark! Some one without is calling!" said he.

A faint shout rushed wildly on the whistling gale.

"Aboy! Help!—Oh! oh! Help! Help!—for God's sake, help!"

"Some one in distress," cried Jack, briskly, as he kicked off his slippers. "Toss over my boots, Violet—quick, mother, light the lantern!"

Ding-dong-dingle-dong! rang the loud-mouthed bell, waking a hundred surly echoes in the grim old tower.

Mrs. Warbold sped to the window.

She tore open the casement by main force.

A flood of rain dashed in her face, and the savage wind rushed in, extinguishing the candle and streaming her soft brown tresses.

"Who calls?" she cried excitedly. "What is the matter?"

"Oh lors, marm! let me in!" shouted a deep, but quivering voice. "As ye hopes for marcy pity a poor sinner! I've seen—I've seen——"

"Seen what? My son is coming to you—it's Mr. Cleats, I think?"

"Right, marm, It is that unhappy wretch—saving yer rev'rence, marm, I've seen the dev——"

But by this time Jack had bounded down the stone staircase, his terrier barking at his heels, and had unbolted the massive door.

He tried to rush out into the darkness, but was literally hurled backwards by the fury of the buffeting gale.

He thrust out his arm, however, and seized the jacket of a white-haired old man reeling helplessly on the threshold, unable to stand against the raging tempest, and drew him into the house.

The massive door creaked round on its rusty hinges, and slammed to with an awful bang.

"Why, Mr. Cleats, what has frightened you?"

The old man tottered to the stairs, threw himself down in a heap, and covering his white face with his trembling fingers, groaned piteously.

THE PHANTOM OF THE FOAMING REEF. See Page 12.

"What have you seen?"

The old man shook his head with dreadful significance.

"If you had seen old Nick himself you couldn't show more terror," said Jack, a little contemptuously.

"Tail and horns!" moaned the old sailor. "Oh—h—h!"

"Where?"

"Avast heaving, Master Jack, lend a hand to heave me up the gangway; I'm as helpless as a stranded porpoise. Oh, that I should ever live to see this night!"

Jack gave his arm to the old fellow, carefully led him up the stairs, and conducted him to the chamber where Mrs. Warbold and Violet received him with looks of awe and wonder.

"Oh! what has happened?" cried Jack's mother.

But the old man looked unutterable things, and sinking down upon the couch, renewed his piteous groaning.

"Shall I fetch the case-bottle, mother?" asked Jack, biting his lips to restrain an involuntary smile; "perhaps a dram of cognac ——"

"Might revive the wital spark in my bussom, which is now as cold as a lump of ice," rejoined the old man, through his chattering teeth. "Thank'ee, Master Jack; the least drain in the varsal world, marm, t'd be a charity."

Mrs. Warbold needed no further prompting, but

immediately mixed for her guest a stiff jorum of hot brandy.

She then kindly induced the old fellow to remove his wet pea-jacket and bucket boots, and drawing the arm-chair before the fire, invited him to light up his pipe and make himself comfortable.

The old chap sipped the steaming grog, gasped, spluttered, shook his head and moaned.

"And now, Mr. Cleats," said Jack, placing a chair for Violet, and carelessly throwing himself along on the hearth, "now let us hear your terrible story."

"Pray do," urged Mrs. Warbold, taking her seat beside the young folks, "we are dying with impatience to learn what could have given you such a terrible fright."

"Fright, marm! Douse my toplights, if the happarition I beheld this blessed night warn't enough to frighten Old Benbow himself; but, belay, I'll twist the yarn, and you shall judge for yourself whether I have reason to thank my stars that I'm now in dock, every timber taut, and a blowin' my cloud, and a tipplin' my toddy with all gratitood to you, marm, for yer hospital kindness. Here's health and dooty!"

The old chap took a pull at his forelock, and then at the grog.

"But let's get under weigh. About dog watch, I put off in my shallop to look arter the floatin' buoy as marks our boundary o' the fishing grounds, for as 't were blowin' great guns and small arms, some o' my mates were afeared as the buoy would slip its moorin's; not one o' 'em would wolunteer for the sarvice, for there was a choppin' sea on, so I went alone. Ye see, my dears, I had to pull agen the underflow, and I'd a'most tugged my arms out o' their sockets betimes I made the Foamy Reef. I found the buoy had slipped her anchor, and had drifted a point to leeward, so I towed her astern by the hawser, and were pullin' back to shore when— O my eyes!"

"When? when?"

"Easy, master Jack; I kept a bright look-out on the Reef with a sort o' foreknowledge that all warn't ataunto, for why? Mother Carey's chickens were wheelin' around my boat, dippin' their beaks in the surf, and screamin' like storm bags—a thing as never bodes good—when, suddenwise, up flares a hazy blue light, like the ocean flame in the Mediterranean, and spreads all around the rocks, lightin' up the spray of the boundin' breakers till it skimmered like a cloud o' diamond dust. I were taken aback, I acknowledge, for though I'm not one o' them misbelievin', baboon-behaved lubbers as larfs at omens and wisitations, I cert'n'y had my humble doubts about Mynheer Van Teufel the Phantom Pirate as haunts the Foamy Reef, and so I resolved to try conclusions, for, 'Dam'me, Clem Cleats,' says I to myself, 'a thorough seaman should be ready to face old Blazes hisself in the coorse o' dooty,' and I plucks up a brave heart, gives a tug at the larboard oar, pulls through an ugly cross sea, and runs my craft astern on the reef. I looks up, and what I beheld, cur'ous to say, were sheerly——"

"What, what?"

"Jes'—nothun, Master Jack."

"And you were scared at—nothing?"

"Steady a bit; raising my peepers a second time, I were amazed to behold a great sea-chest lyin' on top o' the rock, and could hear a noise from the lee-side of it, as of some unseen chap, a knock, knock, knocking on the rock, and then (still inwisible) a long, loud, shrill whistle on a bo'swain's pipe. 'Ahoy! skipper, ahoy!' I sings out. 'What cheer, what are ye doing up there, my hearty?' When— O, lors!"

"Do go on."

"When up popped a black head, fitted with a pair of horns as long as the main-yards, and eyes like fightin' lanterns, and sich glitterin' white fangs, showing like a tier o' white ports, and a pair o' red blubber lips opened as wide as the main-hatch of a man-o'-war, and a woice as loud as all the guns o' Gibraltar roared out——. Well, just a leetle drain, marm; this is rare good stingo."

Jack sloushed the whole contents of the brandy bottle into the old fellow's glass, swamping the floor in his eagerness.

"Yes, yes; this dev——well, mother, this big-horned black fellow——"

"Roared out in the voice of a walrus, 'Sheer off! sheer off, yo dam buckra mortal; I, Mumbo Jumbo, an 'pose yo not clear away, I clapperclaw yo like de debil in more less nor no time.'"

"Must ha' been a nigger!"

"Belay, Master Jack, we all know his colour. But I was that flabbergasted that I shoves off with the oars, and then swooned right away on the gratin's of the boat. I didn't come to my senses till the current had carried me half a cable's length from the reef, when I were roused up by a heavy sea that dashed over the bows, and a-nigh swamped the shallop. I looked back——"

"And the light?"

"Had wanished like a shootin' star or an ice-blink in the No'th'n skies; all were black as a shark's maw, 'ceptin' for the white surf of the breakers leapin' over the reef."

"Did you pull back?"

"My jib, Master Jack, was it for a honest seaman to tempt the devil?"

"Did you hear nothing more? Where you chased?"

"Well, not to prewaricate, I fancied I heard the dip of oars, but I rowed so fast that Old Nick in a symoon couldn't a overhauled me."

"So the light went out, and you were chased—ah!"

And Master Jack fell into a fit of abstraction. At length he looked up quickly.

"I say, Mr. Cleats," he exclaimed, "suppose you and I row over to the reef, and see whether the—the black gentleman will appear again."

"How dare you, Jack?"

"Why, mother, dear, you needn't be angry, there's no danger; the goblin didn't hurt Mr. Cleats, and surely I, a mere boy, would be beneath his dark majesty's notice; I'm not afraid of Mynheer Van Teufel, though he does reside in such strange quarters. Will you go with me, Mr. Cleats?"

"Avast! not for all the treasure of Prester John," growled the old fisherman; "so now, marm, as I've spun out my yarn, and the wind has fallen a little, with your good leave I'll weigh anchor; it is time I turned in, for I must be on the beach by eight bells to-morrow; and do you accept this piece o' partin' adwice, Master Jack—never tempt the devil! And so good night, my dears."

Jack soon had reason enough to remember the old man's warning; but of that more hereafter.

CHAPTER VI.
THE SPECTRE OF THE FOAMY REEF.

THE storm had in some measure abated, but the gale still blew hard in fierce, fitful gusts, with squalls of rain, which spouted and battered dismally against the darkened windows of the lone tower on the cliff.

Jack's bed-room was a quaint little chamber, situated in an abutment of the turret on the side facing the sea.

On retiring thither, the boy, who had been much excited by the old fisherman's strange story, threw open his casement, and gazed intently forth through the deep darkness.

Ever from the beach spread far below, soared upwards the grand, ceaseless roar of the billows, plunging and scattering on the rattling shingles, while the wind soughed past, and alternately raved and howled round the half-ruined dwelling.

For almost an hour our hero had kept his glance steadfastly fixed upon the dark outline of the Foamy Reef dimly discernible against the night sky.

Hitherto all had been darkness and desolation, when suddenly a faint blue light broke forth on the sky line, and shone like a halo round the rifted crag in the far distance.

Jack drew back, and scarcely repressed an exclamation of awe, and his heart throbbed audibly.

A heavy locker stood on one side of the room containing the arms and nautical instruments which had belonged to our hero's father. Jack opened this sea-chest and took out a night-glass.

He returned to the window, and having adjusted the focus to suit his sight, took a long and careful look at the distant reef.

"Some one is moving on the rocks!" he muttered, breathlessly. "Ah! there are more figures than one—three! four! They seem floating about in the weird blue glare. Who or what can they be? Devils! Aye, they are *pirates*, the crew of that ugly craft in the offing!"

Jack sat down upon the coping of the window and rested the telescope upon his knees.

"What can be done?" he asked himself, mentally. "If I could beard these dread spectres, unmask their black tricks, and bring the murderous villains to justice, what a glorious feat that would be!"

He pondered deeply.

"But if—if they should really prove beings of another world—horrible phantoms! To brave them, alone too, on such a wild night! My blood freezes, my hair stirs at the bare thought! Ah! the light is waning! it flickers, it dies out as if quenched in the bosom of the sea—all dark!"

Several moments elapsed, measured as distinctly by the beating of the daring boy's excited heart as by a watch. At last, as if forming a sudden resolution, he sprang to his feet and shut up the telescope with an emphatic snap.

"I'll go!" he exclaimed aloud.

Walking quickly to the door he opened it softly and listened.

Silence reigned in the house.

"Not that way," he muttered, drawing back. "Mother will be waked; she'd die of fright if she knew what I was about. I deserve the worst that can happen to me for my rashness and disobedience. It is so wrong of me to play these pranks. Ah! the light again. I can't help my nature; I'm restless, reckless Roving Jack, and ghosts are not to be met with every night in the twelvemonth! The tide's on the turn; the wind dies off in catspaws. I shall be back before dawn. I'll go!"

Once more Jack rummaged the locker.

"I'll take the dark lantern with me," he thought, "and the night-glass, and here's my father's sword."

He drew the shiny blue blade from the sheath, and looked on it with reverence.

"May the Lord of Hosts grant that this pure steel may never be stained with innocent blood!" he murmured, devoutly. "I will be no marauding soldier, no gold-griping blood-thirsty robber; but, oh! may this arm be nerved to strike in defence of the righteous cause, to smite the base robber on land and sea! May my life's wild romance move every brave, adventure-loving boy to own how much more noble it is to be a deliverer than a destroyer, an heroic robber-hunter than a selfish, cut-throat robber!"

He kissed the gleaming blade, and, sheathing it, buckled the sword about his slim waist.

Then he laid his hands on a case of pistols.

"No; let them rest. In my rash hands they might be dangerous—to myself, to my own honour. After all, they are the tools of the coward; foot to foot, hand to hand, breast to breast, I will fight my foes with my father's sword, which is hallowed!"

The young enthusiast drew himself up to his full height, and folding his arms, burst into a buoyant laugh, as his vivid imagination and his strong, bold heart pictured and confirmed the truth that he was born to a high and noble destiny.

"But now comes the clinch!" muttered Roving Jack, starting from his reverie. "How am I to get down from the window?"

He looked out.

"Phew! it's an awful height—but, 'where there's a will there's a way.'"

He took the blankets, sheets, and coverlet, from his bed, and tying them tightly together fastened one end to a strong nail in the wooden case of the window. He stood for an instant looking down into the dark, dizzy depth.

Then he launched himself forth into mid air.

Hand under hand, knee under knee, tightly gripping the swaying line, he descended a little way.

The strain was great, and the line shook and seemed to be tearing out the nail from the beam.

Jack looked down—down!

He shuddered, clenched his teeth, and a qualm of deadly sickness rose in his throat.

He arched his fingers, loosened the clasp of his entwined feet, and down, down he shot like a stone, the line rushing through his burning palms like a round red-hot bar.

At last he hung, suspending himself by his hands, full twenty feet above the ground.

He set his toes in a crevice between the time-worn stones. He leaped. Stumbling a yard or so, he rolled over on his side half stunned.

He had struck his foot against some obstruction, and was thrown heavily.

He rose, however, and after a rest, descended the cliff by a rugged and slippery rock-way.

The night was pitch dark; the rough breakers poured along the echoing coast with their continuous and tremendous roar.

The place became dark and piercing chill, and the situation was drear, lone and dangerous.

But peril was pleasure to Roving Jack.

Reaching the stony beach, he plodded across the crashing shingles till he came to the very margin of the foamy main.

Here he stood for a moment, looking heedfully on the white frothy mountains of brine as they came rolling, bursting and founting in, bellowing amid the hollows of the rocks, and hissing harshly up and down the pebbly strand.

"I shall have some trouble to launch a boat in such a sea as this," thought Jack, as he ran out of reach of a bounding head-wave that seemed to give him chase with conscious spitefulness; "but it's not so rough under the cliffs in the little bay. But what shall I do for a boat? and if I find one how can I launch her? I am afraid I shall have to give up."

Forging on over the sharp and massive rocks which formed the footstool of the headland, Jack arrived at a little bay, sheltered on either side by projecting cliffs.

Here it was comparatively calm.

Jack had not proceeded far when he perceived a large boat lying on the verge of the advancing tide.

"That's old Clem's shallop," said Jack. "The old chap was so scared that he did not stay to drag it up above the tide line ; in a few minutes it would be floating adrift. I think there's depth enough to float her already. Heave yo !"

Jack applied his shoulders to the stern of the boat, and, driving hard against her, disengaged her from the little hillock of sand, and she shot clear ; and while Jack, drenched to the skin, was scrambling over her bows, she bounced over a mighty breaker, and danced out to the open sea.

"She's away !" cried Jack, exultingly, as he righted himself on the thwart, and seized the oars, for the boat was waddling like a wash-tub in the rough cross seas.

Alone in the frail little vessel on the angry seas —alone in the night and the darkness—launched for an enterprise of deadly danger, Roving Jack felt just a pleasurable sensation of excitement and awe ; but fear was absent from his dauntless heart ; he pulled hard, and panted at the oar, but he gave no homeward glance, and only turned his head to stare impatiently through the gloom towards the dark peaks and crags of the Foamy Reef.

Again the mystic light haloed the rugged crag towards which our brave boy hero was bounding in the old weather-worn shallop, now heaved aloft on a briny mountain, crested with snowy foam, then plunging deep down into the dark and dreadful trough of the sea.

The more immediate and definite danger of having his frail open vessel swamped by the heavy seas that burst in cataracts over her bows, or ground to pieces against the sharp points of the cruel, hidden rocks, countervailed the natural horror that our gallant Jack might feel at the prospect of being brought face to face with pallid ghosts of the guilty dead, or grizzly phantoms and fiends of the storm.

His main thought was only how to save himself from drowning, and with most admirable skill did the young steersman pilot his boat through those raging, rocky waters.

The wild wind shrieked fiercely past, hissing fountains of briny spray drenched him to the skin, while from time to time the keel of the boat grazed against the sunken rocks, and communicated its grating shudder to Jack's half-numbed body, and electrified his stout heart with a keen pang.

But still the intrepid lad forged bravely on, and at length, rising on the crest of a tremendous billow, he was borne abreast of the Foamy Reef.

For a moment he stared aghast at the blue, luminous mist, then with a shiver he closed his eyes and clenched his teeth.

On the top of the minor crags composing the reef a table of rock, rising a few feet above the seething surface of the raging waters, stood, still as a statue, *a tall, dark, and weird form.*

Vanderdecken !—the Flying Dutchman himself !

At least the figure bore a perfect resemblance to that described as belonging to the phantom skipper of the Phantom Ship.

The rough, ungainly, but picturesque Dutch costume, the broad belt and leathern kilt, huge bucket boots, and peaked hat, while from his shoulders, its massy folds waving heavily in the rushing blast, streamed a jet black pall, on which was broidered, in hideously contrasting white, the ghastly symbols of the pirate's bloody trade—the death's head and cross-bones.

He stood, his pale, stern, evil countenance rigid and inanimate, his eyes dully glaring upon vacancy, as though he were oblivious of all but the fiery thoughts surging in his tortured heart—smitten and blighted by the awful punishment that had fallen upon him by which he was doomed, an exile from bliss or hope, to roam for ever and ever and ever the wild and restless salt sea, which he had in life so often stained crimson with warm, human blood.

Jack drew his sword, and unclosing his eyelids, shaded his eyes with his hand, and kept his gaze hungrily fixed upon the strange, ghostly sentinel of the reef. The light flickers, fades—darkness.

A sullen red glare, that faintly streaks the eastern horizon, throws into dark but strong relief the rugged line of the rocks.

The stony platform is void—the phantom has vanished !

Then a blinding, forked flash of livid blue lightning rips the lowering black clouds, and sets the earth and sky in one electric blaze.

Yes, the Phantom has vanished ! Lit by the living glare, the glittering jets of surf fount over the green, sea-slimed rocks, flow down in pure, briny sheets, and drip in falls of flashing, twinkling diamond-drops from the narrow ledge on which the spectre had appeared—but he was gone !

Utter darkness !—the darkness of plague-stricken Egypt—the gloom of the deep grave !

A roar ! All the firmament—volley on volley of rattling thunder, rolling, growling, muttering, dying away !

Jack clutches the thwart of the boat, for the wind, which had fallen, comes now in a strong, hot gust, and close in its wake tumbles along a giant tidal wave, which bashes and shatters against the reef, lashing the waters around it till they bubble and seeth as if the gulf were a boiling caldron.

Knocked down, bruised, battered, half-stunned, poor Jack sinks on the grating of the creaking boat, which dances like a nutshell in a mill-dam.

The heavy sea pours onwards ; then the boat slowly rises on a green, glassy, gliding hillock of brine.

Now she is drifting—smoothly, swiftly, steadily, drifting. Jack leaps up.

His hair rouses, his eyes fix, his lips part ; in a second, however, he masters his emotion.

He set his foot lightly on the gunwale. The boat lurches. He springs wide.

He plunges head foremost into the smooth, treacherous bosom of the billow that was bearing him so calmly to destruction.

Down, down, in the chill depths he glides, and then he struggles to the surface.

He rises amidst the roars of the bursting breakers which have dashed his boat to splinters against the reef.

Gasping, sinking from weakness, then struggling up again to the surface by desperate efforts, Roving Jack fights his way to the reef.

For an instant he has foothold on the point of a sunken rock ; but his foot slips, and again he is dashed away into deep water.

Utterly faint and exhausted, down he sinks, hopelessly it would seem.

Yet he rallies once more, and madly he clutches at the green sleek vegetable fur that coats the rocks. The lithe, tough, slippery sea-bine laps round his hands.

He has a hold ! No, for the weed tears out by the roots, and once more down, deep down, he plunges.

Afloat again, and upraised on a mighty wave as

by the arm of some marine giant about to smash him upon the crag, away he goes.

Clutch! clutch! his fingers slither along the side of a mass of stone.

The sea-weed is stronger here.

He seizes a bunch in his fists.

With the clutch of a vice he fixes his toes on a jutting ledge.

Hold on Jack, for dear life!

The mountain-wave sinks under his feet; it slides and slips like a toppling avalanche, till, at no slight distance beneath him, it falls and bursts among the thickly-strewn rocklets in ten thousand foamy thunders.

For a moment, Jack hangs, suspending himself, and panting for breath, then he frantically clambers to the top of the crag.

He kneels upon the exact spot where, but a few minutes before, the spectre had stood!

And he looks round upon the wild and awful storm-scene with a fainting glance of horror and despair.

CHAPTER VII.

ROVING JACK'S FIRST MEETING WITH JONATHAN WILD.

ROVING JACK soon roused himself from his state of stupor and exhaustion.

Creeping on his hands and knees, he reached the other end of the rock, and found that, though viewed from the lee side it appeared to be quite isolated and detached from the rest of the reef, it was, nevertheless, connected with a rugged little island by a long and narrow causeway, over some parts of which heavy seas were breaking.

A strange suspicion took possession of Jack's mind. He could not suppress a shudder as he thought of the terrible issue that might attend his rash adventure.

At the best, here he was, prisoned on this lone rock, at least three miles from shore, a desolate spot on which he might be left to starve for aught he could tell, for whether or not the rock was haunted (though, to him, there could now be no doubt of the fact) the fishermen and sailors shunned it with dread and abhorrence.

But as his hand rested on the hilt of his father's sword, and as, with gratitude to Providence, he recalled his late remarkable deliverance from such fearful dangers, his bold spirit rose with the occasion, and he determined that he would follow up with unquailing courage what he had begun with such thoughtless temerity.

Scrambling down on to the causeway, he crept along in imminent peril of being swept away by the heavy seas that ever and anon dashed over him till he gained the island.

Here he rested himself for awhile, sheltered under a cavernous hollow, and listened with breathless intentness to the noise of the wind and the waves.

At last, upon turning his head towards the inner wall of the cave, he was startled to perceive a faint ray of yellow light, emitted from certain crevices between the stone.

He cautiously approached the place where this ray of light penetrated the dark cave.

He touched the stones and found them to be loose. Carefully removing one or two, he found that he had opened a space large enough to admit his head. He peered in.

To his surprise, he beheld a rude ladder-stair descending into a vault below, hewn out in the living stone, and lighted by a flaring torch stuck in a sconce in the wall.

He descended, and found himself in a sort of shaft, on either side of which were heavy doors, seemingly formed of massive bulk-heads and other ship timbers.

All were closed and dark except one, through the cracks of which rays of light poured in.

He listened and could distinguish the faint, hollow echoes of distant voices.

He gave the door a slight push and it opened.

Jack drew his sword and boldly entered.

Very softly he trod the slippery floor of a sort of corridor or tunnel, and came at last to a heavily barred trap-hatch in the ground.

Here the voices grew loud, and he could plainly distinguish every word of conversation, carried on in gruff tones, and interspersed with hoarse laughter and savage oaths.

Peeping through a cranny in the hatch he looked down into a large chamber hollowed out in the rocks below the water mark.

It was cumbered on all sides by spars, casks, sea-chests, cabin-fittings, bales of various costly stuffs, vessels and utensils of gold, silver, glass and china, bags and strong boxes probably containing money, and arms in great diversity.

In the centre of the cavern and beneath the swinging lamp which threw its lurid flare upon the strange scene, was a long table at which no less than forty swart, weather-beaten ruffians in leathern kilts or petticoat-trousers gathered at the knee, belts bristling with long knives and clumsy pistols, and with red woollen caps on their heads, were seated, smoking long pipes and drinking strong liquors in horn cups.

"Odsfish!" laughed one of them, an undersized, deformed, but powerful rascal, whom Jack at once recognized as his former friend Barabbas, "and so the old beggar mistook you for the devil, my black beauty?"

This question was addressed to a tall, lank negro, who seemed to be greatly diverting the company by a story he was telling.

"Yah! ah! yah! yah!" yelled the black, snapping his fingers, and displaying a formidable row of flashing white teeth; "yo see, mate, no soon as de ole jackamarass see me wid de cuss long cow-horn stick on head, he sing out, 'Oh, yo! skipper dere, what yo do?' 'What me do? Yah! I Mumbo Jumbo! Why yo no clear out? I go jump on yo, tear yo tousand lilly piece, like one Korimante debil! Yo savey dat, yo dam buccra fisherman! yah! hi! whoo!' Gorramighty, messmate, me sing out like one mad bull, poke wid horn, pour more blue fire in chaffer, makee more blue light, yah! den screechee, screechee, nuff frighten Massa Davy Jone', pose him hear. By gum, sar, dat skear he; he sheer off good; nebba see um no mo', big sea swamp um boat, pose he shark-meat now, dam 'quisitive swab lubber! Yi, ho! tink me larf to split!"

And the negro clutched his sides and burst into shrieks of mirth, chorused by the others.

"And that's old Clem's bugbear!" thought bold Jack, who could scarcely help joining in the laugh himself. "Well, he's a funny devil, no mistake!"

A shrill whistle ringing down the rocky passage caused Jack to turn with a start.

Vanderdecken!

Torch in hand, the apparition of the Foamy Reef approached. He was followed by a number of men.

Jack clutched the hilt of his sword and confronted him with dauntless courage.

"Donner und blitzen!" roared the Dutchman. "What for a stranger is dis?"

"Ha! a stranger!" cried a deep, authoritative voice,

A burly man stepped forward, as he did so unsheathing his whinger.

For an instant even our brave young hero quailed beneath the stern, searching glance of those wolfish grey eyes.

The man was short in stature, thick set, but not ill-proportioned; his face expressive of extreme cunning and determination, his complexion fair and ruddy, his mouth wide and firm, his hair foxy red, his square, hard brow scarred by a desperate gash covered with a strip of black plaister; he was neatly dressed in a suit of sober brown, with brass buttons, a small cocked hat was perched on one side of his head, and a " blue Benjamin " loosely wrapped about his bull throat; he was powerfully armed with a brace of heavy pistols and a whinger; a constable's crown-headed staff protruded from one of his wide, flapped side pockets.

" Who is this kinchin ?" he asked, sternly.

" Vor Hemmel ! How sall I tell zat, Meister Vild, vhen I never zee de jonker before !" returned the Dutchman.

" Who are ye, sirrah ?" cried the other, in a tone meant to intimidate our hero.

But for once he was mistaken in his customer; the noble boy was one whom a gentle voice could easily command, but whom threats served only to exasperate.

" Sirrah yourself ! Who are you ?" retorted Roving Jack, in his boldest accents.

" I am one, sir, who will not brook insolence," returned Jonathan Wild, in an undertone of great ferocity.

" In that respect I think we resemble each other," returned the youth, with provoking coolness, " Neither do I !"

" I am unused to such language," gasped the thief-taker.

" That is because your associates are sneaks and cowards that can be frightened by big looks and bluster."

" Haw, haw !" laughed the Dutchman. " Mein Got ! dat ist vehr goot vor zich a yong knave !"

" Pish ! mere bravado," rejoined Jonathan; " he thinks his case is hopeless. We mean to kill you, my ben kinchen. Ha !"

" I hope not; hark ye, I know you're all pirates——"

" Teufel !" growled the Dutchman, half drawing a pistol.

" Aye; and I'll tell ye what brought me here," continued the boy, in the same quiet, even tones. " You have been performing a pretty farce of devil scare all, to frighten the seamen and fishers from the Foamy Reef. Seeing your blue blaze on the crag I thought it worth the venture to row over and learn what you were made of. Now, as I've satisfied my curiosity, and set some value on my life, if you lend me a boat (my own struck on the reef and went to pieces), I'll go ashore; I'll pledge my word not to betray you."

" Smother me ! Was ever heard better, governor, the cull dictates terms like a conqueror ?" laughed a tall, stalwart ruffian, with a face as dark as a malay's.

" Silence, Blueskin," rejoined Wild, sternly. " Now, my ben kinchen, I like grit, you seem a bold fellow. I mean to question you further, and if I am satisfied with your replies you shall have a free pardon; but if you attempt to brave or bamboozle me, you shall die for it, if there's not another rogue left unhung in England !"

" Ye hear what the gov'nor says, my little dimber damber ?" growled Blueskin. " There's no queering that."

" No; I never forfeit my word," said the thief-taker; " and now, my lad, you must deliver up that toasting-iron."

" Certainly," said our hero, handing his sword; " it can't aid me much against such odds."

" Good. Are you alone ?"

" Aye," returned Jack, adding to himself, " and in precious bad company."

" Enough; Mynheer Wolfgang, admit us to your sanctum."

" Ja, ja ; dis vay, Meister Vild."

The trap-hatch was now lifted, and Jack was roughly thrust down the ladder into the vault below.

He found himself surrounded on all sides by scowling faces, and quite at the mercy of the villanous gang.

One of the pirates advancing from the throng glared savagely into the boy's face.

" Blood and thunder !" he cried, furiously. " 'Tis Roving Jack !"

" Donner ! Do ye know dis yong gallowsh-bird, Barabbas ?"

" Know him ? aye, well enough, captain. But a week since I met him on the jetty; I was near slicing out his viperous tongue. His name is Jack Warbold—they call him Roving Jack. His mother is a whining widow, a cunning, low-born woman, who depends for her subsistence on the charity of his late father's relatives; a——"

Jack interrupted the speech by springing at the ruffian's throat like a young panther.

" Ha, you dog !" growled Wild, hurling the boy off, and then seizing his quivering arm in an iron grasp.

" You see," panted Barabbas, with an atrocious oath, " you see what a young hell-hound it is !"

" Silence !" cried Jonathan Wild. " Go on with your story."

" Aye, aye, sir; there's little more to say than this: the whelp told me to the teeth that I was a pirate, swore he would denounce me to the beaks, and declared that when he became a man he would devote himself to hunting down gentlemen of our gallant trade—that he would be a pirate-hunter !"

" Speak, Roving Jack, is this true ?"

" Partly," replied our hero, with perfect calmness. " This blackguard is a thief and a murderer. He tempted me with fine promises to join his bloody gang, and because I refused to do so he attacked me with knife and pistol; so, with the help of my chum, Hal, I pitched him into the sea; but he who's born to be hanged can never be drowned."

" And so you're a pirate-hunter, eh ?"

" If you'll set me ashore safe and sound, I'll promise not to betray you; I always keep my word."

" And so do I, Roving Jack," returned Jonathan. " But come, I like your mettle. Do you know who I am ?"

" Mr. Wild, I believe, sir."

" Right—Jonathan Wild, the king's chief peace-officer, and, moreover, what you aspire to be, a thief-taker."

" And a thief-*maker*, or rumour foully belies ye," muttered our hero.

" I make you a fair offer, my kinchen; I will take you into my service, will teach you a lucrative profession, make you a high pad bridle cull* or a tip top cracksman†, extending to you my powerful aid and protection. Refuse this offer, Roving Jack, and you die ! if there's another rogue left unhung in England !"

_____
* Highwayman.   † Housebreaker.

Jack was silent.

"Your answer?—but beware! I never break my word!"

"Heaven help me, then!" said Jack, solemnly. "Rather a thousand deaths than such dishonour! There is no power on earth that could make me a base robber!"

"Fool!" sneered Jonathan. "Is this your answer?"

"I can give you no other," was the boy's reply.

"You have thrown away your last chance," growled the arch-villain, as he swished round his whinger, in order to cleave the young martyr in twain.

Clash! The descending weapon was deftly parried by the blade of a small dress sword.

The interposer was a short, slight, but well-built youth, about nineteen years of age, very showily dressed in a scarlet riding-coat, richly brocaded with gold lace, a three-cornered hat, also laced with gold, top-boots, and an ornamented baldrick, from which depended the scabbard of his small, silver-hilted sword.

In his belt were thrust a brace of handsomely-mounted pistols; his linen and lace ruffles were of the daintiest white and finest texture; his fingers were covered with brilliant rings, and a costly diamond brooch glistened in his fringe cravat; his complexion was pale, his eyes large, black, and lustrous; his sleek black hair was close-cropped, and his head small and bullet-shaped.

"This to me, Jack Sheppard?" roared Wild, lowering his sword, and staring at the youth in blank amazement.

"Hark ye, governor," returned the notorious house-breaker, "I've served ye faithfully, haven't I? Will ye do me a favour?"

"Humph!"

"Spare this dimber* little kiddy, just for my sake? I've taken a liking to him! he's such a plucky one."

"Sorry to disoblige you, Jack," returned Jonathan, firmly, "but it can't be done. It would be a bad precedent. I've said he shall die; my word's my bond."

"S'death!" cried Jack Sheppard, with rising anger. "You won't refuse such a small favour to one of your best men? Haven't I always done my duty, and handed over two-thirds of the swag without grumbling? Very well, governor be reasonable. This rash cull deserves a better fate than to be made a box of cold meat of; he's steel to the backbone. I'll stand bail that he won't whiddle*; he's no peach. At all events, give him a chance."

"I have given him a chance—a last chance," returned Jonathan, sternly. "He has thrown it away."

"Pshaw! give him time, governor. The road to the nubbing-cheat,* like the floor of a certain place, is paved with good intentions. There's many a high tobyman that worked capital† and came at last to be a Tyburn Show, that resisted temptation in the onset. Don't spoil a good hand for want of a little patience. Give him time to reflect—say an hour. Life's sweet, and he may come to terms. If he don't, why, then, curse him for a fool, say I. I wash my hands of him."

"Well, Jack, as I desire to gratify you when possible, as you've been useful to me, I think I can yield thus far without compromising my word. I *will* give him an hour for reflection; but if he obstinately persists in refusing my fair offer, he shall die, as sure as Newgate."

"Bravo! that's jannock!" cried Jack Sheppard, delightedly. "You hear what good Mr. Wild says, my plummy kinchen? Why endure an hour's suspense? Strike a bargain at once; join our gallant company. You shall be my pupil and pal, and I'll make a tip-top cracksman of ye, for who can teach you to slum a ken* in finer style than Jack Sheppard?"

"I thank ye, it is kind of ye to wish to save me," said the honest and heroic boy, in a frank and pleasant manner; "but I would rather die a thousand deaths each day than live one hour the slave of this villain as you are, Jack Sheppard."

A shade of pain flickered over Jack Sheppard's pale face, and a faint blush rose to his cheek.

Jonathan Wild glared like a demon.

Once more he whirled round his heavy sword.

Jack Sheppard caught his wrist.

"Your promise, governor," he said, quietly.

"Right," said Wild, curtly, as he sheathed his sword. "I'll keep it. Here, Quilt Arnold, Abraham, clap this kid into bilboes,* gag him, and pitch him down into the black hole."

In an instant the two satellites, one a fierce-looking ruffian, the other a miserable old Jew, seized the boy, handcuffed and gagged him, and tied his feet together.

Barabbas roughly seized the helpless victim by the hair, and dragging him along to a dark recess in the cavern, pitched him down a black shaft, and let fall the heavy trap-hatch upon him.

CHAPTER VIII.

THE BOY MARTYR.

JONATHAN WILD having thus disposed of our noble boy hero, turned to the pirate skipper.

"Well, mynheer, what news from Amsterdam?"

"Fere goot, Meister Vild. De gelt is in de factor's handsh, de vatches and goldshmitz notes vosh take in de 'Raven.' De jewelsh ish reset, Muntmeister. Dat ish a fine cleversh fellow, Van Stein. Vot you call zat he is?—de jeweller—ja—de lapidary? He zend you dish notesh."

"Pay him when you return; but the papers, Wolfgang? The documents you found in that Dutch galliot you took?"

"De papersh? Goot! Vot belonged to de Jacobite, Sir Jocylyn Tremaine and his frow—his vife—de Lady Annabel."

"Yes; have you bought them?"

"Ja, Meister Vild; but noting vos heard of ze frowlein—de childst vosh drown. I vill zhow de papersh to you iv you will come vith me, dere arl in my own shalloon. Come dis vay."

The Dutchman rose and stalked through the cavern followed by Wild.

As soon as they were gone, Blueskin, Jack Sheppard, and the rest, seated themselves at the table, bottles of wine and spirits were placed on the board.

Blueskin, Sheppard, and about half-a-dozen others of Jonathan Wild's dependants, with the pirate crew, throwing off the restraint their leaders' presence had imposed upon them, now broke out into uproarious merriment.

"Captain, tip us a ranting stave," suggested Blueskin.

"Aye, aye! a song, Captain Sheppard! a song!" was the general shout, accompanied by a tremendous thumping of tables, and clattering of tiles and glasses.

Jack Sheppard laughed, tossed off a brimmer of hot brandy, and without hesitation trolled forth, in a fine mellow voice, the following

> " Pale Oliver* " rears his shining face,
>   Above the rushy fen, sirs ;
> The horseman rides with hastening pace,
>   Adown the ' Deadman's Glen,' sirs.
> The roving wind now ramps about,
>   Claps to the cotter's door, sirs ;
> Or clanks the rusty gibbet-bolts,
>   Where Mat swings on the moor, sirs.
>
>   So up, my boys ! up, my boys !
>   Deeds to-night, to-morrow joys !
>   To cheat the day,
>   Let's mount—away !
>   Hurrah ! hurrah, for the road, boys !
>
> "The mill-ken† lurks behind the pale,
>   The Romoner‡ haunts the glen, sirs ;
> And where the road winds down the dale,
>   Ye meet the tobymen, sirs !
> But man must live—they gain the least
>   That labour most, I think, sirs !
> So when poor hunger finds a feast,
>   I feel inclined to wink, sirs.
>
>   Then up, my boys ! up my boys ! &c.
>
> "Beneath the dark and shadowy elms,
>   That skirt the lonely lane, sirs,
> When night the world with gloom o'erwhelms,
>   Our prancing prads§ we rein, sirs ;
> His lordship's rumblers‖ rattle by,
>   Our barking-irons¶ click, sirs,
> ' Stand and deliver, or you die !'
>   Then gelt** and gems we nick, sirs.
>
>   So up, my boys ! up, my boys ! &c.

" Brayvo !" shouted the whole conclave ; "hurraw for Captin Sheppard, and his pal, Blueskin !"

In the midst of the tumultuous applause that succeeded, Jonathan Wild and Wolfgang, the skipper of the pirate schooner, entered the cavern.

"Ze gale shtill blowsh shtiff, Meister Vild," said the Hollander ; "it ish ein teuflesh ugly night. Von't you shtay mit uns, her-re in ze cave, till morgen ?"

"No ; get ready the boat," returned Jonathan.

"Quilt, Arnold, collect our men. Come, Jack, and Blueskin, we must be on our road to London before daybreak."

"Pardon, Mr. Wild ; what of the chick we've caged ?" rejoined Barabbas, maliciously. "Shall we keep him under hatches till further orders, or wring his neck at once ?"

"I had not forgotten him," said Wild, coldly ; "bring him hither."

Barabbas uttered a barbaric whoop, and bounded off to the gloomy recess in the cavern beneath which our hero was lying, bound and in darkness.

The ruffian lifted the trap and hurried down.

Soon he re-appeared, brutally dragging along the gagged, fettered and disabled prisoner.

"Unmuzzle him," said Wild, with a leer ; "let us hear whether he will change his tune ; he has had time for reflection. Speak, Roving Jack, your answer to my offer, repeated for the last time. Will you enter my service, or are you prepared to pay the penalty of your foolhardiness !"

"You can kill me, Jonathan Wild," returned our hero, in a thrilling tone, "but you cannot make me your slave. I can die, but I cannot be a thief !"

"Die, then !" growled the villain, uplifting the pistol, which he grasped by the barrel end.

---

* The moon. † Housebreaker. ‡ Gipsy. § Horses. ‖ Carriage wheels. ¶ Pistols. ** Money.

For an instant he paused, with upraised arm, glaring threateningly upon the calm, dauntless countenance of the noble lad.

He uttered an awful imprecation, and struck our hero down with a fearful blow.

Roving Jack reeled backwards and fell flat ; his battered brow spouted blood, his arms sank listlessly by his side ; he groaned, his eyes closed, and a mortal shudder ran through his frame, then his limbs stiffened, and he lay quite still.

"Myn Got ! dat vos a fery prave jonker !" said Wolfgang, with a dark scowl at the thief-taker. "Is he tead ?"

Barabbas leaned over the prostrate boy, and laid his hard hand upon his delicate but firm breast.

"Humph !" said he, "his heart has ceased beating ; but it's best to make sure of him."

"Chive (stab) him !" growled Blueskin.

With a satanic leer Barabbas drew his long, sharp knife from his belt, and was about to draw its keen edge across our hero's throat, when the pirate captain raised his foot and kicked the bloodthirsty villain half-across the cavern.

"Donner und holle !" he thundered. "Vot for a trick is dis ? Sall you make my varehoush von bleeting shambles ?"

Barabbas stumbled on to his feet, and looked rather sheepishly towards his irate captain.

"Ax yer pardon, captin," he mumbled.

"But shall I stow away the little stiff 'un ?"

"Ja ; pitch him down the " Dead Hold," returned the pirate, coolly.

Barabbas seized the senseless form in his brawny arms, and hurried it along to the end of the cavern, where a flight of steps led to another of the numerous passages cut in the living rock.

Taking down a torch from a sconce in the wall he brandished the lurid flame about his hideous head, and with the air of a gloating fiend, chuckled over his lifeless burthen.

He reached a heavily barred door.

He unbarred and then opened it with a large key that he selected from a bunch hanging at his belt.

As the ponderous door jarred back a small circular chamber appeared.

From the centre of the ceiling hung a pulley and a long chain, one end of which was attached to an iron ring in the floor.

A horrid, sickening stench pervaded the place.

Barabbas laid the body down by the door, and stationing himself close by the wall, caught hold of the chain pending from the block, and pulled at it with all his strength.

A large and heavy trap was slowly raised from the floor, and a deep black shaft displayed, from which arose increasingly a foul, stifling smell.

"So ends the career of a Pirate-hunter !" chuckled the ruffian. "Ho ! ho ! shouldn't wonder if his ghost doesn't join some phantom crew of ' jollies ' (men-o'-war's-men), and give chase to the ' Flying Dutchman !' "

Here he placed his arms round the boy's slim waist and dragged him to the hatch.

" More meat for the worms !" he laughed, fiendishly. "Ho ! ho ! they can't grumble at me for a stingy purser ; they gets their 'lowance. There, you epicures, there's a luscious morsel for ye ; no tough salt-junk that, but a bleater, fresh killed, young, and tender, the flower of the flock ! ho ! ho ! That all this big round world should be nothing but a grazing ground for worms'-meat !"

So saying, he lifted the inanimate form in his arms and dashed it down into the darkness.

A dull thud, a clatter as of bones, and hollow,

ROVING JACK RESCUED FROM THE DEATH HOLE—*See page* 21.

sickly echoes !—echoes, moans, dying echoes—then the trap bangs down !

*   *   *   *

"Adieu, Mynheer Wolfgang," said Jonathan Wild, shaking hands with the pirate skipper, who was conducting him from the cavern by the passage in which he had encountered our gallant young hero. "Do not forget when you see Van Stein to ask him for those papers we spoke of."

"Nein, I vill tink of all, Meister Vild, but soon sall I leave dese Pritish vaters vor goot, vor I mean to hoist ze rover's bunting in the Spanish Main, vhere gelt ish to be picked up as easily as pebblesh on the peach—haw ! haw !"

No. 3.

"Bravo, Commodore !" returned Jonathan Wild, rubbing his hands ; "I often regret that I am a landsman, but still my dominion stretches over land and sea."

"Vere true, muntemeister ; you are king of ze rogues all ofer de world."

"Humph ! I may be yet," muttered Wild ; "at present I hold all England under my sway—other dominions may be mine likewise."

"Hush ! hush !" gasped a red-capped ruffian, rushing into the cavern. "Where is Mynheer ! with Wolfgang ?"

"Here, mine friend Villiams ; have you seen the teufel ?"

"Worse; there's a cutter manned by the 'jollies' making straight for the Foamy Reef."

"Donner!"

"And I here!" growled Jonathan Wild.

Sheppard and Blueskin drew their swords.

"Where away is the boat?" asked one of the pirates.

"Right abreast of the reef," returned the seaman.

"Then they will land, you can't prevent that," said Jonathan Wild, quickly.

"Iv so, Meister Vild, ve can fight 'em here."

"How's the wind?" asked the thief-taker.

"Fallen, sir," returned the man; "but there is still a heavy sea on."

"Well, I will take command of our garrison," returned Jonathan, coolly. "Do you, Wolfgang, man a boat, and when their attacking party is fairly landed, fall upon the reserve that will be left in charge of their boat; leave the rest to me; if a single man escapes we are lost."

"Vere goot, Meister Vild; it sall be zo; but vere ish Barabbas?"

"Here, cap'en," returned the dwarf, returning from the Dead Hold.

"Come vith me, Barabbas, de cavern ish attack; ve must man de pinnace, and fall on ze boat."

"But let it be done quietly," said Wild. "You must embark on the opposite side of the reef from that on which they will land; leave as many men as you can spare to act under my directions."

"Goot, mynheer," rejoined the pirate.

Wirth Wolfgang selected about a dozen men for his purpose, and with them left the cavern by a secret outlet.

"Now, my men, be steady and keep silence," cried Jonathan to those remaining. "Let as many as possible of these meddling fools enter the cave, and when they are fairly in the trap fall on them, and cut them down to a man; your lives depend upon your courage. Hush! no cheering. Lurk in the hollows of the rockway, and, once more—perfect silence!"

"Aye, aye, Mr. Wild," returned the pirates, starting into ambush.

"Jack and Blueskin, keep by my side."

"All right, governor."

"Quilt Arnold, remove that torch to the sconce nearest the entrance; the light will attract the wasps."

The myrmidon obeyed his master's orders.

"Blueskin, Sheppard, follow me," said Wild.

He retreated into a dark angle of the cavernous chamber.

For a moment all was breathless silence and suspense.

"Hillo, hillo, messmates! this way!" shouted a voice from without. "Here's a light! this is the entrance!"

"Belay, my hearty, not so much row," responded another voice; "the devils will hear ye. We must bash in this bulkhead. Stick together, lads. Dennis, ahoy! keep a bright look-out, or we may be attacked in the rear."

Then came a loud and continuous thundering at the door.

At length the barrier gave way, and with a hearty "hurrah" a large number of blue-jackets poured into the cavern.

"Push on, lads!" cried a tall, handsome fellow, who appeared to be their leader; "it was an oversight not to station a party on the other side of the reef; the rock is burrowed like a rabbit warren; no doubt the blackguards have plenty of outlets there. Push on!"

"Hurrah!"

"Halt! What's that?"

"BANG! bang! bang! boom!" ring the echoes.

"The rock has fallen in!"

"The entrance is blocked!"

"We are trapped!"

"Keep together, men!" cried the officers; "at least we can sell our lives dearly; besides, they dare not oppose us."

"Dare not? Ha! ha!" cried a loud, stern voice. "Fire on 'em, my culls! pistol every man!"

A blinding flash, a long, terrific crackling of pistol shots.

Curses, cries, groans.

The pirates sprung from their ambush.

Cooped within the narrow passage fifty fierce men are madly battling.

The reverberating rocks roar back the thunders of the fray.

Foremost among the assailants of the gallant and devoted king's-men is Jonathan Wild, the peace-officer.

He slashes right and left with his reeking sabre, and encourages his subordinate fellow-ruffians by his wild shouts.

Jack Sheppard and Joe Blueskin second him in the onslaught.

For a quarter of an hour the hand-to-hand conflict rages wildly.

The officer of the invading party falls under Wild's sword.

Cut and thrust! clash and crackle! the place is filled with choking sulphurous smoke!

Deadly flashes of flame flit like lightning streaks through the stifling cloud, and torches toss fiercely in the murky air.

Yells, oaths and horrid blasphemy ring down the shuddering aisles of the pirate's hold.

Jonathan Wild slashes down the last of the king's-men.

A dreadful pause, and a sudden thrilling hush.

Then the pirates utter their stunning huzzas.

Immediately after the fiendish crew pistol or stab the wounded, and the dread work of slaughter is complete.

"Well, done, my men!" pants Jonathan Wild, wiping his blood-smeared sword-blade with his handkerchief. "If your captain, Mynheer Wolfgang, has played his part as promptly and effectively as we, there is nothing left to be desired."

"Bravo!" roared Blueskin. "But, blood and 'ouns! it was hot while it lasted. I've got a devilish ugly scratch over the left listener."

"I wish it had been in the mouse-trap!" growled Jonathan. "Hist! you fool!"

"Patience, governor!"

"Silence, all!"

A creaking noise was heard.

"They are raising the portcullis," laughed Jonathan. "Dam'me, but that's a clever device, worthy of the architect of the Old Bailey. This place would make a fine prison! Wonder that all the jugs are not built in the middle of rivers or on sea islands. Humph! that's an idea worth making a note of"

"I'll warrant I'd find my way out of such a hold as this even." said Jack Sheppard, with a laugh.

"Pish! you're a clever carpenter, Jack, I own," returned his patron, smiling; "but that would be work for a stone-cutter; but look, yon poor devil has dropped his nose-feeder. Give me a pinch of rappee; this infernal smoke has well nigh strangled me."

Jonathan took a sniff, and Jack coolly pocketed the silver snuff-box.

At this moment the creaking noise ceased.

The bleak sea breeze rushed into the rocky tunnel, stirring and dispersing the dense gunpowder fumes.

"Haw! haw! Vos ever de like, Meister Vild, dere ish not von of ze togs escape!" cried Wolfgang, entering with his party; "ve are victors, and ve hafe made everyting safe."

"And the bodies?" asked Jonathan Wild.

"Avast! I'm the quarter-master of graves!" chuckled Barabbas. "I'm the sexton of this island. Shiver my topmast! but this place would be a treasury to the surgeons. Ne'er a 'grabber' (body-snatcher) has a better collection of stiff-'uns. The bodies? They'll never trouble the sail-maker; I'll dispose on 'em."

"But why not throw them into the sea?"

"Why, ye see, Mr. Wild, the fishermen might drag 'em up with their hawling nets."

"Right; I commend your prudence," returned Jonathan Wild. "But it is time I was ashore, the light is dawning."

"I vill zet you ashore in ze little creek to the leeward of the village, muntmeister." said the Dutchman. "Vor our part, ve are going on board de 'Raven,' as mine Englisher crews vill call 'die Raub.' Haw! haw! Barabbas and vive or six men zall ztow avay dese bodies, and den—ve must zay varevell, muntmeister."

Jonathan Wild and his attendants then left the cavern with Wirth Wolfgang and all of his men, excepting Barabbas and a few others, who were left to bury the murdered.

"A pretty night's work, by the living Jingo!" laughed Barabbas. "But the fool who thrusts his hand into the hornet's nest must expect to get strung. Smart fellows some of 'em; and not one so homely but he would have turned with loathing from the dwarf, Barabbas. Ha! better a live dog than a dead lion! Heave ho, my jolly hearts! Haul 'em along to the Dead Hold!"

CHAPTER IX.

ROVING JACK IN THE DEAD HOLD.

OH! the unutterable horror and despair of that awakening in the pit of death and darkness!

The rude shock of his fall roused our hero from his state of insensibility.

He lifted his head. He felt blinded, racked with agonizing pain, sick, giddy, faint, bewildered, half-suffocated with that awful stench of corruption.

He was alone in the deep darkness, but where?

He knew not; his mind was a glass darkened and shattered.

A hideous nightmare! it could not be real! No, he remembered parting from his mother and from Violet; their kisses were still warm upon his lips; he was at home in his own snug bed-room; and all the frightful events which swept before his starting eyes could be nothing but the mad phantasies of some horrid dream.

He must shake off the wretched incubus that lies like a ton of lead upon his breast; he must awake—awake to the cheerful light; start from his hell-charmed slumber; break through the hag-spell that

enthrals his soul with such dark and loathsome conceits.

The boy uttered a wild cry; the echoes laughed like mocking demons.

He raised his hands.

The hard steel clinked, and he found his wrists locked together, and his feet bound!

A twinge of exquisite pain shot through his aching head, and the veins of his brow seemed to swell to bursting.

He felt a clammy, warm trickling down his face.

It was a stream of blood!

By slow and painful degrees he collected his thoughts, and recalled all the dread incidents of that eventful night.

The savage face of the miscreant thief-taker seemed scowling upon him.

This fancy nerved the fierce heart of the fiery young hero to a pitch of desperate anger.

"No, you villain!" shouted Roving Jack, shaking his fettered hands through the darkness as if his enemy were actually before him, "you shall never, never conquer me! It is natural I should feel awed by these horrors; but wounds, nor darkness, nor starvation, nor death itself, can ever frighten me into becoming a cowardly slave and a sneaking thief. Oh! if I had you alone, armed to the teeth as you are, with just my father's pure sword in my hand!"

Jack gnashed his teeth with rage.

"I suppose I must die here," he sighed, bitterly. "That is hard, too—so young! To leave no name behind me! all my bright dreams of glory to perish so soon and miserably! And mother!"

Jack burst into tears.

"And—and Violet, who loves me so dearly; but there—there, I must not think of them, I cannot bear it!"

He drew his sleeve across his eyes.

"Blubbering like a puny girl!" he muttered. "Well, it's a comfort there's no one to see my tears; but for that matter, I don't think I need be ashamed of them, they do not spring from fear. But I must keep my mind steady and quiet, for, since there is no escape for me, I will die calmly and bravely as i can."

Jack dried his eyes and rested his head against the cold, dank wall.

He fixed his thoughts steadily upon holy things, and murmured a prayer.

After he had remained thus for some moments, a vague, wild hope thrilled through his heart.

"Yes, I will try!" he whispered, hoarsely. "Soon I shall be too much exhausted by hunger and pain to make any effort. I know my case is hopeless,; yet at least I will find out what sort of tomb this is and what causes this dreadful sickening stench."

Jack turned over upon his side, and managed to writhe along for a yard or two. He stretched out his arms.

"Ugh!" gasped Jack, recoiling with a violent shudder. "It is—a skeleton!"

He shook convulsively, and it was a long time before he could controul his excited feelings.

"Oh! for one ray of blessed light!" he cried, fervently.

Crawling about he laid his hands more than once on round hard sculls, and sharp fleshless bones.

He uttered a fearful cry, his brow exuded a cold clammy sweat, his limbs quivered like reeds in the wind, his lips became parched, his hair roused, and he felt as if he were losing his senses.

He threw himself down against the wall, and buried his face in his hands, crushed by despair and dismay.

At last he roused himself from his stupor, and glared wildly round him.

The stench grew more and more oppressive and the darkness was intense.

All at once there arose from the floor at some distance from him a greenish lambent flame that flickered faintly, and threw a ghastly light upon the awful scene.

Transfixed with awe, our hero glanced around.

The place was a very charnel of dead bones.

On all sides, and in all attitudes, were strewn the mouldering bodies of hapless crews who had been murdered by the fiendish pirates; many of them were still attired in their naval uniforms, but this only rendered their appearance more grim and horrible.

But whence that spectral light illumining the ghastly scene ?*

It lapped along the floor, and in its fantastic waverings resembled the flare of ignited ether.

At last it settled at the feet of a lank and hideously-grinning skeleton propped against the opposite wall, glinting on the gilt buttons and burnishing the tarnished fringe of the gold epauletts.

Then it spread about the dread relict of miserable humanity and flamed upwards in an unconsuming blaze, playing round the smooth bare skull and creeping into the hollow-eye sockets.

As Jack, with fascinated gaze, eagerly watched this skeleton spectacle, he was surprised to see a packet of letters on its knees which had evidently slipped from the breast-pocket.

Impelled by a strange but irresistible impulse, our hero crawled across the cavern, and hastily snatched the papers.

He opened one of them, a saffron-coloured document, and, in faded writing, read by the grizzly light the following words—

"To the Lady Annabel Tremaine.   "Barfleur, Normandy.
           "August 10th, 1716.

"MY HONOURED LADY,—These to apprise you of the safe arrival here of your ladyship's little daughter, Violet——"

Sudden, blinding darkness blots all.

The corpse-light had expired, and the place was once more buried in the deepest gloom.

Overwhelmed with surprise at the words he had read, suggesting as they did such strange surmises, our hero sat pondering deeply, almost forgetful of the surrounding horrors.

Presently he was startled from his reverie by a *quick, stealthy, rustling.*

RATS !

Tumbling and squeaking among the rattling bones, a legion of these detestable vermin surged round him.

One darted right across his face, inflicting a sharp bite upon his cheek.

---

* It is a well-known fact that dead bodies in advanced stages of decomposition emit certain foul gases, which occasionally appear in a state of combustion, flickering round the corpse in a faint blue flame. This natural phenomenon will account for many of the strange tales told of " corpse candles " and " death lights " seen glimmering around graves in old and dank churchyards. A similar laminate gas is engendered by miry swamps and marshy fens, and is often descried by the belated traveller dancing before him on his dark path as if luring him to follow, and which is considered by some superstitious country folk to be a certain tricksy fire-sprite, called " Will-o'-the-Wisp," or " Jack-o'-Lantern."

Jack shrieked and staggered on to his feet, supporting himself against the wall.

Goaded to a pitch of madness, he snatched up a skull, and sent it clattering along the ground.

Squeak, squeak ! and a terrific scampering.

Jack hurled another skull, and another, and another, till he sank with exhaustion.

He fainted.

How long he had remained in a state of unconsciousness he could not tell, but as his senses returned he felt sore, cold, and his tongue was parched with a burning thirst.

He groaned bitterly, and bowed his aching head upon his breast.

No hope, no deliverance ! and death so slow, so cruelly lingering.

His mind wandered, and he feebly muttered his incoherent prayers.

Now, the darkness seems peopled with dusky but yet visible forms, shapeless, yet living; they surround him, and seem to gloat over his dying agonies.

"I am going mad !" muttered poor Jack, in a hoarse, harsh whisper, as he raised his fettered, swollen hands to his head.

" Ha, ha, ha, ha, ha-a !" the cavern resounds with demoniac laughter.

" *Ha, ha, ha, ha, ha-a !*" roar the echoes.

A mystic blue light dawns in the place.

The skeletons move !

They rear themselves on their gaunt shanks, and clack their bony hands together.

"I am mad, mad !" gasps Jack; "Oh, horror, horror !"

A surging, solemn swell, as of the mighty breakers roaring along a rocky strand is now heard, and to its wild organ-like music they dance—the grim, gaunt skeletons !—they dance slowly and grotesquely at first, and they wave their long, fleshless arms, inviting him to join their awful revelry.

Jack now loses all sense of fear.

He laughs insanely at their grim antics.

Now they whirl round him faster and faster and faster, till he becomes dizzy.

One of them is taller than the rest, and seems to be their leader.

He is mantled in a heavy, black velvet pall, fringed with white lawn.

He pauses in the dance, and, approaching the captive, seems to proffer him assistance.

Jack holds out his chained wrists.

The spectre touches them with the hard tip of his bony finger, and an electric thrill darts through the captive's shrinking veins.

The steel manacles are shattered and clash to the ground like broken glass.

Jack shouts in mad triumph, and then points to his scorching lips, and sues for drink.

The spectre presents a skull into which he has poured some ruby liquid.

Jack takes a greedy draught.

Then, with a horrible scream, he dashes the ghastly chalice to his feet.

His face and hands are smeared with—blood !

" Ha, ha, ha, ha, ha-a !" yell the death spectres, and away they go round again, whirling dizzily, dizzily, deftly, nimbly, tossing up their jointed limbs, and nodding their faceless heads.

A delightful sensation of languid repose now

overpowers the captive, and he stretches himself on the ground.

But what strange spell is on him?

His limbs stiffen rigidly; he cannot move hand or foot; he tries to speak, he finds himself voiceless; then he would close his eyelids, but they refuse their office, and with fixed and glazing eyes he glares helplessly up to the murky vault above him.

Yet he can hear, he can see, he is perfectly conscious, but limb-locked by the wicked, cruel spell; he is dead alive—alive yet dead!

Now the horrid skeletons troop round him.

Their merriment is hushed; they kneel at his side, they wring their hands, and show every sign of grief as friends mourning over the body of a loved one departed.

Some even bend down their lipless gums to his cheek as if to kiss him.

Jack *wills* to shriek his horror, but he cannot even *try* to do so. Such is the potency of the death-charm.

Now there is a deep hush; the skeletons depart, and he is left alone.

After awhile they return and swathe the living corpse in the garments of the grave, and place it upon a bier.

Boom!

The hollow echoes respond solemnly.

Boom, boom!

The passing knell of the living dead!

The bier is raised on the clacking shoulders of the ribbed spectres.

Boom! *boom!*

The cavern rings with a grand organ peal—the dirge of the dead alive!

Boom!

The funeral procession is formed; some of the grizzly skeletons march before, and they scatter fresh flowers that wither to dust ere they reach the ground.

Others of the spectres follow.

The black-mantled leader acts as chief mourner.

Still the enchanted retains perfect consciousness.

A dark grave yawns beneath him.

He is lowered amid the hollow moanings of the skeleton mourners.

Cooped in his narrow cell, still conscious, but dumb and impotent to stir a muscle, the living dead glares up at the black cloud that is descending upon him.

It is *the pall!*

He feels the mazy velvet folds wrap round his spell-bound limbs, he hears the last grand chords of the requiem dying away; then—

DARKNESS! OBLIVION!

CHAPTER X.

ROVING JACK RESCUED FROM THE PIRATES.

ROVING JACK starts to find himself still alone in darkness and bondage.

The manacles still fester in his flesh, but the grizzly band of spectres has vanished, though in close contact with him the miserable remains of the pirates' victims are idly strewn.

His mental and bodily agony is extreme, his feelings of horror are worked up to an intensity scarcely endurable.

"A dream!" groans poor Jack. "Oh, may I sleep no more until I sink into the unbroken slumber of death!"

Dreary dreary silence and darkness!

Hush!

"No, it is fancy, mere fancy!" he raved. "Welcome ten thousand ghastly fiends! Let me endure it all again, but do not let me cheat myself with cruel, deceitful hopes. Hark!"

Very faint and far off came the echoes of a cheery shout.

Jack's heart beats wildly.

He tries to call out, but he is dumbed by excitement and anxiety.

Again that shout, nearer now, and louder.

Then the barking of a dog is heard, and the trampling of feet on the floor of the chamber above.

"Belay, Master Hal," cries a well-known voice; "'taint ne'er a bit o' use seeking further. The pirate devils have murdered the poor, rash lad, or mayhap he was swamped last night in the gale, for the sheathings of my old shallop have been washed up the beach since morning."

"I feel sure we shall find him here, whether he be alive or dead, Mr. Cleats," returned a boyish voice; "and look at Snap: he is whining and sniffing yonder. Hand the torch. A trap! by all that's joyous. We shall find him now."

Jack threw himself upon his knees, clasped his hands, and poured forth a torrent of thanksgivings to Heaven for his providential deliverance.

"Yes, yes, dear Hal, my own true friend, I am here!" he shouted. "Quick! raise the trap, and deliver me from this horrid tomb!"

"Hurrah! hurrah!" cheered old Clem and Hal.

But it was no easy task to raise the ponderous trap, for Barabbas had removed the chain from the pulley in the roof above.

With a hearty good-will, however, they set themselves to work.

Every stroke of the axe, and every scrunch of the iron bar—the instruments they were plying so vigorously—were heavenly music in Jack's ears.

At length the ponderous platform was raised.

The first to spring down into the vault was Snap, our hero's faithful terrier.

The good dog leaped upon his master, whining and fawning, and frantically caressing him.

Jack fairly hugged the faithful creature to his heart.

"Steady, a bit, Master Hal; it's too deep to jump," cried old Clem. "Let's reeve this hawser through yonder dead-eye, and then I can let you down into the hold like a barrel of salt junk. Heave-ho! Hold taut, my cheery!"

Hal put a cutlass between his teeth, clutched the torch in his right hand, wove his legs round the rope, and shot straight down into the vault.

He leaped on to the ground, and then, raising the torch, he stared around him in boundless dismay, and uttered a loud cry.

Jack seized his trembling hands, and thanked him fervently.

"Horrible!" gasped Hal, looking round him. "What you must have suffered here, my poor Jack!"

"That can never be told, Hal," returned our hero, solemnly; "but I praise the All-merciful for this unexpected, undeserved deliverance."

Old Clem Cleats, who had also scrambled down into the vault, gave a yell of terror at beholding the ghastly spectacle.

"My jib! if this ain't a scene as would freeze the witals of a wampire!" he whispered, faintly. "This is cert'n'y a case for the coroner. Now, Master Jack, are ye satisfied that the Reef is haunted?"

"Aye," returned our hero, with a sickly smile. "But, dear Hal, do help me out of these hand-cuffs; they eat into my flesh—and—please ask me no questions yet. Get me away as quickly as you can, for I am faint, very faint."

Hal cut the cords that bound Jack's legs, and setting to work with a large iron nail, contrived to force off the hand-cuffs.

The revulsion of the blood from his tortured wrists caused Jack to utter a half-suppressed cry of anguish, and he dropped at Hal's feet, insensible!

Old Clem kneeled by his side, and, tenderly raising his head, poured some drops of brandy upon his lips.

Jack opened his large dark eyes and smiled radiantly.

He clutched his young comrade's hand.

"Is it day or night without, Hal?" he asked, faintly.

"Evening, Jack."

"Then I have been prisoned here for forty-eight hours!" he sighed. "Oh, what ages of agony and grief may be compressed into that short time!"

He was now sufficiently recovered to stand.

"Before we leave this horrible place, secure those papers," said Jack, pointing to the packet which had fallen from the skeleton. "Lend me a hand to escape from this grave; let me once more breathe the pure air, and I shall be myself again."

Old Clem and Hal assisted our hero to mount through the trap.

They followed him close, and reached the cell above the "Dead Hold."

"How did you manage to find this place?" asked Jack.

"We entered through yonder hole in the wall," replied Hal, pointing to a kind of trap-door near the roof. "Beyond it there is a long tunnel, which leads to a cave on the island."

"Did you and Mr. Cleats come alone?"

"Oh, no, Master Jack," rejoined old Clem, "there's a whole boat's crew of your school-fellows on the reef."

"Why, Jack, you see that as soon as I heard the news of your sudden and strange disappearance from home, I went to your house," said Hal. "I found your poor mother plunged in deep distress at your absence. She showed me the window by which you had taken flight, and the ladder you had made with the sheets and blankets; she told me, besides, that you had taken away your father's sword and night-glass."

"Yes," said Jack, bitterly, "I have lost both! It was useless to resist the villains; I was forced to surrender up my father's sword, but I may recover it yet."

"Your mother went on to speak of Mr. Cleats's visit, and of his strange adventure at the Foamy Reef," continued Hal, "and I felt convinced that you must have seen the light on the distant rocks, and gone off incontinently in search of the phantoms."

"So I did—the more fool I," was Jack's cool rejoinder.

"Remembering our brush with the pirate Barabbas, and sharing your suspicions that the phantoms of the reef were in reality pirates, I held a council with our schoolmates, Frank Harley, Ned Ross, Will Ryan, Bert Atherstone, Ben Bouncer, and half-a-dozen others, and a resolution was carried unanimously that we should arm ourselves, take a boat, and row over to the reef in quest of you."

"Hurrah!" shouted Jack, buoyantly, "my brave comrades! With a band of such heroes I might hunt down every ruffianly pirate on the high seas! Go on with your story, dear Hal."

"Just as we were putting off in the boat, Mr. Cleats came along, and tried to dissuade us from our purpose; but seeing that we were determined to carry it out, he kindly offered to go with us, and of course we were delighted to accept his valuable assistance."

"Belay," grunted the fisherman, "I promised the old Dominie that I'd capture the truant. I wouldn't be in your skin for a trifle; there's a pretty rod in pickle for ye, I can tell ye that, Master Jack."

Jack laughed.

"I think I have suffered punishment enough already for my folly," returned our hero.

"When we reached the reef," continued Hal, "we broke up into parties of two or three, and scoured the island in search of you. Mr. Cleats and I, led on by your faithful little Snap, discovered a hole in the rocks screened by some old sheathing boards; we forced an entrance, but not without great trouble, worked our way through a narrow tunnel, and at last reached the door, you see, and, bursting it open, found ourselves in this strange place."

"Well," said Jack, "of course we must acquaint the authorities with the strange discovery we have made, and set the officers of the law on the track of these bloodthirsty, buccaneering villains; and let me tell you, my hearties, there is a cavern in the reef, if we can but find it—for it was so dark when I was cast ashore, and I was so exhausted that I scarce know in what part of the island I took shelter. There is a treasure cave, I say, that contains sufficient plunder for the Forty Thieves to retire on; but let us get into the fresh air, my faintness is returning, and I have seen enough of this chamber of horrors."

"My jib, Master Jack," gasped old Clem, "I should think you have had a lesson for life; arter the terrific ewents of the last few days, you orter be satisfied with your adwentures, and moor in quiet waters for the rest of your nat'ral life."

"Not yet," answered Roving Jack, grinding his teeth, and speaking fiercely; "when I have hanged Jonathan Wild, hunted down the Phantom Pirate and his devilish crew, restored my foster sister Violet to her home and fortune——"

"And set the sea afire!" rejoined old Clem, impatiently.

Jack's cheek reddened, and he lowered his eyes.

"I talk like a braggart," said he; "but, hark! our comrades are shouting for you, Hal; let us join them."

Hal mounted on old Clem's shoulders, and having entered the narrow passage, which he has himself already described, assisted Jack to climb up after him.

Old Clem followed more nimbly than could have been expected from one of his years and weight.

They passed along the narrow and low-browed tunnel; stooping low, and not escaping an occasional bump against the various sharp corners of the rock, they reached the entrance, and issuing forth, found themselves on a narrow rock-way that wound down the side of the crag; immediately before them was a large mass of rock, which completely concealed them from their school-mates, who were clustered on the beach below, and were shouting for Hal, and protesting that further search for Jack would be quite useless.

Our hero leaped upon the rock.

His sudden and startling appearance was greeted by the crowd of boys below with a stirring cheer.

"He is saved! he is saved! Roving Jack for ever! Hurrah!"

Jack ran down the rock, and, rushing into the midst of the group, heartily shook hands with his affectionate and brave young comrades, and thanked them warmly for their kindness and unselfishness.

"But did you really come to the reef on purpose to outface the ghosts, Jack?" asked Frank Harley, eagerly.

"Aye, for what else?" laughed Jack; "but I have no cause to be proud of my foolhardiness, for what would have been my fate if you had not come to my rescue?"

"You would have perished in the cave, I suppose," said Will Ryan.

"Yes; I was thrown down a dark shaft," returned Jack, drawing a deep breath, "bound, gashed, and insensible, and left to die amid the dead bodies of former victims of the fiendish gang."

The boys gave a shout of consternation.

"But have the pirates left the island?" asked Ned Ross, glancing round nervously.

"Aye, that's certain, or you would not have remained on it so long without being attacked," said our hero.

"Sit down, Jack, and take a rest before we start," rejoined Bert Atherstone, the youngest of the party, a slight-built, delicate-looking, but supremely handsome little fellow; "sit down, and tell us your adventures."

"Aye, do, Jack," blustered Ben Bouncer, "and then I'll entertain the company by adding an account of a similar scrape I got into myself. I I suppose you know that when sailing round the coast in my uncle's brigantine I was taken prisoner by a gang of pirates, much in the same way as you were, Jack. All to be set down to my own daredevildom, I must own."

"And were your pirates phantoms?" asked Jack, smiling.

"No; there you have the best of me. Except a sort of hobgoblin I once met, and a glimpse I caught, one winter night, of old Horney, I never saw but two real ghosts in my life. The first was the headless spirit of poor Mrs. Lathers, that was murdered by her wicked husband, the village barber; in one hand she held her severed head, in the other the razor with which the fearful crime was perpetrated. The second apparition——. Oh, laugh on, if you think there's anything to laugh at in such horrible occurrences. Now I won't tell you another word of this interesting and truthful story. But to return to the pirates."

"How many of them were there, Ben?"

"A whole fleet, Jack, I do assure ye; about fifty sail, I should think, perhaps more, but I hate to exaggerate. Well, my sons, these wretches were, as Jack says, not phantoms, certainly, but what then? They were a deuced deal worse — cannibals!"

"Stopper all, Ben Bouncer; stash your lying yarns!" shouted his school-fellows, who immediately set upon him with a rush, bonneted him, and, rolling him over in the sand, pommelled him into silence.

Order being restored, our hero electrified his hearers by the thrilling account he gave of his perils in the pirates' cave.

"And you saw Jonathan Wild?" they all cried, in astonishment.

"Aye! and I shall meet him again in open day, I trust," said our hero, bitterly.

"And Jack Sheppard?"

"Aye! the fellow that broke out of the New Prison some months ago."

"What was he like? Very handsome and dashing, wasn't he?"

"Well, there was a look of shrewdness, daring and good-humour in his pale countenance, but after all he appeared what he is, a sly, idle, dissolute scamp, a born thief! altogether to be despised by every boy who loves real manliness!"

"But Blueskin?"

"The darkest, most evil, and savage-looking ruffian that ever a trusty house-dog barked at! a cut-throat, a drunkard, a bully, a thief! So much for Joe Blake, the Blueskin!"

"But I always thought highwaymen were such slashing fellows!" cried little Bert, with enthusiasm.

"So did I," replied Roving Jack, "until I gave up reading bad, false books, and studied the *real* lives and deeds of such murderous, skulking villains; until I reflected on the baseness and unmanliness of robbing paltry money from others. Selling honour and self-respect for a watch or a bundle of notes! Would you do it? Would I? Never! Ugh! and to call such fellows heroes! Oh, how I hate such humbug!"

"So did I, Jack," responded Hal; "I should like to clear the world of such rogues; they are like vermin in a granary, and ought to be killed off with as little mercy as rats are burned."

"Yes," cried our hero, "the roads are not safe for honest men to walk; women and children are not secure from insult and brutality; the merchant vessels on the high seas are liable to be run down, plundered, burnt to the water's edge, their honest crews murdered, perhaps tortured to death, and the villains who are the cause of all this trouble and distress are to be pictured in dashing clothes and ticketed up as heroes. Ain't it rascally?"

"It is Jack, it is!" responded Hal, right heartily. "But boys are not such fools as they were; there are those who have toiled and suffered in the work of convincing them of the utter nonsense of picturing a thief as a hero; and, now we have the real hero in the right place, we shall have all the fun and sensation of robber-hunting; we shall have all that is terrific and exciting—fire, slaughter, tempest and passion; but, at least, our hero will be noble and kind and honest, and his name shall be Roving Jack!"

"Hip, hurrah! three cheers for our hero! three

cheers for Roving Jack !" shouted the boys, with frantic glee.

"I thank you from my heart, dear, brave comrades !" cried their boy leader, with a proud and happy smile. "Let me ask you to give a cheer for my brave Boy Band of ROBBER-HUNTERS !"

"Hurrah for Roving Jack and his Robber-hunters ! Hurrah !" shouted the boys, tossing up their caps, and dancing about in the excess of their joyous enthusiasm.

"Avast heaving, you young monkeys !" interposed old Clem Cleats. "We must get aboard; it's time we were steering for home."

"First, let us try to find the store-house of the cursed buccaneers," said Jack, who had now quite recovered his spirits, though he still looked very pale and haggard. "Follow me, comrades !"

"To the death, Roving Jack !" was the hearty response.

He led the way along the rugged shore, and, after searching several of the hollows in the reef, came at last to the cave through which he had entered the pirates' hold.

After removing the loose stones, as he had done before on the occasion of his first visit to the cavern, he crept down the rude ladder into the shaft surrounded by heavy doors.

Hal had re-lighted the torch, and kept close by our hero's side.

After much exertion, and with the assistance of the old fisherman, the young pirate-hunter entered the long corridor, at the end of which they found the trap-hatch.

It was some time before they could raise it.

Many of the boys looked down into the robber's den with paling cheeks, and drew back in alarm; but, re-assured by the dauntless manner of their heroic young leader, they followed him down the hatchway.

When they found themselves in the huge cavern, surrounded on all sides by the spoils of so many splendid but fated vessels, the boys looked about them in the utmost bewilderment.

"It was here that Jonathan Wild offered to take me under his protection," said Jack, bitterly; "'twas here I stood like a lamb in the wolf's lair; it was here that Jack Sheppard saved my life—a good turn, which I will requite if ever I should have it in my power so to do. I was tempted, but Heaven gave me strength to pass through my fiery trial; I looked on all these riches, and I thought to myself, 'Will all these ill-gotten treasures purchase one hour of true peace to a guilty conscience ?' But, come, I will take you to the horrid tomb from which I was rescued by kind Mr. Cleats and my true chum, Hal Hetherington."

With this, Jack was about to lead his astonished comrades to the door at the end of the cavern, through which, as he rightly judged, he had been dragged while insensible by the fiendish wretch Barabbas.

At the instant old Clem Cleats came bounding down the hatchway.

"Avast there, Master Jack ! Quick ! quick ! we must clap on all sail, and sheer off these shoals," he panted. "Shiver my topmost, if that black-hulled, rakish-rigged schooner isn't in the offing; she's making for the reef, and flying along close by the wind no end o' knots an hour."

"Away, then !" cried Jack. "If they catch us here, they'll murder every mother's son of us, and we're no match for them now. Our time may

come, my lads; but now we must brush if we would save our precious lives."

The boys scampered up the hatchway, rushed along the tunnel, bounded out of the cave, and paused not till they stood upon the beach.

Turning their eyes towards the horizon, they beheld the tall, slant-masted, lateen-rigged schooner bearing up as swift as a flying swallow.

"Aboard !" roared old Clem. "Run, run, lads ! The boats are in yonder creek. Tumble in with a will, boys, or it will be too late !"

The boys raced to the spot where the boats were moored.

They rushed up to the middle in water, and scrambled in, helter-skelter.

More than one of them, in their hurry, got tripped over the gunwales, and caught a fine ducking.

"Trim the boat, you young dogs !" shouted old Clem, beside himself with consternation. "She'll capsize, you little devilskins !"

"Steady, boys, steady !" cried Jack, in the tones of a born commander.

The boats were cast off.

The boys crowded on the thwarts, seized the oars, and rowed away right lustily.

"Pull together !" cried Jack; "no flurrying ! Courage and quietness, and all will be well !"

"Hurrah !" shouted the young heroes, when they were fairly out to sea.

"The cursed buccaneering hounds will see us, will find that their store-house has been rummaged," cried Jack, passionately, "and they will either ship off the best part of their plunder, or destroy it, rather than it should fall into the hands of the authorities. Never mind, our turn will come."

"Stopper all, you young rascal !" roared old Clem, "and think yourself lucky that you're not now lying five fathoms down, with a slit in your throat. You'll make your mates as mad as yourself. Oh, my little cheery, won't I come and see you toby-tickled to-morrow ? If you live much longer, and don't mend, there won't be a birch broom to be bought for love nor money ! SIT DOWN ! you young dare-devil, and don't glare so. You give me shivering doldrums."

"Look !" cried Jack, quite regardless of the old man's anger in his own intense excitement, "the scoundrels have lowered a boat ! Oh, couldn't we fight 'em ?"

"Oh, lor, no, Jack," cried Ben Bouncer. "Don't mention it. I ain't no coward, ye know—I once had a hand-to-hand combat with two or three dozen of the ruffs—but, 'pon my word, I ain't in a fightin' humour. Sit down !"

The pirate's boat was gaining on them fast.

"Pull away, lads, pull away ! or you'll miss your mess, as sure as Sunday dumplings !" cried Clem, in great alarm.

Suddenly a puff of white smoke jetted from the dark hull of the distant vessel.

A hollow "boom" rolled along the face of the waters, and a heavy shot came spanking past, close to our hero's head.

His comrades uttered a shriek.

Not so Roving Jack; he laughed excitedly.

"Hal, did I bob my head ?" he asked, chuckling.

"No, Jack," returned the other, with forced calmness.

"Think I did, though, just a bit. Phew !"

Another puff of white smoke, a flash of flame, and

BARABBAS SETS FIRE TO THE YOUNG WIFE'S HOME. *See No. 5.*

A heavy pounder came whizzing past the stern of the boat, and sank to larboard in a fountain of sparkling spray.

"Capital!" cried Roving Jack. "Here's luck, and a fine lesson. We shall learn how to stand fire! Hurrah! I *can't* fear the villains, and I *won't*. Death to all bloody buccaneers! Hurrah!"

CHAPTER XI.

OW ROVING JACK WON BACK HIS FATHER'S SWORD.

THE position of the boyish crews now became very critical.

No. 4.

The ship kept up a steady fire.

The pirate boat was approaching nearer and nearer.

It was a wild and exciting scene to the boys.

The sea was comparatively calm; the western horizon glowed rich red, and the sea shimmered cold silver; a few intensely brilliant points glittered in the darkening zenith.

Astern rose the romantic peaks of the dark and haunted reef—astern lay the land, the white cliffs softly blushing with the last roseate tinge of the departing sunbeams.

The black, wolfish-looking pirate craft was creeping down upon them—the pirate boat was gaining upon them at every stroke of the oars.

The short, squat, but powerful form of the hideous Barabbas was clearly discernible.

He stood erect in the stern-sheets, and waved a sword that flashed in the fading sun-glow.

Jack seized a glass which old Cleats had let fall on the gratings.

He looked through it intently, and then lowered it with a gasp of rage.

"Yes; it is my father's sword that the scoundrel wields!" he cried, fiercely. "I was forced to surrender it tamely, but I will win it back. What do ye say, comrades?" he added, appealing to the rest. "You have promised to be pirate-hunters; well, now is your chance for proving your courage and sincerity. We have two boats, they have but one; we are fifteen, and they but ten; you are armed with cutlasses and clubs, Mr. Cleats has a pistol, let's overhaul the pirate fiends, and sweep them off the sea; we can do it! When we come to close quarters the crew of the schooner will be afraid to fire, lest they should strike their own boat, so ye see that the bold stroke is the safest one, for they are better oarsmen than we, and will be alongside in the twinkling of a handspike."

"Belay, you cantankerous young scaramouch!" shouted old Clem, aghast with anger and dismay; "you will destroy us all; if you don't haul in your jawing tackle I'll pitch you into the sea!"

"If you do I can swim, Mr. Cleats, and I'll board 'em alone, for I'll have my father's sword, if it costs me my life!" cried Jack, pushing him aside, and seizing the tiller.

The boat swayed round.

Jack's young comrades, inspired by his lion-like daring, cheered loudly, and pulled hard to meet the pirate boat.

The men aboard the schooner seemed to think that the boys designed to surrender at discretion, and ceased firing.

"Ahoy! boat ahoy!" cried Barabbas, as the boats met together. "I thought we should soon bring you to your senses! Lay to, seize ye, or I'll serve ye as I served that young gallows bird—Roving Jack!"

Our hero sprang up in the boat, cutlass in hand.

"Ha! Master Barabbas!" he shouted, mockingly. "I'll be sworn when you threw me down the dead hold you little thought to see me again so soon! I can play the ghost as well as you. I have risen from the grave to confront ye! I was saved by these brave comrades; and we mean to take vengeance for the murdered victims that lie buried in yonder bloody den!"

"Ten thousand devils!"

"No such thing," laughed our hero; "you are but ten, and, by Heaven, there shall be ten villains the fewer in the world before an hour passes! Run them down, boys! Hurrah!"

Barabbas uttered a savage oath, and fired his pistol at our hero, but missed him.

"Cut 'em to pieces, my mates! Squelch the young adders!" roared Barabbas. "If one of them escapes our worst secrets will get blown! Slice 'em into mince-meat! Port! Smash your eyes! The boys are mad! and we shall be capsized! Now! now, Roving Jack!"

Crash! the keel of the fisherman's heavy boat struck against the lighter craft manned by the pirates.

At the instant that his boat ran astern of the enemy's, Jack leaped upon Barabbas.

The pirates had enough to do to save themselves from drowning by clinging to the gunwales of the boat.

The boys struck at them with their cutlasses and clubs, and fired at them with old Clem's pistols.

The old fisherman himself seeing that it was useless to attempt to resist our hero's influence with the boys, resigned himself to circumstances, and did good service by steering with admirable skill and care.

Jack and Barabbas struggled fiercely for the sword, which the latter was making frantic efforts to wrest from our hero, who had secured it after a fierce wrestle.

The pirate boat capsized; and Jack and Barabbas were seen struggling in the waves.

Old Clem turned the boat, and bade his young crew pull for their lives, as another boat was being lowered from the schooner.

Away went the little vessel, shooting like a ploughshare through the furrowing brine.

Roving Jack swam up with the sword he had won so bravely clenched in his teeth!

His comrades helped him over the side, and, for a moment resting on their oars, made the air ring with a deafening hurrah!

CHAPTER XII.
THE "KING'S HEAD."

JONATHAN WILD, Jack Sheppard, Blueskin and the rest of the thief-taker's gang, upon being set ashore by the pirate, Wirth Wolfgang, mounted their horses, which had been tethered in a cave by the shore, and at once took the road to London.

They rode hard all day, and about five o'clock in the afternoon reached an old and dilapidated roadside inn, at the door of which they drew rein.

They dismounted beneath the swinging signboard, which was emblazoned with the royal arms on one side, and on the other embellished with a highly-coloured portrait of His Majesty Charles the Second, of blessed memory.

The landlord, a spare, weazened old fellow, with little of the "Boniface" in his appearance, received the guests on the door-step.

"Welcome, Mr. Wild," he mumbled, starting, and turning pale as he recognised the thief-taker. "It's long since you honoured the 'King's Head' by a visit."

"Yes; nor should I have called here now but that I have a little matter of business to settle with you, Master Ridge."

"Indeed?" said the landlord, humbly. "You have not received despatches from me lately; but I have been ill, Mr. Wild, very ill, truly, sir. I'm a martyr to the gout, ye see; and that little affair about the smuggling pedlar, I am not responsible for that; I did not peach; he was betrayed by one of his pals. I couldn't save him."

"Humph! it will be well for you if you can satisfy me upon that point, Master Ridge," rejoined Wild, sternly. "But look to the horses, and let me have a cup of canary."

A short, cunning-eyed, red-headed fellow, seated at the door smoking a long pipe, now rose and slunk into the house.

Passing along the sanded passage, he opened the door of the tap-room.

Four ruffianly fellows, flashily-dressed in riding coats, top-boots and laced three-cornered hats, and heavily-armed, were noisily carousing.

"Hist! Warehawks!" cried the tapster, in a husky whisper, as he laid his finger on his lips.

"Blood an' 'ouns! trapped!" shouted the men, starting to their feet, and seizing their fire-arms. "Is it the harming beaks?"*

* Police-office

"Not the county blokes," grinned the tapster.

"Who is it, then?"

The fellow dropped his voice to a thrilling whisper—

"*Jonathan Wild!*"

"S'blood! and I'm in his black books," growled one.

"And I too, by the living Jingo!" responded another.

"He has sworn to bring me to the crap before the sessions are over," gasped a third.

"Then you may as well make your will at once, for, depend on't, he'll keep his word," said the tapster, with a leer.

"Let us escape by the door at the back," suggested the fourth man.

"No; Quilt Arnold and the Jew, old Abraham Mendez, are there, looking after the horses; but hark ye, my ben culls, for a handful of 'beans' I'll tell ye how it may be managed," said the tapster, with a grin.

One of the highwaymen—for such they were—tossed the fellow a purse.

"Quick, Barney!" said the robbers, in one breath. "That's his wolf's growl!"

The man chuckled, tossed up the purse, caught it deftly, and, slipping it into his pocket, stalked to the end of the room and touched a steel spring in the wall; a sliding panel shot down, and disclosed a secret passage.

"In with ye!" whispered the tapster, quickly, "and lie close, if you value your necks!"

The fellows tumbled one after another into the hiding-place, and Barney closed the panel.

He then stirred the fire and bustled about the room, dusting, removing tankards and glasses, and carelessly humming some flash song.

Wild and his companions entered.

They seated themselves, and, calling for bowls of punch, lighted long pipes, and puffed such dense clouds of tobacco smoke that it became a difficult matter to distinguish faces.

The rafters rang with their boisterous shouts of laughter and merriment.

"I tell you, sirrah, you have deceived me!" cried Jonathan Wild, who was conversing apart with the landlord.

"'Fore God, I have not, Mr. Wild," protested the trembling innkeeper.

"Ye lie!" roared Jonathan Wild, stamping his foot. "I say you have deceived me."

The rest of the company assembled stared at the bullying tyrant and the abject victim of his abuse with gloomy looks.

"In what way, Mr. Wild, can I have betrayed your confidence?" asked the landlord, submissively.

"Sirrah, is it nothing that a new gang of bridle culls infest the king's high roads, that they frequent this booze-ken? And yet you have never advertized me of the fact."

"I thought, Mr. Wild, that they were gentlemen of your troops—some of your heavy cavalry, you know. One of them told me that you had provided him with barkers* and dogs' meat†—in fact, had equipped him for the high toby scout.‡ I thought it was all right."

"It is false, you dog!" growled Jonathan Wild. "Did they give you the 'parole?' Did they produce their licence?"

---

* Pistols.   † Horse.   ‡ Highway robbery.

"Why, no; for that matter, Mr. Wild, I took their word for the truth of what they told me," stammered Ridge.

"Enough; I see through your treachery. You have done for yourself, my ben cove—you have broken your contract, and must take the consequences. Seize him, Quilt and Abraham!" thundered the arch-villain. "Clap on the darbies. I arrest him as the accomplice of highway robbers!"

Ridge dropped on his knees in an agony of fright.

The red-bearded, withered old Jew, and the burly ruffian, Quilt Arnold, seized him roughly by the collar.

"Mercy! mercy!" shrieked the poor wretch. "Indeed I am innocent, Mr. Wild! Spare me this once! I'll peach on the rascals! I'll trap 'em for you if you will pardon me this time!"

"Humph!" said Jonathan, producing a pen and ink-horn, and seating himself at a table, "I must have the name and description of every member of this gang who have dared to set my authority at defiance. If you deceive me in the least particular, you shall swing, if there's not another rogue left unhung in England?"*

The thief-taker drew out a large pocket-book, and prepared to take notes.

"A proclamation is about to be issued," said he; "a reward of £200 will be offered for the apprehension of the leader of this gang, of which, had you acted square, you should have pocketed one-third. As the case stands, you may esteem yourself fortunate if you escape punishment."

"Give me time, Mr. Wild, and I'll trap 'em for you," mumbled the luckless innkeeper. "My life on it!"

"I accept the offer," said Jonathan, with a malignant glare. "I will give you one month, and if, within that time, they are not in my hands, I will be on your track, and if you escape me I'll forgive you."

"Agreed, Mr. Wild."

"Their captain's name?"

"DICK TURPIN."

"Ha! I thought as much," said Jonathan, writing. "Describe the fellow."

"He is about thirty," returned the informer, "by trade a butcher, about five feet nine inches high, brown complexion, very much marked with the small-pox, his cheek bones broad, his face thinner towards the bottom, his visage short, pretty upright, and broad about the shoulders."†

"That will do, Mr. Ridge," said Jonathan, stopping to mend his pen. "I will pay you this compliment—you are a shrewd observer," he added, with a grim smile. "But now, proceed—the names of his accomplices?"

"'Pon my word, Mr. Wild, I know but three or four of them. He has others, of course, for he was connected with a gang of gipsies and poachers who infested Epping Forest."

"I am aware of the fact," said Jonathan, coldly. "Give me the names of such of his accomplices as you are acquainted with."

---

* This was a favourite expression of Jonathan Wild's.

† This description of the famous highwayman, Dick Turpin, is an accurate copy from the king's proclamation. What a striking contrast it presents to the romantic, fascinating, fancy portrait of this cruel and brutal ruffian as it has been painted by certain writers of pernicious romances!

"Well, first there's a dashing fellow whom they call the 'gentleman highwayman.'"

"Ha! Tom King!"

"Yes, sir."

"I know the rascal. And the others?"

"Let me see, there's Fielder, Rose, Greg——"

He broke off suddenly, warned by a rapid signal made by Barney the tapster, who stood behind Jack Sheppard.

"Eh? Who are they? *Fielder, Rose,* and who else?" asked Jonathan, as he wrote down the names.

"And—and Gregory," mumbled the innkeeper.

"Curse ye! can't ye speak up?" shouted Wild, in a tone of ferocity. "What name?"

"Gregory," said Ridge, in a louder voice.

"*Gregory?*" responded Wild, 'pricking' it down. "Any more?"

"Yes; there's Wheeler, Walker and Bush."*

"Good; I know them all. And so the rogues have dared to set me at defiance? Ha! ha! and the fools thought to escape me! Egregious presumption! And now to horse, my men; we must be on our road to London, and beware, Master Ridge, how you attempt to play the fool with me hereafter. If these fellows are not in my power within the ensuing month, you shall pay forfeit for them with—your life! I am a man of my word; so, beware, sirrah! Now, lads, to horse!"

Barney led the way to the stable.

When they had departed Ridge slunk off towards the door.

Just as he was passing the threshold, however, the panel in the wall was thrown down, and the highwaymen sprang out.

In an instant old Ridge was seized from behind.

A pair of hard, horny hands were clapped over his mouth, and he was dragged backwards.

"Hist! they are not gone!" muttered one of the ruffians, in a hoarse whisper. "Hold him tight, Fielder; we'll teach the cursed spy to play booty with a vengeance!"

The clatter of the horses' hoofs was now heard without, gradually receding in the distance.

When they had quite died out, the ruffians hurled the landlord against the wall, and, drawing their swords and pistols with threatening gestures and a torrent of foul execrations, surrounded him.

"Gentlemen, it was not my fault," panted Ridge, ducking his head to avoid the blow aimed at him by the exasperated robbers. "What could I do? You know I'm wholly in Wild's power. I might have betrayed you; have shown him your hiding-place, but I spared you at the risk of my own life. Consider that."

"Liar!" shouted one of the thieves; "he thought we had left the house."

"Down with the infernal peach!" roared another.

He upraised a heavy bludgeon, and with a fearful blow struck the unfortunate innkeeper senseless to the ground.

"Hark! Barney comes," cried Fielder.

"We'll settle him too," rejoined Rose.

"No, no, he's jannock. He kept faith with us," Bush interposed, seizing Fielder's hand, for he had levelled his pistol at the door.

"Shove the cursed peach in the hole in the wall," cried Walker, "and shut up the panel."

Acting upon this suggestion, the ruffians flung the inanimate body of the innkeeper into the dark gap, and slid up the panel.

Barney entered.

"Where's the governor?" he asked.

"Left by the front entrance," said Fielder.

"Whither has he gone, then?" asked the man, suspiciously.

"Stash your fool's questions," returned Rose. "Bring us a tankard of hucklemybuff. Go with him, Fielder; I suspect treason."

Barney stared at the robbers, and felt cowed by their sullen looks.

They fingered their knives and pistols, and scowled at him with evil glances.

Barney sneaked out of the room.

Fielder and Bush followed him.

The rest seated themselves at the table with moody looks.

"We must begone," said Gregory. "Wild may return—he may receive information that we are here."

"No," returned Walker; "we must stay for the captain."

"When do you expect him?"

"On the instant."

"Is he alone?"

"No, he brings his new pal with him—Tom King."

Barney now entered the room with tankards in his hands.

The men sternly bade him remain in the room.

They re-lighted their pipes, and clustering together at one of the tables, conversed in low, anxious whispers.

Suddenly a clattering of hoofs was heard.

The men started up, and seized their weapons.

Then firm, manly steps were heard in the passage, and a deep, mellow voice trolled out,

> "Oh, Claude du Val was a gallant wight,
> And the ladies dub him their own true knight,
>   With his fal-lal-lal-lal-la!"

"All's well, my ben culls," cried Fielder; "it's Turpin and Tom King!"

CHAPTER XIII.

DICK TURPIN AND TOM KING.

TOM KING, a handsome, gentlemanly-looking fellow, pushed open the door of the tap-room, and was greeted with a shout of welcome by his fellow-robbers.

"Ben brightmans,* my ben culls," he cried, in a cheery voice, shaking hands all round. "What's the best news?"

"Blasted bad, Tom," growled Fielder.

---

* All these names are genuine. The main incidents in the lives of Jack Sheppard and Dick Turpin as given in this history will be drawn from the most authentic accounts. Our readers will be surprised at the contrast existing between their *real* characters and the ideal rendering of their "gallant" deeds by the romancers. Tom King seems to have been a little less inhuman than the rest. It is our purpose to "nothing extenuate nothing set down in malice."

---

* Good morning.

"What, all amort? Look, here's something will make your eyes sparkle and your hearts jump—

"'Jingle, jingle, pleasant music,
Clinking golden in mine ear!'

Ha, ha! I must say that I and Dick don't scout the pad for nothing. We stopped the royal mail last night, and won a royal ransom. Fingers off, you villains!"

With a ringing, manly laugh, Tom King piled a heap of jewels, watches, and money upon the table.

"Bravo, Tom!" chorused the party.

"And what's the news?" asked the highwayman, throwing himself wearily into a chair. "Heigho! I have set the saddle till my legs are become as stiff as a rusty pair of tongs. Pass over the tankard."

He took a deep draught of the strong drink, and then turned a merry glance on the serious faces of his companions.

"Dam'me! you look as if you were listening to the toll of St. Sepulchre. What's the matter?"

"Jonathan Wild has been here."

"The devil!"

"Yes; and the famous cracksman, Jack Sheppard, and the Blueskin—his right hand and his left."

"Poor rogues!" said Tom, lightly tapping his top-boots with his riding-whip; "the treacherous hound will hang them sooner or later."

"And he has sworn to hang us too," returned Walker, "like onions, in one string."

"He'll never hang me," laughed Tom.

"How do you know that?" growled Rose.

"Kismet! It's fate, my covey," returned the highwayman. "Hark'ee; when Jonathan Wild was a buckle-maker, and wooed Mary Milliner, he joined the gips, and one of the dimber blowens of the tribe taught me this prophecy. Let me think—ah! that's it :—

"The Romany dell,"
Said she to me;
"By the power of the spell
Thy doom I see."
Quoth I, "Shall I leap from the leafless tree?"
"That is not in destiny, Tom," quoth she.
"Queer fate, we can't, my dimber dell
So fearless my fortune, prithee, tell.
How shall my reckless life have end?"
"You'll die by the hand of a trusty friend!"
Quoth she—quoth she.

Ha! ha! ha! there's comfort in that."

"Rather cold comfort, Tom," said Fielder.

"I don't know," rejoined King. "Remember the old epitaph—

"'Die, must we all?
We must all die!
Must we all die?
Die we all must!'

There's no queering that, my boys! Why, then, fancy an old—an aged toby man—an old criminal!

"'Let me die in the glow of my manhood's prime,
For why should I live till the winter-time?
When the hot blood chills, and the frost flakes rest
On my cold worn head, in my ice-cold breast."

No, no; a 'short cruise and a merry one,' as the pirate would say."

But Tom's hollow laugh rung with the echoes of subdued despair.

"S'blood, my boys! Have you seen the captain's new trotter?"

"No, Tom."

"Her name was Whitestockings, the famous racer. Dick borrowed her of Mr. Major, and means to call her Black Bess, for she has not a white hair in her now, though her fetlocks were white when she was foaled."

The men rose, and followed Tom King to the stables, beckoning Barney to accompany them.

They found Dick Turpin grooming a splendid black courser.

As his physique has been already fully described it is unnecessary to enter into further details.

It may be mentioned, however, that he was richly dressed, and, despite his ugly, villanous countenance, had a manly and dashing exterior.

"Good morning, comrades," said Dick, nodding. "What do ye think of my new nag? She's a beauty, eh?"

Dick patted the silken black neck of the noble courser.

"She's a wonder, captain!" responded the others, with unfeigned admiration.

"Mounted on this bonny mare, I can defy all the runners in Bow Street to catch me," laughed Dick.

"Shall I give her a rub down and a feed o' corn, Captain Turpin?" asked Barney, who from time to time cast furtive and uneasy glances about him, for he had shrewd suspicions of what had happened to his master the innkeeper.

"No, my trout; I shall always do her grooming myself," returned Dick, slipping off his gold-brocaded riding-coat, and rolling up his dainty shirt sleeves and ruffles.

The robbers looked on while their ringleader tended his beautiful black mare, and warmly praised her fine points.

After Dick Turpin had groomed and stabled his horse, he took a wash at the stable pump, combed out his foxy brown hair, slipped on his coat, and led the way into the house.

Re-entering the tap-room, the robbers threw themselves down on the settles, and Barney was ordered to refill the tankards, one of them keeping by his side as he descended into the cellar for a bottle of canary.

The captain of the robbers then enquired of them whether they had any further intelligence to communicate.

They gave him an account of the visit of Jonathan Wild and his myrmidons, and how they had overheard the treacherous disclosures made to the thief-taker by Ridge the innkeeper.

Dick Turpin blasphemed most horribly, and enquired what measures they had taken.

They told him how they had half murdered Ridge, and asked him what was to be done with Barney.

With a foul oath, Dick Turpin drew his sword and took his station by the door, threatening that he would cleave the tapster in twain on the moment of his entrance.

Tom King, however, interceded in the poor fellow's behalf, and when he entered protected him from his partner's violence.

Barney also pleaded hard for his life, and swore eternal fidelity to the robber gang.

Dick commanded him to remain with them, and swore that if he left the room without permission he would cut him to pieces.

Quiet being obtained, Dick reverted to the thief-taker.

"Zounds! but I'll be the death of that cursed bloodhound, as I was of the meddling fool who tried to capture me at my cave in Epping Forest," swore Turpin.

"There's a reward out for your apprehension, captain."

"I know it; they have increased the sum to £200," rejoined the robber, laughing; "but after that affair with Thompson, there'll be few found daring enough to tackle me."

"What was that, captain?" asked Fielder.

"Why, my pal, I and Tom once earthed in a fox-hole, a cave at a sequestered spot between King's Oak and Loughton Road. We found there a retreat large enough to receive us and our horses. The place was well screened by trees and brushwood, and was in all respects well adapted for our purpose; many a time we have scared the owls with our jolly chants when we had returned from the road loaded with swag, haven't we, Tom?"

"I believe ye, my hero," laughed King.

"Well, my nabs, it happened that a certain fellow, one Thompson, the king's park-keeper, eager to obtain the reward, with a guide, Larry Lossle—a cursed peach, whom I'll flay alive when I catch him—came to the cave, as bold as brass, intending to apprehend me. I'd had devilish bad luck that day, for I'd scoured the road without finding a single stiver. I was wofully tired, quite dead beat, so I turned my nag out loose, but without his saddle, and, lying down under a thicket, fell fast asleep."

"Was there no one in the cave, captain?"

"Devil any one! Tom was out on the scout, and my wife had gone to Waltham, to suborn some witness to get up an *alibi* for a pal of mine who had been nabbed by old Jonathan."

"And were you caught napping?"

"No; you shall hear. When I awoke, I found my horse had strayed away, and I went in search of him. I met Thompson, and asked him if he had seen my stray nag. To this he replied with consummate impudence, 'I know nothing of Turpin's horse, but have found Turpin himself,' and, without more ado, he clapped a big blunderbuss to his shoulder and fired at me; but, not to be done, I nimbly jumped behind a broad oak, and avoided the shot, and in return I popped my own carbine at him. He fell like a stone, and never moved more!"

"You killed him, then?"

"I tell ye so; one slug went through his heart, t'others lodged in his belly. Then there was the devil's own hullabaloo! the cracks of the blunderbuss and carbine brought a whole posse comitatus of well-mounted, well-armed travellers and park-keepers to the spot. Of course I melted, and, clambering into a large yew-tree, I remained there two whole days and one night, after which I escaped."

"And where did you go to then, Dick?"

"To Romeville, to the central sink of iniquities, London, my rum 'uns; but it was by a deuced near squeak that I reached it, for I borrowed a black horse from a close near the highway, and was pursued by some harvesters working in a field hard by, but amongst 'em I recognised some of the palming crew (gipsies) well known to me, and, throwing them a handfull of loose couters, they gave up the pursuit; but I was forced to dismount the black horse and turn him loose, and forthwith I betook myself to a chesnut which was cropping the grass in a neighbouring meadow, and I rode her till she was shot under me in a ramp with the traps at Barnet fair."

"That happened soon after our first meeting on the road to Cambridge, eh, Dick?" said King.

"You're right; but gad zooks, my pal, you had a narrow escape then. I never recall it without laughing to think I could mistake such a spry cull as the 'gentleman's highwayman' for a beggarly chawbacon! 'Stand and deliver!' cried I; you attempted to expostulate, and I swore to blow your brains out, and should have done it too, but that you called out in the nick of time, 'What, dog eat dog! come, come, Brother Turpin, if you don't know me I know you, and should be glad of your company!' And many a dashing adventure we've had together, since that day, Brother Tom. Here, let's drink confusion to the harming beaks, and hurrah for the Road!"

"Hurrah for the Road!" chorussed the robbers.

At this moment a loud knocking was heard at the outer door.

The thieves immediately snatched up their weapons, and listened breathlessly.

"Ahoy! are ye all asleep here?" cried a manly voice, with, "Come, skipper, let us into your caboose, and be hanged to ye."

At a sign from Turpin, Fielder sneaked out of the room.

He entered the front parlour.

Though the forenoon was well advanced the shutters were closed.

He opened them cautiously a little way, and peeped out.

A smart, handsome fellow, about thirty, dressed in heavy boots, and wrapped in a pea-jacket, stood on the step.

Fielder returned to his companions.

"Oli compoli *," he whispered, "it's only a blue-jacket, a wandering Jack-tar; he's alone, and, no doubt, a prize. I'll warrant his rhino-bag is well filled. Shall's let him in?"

"Dam'me! need ye ask? But who's to play landlord?"

"I will," returned Fielder, slipping off his red rug coat, and putting on an apron.

"House! house! Look sharp, your purser swab, or I'll batter in the bulk-head!" shouted the voice.

"Coming, coming," returned Fielder, shuffling down the passage, and opening the door.

Presently he re-entered the room, accompanied by the sailor.

"What cheer, my hearties?" asked the seaman, in a pleasant voice. "Hope I'm not intruding, but I'm as a castaway on a catamaran, and shan't stay a moment, for, bless your eyes, I have five leagues to sail before I can drop anchor. I'm homeward bound, my cheeries, and hope before nightfall to be moored alongside of the prettiest little pinnace——But, there, you must excuse sea manners, gentlemen; I haven't seen my little wife. Nellie, these two years. Where's the ship steward? Here, my hearty, fetch me a stiff glass of grog, a hunk of cheese, and a loaf of soft tack."

Fielder obeyed this order, and the seaman sipped his grog, and munched the bread and cheese with keen appetite.

"Once more your pardon, gentlemen, if I make one too many."

"On the contrary, sir," returned Tom King, with an elegant bow, "you are right welcome. We are travellers, and have put up for a rest at this roadside inn. Do us the honour of drinking with us."

---

* A cant expression for "All's well."

He handed the tankard, and the seaman took a draught.

"Well, that's hearty," he exclaimed. "And now let us exchange signals. Whither bound?"

"To Plymouth, sir," replied Tom King.

"Now, you don't say so!" cried the tar. "Then, maybe we can sail in company, for I understand that there's a whole fleet of pirates cruising in these waters, and as I carry a rich cargo of pay and prize-money, I don't want to be overhauled by the sharks."

"You belong to his majesty's navy, I presume?" remarked Tom King.

"No, I'm in the merchant service," replied the seaman; "second mate of the West Indiaman, 'Evadne.' My name is Paul Peveril, and I'm bound for a village near Plymouth, called Seaborough, where my wife lives. You may imagine how eager I am to reach home when I tell you that I parted from my lass within a fortnight of our marriage, two years ago, and that I have not seen her since."

"And does she expect you?" asked Turpin, with a sneer.

"No, there's the best on it," returned the honest tar, gleefully rubbing his hands. "My jib! how she will open her pretty peepers when she sees me! I think I can feel her heart sobbing with joy against my own. Oh, she's the sweetest little cherub, hearties, that ever haunted a man's brightest dreams. Belay! what a fool ye must think me!"

The worthy fellow turned aside his head to hide the tear twinkling in his clear blue eye.

"And she has been left alone and forlorn for two years?" laughed Turpin, coarsely. "Let us hope she has not found some other swain to solace her in her loneliness."

"Hulloa, you swab!" cried the tar, with a burst of sudden passion. "What's that you say? What do you mean?"

"No offence, I am sure," rejoined Tom King, quickly. "My friend likes a friendly jest."

"That's all ataunto," returned the sailor, "and so do I, as much as any one; but my wife's name is sacred, and I'll have ye respect it. But avast, it's time I hoisted the Blue Peter and made sail, for I've a long voyage before me."

"Stay, my good friend," said Tom King; "do you intend walking all the way to Seaborough?"

"Aye; I should have taken a berth in a land ship—a coach, as ye call it—but the roads are so cursedly infested with highwaymen that I thought it better to trudge alone, and trust to my own steering for a safe passage."

"Well, sir, if you will accompany us we can provide you with a horse, a jennet I am taking to Plymouth," said Tom King. "We are too formidable in number to fear any attack from highwaymen."

"Why, now, that's kindly," cried Paul in delight. "I'll ride convoy with you, with great thankfulness."

"Come, then, let's mount; but first we'll have a stirrup-cup together."

"Dam'me, but I'll pay for it," said the seaman, pushing back Tom King's hand, which held out a heavy purse.

Paul put his hand into his breast pocket and drew forth a leathern bag stuffed full of gold pieces.

The robbers' eyes glistened as they heard the money chink.

Glasses were filled, and the travellers drank to each other.

Then they issued out in a body into the stable yard.

They mounted their horses, and rode off, merrily chatting together.

Barney crept to the door and looked after them.

He then returned to the tap-room.

Their whispered, parting threats rang in his ears.

In those lawless times criminals could often escape capture for many years, and perpetrate the most atrocious acts with impunity.

Barney knew this, and shuddered as he thought of incurring the robber's vengeance.

He crept to the end of the room and raised the panel.

He dragged out the body of his master; it was stone cold, and to all appearance quite dead!

———

CHAPTER XIV.

HOW THE DASHING HIGHWAYMEN FLEECED THE POOR SEAMAN.

THE merry band of travellers rode on at a rapid trot, and beguiled the road by genial conversation.

The scenery was very beautiful; rich wide patches of golden corn were succeeded by the deep green woodlands, while at intervals across the spangled meads wound the silver chord of some meandering river or brook.

The weather was calm, and the skies profoundly blue.

The breeze blew gently, and wafted the perfume from the burned orchards and vineries.

After riding a mile or two the party came upon a wilder and more rugged part of the land.

Here the forests were denser and more sombre; the trees were closely interwoven, and in some places the underwood was so thick as to render the dingles almost impassable.

In the wildest and lonliest spot which the travellers had yet met with a narrow bridle path diverged from the high road.

Here the travellers drew rein.

"By taking a circuit through the wood we shall save some miles," said Dick Turpin; "but here we must ride in single file. Come, gentlemen, you must put your nags on their mettle, for there is but one halting place betwixt this and our destination."

The unsuspecting seaman urged his companions to take the shorter route.

For some time they rode on in silence, the difficulties of the road precluding conversation.

The trees were close set, and the path so narrow that even a single horseman could scarcely proceed.

At length they reached a rude bridge, formed by a few planks thrown across a brawling brook.

Here they were forced to dismount, for the huge branches of the grand old oaks and mighty beech trees interlaced at so little distance above the ground that it was almost impossible for a rider to clear them; besides which, the road was so bad—so full of ruts and holes that at every step the horses were in imminent danger of being thrown down.

After crossing the rustic bridge, the travellers entered a shadowy dell, down which the path wound its rugged way, sometimes lost amid the dense growing underwood.

Here Dick Turpin, who took the lead, ordered a halt.

"Split my top-mast! but we are cruising in ugly waters, my hearties!" said the seaman, swabbing the perspiration from his swarthy brow; "I think we're land-locked here, for there don't seem to be steerage way for a cockle-boat; and, my eyes and limbs! look yonder, there's a poor fellow hanging in chains!"

Paul, as he spoke, pointed to a gibbet erected on a small clearing in the forest, on which a corpse was swinging.

"Aye, that's the body of poor Mike Mahony that beat out the packman's brains, and robbed him, on this very spot," said Tom King. "You see that crumbling heap of earth and stones? That's where he buried his victim."

"*Poor* Mike, do ye call the pirate cut-throat?" gasped the sailor. "'Scuse me, sir, but I think such sympathy's rather misplaced."

"Did ye ever sail in the sound of Elsinore?" asked Tom, laughing.

"Aye, aye, sure enough; but why do you ask such an odd question?"

"Well, if you remember, every vessel that passes the castle of that town——"

"Is bound to lower her top-masts, and pay toll to the Danish king. I know it; but what, then?"

"A similar custom prevails in this part of the world. Every one who passes that gibbet must pay the dues; must shell out a cap-full of blunt to pay masses for poor Mike, who was a sort of martyr in his way, and died in the full odour of sanctity, being attended at the gallows by a couple of Jesuit priests and a French abbot."

"And who levies the contributions, my hearties?" asked the sailor, laughing, but backing cautiously towards a huge gnarled tree.

"We do!" growled the robbers, "in the name of St. Nicholas!"*

"Dam'me, ye land-sharks, I begin to understand ye!" cried the bold seaman, throwing his back against a tree and pulling a brace of immense, murderous-looking pistols from his jacket pockets. "Now I'm willing to pay the toll, but it shall be in lead and not gold, you scoundrels!"

"Bah! resistance is quite useless, my friend," said Tom King. "You seem a brave fellow, and we should be sorry to hurt you; but we are sworn to keep up the good old custom, so dub up without further bother. Do ye know who we are?"

"I shouldn't wonder if you are Dick Turpin's crew of land-pirates," returned the sailor; "but, be ye who or what ye will, if you mean to board and rob me, ye must fight for it, my men!"

So saying, he presented his pistols right and left, aiming one at the head of Dick Turpin and the other at Tom King's.

The robbers instantly drew their pistols and bludgeons.

"Curse ye, for a fool, ye *will* have it, then!" cried Turpin, and he fired.

The bullet, however, whizzed past the seaman's head, and lodged in the tree behind him.

Paul returned the shot.

But his clumsy, ill-made weapon only flashed in the pan.

Tom King threw himself behind the tree, and slipping quickly round, came close behind the seaman, who had just fired the second pistol, the shot passing through the fleshy part of Fielder's left arm.

Enraged at this fierce resistance, the robbers covered their man with their levelled pistols, and in a moment would have poured a half-dozen shots into his body, but Tom King on the instant smote him senseless to the earth by one blow of his pistol stock.

He then held up his hand.

"Back, you dogs!" he cried, "he is disabled. No needless bloodshed; we can relieve him of his tattler and his sugar-bag without killing him outright."

* The thieves' tutelar saint.

"That's all infernal fal-de-ral. Master King," growled Fielder. "Look at my arm; do ye think the dog shall bite me twice? Stand out of the way while I give him a crack over the mazzard. If he recovers he will inform against us; of course he can swear to us, me and all. Better settle the job at once."

"Aye, Tom, better finish him off," said Turpin. "Slit his weason and pitch him down the dingle."

"Out on ye, Dick!" cried Tom, indignantly. "Will you countenance such a cowardly, brutal deed? No, dam'me, I thought we were gentlemen of the high pad—heroes of the road. I, for one, will not suffer any such foul play."

"As you will, comrade; but your squeamishness will one day be your ruin," returned Turpin, sullenly.

The robbers now bent over the inanimate body of their victim and rolled it over on to its back.

The face was deadly pale and rigid, and the forehead awfully gashed.

They rifled his pockets.

"Phew! here's a good haul," said Dick. "I should think this fob contains two hundred couters, and here's a plummy bunch of onions (Watch and seals)."

"Hurrah!"

"And what's this? A miniature and a lock of hair; and here's a bundle of letters," continued Turpin. "Humph! the miniature is prettily set with choice pearls, and the gold chain is worth something."

"Spare them, Dick," said Tom; "I'll warrant the poor rogue prizes them more than the bag of gold. Ye see it's his wife's portrait; and, gad, sir, a pretty little wench she must be. I almost pity the poor devil, returning empty-handed after his long separation and hard service. But, hark!"

The robbers stood transfixed with anxiety, and listened to a distant sound that resembled the patter of horses' hoofs.

"Zounds!" cried Turpin, "we are pursued!"

"I fear they are on our track," cried Fielder.

"I fear no one but Roving Jack, who, although a boy, has the pluck of a man, and has set his life on hunting us down; but to horse, lads!" cried Tom.

ROVING JACK DEFENDS HIMSELF FROM THE HIGHWAYMEN.—*See* No. 6.

The highwaymen scrambled into their saddles.
"We must disperse," cried Dick Turpin. "If all's well, let us meet to-night at the 'Rover's Best,' in Plymouth."

No. 5.

"Good, captain," cried the robbers; "away!"
They galloped off, each taking separate directions. Shaking the reins and urging on his bonnie black courser, Dick Turpin sped through the mazy forest.

guiding his steed in the most admirable style, and bending low in the saddle to avoid contact with the low-sweeping branches of the trees.

Scarcely had the thieves decamped when a large party of well-armed and well-mounted police-officers and farmers came tearing along till they arrived to the spot where the unfortunate Paul Peveril was lying.

Here they halted, uttering a general shout of horror and indignation.

"This is the work of that infernal villain Dick Turpin!" cried the principal officer, in a breathless tone. "See, gentlemen, the hoof-prints diverge; some of you take one road, some another; remember the reward that is offered for the capture of the black scoundrels; I will add twenty guineas to his share who is the first to lay hands on any one of the cursed gang. Off, gentlemen!"

Of course two or three of the party had dismounted to attend to the wounded man.

A surgeon happened to be one of the party.

Kneeling down by the side of poor Paul, he raised his head upon his knee, loosened the kerchief from his neck, felt his pulse, and pressed his hand over the region of the heart.

"Be the poor lad dead, doctur!" asked one of the farmers, kindly.

"He is not, but the pulse is very low; he is seriously injured, I fear; must be removed at once."

"The blamed ruff'ans!" panted the farmer, grinding his teeeth, and clenching his fists. "And a poor zeaman, too, mayhap returnun to his whoam, and his lass. Odsbodikins! I'd give dwenty pund to zee that doamed Turpun vlayed aloive."

At this moment a stirring tally-ho rang through the leafy forest.

The farmers were whooping as if in chase of a fox.

As for Dick—borne along like the wind by his bonnie Black Bess, whose course no obstruction could stay—he cleared the wood, and bounded across a wide, open, gorsy common, the officers hotly pursuing him, and from time to time discharging their pistols at him.

Tom King, who had taken a nearer cut, and thereby got the start, was seen speeding away in the distance.

He turned in his saddle, waved his cocked hat, and his shout came faintly on the breeze.

"Harkaway, Dick, harkaway!"

Turpin reached the hedge which bounded a neighbouring field; Black Bess flew over like an arrow, and away she rattled along the high road.

Several of the farmers attempted to jump the barrier over which the famous racer had flown like a bird; but either their horses refused to take the hedge or else failed to clear it, throwing their riders into the ditch.

Others, more cautious, sped along the hedge-row till they found a gap, and, having reached the road, tore along in pursuit of the fleeting figure, waning smaller and smaller in the far distance, bawling from their stentorian lungs,

"A highwayman! a highwayman! Stop thief! stop thief!"

Dick Turpin, however, forged a-head, gaining ground at every spring of his beautiful, gallant mare.

He turned his head to look at his pursuers, waved his hat, and laughed in derision.

At length a formidable obstacle to his progress presented itself in the shape of a six-barred toll-gate at the foot of a high, steep hill.

Hearing the rapid clatter of horses' hoofs and the wild shouts of Dick's pursuers, the toll-keeper,

a short, burly fellow, and his son, a gawkey lad of sixteen, came rushing out of the little toll-house.

"Whea! Dick Turpin vor a guinea!" he cried, gleefully. "Darn 'im, we got 'im now! Clap to the gate, Joe. Marther, marther, bring out moy blunderbuss!"

Dick Turpin came gliding along as smoothly and as swiftly as a speeding arrow.

"Now, Bess!" he panted, "my bonnie Bess! Harkaway, lass! Tally ho! Over! over! Ha, ha, ha!"

The next instant he was flying up the hill, and in the next had shot over its brow and disappeared.

CHAPTER XV.

BARABBAS MAKES LOVE TO NELLIE PEVERIL, AND SETS FIRE TO HER COTTAGE FOR REJECTING HIS OFFER.

OUR scene shifts to the home of Nellie Peveril, the wife of the gallant but luckless young tar whose misadventure formed the subject of the last chapter.

It was an humble, but neatly-furnished and pretty cottage, situated in a lonely spot by the sea-shore at some distance from the small fishing hamlet of Seaborough.

Nellie sat on a little settle beneath the rose-covered porch of the cottage, and wearily watched the ocean billows calmly rising and sinking in the evening sunshine.

She was an extremely pretty girl, not more than nineteen or twenty years of age, with soft brown hair, and mildly bright hazel eyes, and her countenance was remarkable for an expression of exquisite sweetness.

A little heap of needlework lay upon her lap, but her hands were listlessly folded, and her head leaned back against the porch in a desponding manner, while her eyes were suffused with hot tears that fell from her long lashes and trickled slowly down her soft, pale cheeks.

"Hope—cruel, cruel hope!" she murmured, faintly, "why do you haunt me only to torture me? Abandon me for ever! Hope, long deferred, that makes the yearning heart sick! Oh, Paul, Paul, will you never return to me? I am so lonely, so persecuted, so helpless—and you are reft from me! If I could believe that you were dead—oh, how gladly, how happily could I die, too! But this suspense—this constant torment of baffled expectation—it is more than I can bear!"

"Then why the devil do ye bear it?" cried a coarse, vulgar voice.

Nellie started, and uttered a slight scream.

"Now, then, what air ye hollerin' about?" said a short, conceited-looking fellow, dressed in a rich livery, stepping from behind the porch and seating himself by her side. "Take another look at me, Nellie Peveril, and see if I'm the kinder figger to hexite any hother sort of hemotion in the female buzzom except love and hadmiration."

"Oh, Tony, how you startled me!" said Nellie, in a trembling voice, as she withdrew from his side. "And pray, what news do you bring me?"

"Fust chop!"

"The squire, then, relents of his unkindness to a poor, bereaved, friendless woman, who has struggled so hard to earn an honest living, and to meet his claim of the rent?" said Nellie, eagerly. "I am but a trifle in arrears, and my husband will soon return —indeed he will. The squire will never be so harsh and cruel as to drive me from my poor little nest, when he himself is so rich, and can live in such comfort and splendour. I may remain; this is your good news, is it not so?"

"No; it is *not* so, never was so, is so, will be so, nor can be so! The squire means to turn you out; he's swore so, and he'll do so."

"Why, then, what can be your good news?"

"It don't come from the old squire, you may be sure. Why, now, you don't expect to hear anything favourable from him? No, my lovely creetur, the eyes in which you have favour are the bright brown sparklers of handsome Master Ranulph, a gallant that even Court ladies have adored. Oh, jemini! you are the beauty of the whole village, and here's a dainty billet-doux for you, as full of sweetstuffs as a box of comfits. I partly guess its contents. The old man turns you out of your home, and the young 'un, by vay of compensation, offers you another. Vell, in course you won't be such a hegrigious fool to loose sich a chance, for who knows but by playing yer cards cleverly you may become Lady Ellen Gayton?"

Nellie rose.

Her eyes flashed, and her breast heaved with indignant passion.

"The brutality of the son is more unbearable than the father's harshness," she said, with cold disdain. "For your master's letter, there is my answer."

She tore the unopened note, and tossed it back to the servant.

"Long ago I should have ceased to be Sir Ranulph's tenant," she continued, her voice trembling with suppressed indignation; "but I have lingered here still buoyed by the hope of my husband's return. Well, I shall leave this place to-morrow, and among my friends in the village I may find some one chivalrous enough to defend me from the persecutions of my dastardly insulter."

The girl swept haughtily into the cottage, and was about to close the door, when Tony darted in, and seized her by the hand.

"Come, now, I say, vhat *do* you mean? My precious eyes! yer puts me in a cold swelter!" he gasped. "Don't yer go for von moment to think, imagine, or suppose as I'm a goin' to deliver any sich imperant messages to the peppery young squire. Vhy, vhat vould he do to me? He'd bundle me out o' vinder or kick me down stairs."

"You need say nothing that would excite his anger against yourself," said Nellie. "Give him back the unopened letter, and say that I shall leave the cottage to-morrow."

"Hark ye, Nell," said the fellow, with a leer; "I've a proposal to make to ye; von vich does honour to my 'ed and 'eart. You vants pertection, then I'll be yer pertecter; you vants money, I'll supply enough to pay yer rent and to buy yerself a new dress besides; haint I gen'rous? Vell, hover and above all this, I hoffers you my 'and! Vill you be mine?"

The gallant Tony threw himself at her feet.

She tried to look angry, but the expression of his countenance was so comic and ludicrous that she could not resist laughter.

"You spurns me, you larfs at me!" growled the enraged suitor, leaping to his feet.

"No, no, no!" cried the girl, frankly, her fair cheek at the same time suffusing with a hot blush of shame and confusion; "you would really marry me! you offer me your hand?"

"Name the day, and rush to my buzzum!"

"But I am already married; my husband will return."

"I'll run the risk o' that."

"Were I not sure that Paul is alive, that he will soon return, could I talk with such levity? And, indeed, if I were free, had I never been Paul's wife,

there is no one but him in all the world that I could love. But enough of this foolish talk. Leave me; yet do not let us part in unkindness. There is my hand, Tony; we are old friends, forget what has passed between us, and deliver my message to the squire; to-morrow I shall quit this place."

Nellie opened the door, and, by an appealing look, urged her unwelcome guest to leave her.

But Tony pushed rudely back, and once more caught her hands.

"I vont leave you, Nellie," he cried, in a tone intended to be endearing; "I've svorn that you shall be mine, and I vont be rejected; you must and shall ved me!"

He wound his arm round her waist, and rudely kissed her cheek.

She struggled to release herself, and shrieked amain.

A growl that might have been uttered by a wolf or a panther caused Tony to relinquish his grasp, and turn in trepidation.

A hideous but powerful fellow, dressed in the costume of a Dutch seaman, stood beside him.

It was the dwarf—Barabbas!

His small snake-like eyes glistened venomously; his long claw-like hands were outstretched, and seemed ready to tear the wretched Tony to pieces; his coarse, rusty black hair streamed back; and his strong though bandine legs were firmly set.

"Barabbas!" gasped Nellie, recoiling with fright, and supporting herself against the wall, in a half fainting condition.

"Aye, it is Barabbas—the ban-dog Barabbas," chuckled the pirate. "But who is this land-shark? What does he here?"

"I come on a mission from Sir Ranulph Gayton," said Tony, assuming a swaggering air; "I'm a gentleman's gentleman. Vhat disgusting monster are you?"

"A monster, ha!" laughed the dwarf.

"A ghoul, a ogre, a wampire!" roared Tony, backing before the advancing ruffian.

"You'll find me more terrible than either," growled the pirate. "Are ye pious?"

As he spoke he drew forth a long sharp knife, and passed his thumb along its keen edge.

"Vhot do ye mean ye hijeous sea-urchin?"

"I mean this, that you had better say your prayers, for I mean to cut your throat."

"I should think cutting throats is yer reg'lar perfession, you butcherly thief."

"True; you'll not be the first calf I have slaughtered," growled the pirate, taking a step forward.

"Help!—thieves!—murder!" shrieked Tony, dodging round the table. "Pertect me, Nellie! If he kills me, I gives you warnin', I'll swear to you as his accomplice in the dreadful hact. Oh! lors! help! murder! mercy!"

The dwarf leaped over a chair, and fixing his grip upon Tony's neck, shook him as a dog would shake a rabbit, and then, dashing his head violently against the wall, clapped the keen, gleaming knife to his throat.

With a piteous shriek the girl threw herself between the struggling men.

"Mercy!" she panted. "Barabbas! spare him! spare his life!"

"Do ye plead for the dog?" growled the pirate, savagely. "He has insulted ye; but perhaps *his* advances are not deemed insults. Maybe he is your paramour. The monkey-jibbed lubber!"

Once more the pirate shook his victim till his teeth chattered like castanets.

"Spare his life, Barabbas! no bloodshed!" frantically implored the girl.

"Humph! you ask the cur's life?" growled the pirate.

"I do. I beseech you, pardon him."

"For your sake?"

"Yes, yes."

"For your sake, then, Nell," returned Barabbas, letting go his hold and lowering the knife.

During a few moments he stood regarding the prostrate Tony with a vindictive, irresolute glare.

Then, as if unable to restrain his passion, he dashed down the knife.

"But, dam'me, I'll tear out his scurrilous tongue, and make him eat it!" he roared, leaping more furiously than ever upon his crouching victim. "A monster am I? Ho! ho! Ware fangs, you liveried, dust-licking mongrel lackey. A monster do ye call me? Ha-a!"

"N-n-no!" gasped Tony. "L-l-let me go! h-help, h-elp! Oh, l-lors! You'll shake me to splinters!"

"Speak, you trencher-swabbing son of a scullion. Am I an ogre?—a ghoul?—a vampire? Speak, dam'me, or I'll rip ye into ribbons!"

"N—no!"

"What am I, then? A Phœbus, an Adonis?—a Lovelace?—a gay and handsome gallant, eh? Do ye admire my perfumed, rippling, luxuriant, love-looks? Are ye dazed by the piercing brilliance of my starry eyes? Are ye awed by my stately, well-proportioned frame? Am I not comely? Am I not a mate for peerless beauty? Speak, you frowsy varlet!"

"Yes, yes!" yelled Tony, for Barabbas emphasised every question by bashing his head against the wall.

"I'm neither a ghoul, an ogre, a vampire, nor sea-urchin, but a dashing, handsome (bump), gracious, goodly (bump), noble, elegant (bump), valiant, courteous, bold, gallant, righteous, ranting lover (bump—bump), eh?—eh? Am I all this?"

"Y-y-es, y-you're all that," groaned poor Tony.

"Out, then, you foul-mouthed, slanderous, insolent, abusive, yelping, snarling mongrel, mangy turnspit; limp home like a lashed hound, and hide your cropped ears in your kennel. Out, you crawling menial!"

Barabbas seized his passive victim in his long, gorilla like arms, doubled him into a hoop, and hauled him far through the open window.

"Ha! ha! ho! ho!" he laughed harshly, as he threw himself into a chair, and folded his brawny arms, "I'll teach the howling cur not to bark at his betters; but come, Nell, my passion is over, the devil is not so black as they paint him. I am not so monstrous after all, am I?"

The girl covered her face with her hands, and shuddered with loathing.

"At least, my rough but well-knit frame, nerved with a lion's strength, should not be ungracious in your eyes," said the wild pirate, in a tone of strange softness. "The roughest rind often encloses the sweetest kernel. If my aspect is rugged, Nell, my heart is softened by the fervent love I bear you, and your name is as deeply impressed upon it as the seal in the molten wax. I love ye, Nell—I adore ye! Beauty is in the eye of the gazer—is but an arbitrary thing of fashion and fancy. Here is an arm your frailty can lean upon; here is a hand that is strong to protect ye."

He paused, but receiving no answer, continued earnestly,

"Aye, familiarity reconciles one to ugliness, or satiates with loveliness. When you have lived awhile with me you will learn to love me. I will *make* you love me, lass, for, savage as I seem, with you I will be as tender and gentle as a mother to her new-born babe. Be generous, Nell; pity and accept me!"

The horrible dwarf stooped low upon his bended knee, and drooped his huge and hideous head upon his broad, heaving breast, and his hot tears pattered on the floor.

"Love—accept—*you?*" gasped the shuddering girl. "A felon—a pirate—a murderer!"

"And if I am," growled Barabbas, starting up, clenching his huge fists, and gnashing his yellow fangs, "is it *my* fault? Why is my hand against every man? Because every man's hand was against me from the cursed hour that I first drew the breath of pain and misfortune. The spawn of the foulest of outcasts, engendered like a toad in a filthy dungeon, my sponsor the brutal gaoler, my shame-branding name, Barabbas! Why should I respect a world which treats me like a loathesome intruder —a foul, ulcerous blotch upon the fair face of creation? No, death and darkness 'whelm the world! the curse of my withered heart blight its whole race of paltry, painted butterflies like an autumn frost! The devil take his own!"

Appalled by this dreadful language, the girl shrank from the excited deformed, and sank pale and faint upon the couch.

"And that was why I loved ye, Nell," whined the strange being, in a tone of thrilling emotion. "When I was spurned, misused, hounded, spit upon by all beside, you were so kind, so gentle with me! You poured the holy balm of your pitying tears upon my rancorous wounds, and I, who was not suffered to love God nor man, was drawn to you as to the only stay to which I could cling for sympathy. But for you, long since, I think, I should have run amuck, like a frantic Malay, and, hewing and slashing left and right, died in glutting my vengeance upon the oppressors! Oh, Nell, Nell! I would pawn my eternal soul to the foul fiend if he would but make me comely and generous in your sight, though but for one year!"

The strange and dreadful creature paused, as if suffocated by his qualms of passion.

Nellie remained awed and silent.

"Do ye mind the time, beloved, when I was set upon by a pack of heartless young hounds, who cursed, beat, and stoned me—called me a hag's imp, a monster, an abortion? How you bandaged my broken arm, mended my torn jacket, brought me food and drink—wept over me?"

Barabbas hid his repulsive face in his broad, hard hands, and sobbed like a little child.

"Avast!" he growled, gulping down the qualm in his throat, and dashing his tears scornfully away. "You will but despise me. Enough; I thought I could controul myself better. But it's over; and now, hearken, Nell Peverill—you *must* be mine!"

"Never!" gasped the frighted girl.

"You cannot help yourself; but listen—Paul, your husband, is dead."

"No, no!"

"I tell you it is so. His ship, the 'Evadne,' struck on a coral reef off the Bermudas. Every soul perished."

Nellie clasped her hands, and uttered a wild shriek of agony.

"But I will be a brave consort to ye, Nell; I will make you a princess! I have taught my fellow-vagabonds to respect me, for I have made them fear me; my influence with them equals Wirth Wolfgang's; if it suited my purpose I could become their chief. We are rich, fabulously wealthy! Our fleet scours the Spanish main, and reaps abundant harvests of golden plunder. See what I have brought you in earnest of richer gifts hereafter."

As he spoke he produced from his wallet a beautifully enamelled casket, which he opened by a spring.

Within it, bedded in blue velvet, sparkled a circlet of exquisitely-set and priceless brilliants, a pair of flashing diamond bracelets, a necklace of red-glowing rubies, and a brooch of large, fine pearls, mingled with green-gleaming

"This is nothing, lass," he chuckled; "I can robe you in radiant light, drape you in prisms of silks and satins, crown you with diadems of gold and jewels; you shall be a queen, and I will be your slave. I will found you a kingdom on one of the palmy islands that gem the Western main; I will surround you with every luxury that can make existence blissful; you shall have slaves over whom you shall wield the power of life and death. I will not even ask you to love me! Be but my goddess; endure my worship, though never so coldly, and I will be content."

"Never, tempter, never! Rather let me die in torture!" cried Nellie, vehemently.

"Yet hear me."

"Not a word; away!" cried the girl, fiercely; "your presence is hateful to me! I cannot endure the sight of one who has played the part of a fiend; who has broken every law, human or divine, whose hands are red with innocent blood."

"You are mad, wench!" growled the pirate, wildly clutching her wrist. "You once cared for me, once were good to me; no soul on earth could have such cause to love you as I have; my only friend, the only creature whom I love, and as hotly as I hate all others of my kind. Well, well, my vehemence distracts you; but one smile will calm me. For what can you sacrifice the brilliant destiny I can create for you? Not for scorn and beggary? and what else awaits you here? The hand of death has shattered your idol, blighted your fool's paradise; your husband is dead, and your home is desolate!"

"Yet it is a home I would not exchange for all the splendours you falsely promise," said Nellie, fervently. "No, I will cleave to my humble home though you kill me on its threshold."

"Is it that?" growled Barabbas, casting his red eyes around with a demoniac glare. "Ho, ho! by the power of thunder, you shall have no home but mine, and woe to the rash fool who casts his shadow between us! Your 'home!' To the flames with the beggarly hovel!"

Uttering an eldritch screech the maddened ruffian pushed her away and flew to the ingle-side.

He took up a blazing log from the hearth, and, before the shrieking girl could prevent him, set fire to the curtains, the thatched roof, the wooden, sundried walls, and soon the place was engulfed in fire and smoke.

Nellie fell upon her knees, and tossed up her arms with a cry of despairing horror.

Barabbas bounded to her side, and once more gripped her arm.

"Your home!" he yelled, brandishing the torch, and laughing fiendishly. "Your home is henceforth in my speeding craft, on my island fastness! I will not be fooled by a puling wench who will love me none the better for playing the cringing slave. Now I will be master! Come, my bride, ere morning dawns, leagues of the trackless sea shall roll between us and this home of my shame and oppression! Come, Nell, you are mine for ever!"

The poor girl flew from him distractedly, and attempted to reach the door.

A gust of smoke intermingled with lurid forks of scorching flame swept across her path.

She recoiled with a dreadful shriek.

She felt the strong sinewy arms of the terrible dwarf curl about her slim, yielding waist; she found herself clutched in his embrace; his hot breath fanned her quivering cheek; his small, blasting eyes glittered red in the blinding glare of the burning cottage.

She closed her eyes with a mortal shudder, her beautiful head drooped upon his broad shoulder—she fainted.

Barabbas took one triumphant glance around.

Then again and again he covered her cold, bloodless cheek with fervent kisses.

But the room was now full of choking fumes, and the fire roared like a furnace, while the heat was intense to a pitch of torture.

Tightly clutching his prize to his heart, the dwarf leaped over a pile of red-hot embers, and bounded through the door.

Just as he had passed the threshold, with a thundrous crash the roof and walls fell in. A pyre of black smoke rolled high into the heavens, and showers of flitting flamelets and bright twinkling sparks filled the murky air.

CHAPTER XVI.

ROVING JACK RESCUES NELLIE PEVERIL FROM BARABBAS.

BEARING his senseless burden as lightly as if it were a pillow of down, the dwarf sped along the top of the cliffs.

Far from behind him came the dreadful cry of "fire!"

He only laughed and capered in grotesque delight.

"She is mine!" he chuckled. "No hand shall tear her from me. No! I will stab her to the heart rather than yield her to another's arms. Perhaps I may win her love; if not, at least she will be near me. Let her curse and revile me; the caged bird sings not less sweetly though his notes be wrung from a raging heart. Ho! ho! I'll gloat on her pretty passions of shame or anger; her voice is always sweet to me whatever be the notes of her song. 'Tis the tone that makes the harmony. Ha! ha!"

Nimbly clambering down a precipitous path by the cliff, he reached the beach, and sped to a little creek where his boat was moored.

He leaped into it.

His foot struck against something soft that lay on the gratings covered by a piece of sail-cloth.

"S'blood! *what's that?*" he muttered, drawing back his foot. "Ah, the bale of velvet I brought from the reef."

He laid the girl tenderly down on the sternsheets of the boat, pillowing her head upon his rough pea-jacket, which he had thrown off.

He seated himself on the thwarts, and, seizing the oars, pushed off the boat.

He pulled lustily, and soon was flying along through the dancing waves.

He laughed, and vented his glee in wild song—

> "Over the far and foamy main
> The rover bears his bride again;
> The red flag flies, the bowl flows free,
> A winsom wooer I know is he!"

Something stirs beneath the sail-cloth on the gratings behind the oarsman.

The light graceful form of a tall slight boy rises from beneath the covering.

Barabbas does not perceive him, but tugs away at the oar, and continues to pour forth snatches of wild melody.

The boy crouches, poising a long hand-pike in his hands.

The unconscious pirate blithely sings,

> "She wept, she sighed, she fairly swore
> She'd smile, she'd speak, she'd live no more;
> Rather than be a rover's bride,
> Would drown her shame in the cold, deep tide.
> Why, then? How, then?
> Ha! ha!
> Young Ralph has knipped her in his arms;
> She fondly yields her rarest charms.
> But tell, O tell,
> What potent spell
> Tamed the proud heart of our wild bird, Nell?
>   Ha! ha!"

WHISH!

The hand-pike descends on the bison head of the dwarf with a horrid crash!

The boat lurches and ships a heavy sea.

The boy springs forward as Barabbas reels and falls flat backwards upon the gratings, quite insensible.

The boy sets his foot lightly upon his breast and stares down upon his livid face, holding the hand-pike ready to strike a final blow if needed.

The young hero who has risked his life to save Nellie Peveril from a shameful fate, is, as our readers anticipate—

Roving Jack!

He seats himself upon the thwart and quietly takes hold of the oars.

He looks seriously upon the unconscious forms of the pirate dwarf and the hapless Nellie, and then gazes anxiously round upon the expanse of sea and sky.

A few white sails flit like moth-wings in the sunbeams, and the dark hull of a schooner glides along the sea-line.

He then turns his glance landward.

The cottage is flaming on the summit of the white cliff, and he can just distinguish the forms of men and women rushing wildly towards the scene of the conflagration.

"Lucky I found the boat," thought Jack. "I saw it put off from the reef, but could not tell where it put in shore, for the windings of the coast are so intricate. The pirates contrived to ship off the best part of their treasure before the preventives could reach the island. What could Barabbas want there? Why is the schooner still hovering in these waters, when it must be known to Wolfgang that a man-o'-war is in chase of him? But, wonder of all wonders, why did Nick Dangerfield, the officer of the coast-guard stationed on the reef, suffer the dwarf to slip through his fingers? Ha! I half suspect that fellow is in league with the pirates and smugglers, for though he is considered a diligent officer, and has overhauled many contraband cargoes, now I think of it, the goods he has recovered are seldom of much value and he never takes any prisoners."

Roving Jack looked eagerly in the direction of the schooner which had hove to.

"I shall be seen and pursued," he thought, "and this is tough work pulling against the tide. I'll lighten the craft by throwing that villain overboard."

Jack drew in the oars with intent of carrying out this purpose.

However, he suddenly changed his mind, and once more tugged away with all his strength.

"No, I'll get him ashore," he muttered. "Al-though I have little scrupie in killing such a villain, I'd rather leave that piece of work to the hangman. Hal and the rest of them are hiding among yonder rocks; we can bind the wretch hand and foot and carry him to the village in Old Clem's cart."

After a half-hour's hard rowing Jack ran the boat ashore in a little sandy bay.

Not without considerable difficulty he managed to lift the huge though stunted body of the dwarf out of the boat. He was as stiff and motionless as a log, his yellow tusks were tightly clenched, his glazed eyes half closed, and his knotty forehead disfigured with a " parlous bump."

With much greater ease our hero raised the slight, though well-rounded form of the fainted Nellie.

Her breast heaved gently, her lips parted, her eyelids quivered, and she showed every sign of returning animation.

Roving Jack placed her gently against a little mound of sand, as far apart as possible from the ruffianly Barabbas.

He then mounted upon a rock, and shading his eyes from the sun, looked cautiously around.

No human creature appeared, though he could hear the distant roar of voices from behind the brow of a neighbouring cliff, whence soared a pillar of dense black smoke from the burning cottage, which was itself invisible from the spot where our hero was standing.

Roving Jack's next act was to apply a whistle to his lips and blow a long shrill recall. In an instant twenty of his bold boy comrades started up from their ambush, and, bounding down the rocks, surrounded him.

"So you've caught the blackguard?" said Frank Harley.

"Ugh! what a hideous monster he is."

"I must say, Jack, that you are a wonderful chap," added Ben Bouncer; "must be descended from the original Jack the Giant-killer. O crimini, he *is* a horrid-looking monster!" he cried, as he cast his eyes upon the hideous form of Barabbas. "He reminds me of a three-headed dwarf I once saw at Seaborough fair; but this wretch is only a patch on that one for ugliness, would you believe it now? He had three mouths, but could only eat with one, drink with the other, and speak with the third; but, then, he used to do all these three things at once; being rather short-sighted he wore a triple pair of specs, all the glasses fixed in a kind of hoop that went round his heads. Oh, I ought to have mentioned that his three shocks of hair were of different colours, so were his three pairs of eyes, which all squinted in different directions; yes, and his noses—one was flat, t'other snubbed, and the last beaky; but this was the oddest thing of all, his arms were placed where his legs ought to be, so that he was forced to walk with his heads downwards! Oh, you should ha' seen him, Jack!"

"Aye, Ben, for he was one of those phenomena that must be seen to be believed."

"Well, it is astonishing what marvellous things one may see and read about for the small charge of 'von penny'—but, hillo; why, bless my life, here's Nellie Peveril!"

"How strange!" cried Hal; "then it must have been this awful rascal, Barabbas, that set fire to her cottage on the cliff, stunned Squire Gayton's servant, and carried off poor Mrs. Peveril! What an outrageous villain!"

"But what shall we do with him?"

"I'll show you what we'll do," returned Jack. "Where's little Berty?"

"Here, Jack, by your side," cried the pretty,

flaxen-haired boy, who was a great pet with our hero.

"Run, Bert, to the Owlet's Roost, and ask my sister, Violet, and my mother, to come and attend to this poor young woman. Look sharp, like a good chap."

"I'll fly, Jack," returned the boy, smiling.

He darted off like a racer.

"Will Ryan, fetch that coil of ropes from the boat," ordered our hero.

"Aye, aye, sir!" laughed Will, touching his hat in seaman-like style.

"Now we must draw the adder's sting," said Jack, stooping by the prostrate dwarf, and drawing the long, sharp knife out of the ruffian's heavy leathern belt.

He then laid hold of the fire-arms.

"My eye, Jack!" cried Ben Bouncer, dodging behind his companions, "do take care with those dreadful pistols; finger 'em gingerly! I once got tampering with my uncle's blunderbuss and the beastly thing busted and blew me clean through a haystack!"

Our hero laughed, but carefully laid the fire-arms aside, keeping the muzzles pointed to the ground.

Courageous people who have no need to "show off," are always the most careful with dangerous weapons; remember that, young readers.

"Now, Will, pass the rope, and help me to lash the rascal hand and foot.

The boys passed the hand-pike under the dwarf's passive arms, tied his wrists tightly together, and then drew the cord round his bowed legs.

"Ned Ross, you know where old Clem Cleats keeps the horse and cart that carries the fish to market?"

"Yes, Jack, in the little shanty under the cliff."

"Well, if you see the old chap, ask him to lend you them; tell him what for. But if you don't meet him, bring them away on French leave. This is no time to stand for ceremony."

"All right, captain, I'll fetch 'em in a jiffey," returned Ned, as he ran off to execute his commission.

At this juncture Mrs. Warbold and Violet arrived on the scene.

They were loud in their expressions of sympathy for poor Nellie, and tended her with affectionate care.

After some time the poor girl recovered her senses; she raised her hand to her head and stared wildly round, then, closing her eyes with a shudder, she clung trembling in the widow's embrace.

"Courage, Nellie dear," murmured the kind lady; "you are with friends."

"Mother, wouldn't it be better for you to take poor Mrs. Peveril to our home at once? Don't let her see the horrid pirate!"

"Yes, Jack, it shall be so. I am glad, my dear, brave boy, that you have rescued her from such a monster; but pray, pray, don't run into further danger!"

"Oh, it's all right, mother," said Jack, laughing, and looking winningly into her mild, anxious face. "But please go home, you women folk, and leave us manly fellows alone with our glory! We must get this rascal to the village and give him into custody."

"Still, my dear son, be careful. You are killing me by these hair-brained ventures."

Mrs. Warbold and Violet then gently led away the poor girl, who seemed quite amazed and helpless.

"Here comes the cart, Jack," cried Bert, as old Clem and Ned Ross arrived with the little wain.

"At your old tricks, Master Jack!" said the fisherman, shaking his white head. "But, certainly, you are a young hero, though I fear you'll never live to be an old one. So you've captured the wretch? Avast! but I know this gaol-bird well; it's the thief Barabbas. Heave him in, boys, and let's steer for the village before any of his brother sharks can come to the rescue. My jib! this is a queer haul you've made, my cheery."

"A real monster of the deep, isn't he, Mr. Cleats?" rejoined our hero, merrily. "You don't often pull up such a queer fish."

"A kind o' devil-fish, I takes it!" grinned the old salt.

They raised the burly body of the insensible pirate and flung it into the cart.

The old fisherman whipped the horse and the cart bundled off, Roving Jack and his Boy Band marching as escort.

"And now, Jack, I've a strange bit of news to tell you," said Hal to our hero, as they walked side by side. "Nellie's husband. Paul Peveril, has returned home."

"That is good news."

"So far as it goes; but misfortunes never come alone. While Nellie was carried off by the pirate, her husband was attacked by highwaymen, and robbed of all his pay and prize-money."

"The cursed scoundrels!" cried Roving Jack, with intense fierceness.

"And the worst part of it is, the poor young couple will now be homeless and penniless."

"Never mind, Jack, we are not robber-lovers, but robber-hunters," returned Hal.

"Talking about highwaymen!" asked Ben Bouncer, stepping up. "I'll tell you an adventure I had with 'em once. I was travelling with my uncle, Major Bouncer, in a post carriage; it was an awful night; such a terrific storm had not been known for centuries. The lightning was so fierce and the thunder so loud that in one part of the country the whole people were blinded and deafened to that degree that they were forced to be fed and led about by persons imported from a distant place for five or six weeks before they could recover their sight and hearing, and the chattering of their teeth caused a slight earthquake."

"Did it rain, Ben?"

"Rain! The next day, Jack, all the leaves in the forest were found to be washed as white as paper; and as for the flowers in the gardens there wasn't a bit of colour in them, and the woodwork of houses, doors, shutters, sign-boards, and the like, all looked as if they had been peeled with a carpenter's plane."

"La! but the highwaymen, Ben?"

"They're coming, Jack. The storm was raging awfully, thunderbolts were flying about like sparks in a forge; steeples and chimney-stacks were toppling down like so many skittles, while it was blowing and thundering ten billion big guns. As for our carriage, it had sprung a leak in several places, and we had to keep baling with all our might and main to save ourselves from drowning. A regular cut-throat night, just the sort of night for highwaymen; they like rough weather."

"Then they must have been well suited on that occasion."

"They were, Jack. Well, I must tell you; my uncle, the major, was very rich; he had just returned from the West Indies, and carried about him bank notes and valuables to the amount of several millions. He was a remarkable man. When abroad he killed so many lions that he was able to supply every man in his regiment with a hide to sleep on;

and once having crept into the open jaws of a dozing alligator, he crawled so far down into the creature's tapering extremity, that his head got wedged in so tight that he was forced to be cut out bodily, and ever afterwards his forehead was pointed like a sugar-loaf. But he was the head of our family—*the* Bouncer, you know. What did I begin about?"

"The robbers, Ben."

"Of course. I like you, Jack, because you listen to my stories without interrupting me, and don't insult me by pretending to think I exaggerate—I detest exaggeration! Why can't a fellow spin a yarn modestly, and keep within the truth?"

"Why, indeed, Ben?"

"Listen, Jack. At midnight we were crossing a lone country road. It was dark as pitch, you couldn't see the nose on your face, when we were surrounded by a band of highwaymen, about five hundred strong."

But Ben Bouncer was not allowed to finish his interesting story, for old Clem Cleats suddenly stopped the cart.

Little Bert Atherstone, who had been running on before the party, came rushing to our hero's side.

"Roving Jack," he whispered, breathlessly, "there is an ugly rascal lurking behind yonder rock; one of the pirates, I'll warrant."

Ben Bouncer gave a shout, and darted off

The rest of the boys seemed inclined to follow his example.

Our hero, however, rushed upon Ben, and seized him by the collar.

"Halt, you cowards!" he shouted, in a reproachful tone. "Are you the same fellows that fought the pirates so bravely? Are you my band of robber-hunters? Am I your chosen captain, and will you flee at the first scent of danger? Halt, for shame!"

"Hurrah for Roving Jack!" shouted Hal, who had not stirred a step from our hero's side.

"Hurrah!" cried the boys, inspired by their leader's daring.

"Hark ye, Master Ben Bouncer," said Jack, sternly; "you're a very amusing fellow, and your bouncing hurts nobody; and as for the terrific accounts you give of your fights with legions of robbers——"

"'Pon my word it's true, Jack," gasped Ben. "Do ye think I'd tell ye a lie? Only, you see, I'm so rash and hot-headed that I don't trust myself; if it comes to a brush with the devilish buccaneers I shall lose all controul of myself, and there'll be murder done when once the lion is roused in my breast; he won't be pacified till he has tasted blood!"

"Stir him up, then," laughed Jack; "we want a lion to tackle these wolves, for we're little better than eagles ourselves. Lead us on to glory."

"The better part of valour, Jack, is discretion; true glory consists in resisting temptation. I feel horribly inclined to slaughter two or three dozen of the ragamuffins, but better thoughts prevail; I'll let the law take it own course."

"And what course will you take?"

"Look, Jack! Wagh! The devils have got the best of it; they're armed to the teeth, and we've nothing but sticks and stones to defend ourselves. I'm off, Jack; it's sheer suicide to linger. Only wait till I'm prepared for 'em, and then you'll see how I'll mow 'em down by hundreds. Run, lads, run; they're after us!"

He broke away from Jack's grasp, and darted off like lightning.

Our hero laughed, and his boy comrades set up a shout of derision.

Ben regarded them not, but continued running at the top of his speed, till, quite exhausted, he was obliged to throw himself upon the sand under the shelter of a large rock.

Meantime a number of wild-looking ruffians were advancing in a body towards the boys.

They carried huge pistols and heavy cutlasses in their hands, and were gesticulating with great ferocity.

"Shiver me, Master Jack," said old Clem Cleats, suddenly halting, "we had better make sail; we can never tackle such a crew as that."

"No," said Jack, thoughtfully, but with perfect coolness, "I'm afraid not; I'll tell you how we'll manage the business. Keep well together, but make for the cliff; you can clamber up under cover of the rocks, or can hide yourselves in one of the caverns till assistance comes, for look, Ben Bouncer is running along the top of the cliff. He will give the alarm, and bring down a party of the villagers to the rescue. Hal and I will jump into the cart and run the gauntlet. Give me a pistol!"

Jack snatched one from old Clem's belt, and then leaped into the cart.

Hal mounted also.

"Fly!" cried Jack. "Never mind us; we can shift for ourselves!"

Old Clem remonstrated, but all in vain; our fiery young hero lashed the horse into a gallop, and dashed away at a rattling speed.

"Potztauzand! Vire on ze yong teufels!" roared Wirth Wolfgang, as the cart came jolting past him and his seamen.

"Down, Hal!" cried Jack.

They crouched in the cart.

Half a dozen pistols were fired at them; but without effect, being at long range.

Some of the bullets passed over the cart; some flattened against the side of the cliff.

Once more Jack sprang to his feet and lashed the horse, which flew along at a terrific pace.

The pirates, with oaths and wild shouts, rushed after them.

Again they fired at the cart.

Still without effect.

"Hurrah!" cried Jack, turning a backward glance, "Old Ben's a trump after all. See, he has fetched the coast-guard, and they are hurrying down the cliff."

"Aye, Jack, and Old Clem and the lads have garrisoned the cave yonder, and are throwing a volley of stones at the pirates. Drive on, for dear life!"

Lash! lash! came the whip on the horse's flanks, and on rattled the cart.

The pirates were gaining on them.

"This is a pretty scrape," said Hal, "we shall be run down as sure as fate."

"If we can hold out a little longer and reach yonder point we shall do," said Jack. "Lie close, Hal; you'll be shot if you expose yourself so much."

The negro of whom mention has already been made, outstripped his companions.

TOM KING STABS THE EXECUTIONER. - See No. 7.

The horse reared, plunged, and fell on his side. The negro had shot him through the heart.

The cart toppled over, and the boys and their prisoner were tumbled out.

Luckily, however, they were rolled in a heap upon the soft sand.

"Ah! yah! yo 'top now!" roared Quashie, running up with an immense sabre flashing in his hands. "Me cotch ye, ha! Me kill yo to deff ye dam young rascal!"

With a savage yell he flew upon Jack, who had risen to his knees.

Our hero felled him by a terrific blow with the pistol butt.

"To the rocks, Hal!" shouted Jack. "I have No. 6.

still the loaded pistol. Run! run! I'll keep the villains at bay!"

Away ran his brave young comrade.

Jack followed.

Soon they were scrambling up the side of the cliff.

Bang! bang! rattled pistols and carbines, and the bullets whizzed by the boys' heads.

Upwards and upwards, from crag to crag, they desperately struggled.

"I vill give von hunders pounds to ze man as vill cotch zat yong tief!"

"Roving shack!" cried Wolfgang. "Donner! zey vill eshcape!"

Three or four of the pirates immediately commenced scrambling up the rocks in pursuit of the boys, who were climbing as fast and as cleverly as monkies.

Hal was the first to reach the brink of the cliff.

Jack uttered a fierce shout.

Just as he had set his foot on the brow of the cliff he felt himself seized from behind.

He turned.

He felt himself grappled by a strong ruffian.

The pirate was a broad-built, burly fellow with a demoniac countenance aglare with ferocity.

He dragged Jack down the side of the cliff.

Our hero staggered.

He felt his foot slipping, and with a qualm of horror glanced down the awful abyss.

The pirate had fixed his grip upon Jack's belt.

Clinging to the rocks with one hand, with the other our hero loosened the belt.

The pirate stumbled backwards, and narrowly escaped being thrown down the rocks.

Uttering a frightful oath, the pirate drew a pistol and aimed it point blank at our hero.

Jack, however, was too quick for him.

He flung out his arm, clapped the muzzle of his own pistol between the ruffian's eyes, and drew the trigger.

The brace of bullets passed clean through his head, shattering his skull and scattering his brains.

The pirate tossed up his arms, bounded off into mid-air, and fell down and down, till, striking upon the rocky base of the cliffs, he was literally dashed to pieces.

Our hero scrambled on to the top of the cliff, and breathless and faint, flung himself down upon the sward.

Hal rushed to his side, and lifted him in his arms with a cry of joy.

"Saved once more, dear Jack!" he cried, with fervour. "Surely some guardian angel watches over you. But see, the pirates are rowing off to the schooner, pursued by the coast-guards."

"Aye, but they'll not be overhauled," said Jack, drawing a deep breath. "Look! the schooner is crowding on all sail, and will soon make a good offing; but the worst plague is, they've got off that ogre, Barabbas."

CHAPTER XVII.

ROVING JACK'S UNEXPECTED ACCESSION TO RANK AND FORTUNE.

PAUL PEVERIL was restored to his faithful Nellie, and, by the kind assistance of Farmer Hetherington, Hal's father, the worthy young couple were established in a new home.

Several months passed away, during which nothing was heard of the Pirates of the Foamy Reef.

Roving Jack and his Boy Band of Robber-Hunters had, therefore, a quiet time.

Somewhat sobered by the terrific adventures through which he had lately passed, our hero conducted himself with unusual discretion.

At home he appeared more grave and steady, and won all hearts by his kind and dutiful conduct, while at school he applied himself with the greatest diligence to his various studies, and being gifted with rare talents, made astonishing progress.

He applied himself in particular to nautical astronomy and the science of navigation.

He also studied foreign languages, and constantly associated with the foreign seamen who frequented the little seaport near which he dwelt.

He was a constant visitor at the cottage of the Peverils, and, as Paul obtained employment as a Channel pilot, our hero, with his trusty comrade Hal, frequently accompanied him on a cruise, and obtained a thorough practical knowledge of all pertaining to seamanship.

At length Paul Peveril obtained a commission on board a man-of-war schooner, and, after much hesitation, Mrs. Warbold consented to write to her late husband's father, Admiral Warbold, requesting him to use his powerful influence in order to obtain for her son and for his young friend, Harold Hetherington, midshipmen's commissions.

In a few days a brief, coldly-worded reply was received from the admiral, expressing his approbation of the step which had been taken, and enclosing the commissions, together with bank notes to a heavy amount for Jack's outfit.

Our brave young hero was nearly wild with joy at the receipt of this letter, and this exultation was damped only by the evident grief his doating mother felt at the near prospect of separation from her beloved child.

When the day of parting arrived Mrs. Warbold's resolution gave way; she burst into a passion of anguish, which she could no longer subdue, and but for the firm, though gentle remonstrances of her son, would have detained him at the last moment.

Jack and Hal accompanied Paul Peveril to Portsmouth, where they embarked in his majesty's schooner the "Foam," and sailed for the West Indies.

It it not our intention to detail the adventures of Roving Jack during the twelvemonth he served on board the man-of-war, for though in themselves they would prove extremely interesting, we have so much to tell of our gallant young hero in his dashing character as a PIRATE HUNTER that we cannot afford space for them here; but in the course of this history we shall find Jack himself frequently reverting to them, and his stories of life in the naval service will be found most enthralling.*

*   *   *   *

It was on a golden evening in autumn that our hero, Roving Jack, and his partner Hal descended from the stage coach which had brought them to Seaborough.

The young middies had just returned after a long and adventurous cruise, and with springing step and bounding hearts walked arm in arm through the dear old village.

"Let's go to the old homestead first; this field leads to your father's farm," said Jack, clasping his true comrade by the arm.

"No," returned Hal, with a bright smile, for he had learned some pleasant news from Paul Peveril with which Jack was as yet unacquainted, "let me see you safe to the Owlet's Roost, lest you should get eagle-hunting or lion-killing by the way."

"As you will, Hal," returned Jack, with a gleesome laugh. "You always think more of me than you do of yourself; but if you have the start of me in this case I'll best you next time."

---

* Every British Boy who loves the sea—and what true boy does not?—should read the most interesting work, entitled, "The Boy Sailor; or, Life on board a Man-of-war," which contains a full and graphic description of the discipline and economy of the British naval service. The prologue to this wild and exciting story relates some truthful and remarkable anecdotes of the dreadful deeds and strange superstitions of the old Cornish wreckers, while the narrative itself includes a complete history of the glorious career of England's great hero, Lord Nelson.

"You don't know what's in store for you, messmate," returned Hal, smiling. "I would not lose the pleasure of seeing your reception at home on any account."

"How? Something unusual has happened?" asked our hero, with a slight start.

"Why, Jack, you will be received by your Boy Band of robber hunters, the heroes of the 'Foamy Reef,' who claim you as their captain. Jack, have you changed your mind?"

"In what respect?"

"Are you still determined to be a robber-hunter?"

"On land and sea!" returned our hero; "but it will be a long time ere I shall obtain the command of a vessel."

"Perhaps you will soon have one of your own?"

"A privateer? No; that is a service I don't like; a privateer is little better than a pirate. Well, to 'build castles in the air,' ye know, Hal, I should like to get a roving commission from the king to hunt down pirates and robbers on land and sea; but, belay, we are reckoning chickens 'before they're hatched.'"

Hal smiled, and then hurried his companion onwards.

"Are all the folks asleep?" asked Jack, looking round wonderingly at the deserted houses and silent streets, "or have they fied from the old village? Even the 'Blue Anchor' stands desolate. What can it mean?"

"The harvest feast at my father's farm is held to-day, Jack," returned Hal, rubbing his hands.

"Come," said our hero, turning slightly pale with excitement, "I long to be at home. Let us mount the rugged lane, and get through the old turnstile atop of the hill yonder, and then we shall sight the old tower."

"Aye, let's hasten, Jack!" cried Hal, bounding with glee, and racing up the hill.

Suddenly the air rang with a gust of mellow bells bursting into a loud, long and merry, merry peal.

Then came a shout from the field above, as little Bert Atherstone's beaming face peered over the turnstile.

"He comes!" screamed little Bert, clapping his hands, and capering about.

"He comes!" responded a hundred blending voices. "Roving Jack, hurrah!"

Our hero paused as suddenly as if he had been struck by a bullet.

He raised his hand to his head, and leaned backwards against the pale that fenced the narrow lane.

Hal seized both his hands and wrung them with affectionate joy.

"Can you read the riddle now?" he cried.

"Yes," returned our hero faintly; "the old admiral is dead. I am now Sir John Warbold, and lord of the manor!"

"But why don't you shout?—Why don't you rave with delight as I do?" cried Hal. "Fancy, fancy, Jack, you are ennobled, and in possession of boundless wealth, for your family is one of the richest in all England, and you are its only representative. Why, in wonder's name, do you look so pale and grave?"

"Extremes meet, Hal; the sudden shock of great and unexpected joy is almost as hard to bear as the stroke of a dire calamity," replied the young nobleman, returning the pressure of Hal's honest hands, while the tears glistened in his eyes, and his voice thickened.

Then his tones changed; his superb form dilated,

his eyes flashed with heroism; he gripped his dirk, and lifted his cap from his curly locks.

"Now will I be a robber-hunter with a vengeance!" he cried. "Death to all sneaking highwaymen and bloody buccaneers!"

They now stood on the brow of the hill.

A heart-stirring scene presented itself.

The field before the long, stern tower was crowded by the villagers, dressed in holiday attire, with bands of music, banners, and wreaths of bright flowers.

The castle itself was adorned with flaunting flags and rich hangings, while the pathway which led to the gate was spanned by triumphal arches bearing mottos of welcome and congratulations such as—

"Welcome home, Roving Jack."

"All honour to the Pride and Lord of the Manor."

The bands struck up a stirring march, and, in an instant, our beloved young hero was surrounded by a crowd of his friends and tenants, who rent the air with stunning huzzas.

Before he could surmount his bewildering emotion sufficiently to utter a single word, he found himself lifted on to strong shoulders, the band parading before him, his brave boy band of robber haters and pirate hunters tossing up their caps, waving handkerchiefs, and streaming flags, and uttering the most deafening shouts of rejoicing.

"Hurrah for our dear young master, brave Sir John Warbold—the honoured lord of the manor!" shouted the tenantry.

"Hurrah for our captain! Long live Roving Jack!" responded the young robber hunters.

So they bore him in triumph along.

"Clear away, you young dogs!" shouted the cheery voice of old Clem Cleats. "Bless my heart, let me grapple him, let me welcome his honour—ha, ha!" and the hearty old chap fairly hugged the handsome boy in his sinewy arms.

Jack laughed, and shook hands right and left, and pacing on to the strains of martial music, advanced to meet a gilded chariot, drawn by milk-white horses, which came rattling from the gates of the old house.

His mother, dressed in a rich robe of black satin, and his foster-sister, Violet, also richly attired in deep mourning, now descended from the carriage.

The crowd swept respectfully back, and looked on in deep silence and with uncovered heads as the fond mother tearfully embraced her darling son.

"Isn't this jolly?" cried Ben Bouncer to Ned Ross. "I suppose you know that I shall some day enjoy a treat of this sort?"

"When will that be, Ben Bouncer?"

"When I succeed to the princely titles and vast territories to which I am heir," returned the incorrigible Ben. "The Bouncers are a large and magnificent house; their representatives are to be found in all quarters of the world. Perhaps you mayn't have heard that I'm next a-kin—a heir apparent—to Lord Maximus Bouncer, Baron Munchausen, Brag-Master General of the British Empire, and Arch-Duke of Gascony."[*]

Having heartily returned the caresses of his mother and his foster-sister, our hero mounted the carriage, and, standing erect, waved his hand as if to request attention.

He was hailed with three stirring cheers.

---

[*] The people of Gascony, in France, are reputed to be great "bouncers." One of their redoubtable warriors boasted that he had slain so many enemies that he commonly slept on a large bed stuffed with their mustachios and whiskers. The word, "to gasconade," which means to brag, is derived from this reputed propensity of the Gascons.

"My dear, kind friends," said Roving Jack, while happy tears sparkled in his proud, flashing eyes, "I am conscious of my own unworthiness—I know that I have done nothing by which I could deserve these expressions of your generous sympathy and warm affection—I know that this demonstration proceeds from the spontaneous impulse of your own kind nature, from the outburst of generous pleasure felt by your kind hearts at beholding a poor, humble boy, born amongst you, suddenly raised to a position of unhoped-for wealth and distinction. Yet be assured that I will for ever strive my uttermost, both as lord of this manor, and as your favoured friend, to win your cherished love and esteem, and, as far as lies in my power, to help those in distress, to make peace between those who are at enmity with each other, to improve the lands, and to bring prosperity and comfort to the humblest homes in Seaborough. God grant me strength and wisdom to fulfil this vow!"

"God bless the noble lad!" cried the men.

"The flower and pride of the village!" responded the women.

"Hurrah for Roving Jack, the Lord of the Manor, the Prince of Jolly Good Fellows, and the King of the Robber-hunters!" shouted the brave Boy Band.

CHAPTER XVIII.

ROVING JACK'S CAREER IN LONDON — THE OLD BLACK LION IN WYCH STREET.

LET our youthful readers imagine themselves transported to the quaint old street near Drury Lane bearing the familiar name that heads the present chapter.

In those days, every shop had its sign, and on either side of the narrow thoroughfare were hung the various quaint symbols of the various trades carried on in the tall, dark, strangely-gabled houses.

At one corner was the figure of a man in armour, opposite to which swung the tabard of a dirty, disreputable-looking tavern called the "Black Lion," famous as the haunt of Jack Sheppard, Blueskin, and various other scoundrels of the same class, who have won by their crimes such an evil notoriety.

Beyond this hung an immense glove, carved in gilded wood; beyond that a monstrous key, with other like devices bespeaking the occupation of the various inhabitants.*

It was in the dusk of the evening, before the dim oil lamps—or, rather, lanterns—which then served to illumine—or, rather, to make visible—the darkness of the dirty streets, had been lighted, that two distinguished-looking youths paused at the door of the "Black Lion."

One of them, a supremely noble and handsome boy, was richly dressed in a mourning suit of black velvet, a three-cornered hat trimmed with crape, black silk stockings, and shoes with diamond buckles, and wearing a small sword by his side.

His companion was attired in a gayer style, wearing a sky-blue coat richly brocaded with gold lace, a laced cocked hat, ruffles, and a silver-mounted sword.

"Upon my life, Jack, I think you had better forego this adventure," said the latter of these young gallants. "You are known to some of the villains, and will surely get into some scrape."

* It has been the careful aim of our artist, in picturing the various scenes of our hero's career in old London, to make his local sketches as accurate as possible, so that our young readers may be able to know what London was really like in the olden times. From time to time pictures will appear of Old London Bridge, Smithfield, Newgate, the Tower, &c.

"I care not," said our hero, for it was he. "I was anxious to see that fellow, Sheppard; I can discern some germs of good in him. He did me a good service once, and I should like to rescue him, if possible, from that awful rascal, Jonathan Wild, who evidently designs to bring the poor lad to the gallows."

"Of course, where you lead I follow," was Hal's reply, given in a tone of reluctance. "Only I don't see what good can come of it. Jack Sheppard's case is quite hopeless, even if you could induce him to give up his present mode of life, which I gravely doubt. He is a condemned felon, only at large because as yet the officers of the law have failed to catch him."

"I can supply him with money, if he will pledge himself to reformation, and smuggle him across the waters in my new frigate 'The Avenger,' and give him a chance of redeeming his past errors and crimes by a life of industry and honesty in a new country."

"It will be a case of 'love's labour lost,' depend upon it, Jack."

"At least, I will wipe out the obligation I am under. No one shall say that I suffered a good turn to pass unrequited."

"Yet I think it is folly to run the risk of being hustled, robbed, and perhaps murdered——Ha! Step aside, Jack, the villains are watching us from the window."

"Then we'd better put a bold face on the matter," returned Jack. "The rogues might dog our steps if they saw us retreat now, and this is a cut-throat neighbourhood."

So saying, Jack mounted the steps of the tavern, and entered the low, dirty passage.

The landlord, by name Joe Hind, a burly slovenly fellow, came shuffling out to meet them.

For an instant he stared at them with surprise, as if their appearance was that of unwonted visitors.

"Mohawks!" he muttered, "or roving bloods on the quest for some pretty bona roba."

Then he bowed obsequiously, and said, with a frowning smile—

"Welcome, noble young gentlemen. My poor house is honoured by such a presence."

Bowing and grinning, he led the way down the passage.

"Do you require a crib—a room in private?" he asked.

"No," returned Roving Jack, coolly. "We are willing to join in with the rest of your company."

"Gad! that's all bob! my dimber gentry coves," returned Hind, winking. "You're fly to the humours of the ken!"

"We are not greenhorns," said Jack, smiling.

"Blast me, all on the square, my flash culls, I perceive—ha! ha! This way, my bloods."

He laid his hand on the panel of the door of a large room, from which rang forth sounds of boisterous merriment, above which a manly voice was heard hollering out,

"Now Phœbus sinks into the west,
And welcome joy and welcome jest,
Midnight shouts and revelry,
Tipsy dance and jollity."

Hind opened the door, and thrusting in his head, laid his finger on his nose.

"Ha! the traps!" cried one or two villanous-looking ruffians, seizing their weapons.

"All's bowman, my covies, it's only a brace of stray pigeons."

"Fit for plucking, eh!"

"Stash your clatter, they're down to the rigs;

bold slips though young 'uns, so draw it mild, my blades."

He then turned to his guests.

"You'll find a crew of roaring boys, real blades of the huff, my dimber kiddies," he said to Jack, as he threw open the door. "If you behave prettily and ain't above throwing a sop in the pan, perhaps you will be accepted as candidates for the liberties and privileges of this dominion. Don't forget the garnish."

Roving Jack and his friend walked into the room with an air of ease and self-possession that could scarcely have been expected from their age and inexperience.

They found themselves in a large room crowded with vile and desperate characters of both sexes.

At the head of a long table sat a tall, handsome fellow, of very dashing exterior, richly dressed in a crimson silk coat, covered with gold lace; his laced hat, a riding whip, and a brace of finely-mounted horse-pistols, lay on the table before him, while upon his knee was seated a young female of witching beauty. She had delicate features, large, lustrous, laughing black eyes, and brilliant complexion, and long rippling ringlets black and glossy as the raven's wing.

She was very showily dressed, and her charming person was adorned by some very valuable jewellery.

Gangs of house-breakers, pickpockets, footpads, gipsies, gentlemen of the highroad, and girls of bad character crowded the reeking den.

With firm and graceful step, Roving Jack walked lightly across the room to a vacant seat by the table.

The men present greeted him with a stare of suspicion and a suppressed growl of envy and malice.

But the young "ladies," on the contrary, expressed their admiration of the two gallants, by the boldest comments.

One girl, a lovely blonde, extravagantly dressed, her saucy blue eyes dilating, and her piquante cherry lips parting in a dimply smile, that displayed a row of tiny teeth as white as seed-pearls, exclaimed aloud,

"La! Poll; what lovely eyes!"

The tall, dark, commanding, but very handsome woman to whom this remark was addressed, was attired in a green silk riding-habit, embroidered with silver, a man's velvet jacket, a muslin cravat, edged with the finest point lace, and a three-cornered laced hat cocked jauntily on one side of her head.

"Devilish pretty fellows, both on 'em, Bess; but, for my part, I prefer the fair one—the cove in sky-blue—look at his leg!"

"You're a fool, Poll," returned the other, coquettishly, tossing her pretty head. "The gallant in the black suit is all my fancy; the other is not to be compared with him; he's a perfect duck. Ah, me! In mourning, too! He looks so tender and interesting. I should like to kiss him."

"Come, come, Bess; what would Jack Sheppard say if he heard you?"

"Oh, Jack's well enough," returned the girl; "but this is real gentry."

"Much! I'm sure! Your modesty is refreshing, Edgeworth Bess; do you think such a gallant slip as that is gull enough to stoop to pick up nothing?" returned Poll, contemptuously.

"Come, I say, Mistress Maggot; civility, if you please!" cried Bess, raising her voice to a shrill pitch, while her cheek flushed crimson with passion.

"Oh, my dear! pray don't let's quarrel," said Poll, coolly.

"Well, don't you make me mad, Poll Maggot," returned Bess, with difficulty restraining her temper; "I don't want to break out; I've had fits; it upsets me; but don't you suppose that because Jack Sheppard's my fancy man that there ain't none of the true blood's and Corinthians that favours me. Who gave me that bracelet do ye think?"

"Some cracksman or bridle cull (highwayman), I suppose."

"Guess again."

"Perhaps it was the old Jew, Abraham Mendez," sneered Poll, "who stood your friend when you were sent to Bridewell for filching the old French marquis's gilt screen and reader," (gold snuff-box and pocket-book.)

"What, you wretch!"

"Don't be cross, my dove," retorted Poll; "poor old Abe deserves your gratitude, for he saved your dainty bodice a precious tight lacing, you know; and though he is old, and frowsy, and blear-eyed, they say he has saved quite a fortune since he has been in Jonathan Wild's service. If anything should happen to Jack, I'd advise you to make a Fleet match with the old Israelite; he can't last long with so many diseases; and then, Bess, you may gratify your ambition, and cut a shine as a fine lady."

The face of Edgeworth Bess blazed scarlet with fury, and for an instant she seemed inclined to spring upon her companion; but, cowed by the cold, scornful glance of the tall and powerful virago, she relapsed into a hollow, giggling laugh.

"I know the meaning of your jeers, my love," she said. "It isn't my fault if Jack likes me better than yourself. I never was jealous of you, I'm sure. But if you want to know how I came by this pretty bracelet, I'll tell ye. Sir Ranulph Gayton, the prince of the gay rufflers, and leader of the Mohocks, gave it me. There now!"

"Jack will be delighted, madam, to hear of your good fortune," said Poll, stiffly.

"That for you, and Jack, too!" retorted Bess, snapping her fingers in her companion's face.

"And that for yourself, minion!" returned Poll, inflicting a sounding box on the ear, which knocked poor Bess on her back.

Bess sprang up, and, but for the intercession of the bystanders, would have assailed her like a tiger.

Poll put her arms akimbo, and laughed derisively.

"Let her come to me; a tender lamb," she sneered.

Bess raved herself hoarse with shrieks and imprecations.

But uttering a burst of choice oaths, several of the ruffians seized the pretty frail fury in their strong arms, and, despite her kicking and struggling, at a sign made by the dashing gentleman at the head of the principal table, carried her out of the room, and turned her adrift in the streets.

As for Poll, she laughed her cold contempt, and, reseating herself, cocked her hat more fiercely than ever, and tossed off a glass of gin.

This short and sharp altercation between these two ladies, fair and gentle, had little effect in disturbing the composure of the general company.

There was a sudden break in the loud conversation and the flow of jest and laughter just for a moment, and some eyes were carelessly turned upon the girls.

The women folk, however, showed an inclination to take part in the quarrel, and support their respective favourites, and a general row would undoubtedly have been the consequence had not the president issued prompt and stern directions to some of his immediate supporters to maintain order.

Meanwhile, Roving Jack and Hal Hetherington had initiated themselves into something like favour with the honourable conclave by ordering bowls of punch all round.

"Dam'me, this is a true blood!" cried the chairman, extending his hand. "Tip us your bunch of fives, and welcome to Bermuda! What say, my young kestrels, to claiming the privileges and immunities of our society? Only costs you a handful of smelts, and then you may have the freeman's key to all the lurking cribs of the old Mint, to the liberties of Alsatia, and the protection of all the boys and roving blades in the Friars, who will be bound to defend you from writ and warrant, harming beck and bum-bailey."

"Blood and 'ouns! What are you talking about, Tom King?" cried a highwayman at the table, starting with alarm. "Who would dare initiate the culls without the authority and sign manual of the King o' the Rogues—Jonathan Wild?"

"Jonathan Wild be d——d!"

"Tom!" shrieked the lady who reclined in his arms, as she cast a trembling glance around, "are you tired of your life?"

"Fudge!" returned the highwayman, with a merry laugh. "You all seem to fear that bumptious covey-catcher as if he were Beelzebub, and his tipstaff a pitch-fork; but come, my dimber gallants, tip up the stivers, and, as vicegerent at the council-board, I'll take upon myself to bestow upon you the freedom of the sanctuary. Joe Hind, pass over the register. Your names, my bucks; and which of you lily-livered curs here will stand godfathers to these bantam chicks, in defiance of old Jonathan, who is a bandog, a dubsman, a spy, a whiddler, a peach, and a ten times anathematised traitor and usurper!"

"Hush, hush!" cried some of the thieves, in great dismay.

"We won't listen to any treason agen the guvnor," cried others. "Stash yer gaff, Tom King."

"Don't kimbaw the flash coves any longer!" shouted a savage ruffian, swaggering up to the table and brandishing a monstrous whinger. "What business have they here? It's a trap. Chive the cursed spies! Down with the harming cheats!"

The men rose from their seats, and fiercely seized the weapons.

The women screamed in terror.

Roving Jack was on his feet in an instant.

The burly scoundrel who had raised this sudden storm, a broad-built fellow, with enormous mustachios, fiery nose, and deep-set, ferret eyes, dressed in an old discoloured and patched military uniform, advanced the point of his sword to Jack's throat.

Striking the weapon aside with his left arm, our hero planted his fist with a loud clap upon the huge ruffian's blossomy nose, and floored him flat on his back.

Jack instantly snatched up the weapon of his fallen foe, and presented it to the rascal's breast, at the same time raising his left hand.

"Fair play's a jewel," he cried, in a dauntless, cheerful tone. "Hear my explanation, ladies and gentlemen——"

"Ben coves and dimber-morts," supplemented Tom.

He leaned over the table, and emptied a flagon on the head of the recumbent ruffian, who writhed and swore most awfully, but made no attempt to rise.

Jack's noble face, dauntless attitude, pleasant, boyish voice, and the gratification generally felt at the discomfiture of the detested bully, caused a re-action in our hero's favour.

"Ha, ha! hear the game kinchen; let him say his say," was now the cry, mingled with shouts of laughter at the bully's expense.

"Ladies and gentlemen," said Jack, "I and my companion have come hither with no hostile intent, our purpose being to meet one of your associates, who has rendered me a service which I am anxious to requite."

"Name?" shouted the gang.

"Jack Sheppard," returned our hero.

"Where is Jack? Where's the Blueskin?" asked the thieves, looking about in search of those worthies. "Here, Poll Maggot, do you know this younker?"

"Know him? Yes, bless his heart!" returned the stalwart Poll, advancing, and ogling our hero with such an amorous glance as brought the blood tingling to his smooth fresh cheek, and caused him to lower his eyes with a frown. "He's a noble young gentleman; only last night he saved poor blind Mab the ballad-girl from the insults and rough handling of the Mohocks. Never a knight-errant fought for distressed damsel more gallantly. Oh, he's a good boy, and let me see who'll dare to hurt one hair of his pretty curly head. Come under the shadow of my wing, poppet. Now who dares attempt to harm ye?"

Poll slid her large but comely arm round Jack's waist, and hugged him, blushing and struggling, to her side.

In her right hand she twirled a stout cudgel, and defiantly whistled a military air.

Thus released from the pressure of Jack's foot and the keen point of the sword pressed to his throat, the bully stumbled on to his feet, and, with swelling front and swashing air, swaggered up to Poll.

"Darkness and devils!" he thundered, "let me get at this insolent pap-fed cully; I'll hack the pigmy chit into wafers! Blood and woun's! shall a veteran's beard be plucked by paltry kids and women? Broil me first! Toss me over my pinking iron, sirrah, and draw your own cheese-toaster, and then prepare yourself to die untimely death, you silken spaniel whelp!"

"Who is this ass in lion's hide?" asked our hero, laughing with genuine amusement at this bombastic tirade. "His bray is tremendous."

"Hurraw!" shouted the robbers. "A plucky kinchen! a brave slip! A ring! A ring! Let the kiddy quiet the swaggering, cowardly cur—he can do it. Let 'em fight it out!"

Our hero laughed merrily.

He broke from Poll's embrace and flung the long basket-hilted sword at the bully's feet.

"Let me know my adversary's name," said Jack, smiling, as he drew his slim, blue, gleaming steel. "I am bound by the rules of my order not to fight with any but gentlemen; and I mean to unsheath my sword in no cause that is not a good one. Yet I think that the distinction between an oppressor or a scoundrel in a silk coat and one in fustian is not worth regarding; so let me know what name is to be inscribed on his coffin-plate, speaking in his own heroic vein. Pray, madam, release my arm; you put me in imminent peril, for, you see, this treacherous hound is capable of taking the basest advantage."

This last request was addressed to Poll Maggot, who had caught his sword arm, and was dragging him back.

Nor was it uncalled for, as the dastardly bully had snatched up his sword and made a desperate lunge at him.

Tom King, however, had parried the treacherous thrust.

"Kill the skeldering cur!" growled Tom. "He calls himself Captain Hector MacDubber; he says he was a soldier, and fought under Marlborough at Ramilies and Malplaquet; but the lying poltroon was drubbed out of his regiment for desertion and cowardice, and the only wounds he can show are the scars of the cat-scratching on his lubberly shoulders, or the brand on his side. Pah! never stain clean steel with his gutter blood. Leave him to Poll's cudgel, my gallant juvenile."

"By all the fiends of war, you shall pay for this, Tom King!"

The highwayman affected a start of terror at this threat, and then, with a hearty laugh, coolly raised his heavy boot and kicked the bragging dastard across the room.

"Corpo de Bacco! Thunder and blood!" roared the captain, once more scrambling on to his feet.

He rushed at our hero with a frantic lunge.

Jack quietly avoided the stab, and, walking calmly up to him, made a straight, swift thrust.

The valiant captain tossed up his arms, and his huge sword fell clanking on the floor; he staggered for an instant, and then fell flat on his back, yelling most dismally.

His dingy shirt and ruffles were drenched in blood.

"Pinked! by Jehoshaphat!" cried Tom, bending over him.

"Help! Murder! Watch!" roared the coward, writhing and glaring about him in mortal dismay. "A surgeon! I am murdered! A priest! Ah! my guilty conscience! I must confess, I cannot die yet. Will no one have pity on me? O-oh!"

Tom King had lifted the fellow's right arm, and found that his wound was merely a flesh cut a little above the elbow.

Upon making this discovery he turned a significant glance upon the surrounding faces, dropped the limb, and, standing over the prostrate bully, worked his black silky moustache, looked down upon him with such a serious phiz that the latter read a confirmation of his worst fears, and was beside himself with terror.

"The miserable young villain!" groaned the captain, raising himself on his hands. "My blood be upon his head. Justice! Justice! I take you all to witness that murder has been done. Arrest him! What, you laugh! You heartless fiends, to laugh at dying agonies: but I'll have some vengeance on ye. What, ho! watch! Murder! Murder!"

"What the devil is all this hullabaloo?" panted Joe Hind, the landlord, rushing in. "We shall have the shoulder clappers down in the twinkling of a bed-post."

"I am murdered, Joe!" moaned the unfortunate captain. "I am a dead man!"

"Well, if you are, you needn't make such a row about it."

"Blood for blood!" roared the captain. "I'll hang you all! Fetch the watch! Bring a surgeon! I bleed to death! Murder!"

"Silence the howling cur," cried Joe Hind, in great alarm, "and get the gentry coves out of the house. Gag the shrieking pig; beat his brains out!"

Profiting by this admirable suggestion for quieting the terror-struck dastard, Poll Maggot stepped coolly up to him and stunned him by a blow on the head with a cudgel.

"Carry him into some snoozing-crib, Joe Hind, and let old Nightshade, the apothecary, look to

him," said Tom King. "And now, my pals, let us resume our revels. Never heed that lubber, his wound is a mere scratch; and as for his thick skull, Poll's cudgel suffered most in the concussion. Fill up the punch-bowls, Joe; let us drink the health of this gallant young roysterer."

Captain Hector MacDubber being borne from the room, the late fracas was soon forgotten, and the robbers abandoned themselves to a noisy carousal.

"Hark ye, young sirs," said Tom King, to our hero and his companion, "I will make bold to speak roundly with you. Though I admire your courage and commend your desire to keep faith with Jack Sheppard, I think you have been guilty of a great piece of foolhardiness in venturing into this province without a pass from the great Jonathan; but you are safe for this night, at least. I am lieutenant of a gallant troop of dragoons; our captain is the famous Dick Turpin. We are strong enough to protect you from violence, but I should advise you to get out of these quarters as soon as possible, and appoint some other rendezvous to meet Jack Sheppard."

"I am about to leave England," returned our hero, "and I have determined upon seeing Jack before I set sail. I have ascertained that he will be here within an hour, and for any danger that may threaten I am willing to outface it."

"Say you so, my prince? Then, push about the bowl, and let's get glorious!

"Oh, wine! all the muses
Have still sung thy praises,
And through time's long ages
All poets and sages
Have tippled——'"

Here he suddenly stopped and glanced at his mistress, who had slipped from his knee and placed herself between Jack and Hal, and was striving to allure them with her siren smiles and tender speeches.

"Ah, Kate," laughed Tom, "have ye found 'metal more attractive?' Do ye want to see me spitted like the poor captain by this ruffling bantam? Oh, woman! woman!"

And once more the gay fellow burst forth,

"Do not say I am deceived,
That Chloe's false and common,
All along I have believed
She was a—very woman!"

At this moment there was a sudden and general shout—

"The Blueskin!"

Our hero started.

He turned his eyes towards the door.

Booted and spurred, and wrapped in a long riding-coat, the celebrated associate of the still more notorious criminal, Jack Sheppard, entered the room accompanied by Edgeworth Bess.

The company made way for him, and, seeing Tom King at the head of the table, he marched up to him and shook hands.

"Ha, ha! my knight of the snaffle, welcome to Romeville!" he said.

Then he turned his glance upon our hero.

He sprang back.

"Hulloa! what strange kinchen is this?" he thundered.

"A friend, Joe Blake," returned Tom King; "he's a good boy, and under my protection."

"S'blood! Do you know who he is?"

"No, and care not; he's a young hero."

"'Tis Roving Jack!" roared Blueskin, unsheathing his whinger.

"Roving Jack!" yelled the robbers, each starting to his feet.

Every sword leaped from its scabbard; pistols

were drawn, and the crowd surrounded the daring boys with menacing looks and a torrent of execrations.

Blueskin would have attacked our hero, who, with Hal, had drawn his sword, and stood prepared for the assault.

But Tom King interposed.

"I care not if he be the queer-chief (chief-justice) himself! He is under my protection, I say, and no one shall harm him!"

"Cut him down, Blueskin! Down with the infernal spy!" shouted the robbers.

Thus incited, Blueskin uttered a tremendous oath and raised his sword.

Tom seized him by his laced cravat and dragged him backwards.

"I say you shall not touch the kid!" cried Tom. "I am sworn to his quarrel, and will defend him with my life!"

Blueskin released himself from Tom's grip, and then flew upon him with a frightful oath.

Their swords clashed.

The next instant by a dexterous twist of his wrist Tom King disarmed his antagonist, and sent his sword flying across the table.

Meantime, Jack and Hal were defending themselves vigorously from a furious assault of swords, knives, and bludgeons.

There was a terrific uproar.

Women shrieked, men thundered their oaths, swords clashed, benches and tables were overturned, lights were knocked out, and all was pell-mell, havoc and confusion.

Jack and Hal had leaped upon the settle, and, finding that their slight dress-swords were of little use in defending them from such numbers, snatched up chairs and stools and dashed them down upon the heads of their assailants.

Blueskin drew a pistol and levelled it at our hero.

Tom King grasped his arm.

The two strong men wrestled desperately, and snarled at each other like fighting tigers.

The pistol went off.

The bullet lodged in the ceiling, and patches of lath and plaster scattered down.

Joe Hind roared his entreaties to keep the peace, but was utterly disregarded.

The daring boys had thrown all the missiles within reach, including bottles, candlesticks, flagons, and punch-bowls, and were fain to betake themselves to their swords.

Another instant would have decided the contest by the destruction of Tom King and the dauntless young robber-hunters; but a slight-built youth bounded like a harlequin over the heads of the crowd, and perched himself upon the table, sword in hand.

"Hold!" he cried, in a loud, ringing voice. "Back, all of you! If the kinchens are spies we can strangle 'em according to the laws of the province. But, the watch is alarmed, and in another moment we shall have 'em battering at the door in the king's name. Back, you curs! Are a couple of kids worth all this pother? Silence, I say!"

"Right, Captain Sheppard!" growled one of the ruffians. "You're not the lad to shield a cursed peach! Silence all!"

Comparative quiet being obtained, Jack turned to our hero, and questioned in a low tone.

"Fool! What brought you here?"

"No treachery, Jack Sheppard; I am by choice and profession a robber-hunter; but——"

"Hush, fool!" cried Jack, sternly; "answer my question!"

"You saved my life when I was attacked by Jonathan Wild in the cavern on the Foamy Reef; I vowed at the time that I would seek you out, and offer you my assistance to escape from the cursed thief-taker—who has sworn to hang you—from your vile associates and evil courses. My ship is equipped and ready to make sail; I can remove you to a foreign land where you may spend the rest of your life in honest industry and happiness. If you refuse that offer you will at least accept a hundred guineas, which I have brought as some recompense for the good turn you did me."

"Phew! we'll speak more of this hereafter, Sir John," returned Sheppard, respectfully; "and now I will do my best to save your life, for you are in deadly danger."

He then turned to address the impatient robbers, who stared on this scene with wonder.

"It's all bowman, my pals," said Jack, with a light laugh. "This slashing lad is an eccentric; I saved his life on one occasion, and he has brought me fifty guineas according to promise. I had no thought that he would have had the pluck to keep our appointment at this place; but we roaring boys of the high pad know how to respect courage, and the gallant young gentleman is willing to distribute another fifty guineas amongst you by way of garnish."

Jack Sheppard held out his hand, and our hero slipped a heavy purse into it.

The housebreaker then took out a handful of guineas, and threw them among the crowd.

"Hurraw!" shouted the thieves.

There was a desperate scramble.

"This way, gentleman; follow me close," said Jack Sheppard, proceeding towards the door.

Tom King brought up the rear.

Blueskin, however, opposed their exit.

"Blood and thunder!" he shouted. "Are you mad, captain? Will you let the ban-dog whelps escape?"

"I have given my word, Blueskin."

"Your word! I say it shall not be; they have thrown themselves into the trap, and we'll wring their kite's necks."

"Harkye, Blueskin," said Jack Sheppard, coolly, "if you attempt to thwart me in this matter, our partnership ceases from this moment; I break with you for ever!"

Blueskin uttered a savage growl, and stamped his foot with disgust.

Joe Hind, who stood trembling by the door, immediately threw it open.

Roving Jack, Hal, Tom King, and Jack Sheppard passed out, and proceeded along the dark passage.

Before Joe Hind could prevent him, Blueskin sneaked through the half-closed door.

HAL HETHERINGTON TO THE RESCUE.

CHAPTER XIX.

JACK SHEPPARD ACCEPTS ROVING JACK'S PROPOSAL TO JOIN HIS BAND OF ROBBER-HUNTERS.

JACK SHEPPARD ushered our hero and Hal into a large, dirty, dingy chamber.

Tom King, with drawn sword, took his station without the door.

Roving Jack beckoned him to enter.

The highwayman bowed gracefully, and carelessly swaying his laced hat, tramped in.

Sheppard instantly closed the door, and locked it.

"We are safe from intrusion," he said; "and in case of accidents there is a window which opens in Wych Street, and from which I see lights burning in the little bed-room at old Wood's, the carpenter's, where I have often slept sweetly, after a day of honest labour." Jack drew a deep sigh, then, reddening with the false shame of a genuine criminal, "Pish! I was green then," said he. He drew out his pistols, laid them ready upon the table, and then, after peering cautiously round the room, drew chairs to the table, and invited our hero and Hal to be seated.

"And now, Sir John Warbold, may I hear your proposal?"

"Your hand, Jack Sheppard," said our hero, frankly. "And yours, Tom King; you have generously and gallantly defended an enemy of your class because he was out-matched by numbers, and had come with the flag of truce in his hand."

"Dam'me, every messenger who brings such peace offerings may be sure of a welcome," laughed Tom King. "Your pardon, Sir John."

"Now, Jack, I mean to ask you a plain question. Are you happy in your present course of life?" continued our hero.

"Happy?" said Jack, in surprise.

"Bah! who *is* happy?" asked Tom King. "Happy is a maudlin word."

"Confound your clatter!" cried Sheppard, impatiently. "Let his honour speak."

"I repeat the question, then, Jack."

"No, I am *not* happy," said Sheppard, as he threw himself into a chair and toyed with the jewelled rings on his fingers; "and yet I ought to be—I always wished to be considered a fine, dashing fellow; to be a sort of hero. I have reached the height of that sort of renown that may be won by such as I; for I am the finest cracksman of the day; I am lord of the lock and king of the key; no prison can hold me; no crib is safe from me; I can boast of more daring deeds, have taken more swag, than e'er a reeving blade of 'em all—yes, I've gained my wish—I am famous."

"*In*famous, Jack."

"Ha!" growled the young housebreaker, instinctively clutching a pistol. "But your motives are friendly; pray, sir, proceed, but don't play the chaplain; this is not the Stone Hall of Newgate, and I am rather short-tempered."

"I have no wish to sermonize," said Roving Jack. "Do you know, Sheppard, that you and I are somewhat alike in disposition?"

Jack Sheppard laughed.

"How can that be?" he asked.

"You are of a restless, roving, adventurous turn, so am I; you love danger and excitement for its own sake; you like to surmount the most desperate obstacles by your own subtlety, pluck, and perseverance; you are greedy of fame; in all this we resemble each other. But, Jack, you made a false start; there are two roads; you took the wrong one; the one you have taken will lead to Tyburn; and, as for your 'fame,' it may live in the vile ballads and romances that please the depraved, but every honest youth will scout the idea of such as you being a *hero*. The devil himself is famous in your fashion."

Jack Sheppard's broad, black brows met in a sullen frown, and his pale cheek flushed with subdued anger.

"Hark ye, Sir John," said Tom King; "as you are strong, be merciful. Born as you are to wealth, ease and honour, you cannot appreciate the power of those temptations that beset poor rogues in a lower sphere than yourself."

"I can and do, Tom," said our hero, warmly; "and though I am now in possession of wealth, as you mention, the time has been when I was but a poor friendless boy with very uncertain prospects, and Jack will tell you that I was once subjected to a severe trial."

"That's true," said Jack Sheppard; "old Jonathan made sure he had killed ye."

"I plead no merit, Jack; in my case you would have acted as I did."

"Yes; I would be honest if I liked, no one should prevent me," muttered Sheppard, in a sullen tone.

"You should have been a soldier, a sailor, or an explorer of strange and savage lands; then, Jack, with your skill, pluck and endurance, you would indeed have been a hero."

"But I turned—*thief!*" muttered Jack, folding his arms, and bending his head.

"Come, Jack, it's not too late to repent," said our hero. "As I mean to aid the law in battling with strong-handed robbers on land and sea, I will take licence to save one now and then, who, I think, is worthy of a better fate than that which must attend such base and wretched courses. Let the past go, Jack! Live to redeem it; we will sail as comrades, and see if we can pluck up 'drowned honour by the locks,' if we can carve out fame in the cause of right and chivalry!"

"Blueskin wouldn't hear of it," mumbled Jack.

"Bah! are you a coward that you cannot face his vulgar jibes and mockery?" said our hero. "I thought you were one who could never be turned from your purpose?"

"But I haven't made up my mind to anything yet," said Jack Sheppard, sulkily.

"But you will make up your mind, Jack, I am sure, to join me in my venturous cruise," returned our hero. "I like you. Come, then, are we friends?"

"Till death!" returned the house-breaker, gripping his hand. "I am a thief. You do not despise me?"

"As a thief I do; be you as bold, as generous as you will; but you cannot be either. It is hollow mockery and folly. Can a man be generous with what does not belong to him? Can a man be bold who is too much the coward to face hard work, but must filch like the sneak, the 'thief in the night?' I like you, Jack, because I believe you to be a wild, brave spirit—lost and castaway. Come, then, join my band; but that is nothing. What is my band? What am I? Come out into the straight, plain paths of common honesty, and be a man! Where did you get those ruffles, that glittering brooch, that waistcoat of silver brocade?"

"I—I——"

Jack's face flushed crimson.

"Stole them, or the money that bought them. Woman! baby! will you be lured by such paltry, tawdry baits? Would you not be more proud and princely in the roughest guise, if your heart were free, and your hands clean of crime? A thief, Jack, a thief, a thief!"

"Why don't I kill ye?" hissed Jack Sheppard, clutching his sword hilt.

"Because you know I tell you the truth from grateful and friendly motives," returned Roving Jack, boldly smiling. "Do ye think that I want to cant and preach; that I, your very counterpart in some respects, wish to blame you for your pluck and deviltry? Not a whit; but; oh! Jack—a thief! a paltry, sneaking thief!"

"But I can't leave them; they think so much of me; and Edgeworth Bess," muttered Jack Sheppard, irresolutely.

"She will betray you, Jack."

"The Romany fortune-teller said she has threatened me in her passion," returned Jack, with a careless laugh; "but I'll never believe it of her."[*]

"Egad! woman is at the bottom of all mischief," said Tom King, a dark cloud settling on his manly brow. "But for one of those 'tinted' sepulchres, so comely without, so loathsome within, I should not now be a gentleman of the high toby. Well, let the world wag, for, as the pirate says—

"' I am what I am,
And I don't care a d——n,
For I sail 'neath the Jolly Oliver.. [†]

---

[*] Our young readers will remember that Jack Sheppard was betrayed by the girl whom he had rescued from prison.

[†] The black flag of piracy.

"Ha, ha But, dam'me, I *loved* the girl."

Tom stamped his foot with impulsive energy, and there was deep sincerity and tragic earnestness in his tone.

"I'll tell you the story some day, Jack Sheppard; but there, there, it's all rot! A man loves—his idol crumbles to dust! He toils—his cunning hand withers! Nevertheless, Jack, I'll tell you thus much of sober truth—there must be some 'hereafter,' and we shall cut a sorry figure when the great reckoning comes; but 'shadows avaunt! Richard's himself again!'"

Tom King laughed a hollow laugh, and then, clapping our hero on the shoulder, he added,

"I accept your offer, Roving Jack. I will join your band, I will fight on the right side, and the first shot that levels me with the dust I sprang from shall be welcome."

"You will not say so, Tom King, when you feel that you are once more restored to self-respect, and can look the world in the face as an honest man," returned our noble boy hero, joyously. "One cruise with me, and then I think I shall be able to obtain a free pardon for you; in that case, all will be well, and the stains of the past will be cleansed away for ever. Won't you join us, Jack?"

"Yes, Sir John, I will!" returned Sheppard, starting up, and clasping his hand; "but take back this purse; I will receive no gelt from you till I have earned it."

"You have earned this already," said our hero, smiling, and dropping two valuable rings into the purse. "Take it, and if you should find yourself in want of money, freely apply to me. And now it is settled that you will join my band?"

"Done, Roving Jack."

"And you, too, Tom King?"

The highwayman trolled out—

"This world's a wide sea, and a rover,
    It's battles and breezes I've breasted
Some fortunate isle to discover,
    Where my home-loving heart might be rested."

"Aye, I'll be your captain of mariners."

"Meet me, then, to-morrow night; but, hark!"

A shriek was heard in the passage without.

Then the light patter of flying feet.

"Tom!—help!—let me in!" cried a voice without.

The highwayman and Jack Sheppard sprang up, and seized their weapons.

"'Tis a woman's voice," said Hal.

"Aye, Kate's," returned Tom King, stepping to the door, and unlocking it; "some cursed mishap; the traps are down, for a wager."

Tom's mistress sprang into the room.

Trembling and breathless, she threw herself into his arms.

"Save me! save me!" she gasped.

"Tut, tut; calm yourself, my dainty dell," returned Tom, drawing his sword, "you are saved already. What has happened?"

"No, no! slap to the door!" cried the girl, breathlessly. "Ah! they are coming! Whither shall I fly?"

Jack Sheppard rushed to the door, closed it, and turned the key.

"The brown bills?"

"Yes, Tom; that wretch Quilt Arnold, and the horrid old Jew, Abraham Mendez, with a whole posse of watchmen, are in pursuit of me."

Voices and hurried steps were now heard in the passage.

"To the window!" cried Jack Sheppard. "Now, Sir John, will you aid us to save this poor wench from the lash?"

"With all my heart," replied our hero; "I cannot bear to see her dragged away by those brutal ruffians, and, right or wrong, I'll help you to save her."

"Gallant heart," cried Tom King. "Keep the door, then. Now, Kate, give me your scarf."

"Must I clamber down from this window?" said the girl, shuddering.

"Aye, lass; but that is easy," returned Tom, binding the scarf about her waist. "Catch hold of my hands, and I will let you down."

The girl obeyed, but not without hesitation.

The thundering at the door, which Jack, Hal, and Sheppard had barricaded with chairs and tables, urged her to exertion, and she let herself down.

Tom King held the end of the scarf, and encouraged her in whispers.

She reached the ground in safety.

"After her, Tom," said our hero, in an under tone. "She may be waylaid in the street; besides, you may be recognised and captured."

Tom raised his hat, and smiled his adieu.

He then nimbly clambered through the window, and dropped lightly on to the pavement below.

"Curse ye—open the door!" roared the surly voice of Quilt Arnold. "Open, I command ye, in the king's name!"

Bash!—bash!

"Hold!" cried our hero, as Sheppard closed the windows. "No violence; we will let you in." He threw open the door.

But so suddenly, that the little, ugly, weazened, red-bearded Jew stumbled forward, and pitching over a chair, rolled half-way across the chamber.

Howling, cursing, and rubbing his ankle, he scrambled on to his spindle legs.

"Where's the blowen? You have let the baggage escape!" cried Quilt Arnold. "Mr. Wild shall know of it. I'll arrest you all for this rescue—ha! Jack Sheppard, you here?"

"Aye, my nab; so be civil," returned the robber.

"Holy Abramsh, who ish dese shentlemensh?" snuffled the old Jew.

Quilt Arnold glanced with astonishment at the gallant forms of our hero and his friend.

"If I mistake not, sir," he said, in a respectful tone. "I have the honour of addressing Sir John Warbold?"

"Aye, Master Quilt Arnold," returned our hero, sternly; "and this is not the first time we have met. Have you forgotten the pirate's cave, at the Foamy Reef?"

"Hush, for mercy, Sir John!" muttered Wild's satellite, with a start. "Do not betray me."

He then drew our hero aside.

"Hark ye, Sir John; per'aps you have some wish that the bona roba should escape?"

"With what crime is she charged?" asked Roving Jack.

The thief-taker grinned.

"Not with cly-faking, I must confess; she's not a cut-purse exactly; but Mr. Wild has reasons of his own for wishing to apprehend her; and you know, Sir John, that by virtue of the new statute, he can at any time clap his hand on the shoulders of a girl of her class."

"I understand," said our hero. "But tell Jonathan Wild that it was *my* wish that she should not be apprehended."

"Should be sorry to be the bearer of such a message, with pardon, Sir John," returned Quilt, gravely. "You don't know the man."

"I *do* know the man!" returned our hero, fiercely. "I know him for a bloody and treacherous miscreant; and I have sworn to send him to the gallows, if there's not another rogue left unstrung in England!"

Quilt Arnold leered malignantly.

"These are dangerous words, I do assure ye," said he; "however, since it is your honour's wish, the pursuit shall be stayed, though Mr. Wild's anger will fall heavy on me, and these poor fellows will lose the reward offered for the girl's apprehension."

"They shall not suffer any loss on my account," returned Roving Jack. "Divide this amongst them."

The old Jew, who stood by, looked on with glistening eyes, and twitched his long, claw-like fingers.

He shuffled up to our hero, and plucked his black velvet sleeve, at the same time shrilly whispering in his ear—

"Von vordsh, Shir Shon—dish vaysh."

Our hero took a step in advance, the old Jew cringing by his side.

"I am shuresh you have not comesh to dish dish-repetable plashe for nothing, Sir Shon; dere ish shome pretty girl in de cashe."

"A shrewd guess," replied our hero, smiling; "but the deuce of it is that the minx does not care a fig for me, and I am determined to possess her."

"Shtrike me! datsh spoken like a prave young shentlemansh!" returned the old sinner, rubbing his hands, and chuckling with delight. "Ferry goot, Shir Shon; I'll do it sheap, I'll have the skittish fench carried off for you."

"Bravo, old Judas!" laughed Roving Jack; "but she has a lover, a meddlesome rogue; I wish he were put out of the way."

The old Jew's eyes glittered with bloodthirsty eagerness.

He threw a glance around.

Then he crept close to Jack's side.

He drew his skinny fingers across his own throat.

"Umsh!" he grunted, inquiringly.

"You wouldn't object to undertake such a job?" said Roving Jack, carelessly.

"I am sho poorsh, Shir Shon," whined the old wretch, "I can't afford to be too shcrupiloush. He! he! fere shall I find dish varlet? He shall not trouble your vorshipful honoursh any morsh; but, by Moshesh peard, you must not grudge putting down someting handshom for such a shob ash dat."

"Pretty peace-officers," laughed Jack; "but, enough," he added, impatiently turning towards the constables. "You see, gentlemen, the girl you are seeking is not here; are you satisfied of the fact?"

"Quite satisfied, yer honour," returned the poor old "Charlies," grinning, and touching their caps.

"Had you not better allow us to escort you home?" suggested Quilt Arnold. "This is a dangerous locality; you may be attacked by footpads."

"Thank you, I am not alone," returned our hero, "nor yet unarmed; I have no fear of the rascals!"

"As you please, Sir John; I wish you good night, and a safe passage home," returned the thief-taker.

"Joe Hind vill tell you fere I can be heard of," whispered the old Jew, "I vill do de shob for your vorships; the prish ish von toushand poundsh!"

"When I want your assistance I will apply to you."

"It ish not shafe to trusht anypody in such

mattersh, exchept a reshponshible pershonsh like myshelf. De ting shall be done in a quiet, pianesh-like mannersh. Keep de shecret, Snir Shon."

The old Jew winked, and stroking his red beard, shuffled towards the door.

"Good night, yer honour," chorused the watchmen.

"Good night, friends," returned our hero.

"What was that rascally old Jew talking about?" asked Hal, when the thief-takers had left the room.

Roving Jack laughed.

"Would ye believe it, Hal? The outrageous old villain offered to carry off a pretty girl for me, and to cut the throat of my rival in love!"

"Benevolent, serviceable old creature," laughed Hal. "But, seriously, is that true?"

"Fact, I assure you."

"And what was the price he asked for this precious bit of service?"

"Only 'ven toushand poundsh,'" returned our hero. "But is it not scandalous that the arch-villain Wild should hood-wink the government and surround himself by such desperate agents to carry out his devilish schemes? I am resolved to do my best to unmask the wretch."

"Let sleeping dogs lie!" growled Jack Sheppard. "The governor's a dangerous customer; even I am hardly a match for him; he is the king of all the rogues in England."

"Two Jacks will be a match for this king of clubs, I'm thinking," said our hero, with curling lip; "but come, Jack Sheppard, you are mine now, accompany me home, and I will provide you with a suitable disguise, and you can lie close till my ship sails."

"I cannot leave this place to-night," returned Sheppard, firmly.

"If you linger you are lost," urged our hero.

"Do not fear for my resolution, Sir John," returned Sheppard; "I have passed my word, and that is enough."

"At least I shall see you in the course of to-morrow," said Roving Jack, reluctantly giving up the point; "I shall want to employ you in a certain mission which will require all your tact and diligence."

"May I ask what sort of business it is?"

"This is neither the time nor place for explanation," returned our hero; "but I will tell you thus much—I am anxious to discover the whereabouts of the parents of a certain young lady who has been separated from her family since her early childhood."

"And do you know the name of her parents?" asked the robber.

"Her father is, or was—for I know not whether he is dead or living—Sir Jocylyn Tremaine."

"Sir Jocylyn Tremaine!" repeated Sheppard, starting in surprise.

"Have you ever heard the name before?" asked our hero.

"Yes," returned Sheppard, "it is one of old Jonathan's secrets. Is it your purpose to restore the young lady to her friends and fortune?"

"Exactly so."

"Then let me tell you, Sir John, you are embarking in a very perilous enterprise," returned Sheppard, seriously. "However, we will speak of this to-morrow. But they are calling me; I must return to my associates for the present; get you away as quickly as possible, to-morrow I will visit you at your residence, Sir John."

"Do not fail; and so, good night, Jack Sheppard."

CHAPTER XX.

LONDON IN THE OLD TIMES—JACK'S ENCOUNTER
WITH THE HIGHWAYMEN.

AT the time of which we are writing London was
one great haunt for highwaymen and footpads.

It was almost an act of desperation to venture
forth into the narrow and ill-lighted streets after
sunset; and if any of our young readers were to
turn over the pages of some London newspapers
of the middle and latter part of the last century
they would be utterly astonished at the frequency
and atrocity of the outrages committed by the
so-called "dashing" highwaymen, and would most
certainly congratulate themselves on the improved
condition of the metropolis in this respect. Take
a few examples :—

"1738, September 11. A gentleman was stopped
in Holborn about twelve at night by two footpads,
who, on the gentleman's making resistance, shot
him dead, and then robbed him. Some of the villains have since been apprehended."

"1760, February 24. An apothecary in Devonshire Street, near Queen's Square, was one night
last month attacked by two ruffians in Red Lion
Street, who, presenting pistols and menacing him
with death if he resisted or cried out, carried him
to Black Mary's Hole, when, by the light of a
lantern, perceiving that he was not the intended
person, they left him there without robbing him.
This mysterious action has not yet been cleared up,
though they are suspected to be the same fellows
who lately sent threatening letters to Mr. Nelson,
an apothecary in Holborn, and another tradesman."

"1763, July 23. One Richard Watson, toll-man
of Marybone turnpike, was found barbarously murdered in his toll-house; upon which, and some
attempts made in other toll-houses, the trustees of
turnpikes have come to a determination to increase
the number of toll-gatherers, to furnish them with
arms, strictly enjoining them at the same time not
to keep any money at the toll-bars after eight
o'clock at night."

"1763, October 17. A man was lately robbed and
barbarously murdered on the road to Ratcliff Cross.
Finding but twopence in his pocket they first broke
one of his arms, then tied a great stone about his
neck and threw him into a ditch, having first shot
at and mangled his face in a shocking manner.
The unhappy man had, notwithstanding, scrambled
out of the ditch into the road, but expired soon
after he was found; and two days after another
man was found murdered in the Mile End Road."

In 1726 an ordinary of Newgate writes thus, re-
ferring to one of his impenitents :—

"He stopped the Earl of Hanborough during
broad daylight in Piccadilly; one of the chairmen,
pulling out a pole of the chair. knocked down one
of the villains, while the earl came out. drew his
sword, and put the rest to flight, but not before
they had raised their wounded companion whom
they took with them.

"Their next robbery was at the house of a grocer
in Thames Street. The watchman passing by as
they were packing up their booty, Bellany seized
him, and obliged him to put out his candle, lest
any alarm should be given. Having kept him till
they were ready to go off with the plunder, they
took him to the side of the Thames and threatened
to throw him in if he would not throw in his lantern and staff; it need not be said the poor man
was obliged to comply with their injunctions."

"1761, December 31. Murders, robberies, many
of them attended with acts of cruelty, and threatening letters, were never, perhaps, more frequent
about this city than during the last month.

"The police system was in a most inefficient state.
Besides, the streets, lanes, and courts of many parts
of the metropolis were narrow and irregular, such
as may still be seen in the neighbourhood of Clare
Market, Chancery and Fetter Lanes, and encumbered with buildings offering facilities for unforseen
attacks, and for the escape of malefactors.

"Accordingly, it may be truly said, there was a
time, and not very long since, when no man might
securely travel in the vicinity of London, singly or
in company, without fire-arms."

Every horseman who appeared on the horizon
was suspected to be a "Golden Farmer," or a
"Dick Turpin ;" and every pedestrian, especially
if the unfortunate wight carried a stick—which
was, of course, considered to be a bludgeon—was
looked upon as a foot-pad, and the wayfarer prepared either to resist or "Stand and deliver," as
suited his pluck.

Now all this is changed.

But quitting this digression, though it is by no
means without a certain bearing upon our story,
we return to our hero.

When Roving Jack and Hal Hetherington
emerged from the glowing portals of the hell in
which they had passed the evening, they found
themselves in the dark and narrow thoroughfare
called Wych Street.

The night was black and murky.

The clocks of St. Clement Danes' and St. Mary's
were striking one.

The street was dark, dead and deserted.

At each corner of the street the dim greasy flare
of a lamp threw a patch of flickering light upon the
pavement; elsewhere darkness prevailed.

It had drizzled rain, and the pavement was dank
and miry.

Roving Jack and his companion, arm in arm, pro
ceeded up the silent street in the direction of Drury
Lane.

"This has been a night of adventures," Hal
remarked; "but I think thus much good will come
of it, that Sheppard is a cunning dog, and will no
doubt greatly assist you in the search for Violet's
parents."

"I hope so," replied our hero. "And what is
more, I trust we shall yet be able to save him, and
that slashing fellow, Tom King."

"I fear you will fail in that attempt," replied
Hal, "for Jack Sheppard is evidently altogether in
Wild's power. And as for Tom King, he has been
too long accustomed to his desperate and profligate
mode of life to reform; but we shall see what we
shall see."

"Spoken like an oracle !" returned Jack; "but
yonder is our coach. I'm glad enough to reach it,
for, to tell you the truth, Hal, I am quite outworn
with fatigue and excitement."

As they were speaking, a handsome carriage
rattled up.

The footmen, who wore very splendid liveries,
opened the carriage-door, and Hal was the first to
get in.

The young baronet had already set his foot upon
the step, when, turning his head, his attention was
attracted by the face and figure of a man who at
the instant was passing on the other side of the way.

He was a short, thick-set fellow, with a foxy red
beard, and a face expressing the utmost determination and cunning, but not a little disfigured
by more than one terrible sword-gash.

He was close wrapped in a horseman's coat, and
wore heavy riding-boots.

Instantly upon seeing him, our hero started and whispered to his companion,

"'Tis Wild! Stay one moment, Hal; I'll watch the rogue down Wych Street, and see if he will enter the ' Black Lion.'"

" But I will go with you."

" Set still, you will attract his notice," returned Roving Jack. "I'll return on the instant."

Our bold young hero dogged the steps of the thief-taker, and tracked him to the " Black Lion," where, as our hero had expected, he had entered.

Crossing the road, Roving Jack peeped in at the little window of the parlour.

In the middle of the room stood Jonathan Wild, a sullen glare on his savage and astute countenance, listening to the eager recital of the tall and dark-faced ruffian, Joe Blueskin.

" And he has dared to listen to such a proposal ?" growled Jonathan Wild.

"Dared !" returned Blueskin, with a scowl. " Zounds ! what is there that Captain Sheppard dares not do? But my notion is simply this, that we mustn't lose our best hand, eh, guv'nor ? Wherever was there such a cracksman as our little pal, Jack ? and what should I do without him ? Why, 'od rot it ! I think I should give myself up, or save old Marvel* a job by chalking myself across the weason with my own cheese-knife. And Edgeworth Bess, and Mistress Maggot, what would they do without their fancy man ? We should all break our hearts."

" You may console yourself on that score, Blueskin," sneered Wild. " Jack Sheppard shall never leave England."

" Perish me ! no, guv'nor, it's not to be thought of."

" And so that young bloodhound, Roving Jack, has inherited the fortune and title of Sir John Warbold, the old port-admiral ?"

" That I and Jack fleeced so neatly in the St. Alban's Road," grinned Blueskin. " Aye ; but how long shall the troublesome young braggart enjoy them ?"

" Only so long as it suits my purpose," returned Wild, sternly. " So his term is short, Blueskin, I warrant ye."

" Send I may live ; but I'm glad you're o' that mind, guv'nor," chuckled the robber. " He has done mischief enough already. I'm ready to cut his throat whenever you like to give the word. It'll be a labour of love."

The ruffians now receded from the window, and our hero was unable to catch the rest of their conversation.

Roving Jack now thought it prudent to return to the carriage.

With this intent he proceeded a few steps towards Drury Lane, when his progress was suddenly arrested by the appearance of three showily-dressed fellows, masked, and armed to the teeth, who sprang forth from the black shadows of a gable, and with naked swords gleaming in their hands, confronted him.

" Stand !" shouted one of them.

Roving Jack threw his back against the wall, and drew his sword.

" Back, you villains !" he cried. " The first man who advances one step dies on the spot !"

" B—t ye ! give up your money, and quickly, too, or I'll rip your heart out !" growled the tallest of the three robbers, and apparently the leader.

" Aye, Dick ; let's have no palavering," rejoined another, savagely. " Wild passed just now, we have no time to lose."

* The hangman.

" Come, sirrah, your purse, your fawneys, your coat !" cried Dick Turpin, for it was he who took the lead. " Quick, I say ! another moment's hesitation and I'll lodge a couple of slugs in your piggish head, you obstinate fool !"

" Rescue ! thieves ! watch !" shouted our hero, lustily, while he darted upon the robbers.

Dick Turpin uttered a tremendous oath.

He sprang towards our hero with a furious lunge.

Roving Jack cleverly parried the thrust.

The slim blades clinked and clattered as they intertwined in the mortal conflict.

Our hero, who had constantly practised the art of fencing under the best masters he could procure, fought with the utmost skill and bravery.

The highwaymen slashed and lunged, cursing and swearing by the deepest and most dreadful oaths, that they would kill their courageous opponent.

Roving Jack shouted in bold tones his cry for help against such heavy odds.

One of the highwaymen, hearing the distant sound of springing rattles, and the shouts of Hal and the two footmen, who were hastening to our hero's assistance, took a step backwards, and drew a pistol and levelled it at him.

But in an instant Jack was alive to his danger.

Recklessly dashing through the advanced swords of the other two highwaymen, our hero reached the fellow whose fingers were already curling round the clumsy lock of the long pistol, and with a fierce thrust ran his sword to the hilt through his body.

Blood flew from the ruffian's mouth, his arms tossed up, and as Jack drew back his sword, the robber rolled down as dead as the stone that was stained with his gore.

For several moments the rascally Joe Hind, the landlord of the " Black Lion," had been a witness of this exciting scene.

He stood on the step of his house, and held aloft a flaring torch, which threw its lurid light upon the combatants.

Yet he forebore to interfere, though Jack called to him, and adjured him to come to his assistance.

When Dick Turpin saw his comrade fall dead at his feet his surly and savage temper broke all bounds, and, literally foaming with rage, he sprang upon our hero, receiving a desperate cut on the cheek, however.

Seizing his laced cravat he attempted to drag him down, while he shouted to his comrade to snatch the watch and jewels and to cut away the pockets of the struggling boy.

With his right hand our hero slashed at the robber who was attempting to carry out his leader's directions, while he contrived to wind his left arm round Dick Turpin's waist, and advancing his knee pitched him over, and threw him heavily upon the curb.

With a yell of fury the highwayman drew a pistol.

Roving Jack, planting his knee upon the breast of his prostrate foe, clutched his wrist.

A desperate and protracted struggle ensued for the possession of the pistol.

The other robber, freed from Jack's attack, now stole behind him, sword in hand.

The point of the weapon had already touched the velvet coat of our unconscious hero, who was too much absorbed by his tussle with Dick Turpin to think of anything else, when a loud report ran down the street.

A bullet whizzed past our hero's shoulder, and cracked into the robber's skull, scattering his brains against the wall, and stretching him stiff upon the pave.

Hal Hetherington ran up, a pistol still smoking in his hand.

The footmen followed.

Then came a large rabble, consisting of the watch with their staves and lanterns, and a crowd of the inhabitants, some shoeless and stockingless, others in their shirt-sleeves, and not a few scarcely sufficiently attired to meet the claims of decency; in their hands they carried weapons of every variety, carbines, pistols, blunderbusses, cudgels, with a sprinkling of pokers and mop-sticks.

Hal rushed to our hero's assistance, and seized Dick Turpin by the collar.

"Hold him fast, Hal !" panted Jack, disengaging himself from the robber's grip, and rising on his knees. "It—it is—th—the villain Dick Turpin !"

"TURPIN !" shouted the crowd in astonishment.

"Yes, yes !" gasped Jack, who was completely exhausted, and gasped for breath. "Seize him, ye fools !"

Jack's impatient exclamation was certainly quite pardonable under the circumstances.

The poor impotent old Charlies stared at the redoubtable highwayman with evident disinclination to tackle him, while the crowd, who had just been roused from their quiet sleep, stared in bewilderment.

"Will you let him escape ?" shouted Hal, who with the two footmen, were struggling to hold the powerful fellow.

"Not trapped yet," roared Dick Turpin, hurling Hal one way and the footmen another.

He bounded across the road and sprang into the "Black Lion."

No sooner had he disappeared than the crowd seemed to be suddenly roused from its apathy.

Bang ! bang ! flew the bullets after the fugitive, rattling against the wooden posts of the door, and smashing several window panes.

"We'll capture him yet," cried Roving Jack, waving his sword. "Come, my brave folks, remember the reward offered for the miscreant; I will add to it myself five hundred pounds to the first man who catches him."

"Hurrah !" shouted the watch and the mob, in deafening tones. "A highwayman ! A highwayman ! After him ! Stop thief !"

Rattles whirred and crackled ; staves and brownbills clattered ; the mob hustled and yelled, and, close following Jack and Hal, poured into the narrow passage of the old tavern.

"Hulloa ! hulloa ! What means all this ?" cried Joe Hind. "Here's a pretty rumpus. What's amiss, neighbours ?"

"Amiss, you rascal !" cried a kindly, respectable-looking man, in a brown coat with brass buttons. "This young gentleman has been assaulted, robbed, and well-nigh murdered by highwaymen; the villains have taken refuge in your godless house, which is a very synagogue of the devil, a sink-pool of vice and villany—the harbour for cut-throats, thieves, and prostitutes. It was here my poor apprentice lad, Jack Sheppard, was first seduced from the paths of honesty ; it was here—"

"Tut, tut, neighbour Wood," returned Joe Hind ; "I can't be held responsible for the character of every guest who orders a bowl of punch or a flagon of hucklemybuff. Come to the gist of the matter."

"Truly the Psalmist hath said——"

One of the bystanders uttered a somewhat profane expression with respect to the sacred monarch, and hastily pushed past the worthy old carpenter.

"Don't you see, neighbours, that while we are confabbing here the rogue is escaping. and with him our chance of the reward ? A hundred pounds is something to me, and earning that I'd risk my life to capture the scoundrel."

"Well said," cried Roving Jack ; "and so, Mr Joe Hind, you had better give the fellow up quietly, else we'll ransack this den, and tumble its four walls about your ears."

"Aye, that we will," cried a valiant button maker. "This vile house is the curse and pest of the neighbourhood. What say, neighbours all ? We have found all our applications for the removal of this crying nuisance are vain. That scoundrel, Jonathan Wild, for his own ends, screens the rogues who infest this hole. Let's take the law into our own hands, and smoke the vermin out of their nest !"

"Aye, let's fire the house !" cried others, "let's burn it to the ground."

"Hurrah !"

And several of the enraged inhabitants, who carried lanterns and links in their hands, were actually preparing to put their threat into execution.

But, by the intervention of our hero and the watchmen, they were dissuaded from such a violent measure ; then they returned to their former cry and shouting,

"A highwayman ! Down with the scoundrel !" rushed along the passage, and burst open the doors of the various chambers in search of the fugitiv robber.

Joe Hind was knocked down and trampled under foot.

Our hero and Hal, followed by the watch and the most determined of the rest of the party, burst into the tap-room which had so lately been crowded by the desperate and debauched frequenters of this flash ken, but it was now quite deserted.

Tables and benches lay overturned.

Windows and doors were thrown wide open ; and men and women were seen scrambling over walls and roofs.

The exasperated besiegers did not scruple to discharge their fire-arms at the escaping thieves and bona robas, and more than one shriek or yell told that some of the shots had taken effect.

"What ho, there !" thundered a stern and terrible voice. "Keep the peace, I say !"

The commander-in-chief of the thief-takers and the autocrat of thieves sprang into the room, savagely scowling and brandishing a heavy bludgeon.

"What means this outrage ?"

"Heed him not !" shouted Jack. "Knock the villain down ! Yonder flies Dick Turpin over the roofs of the outhouses ! After him ! Five hundred gold guineas for the bloody wolf, dead or alive !"

With an oath the thief-taker rushed up to our hero.

"Audacious whelp ! Do ye know me ? I am Jonathan Wild !"

"And I am—Roving Jack !" responded our hero, sending his fist smash into the ruffian's face and knocking him backwards.

"Down with the traitor, the double-dealing wretch who lives upon the blood of his misguided victims !" shouted Jack, indignantly. "Hang him up ! Beat out his brains with his own tipstaff ! He is the law's disgrace, and it is no breach of law to slay such a hyena !"

The mob uttered a shout of execration, and flew upon the thief-taker.

But Jonathan Wild was a man of indomitable courage, and fought like a rampant lion.

Whirling round his heavy sword, he carved a way through the crowd and escaped from the house.

Meantime, the mob scrambled through the windows, and hurried in pursuit of the thieves; the noise of the riot alarmed the whole neighbourhood, and soon the streets were filled by the excited populace; alarm-bells were rung, and a troop of dragoons paraded the streets.

Several persons were arrested, but, upon hearing heir statements as to the cause of their exasperaion, were dismissed by the magistrates.

This outburst of popular indignation was a deadly blow to the influence of Jonathan Wild; his conduct was decried in the daily prints; he was censured by the higher powers, and lost no little authority amongst his peculiar subjects, the thieves.

It was long before he recovered his former power, but at last he succeeded in so doing, and established his ascendency on a firmer basis than ever.*

CHAPTER XXI.

HOW TOM KING KILLED THE EXECUTIONER.

ON the day succeeding that on which our hero stormed the "Black Lion," Tom King dressed himself gaily and betook himself to the Mall in St. James's Park, then a very fashionable resort.

Tom seemed to be in an unusually thoughtful mood.

He walked amid the gay and dazzling crowds of gentlemen and ladies promenading the long avenue with an air of abstraction.

More than once the eyes of beauty rested approvingly on his handsome and dashing form, but, for a wonder, Tom was insensible to their admiration.

At length he threw himself disconsolately upon a chair.

He traced figures on the smooth gravel with his gold-headed walking cane, and muttered vacantly.

The sudden pressure of a heavy hand upon his shoulder caused him to start.

An ugly-faced, but strong-limbed, well-built fellow, stood before him, in a handsome riding-dress.

"Why, comrade, what cheer?"

"Ha! Turpin," returned Tom, biting his lip, as if his friend were for the nonce scarcely welcome, "I thought you had left town for Yorkshire."

"Why, comrade, but for you I should now be on the road," replied Turpin.

"But for me? How's that, Dick?"

"Aye, I went to the 'Black Lion' in search of you but found you had left. Joe Hind told me of your madcap adventure with Roving Jack," returned Turpin; "and I was so galled to hear how you and Jack Sheppard rescued the infernal young spy from the bridle-culls and spruce prigs, that I laid a plan with Marks and Peterson to waylay the young bloodhound in Wych Street—but, phew! he is the very devil!"

"What! He routed you—put you to the right about, and got off scot and lot? Ha—ha—ha!"

"'Tis rather an ugly jest your laughing at, Master Tom," growled Turpin, with a villanous frown; "Marks and Peterson were both killed; Roving Jack then headed a mob of cursed shopkeepers and watchmen, and hang me if they did not burst open the jigger † of Joe's boozing-ken, and his knowing customers were forced to scatter like so many rats at the snarl of a terrier. For

---

* The riotous attack on one of the flash kens by the respectable inhabitants of a thief-infested neighbourhood is founded on fact.

† Door.

---

my own part, the chase grew so hot, that I was obliged to mount my bonnie mare, and ride off to Black Mary's Hole, where I passed the night, booted and spurred, and the mare's girth for a pillow."

Tom King laughed heartily.

"Dam'me, that boy's a startler!" he cried; "he saved my dimber, Kate Dulcimer, from the harming beaks; and they say he defied Jonathan the Great to the teeth; and even struck him!"

"And dimber Kate got off, then?"

"Yes," returned Tom. "I escorted her to her lodgings in Spitalfields, and left her there."

"Humph! Then you've not heard the news?"

"Of what? Of whom? Of Kate?" asked Tom, quickly.

"Aye; she has been nabbed by that infernal Wild, carried before the beak now sitting at Bow Street, and sentenced to be publicly whipped at Smithfield."

A fierce and dreadful oath burst from Tom's lips.

He sprang to his feet, and laid his hand on the hilt of his sword.

Dick Turpin laughed.

"'Twill do her no harm," he said, with a leer. "I owe her a grudge—she hates me like venom. One day, when I attempted some endearing pleasantries, the vicious jade tried to stab me. Egad! sir; but the beadles will tame her wild blood, and teach her submission; she will learn a lesson she greatly stands in need of. You're an easy fool, Tom; you don't understand such cattle. A woman loves the man she fears, and scorns the fool who does not rule her sternly. Dam'me, were she my dell instead of yours, I would bend or break her, I warrant ye!" *

For an instant Tom glared upon the coarse and ugly face of his partner in guilt with a look of deadly anger.

Then he turned away, sneering his bitter disdain.

"And I am leagued with this beastly cur!" he muttered, sternly; "but I will break the leash, and henceforth hunt alone."

With this, he rose, and stalked haughtily away.

Dick Turpin bounded after him.

"Hulloa, comrade!" he laughed; "don't let's split about the paltry wench—where away so fast?"

"To Smithfield," returned Tom King, coldly; "and I hope you are bound for Tyburn."

Turpin growled an oath, and while with one hand he grasped his sword-hilt, with the other he seized Tom's arm.

---

* The "gallant" Dick Turpin was one of the most brutal ruffians that ever disgraced humanity. On one occasion he put a poor old woman upon the fire in order to extort from her the secret of where she kept her paltry savings. On another, having, in conjunction with his villanous gang, broken into a gentleman's house, he dragged two fair and gentle young ladies from their beds, tied them to the bed-posts, and lashed them with his belt and riding-whip till they fainted; and this in the mere wantoness of cruelty. In the course of the present eventful history our readers will meet with many instances of the dastardly violence of this shocking blackguard, who has been elsewhere extolled as the pink of "gallantry." We have brought out the better qualities of such men as Tom King and Jack Sheppard, not to create sympathy for a pair of arrant rascals, but in some measure to relieve the dark and revolting picture that truth compels us to draw of the deeds of the "gentlemen of the road."

THE FIGHT BETWEEN DICK TURPIN AND ROVING JACK.—See No. 9.

"Hold!" he cried, fiercely. "We don't part thus, Tom King; I am captain of our troop, and I will neither brook mutiny nor desertion."

"Captain! you base and brutal hound!" roared Tom, collaring him, with a terrible scowl. "The devil himself would disown such a dastardly slave! By the living thunder, if you attempt to 'captain' it over me, I'll larrup ye into tatters with my norse-whip."

Dick Turpin half drew his sword, swearing frightfully; then, as if changing his thought, he put it back.

"But not here," he hissed. "If we attract attention we shall be recognized and captured; but you shall answer for this when time and place serve."

"When and where you will," returned Tom, coolly. "But, if you are wise, and do not court a pitiless drubbing, you will keep out of my way, *Captain* Turpin."

With a scornful laugh the robber shook off his confederate, and walked quietly off.

For an instant Dick Turpin stared savagely at the retreating figure, and, thrusting his hand into his flapped pockets, clutched his pistols spitefully.

Tom King proceeded at once to Smithfield.

Upon arriving there he found a large and motley

crowd assembled in the open space around the pillory and whipping-post.

Though, for the most part, the throng consisted of low-bred, skulking loafers, there was nevertheless a considerable sprinkling of dashingly-dressed fellows, for in those dark and cruel times to witness such a scene as that about to be enacted was considered a pleasant pastime by certain ruffians of the "higher" classes, who, it is recorded, paid heavy sums to obtain permission to be present at the women-floggings, of such frequent occurrence at Bridewell. So much for the chivalry of the "good old times."*

Tom King pushed his way through the dense throng, and took his station near the whipping-post, where two rough-looking fellows, the executioner's assistants and a little knot of constables, were grouped awaiting the arrival of the hapless culprit condemned to the shameful and cruel punishment of the lash, at that time inflicted upon weak and delicate women even for very slight offences.

"Do you know this wench, Sir Ranulph?" asked a gaily-attired, but profligate-looking young fellow, of a companion who stood by his side.

"What, dimber Kate?" he replied, laughing. "Why, she is one of the brightest stars that illumine the otherwise murky firmament of Alsatia. She is one of a trio of rare beauties; there's Dimber Kate, and Edgeworth Bess, and Mistress Poll Maggot. They are known as 'The Graces.'"

The speaker was a very handsome man, about thirty years of age, tall, dark, and of manly proportions; his hair was long and fell upon his shoulders in luxuriant curls, for, contrary to the prevailing custom, he discarded the peruke; he had a fine, intellectual brow, keen and sparkling eyes, but there was a sinister expression about his sensual lips which detracted considerably from his beauty.

"You seem to be well acquainted with the humours and the celebrities of the great republic of Rascaldom, Sir Ranulph."

"Aye, cracksmen, rooks and divers, autem morts and bona robas; I know them all!" laughed the young roué. "I am sorry, Sir Maurice, that I cannot induce you to enlist in my slashing company of Mohocks."

The young libertine smiled affectedly.

"Gad, Sir Ranulph, your divinities are not in my

taste!" he answered, in a languid tone. "Your sports are too rough."

"Not to say ruffianly, ha!" laughed Sir Ranulph. "But a man must live with the times, and he who would be considered a 'blood' must play the blackguard; custom demands it, and custom is omnipotent."

"Aw, truly. Well, thus far I'll yield to your importunities, Sir Ranulph: I will pay a visit to this sanctuary, and you must present me to some of your fair divinities."

"Some of them are really divine. There are two girls, odd to say, prudent and virtuous too, who are paragons of beauty, though of the opposite types. There's the dark-eyed gitana, Gipsy Jael, and the mild, angelic, golden-haired little songstress, 'Blind Mab.' You are to be pitied if you have never seen these rare creatures."

"Indeed! You surprise me."

"But the Venus of Alsatia—though I should rather say the Diana, for she is as coy and chaste as the huntress deity herself—is a beautiful girl with whom I am madly enamoured. She is the daughter of a wretched old rogue who keeps the 'Bear and Ragged Staff,' a low tavern in Salisbury Court. Her name is Bertha Gray."

At this moment a cry was heard,

"Here she comes!"

Then followed howls, oaths, and shrill cat-calls.

Towering above the heads of the people, being mounted on a high, sturdy charger, rode a thick-set fellow, dressed in a brown coat and wearing a three-cornered hat, heavily armed with a long sword, and pistols in his belt and holsters.

"Jonathan Wild;" was eagerly whispered by several in the crowd.

There was a bustle about the whipping post, the police officers thrust the people back, and the executioners began to make their preparations.

Tom King pressed forward.

A file of brown bills—a sort of halbert or hatchet mounted upon a long pole—now appeared winding through the crowd, who was far from expressing any sympathy with the unfortunate prisoner round whom it was surging.

At last the crowd divided.

Jonathan Wild and one or two other horsemen rode into the little open space.

Then followed some of the prison officers, then two low-browed, surly-looking gaolers leading along the unfortunate frail one.

Poor Kate looked unusually lovely in her distress, for all her strong womanly instincts of shame and timidity were roused, and her pretty face wore such an expression of mute terror and appeal as would have filled with sympathy any heart not thoroughly brutalized.

As it was, there were some in the crowd who loudly expressed their pity.

When the gaolers released their hold of the poor girl she staggered and almost sunk to the ground.

The executioner, who had accompanied the procession, seized her roughly.

Her hands were tied and caught up to the whipping-post, her dress having been rudely torn from her shoulders.

There she stood, pale as a statue, half nude and quivering like a reed, her eyes closed, and her budding lips ashy white with terror.

Her helplessness and the statuesque beauty of her lovely form caused a deep impression among the bystanders, who remained with bated breath watching the scene in deep silence.

The executioner stepped into the open space, and

* In a curious document left by one Henry Machyn, who lived a little more than a century prior to the date of our story, are to be found some very curious entries illustrative of the manners and habits of our forefathers. For instance:—

"The 1st of July, 1552, there was a man and woman on the pillory in Cheapside; the man sold 'pots of strawberries, the which were not half full, but filled with fern."

"The 30th day of June, 1553, was set a post, hard by the Standard in Cheap, and a young fellow tied to the post, with a collar of iron about his neck and another to the post with a chain, and two men whipping him about the post, for pretended visions and opprobrious and seditious words."

"The 7th of March, 1554, rode a butcher about London, his face towards the horse's tail, and another behind, and veal and a calf borne before him on a pole, raw."

"30th May were two set on a pillory, a man and a woman, but the woman had her ear nailed to the pillory for speaking false lies and rumours; the man was for seditious and slanderous words."

"The 22nd of February was Shrove Monday. At Charing Cross there was a man carried of four men, and before him a bagpipe, playing a shawm, and a drum playing, and twenty links burning about him, because his next neighbour's wife did beat her husband, therefore it is ordered that his next neighbour shall ride about the place.

"The 9th day of October, 1555, a serving man (the painter's brother that was burned at Staines) was buried in Moorfields beside the dog-house, because he was not to receive the rites of the church."

cooly took the martinet or cat into his long wiry hands.

Crouching backwards he deliberately swayed round his right arm.

The lash fell with a seething sweep.

Poor Kate uttered a wild and piteous shriek of intolerable agony.

Then her soft, snow-white flesh appeared seamed with streaks of bloody red, and she writhed desperately with her bonds.

Once more the hangman stepped coolly back, and took deliberate aim at his wretched mark.

Already the cruel lashes were twirling in the air, when Tom King burst through the crowd.

He stole behind the hangman, and, quick as thought, whipping out his sword, *ran him straight through the body !*

The unfortunate wretch sank in a heap upon the stones.

Tom King set his foot upon the body, and, drawing a pistol with one hand, while with the other he clutched his reeking sword, glared defiantly around.

For an instant an electric thrill of horror and amazement at this unparalleled and daring crime seemed to course through the veins of the appalled spectators, who stood petrified as by the glance of Medusa.

Then burst forth a wild, thunderous roar of consternation.

"Treason ! murder ! Strike down the assassin ! Seize the bloody villain !" was shrieked and shouted on all sides.

Swords flew glittering from scabbards, bludgeons and staves were upreared.

Jonathan Wild, Quilt Arnold, and other police-officers sprang forward.

Tom, however, extended his right arm and pointed his pistol blank at Wild's head.

But the indomitable Jonathan, nothing recking, dashed at the assassin.

Tom fired ; the slug from his pistol struck Wild's hand, which fell powerless by his side.

As for the girl bound to the whipping-post, she had turned her blanched, distorted face at the moment the dreadful deed was perpetrated, and, uttering a dreadful scream, sank down in a deep swoon.

Tom King rushed to her and passed his left arm around her waist.

"What are ye howling about, ye cruel, heartless ban dogs ?" roared Tom. "Do ye blench at the sight of this brutal hangman's blood, and have you no eyes for this ?"

So saying, he lifted the fainted girl's long and luxuriant tresses, and wrung out clots of her gore.

"She was frail—she had fallen ! But she had committed no crime against national law ; and was she an object deserving of such a bestial, bloody punishment as this ? Off, you snarling curs ! Or, if there is a man among you, let him stand to my side !"

Swift as thought he severed the rope that bound the girl's arms to the stake, then seizing her firmly on his left arm, he bounded into the midst of the startled crowd, slashing right and left with his sword.

He had thus cut his way into the heart of the throng.

He now found himself pressed on all sides by a number of low, ruffianly fellows.

A slim, pale-faced youth touched him on the shoulder.

"You, too, Jack Sheppard !" growled the robber, turning fiercely.

"Whist ! I'll save ye !" muttered Jack. "These fellows are friends. We'll pretend to seize you ; you must struggle amain—barking dogs don't bite —we'll hustle you out of the crowd."

"I twig ! To it then !" returned King.

"Here he is ! hold him fast !" roared Jack, catching hold of Tom's collar.

"Stop the villain ! cut him to pieces !" thundered Blueskin.

"I have him ! I have him !" yelled another.

So, tumbling, and scrambling, and affecting the utmost zeal for his capture, the mob of confederates pulled, dragged, shoved, and hustled Tom to the barriers of the execution place, while he pretended to be resisting with the utmost desperation.

At last he reached the wall of St. Sepulchre's church, and, hurling the nearest pursuers backwards, he sprang over it, and dodging behind the grave-stones made for Snow Hill.

Jack Sheppard leaped over the wall and fired after him, of course taking good care not to hurt him.

Blueskin followed this example.

During the sham struggle Jack had informed Tom that a horse was standing at the door of a certain tavern at the foot of Holborn Hill.

Thitherwards Tom King sped at lightning speed, the mob howling behind him, and throwing all kinds of missiles, but intentionally allowing themselves to be outstripped in the race.

Tom King found a splendid chestnut horse tethered to the sign-post of the tavern Jack Sheppard had referred to.

Breathless and flushed with exertion he seized the rein.

A hostler rushed out from the stable yard, shouting,

"A highwayman ! A highwayman !"

He tried to seize the fugitive.

Tom felled him by a blow of his pistol stock, and then clambered into the saddle.

Away he flew, and mounting Holborn Hill, turned up Gray's Inn Lane and made off in the direction of Islington, which was at that time a pretty village surrounded by orchards, corn fields, and meadow lands.

In less than half an hour he reached a lonely hovel called Black Mary's Hole.

A wretched-looking old crone hobbled out to meet him.

"Welcome, gallant captain," she mumbled. "Come in, come in, and hide yourself and your pretty mort, you are safe here ; but you look generous, and won't fail to pay handsomely. He, he !"

"Aye, aye, mother," returned the highwayman, impatiently, as he tossed her a heavy purse. "But attend to the girl and bring me some brandy ; and now I must look to the horse."

He left the hovel.

For an instant he stood motionless, with clenched hands and gnashing teeth.

"'Tis the first time I have embrued these hands in blood," he muttered, hoarsely, "but it will not be the last, for that cursed thief-taker shall not live another day ! This very night I'll seek him out and send a bullet through his black heart, and then come what will ! I am tired of life ; I care not what befall me !"

The highwayman threw himself dejectedly upon the sward, a prey to the keenest remorse and darkest despair.

CHAPTER XXII.

HOW ROVING JACK AND HIS FRIENDS SUPPED AT THE "BEAR AND RAGGED STAFF"—THE MYSTERIOUS GUEST AND HIS TERRIBLE STORY.

ROVING JACK sat at a gilded table in a magnificently-furnished apartment, hurriedly writing.

His inseparable friend, Hal Hetherington, lounged at the open window and listlessly watched the various groups of gaily-dressed passengers that sauntered past.

The young baronet had affixed his seal to the last of the numerous letters he had been writing, and pushing back his chair, said, with a sigh of relief,

"At last, Hal, I am free! I think I have done a good morning's work; I have held quite a levee; have received notaries, conveyancers, tenants, and land bailiffs. 'Faith, my friend, I had no notion that the possession of a large fortune entailed so much toil, trouble, and responsibility. But now, as 'all work and no play, makes Jack a dull boy,' suppose we go in search of some pleasant diversion for our 'care-tired thoughts.' Whither shall we betake ourselves?"

"What do you say for a stroll to Sadler's Wells, or a night at Ranelagh?"

"Aye; or, now I think of it, Hal, I had determined last night to pay a visit to a certain tavern in Salisbury Court, kept by a fellow named Morgan Gray."

"And what can be your business with him?" asked Hal, seriously. "Remember our adventure at the 'Black Lion.'"

"I do, with triumph, Hal, for we came off victors," returned our hero, laughing. "But I will tell you what induces me to visit the 'Bear and Ragged Staff.' I am acting upon certain information received from Jack Sheppard, who tells me that Wirth Wolfgang the pirate when in London frequents that tavern, and that the pirate is in possession of very important documents which belonged to Sir Jocylyn Tremaine, who was no doubt the father of Violet."

"And do you expect to find the Dutchman there?"

"No; for he is now cruising in the Spanish main, where, they say, he has joined the fleet of that redoubtable rascal, Captain Kidd; but this innkeeper, Morgan Gray, is reported to have been a confederate with Wolfgang in many nefarious transactions; and there is also a strange character to be met at that old tavern whom I desire to see."

"And who is that?"

"An old fellow who pursues the vocation of apothecary, alchymist, and astrologer. He is said to be an extraordinary personage, and is held in awe by all the rogues in Alsatia, who believe him to be a terrible master of the black art, and in close league with the arch-fiend himself.'

"What is his name?"

"He is known as Docter Daniel Nightshade; it is suspected, from his slightly foreign accent, that he is a German adept who has fled his country to escape the consequences of some dark deeds."

"Your account has whetted my curiosity; I like to encounter such originals," returned Hal, smiling. "There is 'method in their madness,' and these visionaries are ofttimes men of deep learning."

"Come, then, let us make a start," said Roving Jack.

After an hour's walk they reached the "Bear and Ragged Staff."

It was a fine old hostelry, and had in former times been a place of high repute, but it had long fallen into a state of dilapidation and decay.

They entered the bar.

They were surprised to find two handsome and distinguished-looking cavaliers conversing with a modest and beautiful girl, who, with drooping head, and hotly-blushing cheeks, listened unwillingly to their loose banter and fulsome adulation.

"That pretty maid is Bertha Gray, the innkeeper's daughter," whispered our hero to his companion, "who's beauty has turned the heads of all the gay sparks in the town."

"She is indeed a lovely creature!" Hal answered, softly. "Who could dream of melting such purity in a place like this? But true gold is only refined by contact with the fire."

"You say truly," rejoined our hero. "But who are these gay rufflers?—persons of distinction, I should imagine."

"Why, yes; don't you recognise them?"

"Now I observe them more closely, I do," returned Roving Jack; "one is Sir Ranulph Gayton, the other, the elegant Sir Maurice Lacy."

At this moment the first mentioned of the fine gentlemen turned a careless glance upon the new comers.

Then he started, smiled courteously, and said, with a graceful bow—

"Surely I have the honour of addressing Sir John Warbold?"

Our hero returned the salute in an easy and gallant manner, answered in the same strain, and then politely introduced his staunch friend, Hal.

Bertha Gray seized this favourable and welcome opportunity of escaping to the little room behind the bar.

Her father then issued forth to receive his new guests.

He was a thin fellow, with a sallow face and wrinkled, sullen brow; his eyes were small and piercing, and his lips were curved with a changeless, bland, but sinister smile.

"Welcome, noble gentlemen," he whined, in a cringing tone. "It is seldom my poor house is honoured by such distinguished guests."

"Tush, Morgan! cut short your old set speech, it's getting musty," Sir Ranulph interrupted, in a tone of impatience. "The case stands thus, Sir John; I and my friend, Lacy, have arranged to sup here, after which we are going to the king's house to see the new comedy; will you join us?"

"Nothing could give me more pleasure," returned our hero.

"Come, then; Morgan tells us that there will be one other guest, who is a constant visitor to this ordinary; as I am fond of studying character, and as this man is said to be very learned and deep skilled in forbidden lore, I have consented to his being admitted to our table—that is, if you have no objection."

Our hero had not; and the four gentlemen adjourned to a large and handsome chamber, much better furnished than any other in the house.

Here they found a table, spread with the daintiest viands.

They seated themselves in merry mood.

The host appeared, the dishes were uncovered.

Suddenly, short, quick steps were heard upon the creaking stairs.

The door was pushed open, and a little old man entered the chamber.

He was closely wrapt up in a prodigious cloak,

over which nothing was to be seen but his nose and eyes; but such eyes!

They looked like two squibs in full fire, and the point of his nose seemed red-hot by being so near them.

The gallants exchanged smiles and significant glances.

Even the haughty Sir Ranulph involuntarily cleared the way for the new comer to draw his chair up to the table.

He sat down without taking any notice of this civility.

He undid his cloak, and tossed it to Morgan Gray.

Everybody stood in such awe of the little old man that one might suppose him to be Beelzebub in disguise.

Morgan Gray attended to his orders, which were uttered in a strange, hollow voice.

The supper proceeded for some time in silence.

Roving Jack was the first who began to enter into conversation with the object of his curiosity, who at length fixed his tremendous eyes upon Roving Jack's face with so long and persevering a stare that our hero had some thoughts of chucking the little individual among the logs upon the hearth for his impertinence; but there was something in the creature's stare that kept even him, bold as he was, silent.

"No," he said at last, unscrewing, as it were, the glance he had run into our hero's eyes, "no; there is no other symptom about you; but, by heavens, sir, talking idly, with so stately a dish as that at your very nostrils, is a most dangerous sign. In Germany I have given number four to many a man on less decided grounds."

"*Number four!*" gasped Roving Jack. "What do you mean?"

"A strong room — grated windows — bread and water."

"What!" our hero interrupted, "put a fellow in prison for it?"

"Prison?" said the little man, drawing back. "Bah!"

Our hero felt inclined to pitch the insolent charlatan out of window, and he was rising for that purpose, when the frightened landlord interfered.

"Let me but finish my supper, gentlemen," said the little man.

Here the clatter upon his plate, and the fulness of his mouth, prevented his further observations from being heard.

However, as the wine circulated freely, they became a little more animated, and when one or two ghost stories had come to a conclusion, the old man broke in upon the conversation.

"Let us have no more ghosts, gentlemen; but there is an anecdote I will tell you—true as gospel, though very supernatural; no ghost fading away behind high altars, no spectre carrying a lamp or dagger, but an incident, of the effects of which I myself am a witness.

They pressed him to let them hear the story, and drawing near the fire, he thus began:—

"I believe in the DEVIL! Yet I can claim very little credit for this belief, on the score of his being impalpable to the grosser sense. *I have seen him, touched him, smelt him!*"

The little old man's voice grew deep and solemn.

His eye flashed with a gloomy, almost supernatural light; and when he perceived that the attention of his auditors was fairly fixed, he proceeded.

"Yes; I have seen him, touched him, smelt him

——Ha! Gracious Heavens! What sound was that?"

Sir Maurice nearly sprang off his chair in alarm.

Somehow or other even brave Jack, with his friends, all edged in their seats a little nearer to the fire.

"I see," continued the strange old man, with a satisfied smile, "I may go on now:—

"Adrian Reinhold was certainly the handsomest officer in the Bohemian Light Hussars!

"But the portion of his charms which Adrian himself admired most warmly was—*his hair!*

"Long brown ringlets, that would have done to sweep gracefully over the shoulders of Cleopatra, hung down over his epaulettes.

"In theatres, at balls, wherever Folly collects her votaries, Adrian waved the honours of his head.

"One night he was seated at the hazard table; luck had been long against him; he had lost nearly everything he had, and still resolutely played on.

"The lamps one by one were extinguished as the several tables were deserted; at that moment *the clock struck twelve!*

"'Curse on the dice!' exclaimed Adrian; 'and you, sir,' he added, turning to a good-natured looking man who had been leaning over his chair, ''tis you have brought me bad luck.'

"'I was just going to advise you,' replied the stranger, with good humour, 'not to force Fortune; she will be favourable to you some other time.'

"'No, sir,' cried Adrian, 'you are the cause of all my losses. I have lost every throw since you came near me; so move off from my chair, or take a seat and play.'

"'I have no pleasure in play,' replied the other, 'I always win!'

"Adrian looked at him in blank amaze.

"'No pleasure! and always win!'

"'Yes,' he answered, 'always win.'

He at last sat down.

"'This ring is worth ten thousand florins,' said the stranger, 'but to show you how sure I am to win let it stand for one.'

"He called and threw.

"'I never fail, you see,' he went on, replacing the ring on his finger and depositing the gold in his pocket. 'To lose occasionally would be delightful, but alas! alas!'

"To hear the melancholy tone in which he spoke one would have thought the stranger had met with some great misfortune.

"The mouth of Adrian would have been death to an army of flies.

"He could scarcely close it again.

"The stranger drew him into a corner of the room.

"'My good friend,' he said, 'I am afraid you have some grounds to accuse me of being the cause of your bad luck to-night; people, indeed, seldom win when I stand at their backs. Let me make up your losses.'

"As he said this, he pressed the gold he had won, as well as the ring, on the astonished Adrian.

"'Oh, no; quite impossible,' hesitated the handsome youth, passing his hand through his beautiful hair, 'couldn't indeed, but I'll throw you for——'

"'Nonsense, my good friend, you would lose to a certainty,' said the other; 'let us make an exchange.'

"'Oh! with all my heart.'

"'I have been struck with your splendid curls. Will you will cut me off one of them?'

"'One of my curls! Imposs——'

"But he thought of the gold and the ten thousand florins' ring.

"'Will any curl serve your purpose?'

"'Oh, yes, behind the ear, anywhere.'

"The bargain was soon concluded.

"Adrian pocketed the money, and put the ring on his finger, while the stranger carefully deposited the glittering lock in his pocket-book.

"Something, however, very unpleasantly passed in the expression of the stranger's face.

"'Pray, sir, may I inquire what you will make of my hair?'

"'Oh, merely a spring to catch fools with. I coil it into a mystic rope. If you require more money at any time you shall have it on the same terms; but remember, wherever my scissors touch, the hair never grows again!'

"A thought of horror rushed through Adrian's soul.

"'But how am I to find you if I require you?' inquired Adrian.

"'Only *wish* for me; I shall be at your side in a moment.'

"'But your house?'

"'You shall see it next time we meet.'

"The happiest man in Prague that night was Adrian Reinhold.

"He left the army, and gave himself up more than ever to the cultivation of his beauties, and the winning of a beautiful widow.

"The lady seemed always to like him in proportion to the offerings he made her.

"Sweeter smiles than ever were lavished on our hero, and a wild look of anger cast on him by Count Drethelm, his rival.

"His money now was all gone; his debts were very pressing.

"'How I wish I could see him again!' he said, one evening, despondingly.

"'*You want me? I knew how it would be,*' said a well-known voice. 'Come with me to my house.'

"Adrian was too much frightened to ask how he had come in.

"'Shall you need a great sum?'

"'Prodigious! almost too much, I fear!'

"'Oh, never mind the amount; you have plenty of locks to spare. Come along.'

"Through street, square, and alley walked the two.

"They came at last to a noble house.

"The sides of the door were ornamented with two prodigious sphinxes carved in stone; and when Adrian looked on one of them he fancied that a human eye glanced on him from the granite head.

"Swallowing his fear he followed his friend.

"'You know who I am, I suppose?'

"'No,' replied Adrian, confused, and dreading he knew not what.

"'But though you don't know my name, you know I am——'

"'A very wise philosopher, sir. And, sir, as you seem so learned, can you tell me whether the report be true that there is a treasure buried in my garden?'

"'I know it well,' answered the other. 'It is under the old willow at the bridge. So spare not whatever I give you.'

"'But how is it to be found?'

"'On a saint's night, by moonlight.'

"'Must I be alone, for I have always had a horror of that very spot?'

"'I shall be with you; fear not!'

"As he said this, the stranger laid his hand upon his shoulder.

"It seemed like a mountain of ice.

"Adrian shuddered beneath its weight.

"'But to business. This sack contains a hundred thousand florins; will it do?'

"Adrian's heart again beat high.

"'Charming! Oh! it's worth every hair on my head!'

"'Half of them will do,' answered the stranger, with a smile. 'You will probably need me again to-morrow. And now, good night.'

"Adrian went home, carrying the sack in his arms.

"In the morning he emptied the shining gold upon the table.

"Horror and death! from the bottom of the sack rolled out a *human skull!*

"Gathering courage he took the dreadful object in his hand.

"He flung it with all his might into the garden.

"*It groaned as it flew through the air!*

"A jeweller was waiting with a case of jewels, money paid, and with many protestations of admiration the jewels were dispatched to the widow.

"Two notes came in answer.

"One from the lady to say that she had dismissed Count Diethelm; and one from that gentleman himself, containing a challenge to the favoured swain.

"'What! young, rich, happy, in love, to be shot by a bloody-minded fellow like the count!' the thought was dreadful.

"'I will visit my friend,' he exclaimed, in his distress, 'he will help me.'

"Through street after street paced Adrian.

"He reached the barrier.

"There were but four houses beyond it.

"He knocked at a little low door, and made his enquiries of a withered-looking old man.

"'Who lives next door to me, sir?' said the man, taking his pipe from his mouth.

"'I meant, my friend, to ask you where is No. 203?'

"'You see it from this door.'

"Adrian looked in the direction pointed out by the old man.

"He saw a bare expanse of country before him, and on an eminence at a little distance a building of some sort which he could not distinguish clearly.

"'That's it,' said the old man, with a grin, seeing the direction of his eye. 'It is the gallows, sir; I put the tenant into it last week.'

"With a shudder Adrian rushed from the spot, and entered his own house again.

"With increased anguish he saw on the table of his room the skull which he had thrown out of window!

"He covered his face with his hands; but while he was sunk in this state of almost senseless despondency, the door noiselessly opened.

"Adrian opened his eyes and saw the intruder sitting quite composedly in the opposite chair.

"'Away! away!' cried Adrian, 'you have deceived me!'

"'A little, I grant you,' answered the stranger; 'but, come, do you want any more money?'

"'No, no,' cried Adrian. 'Why did ever you oppress me with your offers?'

"'I—I oppress you? You must be joking. You knew who I was the moment you paid the jeweller; to that I have a witness.'

"'Where?' said Adrian, with a start.

"'The skull now smiling on us from the table,' replied the other, with a laugh. 'Our friend, you see, has lost his eyes; but he is a very good witness notwithstanding. Cheer up, man, I am ashamed of you. If you want any help place but your hand upon the skull and name my name, I shall be at your side like thought.'

"When Adrian recovered his self-possession he was alone, in presence of the hideous witness.

"'His name,' he said; 'I know not his name. Oh, that I had never known him! and he is gone, too, before I had time to tell him about the challenge. Oh, if I am shot! If I die in such a cause, with such a treasure in the garden! Oh! life is too delightful to be risked.'

"In despair he rushed forward and seized the skull.

"'Wild, dreadful, mysterious being! I abjure thee by——'

"'Why, you are quite romantic to-day,' said the stranger, suddenly appearing; 'you invoke me as if you were acting a tragedy. Your will?'

"'Help! help! life!'

"'All of them. The count's pistol shall miss it's aim. Be confident and bold!'

"Adrian looked up. He was alone; a loud crack, as of a pistol shot, startled him, and when he turned to the table he saw the skull with its brow shattered to pieces, and, rolling down the ghastly cheek-bone, a drop of blood!

"In the morning Adrian met the count, and on the signal being given Adrian fired, and his adversary fell dead from a wound in the forehead, exactly in the spot where the brow of the skull had been broken.

"'I fired in the air!' exclaimed Adrian.

"'He is dead, notwithstanding,' whispered the stranger. 'You must fly! I am ready to help you.'

"'Curses on you!' cried Adrian, wringing his hands, 'and double curses on me if I ever again apply to you for your help.'

"'We shall see,' said the stranger, as he slipped off among the trees.

"Adrian was arrested, and sentenced to imprisonment for life.

"It was discovered that a sum of money would open the prison door.

"But without the stranger's assistance where was the money to come from?

"At last, however, a note from the widow, offering to share his flight, decided him.

"The mysterious stranger as usual made his appearance.

"'You wanted money; see, I have brought you some.'

"Adrian did not speak.

"'Tush, man, this is childish. Am I not your friend? I am sorry to observe your locks are thin and bare, ha, ha!'

"But the scissors were relentless; the last lock of hair was clean clipped off, and Adrian was again alone.

"The money, however, set him free.

"His extravagance and gambling still continued.

"When his last florin had disappeared he slipped back into his own country, attended only by his poor old servant William, who had never forsaken him.

"Watching for the mystic time, they proceeded one blustering night, when the church celebrated the martyrdom of a saint, into his well-known garden.

"A watery moon feebly struggled through a mass of clouds, and the wind every now and then howled fitfully among the leafless branches.

"Stealthily they crept through the weed-covered, neglected garden.

"Adrian put his spade in the ground, while William stood by almost paralysed with his terrors.

"'The light more this way,' said Adrian; 'and don't tremble so.'

"Adrian dug on; all was silent except the wind, and an owl high among the branches of the willow whooping its perpetual cry.

"'That is a bad omen, dear master,' said William. 'Oh! let us leave this place.'

"'Hush!' he said, 'I feel something hard; it sounds like iron. We shall reach it soon.'

"'Only listen to that owl,' said William; 'it is now sitting on the hand-rail of the bridge. Hear its to-whoo! to-whoo!'

"'Leave the cursed owl alone!' cried Adrian. 'Here is the chest at last! help me to get it out. 'Tis not heavy.'

"'Not here! Oh, for the sake of Heaven, don't open it here!' exclaimed William. 'The owl has come closer than ever! Its eyes are glowing like fire! Let me go!—let us go!'

"'Silence!' cried Adrian, harshly, and forced open the lid of the chest.

"At the bottom of the box lay, coiled up into a rope, with a running noose at the end of it, all the beautiful long hair which had been such a source of wealth and misery to its owner!

"The owl screamed louder and louder; the branches of the willow shook and rattled as if a storm passed by; strange sounds of joy and laughter filled the air; and, overcome with fear and cold, William sank senseless on the ground.

"When he came to himself, he looked up at the old willow, and from the lowest branch he saw Adrian swinging in his last struggles——"

"Did he hang himself in his own hair, sir?" inquired Morgan Gray.

"He tried it, sir," replied the little gentleman, with a knowing shake of the head, and buttoning up his great cloak as if to depart; "but he cannot try that experiment again. His hair is never allowed to be a quarter of an inch in length."

"What? Adrian is alive, then?" asked Roving Jack.

"Aye, and will soon be well, I hope. He is let out of number four."

"What, he is mad?" said Jack, pointing to his forehead."

"If you will visit me to-morrow you shall see him."

With this the old fellow wrapt his cloak closer round him, bowed to the party, and the next moment he was heard galloping along the road, and his horse's tread was lost only when he turned the corner of the street.

"Who is that gentlemen?" said Sir Maurice, to the landlord.

"Don't you know the great Doctor Nightshade?" answered Morgan Gray. "Why, sir, though he lives in the Mint, and pays tribute to the Master of the Mint, in order that he may pursue his dark studies unmolested—for more than once he has been threatened with a prosecution for his unhallowed practices in the Black Art—he is the best mad doctor; his cures are extraordinary. He once cured a pirate chaser, and that confirmed his reputation."

"A mad doctor!" muttered Roving Jack. "And the little devil would put me into number four—phew!"

The clocks tolled eleven.

"Confound the old warlock!" laughed Sir Ranulph Gayton. "We have been so enthralled with his ridiculous story that we have not noticed the flight of time—and now we are too late for the comedy!"

CHAPTER XXIII.

A QUARREL BETWEEN JACK SHEPPARD AND JONATHAN WILD.

"I DON'T like to leave Bess neither," said Jack Sheppard, internally; "and though I am in hourly danger of being captured and brought to the gallows, I cling to the scene of so many exciting adventures with an infatuation that I can't shake off. But this place is getting too hot for me; I have had more than one quarrel with old Jonathan, and I cannot depend upon him protecting me much longer. No, I'll give them all the slip—I'll send word to Field at our lumber ken, and make over my share of the swag to him and Blueskin; and the money I got from Roving Jack I will divide between Bess and Poll; and then I will join the crew of Pirate-hunters, and begin the world anew."

While thus soliloquising, Jack stood beneath the dark shadow of the boundary wall of the old Fleet prison.

He had doffed his showy dress in which he generally appeared in public, and was now attired in dark and homely clothes, and looked like a respectable apprentice or tradesman's son.

"Twelve!" muttered Jack, starting surprisedly, as the bell of St. Sepulchre's sullenly chimed the midnight hour. "He is late—perhaps he has changed his mind, and will deceive me."

A cloud of anxiety gathered on his brow.

Then he burst into a laugh.

"How Blueskin will storm when he finds that I have failed to keep my appointment at Field's; to-night we were to speak to the case at Plaistow—but who comes here?"

The stern, heavy tramp of footsteps caused Jack Sheppard to turn hastily.

A burly fellow, in a drab coat and top-boots, paused in his walk, and fixed a quick, hawkish glance upon the robber.

"Never! it can't be you, Jack!" he cried, in surprise.

"I wish it couldn't," mumbled Jack, thrusting his hands deep into his pockets, and glancing down, half sheepishly, half sullenly.

"Hulloa! failed? What, has there been a smash?" asked Wild, in a tone of annoyance.

"Yes, of the whole concern—dissolution of partnership, and retirement from business," said Jack, grinning. "It's better to be plain with ye, ain't it, governor?"

"Then, why are you not plain with me, sirrah? What do you mean? Have you quarrelled with Blueskin? Has Field played the snitch?"

"I have quarrelled with no one but myself, governor," said Sheppard, coolly; "but I have been reflecting upon my folly in joining a firm where one partner has all the profit and honour, while the others share nothing but the shame, dishonour and danger of the trade. I want to escape the gallows if I can."

Wild looked grimly at him.

"The wish is not unnatural, Jack," he said, with a leer, "but, in order to its accomplishment, you must divest yourself of every idea of your own free agency. You are sold, Jack, and bought; you are mine. Mine to save you or to hang you according as I find you obedient or rebellious. The noose is already round your neck; I can loosen or tighten it at pleasure."

"Jonathan Wild, you are an infernal villain!" growled Sheppard, between his clenched teeth.

"Granted so," returned the thief-taker, chuckling; "and really, Jack, as the world goes, it's scarcely worth while to deny such a trivial charge. A villain I may be, Jack, but I am also—a power! one you cannot resist."

"The power of evil *can* be resisted, though," returned Jack, with a sneer. "For, as my pious old master, the carpenter, used to say, 'Resist the devil, and he will flee from thee.'"

"Humph!" chuckled Jonathan. "Then I am a mightier devil than my master, for I flee from no opposition, and as for resistance, ha! ha! What are you thinking of, Jack? You know that within an hour I could lodge you in the strongest dungeon in Newgate."

"But you are not quite sure how long you could keep me there," returned Jack, with a smile.

"The next time, Jack, that I think it necessary to clap you into the stone jug I will take such precautions as will try your skill to the utmost."

"Do so; I should like to startle the world by my next deed of prowess," returned Jack. "I mean to become famous as the Prince of Prison-breakers."

"You will have every opportunity afforded you of gaining such a reputation; it will be your own fault if you fail," sneered Jonathan.

Then sternly scowling and assuming a bullying air, he growled in a tone of great ferocity,

"Away with this jargoning! What news from Plaistow, sirrah? Have you spoken to the case?"

"No!" shouted Jack, with flashing eyes.

"And Blueskin?" asked Wild, trembling with wrath.

"What he and Field have been about to-night I neither know nor care," returned Jack, doggedly. "For my own part I did not want to have a hand in the plant; I am not in need of the ready just now, and I had other fish to fry; so there you have it."

"Dog!" growled the thief-taker, savagely wielding his truncheon.

He struck Sheppard a desperate blow on the temple.

"You scoundrel!" gasped Jack, "and I am unarmed, too; but come on, I will die rather than be your slave any longer."

With this he sprang at the thief-taker's throat, and tried to hurl him to the ground.

But Jonathan Wild was a terribly powerful man; Jack but slim and slight as a harlequin.

Uttering a chuckling laugh of disdain, he dashed Sheppard back against the wall.

Jack was half stunned by the crushing of his head against the stones, while the sharp edge of the little silver crown that tipped the truncheon had inflicted a deep cut on his forehead, from which the blood ran down in a stream over his face.

"Ha!" sneered Jonathan Wild. "You see how useless it is to cope with me. Am I not your master?"

"No, devil! you have not conquered yet," returned Jack, in a courageous tone.

He swiftly drew out a pocket-knife, and opened the blade, and then made a spring upon the thief-taker.

THE WRITING ON THE WALL.—SEE No. 10.

But, nimble as he was, Jonathan Wild appeared too wary for him; he parried the thrust with his iron arm, and, after a brief struggle, once more crushed the writhing youth in his grip of steel, and flung him with all his force against the wall.

The evil passions in the villain's heart seemed now to be roused to their intensest pitch.

His grey eyes glinted with greenish light like those of a hyena, his teeth clenched, and his wide mouth looked as hard as a prison grating, while a red flush, like the reflection of the fires of Tophet, glowed on his fiendish face.

He uttered a foul and savage execration, and, springing backwards once more, brought the truncheon down upon his victim's head with terrible force.

Sheppard staggered and sank backwards against the wall, half insensible.

In another instant Wild would have beaten his brains out, but was stopped as he made a rush upon him by the cold, gleaming steel barrel of a pistol which was upon the instant clapped to his head.

He recoiled.

Before him, and supporting the victim of this murderous attack, stood a dashing gallant dressed in a sky-blue silk coat, richly brocaded waistcoat, laced hat, and high boots.

The thief-taker seemed struck motionless; his left hand was tightly clenched, and his right upraised to strike. He stood like a "painted devil."

His savage temper was so strong that it seemed for awhile to overmaster his prudence and sense of danger, and he seemed determined to reek his malice in spite of every risk.

"If you strike I fire, Jonathan Wild!" said Hal Hetherington, sternly, for he was the timely interposer.

The thief-taker took a backward step.

He lowered his arm, and then coolly replaced the blood-smeared truncheon in his capacious pocket.

"Thanks, fair sir," he said, with a satanic grin. "You have saved me from committing an act which I should have sorely repented. This young scoundrel belongs to the country; his life is forfeit to the law, and he shall not receive his quittance from the earth he as polluted by his crimes so suddenly and easily; he shall undergo all the shame and protracted agony of a public execution—he shall hang on Tyburn tree."

He paused, laughed malignantly, and rubbed his hands.

"Perhaps, sir," he continued, "you are not aware whom you are defending from one whose duty it is to arrest him. This young scoundrel, sir, is the notorious cracksman and prison-breaker—Jack Sheppard!"

"And you are the false and double-dealing traitor, Jonathan Wild," returned Hal, sternly. "But for your machinations, this misguided youth might now be an honest and worthy member of society. You shall not take him."

"How, sir? · Are you a champion of thieves and rascals, sentenced by the just laws of your country to suffer the penalty of their offences?" returned Wild. "Well, you will have to answer elsewhere for your strange and unwarrantable conduct; meanwhile I will summon my assistants, and at once lodge the rascal in Newgate."

He blew a whistle, and a number of his myrmidons came rushing to the spot.

At the same moment our hero, with Sir Ranulph Gayton and Sir Maurice Lacy, appeared upon the scene.

"What does this mean, Mr. Hetherington?" asked Sir Ranulph, in surprise. "Ha! and have you captured that rogue, Sheppard? Faith! you have done the state a good service; he has long set the law at defiance, and scarce a month ago he and his gang stopped my coach on the Dover road. Hold him fast, he is a determined young dog."

"I crave a favour, Sir Ranulph," said our hero, smiling. "Jack Sheppard has promised reformation, and I believe that I can depend upon him keeping his word; for a reason, I will hereafter explain to you, I desire to save him. Permit me one moment's conversation with the thief-MAKER."

Roving Jack's bold eyes glared fiercely, and he stepped aside.

Jonathan Wild frowned darkly, and gnawed his lips.

He followed our hero, nevertheless, and stood looking upon his hands and face with a gloomy stare.

"I will make a bargain with you, Wild," said Roving Jack. "You must be aware that your life is in my hands; that a word from me would consign you to the same fate as that to which you have brought so many of your wretched dupes. I know you are a rogue in grain, as treacherous as a fawning tiger; but I fancy that you will have some respect for your own interest and safety. This unhappy young fellow has been a source of profit to you, has served you faithfully."

"Ha! do you dare, sir, to impeach——"

"Tush! now you play the fool, Wild. I know you to be a villain, but I did not think you were a fool!"

"This insolence——"

"How, you low-bred rascal, do you talk of insolence to me? you, a beggarly fence and thief?" cried Sir John Warbold, in a fierce and haughty tone, his cheek flushing, and his lip curling disdainfully. "But enough," he added, resuming his calmness. "Remember the night we spent together in the pirate's cave; remember what damning proofs of your guilt I can bring forward."

"Proofs!" sneered Jonathan. "What proofs? You were alone, and there are a hundred witnesses here in London whom I could call to prove an *alibi.*"

"I have no doubt that many of your roguish majesty's rascally subjects might be found ready to swear anything in your service," rejoined our hero, scornfully; "but look at this mute witness."

He drew out a pistol from his pocket, and pointed to the initials J. W. and the royal arms engraved upon the stock.

"This was found on the Foamy Reef on the morning after your visit, and there is an old fisherman who saw you land with Wirth Wolfgang and his crew of wretches. Nor is this all; I am acquainted with some of your darkest secrets."

"Secrets!" said Wild, starting. "Bah!"

"Answer me this. What became of the Jacobite fugitive, Sir Jocylyn Tremaine?"

"Then you know of the—the——" gasped Wild, thoroughly taken aback, and turning livid pale.

Roving Jack turned a quick, steadfast glance upon the villain's quailing eyes.

"The —— *murder!*" he whispered, impressively, "And where is Lady Annabel?"

"She—she is alive!" returned the thief-taker, who, with all his dogged daring action, was morally a coward, a fact afterwards proved by his craven conduct in the dock and on the scaffold.

"Good; we will revert to this subject on the first favourable opportunity," rejoined our hero.

Jonathan Wild stamped his foot with vexation at being so thoroughly non-plussed; but, then collecting his resources, he said, with a gruff laugh,

"But what proper stuff you are talking, Sir John; the man you mentioned was a rebel and a traitor, and his life was forfeit to the state."

"Is it not rather strange, then, that you did not claim some recompense for the meritorious action of destroying him?" asked our hero, coolly.

"I had no hand in it."

"Not directly, perhaps, yet——"

Wild interrupted him with a ferocious oath.

"Come, sir," he said, "this is nothing to the purpose; these people are gaping like cod fishes with wonder at our palavering, they will overhear us. You said something of striking a bargain with me; your false charges, though they could result in no injury to me, would, if publicly made, lead to some passing annoyance. What do you want? To save Sheppard, is that it?"

"That is my first demand."

"Ten thousand curses seize the rest! Come to my house, and there we can confer upon any other business."

"I *will* come to your house, Jonathan Wild," returned our hero, sternly: "but your triumphant leer at hearing this resolution is quite uncalled for; be sure I shall take complete measures to secure myself from your treachery by placing in the hands of a trusty and authoritative agent the proofs of your villany, to be brought against you if you attempt any foul play."

"Enough! enough! Will you put an end to this foolery?"

"With a final sentence. You are mine, Jonathan Wild! The meanest of your dependents is not more wholly a slave to you than you are to myself. If you attempt to brave, or thwart me (to use your own expression), my word is my bond, and you shall die if there IS NOT ANOTHER ROGUE LEFT UNHUNG IN ENGLAND."

"Gentlemen," said Wild, nervously, turning away to address the astonished by-standers, "Sir John has interceded on behalf of this wretched young criminal, whom he desires to save from punishment, and though it is a breach of my plain duty, as I am pleased to have it in my power to oblige so benevolent and distinguished a personage, I will give Sheppard a last chance for his life."

"Ha! ha! governor," cried the house-breaker, gleefully, "so you've met your match at last!"

"Silence!" rejoined our hero, "away! and think yourself fortunate that you have escaped from your well-merited doom. I will send you some money, and enable you to evade your pursuers, and to redeem your character; but you must leave the country."

"Heart's thanks, Sir John," returned Sheppard, "but not till I have settled accounts with yonder villain."

He turned, and rapidly turning the corner of the street, disappeared.

As for Wild, he was struck dumb with mortification and baffled revenge.

"This is most extraordinary!" cried Sir Ranulph. "In heaven's name, what motive can you have for wishing to wrest such a notorious criminal from the hands of justice?"

"I don't wonder that you think my conduct strange, Sir Ranulph," was our hero's reply, "but, I will explain all as we walk along, for it is very late, and we must turn our steps homewards. Good night, Mr. Wild; we shall meet again."

"Accept my excuse, Sir John," replied the nobleman, "but we must part here for the nonce; I have a word to say to Mr. Wild respecting the recovery of some of my stolen valuables, and it is not my intention to return to my house to-night; but Sir Maurice will accompany you."

Our hero and his party raised their hats and retired.

Sir Ranulph drew to the side of Wild.

"We have witnessed a rather odd scene, eh, Jonathan," he said.

The thief-taker smiled grimly.

"I and Sir John understand each other," he replied, with a shrug.

"Is it possible? You have done business together, eh?"

"Yes, and I hope to do more, for he is a good paymaster."

"Amazement! The gallant Roving Jack too, the robber-hunter, ha ha! Well, with all his chivalrous bearing, I always thought him a deep dog. Is his affairs similar to mine? Has he been bewitched by some of the Alsatian Helens, or does he wish to wreak his vengeance upon some private enemy?"

"'Tis a secret, Sir Ranulph."

"Right, right; I have no wish to pry into your secrets, Jonathan, so long as you respect mine. But, dismiss your followers."

The thief-taker turned towards his satellites and waved his hand.

At the signal they fell back, and slowly followed the pair, keeping out of ear-shot.

"And now listen," said Sir Ranulph. "I have brought you the money according to promise."

Wild seized the purse that the other offered, and, with glistening eyes, slipped it into his pocket.

"Now, I find, that with all my endeavours to vanquish my cruel charmer's aversion to me—of course, I allude to Bertha Gray—I cannot——"

"Permit me to interrupt you, Sir Ranulph, for one moment. Can you tell me by what route Sir John Warbold will return home?"

"Why do you ask?"

"Oh, from no evil motive. I forgot to inquire of him on the subject; it has a bearing on the little affair between us."

"Well, then, he will cross the river in a wherry, embarking at London Bridge; but, to come back to the business in hand——"

"Once more I must ask your indulgence, Sir Ranulph. You see that fellow lurking under the shadow of yon portico? I must speak a word with him; I'll return in an instant."

He crossed the road, and gave a low, peculiar whistle.

A tall, dark-faced ruffian glided from his ambush.

"Blueskin!"

"I'm here, guv'nor," growled the robber. "I know you'll be angry, but, send I may live, it wasn't my fault."

"I know what you would say, Joe; the plant you were engaged for has miscarried——"

"Aye, but, dam'me, Mr. Wild, I can't think what has happened to that frisky lad, Jack Sheppard. He promised to meet me at Field's; we were all three to go reg'lars in the job; but when I got to the lumber ken I found he was not there. I waited for hours, but he didn't show up. What has happened?"

"No matter now; I am satisfied that you were not to blame. The plant will keep; but, harkye, Blueskin; I have a proposal to make to you."

"Spit it out," was the elegant rejoinder.

"Will you earn a hundred guineas?"

"Oh, no, 'tain't likely," returned the ruffian, laying his finger on his nose, and winking significantly.

"Roving Jack is at the bottom of Sheppard's defection; he has seduced him from his allegiance by tempting offers of reward and security."

Blueskin apostrophised our hero in a style more emphatic than flattering.

"He must not live another day," said Wild; "either he or I must fall. He has laid a deep plot to trap yourself and a dozen others."

Again Blueskin interrupted with a terrible imprecation.

"Harken! he is now on his way home; you must overtake him, and make cold meat of him; if you'll do it I'll add another fifty guineas to the sum I've offered."

"That's all bob, guv'nor; but this is a fancy affair I could a'most do for nothing. So help me, Nick, I'll do for him."

"Aye! but it's a ticklish job, and will require all your skill and wariness. Moreover, there's no time to be lost; he will cross the river from London Bridge. I know the waterman at that station; he is Sam Sculler, one of my men; and I shouldn't wonder but you will find Chiving Dick hiding under the arch; he is keeping out of the way on account of that affair of the farmer whom he killed in Holborn; take him with you, and tell him that if he succeeds with your help and the waterman's to kill our arch-enemy, the robber-hunter, I will extend my protection to him, but that, if there's any bungling, he shall mount the nubbing sbear, if there's not another rogue left unhung in England."

"Done, guv'nor," returned Blueskin; "I'll meet

you to-morrow to say the job's finished, and then you must tip up the shiners. But there's one thing."

"Well."

"You must forgive my little pal, Jack Sheppard, for he's the lummiest kiddy on the pad, and I loves him like a son!"

"Ah! you've brought him up in the way he should go," returned Wild, with a brutal grin, "and I'll take my oath he shan't depart from it."

"That's settled," returned the robber, grinning; "and, as for Roving Jack, he sleeps to-night in the bed of old Father Thames!"

"Quick, then, or you will be too late. London Bridge! If you cannot do the trick to-night, lay a trap for him in the morning; but return defeated at your worst peril!"

Blueskin laughed and tapped the hilt of his sword, and then, taking to his heels, ran off at full speed in the direction of the Strand.

"Pity I must remove such a useful rascal," muttered Jonathan Wild, as he re-crossed the road to Sir Ranulph; "but, with Roving Jack, both he and Sheppard must perish. 'Dead men tell no tales.' Hackneyed sayings are mostly wise ones."

————

CHAPTER XXIV.

THE THIEF-TAKER'S POLICY—SIR RANULPH AND WILD PLOT THE ABDUCTION OF BERTHA GRAY —THE PHILTER.

"WHO is that fellow?" asked Sir Ranulph, of Jonathan Wild, when the latter had approached. "I cannot help thinking—though certainly I caught but a transient glimpse of his face as he passed under the lantern—that he is one of the gang of rascals that stopped my coach; his height, his lurching gait, his swarthy, villanous face. Zounds, Wild, I am sure it is the very scoundrel!"

"You have guessed rightly," answered the other, with a cunning smile; "he is the Blueskin."

"Then why, in the name of vengeance, did you let him pass unmolested? Why did you not at once arrest him?"

"You see, Sir Ranulph, if I had done so all chance of recovering your property would have vanished; these rascals stick together, and are a powerful confederacy. The present system of police is very defective, and I am obliged to temporize with them."

"Ha! I perceive."

"Again, it is good policy to take advantage of their mutual enmities and jealousies; indeed, I have intrigued so skilfully, flattering here, bullying there, hanging one, reprieving another, that I can tell you, sir, nosing—that is, peaching or informing —has become the order of the day, and there is scarce a thief in England, and certainly not one in London, on whom I could not clap my hands at any time."

"Your system is a strange one."

"But success is the touchstone of merit; at least, in such a case as this. The amount of plundered property that I have restored to owners within the last twelvemonth is something enormous."

"Wild, you are certainly a wonderful personage."

"I try to do my duty, sir," returned the thief-taker, with commendable modesty; "but let us speak of your little love affair. You were saying that the foolish wench had repulsed your advances; you were about to add that, being determined to gratify your passion, you intended to carry her off; am I right, Sir Ranulph?"

"Aye, but it must be done at once, Wild," returned the young libertine, earnestly; "could it not be managed to night?"

"The night is passed, Sir Ranulph," returned Wild. "Hark, the clock is now striking one; have you any special reason for wishing that the bird should be caught and caged so soon, because ——"

"Come, Wild, make no opposition; show but zeal and promptness in serving me, and you will find me no stickler as to terms. Can it not be done at once?"

"Humph!"

"Your answer?"

"The light is breaking; it is some distance to Salisbury Court; I must send for tools with which to effect an entry into the old inn. I have already set a waiter to keep watch; I know in which bed-room the girl sleeps, and that she is its only occupant."

"Might not plans so well matured be carried into present execution?" urged Sir Ranulph.

"But it was arranged in the first place that your sedan should be in waiting," returned Wild. "Besides, it will be almost impossible to convey the girl to your honour's residence until to-morrow."

"These are but slight obstacles easily surmounted. As for the sedan, you can manage without that; you can render the girl insensible by placing a handkerchief to her mouth, wetted with a few drops of a philter I bought from Doctor Nightshade; then you can place her before you in the saddle, and wrap her close in a mantle; it will be thought that you are travellers, and that she has fallen asleep, worn out by the fatigue of a journey."

"It shall be done, Sir Ranulph. We have certainly lost too much valuable time, but my assistants are skilful cracksmen, and we can do the trick with ease and expedition."

"Bravely spoken; but, beware, Wild, no ruffianism. If you harm one hair of her lovely head you shall not escape my vengeance."

"Fear not; a too ardent love for the fair sex was ever my peculiar foible," returned the villanous-looking fellow, with a leer; "but where is the philter you spoke of, Sir Ranulph?"

"It is here," returned the young nobleman, producing a little blue phial.

Wild took it, and carefully unstopping it, applied it to his nose.

In an instant his grey eyes swam dreamily, his jaw fell, and he staggered backwards, and would have fallen had not Sir Ranulph caught his arm.

For some moments he stood dull-eyed, and unconscious as a sleep-walker; and it was not until he had rubbed his hands across his eyes, and had made several deep inspirations that he recovered himself sufficiently to speak.

"S'death!" he cried, at length; "'tis a potent chemical. I must be careful how I apply it."

"Aye, for Heaven's sake, use discretion," rejoined the young noble. "Old Nightshade told me that a single drop was sufficient to render a woman or a child insensible for hours."

"Humph! this is a valuable acquisition," said Wild, grinning; "I should find such an elixir most useful on many occasions."

"Once more, be cautious," rejoined the other.

"I will, Sir Ranulph; but whither shall we take the girl? At once to your residence?"

"Oh, by no means! Surely you can find a place whereto you may remove her for the present. I shall expect you at my house to-morrow, and, then, if all goes smoothly, I will bear off my beauteous prize to one of my favourite manors, situated in a sequestered spot on the sea coast of Devonshire."

"Not far from the Owlet's Roost?"

"Ha! that is the birth-place of that extraordinary boy, Roving Jack. I should have thought him the last person in the world to be in league with you."

"Pshaw! why not? We are both of the same profession—he is a robber-hunter, I a thief-taker. What is the difference?"

"Clearly. The fact did not occur to me," rejoined Sir Ranulph, with a laugh. "But goodnight, or rather morning, Mr. Wild."

"Your servant, Sir Ranulph," replied Jonathan. "Fear not for the successful issue of this enterprise; home! and dream blissfully of your pretty charmer, for she is yours on my word and promise. Trust me; I never fail!"

CHAPTER XXV.

PREPARATIONS FOR A FOUL DEED

JONATHAN WILD'S house was situated in the Old Bailey.

It was a large and gloomy-looking structure, and had much the aspect of a prison.

After parting with Sir Ranulph Gayton, he hastened thither, accompanied by Quilt Arnold and Abraham Mendez.

The rest of his followers he dismissed.

"Quilt," said the thief-taker, as they proceeded, "I have an important job in hand to-night, and am close pressed for time; you and Abe must accompany me. Are you prepared? It will be a profitable affair."

"I am ready, Mr. Wild; and I partly guess the nature of your business," returned Quilt, "and, as you say, there is no time to lose."

"Dat ish truesh, Mishter Arnoldsh," chuckled the Jew.

"Then you are aware of what has passed between me and Sir Ranulph, eh?" enquired Wild, with a suspicious look.

"Only by guess," returned Quilt. "You remember I was present when you sent Nimble Nat on the touting lay to the 'Bear and Ragged Staff,' and it is well known to all the lummy ones that the gay blood is smitten with Morgan Gray's dimber little daughter."

"And, py de peard of Moshesh, dat is no vondersh," laughed the old Jew. "De covessh ish fery peautiful, almosh ash pretty ash Edgevorth Bess."

"Ha! ha! I always thought, Nab, that you had a sneaking kindness for Jack Sheppard's autem mort," said Quilt.

"Do you tink I am inshenshible to de sharms of peauty?" chuckled the hideous old rascal, shaking his bushy red beard.

"Silence, both of you," rejoined Wild, sternly. "Stay here, Abraham; you, Quilt, come with me."

They were now standing on the steps of the thief-taker's house.

Wild took from his pocket a large key, and applied it to the lock; the bolt shot back with a loud clash, and the thick, iron-banded door swung heavily on its strong hinges.

They entered the hall, which was spacious and flagged with stone.

A lamp burned in an alcove; if the exterior of the house was sombre and prison-like the interior was still more so.

Wild closed the street-door.

He took up the lamp, and handed it to Quilt Arnold.

He then produced from his capacious pocket a large bunch of keys, and their "clank-clash" rung thrilling through the echoing hall.

He opened a second door, which was furnished with double locks and heavy chains and bars.

Passing through this, he ascended a wide and vaulty staircase, the lamp twinkling weirdly like the elfin flame on a dark moor at midnight.

They paused when they reached the first landing, a sort of gallery, with rows of large and strangely-guarded doors, and having all the appearance of a corridor of cells.

"To the armoury?" inquired Quilt, upraising the lamp so as to throw its light upon a number painted on one of the doors.

"No, to the magazine; we shall have to crack the crib, Quilt," returned Wild, with a grin. "I am rather pleased with the job, for I am out of practice; my hand begins to lose its cunning."

He unlocked another door, and they entered a large dark chamber bare of furniture, but surrounded on all sides by glazed cupboards and cases.

This was Wild's museum, which will be hereafter particularly described.

As they passed over the creaking floor of the dark and stoney chamber, the faint light of the hand-lamp glinted on many a white, grinning skull, and showed up the deep indelible crimson stains on more than one garment or sparkled on various shackles and other fetters contained in the glass cases of the ghastly museum.

Quilt Arnold cast a shuddering glance about him, and kept close upon the heels of his master.

Jonathan Wild at once noticed this display of awe and terror on the part of his companion, and, with instinctive malice, he sought to increase it.

"It is strange, Quilt, what a startling effect common sounds or objects present under the witching spell of night and darkness, the mysterious hour of dreams and spectral illusions; many a bold heart has thrilled with a pang of mortal dread at the soughing of the wind through leafless branches, or the light rustle of a sere leaf on a dry path. Besides, we have such manifold testimony to the occasional re-appearance on earth of those spirits that have past the shadowy bourne of death, that there must be some truth in the existence of such facts."

"I—I—don't believe a word of it, Mr. Wild," returned Quilt, edging closer, his teeth chattering and his hair stirring.

"Well, I myself lend such tales no absolute credence," rejoined the malignant thief-taker, in a careless tone, "yet sometimes I scarce know what to think. You know, for instance, that this very chamber is said to be haunted by the ghost of that spice high toby gloak, poor Tom Hall, that was crapped last sessions. Well, one night as I was passing through this room, there appeared before me a form, thin, pale and mist-like——. Ha! do ye see that? Look!"

"W-where, where, Mr. Wild?" half shrieked Arnold, shutting his eyes, and actually staggering with fright.

"Hum!" muttered Jonathan, reflectively. "It may have been but a shadow. Bah! what care I? Man or devil, I fear it not! Come, Quilt, every moment is precious."

So saying, he flung open a door which gave admittance to a tolerably large room, the walls of which were hung with jemmies, centre-bits, picklocks, and all kinds of burglarious implements in great number."

"Bring that bag, Quilt," said the thief-taker, "put in this crowbar, a gimblet, and a few files. We shall scarcely want them. 'tis such an easy plant, but it's as well to be prepared ; and now let's away."

They re-passed the gloomy chambers, re-locking the strong doors.

As they emerged from the house the clocks tolled three.

"Hasten, I fear we shall be too late. What an exacting fool is Sir Ranulph to insist upon having the job done at this late hour. Come on. Well, Abe, what's the matter, you seem all aghast? Have you seen the ghost of Tom Hall staring from my window ? Speak, you idiot !"

"Mishter Vild," returned the Jew, in a low, eager whisper, "I fear ash ve are vatched. I shaw a dashing-looking shentleman loafing pehind the church wall, but when I twigged the touter he shneaked off. I tink it vosh——"

"Ha ! the devil !"

"No, Mishter Vild ; but—TOM KING !"

CHAPER XXVI.

THE ABDUCTION OF BERTHA GRAY.

"YOU were not mistaken, Nab," said Wild, as with his two satellites he walked onwards through the cold, bleak street, on which the twilight of dawn was dimly glaring. "We *are* watched !"

They had not proceeded far before Wild stopped at a little door under a narrow by-lane.

"This is one of my lumber kens," he said. "There is an outlet by the back by which we can slip off, so that Master King may watch till a blue moon rises if he likes ; neither he nor Turpin can escape me for long ; their whole gang shall swing if there's not another rogue unhung in England."

They entered the house, and passing through a kind of store-room came out by a back door into a little paved yard, in which there was a gate that opened into the street.

Once more hurrying their steps they pushed on towards Salisbury Court.

At the corner of this alley they encountered a man leading a strong grey charger.

"Well, Nimble Nat, have you had a quiet watch ?" asked the thief-taker.

"All's bowman, Mr. Wild," replied the man. "There's no one down ; the house is as dark and quiet as if all its inmates were dead."

"Good. Hark ye, Nimble, station yourself here with the trotter ; when we have secured the girl we will bear her to the archway, and give a low whistle ; if the coast's clear answer to the signal, and then I will bring her out, put her into the saddle, and carry her off like a Sabine virgin."

"All right, gov'nor, I'll keep my eyes open you may rest assured."

Wild and his two satellites entered the court.

The old inn stood on one side.

They found it as dark and silent as Nimble Nat had described.

"Step softly," whispered the principal villain ; "she sleeps in a little room, no better than a loft."

"Put, my tear Mishter Vild, take care ; there ish a pig tog shained in de yardsh," said Abraham.

"Aye, curse the beast ! I had forgotten him."

"He dosh not park ; perhaps he ish ashleep."

"Ha ; I'll try the philter ; lend me your wipe, Arnold, I shall want my own to quiet the wench with."

Mr. Quilt handed to his superior his tattered silk mouchoir.

"Give him a good dose," he muttered with a chuckle.

"Never fear," returned Wild.

He poured nearly half the contents of the phial upon the handkerchief.

Very cautiously and quietly they scaled the gate, and crept across the yard.

They had not proceeded far before they were startled by a fierce, though a half-drowsy growl, and rattling his chain a large mastiff sprang out from his kennel.

In an instant Wild was upon him, and had thrust the wetted handkerchief into his mouth.

The animal stood as if bewildered and benumbed, then with a suppressed snarl he tottered and fell plump over on his side, and remained so still as if he were death-struck.

"Excellent !" chuckled Wild, "with this magic elixir we might spell-bind and bear off all the houris in teh Grand Turk's harem. Come."

His attendants followed him close.

"By all that's infernal !" growled Wild, starting back, "there is a light burning in her room ; she must be awake !"

"Holy Abramsh, vot shall ve do now, Mishter Vild ?" returned the Jew.

"Hush ! Here, Quilt, take the handkerchief, but don't use it unless she sees you and raises an alarm. Now, clamber up to the window and see what she's about."

Arnold mounted on the slouching shoulders of the trembling Jew and peeped into the room through a hole in the blind.

"Well ?" asked his master, as Quilt slipped quietly to the ground.

"It's a queer go, and no mistake, Mr. Wild," returned the other ; "she is sitting at a table, writing, with a pile of books and maps before her."

"Shtrike me blindsh ! vot a shtrange ting !"

"Ha ! I see," said Wild, quickly, "her chosen lover is a young law student of the Temple, who, being himself a book-worm, is desirous that she should acquire some learning before he marries her, and the fond fool wastes her nights in study for his sake !"

"Vot a pecooliar creatursh is vomansh !" muttered the Jew, uplifting his lank, yellow hands, and sighing sentimentally.

"Well, we have come, and we have seen, and we must conquer !" returned Wild, in a tone of determination. "The handkerchief, Quilt ; and now let me mount up the casement."

Jonathan Wild sprang lightly upwards, caught a grasp on the sill, and raised himself on to his knees.

Peering into the room, he perceived the beautiful and innocent girl, pale and tired, and poring intently upon her love-prompted studies.

A thrilling moment passes.

The girl sees not those demoniac eyes that glare upon her devoted head.

"Tick-tack !" plies the little clock on the mantle. "Chip-chirrup," sings the cricket in the fireless grate.

Bash ! clatter ! clingle !

A piercing shriek !

Wild has bounded into the chamber, and the hapless girl is vainly struggling in his strong, fierce grasp.

He claps the handkerchief over her mouth.

A mortal shudder runs through her tender limbs, and she sinks in a deep swoon.

The jar of a door opening in the lower part of the house.

A step on the stairs.

Wild blows out the candle.

The door is tried.

It is found fastened.

"Bertha, my child," cries a quivering voice from without, "are you ill? Did you call? I thought I heard you scream."

Wild imitates the deep breathing of one in a fast slumber.

"No, she sleeps; perhaps she was dreaming, or I must have been mistaken," mutters the voice. "Bertha! She does not answer. How deeply she sleeps; no wonder, after toiling so hard all day. Well, I'll not wake her. Angels guard the poor child! Good night, my Bertha."

Steps descending the stairs.

The noise of a closing door.

Again death-like stillness.

"Tick-tack," plies the little clock on the mantle. "Chip-chirrup," sings the cricket in the fireless grate.

Wild bears his unconscious burden to the window.

He hands her down to the ready arms of his satellites.

Wild once more stands in the little court-yard, and beside his attendants.

"Capitally done!" he exclaims, triumphantly. "But, gad! what a narrow squeak!"

The ruffians carry their doomed victim through the yard, and lift her over the gate.

They reach the dark entry of the court. Wild gives a low whistle.

It is answered.

"It ish all right, Mishter Vild," mutters the villanous old Jew, gleefully rubbing his hands.

Nimble Nat is ready with the horse.

Wild mounts the saddle, and, placing the unconscious girl on the pommel before him, flings his heavy horseman's cloak around.

"Bravo, my lads!" he cries; "each has acted his part to admiration! You shall be well rewarded. And, now, disperse; I can manage the rest alone."

The three minor villains watch their principal as he spurs his horse, and dashes away.

CHAPTER XXVII.

THE MURDER OF BERTHA GRAY.

JONATHAN WILD galloped his charger, and bore off the unconscious Bertha Gray through the cold bleak streets.

A group of noisy, drunken revellers staggering home; a lurking thief; a shivering, homeless beggar slinking by; some fine beau or belle returning from ball or ridotto, carried deftly along by trotting footmen in sumptuous liveries, and preceded by a link-bearer; a solitary ancient watchman in his long grey coat, toddling feebly, bearing his lantern and staff, and making the walls re-echo to his quaint, plaintive cry, "Past four o'clock, and a cloudy morn;" such were the only passengers he met with.

At the entrance of a dark alley in the purlieus of Seven Dials, Wild dismounted, and lifting the girl from the saddle, carried her down the dark and narrow entry.

He opened a little door in the wall with a key he took from his pocket, and bore his victim into a dark room.

He was evidently well acquainted with the place, for though not a single ray of light penetrated into this chamber, he placed the girl gently upon the floor, and lighted a lantern.

The room thus illuminated presented a wretched and squalid appearance; a low truckle bed, screened by a patched and tattered curtain, a rickety table, an old leather-bottomed arm-chair, were the only articles of furniture it contained.

Window there was none, but a sort of trap-door in the wall might, if opened, admit the light; but now it was fast closed and secured by a padlock and chain.

The walls were disfigured by many scrawlings in charcoal—verses from vile doggerels, caricatured portraits and drawings of gibbeted criminals.

He stood with folded arms, gloomily regarding her.

"S'death! 'tis a potent drug," muttered the villain. "I wonder how long she will remain thus?"

He felt her pulse, and thrust his hand into her soft bosom to discover whether her heart had stopped beating.

"Life seems almost extinct," he continued, in a low and anxious murmur. "I will see what can be done to break her trance."

In one corner of the room was a pitcher of water and a small hand-basin.

He brought these to the bedside, and, pouring the water into the basin, bathed her forehead, and sprinkled her face.

But this had no effect.

The girl yet lay as still as an effigy in a tomb—as cold and marble pale.

Jonathan Wild seemed puzzled and perplexed.

"If I have been tricked! If that old leech Nightshade has given us—poison!" he muttered, excitedly. "Could I be sure that she would rouse from this mortal lethargy within a few hours, it would be well as it is; but, if she is dead, how shall I face Sir Ranulph?"

As if impressed by a sudden thought, he seated himself beside the bed.

He lifted her smooth, white, rounded arm; it remained drooping and passive in his grasp.

He then turned another glance upon her beautiful but inanimate face.

"She is indeed a lovely creature," he said, with a peculiarly hideous smile. "I do not wonder that the libertine is smitten with such charms; but I must try and restore her to consciousness."

He drew a clasp-knife from his pocket, and, opening it, made a slight incision in the fleshy part of the white moulded arm.

After some time the little gash crimsoned, and a clot of thick blood oozed forth, which trickled heavily and slowly down the fair and tender limb.

Still Bertha stirred not.

The blood liquefied and flowed brighter and more freely.

Then the lashes unclosed, and the mild, pure blue eyes dilated with alarm and wonder.

Bertha started up.

"What place is this?" she shrieked. "Blood! Oh, I am murdered!"

Her pealing screams rang fearfully through the grim chamber.

"Silence, fool!" growled Wild, turning pale. "Silence, I say; do not force me to quiet you by violent means; you imperil my safety and your own life. Hush! Calm yourself. Do you not know me?"

The girl glared wildly into his face.

Then she recoiled with a shudder of horror and detestation.

"You—you are that demon—Jonathan Wild!" she gasped, in accents of intense terror.

"Demon—ha!" growled the thief-taker. "Insolent minx; but, there, do not be frightened, I war not with women; I have done you a service, for which, hereafter, you will thank me."

"Ah! now I remember all," cried the poor girl, distractedly. "I was at study—you burst into my chamber and seized me—I fainted. You have carried me hither, but with what intent? What have I done to incur your hate?"

"Hate—pish! Had you said *love*——But, there, there, I tell you, you are safe from insult and from injury; and now listen calmly to my explanations."

The girl remained mute and trembling.

"Your fortune is made, Bertha Gray," continued the villain, with an odious leer. "Your bright eyes have inflamed the heart of the handsomest and richest gallant upon town."

"You allude to Sir Ranulph Gayton," murmured the poor girl, faintly.

"Ha, ha! You acknowledge, then, that my description of him is accurate," returned Wild, chuckling.

"A scoundrel, a gamester, a libertine!" cried the girl, passionately.

"Granted he is all this, my pretty Bertha. He is of high birth, is rich and generous, and, if you are wise, you will accept the good fortune. Come, speak truth, and say your gallant lover has earned your——"

"My scorn, my detestation!" cried Bertha, with great vehemence.

"Proper stuff!" growled Wild, impatiently. "But, listen; I am unused to these displays of womanish petulance. I admire the sex; if I have any weakness it is a devoted attachment to beauteous woman, but I will not be thwarted in any design. Sir Ranulph loves you, and you must be his."

"Oh, spare me!" sobbed the girl.

"One word for a thousand!" growled the thief-taker. "I will not endure to be brow-beaten and rated by a puling wench whom I wish to serve."

"Oh, Walter, my own brave Walter, why are you ignorant of my distress? Why can you not save me?" cried the hapless girl, tearing her hair in distraction.

"Faugh!" returned Wild, scowling blackly. "A girl of your beauty and sense to lavish your favours upon a beggarly student, without friends, fortune or prospects; a scribbler of jingling rhymes—I am losing patience; you must prepare to go with me, in silence and submission."

"Oh, no—no!" cried the girl, eagerly. "I will return home; I will breathe to no mortal living—not even to *him*—the secret of this night. It is early yet; my absence may not have been discovered. You shall have my full forgiveness and gratitude, my blessings and prayers. Spare me, Jonathan Wild! By your mother's honour, I implore you save me from this shame, to me far worse than death!"

Wild looked grimly at her.

Then he turned aside.

"Well, well, Bertha; we'll see what can be done," he muttered.

He took out his handkerchief, and the phial containing the fatal chemical, and poured a few drops upon it.

"Traitor!" screamed the girl, leaping to her feet, and dashing the phial to the ground and shattering it to pieces, "I know your design. Now I remember all; but I have destroyed your hellish charm, and you shall not bear me from this place alive."

"Ha, jade!" growled the ruffian, brutally seizing her in his arms.

She struggled violently, uttering the most piercing shrieks.

A thought flashed through her brain.

In the struggle her hand had come in contact with the stock of the pistol that protruded from Wild's coat pocket.

In an instant she grappled the weapon, and drew it forth.

She leaped back with an hysterical laugh, and presented the gleaming barrel point blank at his head.

"Foiled, villain!" she exclaimed triumphantly. "Advance one step, and I will kill you! Now oppose my exit, if you dare!"

For a moment Wild was taken a-back.

Then rousing all the determination of his dogged nature, he sprang boldly upon her.

She fired.

Too late, for he had already closed with her, and the bullet flew past his head, grazing his cheek.

"Help! help! murder!" she shrieked, frantically.

Wild dragged down her hand, and wove his arm around her face.

THE MURDERED TRAVELLER.

She clenched it with her strong, white teeth, and bit him to the bone.

"Damnation!" yelled the ruffian, mad with rage and pain.

Whipping out his clasp knife he plunged it to the haft in her palpitating bosom, which was dyed with gushing crimson.

She staggered and dropped like a stone at his feet.

There was a long and awful pause.

"It is done!" gasped the murderous villain. "I would it were undone! It is the only act in my life which I repent."

Then he dropped over her and raised her head; her eyelids quivered, then she sank back and her lip fell.

"She is dead!" muttered Wild, gloomily; "it was her own fault."

He rose and retreated a few steps, but kept his eyes fixed upon the body with a wild, vacant stare.

Then he started.

"The pistol-shot—her cries! The watch will be alarmed! Yes, yes—steps! I must fly! There is no time to dispose of her now. I must escape, and anon find some means of diverting the consequences of this cursed mischance. I must away."

With trembling fingers he unfastened the huge padlock which protected the trap in the wall before described, and with the heavy chain it clashed down.

He then tore down the hatch, and crawled into the dark opening.

He looked back for an instant with a fascinated gaze upon the body, then, with a muttered exclamation of chagrin, he re-closed the trap behind him and disappeared.

Many moments elapsed, and the unhappy girl remained quite motionless.

At length a piteous groan fluttered from her white lips.

She feebly raised herself upon her arm.

She raised her bloodstained hand, and clutched her forehead, wet with the dews of her death agonies.

"Walter!" she gasped, feebly, "remember me! Avenge me! Yes, it shall be known by whose hand I die!"

Exerting all her strength the dying girl dragged herself along the floor, and sank down by the wall.

Then dipping her hand in the fatal life-tide welling from her wounded breast, she feebly traced the dread letters upon the wall. When she had completed the sentence her hand fell, she sank powerless, and with a low moan her spirit parted.

And there, traced in her life's blood, stared the damning accusation—

"MURDERED BY WILD!"

CHAPTER XXVIII.

THE DECOY—THE STRUGGLE IN THE WATER.

ROVING JACK and Sir Maurice Lacy, with Hal Hetherington, after leaving Jonathan Wild, turned their steps in the direction of the river.

They reached the stairs of London Bridge, at that time the only one in the metropolis.

It was covered with houses, and the arches, nineteen in number, were supported by huge piers laid upon starlings or jetties that stemmed the strong and rapid tide.

A more detailed description of London Bridge is reserved for a future chapter.

The night was black and murky, and from the houses, perched dim and shadowy in the gloom aloft, the lights of windows shimmered down and glittered brightly in the dark and sluggish stream.

Upon the water-steps, which were lighted by a flaming cresset, a waterman stood with folded arms, smoking a pipe, and drowsily watching.

He was dressed in a woollen cap and short doublet, with a badge on his arm.

As the three young gentlemen tripped gaily down the steps, the waterman stepped forward.

"Want a wherry, your honours?" he asked.

"Aye," returned Roving Jack, stepping lightly into the boat, "to Southwark."

He was about to seat himself upon the thwart when he felt a clutch on his arm.

He turned carelessly, thinking it was Hal or Sir Maurice who had touched him.

He started with surprise to behold a strange man, his face pinched with hunger and want, as pale and cadaverous as death; he was very tall, in fact little under seven feet, as thin as a taper.

He was wrapped in a loose and ragged grey coat, and an immense Spanish hat slouched over his eyes.

"Sir," he whispered hoarsely through his clattering teeth, "assist me with a little money; I am dying of starvation."

The man's haggard looks and faint accents so fully confirmed this statement that the three young gallants uttered an exclamation of pity.

"A living skeleton!" exclaimed Sir Maurice.

"Can it be possible! and in this great and wealthy capital?" rejoined Hal.

Our hero looked the stranger searchingly in the face.

"Yes; but who are you, friend?"

"Don't ask me, sir; a poor hunted wretch, who for a whole week has tasted nothing but a few stale crusts, fleshless bones, and other garbage thrown down from the houses on the bridge."

"Ha! then you are a fugitive hiding from the pursuit of justice?"

To this question the fellow returned no other answer than by reiterating his supplication.

"I starve, sir; for God's sake assist me."

The waterman drew our hero aside, and whispered in his ear.

"The rogue doesn't deserve your help, sir," he said; "he is Chiving Dick, one of the gang of foot pads who robbed and murdered the farmer on Holborn Hill. Jonathan Wild is after him, and the hunt is so hot that the poor villain has been forced to hide himself beneath the dry arch of the bridge; this is the first time he has ventured forth since last Wednesday."

"Well," said Roving Jack, "let the officers of law catch him, and hang him; but, meanwhile, I can't for my life resist the appeal of a poor wretch in such a condition as his."

So saying, he placed some guineas in the fellow's extended hand.

"Dam'me!" cried the fellow, with a chuckle of delight, and a brightening gleam in his dark, fierce eyes, "this is the kindest thing that ever I heard on. May fortune favour your honour in war, love, and hazard. I've hardly breath enough to thank ye; but your gift will give me life to serve ye, and, henceforth, I'm your slave! I'd strangle a babe or rob the altar for your honour!"

"I'm afraid you'd do either upon less occasion," returned our hero, coldly.

He seated himself in the boat with his companions.

The boat was pushed off, and disappeared in the darkness.

"Pull away, waterman!"

Chiving Dick peered through the gloom, and watched the boat as it glided through the dark waters.

A hand was clapped upon his shoulder.

He uttered a cry of alarm, turned round, and with a bitter oath, seized the man who had laid hands on him by the throat.

"Ha, ha! startled, my pal! Don't ye know me? I'm a fellow chip."

"What!—Blueskin!" cried the other, with a sigh of relief. "I thought you were one of the nailers."

"'Suspicion always haunts a guilty mind,' as roaring Tom King, the toby gloak, would say," laughed the robber; "but I am in haste. I'm glad I've met ye, Chiving Dick."

"Ha! maybe you come on an errand from Jonathan Wild," returned the other, suspiciously.

"You've hit it," said Blueskin; "I come direct from the city marshal."

"Stand clear, then," growled the robber, stepping backwrdas, and drawing a long, broad-bladed dagger. "I don't mean to be taken alive, and, though half my strength is frozen and starved out of me, the other half will serve against a single adversary; so look out for yourself, Joe Blueskin!"

The swarthy ruffian laughed gruffly, and drew a huge horse-pistol from his belt.

"The odds are mine, pal," he said. Your tool is a very pretty one, and you can handle it well, but it is not worth a wheatstalk against this—but I bring you good news. A reprieve from old Jonathan is to be purchased upon an easy condition; he has promised to get you off if you will assist me in settling a certain flash cull, known as—Roving Jack."

"You are fooling me."

"No, 'pon my soul. I thought to have overtaken the fellow. Has any-one embarked from the stairs within this half-hour?"

"Yes, yes; in Sam Sculler's wherry. Three 'bloods,' one of them in a mourning suit of black velvet."

"That's right. Which way have they gone?"

"To Southwark."

"Quick, then; jump into that boat," returned the robber. "We must give chase."

Chiving Dick stood irresolute.

Blueskin got into a wherry, unmoored her, and struck the oar-blade against one of the piles.

"Will you come?" he asked "If you won't help me in the case, I warn you that Wild has sworn you shall mount the nubbing cheat if there's not another rogue left unhung in England."

"But there are three of them."

"No matter, we are equally matched, for Sam Sculler is one of Wild's lieges, and though he has no weapons, neither of the gentry coves, as I think, carries a barker."

"Yes, I'll go," returned Chiving Dick, quickly.

He sprang into the boat.

"Take an oar," said Blueskin; "and pull like blazes. How long have they started?"

"Scarce five minutes."

"Then we shall overhaul them," returned the robber. "The governor has promised me a hundred pounds if the job is done cleanly."

"But must we kill all the three?"

"In course, my covey," returned the other; "unless we can nab the young blood-hound alone when he lands; but we must not stick at trifles; rather than lose our game we must run down the boat; the tide is strong, and the best of swimmers could scarcely manage to reach the shore. But we'll slit their throats first, and let 'em drown arterwards; tug away!"

The boat shot through the black and lopping tide.

Neither of the men spoke for some moments.

Their excitement was intense.

"Hold-water!" whispered Blueskin at length.

"Whist!"

The men rested on their oars, and listened intently.

"Hear anything?"

"Yes, the dip of the sculls," returned Chiving Dick, excitedly. "We are close in their wake."

Blueskin gave a low and peculiar whistle.

The signal was answered from ahead.

"All's bob," chuckled Blueskin; "are you ready?"

"Aye," muttered the other, trembling not with fear but with cold and hunger.

"Be resolute," said Blueskin. "If we can manage this job, old Jonathan will come down handsomely, and you may snap your digits in the queer-chief's face, though you were guilty of regicide, for Wild's a trump and never breaks his word."

"Hush!"

"Confound you, take the tiller, we shall run astern of this hulk," muttered Blueskin.

His warning was timely, for the strong tide drove the boat violently against some craft moored in the mid waters with a terrific bash, and nearly overset her.

"Boat ahoy! help, we're swamped! ahoy! help!" cried Blueskin, in a loud ringing tone.

Then he whispered in the other's ear,

"I know the kid; he can never resist that, he will come to the rescue; though he's as hard as the devil's horns in hunting down us reeving culls, his heart's as soft as a woman's, and he always responds to an appeal for help or charity."

"Aye, I know it," returned Chiving Dick, in a hoarse tone.

"Look ye; when their boat runs alongside, leap in and settle 'em all three; the sculler will help us. Can you swim?"

"Like a trout."

"So can I; and in case of accidents, I'll divest myself of my coat and jack-boots."

With this he threw off his rug coat, and drew his legs out of their heavy encasements.

Again Blueskin gave a loud shout for help, at the same time splashing the oar in the water.

"It's all right," he chuckled; "Sam Sculler has put about. See, they have lighted a link, and are pulling this way."

"Ahoy there, what cheer?" cried a voice, which the robbers immediately recognised as the waterman's.

"Help! ho help!" cried Blueskin, steering the boat close under the deep shadow of the huge barge,

The other boat now ran swiftly alongside.

The waterman leaned upon the bows and held the torch close over the water.

Roving Jack stood up in the stern-sheets.

Blueskin shouted a few rapid words in a slang that was unintelligible to the gentlemen, but not to the waterman, who, at hearing them, started and turned deadly pale.

He answered, however, in the same jargon.

"What does this mean, sirrah?" cried our hero, sternly, for his suspicions were aroused that all was not right.

"Nothing, your honour; at least no harm," returned the man, with forced calmness; "we scullers have a peculiar cant of our own."

"Ha, then it was a waterman who shouted; his wherry in distress, perhaps?"

"Yes, sir; run astern of yon craft; the fellow is clinging in the chains, most likely," returned the sculler, in an excited, anxious tone.

Once more Blueskin roared out some unintelligible order.

The sculler replied, then turning to Roving Jack, he said,

"Pray be seated, sir, else the boat will be overset; we must rescue the fellows one by one and put them on to the barge, there's not room for them all in the boat; they are clinging to the hawser that moors the vessel."

"How many are there?"

"Can't say; two or three, I think," returned the sculler; "but it is so dark I cannot discern them. Pray sit down."

Our hero complied.

The waterman crept behind him, making some excuse, and as he did so drew a knife from beneath his doublet and placed it between his teeth.

Blueskin now seized the oars.

"Mark ho!" he whispered to his companion. Now's the time; Sam will finish the spy and we must tackle the other two."

"TREACHERY!" roared Chiving Dick. "Ware steel, Sir John; your life is in danger!"

Our hero, Hal, and Sir Maurice instantly drew their swords and seized the waterman.

"Ha!" cried Roving Jack, in a terrible voice, "the villain has drawn a knife; we are beset by assassins."

"Mercy!" shrieked the sculler, struggling in our hero's grip.

"Betrayed!" growled Blueskin, seizing Chiving Dick by the throat.

The boats rocked fearfully, and were in instant danger of a collision.

Uttering the foulest imprecations, Blueskin attacked Chiving Dick with wolfish savagery.

The latter had the advantage in height, and, under ordinary circumstances, was more than a match for his antagonist in agility, but he was faint and weak from famine, and as he upraised his long knife his hand quivered as if he were palsy-struck.

The boat lurched and the water dashed over the bows, drenching the combatants.

Chiving Dick got his left hand upon Blueskin's collar, and, forcing him back with his right, was about to drive a knife into his side, when Blueskin clapped the muzzle of his pistol to his breast and deliberately shot him through the heart.

But he did not relinquish his grasp, for his fingers tightened in his mortal agony, and both the men rolled over and plashed into the water.

Down, down they sank, Blueskin fighting desperately to release himself from the other's death-grasp.

The strong tide swept the struggling men away, and again they sank, but Blueskin contrived to free himself from the other's clutch, and rose to the surface of the stream. Turning his head, he beheld the torch in the distant boat flaring luridly through the darkness.

He struck out vigorously, and with a spurt dashed swiftly after the boat.

Meanwhile our hero had pitched the waterman overboard.

Hal and Sir Maurice were rowing fast, while Roving Jack, with the torch in one hand and his naked sword in the other, kept a sharp look-out.

Blueskin swam up.

He seized the gunwales of the boat and tried to capsize her.

Our hero made a thrust at him with his sword but did not reach him. Hal, however, struck him with the oar.

The daring ruffian let go his hold and sank back into the stream.

"Did you see the villain's face, Hal?" asked our hero.

"Yes, it is Blueskin!" returned his friend.

"Zounds! the notorious scoundrel, who, in conjunction with Jack Sheppard, robbed my friend Sir Ranulph of fifty guineas, besides his valuables," rejoined Sir Maurice.

"Well, his career is finished," returned Hal. "I saw him go down; he has perished by water, despite the old proverb."

But Hal was mistaken, for Blueskin, who was a wonderfully good swimmer, glided to the side of the boat and once more attempted to capsize her.

This time our hero thrust the torch into his face, scorching his cheek and setting his beard a-fire.

The robber uttered a yell of pain and once more dived down beneath the surging waters.

In a few moments Roving Jack and his companions ran the wherry in shore without further adventures.

CHAPTER XXIX.

THE DISCOVERY OF THE BODY OF BERTHA GRAY—THE DEADLY CONFLICT BETWEEN JONATHAN WILD AND WALTER REVEL.

ABOUT an hour after the abduction of Bertha Gray one of the hostlers employed at the "Bear and Ragged Staff," a short, thick-set, grizzly-haired fellow, by name Bob Bannister, aroused from a deep drunken slumber, to find himself lying upon a truss of straw in the stable of the old inn.

He rubbed his bloodshot eyes, and with aching head and fevered body glared stupidly about him.

"Od's bobs! this is queer!" he muttered. "The candle has guttered down in the lantern, and the door is half open. I must ha' been gloriously boozed last night; the punch at old Hind's is precious heavy, it has taken a strange effect on me. How came I here? Bah! my memory ewaporated in the steam of the punch. I don't know nowt about it. Well, it's wery evident I warn't seen by any o' the folks in the house when I came home. Ha! let me alone for a deep dog even at the wust o' times. I s'pose I managed to open the little wicket in the coach-yard; but gad! where's the keys? Gone! And if——"

He looked round with a startled air.

"No, the hosses is all right," he added, with a sigh of satisfaction; "but, dash my wig, I mun look arter the keys."

He walked rather shakily to the coach-yard.

He found the wicket ajar, and the keys lying a little way from it among the straw.

"Here's a provident'al marcy!" he chuckled, as he fastened the gate. "It might ha' been a case o' locking the door arter the shed's stolen; but I allers was lucky."

He entered the stable-yard again.

"A—wagh!" he yawned, stretching himself and stamping his foot, for autumn was waning, and the mornings began to get cold, "I wonder why old Jowler's so quiet; it's seldom he hears a futster without rattlin' his chain. High! dog, come out, sirrah!"

But Jowler did not respond to this call.

The old hostler walked to the front of the kennel.

He started back with a blank look.

The dog lay on its side, apparently dead.

"Hillo! here's summut wrong!" murmured Bob. "Why, smother me!" here's a hankercher clenched in the poor brute's jore! He's been a gone and got pizoned!"

He laid his hand upon the animal, and found that its body was warm.

"He don't seem to be dead, neither. Well, this is a start; p'raps the 'ouse has been broke into in the night. Yes, by jingo! Miss Bertha's winder is pushed in! Oh, lors! a trembles like a haspic!"

He ran and fetched a ladder, and, propping it against the wall, mounted to the window.

He started aghast, and his trembling shanks almost failed him; had he not tightly clutched the rowels he must have fallen to the ground.

The room was untenanted; it was evident that the bed had been left untouched, while the table was strewn with books and papers, which were soaked with ink that had been overturned.

The candlestick lay upon the floor.

His first impulse was to give a shout of alarm; but suddenly restraining himself he got down from the ladder, and stood shivering with dismay.

"I have it! she's been kidnapped!" he exclaimed, aloud. "Some o' them doomed mohocks has been and gone and carried her off! Oh, lors! what a go!"

Mechanically, and without any definite purpose, he unlocked the yard gate, and glanced up and down the quiet street.

A tall, pale-faced young fellow, wrapped in a black cloak, stood at the corner.

Upon seeing the hostler he uttered an eager exclamation, and walked towards him.

"Vhy, bless my eyes, if it ain't Master Walter Revel!" cried the hostler, in amaze. "Come, I say, sir, do you know owt o' this pretty business?"

"No—yes—no," stammered the young man, in breathless accents. "What has happened? Speak, for God's sake, speak!"

"Confound it all, sir, none o' yer gammon," cried the other angrily. "You knows more about it than I do, or else vot brings ye here at sich onheerd on times in the mornin'?"

"Gracious heaven!" gasped the youth, raising his hand to his brow; "my dream—my horrible dream—is verified. Bertha ——"

"Is fled! her room is empty and all in disorder."

The youth stayed no further question, but rushed into the yard.

Bob Bannister followed close after.

"Look, sir, the grate is broken open, and the bird's flown," he cried, pointing to the window.

Walter sprang up the ladder and clambered into the room.

He crossed it and tried the door.

It was locked on the inner side.

He gazed wonderingly upon the books and papers scattered about, and then, once more descending to the yard, leaned against the wall as if stunned and paralysed by the calamity.

"It's the work o' some o' them cussed gentry coves as so hadmired the young mistress's beauty, you may depend on't. I'm right, sir, and I'll lay a wager the scoundrel will prove to be that rake-hell Sir Ranulph Gayton."

"She is murdered!" groaned Walter, clasping his hands and uttering a cry of poignant arguish.

"The Lord forbid, sir!" gasped the hostler, uplifting his hands. "What makes you think so?"

"Listen, Bannister," returned the student, in quivering accents of awe and horror, "although I can scarcely expect you to believe my strange story ——"

"Go on, sir," rejoined the other, his knees shaking and his eyes staring, "I'll believe every word as falls from your lips."

But it was some time before the student could sufficiently control himself to speak. At length he commenced:

"I spent the night in study; I was sitting in my chamber, poring wearily upon my books—midnight was past and darkness and light were at war in the east—suddenly a strange, indefinable dread took possession of my soul; I dropped the volume I was reading from my hand, and I sprang to my feet. At first I thought the sensation might be attributed to nervous excitement, caused by my intense application to study, and I took a few turns through the room in order to calm myself, but still the most fearful sense of impending evil oppressed my soul. I could not shake off my foreboding terrors. However, I re-seated myself and tried to resume my task; all would not do, the printed lines seemed to intermingle and float away. I resolved to give it up for the night and return to my bed, when, just as I was crossing my chamber, I was suddenly arrested by hearing a wild, wailing cry. I heard it as distinctly, Robert, as I now hear my own voice; every word thrilled like an ice-barbed arrow through my heart—'Walter, come to me! Save me!'"

"O Lord!" gasped the hostler.

"At once I recognized the voice as Bertha's. I snatched down my sword from the wall, I ran to the window; all without was still; the Temple Gardens lay beneath me dark and hushed; the stithy ripple of a fountain was the only sound I heard, and no living object appeared in view from the path just below to the distant river that crossed the vista of trees like a broad span of dull silver. 'A trick of fancy,' I thought, 'my brain is excited by over study.' I turned from the casement and gazed nervously at the opposite wall of the room, when, to my unutterable horror, I beheld written, in a faltering hand, and in characters of WET BLOOD! these dreadful words—'Murdered by Jonathan Wild!' I rushed to the place, but as I approached the letters faded away, and the glare of my lamp fell upon the bare shining panels of oak."

"Great Heaven!"

"I was resolved not to neglect this mysterious warning. I rushed from the house, and hastened hither."

"And what is to be done now, Master Walter?" asked the old man. "Shall we alarm the house, call up the master, and go in pursuit of the wretches?"

"Stay—where is Jowler?" asked the young student hastily, turning to look for the mastiff. "It is strange that he did not arouse you all with his baying."

"Look at the poor fellow, Master Walter," said the old hostler, pointing to the hound; "they've pizoned him."

"Are you sure he's dead?" asked Walter.

"Fear so," returned the man, sighing; "but his carcase feels warm."

"That is nothing, a dead body will remain so for many hours," returned the student, stooping over the noble creature. "Yes, I can feel a slight pulsation; bring some water."

The hostler filled a pail from the pump and brought it to the student.

Walter poured some upon the insensible animal, and tried to drag the handkerchief from between his fangs.

The dog gave a low, sleepy growl.

"He's a comin' to, Master Walter," cried the hostler, eagerly; "give un another sloush. I'll warrant, if we can bring him to life again, he'll track the villains to the death."

Again Walter dashed the cold water over the animal.

He stirred.

A deep snarl showed that consciousness was returning.

At length the noble brute opened his eyes, stretched himself, shook his grand head, rattling his chain as he did so.

Walter and the hostler patted him, and encouraged him by caresses.

He got up, and gave a long, wild howl, and trotted the length of his chain.

"Let him loose," said the student.

"Aye, Master Walter, I'll warrant he'll soon take the scent," replied the man, grimly.

He undid his chain.

The dog, thus freed, walked about, shaking himself, and uttering a low, peculiar whine. Then he thrust his black muzzle into the pail, which was still half full, and lapped the water.

Then, encouraged by the men, the sagacious brute, who seemed to recall the incidents of the night, set up a deep, fierce bay, and sniffing the ground, bounded to the gate which was partly open and sped out into the street.

"Let's arter him, Master Walter," said the hostler, quickly. "Depend on't he'll follow up the trail till it brings him to the willain's heels. Arter him, sir!"

"Yes, I will follow," Walter returned; "but you must stay here and call up the people in the house."

"No, sir, let me go wi' ye?"

"I will go alone," rejoined Walter; "remain where you are, you will be wanted to explain what has happened."

With this he rushed off, and running as hard as he could, overtook the dog, which was nearing the end of the next street.

Here he stopped.

He began sniffing about, and seemed for a moment to have lost the scent.

He soon recovered it, however, and uttering a slight growl of satisfaction, resumed his rapid trot.

Walter kept close in his wake.

With the wondrous accuracy of unerring instinct the creature traced the path that Wild had taken, through all its deviations, and closely followed by the excited student, reached the dark entry in Seven Dials down which the miscreant had carried his hapless victim, and stopped before the low-browed door in the wall.

It must be remembered that it was still early morning.

On their way Walter had not encountered a single passenger.

The dog scratched at the door, and Walter's cheek went pale, and his blood ran chill, at the faithful creature's heart-rending howls and cries.

Silencing the dog as well as he could, he tried to burst open the door.

It resisted his most strenuous efforts.

He looked about for a window.

None appeared.

The door was deep-set in the brickwork of the massive archway, but there was no sign of its communicating with any of the neighbouring houses.

Walter peered through the key-hole, but it was covered on the inner side by an iron guard.

He listened.

All was silent.

Still the dog kept up his piteous, ominous howlings, and would not be restrained.

Maddened to desperation, Walter threw a rapid glance around him.

A pitch-fork lay beside a dung-heap a few paces down the squalid alley.

He ran and snatched it up.

Returning to the door, he thrust the fork between the frame-work and the door-posts, and using it as a lever tried to prize open the door.

At last it yielded to his efforts, and the wood split, and the iron bolts were torn from their sockets.

The lock still held fast.

Walter, however, stepped backwards, and then springing at the door with a bold, strong bound, burst it open.

The dog immediately sprang in.

Walter drew his sword and entered.

A sharp and narrow passage led to a flight of steps descending into a chamber, which was quite dark, except for the faint rays which poured in from the door.

Scarcely had Walter groped his way for three paces when his foot slipped.

A mortal shudder thrilled through his veins.

His becoming accustomed to the gloom he could distinguish bright crimson clots on the floor.

He uttered a cry of agony.

He looked before him.

A dark mass lay heaped upon what he supposed to be—for it was only just visible—a low truckle bed.

Above it, with cold gray morning beams dimly illuming it, stood the awful sentence—"Murdered by Wild!"

Throwing himself beside the bed his eyes rested upon a dead face glaring ghastly white through the darkness.

It was the face of his own beloved Bertha, and her hands were wet with the blood!

The hound had placed his heavy paws upon her breast, and was licking her cold, clammy brow, and moaning piteously.

Walter stared wildly down upon the wreck of all his love and hopes, and, crushed by the anguish of that awful moment, he uttered a piercing cry, and dropped senseless.

The trap door in the wall was cautiously raised.

A villanous face appeared.

Jonathan Wild crept into the room.

In an instant he was attacked by the mastiff.

He had scarcely time to draw his whinger and throw his back against the wall when the brute flew at his throat.

He slashed at the animal, and inflicted some fearful wounds.

But the brute seemed quite insensible to pain, and springing upon the murderer knocked him down, and fixed his fangs in his arm.

Jonathan Wild was loath to fire a pistol lest the report should cause an alarm.

Yet reflecting that the yelping and baying of the hound was quite as likely to do so, he drew a long petronal, or horse pistol, from his belt, and discharged its contents into the broad breast of the noble hound, killing him instantly.

Then he leaped to his feet, and uttering a savage oath of chagrin and dismay flew to the door.

The dirty court, which was situated at the back of four streets, inhabited by criminals of the lowest and vilest class, seemed as yet undisturbed, except by the barking of numerous dogs pent in the narrow stone yards, and the crowing of cocks.

He breathed more freely.

Re-entering the gloomy chamber, the villain approached the body of his victim.

He started aghast at beholding the bloody inscription upon the walls.

Then his glance rested upon Walter Revel.

"Humph! this is fortunate," he thought; "the poor fool has swooned with horror. Well, it will be an act of mercy to put him out of misery; he must die, there's no alternative."

He leaned over the prostrate body of the student, and drew back his head.

Walter seemed to recoil with a shudder from the polluting hands of the murderer, and quivered as if the foul fiend had touched him.

Then his eyes opened.

They fixed with an intense glare upon the assassin's face.

He uttered a yell of desperate fury, and sprung up.

He hurled Wild backwards.

He then managed to snatch up his sword.

He tried to speak, but, choked with utterance, failed, and he attacked the villain with the utmost desperation.

Both the men were skillful swordsmen, but Wild had this advantage, that he knew the ground, while the student stumbled in the gloom, and more than once had nearly fallen.

Wild pressed him close.

Driving him across the room by a fierce and determined attack he contrived to force him in contact with the table.

Walter fell over it, and before he could rise Wild clove his head in twain by one downright blow of his heavy weapon.

"He fell in fair fight," gasped Wild, wiping the sweat from his brow; "yet, altogether, this night's work has been a bloody and bungling piece of business. For once I am baffled; but now I must stow away the bodies!"

*　　*　　*　　*　　*

With a shout of execration a mob of citizens and watchmen, headed by Morgan Gray, Tom King, and old Bannister, burst into the chamber in which the dreadful tragedy described in the previous chapters had been enacted.

The bodies were gone, the ground reeked with gore like a shambles; but the writing on the wall was effaced and smeared away.

CHAPTER XXX.

A TRUE ACCOUNT OF TURPIN THE HIGHWAYMAN.

BEFORE proceeding to narrate the adventures of Dick Turpin and Tom King on the high road, perhaps it will not be amiss to give some account of those rascals, drawn from the most reliable sources.

"The name of Richard Turpin cannot but at once occur to the general reader as standing in the foremost rank of the heroes of the road.

"We cannot, consistently with the real facts of his career, or the truth to which we are bound to adhere, give any hopes at the starting of his story of presenting that brave, generous, and engaging character which certain romancers have pictured; or set forth robbery and villany, as perpetrated by him, in any other guise than as the deeds of a cruel, plundering, and wholly unprincipled villain, who ran a career of dastardly crime, cowardly violence, or at least of reckless desperation; who lived in terror, peril, constant insecurity and brutalizing vice; and who died with the disgusting bravado of a senseless fool, or as the beasts that perish."*

Richard Turpin was the son of John Turpin, of Hampstead, in Essex.

Having received some school education, he was apprenticed to a butcher in Whitechapel.

Here he served his time, but chargeable with many misdemeanours during that period.

When still but young, he married the daughter of one Palmer, and set up for himself in Essex.

Not having any credit in the market, and people being in general distrustful of him, he did not scruple to maintain himself by dishonest and indirect courses.

He even helped himself to the cattle and sheep of neighbouring gentlemen and farmers.

On one occasion he stole a pair of oxen of Mr. Giles, of Plaistow, which he conveyed to his own premises and there killed them.

However, some of the servants of Mr. Giles had in a measure detected him of the theft; and having heard that Turpin usually sold the hides of his beasts at Waltham Abbey, they went thither, and were convinced, on seeing the skins, that they were the hides of the identical animals stolen.

The men immediately returned to Turpin's house.

On perceiving them, Turpin shrewdly concluding what was the purport of their visit, contrived to elude their grasp, after they had obtained access to him in his house, by leaving them in a front apartment of his dwelling, while he made his escape through a window in another direction.

Having thus effected his escape, but with a blown character, the thief did not choose to run the risk of any more such home visits.

Being now thrown loose upon the world, unprincipled at the very best, and ready to strike out into any wild or wicked adventure which should offer, is it to be thought strange that he in a very short time was found figuring in a lawless gang of smugglers that lurked about the hundreds of Essex?

On the failure of this enterprise, he joined himself to a band of deer stealers.

Almost immediately on Turpin's uniting himself with this last vile association, they made Epping Forest and adjoining parks the scenes of their depredations, having in a brief space got a considerable amount of money.

Here it was that Turpin got acquainted with Gregory, Fielder, Rose, and Wheeler, who were designated the Essex gang.

But even their system of deer stealing did not prove profitable enough, or so rapidly as they considered necessary, they being besides narrowly watched by the park-keepers, and liable to sudden arrest.

Something new, and of a summary nature as regarded the enriching their pockets, was to be discovered; and what more promising or more natural in the onward march of such scoundrels, as a career of plunder, burglary, and highway robbery?

It was at Turpin's suggestion that the gang commenced their course of outrage and depredation upon the dwellings and persons of the unoffending, the insecure, and those who had anything to lose.

Abroad and around the country the villains went, under the cloak of night, their system being, whenever they found a house in which anything worth their seizing was known to be there kept, and felt assured that they were the stronger party, for one of them to knock at the door, and the moment it was opened for the rest to rush in and plunder it of whatever suited them, the inmates, by threatenings, bonds, and other modes of barbarous usage, having been in the meanwhile tamed and mastered.

We will not weary the reader with a recital of anything like the whole of such outrages of the kind indicated, as were perpetrated in the course of a short time by those miscreants.

A few instances must suffice.

Turpin informed his associates in crime that he knew an old woman at Loughton, who, he was certain, had several hundred pounds by her.

Away the band went and obtained an entrance

into the hapless creature's house in the manner mentioned above.

The first thing they did, on getting access into the house, was to bind the old lady and her maid.

They next demanded the whole of her money, and on being told by her that she had none in the house at the time—being very loth to part with her gold—they threw out such horrid threats, and were proceeding to such acts of monstrous cruelty, even going so far as to place her on her own fire, as forced her to discover where the cash was kept that she had by her at the moment, all which they fleeced her of, the sum amounting to upwards of £400.

The next person they robbed was a farmer, whose dwelling they entered, and whose people they subdued in like manner as had been done at the old woman's premises, £700 being the booty which they carried away at this adventure.

It was their custom to wreak out their vengeance against whatever persons should at any time attempt to baulk their schemes and efforts.

Accordingly, they not only committed robberies on a large scale, but often maltreated the helpless ones who had the misfortune to fall into their hands, savagely flogging and otherwise cruelly dealing with their victims.

Frequently would the villains continue in the house for a time to eat and drink at their will, while the inmates were forced to remain in quietness and silence.

On other occasions not only was murderous flagellation inflicted upon women; but they were made to submit to worse than loss of life.

One of their most frightful and monstrous exploits took place at the house of Mr. Lawrence, near Stanmore, in Middlesex.

Here they seized several persons, and treated them in the most ruffian-like manner.

They tied a boy's hands, whom they found putting up sheep after nightfall, with his own garters, and with a pistol held at his head made him do their bidding.

They seized Mr. Lawrence, threw a cloth over his face, and after Turpin had ripped up his small clothes with a knife, taking from the pockets all the money found upon the gentleman, they forced him to go through with them several parts of the house, in order to name to them what was to be found in the same that was worthy of notice; and when they fancied that their victim gave them not all the information they required, they barbarously struck him on the head with their pistols and dragged him from one place to another by the hair of his head.

After other pieces of barbarous usage towards this gentleman, and several of his household, the burglars retired laden with spoil, including plate and linen, warning the terribly-abused people, who were locked up in the parlour by this time, that they, the robbers, would return in a short time to see if any of the family had dared to stir from their place of confinement, when the punishment for so doing—before ample time had been allowed for the safe bestowal of the stolen property—would subject every one of the inmates to a sudden and terrible death.

In short, the gang had become the horror of the districts in which they prowled.

We have thus brought the history of this villain up to the point where our story commences. and forbear for the present to apply to the records of

his life and trial, lest we might, by anticipating some of the most remarkable of his adventures, detract from the interest of the present romance.

The first meeting between Dick Turpin and Tom King has already been narrated by the former.

We resume our story.

CHAPTER XXXI.

THE HIGHWAYMEN PLOT AGAINST SIR RANULPH GAYTON.

IT was a glorious autumn night, and the full harvest moon sailed in her silver galley over wold and waste, town and hamlet, when a party of dashing highwayman spurred gaily along the high road.

The party consisted of Tom King, Rose, Bush and Fielder; they were dressed in a very dashing style, wearing rich-coloured silk coats, elaborately embroidered with gold brocade; cravats and ruffles of the finest point lace streamed in the air from their necks and their wrists.

They were powerfully armed.

THE STAGE-STRUCK CHUMMY PREPARES TO JOIN ROVING JACK.

The silvern glory of the moonlit scene, the fresh keen breeze blowing over heath and meadow, had an exhilarating effect upon the spirits of the party.

Tom King, especially, was in high glee.

He shouted and ranted, and sang, cracked his whip, and made his horse curvet in the most gallant style.

'Gad, but I envy the palming crew," said the highwayman, laughing merrily. "The gipsies must lead a free and jolly life

"'All among the green leaves
Our craft we ply——'

"Ha! ha! Dick and I were never so happy as when we used to go deer-stalking in the king's preserves at Epping. After all, chasing the wild stag is better sport than bullying a fat farmer out of his money-bags, or robbing a timid girl of her trinkets."

"But not so profitable, Tom."

"And there you have it; and, dam'me, on such a night as this there is worse pastime than scouting the pad. Heigho!

"'When the devil was sick,
The devil a priest would be,
But when the devil got well,
The devil a priest was he.'

"Ha! ha! ha!"

"What's the joke, Tom?" asked Fielder.

"Why, Ned, I was thinking how I had promised to join Roving Jack's crew of robber-hunters; 'faith, sir, and I should have done so had I not been forced to make myself scarce after that affair of the rescue of Dimber Kate. Pah! What are a man's resolutions?

"'A thousand times I swore to mend,
    A thousand times my vow was broken——'

"Conscience avaunt!"

"That rash boy will never live to wear grey hairs under his bonnet," said Bush.

"No," rejoined Rose; "he is marked. Jonathan Wild has sworn to do for him."

"And he'll keep his word," said Gregory.

"The cursed bravo!" growled Tom King. "Here's a pretty world! That wretch is a blacker villain than can be found in the worst gang of cutthroats in the high toby, and yet he perpetrates his foul crimes with perfect impunity. He was the murderer of poor Bertha Gray."

"Do you think so?"

"I'm sure of it; but, there, let us not mar the peaceful enjoyment of this country jaunt by one backward glance at the cursed Gomorrah we've left behind us. Ugh! how I hate the town; how I wish it had been my destiny to spend my life in the merry green woods—a shepherd or a cottier—aye, or, better still, a gipsy.

"'When the broad moon floats
    O'er forest and fell,
And the grey owl gloats
    In his ivied cell,
Or flutters his wings
    For a dreary flight,
Through the heart of the woods,
    In the dead of the night,
'Tis then that the gipsy,
    As merry and free,
But never—ah, never,
    So sullen as he,
Starts up from the sward
    In his strength and his glee,
To laugh and revel,
    Ha! ha!
To quaff and to carol,
    Tra-la!
While his brown maid sings,
    When the watch-fires burn,
And the roused deer springs
    From the tangled fern,
Oh, a king of the woods is he!'"

"Hullo! what is it, Giselle? Woh-ho, sweetheart!"

This was addressed to his beautiful chesnut mare, who suddenly stopped, and, stretching out her graceful neck, twitched her fine ears and snorted.

"Halt!" cried Fielder.

The highwaymen drew the rein.

"The patter of hoofs."

"Aye, let's get under shade," said Tom.

"Yonder clump of trees will serve our turn."

"Hark!"

"There is but one rider."

"A farmer, perhaps, spurring home from fair or market, with a heavy bag of beans (guineas) at his saddle-bow."

"Of which we must ease him."

"Hist! He's coming up the hill."

The robbers trotted their horses down a little dingle by the roadside.

The sagacious, well-trained animals kept perfectly still.

"He's coming."

"Look to your brads."

"Aye, aye, Tom."

Presently a horseman appeared galloping down the hill.

He approached within a few hundred yards.

"I'll sally forth to the encounter," said Tom. "Stay here."

He shook the rein, and his steed sprang out from the covert.

He pulled up in the middle of the road.

The rider drew rein, as if startled by the sudden appearance of Tom.

"Stand!" shouted the highwayman.

"And deliver—my message," laughed the other, riding up, and extending his hand.

Tom grasped it cordially.

"What! Slashing Nat Wetherby," he cried.

Then, turning his head, he shouted to his companions,

"All's bowman, my pals; 'tis only our touter."

The highwaymen rode out from their ambush.

They greeted the new comer with great heartiness.

"Well, Nat, and what's the best news?" asked Tom. "Where's the captain?"

"He awaits you at the 'Jolly Harvesters,' about a mile from hence."

"We'll ride on, then."

"Yes; but remember you are travellers, taking the road in company, for mutual protection against the highwaymen."

"What, has he found a purchase?" (a prize).

"Yes; a rare one."

"Ha! let's hear."

Nat Wetherby burst into a long and loud fit of boisterous laughter.

"What are you laughing at?" asked King.

"I'll tell you, Tom; and if you can join me in the laugh I'll call you a philosopher."

"Does the news affect me?"

"That remains to be seen. Weave a cypress wreath, Tom," laughed Nat Wetherby. "If you have tears, prepare to shed them now."

And the wag drew forth his laced handkerchief, and applied it to his eyes.

Then he once more burst into a merry laugh.

"Tom, you have lost your charmer," and he commenced singing in a doleful tone—

"Once I loved a maiden fair,
    But she hath deceived me,
    Vows, alas! as false as glass."

"Hold! you dog!" cried Tom, hastily. "What do you mean?"

"What I say. That your dimber mort——"

"Kate Dulcimer?"

"Has eloped with Sir Ranulph Gayton."

"Oh! my prophetic soul!" cried Tom, clutching his brow, and sinking back in his saddle. Then he laughed, and shaked his silky moustache.

"Phew! the devil!" he exclaimed meditatively.. "Well, let her go, the fickle ingrate jade!" then he drew a sigh and muttered, "Time was when I could not have borne such a loss so easily. Agnes! Agnes!"

"Eh, Tom, what smitten?"

"Not I," returned the fellow, with a careless laugh. "I comfort myself like the olden cavalier—

"'Why should I my cheek with care,
    Pale because a woman's fair?
Why should I die in despair
    'Cause another's rosy are?
Be she fairer than the day,
    Or the flowery meads in May,
If she be not fair for me,
    What care I how fair she be?'

"But now let's talk of the purchase."

"Aye; that's the word," rejoined Fielder.

"Hark ye, then," said Nat Wetherby. "When Sir Ranulph heard of the murder of Bertha Gray, whom he courted, you remember, he was greatly shocked, and for some days remained close at his mansion; the body of the poor girl and that of her lover was found in a sort of chamber in an old archway not far from Seven Dials. The place, I fancy, is one of Wild's hiding cribs; at all events, suspicion fell upon him; but none dared accuse him. He made it appear so plain that he had been far away from the spot where and at the time when the crime was committed, that both the coroner and the magistrate before whom the witnesses were examined never attached the slightest importance to several strange circumstances in the case which convinced me—for I was present at the examination —that he is really the murderer."

Tom interrupted with a fierce oath.

"I am to blame for all !"

"You, Tom ?"

"Yes, I."

"How can that be ?"

"On the night of the murder I went to Wild's house."

"For what purpose ?"

"For a purpose which, if carried out, would have prevented this foul tragedy," rejoined Tom, gloomily.

"What did you want with Wild ? "

"To kill him !" returned King, sternly.

"And, gad, Tom, you could not perform a better action," returned Nat; "but shall I go on with my story ? "

"Aye, we listen."

"Sir Ranulph, as I told you, was for some time quite beside himself with grief and rage, but he dared not make a stir in the matter, for there is little doubt that Bertha was carried off from her father's house at his instigation."

"If I thought so, I would terribly avenge her !" said Tom King.

"You will have a fine chance of avenging both her wrongs and your own," returned Nat, "for Sir Ranulph consoled himself for the loss of one mistress by carrying off another."

"Ha! my Kate. Well, he may have her; he has done me a service by taking her off my hands," cried Tom. "For her sake I have risked the most deadly perils, and on her I have lavished a fortune that might have bought me ease and security—let her go ! "

"As you please about that, Master Tom," returned Nat, "but she must leave some of her sparklers and gelt behind her, by way of a souvenir."

"What ! is Sir Ranulph's coach on the road, then ?" asked Tom, quickly.

"Aye, and we mean to stop it to-night," returned Nat, "so you can pink your rival and recover your mistress."

"Capital !" cried Tom, waving his hat and laughing joyously. "It will be a feat worthy of Claude Duval; one just to my taste. Spur on, lads, and hurrah for the road ! "

The robbers dashed swiftly on, and in a very short time reached a small, low-built inn, known by the sign of the "Jolly Harvesters."

It was little better than a large shanty, being built entirely of wood.

It stood on a lonely spot at the foot of a little wooden bridge, that crossed a brawling, stony brook.

To it was attached a forge, and behind it were some cattle-sheds and granaries, long disused.

Not far away, and upon an elevation a few yards from the road, stood an old windmill in ruins. There were no other houses near the inn, nor in fact was there any other habitation in sight, the situation being a long low valley, the hills on either side fringed with dark dense forests of fir.

At the door of the inn a splendid black courser was pawing the ground, while her rider, dismounted, stood at the door, a glass in his hand, conversing with the landlord.

The latter was a short, thick-set fellow, stout, but unhealthy-looking; his cheeks were flabby and sallow, and his black eyes had a cold, cunning expression, which was very repellant.

The beautiful black steed raised her head upon seeing Tom King and his party, and whinnied as if in salutation.

"Ha, Bess !" cried Turpin, whom our readers have doubtless recognised in the horseman, "are ye glad to see your old comrades, my beauty ?"—and he fondly patted her sleek raven neck. "Once more you will lead the race, as you did of old, for we have a long run before us."

"Ben darkmans, captain," cried Tom King, riding up, followed by the rest.

Dick Turpin shook hands with him.

"So, comrade, our little disagreement is forgotten ! Is it peace ?" grinned Turpin.

"Aye, dam'me, I never had sufficient strength of mind to bear malice for a week together," returned Tom King. "But let us drink a cup to the forgetting of old grievances."

They entered the inn.

"It must be only a stirrup cup, Tom," said Turpin, "for Master Rummer informs me that Sir Ranulph's coach has got an hour's start."

"Say you so, my prince ? Then, bring us a bottle of your best white wine, landlord, and let us drink to the success of our adventure."

The wine was brought.

The robbers filled their glasses.

"Hurrah for the road !"

"How is Sir Ranulph attended !" asked Tom of the landlord.

"By two footmen and his land-steward; but he's an old man," returned the other.

"Mount, then, lads !" cried Turpin. "We must overtake them ere they reach the next town."

The robbers mounted their steeds.

The moon had now reached the mid-heavens, and shone brilliantly in a cloudless sky.

Away sped the horses at a rattling pace.

Turpin forged ahead on his gallant black mare.

Tom King kept close on her flanks.

The others followed in a ruck behind.

The forest rustled past them; the broad meads and corn-crofts swam dizzily by.

They reached the toll-gate.

They inquired of the toll-keeper in a careless manner who had passed through the gate since noon.

By his replies they found that Sir Ranulph's coach was not more than a quarter of a mile in advance of them.

"Have a care, gentlemen," said the toll-keeper. "That scoundrel Dick Turpin and his gang have been seen on the road, and, though you are a strong party, I should advise you to be careful; you should, by no means, separate even for a moment, for the villains are reckless dare-devils that will stick at nothing."

"But is not Sir Ranulph Gayton in some danger of falling into their hands ?" said Turpin.

"No; he is well-armed; besides, he carries with him something that renders him as safe from assault as if he were escorted by a troop of dragoons."

"And pray what may that be ?" asked Turpin.

"A pass of safe-conduct from Jonathan Wild,"

returned the toll-keeper. "With that in his possession no thief will dare attack him."

Tom King laughed.

"I would rather put faith in my own true steel or unerring fire-lock than in the influence of all the rascally thief-takers in Christendom," he said. "But, thanks for your warning, friend, and a good night. Come, gentlemen, let us be going."

The robbers spurred their horses and galloped on.

"Halt!" cried Turpin.

The command was instantly obeyed.

The sound of carriage wheels was distinctly heard.

"We are nearing our guest," said Tom King.

"Aye, look yonder," rejoined Turpin, pointing with his whip.

The men looked in the direction thus indicated by their leader.

A carriage was seen through the trees, passing along the high road.

"No spot could be more favourable for our purpose than that where we shall overtake them," said Turpin. "The road winds through the forest, and becomes narrower and more difficult every yard of the next two miles."

"But how shall we reach them, captain?" asked Fielder. "Shall we follow up the chase?"

"Or make a detour?" suggested Tom.

"We will turn down this lane," said Turpin, "which will lead us into the main road. If we ride hard we shall outstrip them.

"Away, then!"

The party turned into the lane.

They galloped on at a rattling rate till they had neary reached the end of it.

Here Turpin gave orders to them to draw rein. They did so.

"Shall we mask?" asked Fielder.

"No, dam'me!—let us face it out," cried Tom King, recklessly.

But Turpin drew a black mask from his pocket. He put it on.

The others imitated his example.

Tom King shrugged his shoulders.

"Well, I for one will go undisguised," said he.

"Don't be a fool, Tom," growled the other. "You shall mask, I say."

"Well, captain, I defer to you as in duty bound," returned Tom King.

He then covered his handsome face with a black velvet mask.

"Before we proceed to work," said he, "I must request that there shall be no ruffianly violence. Sir Ranulph is my mark; I have an account to settle with him, so you must leave him to me; and as for Kate Dulcimer, she shall remain with him or return with me, as she pleases."

"A curse on your fads and caprices!" cried Dick Turpin, savagely. "Do you think I'll suffer you to imperil the necks of the whole band by such squeamish fooleries? If the girl is suffered to escape, of course she will blow on us. She must return with us, or, what is better, must be quieted. What compassion can you have for the wanton, heartless jilt?"

"Not much, I own," returned Tom; "but I warn you, Dick, whoever harms her makes me his enemy."

"Hark, captain, the coach is at hand!" interrupted one of the robbers.

"Make ready, boys!" whispered Turpin.

CHAPTER XXXII.

THE HIGHWAY ROBBERY—THE DUEL IN THE WOOD.

THE lamps of the coach were now seen twinkling through the dark, wet leaves of the close-growing trees; and sweeping round a sharp turn in the road, the cumbrous vehicle, drawn by a pair of fine horses, rapidly approached.

Dick Turpin and Tom King immediately leaped their horses over the thicket, and posted themselves in the middle of the road.

"Stand!" shouted Turpin.

The fat coachman uttered a shout of alarm, and ducked his head, as if he thought himself in danger of being instantly shot.

"Highwaymen!" cried the servants, leaping down from behind.

Dick Turpin and Tom King rode up one on either side of the road, pistol in hand.

Fielder and Rose emerged from the bushes some yards in the rear of the carriage.

Bush, Gregory, and Nat Wetherby advanced in front.

Thus beset, the footmen drew their pistols, and glared about them in great dismay.

One of them, however, summoning courage, aimed his pistol at Dick Turpin.

He fired.

The report rang through the dim glades of the silent forest.

The bullet grazed Turpin's cheek.

Damning and raving, the captain of the highwaymen presented his pistol.

His finger was already curling round the trigger.

Tom King struck up his arm with his riding whip.

The pistol went off, and the bullet sped through the air, shattering a branch far overhead.

"Come, Dick, no bloodshed," said Tom.

"If we meet with any further resistance, we'll cut the throats of the whole party; but if they are reasonable we will not proceed to extremities."

Turpin growled an oath, but lowered the second pistol, which he had drawn.

One of the footmen tried to scramble up the bank.

"Not so fast, young man!" laughed Tom, pointing his pistol at him. "We do not part yet; seize them, lads."

Fielder and Rose immediately dismounted, and roughly collared the trembling men.

"Gag the infernal caterpillars!" roared Turpin. "Pinion them and pitch 'em into the dyke."

Fielder took a coil of ropes from his saddle bow, and with the assistance of Bush and Rose bound the servants hand and foot, and gagged them with their own cravats, in each of which they had tied up a large stone.

Meanwhile, pealing shrieks rang from the carriage.

Sir Ranulph burst open the door, and sprang out of the coach, a naked sword gleaming in his hand.

"What outrage is this, villains?" cried the young nobleman, sternly.

Tom King lifted his hat and bowed gracefully.

"Your servant, Sir Ranulph," he said. "There is no outrage intended. We are gentlemen, knights of the road, paladins of the high pad, and quite incapable of any act of brutality or low ruffianism. You have borne off my sweetheart; of course it was my bounden duty to give chase and do my best to rescue the lady. You will think it only reasonable that I and my companions should be paid our travelling expenses, and will not refuse me the satisfaction that the rules of society compel one gentleman to afford another in a case of this sort. I shall have the honour of crossing swords with you."

"I agree to that," said Ranulph, grimly, "upon the sole condition that in case I should come off victorious I shall suffer no injury from your fellow ruffians."

"That I cannot guarantee, Sir Ranulph, unless you use more respectful language. These gentlemen are men of honour, and will not brook insult," said Tom.

"The devil seize this buffoonery," roared Turpin. "Blow his brains out, Rose, and stop this infernal palavering,"

As he spoke he was dragging the trembling Kate from the coach.

Rose was about to carry out his leader's orders, and had already levelled his pistol at Sir Ranulph's head.

"At your peril!" shouted Tom, in a terrible voice, seizing his wrist.

At this moment a sturdy man, somewhat advanced in years, but strongly built, and evidently a very powerful person, leaped out of the coach and grappled Turpin.

The robber swore awfully.

A fierce struggle took place.

The old gentleman was struck down senseless by a fearful blow with the butt of Fielder's pistol.

Meanwhile Wetherby, Bush, and Rose, were busily engaged in cutting the traces of the carriage horses, and rifling the contents of the carriage.

The coachman had been dragged from the box, gagged, and bound hand and foot, and flung down upon the bank beside his fellow-servants.

Sir Ranulph and Tom King had engaged, and were exchanging fierce and rapid passes.

With a shriek, Kate Dulcimer threw herself between the combatants.

"Oh, do not kill him, Tom!" she panted.

Tom drew back.

"Are you his advocate, eh, Kate?" he asked, with an ironical laugh. "Have you forgotten all your fervent vows of eternal love and fidelity?"

He wound his arm round her waist.

"Come, lass, make your election. Will you be this heartless libertine's mistress, or will you return to one who has ever been an indulgent, good-natured lover, who has squandered a fortune, and risked his life for you? Come, speak boldly, for you have nothing to fear from my jealousy."

"I will return with you, love," murmured the girl, clinging to his broad, manly breast.

"'Sdeath, ruffian!" shouted Sir Ranulph, passionately. "Release the girl!"

He made a desperate lunge at the highwayman.

The point of his sword entered Tom's left arm.

The robber uttered a curse and pushed Kate aside.

"You shall bitterly rue that treacherous thrust, you dastard," said Tom. "Come this way!"

And he walked off towards the wood-side.

Sir Ranulph followed, sword in hand.

Kate would have rushed after them.

She was seized by Turpin.

"Your jewels, your money, jade," thundered the ruffian, shaking her brutally.

"Help!—save me, Tom, save me!" she screamed, struggling to release herself from the brutal grasp.

But King and Sir Ranulph had disappeared in the forest.

"Silence, you baggage!" roared Turpin, buffeting her upon the face.

She shrieked, and fainted.

The robbers stripped her of every valuable article —her fan, her rings, her watch and chain, her purse—they even tore off her silk mantle, and her shoes.

Turpin then lifted her roughly, and dashed her across the road on to the bank.

"Quick, lads!" he cried to his men. "Is everything bagged?"

"Yes, captain," returned the others.

"Have you fleeced the flunkies?"

"Yes."

"And the coachman?"

"All right, captain."

"What the devil has become of Tom King? Where is Ranulph?"

"They have gone into the wood to settle their quarrel. Hark! That is the clash of their swords."

"Tom King is an egregious ass!" growled Dick Turpin. "Hand me that carbine, I'll precious soon finish this affair!"

Dick Turpin rushed up the bank, and entered the wood.

Guided by the clashing of the swords, the robbers soon reached the spot where the duellists were contending.

Each was stripped to the shirt; they were fighting fiercely, and with admirable courage, skill, and coolness.

Dick Turpin aimed his musket at Sir Ranulph.

"Hold, captain!" cried Nat Wetherby, catching his arm, "*you'll shoot Tom King!*"

"Ha!" gasped Dick Turpin, grounding the carbine, while a strange presentiment sent a thrill through his heart.

Just on the moment Sir Ranulph made a feint in order to give a final and fatal lunge at his adversary.

He was not quick enough.

Tom King sprang lightly forward.

His sword passed through Sir Ranulph's shoulder.

The young noble staggered, groaned, and dropped apparently dead.

"I treated him like a gentleman, and I must say he fought gallantly," laughed Tom, wiping the blood from his sword, which he sheathed. "He is my prize; and gad, sirs, I deserve my winnings."

With this he stooped over his prostrate foe, and tore the brooch from his cravat, he then possessed himself of his rings, watch, snuff-box, silver-hilted sword, and rifled his pockets of purse and papers.

"'S'truth, my rum 'uns, this has been a good purchase," laughed Dick Turpin, rubbing his hands.

"Hurrah!" shouted the robbers.

"Stash your bellowing, idiots!" cried Nat Wetherby. "We have had row enough already. We shall have the harving beaks down as true as Tyburn."

"What shall we do with the body, captain?" asked Fielder.

"Let him lie where he is," returned Turpin. "I'll tell you what, Tom, the old land-steward is killed, and it seems to me that we had better settle the whole lot, throw their bodies into the river yonder, and run the horses loose in the forest."

"Dick, you are a bloodthirsty ruffian!" said Tom, contemptuously. "We are masked, we have not been recognised, except by Kate, and she shall go with me."

They returned to the spot where the servants, gagged and bound hand and foot, were lying helpless.

Poor Kate lay insensible upon the bank.

"Hullo!" growled Tom, as his eyes fell upon the poor girl, "what's this?"

"You shall have your share of the swag, Tom," said Dick, rather alarmed at the fierce glare of his companion's fine eyes, and wishing to avoid a quarrel. "If you are fool enough to wish to restore the hussey her trumpery you shall have it; we'll meet to-night at old Hind's cave and square accounts."

Tom King made no answer.

He kneeled beside the poor girl, and raised her in his arms.

"Fling that old cove's carcase into the ditch," said Turpin.

Rose and Bush raised the old man in their arms, and bore him away through the trees. (*See Illustration of last week.*)

Tom King, in sullen mood, lifted Kate on to his saddle, and, mounting behind her, shook the rein.

"Where away so fast, comrade?" cried Dick Turpin. "See, Rose and Bush are returning. Mount, my comrades, we'll ride together as far as the cross-roads, and then we'll disperse to meet again at Joe Hinds, where we can share the swag over a bowl of rum slim. To horse, my Trojans!"

The gang of villains rode together to a spot where five or six roads branched off in all directions.

"Here we part; not more than two of us must take the same direction. Do you ride with me, Tom King?"

"No," returned the other, sullenly; "I go alone."

With this he spurred his horse, and, without saluting his comrades, dashed away.

"Tom is riled about his doxy," laughed Nat Wetherby. "You shouldn't have handled her so roughly, captain."

"Let him go hang!" growled Turpin. "Come, Nat Wetherby, you must accompany me. Ben darkmans, gentlemen all, we meet to-night at the 'Black Lion.'"

CHAPTER XXXIII.

DICK TURPIN AND NAT WETHERBY—THE PURSUIT.

DICK TURPIN and Nat Wetherby had selected a path which, diverging from the high road, penetrated into the thickest part of the forest.

For some time they maintained silence, and rode at a rapid pace.

Ever and anon they cast anxious looks behind and around them.

They listened heedfully to every sound.

Turpin, who was a daring ruffian, appeared the more collected of the pair, and more than once roughly abused his companion for his evident nervousness.

"S'death, comrade, you start at the crackle of every breaking bough, the rustle of every drifting sere-leaf, as nervously as a joskin when he passes a gibbet on the heath by night," laughed Turpin. "What ails ye?"

"I don't know; I am not myself, I own, captain; I feel qualmish and cold at heart," returned the other, hoarsely.

"A twinge of conscience, ha?" laughed the other, brutally sneering.

"Conscience!" returned Nat, vacantly, and starting in his saddle.

"Pish! 'tis a bug-bear invented by the priests to awe their dupes," laughed Turpin. "Co[n]science! 'tis but another name for weakness an[d] cowardice!"

"And yet, captain, I think we have gone to[o] far," returned Nat Wetherby, remorsefully. "It [was] bad enough to be guilty of assault and robbery but we might have avoided the crime of murder."

"To what end, you squeamish fool?" growle[d] Turpin. "We weigh one weight, don't we? W[e] work capital, and if we were taken should [be] brought to the crup as sure as fate; why then? The[y] can but hang us if we massacre a hundred adve[r]saries. You are almost as bad as that chicken hearted Tom King, who isn't fit to fly any high[er] rigs than the area sneak, or the spruce fakemen who's more fit to be an old maid's chaplain than bold toby gloak. A plague upon such milk-sops

"Hark!" interrupted Nat, suddenly reaing h[is] horse.

"What now, you rabbit?"

"I thought I heard a voice."

"Ha! ha!" laughed Turpin, "the croak of [a] bull-frog in the marsh, maybe."

"Listen!"

"Pshaw! 'tis that raven yonder. The sly thi[ef] scents the carrion we left on the road."

"That dismal croak is a note of il omen to on[e] or both of us, Dick," returned Na[t] gloomily.

"Rather; if you can be sca[r]ed by such ol[d] woman's rubbish, what will you do if you have t[o] confront real danger?"

"Well, I own myself a fool," returned Na[t] Wetherby, drawing a deep sigh; "but I feel as i[f] I had walked over my own grave. I never had suc[h] strange sensations before."

"Drown 'em, man. Here's somethi[n]g will giv[e] you Dutch courage, at least," laughed Turpin.

He drew out a case-bottle of brandy and hande[d] it to his companion.

Nat took a deep draught.

"Ha! that's better!" he said, with a laug[h] "Richard's himself again!"

Turpin also took a pull at the strong waters, an[d] then replaced the case-bottle in his belt.

Again they spurred on through the dense wood.

"Come, it's all bowman, comrade, there's no on[e] down. Let us enjoy ourselves; we'll light up ou[r] pipes and chant a roaring stave," rejoined Turpi[n] "Warble, my frisky cock-o'-the-woods, you hav[e] the voice of a nightingale, and can put all th[e] feathered songsters to shame. What shall it be—

"'Nose, nose, and who gave thee that jolly red nose?
Nutmeg and ginger, and cinnamon and cloves,
And they gave me this jolly red nose.'

"Bah! you are as mute as a pickled herrin[g] Tune up, my noble."

"I am in no mood for singing," returned Na[t] Wetherby, in a moody tone. "But, dam'me, here'[s] for a shy at the blue devils."

And he trolled forth boisterously—

"'In durance vile lay Claude Du Val
His stout heart never failed——'

"Dick, did ye mark that?"

This sudden exclamation was caused by a strang[e] circumstance.

An enormous bat, wheeling out from the tree[s] darted across the path, and in his blind, headlong flight dashed his leathern wings against Nat's head, knocking off his hat, and then with a tiny shriek o[f] anger or alarm, it flittered into the cover.

Nat sat still in the saddle as pale as a sheet.

Dick Turpin burst into a roar of gruff laughter.

"Why, comrade, you look as if one of the devil's black cherubs had run foul of ye. Surely, you're not such a gull as to think that there's anything in the flight of a poor bat."

"They say that to be struck by the wing of a flying bat is a sure sign of death," returned the highwayman, faintly; "but I put little faith in these tokens; but in the presentiments of the mind I have firm belief. I am doomed, captain; my hour is at hand!"

While he was speaking, Dick Turpin's attention was suddenly diverted by the startled attitude of his beautiful black mare.

Black Bess stood with her fore-foot advanced, her graceful, glossy neck extended, her thin nostrils dilated, and her fine ears erect.

She snorted and pawed the ground.

"What is it, lass?" murmured her rider, patting her sleek neck.

"Hark! the trampling of horses! We are pursued!" cried Nat Wetherby.

"Then look to yourself, Nat, your roan jennet is no contemptible pacer; but Wild's men are generally well mounted; or, maybe, our pursuers are farmers, or country gentlemen mounted on their hunters. You had best make yourself scarce."

"And you, captain?"

"I can well afford to trust myself to Bonnie Black Bess. Mounted on my gallant mare I can defy all the runners in Bow Street to catch me; but hark away, lad, the sounds grow louder and nearer. I hear the yelping of a dog; they have struck the right scent."

The two highwaymen spurred their horses and scoured along like the wind.

CHAPTER XXXIV.
THE FIGHT BETWEEN DICK TURPIN AND ROVING JACK.

NAT WETHERBY had attended to Dick Turpin's warning, and was now galloping down a narrow bridle path in the thickest part of the forest.

The highwayman listened to the distant patter of the hoofs with a grin of satisfaction.

For his own part he seemed to be little inclined to hurry himself.

Fully confident in the wondrous powers of his gallant steed he drew rein and lingered, as if half inclined to wait an opportunity of catching a glimpse of his pursuers.

Then he rode on at an easy trot.

The morning was breaking coldly in the east, while the moon still shone with undiminished splendour.

The air was keen and frosty, and along the hardened ground every little noise rang out as loud and distinct as the stroke of a bell.

"S'blood! he is overtaken!" cried Turpin, suddenly. "To the rescue, Bess!"

The sound of voices and the discharge of fire-arms was now heard from within the thicket.

Dick Turpin dashed through the trees, reckless of all obstruction; now bending his head down to the saddle-bow to escape contact with the trailing branches, now leaping deep ruts, or high piles of felled timber.

He reached an open space in the woods.

It was a level plain, as smooth as a lawn, about five acres in extent.

The shouts within the forest on the opposite side of this little plain grew louder and fiercer, and the discharge of fire-arms more frequent.

Suddenly a rider burst out from the thicket and dashed like an arrow across the plain.

He was immediately followed by a young cavalier in black velvet, whom Dick Turpin instantly recognised as Roving Jack.

Our hero pressed close upon the highwayman.

He was splendidly mounted upon a superb white horse of Arabian breed.

A crowd of riders, mounted on inferior horses, galloped in the rear.

Nat Wetherby and our hero exchanged shots.

They were riding at such a terrific pace that it was impossible for them to take steady aim.

A second time they fired at each other.

This time the discharge was not so harmless.

Our hero received a slight wound in his left shoulder, while Nat Wetherby was also hit in the side.

Uttering a savage execration the highwayman turned his horse.

He drew his sword, and spurring deep, dashed his horse against our hero's.

Roving Jack was not unprepared for the charge.

He had unsheathed his sword, and parried the downright stroke the robber aimed at his head.

Upon seeing our hero thus engaged with Nat Wetherby, the other ruffian, Dick Turpin, gave a yell of triumphant malice.

He would have fired at the daring youth, but was afraid of hitting his own comrade.

The swords clashed, and the combatants growled their mutual defiance.

Sword in hand, Dick Turpin rode up.

Our hero, who had distanced his companions in race, was thus left alone to contend with both ruffians, but was in nowise daunted by the odds against him.

"Ho! ha! Sir John Warbold," laughed Dick Turpin, "we meet again; this time you shall not escape me!"

He made a dash at our hero.

Just as he did so Roving Jack had taken advantage of an unguarded moment in which Nat Wetherby left his breast undefended, and, with a swift, fierce thrust, drove his sword through his heart.

The highwayman uttered a groan.

As Roving Jack drew back his sword the dying robber clutched at it convulsively, dreadfully gashing his hands.

Then he reeled in the saddle, and fell to the earth.

His horse uttered a shrill neigh, and darted off into the thicket.

"Ten thousand devils!" roared Dick Turpin; "but you are still outmatched, you infernal bloodhound! You shall pay dearly for this."

"Come on, Dick Turpin," said our hero, cooly; "you have no time to lose, my comrades are hard upon us, and we shall be interrupted."

Roving Jack and Dick Turpin fought like paladins, their horses trampling the ground, and even joining in the fray by biting each other; the body of the slain highwayman was crushed beneath their hoof.*

Both Turpin and his adversary were excellent swordsmen.

The highwayman kept up the conflict in the most daring style, although Roving Jack's companions and attendants were riding up at a rattling pace.

At length finding that, with all his desperate efforts, he failed to make a single home-thrust at our hero, he swore and raved with passion.

Roving Jack fought very warily.

Finding that his adversary was a very powerful and skilful foe, he acted almost entirely on the defensive.

At length it became evident that if Dick Turpin

* See Illustration to No. 8.

protracted the fight any longer he must certainly be taken.

He backed his horse.

" This will settle it," he growled, with an oath.

He drew a pistol from his holster and levelled it at Jack.

Hal Hetherington, who was now riding up, aimed at the robber's hand, and fired.

The bullet struck Turpin's pistol, which went off in the air.

" You have escaped for this time, my kinchin," growled the robber, shaking his fist at our hero, " but we shall meet again."

So saying, he turned his horse.

" Now catch me who can !" laughed the highwayman, waving his hat to his pursuers. " Harkaway, Bess."

And the rascal galloped with the speed of the wind.

An involuntary cry of admiration burst from the lips of the spectators as the beautiful black courser bounded away with such grace and power, darting like a shaft through the briary underwood.

" After him, lads !" cried Roving Jack, " and if you can but get within pistol range shoot the miscreant dead."

" Tally-ho !" yelled the farmers, as if they were hunting a fox.

Away they rattled.

Our hero, whose horse was almost equal to Turpin's, forged ahead, followed at some distance by Hal Hetherington and the rest.

The whole party scrambled recklessly through the wood.

They reached the high road, and leaped their horses down the bank.

Here an exciting chase commenced.

Dick Turpin, who was wondrously proud of his jockey-ship, and, moreover, a most daring villain, actually walked his mare at a slow, graceful, ambling pace, and looking backwards, called upon his pursuers to mend their speed, and laughing and jeering at them for laggards.

But he had well-nigh found cause to repent of his rashness.

Our fiery young hero was in no mood for fool's play ; he came rushing along like the wind, and when but a few lengths behind the highwayman blazed away at him with his pistol, knocking off his hat and grazing his forehead.

Turpin swore most awfully.

For an instant he seemed to be inclined to turn about and attack our hero.

However, he changed his mind, and urged Black Bess to the top of her speed.

Away she flew like lightning.

Roving Jack spurred and whipped his white arab, and the two horses ran neck and neck in a dead heat.

The ride had rather the character of a race than a chase—the black and white steeds straining every nerve to outstrip each other.

At length, with all his exertions, our hero's horse gradually fell off, and now hung feebly at the black mare's side.

Soon the bonnie Black Bess was ahead by many a length, and the arab, apparently exhausted, was losing ground at every pace.

" Stop thief ! a highwayman !" roared the pursuers, seeing a cart in the road. " Knock down the villain ! 'Tis Dick Turpin !"

" Harkaway !" laughed the highwayman, waving his hat, as, with a light bound, his beautiful steed leaped over the cart. " Adieu, gentlemen ; sorry I can't wait for you ; but my time's precious, and you so slow—ha, ha, ha !"

CHAPTER XXXV.

EDGEWORTH BESS ENDEAVOURS TO PREVENT JACK SHEPPARD FROM JOINING ROVING JACK'S BAND.

MR. JOE BLAKE, alias Blueskin, had a house in Fetter Lane, which he rented of one Field, of whom mention has been made in previous chapters.

It was an old store-house adjoining a stable, and was used by Blueskin and his partners as a " lumber ken," or a receptacle for plunder.

Thither, one chill evening, when the watch had just commenced lighting up the dim oil and cotton lamps that tempered the gloom of the ill-paved, dirty streets of old London, that a pretty girl, flashily dressed in wide-hooped petticoats and furbelows and close wrapped in a hooded mantle, came lightly tripping. She stopped at the door, and cast a rapid, anxious glance at the dark house.

No light appeared at any of the windows, and the girl listened tremblingly for some moments ere she could summon resolution to knock at the door.

Though she tapped but gently her summons elicited a deep roaring bay of a dog and the clanking of a heavy chain in the passage.

Then she could hear the muttered blasphemies of a surly voice, and a scramble and bash as if the noisy watch-dog had been rewarded for his vigilance by being kicked across the passage.

The girl stepped backwards in some trepidation.

A little trap door just above her head was pushed open, and a dark, scowling face appeared, with a hand which grasped something long and gleaming that showed in the darkness very much like a pistol.

" Who the devil are you, and what do ye want ?" growled a voice.

" Oh, it's all right, Blueskin," returned the girl, in a whisper, " it's only I. Come down, I want to speak to you."

" What, Edgeworth Bess ?" cried the ruffian, in accents less surly than those in which he had put his former question. " Stop a bit, my dimber mort, I'll let you in directly."

The trap-door was closed and bolted.

Edgeworth Bess waited for some time impatiently.

Then a footstep was heard in the echoing passage.

Then the deep growl of the dog, and the rattle of his chain.

Again Blueskin swore fiercely at the savage brute and kicked him.

He cautiously opened the door.

"Come in," he said, hurriedly.

The girl obeyed.

"Keep off the dog, Blueskin," whispered the girl, nervously.

Blueskin had a lantern in his hand.

Its light streamed down the wide, dusty passage, and fell upon the bandy-legged monster chained to a staple under the staircase.

It was an immense and hideous-looking bull-dog.

"Don't be frightened, my charmer," grinned Blueskin, "he's muzzled, you see. Give me your arm; mind how you step; the staircase that leads to my sky-parlour is rayther rickety. Down, you beast!"

This was addressed to the dog, who would not be appeased, but, springing to the length of his chain, showed his horrid white fangs, and snarled ferociously.

Edgeworth Bess clung to the robber's arm, and he handed her carefully up the shaky stairs.

They entered a large, dusty room, piled on all sides with chests and bales.

It was lighted by a stinking, smoking oil lamp that swung by an iron chain from the ceiling.

The walls were hung with various implements of burglary—crow-bars, centre-bits, screws, gimlets files, pick-locks, and the like, and a very formidable array of weapons, including knives, swords, and bludgeons in great variety.

Blueskin politely set a stool for the young lady to sit upon, carefully dusting it with the flaps of his long, loose coat.

He then placed the lantern upon the table against which he leaned his stalwart body, and, folding his arms, gazed curiously at the girl.

Edgeworth Bess had thrown back her mantle, displaying her moulded bust, while the light from the lamp above her head glowed brightly on her golden locks.

Her pretty face was pale, and her cheeks bore the traces of recent tears.

"Blow me, this is a pleasure, my beauteous Bess," said the robber, gallantly. "And to what fortunate circumstance may I ascribe the honour of this charming visit?"

And he made a sweeping bow.

"Oh, Blueskin, I shall break my heart, I know I shall," returned the lady, wringing her little white hands.

"'Pon my soul, Bess, you hardly deserve pity if you do," returned the dark-skinned ruffian, with an amorous leer, "seeing how many other hearts you have broken."

"Oh, don't you go talking such provoking rubbish," cried the girl, petulantly. "I wish all the false, fickle, treacherous, lying fellows were all hung on one gibbet, that's what I wish."

"Why, my dear, what has excited your anger against your poor slaves of the sterner sex?" laughed Blueskin.

"There's my Jack!—ugh!—I could tear his eyes out!" cried Bess, passionately.

"Why, how has he offended you?"

"He's always getting into some scrape, he is."

"What! thunder and devils! Has the plummy kid got lumbered, then?" cried Blueskin, quickly. "Has old Jonathan nabbed him at last?"

"No, no; I wish he had," sobbed Bess.

"Come, that's nonsense, Bess," laughed the robber; "we all know how you doat upon little Jack; but, come, you may confide in me, what's amiss now, my dear?"

"He's going to desert me; he's going to leave us all, Blueskin."

"Ha!"

"Yes; and he's so obstinate, I know he'll keep his word," returned Bess, sighing.

"Not if we can help it, my dainty dell," returned Blueskin, laying his finger on his nose, and winking knowingly. "I have had some hint of this before; he's going to join that mad cull, Roving Jack, who calls himself the robber-hunter."

"Yes; the ship is now lying off Portsmouth, and is ready to sail," returned Bess.

"And has Jack started for Portsmouth, then?"

"No, Blueskin; he will set off early in the morning."

"And where will he pass the night?"

"With me and Poll Maggott at my lodgings in the Dials; we are to have a parting supper together, and he's going to share the hundred pounds the gentry cove gave him between us."

"Ho! ho!"

"And listen, Blueskin, we must prevent him from going, mustn't we?"

"In course, it's not to be thought on," returned the robber. "He must be prevented."

"But I don't see how that's to be managed," said the girl, despondingly.

"Nothing is more easy."

"I suppose you think my influence ought to be strong enough to turn him from his purpose? But, lor' bless you, Blueskin, my tears and reproaches are of no avail. He only laughs at me. If once Jack makes up his mind to do a thing, however desperate or stupid, he always carries out his intention."

"I'll talk with him."

"Oh! no, indeed, you must not," returned the girl, in alarm. "He made me swear that I would not let you know of his design. He swore that if you came to my lodgings that he wouldn't see you, but would start off at once."

Blueskin growled an oath.

He took two or three strides through the room.

Then he stopped and slapped his thigh.

"I have it, my blowen!" he laughed. "Now listen, I'll tell you what to do."

"Well, Blueskin?"

"In the first place, he must not know that you have seen me to-night."

"No; certainly not."

"You must go home, and, with Poll Maggot, make ready for his coming."

"What then?"

"You must use all your blandishments to put him in good humour, and when he talks about leaving you, only implore him to write to you often, and to hasten his return."

"Yes; I see your drift."

"I'll call in, quite casually, as if to lay out some new plant. I will contrive to worm the secret from him, that he is going to give up business, and to live on the square. At first I'll oppose his plans; but, after a bit, I'll pretend to fall in with them, and then we'll have a bowl of punch to drink to his good fortune."

"And so make him drunk. I'll tell you what, Blueskin, he's too downy to fall into such a trap. Your plan won't answer; drunk or sober, he'll go, depend on it."

"I say he shan't," growled the robber; "and, to

make sure, I'll drug the stingo and put him into a trance that will last for a day or two."

"Oh! no, I will not consent to it."

"You must. If you are willing to lose him, I arn't. I love little Jack better than ere a woman of you all; and we'll have many a brave adventure together yet."

"But suppose the flash cove should wait for him, or should even seek him out?" suggested Bess.

"I know how to provide for that; when we've disabled Jack from playing the fool's trick he contemplates, we'll lock him up in a strong room, and I'll at once write a letter, in Jack's name, to Sir John Warbold, refusing to join the mad-brained expedition, and dispatch it at once."

"I wish we could manage without drugging the poor fellow," said Bess; "perhaps we may do him some injury."

"Not a bit of it. Old Nightshade, the doctor, will supply me with a potion that will do the trick quite harmlessly. I'll go to him at once."

"And I'll return home, where Poll Maggot awaits me," returned Bess, rising.

"Do so, my dimber dell, and I'll visit you in an hour or so."

"Have you heard the news about Tom King?"

"No."

"Why, then, he was to have joined this precious crew of harming cheats, but Roving Jack has disowned him, and will not accept him as one of his band."

"How's that?"

"Why, it seems that Tom King was with Dick Turpin and the rest of the gang, when they stopped Sir Ranulph Gayton's coach, and killed one of his attendants."

"Phew! that fellow will swing before next sessions."

"Yes, he's a rash fool. Jonathan Wild has set Quilt Arnold on his track, and if what I hear is true, that minx, Kate Dulcimer, has sold him to the ban-dogs."

"Ha, the jade! Well, I'll give him a hint of his danger; Jack Sheppard likes the gloak, and will be pleased if I can save him."

"And now I must be going. Remember, Blueskin, you must not let Jack Sheppard know that I have seen you to-night, or you will spoil all."

"I'm mum, my pretty maid," laughed Blueskin; "trust to my discretion."

"For the present, then, good-bye."

Edgeworth Bess rose.

Blueskin took up the lantern.

"Let me escort you," he said; "mind the stairs."

So saying, he led the way down the rickety steps.

A deep growl resounded in the darkness below.

"That cussed dog!" panted the girl, clinging tightly to the robber's arm.

"Grabber is in his sulks to-night," laughed Blueskin. "That dog smells treachery; that lully prigger, Field, has been here to-night, and this brute can't abide him."

The dog sprang out from his dark corner

Edgeworth Bess shrieked.

Blueskin laughed gruffly.

Then, bestowing a curse and a kick upon the brute, he led the shuddering girl to the door.

"Good night, Blueskin."

"Ben darkmans, my ben mort," returned the robber; "you will see me before morning."

The girl drew her cloak round her comely shoulders.

She tripped away.

"There goes Jack Sheppard's fate!" muttered the robber, moodily. "I wish the kiddy warn't so

fond of the petticoats; they'll be the ruin of him some day. Howsoever, I'd rather see him at Tyburn show, any day, than have him follow the fortunes of that cursed young wolf's cub, Roving Jack. And now, 'fast bind, fast find,' and then for old Nightshade!"

Re-entering the house he unmuzzled the dog.

He then fastened bolts and bars, slipped a pistol into his pocket, and a heavy bludgeon under his arm, and passed out into the darkness.

CHAPTER XXXVI.

EDGEWORTH BESS, POLL MAGGOT, AND BLUESKIN, PLAY JACK SHEPPARD A TRICK.

EDGEWORTH BESS and Mistress Poll Maggot, tricked out in extravagant finery, and seated at a table furnished with delicacies, and glittering with vessels of silver and gold, the plunder of many a wealthy house, anxiously awaited the arrival of Jack Sheppard.

Bess had taken her companion into her confidence, and related the particulars of her visit to Blueskin's abode.

The amazon laughed heartily at the trick it was designed to practice upon Jack, and warmly commended Blueskin for his cleverness.

"Jack must be a fool to suppose that he would ever be suffered to give up the mooching lay," laughed Poll. "Why, Jonathan Wild would never permit such a thing."

"Oh, Poll, don't speak of that wretch; it gives me a shudder to think of him."

"But Jack has broken with the thief-taker, hasn't he?"

"Yes; more's the pity."

"Ha! you may well say that," returned Poll, seriously, "for Wild is an ugly customer to have for an enemy."

"He has sworn to hang poor Jack."

"And by letting him go with this gentry cove you might save him," said Poll. "After all, I am inclined to think it would be the best course under the circumstances."

"I beg to differ in opinion there, madam," returned Edgeworth Bess, tossing her head. "If you have not more affection for him than to be willing to part with him so easily, I have. Jack Sheppard is——"

"A generous lover," sneered Poll, "and you are naturally unwilling to lose him. Quite right, my dear. Don't be cross; but, hark! some one is rattling the shutter."

"Oh, it's Jack!" cried Bess, excitedly. "Ah! how I wish it was all over."

Poll Maggott opened the door.

Jack Sheppard strutted in.

The young housebreaker had attired himself in his gayest dress, and moved in a mist of ruffles, a constellation of brilliants, a halo of gold, and a rainbow of silk.

In his right hand he carried a gold-headed cane; diamond buckles sparkled at his knee and on his shoes, while, from the gold-laced pockets of his crimson satin coat, protruded the finely inlaid stocks of a pair of pistols; he wore a long, slight, silver-hilted dress sword.

"Ladies, I salute you," said Jack, with a courtly bow, as he doffed his three-cornered hat.

"Oh, you dimber little cull!" laughed Poll Maggot, backing to obtain a better view of his slashing exterior. "Was ever such a pink of a prince in a fairy tale? Tell you what, Edgeworth Bess, let's toss for the first kiss."

But the fond Bess was already clasped in her lover's embrace.

Poll Maggot, however, tore her away, and fairly hugged the slim fellow in her broad, comely arms.

"And now, ladies," said Jack, "let us sit down to supper; let us take a parting cup together, and mingle it with our tears, for I warn you that I have not long to stay, and that our parting will be a long one.

"'Hurrah for the outward bound!
My home's on the howling main,
And many a sigh shall swell the gale,
E'er I return again.
Fare ye well,
Fare ye well—ri-tol-de-riddle, tol-de-ray.'

"Oh, lor! I'm but a land-lubber swab, make the best o' me; I take to the water about as kindly as a blind kitten. But, come, it's a sad heart that never rejoices,

"'So to-night we'll merry be,
To-morrow we'll get sober.'"

And Jack threw himself at the table, and leaning his head on his hands, sighed heavily.

His mistresses posed themselves one on either side of the misguided young profligate, and twined their arms about him.

"Faith, my darlings, it costs me tough wrestle with myself to tear myself away from you; but it must be done——"

"You'll never have the cruelty to leave me, love?" simpered Bess.

"I must, Bess; but you'll think of me sometimes, won't ye?—and you, too, Poll?"

"Oh, you heartless little monster!" murmured Mistress Maggot, smoothing his laced cravat.

"If you go to sea, Jack, I declare I'll drown myself!" cried Bess, hysterically.

"I won't," said Poll, stoutly; "but I'll tell ye what I *will* do."

"What will you do, Poll?"

"Why, Jack, I'll go to sea myself; I should make a rare good sailor, I warrant ye."

Jack Sheppard laughed heartily at this resolve.

The supper passed off very merrily.

The ladies exerted their powers of fascination to the utmost, while Jack, assuming an air of reckless gaiety, sang and jested in the most buoyant manner.

But he would not be diverted from his purpose, either by upbraidings, tears, or entreaties; he declared his fixed purpose of starting for Portsmouth at daybreak, and then he divided the hundred pounds he had brought with him between the two sirens.

Suddenly a knocking was heard at the shutter.

"Who's that?" cried Jack, starting suspiciously, and gripping his pistols.

"La, dear, I'm sure I can't tell. Who can it be?" asked Bess, opening wide her pretty blue eyes in well-affected wonderment.

"A rival admirer, perhaps," grunted Jack.

"You'd better go and see who it is," said Poll, sharply.

Bess rose, and went to the window.

"It's only old Blueskin, my dell," said a gruff voice without. "Open the jigger."

"No, no!" cried Jack Sheppard, rising hastily. "Sit down, Bess, it's Blueskin; I don't want to see him."

"Why, dear? Surely you would like to bid adieu to your old pal; he's the right sort."

"Hold your jaw," returned Jack Sheppard, fiercely. "I say he shall not come in."

Bess and Poll exchanged meaning glances.

Jack Sheppard rose, and with a gloomy look, took up his hat and walking-stick.

"Farewell, Bess; good-bye Poll," he said, stepping towards the back door. "I'm off. I am not going to be baulked by any of ye, and I don't want to be badgered by old Joe. I shall leave by the gate at the back of the house; don't let him know I've been here."

Bess sprang up, and rushing to Jack, gave a slight scream, threw herself in his arms, and appeared to faint.

"What the devil——" growled Jack, in great perplexity.

Meanwhile, the hoarse voice of Blueskin was heard singing without—

"And up she got, and donned her clothes,
And ope'd the chamber door——"

Again there was a loud rattling of the shutters.

"Hulloa, hulloa! What are ye about?" growled Blueskin. "Let me in, Bess; my little pal Johnny Sheppard is here, and I want to speak to him."

Poll laid her hand on the bolt of the door.

"At your peril, you baggage!" cried Jack Sheppard, angrily.

"At my peril, then," was the cool response. "Come, Jack, don't be a fool now. What harm can there be in your seeing the poor, faithful fellow? Surely if you can resist our persuasion, you will be proof against anything he can have to say. I'll let him in."

Mistress Maggot forthwith opened the door.

Blueskin swaggered in.

"Why, gads my life! you jades, what sort o' treatment do you call this?" cried the robber. "What have I done to be shut out like a dog—but, hulloa, you are yet alive, captain! Tip us your flapper, my ben pal. What have you been doing with yourself this weary while? I thought you were laid up in lavender."

"Stand off, Blueskin!" said Sheppard, coldly.

"What, won't you tip us your bunch of fives?" returned the robber, seating himself, and commencing a vigorous attack upon the remnants of the supper. "And I heard it whispered, too, that you were about to leave us all, and were going over to the enemy."

"And were glad to hear it, I suppose?" asked Sheppard, sneering.

"Glad? no, not glad," returned Blueskin, bluntly. "I don't care a curse; you're no loss to the profession."

This was not a bad stroke of policy.

Jack's wretched, perverted sense of vanity was piqued, and his curiosity aroused.

"No great loss, eh?" he asked, with a frown. "What do you mean?"

"You have proved yourself a gull," returned Blueskin, contemptuously. "If you had been a lad of pluck and mettle, you would never have listened to Roving Jack."

"And if I were a fool and coward I should listen to you," returned Jack Sheppard, sullenly. "But I am neither. I have made up my mind to break through the meshes that you have thrown round me. To-morrow I go aboard, and the next day will find me far at sea. I hope never to return."

"Nonsense, captain, you don't mean it."

"I do, as you will find. So tell me at once, do you mean to try opposition?"

"'Spose it wouldn't be o' no use," grumbled Blueskin.

"You may take your oath of that."

"Let me go with ye, Jack?"

"That is impossible," returned the other, shaking his head; "but, at least, we'll part in kindness."

"Aye, dam'me, let's not darken to-night by the clouds of to-morrow," laughed Blueskin. "Come, Bess, brew us another bowl of punch, and let us drink a merry cruise to Captain Sheppard, a prosperous voyage, and a safe return."

Blueskin turned his head aside, and winked at Poll Maggot.

A smile passed over her broad, handsome face, and her white teeth flashed brightly.

"Dam'me, now, that's jannock!" cried Jack Sheppard, heartily. "And 'struth, my pal, and my dears, I'm loath enough to leave ye; but the best of friends must part, and so let us part merrily, and, maybe, we shall meet again joyously some fine day. Your hand, pal Blueskin!"

The robber clasped his comrade's hand, and shook it as if he intended to dislocate the shoulder.

"Ah! Jack," he said, with a sigh, "you should appreciate my self-sacrifice. It's hard lines. What will become of me when you are gone? I shall have no heart for business. I had such a sweet plant in my eye, too, at Chelsea. Old Field has got the slaveys in a line, and there's such a plummy fakement to be spoken to—but, heigho! I have no more resolution left to carry me through such a job than my bedridden gran'dam. This parting has taken all the pluck ont of me."

"Stash that! I'm not going away till morning, so let us make a jolly night of it."

"Brayvo!" roared Blueskin, thumping his fist on the table, and making the glasses leap. "Polly, put the kettle on, and Bess, my dimber romany dell, lisp us a fine chant."

But Edgeworth Bess excused herself from singing, declaring her heart was too full for merriment.

"Oh! Jack, where are the days that once we saw?" laughed Blueskin. "Ah! the merry adventures we've seen together. Do you mind the night at Dollis hill?—ha! ha! ha! And the jolly rides we've had on the high road under the gleam of pale oliver? After all, the high toby lay is a livelier game than the ken-slumming plant, for, as poor Charley Hitchin used to sing—

"'Of all gallants to frisk a gull,*
Commend me to the bridle cull,†
So roaring, ranting, wild and free,
There's none on road or plain like me.'

"Well, here's a merry cruise, lad!"

So saying, he dipped deep into the punch-bowl.

"Thanks, Joe," returned Jack. "And never think that I shall forget you, girls. No; Roving Jack intends to chase and capture the pirate, Captain Kidd, who, they say, has amassed immense treasure. I'll send you gold galore, and silks and satins, diamonds, rubies, and orient pearls. Sir John has sufficient interest to procure me a free pardon, and who knows but the day may come when the name of Jack Sheppard will hold a proud place in the list of England's worthies?"

"Well said, Jack!" cried Blueskin; "this is plummy, it almost reconciles me to the thought of losing you."

"I wish, Joe, I could persuade you to give up the faking lay," said Jack Sheppard, who was getting elated, and smiled benignantly on the admiring circle; "you will have the shoulder-clappers down sooner or later, and, though I don't care a snap for old Wild, he's hard nails on you, and you won't queer Tyburn, my covey. Sorry should I be on my return to find you swinging in chains, or grinning in some ivory-turner's‡ museum."

"Don't talk like a death's head, Jacky. Come, you don't booze. Smother me! but there's sense in what you say; Wild is hard down. Only to-night I escaped him by a close shave; I tipped old Abraham the garnish, and promised him a handful

of couters, or I should have been nailed by two constables and the head borough."

"Ha, ha! old Nab's a jewel! How did he get you off?"

"He swore, by 'the peard of Moshesh,' that I was the wrong man. But I'll tell ye what, my ben kiddy, I don't half like that fellow Field, he's got all the air of a sneaking noser.*"

"Never could abide that old mousetrap," laughed Sheppard; "but, thank my stars, I shall now sail clear of the whole ruck, curse 'em all! There's not a bit o' true steel among 'em."

"Present company in course excepted," grinned Blueskin.

"You! why, dam'me, yes, I should think you are a hand of trumps," laughed Jack; "either of you would rather die than betray me. Wouldn't you, Bess?"

"Be burnt at the stake, love," returned his mistress.

"And yet Black Mary said—and she's a genuine witch, if ever there was one—she said you would turn traitress."

"The old hag, she ought to be ducked in a horsepond! Wait till I catch hold on her, I'll warrant I'll limb her, the faggot!" cried Bess.

"I'm sure I wouldn't neglect a friendly caution, come from whence it would," said Poll Maggot.

Edgeworth Bess looked daggers at the speaker.

"No rows," growled Sheppard, knocking his fist on the table; "kiss me, Bess, and look pleasant, for maybe it's the last time I shall bask in the sunshine of your smile."

"Ahem!" coughed Poll Maggot, with a little sneer of contempt.

Edgeworth Bess emitted a choking sob, and pillowed her pretty head on Jack's shoulder.

Jack smoothed her glancing locks of gold, and looked fondly upon her.

He heaved a deep sigh, and then, suddenly lifting his piercing black eyes, said,

"What the devil are you putting in my glass, Joe Blueskin?"

"A leetle pounded sugar, that's all, my boy," returned the other; "my brimmer wasn't quite sweet enough. Fill up again; pass over that lemon. Bess hasn't put in quite enough of the acid to make the mixture toothsome. Ha! that's it; now let's have a toast."

"Hark!" cried Sheppard; "who'd a thought it?"

"What now, love?"

Sheppard pulled out a splendid gold watch—he carried several about him.

"Old St. Martin is right," he said, "it has struck three. I must hoist the blue peter, for I've a long ride before me. My horse is stabled at Joe Hind's."

The clocks were now striking in chorus.

Jack Sheppard buckled on his sword, and flung his riding-cloak around his shoulders.

There was a perfect shout of remonstrance.

Blueskin swore.

Poll Maggot scolded.

Edgeworth Bess sobbed and pleaded.

Jack was immovable.

"Well, dash my wig, if you will go, and there's no detaining you, wait one moment, I'll escort you out of the town," cried Blueskin.

"No; I shall be safer alone."

"Only as far as Joe Hind's, then?"

"Oh, dear, darling Jack, sit down, just for half an hour," sobbed Bess. "Do not leave us thus abruptly; let us drink one parting glass together."

"Ten minutes," said Jack, seating himself, and

---

* Rob a soft fellow.   † Highwayman.   ‡ Surgeon's.   * Approver.

sighing; "no longer; and, unless you promise not to embitter this parting by trying to detain me, I'll go at once."

"So help me bob we won't, Jack!" cried Blueskin. "Send I may live!"

"Hand my glass, Poll."

Mistress Maggot complied.

Edgeworth Bess had seated herself on her lover's knee, and had passed her arms round his neck.

"A bumper!" said Sheppard.

They all filled and raised their glasses.

"Here's—Roving Jack!"

And the ill-fated youth emptied the glass at a draught.

"Roving Jack!" chorused the rest.

They exchanged significant glances.

"Pah!" spluttered Sheppard, "surely there's something in——"

"Come, Bess, a chant," interrupted Blueskin, quickly, casting a meaning glance towards her; "let us cheer up our dull hearts with a sweet stave."

"Aye, wench," murmured Jack Sheppard, kissing her lips, "sing, your music will linger on my ear and in my heart when I am far away."

Bess pressed his hand fondly, and then, in a charming voice, as sweet and clear as a flute, she warbled pathetically—

> "Ah! remember me, love!
> Though the boundless sea, love,
>   Roll our arms between.
> Take my heart with thee, love,
> Leave thy heart with me, love,
>   Though ocean intervene.
>
> "Ah! remember me, love!
> Though some fairer be, love——"

"Hist!" chuckled Blueskin, "he's fast as a top!"

Jack Sheppard's head was drooped upon the fair shoulder of his mistress.

His eyes were closed, and his pale face was fixed and rigid; his arm drooped listlessly by his side, he seemed to be sunk in a deep trance.

Edgeworth Bess gently disengaged herself from his embrace, and rose to her feet.

No sooner had she released her hold upon him than his head dropped forward.

He would certainly have pitched down upon his forehead had not Blueskin darted across the room and caught him in his arms.

"Lend a hand, Poll," he whispered.

The stalwart beauty walked across the room, and caught up Jack's legs, while Blueskin threw his arms round his body.

Thus they carried him to a bed, screened off at one end of the room, on which they laid him down.

He sank as motionless and as seemingly lifeless as a corpse.

Blueskin pulled the screen before the bed, and with Poll Maggot returned to the table.

He drained out the dregs from Jack's glass, and refilled it with brandy from a black bottle which stood on the mantel.

He took a deep draught.

He then fixed a steady glance upon the fire.

Silence was for some time maintained by the little party.

Hardened as they were, each felt a pang of remorse.

Jack Sheppard, though a pernicious rogue and pest to society, had proved true and generous to them, at least.

They knew well enough that they had destroyed his last chance for life.

They were well aware that by preventing him from taking the only opportunity that had offered from escaping the consequences of his past guilt, they had left him to the mercy of the merciless law.

Blueskin was the first to speak.

"Come, my dimber dells," said he, "we can't lose our little pal now, he's booked finely."

"Better as it is, his name will be immoralized."

"But he will be hanged!" said Poll Maggot, grimly.

"Bah! what will be, will be; there's no queering fate, Poll. Bring me a pen and ink, I must send a letter to Sir John Warbold."

"Ah! that is a proper gallant," sighed Poll; "he's the handsomest youth that ever I saw out of a picture-frame."

At this commendation of our hero, Blueskin grunted his disgust.

Edgeworth Bess brought him pen, ink, and paper.

The robber nibbled the quill, and scratched his head reflectively for some minutes.

Then, with a fixed and solemn look, he pushed the paper with his left hand half across the table, and describing some imaginary circles and flourishes in the air with his right, finally dashed off a word or two.

Then he pondered deeply, and read over what he had written, and gave a portentous shake of his head.

He rubbed his nose meditatively.

Again he made a desperate plunge at the paper, stretching out his left arm, and resting his head upon it, in much the same manner as a swimmer does when he swims on his side.

A blot!

An oath!

Blueskin applies the paper to his tongue, and licks off the black stain.

He dries the paper over the candle.

He then scratches out the blot with the blade of his dagger, still rusty and knotched from the last throat it had cut.

He scratched a hole through the paper.

Uttering a curse, he tore the letter to pieces.

He then took another sheet, and, after some further efforts, succeeded in finishing his task.

The letter, of course, purported to come from Sheppard, and contained a brief but decided rejection of our hero's offer.

The epistle having been carefully folded and sealed with the knob on the haft of the dagger, Blueskin placed it in his pocket-book.

Then, rising, he tossed his hat and took up his bludgeon.

"Hark'ee, Bess," said he. "Dimber Jack won't open his ogles for forty-eight hours. I shall dispatch this by the mail at once, and, long before Jack can take any steps to undo what has been done, or to reach Portsmouth, the pirate-hunter will have sailed."

"But what shall I tell him when he recovers?" asked Bess, nervously. "He will kill me."

"Pshaw! you must say that he took too much punch, and got so boozed that we were forced to put him to bed."

"But he won't believe me."

"Then you must trust to your woman's wits—turn on the ogle taps; a few tears will soften him in no time," laughed Blueskin. "But I'll return before he wakes, and, with Poll and I to back you, you needn't be afraid of his anger."

"Pray don't fail me, Blueskin. Jack's the very devil when he's roused, and he'll go mad if he finds out how we've bilked him."

"Never fear, my doxy," returned the robber, laughing; "I'll be here, and so, ben darkmans, my dimber morts."

CHAPTER XXXVII.
THE BOW STREET RUNNERS IN SEARCH OF JACK SHEPPARD.

"WARHAWKS!"

This signal of danger was whispered by a dashing looking fellow in a laced hat and richly-brocaded silk coat, who, upon the door being opened, was discovered by Blueskin and the two girls leaning against the porch, and looking intently down the street.

"Hulloa! why, blow me, if it arn't Tom King!" cried Blueskin, in great amazement.

The highwayman pushed him back into the room, and, entering quickly, clapped to the door and bolted it.

"What's the row?" asked Blueskin.

"Your pardon, ladies, for this abrupt intrusion," said Tom, doffing his hat and gracefully bowing, "but the emergency of the occasion precludes ceremony. Tell me, is Jack Sheppard here?"

"What do you wan't with him?" growled Blueskin, suspiciously.

"Only to put him on his guard, that's all; he is in danger, and you, if you're wise, will make yourself scarce, Joe."

"Jack Sheppard is gone," grumbled Blueskin.

"Gad, that's well," returned King. "I'm right glad to hear it."

"Why, what's amiss?"

"Quilt Arnold, Mendez, and a whole posse of Bow Street runners will be hammering at the door in the king's name, and that in the flashing of a pan."

Edgeworth Bess gave a scream.

Poll Maggot a long, low whistle.

Blueskin stamped his foot and swore tremendously.

"I understand," said Tom, frowning. "You have deceived me; he is here."

"Yes, yes," cried Bess, eagerly. "Save him, Tom; he will be taken."

"Where is he, then? Quick; there's not a moment to be lost."

Poll Maggot rushed across the room.

She threw down the screen.

Jack Sheppard appeared lying stiff and pale upon the bed.

"S'blood! what is this? Is he dead or drunk?" cried the highwayman, tramping to the bedside.

A murmur of voices and a rush of many feet was now heard without.

Then came a loud knocking, as by staves, at the door.

"Open the door!" roared a surly voice. "I charge you, in the king's name, you huzzies."

Blueskin scowled fiendishly.

He drew a pistol and cocked it.

"Douse the glim!" muttered the highwayman.

Poll Maggot blew out the candle.

Blueskin lifted Jack Sheppard in his arms and carried him towards the back door.

A tremendous thumping, accompanied by oaths and savage threats, now shook the house.

"Answer them, Bess," whispered Tom King. "Keep 'em at bay till we have made our escape."

"Who's there?" cried Bess, in trembling accents.

"De kingsh officersh, you paggage," mumbled a weazen voice. "And, py de judgemensh of Sholomansh, if you ton't let ush in, you shall pe shent to Bridewellsh."

"Off with ye," whispered Poll Maggot to King and Blueskin.

She took a key from her pocket, and tossed it to the highwayman.

"At the end of the yard there's a shed, and over it a loft, with a door in the further wall, which adjoins the house opposite," whispered Poll, very collectedly, for her coolness formed a strong contrast to the helplessness of Edgeworth Bess. "Go that way; Moll Trollope lives there; she'll conceal you, or let you out in the lane yonder. Don't try the gate in this yard, I'll warrant it's guarded by the traps."

Tom King smiled approvingly.

He softly opened the door.

Poll Maggot let the men out.

She watched them as they cautiously stepped across the yard.

She quietly slipped back the bolt.

"Curse ye, open the door, you jades!" roared Quilt Arnold, from without, "or we'll batter it down."

"Yesh; ve'll knock de housh apout your earsh, py de holy patriarchsh."

"Is that you, Mr. Abraham?" questioned Poll, in the voice of a virago.

"Yesh, itsh me, Mishtress Maggot!" cried the old Jew; "open de toor at vonsh, you faggot."

"What do you want?"

The answer to this question was a tremendous bash, which sent the door flying open.

Quilt Arnold, Mendez, and a crowd of Bow-Street runners rushed in.

Edgeworth Bess sank on her knees, hid her face in her apron, and gave a loud shriek.

Not so the redoubtable Poll.

Snatching up a large cudgel, she flourished it in the face of Quilt Arnold and the shrinking Jew, at the same time shouting defiantly,

"Approach if you dare! What is your business?"

"We come with a warrant to arrest Jack Sheppard," returned Quilt, recoiling from the amazon's twirling staff.

"It's a lie!" was Poll's polite rejoinder, "he is not here."

"Then you have helped him to escape," returned Quilt, stamping with rage. "What's this? Ha! you have had a party to-night, eh, my beauties? Here are four plates, four glasses. I know who have been your guests; Sheppard and Blueskin."

"If you think so, find 'em. I tell you they are not in the house," returned Mistress Maggot, composedly, as she seated herself and folded her arms, but not relinquishing her hold upon the cudgel. "If you have a search-warrant do your duty; but don't overdo it, for I warn you if there is any damage done to the furniture you shall pay for it."

Quilt laughed contemptuously, and with his attendants immediately commenced a rigid examination of the premises.

But the birds had flown.

Boiling with rage and disappointment, and further exasperated by the shrill and shrewish laughter of Mistress Maggot, who seemed to enjoy his discomfiture, Quilt tore open the door at the back, and, followed by the others, rushed out.

"Hulloa! without there!" he shouted to the sentinels posted outside the gate. "Have you seen or heard anything of the vagabonds?"

"No, Mr. Arnold, there's not a mouse stirring," returned a voice.

"Ha! yonder is a shed. Look to your arms, lads. Confound you, Nab, light the way."

"Fery vell, Mishter Quilt," whined the old Jew; "but, pon my shoul! itsh too pad to always thrusht me into the post of mosht danger."

"And honour, old Israelite," returned the thief-taker. "So, as I expected, the door's locked. Smash it in with your bill, neighbour."

An old watchman toddled forward and gave a feeble stroke at the door with his long halbert.

"Yah!" grunted Quilt Arnold, in supreme disgust. "You withered old mummy, give it to me."

He snatched the weapon, and after two or three sturdy strokes succeeded in breaking into a sort of shed in which coals and wood were kept.

The party entered cautiously.

They held aloft their lanterns and peered searchingly into every nook and corner.

Their search, however, was quite fruitless.

Quilt Arnold vented his spleen in a volley of choice oaths.

He examined the walls to discover whether there was any door or outlet of any kind.

He could find none.

He was fain to leave the shed.

"Hulloa, Mister Quilt, there's a loft above," cried a voice from the side of the shed farthest from the wall.

"Zounds! we shall nail 'em yet," cried Arnold, eagerly.

"And here's a ladder, sir! and, hang me, look at this!" cried the man.

He held out a piece of lace which he had detached from a rusty nail.

"One of the scamp's ruffles have caught here. Beau Sheppard, for a wager," laughed the fellow.

"The birds are in the trap," chuckled Quilt, rubbing his hands; "but, for your lives, use caution, Jack and Blueskin are desperate blades."

"And only one on us can mount at a time, Mr. Arnold," rejoined the man, scratching his head, and casting a somewhat dubious look upwards. "This is darned ockard, I do say."

"Pooh! you see the wall opposite?"

"Sure, Mister Arnold, what then?"

"Why, just clamber a-top on't; you have a bull-dog?"

"A brace on 'em," grinned the man, producing a pair of huge and heavy pistols.

"Good; mount the wall, then, and if either of the thieves show themselves send a slug into him."

"Trust me to do that in a click; Mr. Wild said he didn't care whether we brought 'em dead or alive, if so be we took 'em."

"Silence! Now, Nab, are you ready?"

"Shtrike me, Mishter Arnoldsh! vot do'ye meansh?" asked the Jew, in a quivering voice.

"Mount the ladder, sirrah, and show a light."

"Fery goot, Mishter Arnoldsh; after you," returned the Jew, bowing till his red beard swept the ground.

"Up with ye, or, by the devil, I'll report you to Mr. Wild as a coward."

Mumbling an execration and shuddering with ill-suppressed fear, Mendez climbed the ladder.

Quilt Arnold kept close behind him.

The old Jew was evidently afraid to advance.

The more daring ruffian pushed him forward.

Out went the light; there was a yell and a bash, Quilt Arnold felt himself falling; he clutched something in his descent—it was the ledge of an open trap-hatch.

CHAPTER XXXVIII.
JACK SHEPHARD DISCOVERS THE TRICK OF BLUESKIN AND HIS MISTRESSES.

THE noon-day blaze of the sun pouring in through the broken panes of the window of a squalid garret fell full upon a low truckle bed, on which lay ex-tended the insensible form of the fated Jack Sheppard.

Whether the beams of light had any reviving influence, or whether the spell had begun to lose its power, certain it was that he showed signs of returning animation.

His breast heaved slowly, his eyelids quivered, his lips shook with spasmodic twitchings, and at length he turned heavily over, and drooped his arm over his head as one awakening from profound slumber.

At length he unclosed his eyes, and lay glaring fixedly at the low pent roof in a half-conscious state.

He remained thus for full an hour, during which the expression of his face became by degrees less fixed and death-like, his breathing quicker, and his movements freer.

He started up.

He clasped his hand upon his pale brow.

In bewilderment she tared about him.

"How came I here?" he gasped, faintly. "I am numbed and giddy. Ha! some treachery in this. Perhaps I have been poisoned or drugged; my brain is in a whirl, my tongue is parched, my heart beats wildly. Let me remember! let me remember!"

He sat on the bed, and, leaning his elbow on his knees, buried his face in his hands, and strove hard to collect his senses.

He tried to rise.

But he was faint, and staggered back.

Once more, with a groan, he stretched himself upon the bed, weak and exhausted, he knew not from what cause, but as feeble and weary as if he had laid upon a bed of anguish for weeks or months.

"Let me remember," he murmured again; "let me remember."

But it was in vain that he tried to recall the incidents of the eventful night he had spent at the lodgings of Edgeworth Bess and Poll Maggot, the supper, the arrival of Blueskin, the vile trick which had been played by them. His mind was a broken mirror, the images it reflected were all distorted.

After awhile, however, he became more composed, and a dreadful conviction flashed through his brain.

He started up.

"Yes, I know this ken," he growled, clenching his fists, and glaring round him fiercely, though his limbs still quivered with weakness induced by the baneful potion he had taken. "I have been betrayed! and by Edgeworth Bess! They have destroyed me! my curses blight the traitors!"

He rushed to the door.

He found it locked.

"What does this mean?" he murmured, aghast at this discovery. "Surely they have not sold me to Wild?"

He thrust his hands into his pockets.

"My pistols gone too! This is some infernal plot for my ruin!"

SIMON SMUT DISCOVERED ON BOARD THE "AVENGER."

He wandered to the window.

"Aye, it comes back to me now; they have drugged me, and brought me hither to prevent me from joining Roving Jack."

He folded his arms, paced through the chamber, and gnashed his teeth with rage.

"Perhaps it is not yet too late!" he cried, suddenly, a bright beam of hope flashing in his dark eyes; "at all events I will get out of this place."

He smiled contemptuously as he shook the door.

To an ordinary prisoner, however, the barrier would have proved a rather formidable one, for it was of uncommon strength and thickness, and secured by a heavy lock.

Jack Sheppard casts his glance around, and presently discovered a rusty nail lying upon the floor.

Forcing this between the lock and the woodwork, he pushed back the bolt and forced open the door.

He crept out upon the little landing-place, and leaning over the balusters listened to the mingled roar of many voices that soared up from the depths below.

He began to descend the stairs.

He had not taken many steps, however, before he changed his mind.

Remounting the stairs, he entered the room where he had been confined.

"Temptation or treachery, perhaps both, await me below. I will not mingle with any of my old pals; I will get away from this den of infamy —this pest-house— where I first was polluted; and I will start at once for Portsmouth, and get aboard 'The Avenger!' Ha, I like that name."

He took the blankets and sheets from the bed and tore them into strips with his teeth and hands, and then formed a line with them.

He burst open the window, and, creeping out on to a narrow parapet, gazed down from his fearful height with an unquailing eye.

The abutment of a neighbouring house broke the descent, and, crawling along the parapet, he came directly over the lower roof; he fixed the line round a chimney stack, and let himself down on to the leads below.

Not without great danger and difficulty he managed to scramble down on to a high wall adjoining the abutment.

He soon ran along this, and, clambering down by an iron gate, reached the street.

Turning, he shook his fist and invoked a curse upon his late prison-house.

He then walked swiftly away.

Finding that his purse, containing a considerable sum of money, had not been taken from his pockets, he entered an ordinary.

He called for something to eat and drink, and while regaling himself he took up one of the daily newspapers which lay upon the table.

Much to his chagrin, he read that the "Avenger" had sailed from Portsmouth that very morning.

"'Tis no matter," muttered Sheppard, as he rose and left the house, "I will let nothing turn me from my purpose. I will go to sea; but these fine clothes, these jewels—yes, I must get another sort of rig-out. Good, old Isaacs', the Jew fence, will buy them of me and supply me with something more suitable to my present condition."

CHAPTER XXXIX.

BEN BOUNCER'S NARRATIVE OF HIS VISIT TO LONDON—THE CHIMNEY SWEEP WITH "LOFTY HASPIRATIONS."

"AND what do you think of London, Ben?" asked Hal Hetherington of Master Bouncer.

The pair were strolling arm-in-arm along the quays of Portsmouth harbour, whither they had repaired in order to join our hero and his crew of boy pirate-hunters on board his new and splendid vessel "The Avenger."

Ben sagely shook his head.

"I must confess, Hal," said he, "that its general appearance did not quite come up to my expectations."

"Indeed!"

"I did not expect to find its streets paved with gold, nor its houses built of silver and ivory, as I was informed they were by that foolish old Cleats, who has a most ridiculous and annoying habit of exaggerating and perverting facts. For my part, I always like to stick to the truth, and when recounting my own adventures, some of which are certainly very remarkable, endeavour to state things that never can raise a doubt in the minds of my hearers, even though I may suppress the most striking circumstances connected with them."

"You needn't be so reserved with me, however," returned Hal, biting his lips to suppress a smile. "I dare say you met with some extraordinary adventures while you were in town."

"It was not my fortune to meet with many that are likely to interest you very much," rejoined Ben, with the air of a public lecturer; "but, certainly, one or two strange things did happen to me."

"Pray relate them."

"Hem! I would rather not, Hal," said Ben, modestly. "I do not wish you to doubt my veracity; and really one or two of the events I could mention were most astonishing."

"Oh, no doubt! Of course you visited all the 'lions' of the place: for instance, the Tower, the Palaces, St. Paul's, the Monument—"

"The Monument!" repeated Ben, suddenly stopping in his walk and assuming a very grave look. "Yes, I did ascend the Monument."

"And were very much impressed by the magnificent prospect you beheld from that commanding site?"

"But more so by the extraordinary manner in which I made my descent from the top of it."

"Why; did you jump off, then?"

"You shall hear. You remember the mist that overwhelmed the town about a fortnight ago?"

"Very well; it was so dense—"

"That one miserable man, as I heard, in thrusting his head out of window, got it stuck so tight in the fog that he could not withdraw it, and was forced to remain all night fixed like a poor rogue in the pillory."

"How shocking!"

"Well, on the night of the fog, I was on top of the Monument; I had lingered after sunset from a desire of seeing the great city lit up at night. The fog came on suddenly; I was blinded, and groped my way about with as much difficulty as if I had been wading in a mud bank."

"And did no one come to your rescue?"

"A man came through the trap, as I afterwards learned, and attempted to shout for me, but the fog completely stopped his utterance; and though he forced his way round and round the gallery, and must have passed within an inch of me, I could neither see nor hear him."

"But didn't he carry a light?"

"Yes, he had a torch in each hand, but they were of no use, as you couldn't see their blaze at half-arm's length; in fact, I had a tinder-box, and amused myself by trying to strike a light, and for aught I could see should never have known whether or not I had succeeded, if I had not set fire to my sleeve, and burnt my hand terribly; and though I was scorching, I could not see the flames."

"Phew!"

"At last I grew weary of being confined in that solitary place, half a mile up in the air; so, to test the strength of the fog, I made a desperate bound upwards, and found I could not get down again. Maddened with alarm at my strange position, I groped, and waded, and struggled, I know not how long; at last the fog began to clear, and I found myself gradually sinking, like a small pebble through a quagmire, till I struck against something hard; I held on for dear life, the fog cleared away as suddenly as it had come on, the sun burst forth, and, to my utter astonishment, I found myself perched on the steeple-top of a neighbouring church."

"Is it possible! and did you visit the Tower?"

"Yes, by traitor's gate; they happened to be lowering the portcullis just as my boat was passing under it; down came the massive grating, and its great iron spikes cut the boat in half."

"And how did you escape?"

"Why, seeing what was coming, I laid down flat upon my face on the thwarts, right between two of the spikes, and got fixed, and was crushed down to the bottom of the moat. Of course the portcullis was instantly raised, and up I went with it, and there I hung between sky and earth till the bars were filed away and I was liberated; but my face was so masked with mud that it had to be scraped with a spade and a rake, and the spikes made such furrows under my arm-pits as to bare my ribs; I didn't get over that accident for nearly a week."

At this moment the interesting conversation was interrupted by a little queer-faced fellow, grimed with soot, and carrying a brush in one hand and small shovel in the other, who ran across the road to meet them.

He made a most profound bow.

"Excuse me, gentlemen," he said, showing his white teeth with a broad grin, "if I takes the liberty to inquire if you are acquainted with a hillustrious person as calls himself 'Roving Jack?'"

"Pray what motive can you have for asking such a question?" said Ben Bouncer, haughtily. "You look like a sweep."

"Yes, sir; perfessionally I am a purifier of the domestic hearth," said the chummy. "But, ah, sir!" he continued, with a burst of enthusiasm, "I am one of lofty haspirations."

"And to what do you aspire?" asked Hal, smiling.

"Vell, sir, I'm a candidate for fame and glory. I have a soul, sir; a soul."

"I hope so,"

"Yes, sir; a mind as soars above chimbly-pots—cos why? I rides the vinged hoss—I'm of a littleary turn, vel versed in the classics, and fired with the hambition of becoming a second Halexander! For as the svan of Havon sings so sweetly—

"'To be, or not to be, that is the qvestion!'

"But the qvestion vot he couldn't hanswer I has; for I means to be, and vill be, von of the heroes of Roving Jack's crew."

"And what is your name, friend?" asked Ben Bouncer."

"I'm proud to say, sir, as I'm the last representative of a werry hauspicious fam'ly. My father, sir, vould climb you the highest flues vith the greatest hease; and my mother vonce danced to the top of a May-pole on a slack rope."

"But your name?" urged Hal.

"I'm a Smut, sir; the last of the hillustrious line—Simon Smut, at your sarvice."

"And you wish to join our crew?"

"Sich is my desire," returned Mr. Simon, with another profound bow. "I have read the proclamation, and, considering as I hanswers to the description given of the sort of men Sir John vants to man his wessel, 'Smart gallant fellers,' as the proclamation states, I have ventured to present myself to you, sir, who I believe to be von of his officers, as a wolunteer."

"Were you ever at sea?"

"Yes, sir; I've been half sea's over many a time, returned Sim, with a wink, "and have often sailed the briny hoceau in a pleasure-boat."

"But do you know anything of seamanship?"

"Modesty is becoming, as the little school-boys writes in their copy-books. I never vas wanity-glorious, and so I vill confess that my knowledge of seamanship is rayther theoretical than practical."

"You don't know the stem from the stern, I suppose?"

"Oh, yes, I do, sir; the stem's at von end of the wessel, and the starn's at the t'other; and I could larn the t'other from vich, vith a werry little practice."

"Can you box the compass?"

"There you've got it, sir," returned the gallant Sim, putting down his soot-bag, brush, and shovel, spitting in his hand, and throwing himself into a fighting attitude. "Bless you, sir, I can box anything or anybody. Only the t'other day, sir, I vos set upon by a big ruffin as vonted to nail my perfessional implements. Says I, 'Who and vhat are you?' He shrieks vith dismay, I follered up my adwantage with a stinger on the conck, and the ruffin fled, none knew vither."

"Did you ever go aloft?"

"Can you ax, sir, ven I vos the fust to climb that tall shaft yonder, the highest chimbly in Portsmouth."

"You don't dislike the smell of powder?"

"Pah! ain't I been used to the smell of soot and smoke since I vos a climbing hinfant? On von occasion werry nigh smothered in a crooked flue, in vich I was jammed up for a veek."

"Ha! not so extraordinary as a case I knew of one of those poor little climbing beggars," said Ben Bouncer, gravely.

"What was that?"

"Why, Hal, the poor little imp got stuck in the chimney much in the same way as our friend describes; he could neither get up nor down; he was there for three weeks."

"I wonder he wasn't starved to death, Ben."

"He would have been, but for a dodge I hit upon—for this happened in my uncle Major Bouncer's house, where I was staying."

"What did you do?"

"I kept frying beef steaks and onions on the fire below him, and the poor little wretch subsisted on the nourishing smell."

"And how did you get him out at last?"

"You know, Hal, that it is the property of the magnet to attract iron and steel?"

"Certainly; but what has that to do with the case in question?"

"Remembering that the young sweep had an iron shovel with him, I obtained a large and powerful magnet, and getting on the roof, I held it over the chimney-pot, telling him to hold fast to the handle of the shovel. The magnet drew up the shovel, and the shovel drew up the chummy, and so I got him out."

"But what do you think of this volunteer, Ben?"

"A very entertaining fellow," returned Mr. Bouncer, condescendingly. "Let him join the marines, a class of men I have a great respect for, and to whom I like to relate my truthful narratives."

"Well, Mr. Smut," rejoined Hal, "I will mention your request to Captain Warbold, and use what influence I possess in your favour. At the same time, I can promise nothing, for our captain is very particular in his selection, and, as a general rule, will have none but picked men. However, call at the 'Anchor' this evening, and you shall learn his decision ; and so good morning."

Sim made a courtly bow.

The young gentlemen smiled their acknowledgements, and passed on.

"It is a dream !" murmured the chummy, with a dramatic start ; "but no, vot sings the sveet bard of Avon,

"'There is a tide in the affairs of men,
Vich taken at the flood leads on to fortun'.

"And that flood is the high tide to-morrow, vhen I shall bid my native shores adoo and tread the deck of the Awenger ! But, O lors ! here comes that windictive female, Poll Potts. Vither shall I fly to escape her ? Vhy did she fall in love with me ? Well may the philosopher say as all is wanity and wexation ; my manly beauty has proved the cuss o' my blighted life. O lors ! she sees me !"

Tossing his bag on to his shoulder, and snatching up his brush and shovel, chummy gave one parting glance behind him and took to his heels.

CHAPTER XL.
SIMON SMUTS SERVICES REJECTED BY ROVING JACK.

BREATHLESS and panting, the aspiring Sim arrived at the door of a shop where fried fish, pickled eels, and other like delicacies were sold.

He rushed through the shop, and bounding into the parlour at the back of it, threw himself down in a state of exhaustion.

A fat, and jolly-looking dame, busily engaged in frying fish over a roaring fire, turned her broad, scarlet glowing face towards him.

She laughed heartily at his affrighted looks.

"Why Sim, my son, what has scared ye ?" she asked.

"She haunts me everywhere !" gasped Sim.

"Who does ?"

"Poll Potts, that awenging spectre ! She's fallen despritly in love vith me ; she pulls my hair out by handfulls, and calls me a perfigious little monster, and vows if I don't marry her, she'll commit suicide. O lors ! vhot *does* she tell sich lies for ? she von't do it, she never vill, I know she von't. I vouldn't mind marryin' her if she'd drown herself right off immediately after the ceremony. Vither shall I flee to escape this new misery of my life ?"

"It sarves ye right, Sim ; didn't you compoze them beautiful verses for her ?" returned his mother, shaking her head and the frying-pan at the same time. "A throwin' your pearls afore—"

"Don't, mother !" sighed Sim, "I can't bear it. What a cuss it is to be troubled with a hirrepressible gen'us,—bein' smit by that pecooliarity of her features, and that obliquity of her wision as renders her so interestin' as a study of natur'. I indited that lovely poim, 'She sqvints, my lady sqvints,' in praise of the cast of her eyes. I vould rather have writ my own death varrant if I'd a knowed vhot consequences vould follow that rash act ; vhy, the creetur is raving mad in love vith me, and hunts me like a partridge on the mount'ins."

"Never mind, Sim, she's a good customer ; she comes for pickled eels at all hours of the day as an excuse for seeing you," laughed his mother. "Surely you ain't afraid of the woman ?"

"Voman !—she's a fury ! but I have made a stern resolve, mother, vich vill surprise you. I vill stand this no longer ; I am going to sea, mother !"

The good dame seated herself upon a stool and held up her hands in dismay.

"To sea, Sim !" she shrieked. "To break your poor mother's heart."

His little brothers and sisters clustered round the young desperado, and the dog and cat howled and mewed in sympathy.

"To sea !" roared Sim, clapping a saucepan on his head. "To brave the dangers of the dreadful deep ! To fight the bloody buccaneers !"

He snatched up the tongs and waved them round his head defiantly.

"Afore my breast I throws my warlike shield (the saucepan-lid), and damned be he as fust cries 'old, enough ! Yes, mother, I'll escape the inkybus ; I flee her as I vould the leopard (perhaps he meant 'a leper'). I vill seek death in the fire and smoke of the battle, and perish the wictim of a windictive voman !"

"Sim !" shrieked the fond parent, plunging her arms about him as he rushed to the door.

"Unhand me, mother ! I am desprit !" cried the persecuted youth, breaking from the maternal embrace.

He bounded wildly from the house.

"The boy is mad !" cried the frantic parent, rushing after him.

But he paid no regard to her remonstrances, but without stopping an instant hurried at once to the "Anchor."

Here his ardour was somewhat cooled by the warlike appearance of his future messmates.

A group of dashing young fellows, many of them mere boys, were gathered about the door of the inn.

They were all armed to the teeth, and were evidently bound for some dangerous service.

At length, however, the valiant Sim mustered up courage, and sweeping some of the soot from his face with his sleeve, he entered the house.

In a short time after he came running out with an air of distraction.

Clenching his fists, gnashing his teeth, and betraying other signs of agitation and disappointment, he walked at a furious pace to the sea-beach.

There, throwing himself down upon the sand-bank, he folded his arms and scowled fiercely at a splendid frigate that lay at anchor in the offing.

"Rejected !" he muttered fiercely. "Rejected ! and so the harrogant young skipper refuses to accept me for von of his crew—says he has no employment for me, no chimbleys to sveep, and larfed when I quoted from the sweet svan of Avon ; but Smuts arn't to be shook off so easy, there's nothin' as sticks closer than a smut. I vont be baffled ; I'll sail with him vether he likes me or not. I'll hide myself in the hold of his wessel, and when he gets out to sea he can't get rid of me unless he pitches me into the vaves ; and blow me, though that's a wulgar oath, I don't care if he does, for in the briny depths of old ocean I may find a refuge from that odious Poll Potts."

"Ah ! you are thinking of me, my adored Simon ! my name is on your lips !" simpered a shrill voice at his side.

Sim started as if he had heard the roar of a tiger.

Beside him sat a tall, scraggy woman, with a shrewish expression of countenance ; her hair was of a very curious hue, and her eyes remarkable, from the circumstance that each seemed to be looking in a different direction.

In an instant, having stared at her aghast and petrified, then with a despairing yell he bounded off like a madman, hotly pursued by the indignant Miss Potts.

CHAPTER XLI.

OUR HERO SETS SAIL.

IT was a grand and stirring scene.

The pirate-hunter's noble frigate lay at anchor in the bay.

The sunbeams burnished her loosened sail, and her long pennant fluttered gaily a rippling red streak in the pure purple sky.

Upon the quay was clustered a motley party, consisting of persons of all ages and both sexes, who were bidding an affectionate farewell to our brave boy hero and his dauntless young comrades.

Violet clasped her foster-brother's hand, while his mother clung to his heaving breast and sobbed bitterly.

"Courage, dear mother!" murmured our hero, kissing her pale lips. "Have faith in the Providence that worketh all things for good; remember, you are a seaman's daughter and a seaman's wife, and if I should fall in fight, or perish by storm, our separation will even then be but brief, for there is reunion in a world that knows 'no shadow of parting.' Cheer up, dear mother."

But the widowed mother only sobbed more bitterly, as she clung in an agony of grief to her noble boy.

"Ah, if you were not so rashly brave," she said. "But, my dear son, you will, you will promise at least not to recklessly throw away your cherished life; you know how wild and daring you were as a boy."

"But so far I am changed, mother, that I hold it a sin to risk my life needlessly, or in any cause but a very good one," returned our hero, smiling. "But come, dear mother, let us look at the sunny side; fancy how proudly you will receive me when I return laden with wealth and honour,—but hark! the signal gun; time and tide wait for no one, dear mother. I must begone."

During this conversation between our hero and his mother, Hal Hetherington had been taking his farewell of Violet.

The girl listened to his incoherent, modest, yet fervent words, with downcast eyes and a rosy blush.

Again the gun was fired.

Once more the son embraced his mother and his foster-sister.

And then, laughing with forced gaity, he tore himself from their arms and sprang into the boat, which was rowed by his gallant boy comrades.

He stood up in the stern sheets, waved his flag, and tossed up his hat.

His weeping mother and sister followed him with their eyes till the boat reached the side of the frigate, and the roar of cannon, the huzzas of his men, and the floating of the rippling flag from the mast head, proclaimed that he had gone on board the frigate.

Amongst the adventurous spirits who had joined Roving Jack were many of his old school-fellows: Will Ryan, Ned Ross, little Ben Atherstone, and others, with whom we have made acquaintance in the course of this history, not to mention the great Bouncer!

Paul Peveril and old Clem Cleats, the fisherman, had also joined our hero's crew.

It happened that a squadron of king's ships sailed from Portsmouth as convoy to a large fleet of merchant vessels of all kinds.

Our hero was acquainted with the captains and officers on board most of these men-of-war, and he resolved to sail in company with their fleet.

At the very commencement of the cruise of the "Avenger" our hero distinguished himself by the daring act of gallantry and humanity which forms the subject of the next chapter.

CHAPTER XLII.

THE SHIP ON FIRE—ROVING JACK'S HEROISM.

OUR hero sat writing in his cabin long after every one else had turned in, with the exception of the anchor watch.

It was a wretched night. The quick, heavy tramp of the watch on deck formed a sweet accompaniment to the peppering of the rain against the sash.

Pen in hand, our hero, who was very tired, fell asleep.

He was aroused by the sudden report of a gun upon the larboard quarter.

He immediately concluded it to be the commodore of the fleet making daylight.

When he came below he noticed one of the men-of-war, the "Intrepid," was lying on the starboard quarter.

He was mistaken, however, for the gale was harder than before, and it wanted at least five good hours of the time.

"Ready with the gun, there, for'ard! Fire! Hand up the engine from below! Call the captain! Pipe both cutters away!" such were the orders he heard loudly issuing on deck.

They were followed by a rush up the hatchway ladders, and over head as if a man had fallen overboard.

"Hook the yard tackles! Turn the hands up! Out large cutter!" thundered Roving Jack, who had now reached the top of the companion.

He sprang upon the hammock-nettings, and looked around.

A splendid but an awful scene presented itself.

Broad on the larboard quarter lay the "Georgian" transport, the whole of one side, from the brake of the forecastle to the gangway, enveloped in a large sheet of flame.

The fire extended as high as her main-top, and cast round a brilliant but dazzling and almost painful glare.

The blue lights that were continually burning throughout the fleet served to heighten the effect.

They rendered the countenances of the men as ghastly and spectral as though they had been inhabitants of another world suffered to burst the confines of the grave, and summoned, during the waning of the elements, to gaze on the misery of the helpless wretches, whose fearful shrieks sounded most appalling as they reached them at intervals, now, during the lulls, clear and piercingly distinct.

Then again faintly as they died away to leeward, smothered in the howling of the blast.

Away sprang the quarter-boats.

Then the large cutter was fairly hoisted out.

Roving Jack, Hal Hetherington and Will Ryan, with a number of men, jumped in.

Each took an oar, for, on occasions like these, "no more cats are wanted than catch mice."

On reaching the transport, our hero recognized in the "Intrepid's" barge an old messmate, Warner, who was first lieutenant of that ship.

Short greetings, however, pass in a heavy sea alongside a burning ship.

Indeed, all had enough to do in receiving the poor wretches, who hastily crowded into the boats shivering and shaking with fear, and depositing them in safety on board an Indiaman (being the nearest ship), where fires were lighted in the galleys, and restoratives used to many of the women, who, in a perfect state of insensibility, had been wrapt up in blankets, and lowered down the sides with a rope's end.

One in particular, our hero remarked, who seemed much more stunned by external injury than by inward fear.

Although the men on shore, usually on the look out for accidents during a gale of wind of this description, were all away assisting a couple of craft that had got upon a sand-bank, yet the master of the "Georgian" had reckoned so confidently on receiving assistance from the king's ship and the Indiaman, that, having (besides his long boat, which was, of course, stowed on deck, and, moreover, too much damaged by the fire to be of any service) only one quarter-cutter, and an old crazy dingey, which would not have lived a minute in the sea that was then running, he had with his own hand cut them both away on the first alarm of fire, before a single soul had time to enter either.

When Roving Jack returned in one of the boats, which had rowed him back for the third time, with some fresh hands to help in getting out anything that could be saved, our hero found the gallant master of the transport, and about a dozen of his men, working away like horses.

They seemed totally heedless of their danger.

They actually endeavoured to cut away the part of the upper deck and starboard bulwark which was on fire.

The ship presented a most singular appearance.

One side only had been at all burnt.

The flames had been driven aft too rapidly by the violence of the wind to allow of their approaching in a lateral direction.

The mass of burning rigging came thundering down on deck from aloft.

Had these been suffered to remain they would have speedily set it all on fire.

But they were immediately either hove overboard with crowbars, or extinguished by the buckets full of water that were incessantly dashed about in every direction.

But it was all in vain—the flames raged fiercer than ever—the gale was raging—the only cable which remained was stranded in two places.

A council of war was now held between Warner, the first lieutenant of the "Intrepid;" our hero, Capt. Warbold of the "Avenger;" and Sanderson, the master of the transport; O'Kasey, the second mate of the Indiaman; Hal Hetherington, and Paul Peveril, lieutenants of the "Avenger," as to the utility of risking their lives by staying any longer.

Under all circumstances there could be but one opinion on the subject.

Then, and not till then, did Sanderson quit the deck, saying to Roving Jack, as he swung himself by a rope into the stern-sheets of the barge,

"You will bear witness, Sir John, I have done my duty to the last."

And sitting down he covered his face with his hands, to hide the emotions he felt on leaving the ship, for the last time, that he had faithfully commanded so many years.

There was some difficulty in regaining their respective ships.

Indeed it was full time they did so.

The gale was now nearly at its highest pitch. Many of the smaller vessels had parted, and were driving on board each other.

The sudden boom of minute-gun after minute-gun might be heard in all directions. Several times the boats had the narrowest escape of being swamped.

Although cold and wet in the extreme, Roving Jack and his noble boy comrades felt so excited that instead of going below they remained in the poop, gazing on the still burning wreck, in company with several officers from the other ships, when they were suddenly startled by the shrill sound of a woman's voice, shrieking in the wildest accents of despair.

"My bairn! my bairn! my child! my child! Gin ye're the hearts o' men, ye'l save my bairn! It's all that God has left me!"

And the female whom Roving Jack had before noticed as being injured, rushed aft; her long dishevelled hair streamed in the wind; her pallid countenance streaked with the blood that issued from her forehead. She dashed herself down on the deck before Roving Jack, threw one arm round his knees, and pointed with the other, in almost speechless agony, to the wreck.

Our hero, with quivering lip, looked at the weather, and shook his head—then at the "Georgian"—lastly at the poor creature who lay extended at his feet.

He shouted in a voice that needed no speaking-trumpet to assist it.

"Volunteers for the wreck! I'll go myself!"

He turned round to Paul Peveril, the chief mate.

"Not while there are six officers in the ship by heaven, sir!" bluntly replied the gallant seaman.

"Clear away the larboard cutter!" roared old Clem Cleats, the boatswain.

He scrambled over the hen-coops.

"O'Kasey, and five of the forecastle men, and myself."

Roving Jack broke away from those who would retain him, and sprang into the boat.

"Bear her off with your oars, boys!" he shouted, waving his cap.

"Lower away roundly! Let go-o!" sung out old Clem Cleats, directly the boat's bottom touched the water.

The after-tackle unhooked of itself, and was instantly rounded up, high over their heads, but they were forced to "out knife and cut the other ones."

At last they shoved off.

They bent to their oars in silence.

There were fearful odds against them.

In the words of the song, "The sea was mountains rolling;" and though the cutter was fitted with air-tight lockers, had anything happened to capsize her bottom upwards and cast them out, it would have been but poor fun to know that she swam while they themselves were sinking.

The lower rigging of the Indiaman was crowded as high nearly as the futtock-shrouds.

The eyes of all were intently fixed on them. Above two hundred voices shouted in a breath—

"Give way, my fine fellows! give way, shipmates! For your lives, give way!"

But there was one on board that ship regarding their progress with the most painful anxiety, and shuddering at every wave that reared its crest on high threatening to overwhelm them, and blast her fond hopes that they might succeed in saving her child.

They saw her bending over the hammock nettings, her hands raised to heaven, and heard her voice through the roaring of the gale, as she fervently exclaimed, in a tone never to be forgotten till their dying hour by those who heard it—

"Bless ye! bless ye! The Father o' the fatherless preserve ye in his mercy! Bless ye! bless ye!"

Whether the prayers of the widowed mother were heard aloft or not, this much is certain, that had not another and a mightier arm than theirs been stretched forth upon the waters, vain would have been the courage or seamanship of the best amongst them, officer or man.

There being six hands in the cutter, besides Peveril and O'Kasey, Roving Jack let the latter take the bow-oar.

Coiling up his legs, he stowed himself away in the head-sheets as comfortably as circumstances would allow.

They were now within a couple of ships' lengths from the transport.

Her mainmast, which was more than half burned through, and entirely unsupported, went with a tremendous crash.

Its scathed and scorched top-mast, entirely bare of rigging, save a mass of burning cordage just below the cross-trees—the flames of which were extinguished in their passage through the air—was still on end; and as the spar fell with its head aft, bearing a little to the larboard hand, it regularly cut asunder the mizen topsail-yard, shattering the top, striking the cross rick-yard with such violence as to carry away the slings and bring it down with a run athwart the deck, and breaking through the old, chafed, and worn mizen rigging, like so much pack-thread, it lighted on the taffsail, which was ground and crushed in an instant level with the deck, and there rested quietly with its head projecting some few feet over the stern.

Not ten seconds after, a pale, blue, phosphoric light, similar to what is seen settling on the flying jib-boom end or mast-heads of ships within the tropics, sailed flickering along above the deck, and gradually descending as it travelled aft, finally took up its station on the main-top mast-head, and remaining stationary there, shone steadily out, as if to direct where to pull.

They were now rapidly nearing the "Georgian."

Peveril, who was steering, sang out to old Clem Cleats to stand by with the boat-hook, and stave off any floating pieces of wreck, lest we might get a hole knocked in the cutter's bows, at the same time remarking she was pretty full of water.

"Sure, thin, sir, hadn't we better be afther taking out the plug, and letting it all rin?" exclaimed one of the men, a countryman of O'Kasey's, actually putting his hand down and feeling for the cork.

"Take the devil out of h—l, and let him run if you like, sir; but leave that plug alone!" hastily roared out the choleric old Cleats.

It required a quick eye and a steady hand on the part of the coxswains to avoid a bumping match, in which case Roving Jack's boat would, most inevitably, have come second best off.

Our hero seized the tiller, and handled the cutter beautifully, although more than once she was very nearly thrown broadside on to the sea, which they fully expected was going to make a clean breach over all.

O'Kasey volunteered to board the transport, if the boat's head was brought right under the fallen spar, so as he could scramble up by the tangled maze of rigging that remained.

Roving Jack insisted upon following him.

The Irishman kicked off his shoes.

Roving Jack tried to do the same.

But they were originally a tight fit, and from being successively soaked, scorched, and wetted again, stuck to his feet as though they had been nailed on, and, something like the negro's pig, the more he pulled the more they wouldn't come.

"I'll cut 'em for ye," said O'Kasey.

Suiting the action to the word, he divested him of these dangerous appendages, at the expense of having the point of the knife run about half an inch into poor Jack's great toe.

It was no time to stand upon trifles, however.

"There you are, boys. Jump while you may, and catch like cats!" shouted Roving Jack.

"Hurrah!" responded his gallant crew.

O'Kasey shut his eyes.

He stepped on to the gunwale.

Then he bound lightly off like a Dublin harlequin.

Roving Jack kept his wide open, and, singling out a rope, made a desperate spring upwards.

One convulsive, a strenuous exertion of his arms, and he was astride of the spar, and on the transport's deck in the course of half a minute.

A great oversight had been committed.

They had not ascertained before they left the ship where they were likely to find the child.

Luckily they spied it under the lee of one of the carronades, where it had been left, and forgotten, in the hurry of the moment.

Wrapped in a blanket, unhurt by the falling of the mast, and soundly sleeping in his innocence, amid the roaring of a gale which blew loud enough to wake the dead.

"Can you swim, yer honour?" said O'Kasey addressing Roving Jack.

"Yes," returned our hero.

"Arrah, hould the baby, thin!"

"Can you?"

"Divil a stroke!" he replied, and running out to the mast-head, he fearlessly flung himself overboard, trusting to the men in the cutter to pick him up.

Roving Jack looked round for a grating to lash the child to, in case of anything happening to himself.

None was to be found.

He was nearly scorched to death by the flames, and suffocated by the smoke.

He lost no time in following the young Irishman's example.

Providentially, he, the child, and O'Kasey were all three hooked out, and hauled into the cutter without any material damage.

How they ever got near the Indiaman again was a wonder.

Even as it was, they fetched a good half cable's length astern of her.

The other ships were still further to windward, so she was their only chance, and a very poor one too; at least our hero thought so.

The men were terribly winded.

The boat was half full of water.

This, of course, made it so much the heavier to pull.

It was perfectly impossible to bale any of it out, for the biggin was anywhere but where it ought to have been, and, as to hats, it was a matter for thankfulness that the hair was not blown off their heads.

In this dilemma, the same bright idea struck the

acute Irishman, and, laying his oar across for a moment, he addressed himself to Cleats, with—

"The plug, yer honour !" but old Clem was still inexorable.

Instead of making any headway they could scarcely hold their own.

Captain Merivale had, however, provided against such an emergency on board the Indiaman.

Some coir rope was stopped with a bit of spun yarn to the life-buoy, having a spare end of from ten to fifteen fathoms long, the rest being coiled clear away on the hen-coops, in readiness for veering.

The laniard of the buoy was then cut, sufficient scope of stray line being first paid out, to allow it to reach the water, and drift away without checking.

It came floating down to them in glorious style.

The end of the coir, which was floating on the surface, and, waving about like a snake, was easily caught hold of, and a pretty severe turn taken with it round one of the thwarts.

A hawser was then sent down to them by means of a snatch-block, and the end on board was then brought to the capstern.

"Heave round !"

Away went the cutter foaming and flashing through the waves.

Had not the boat been well and strongly built she would have been torn and riven, as O'Kasey expressed it, into "smithereens ;" for, long before they were under the ship's stern, the water was up to the rowlocks, and more than once they were literally dragged under a sea, but, thanks to the lockers, with no further damage than a few cold salt-water duckings.

At last they had the infinite satisfaction of seeing the child up to the clewer-end, borne in a basket and restored alive to the arms of its mother, who was crossing over the taffrail in almost frantic energy.

"Thank God !" murmured our hero, as the deck of the Indiaman was once more beneath his feet.

Deafening were the shouts that welcomed our boy hero.

He was wet and exhausted.

Neither he nor his gallant fellows would stay to hear the fine speeches prepared for them, nor the flattering appearance of the lady passengers, many of whom were up in the cuddy shedding tears, as Clem Cleats said, "enough to fill a jolly boat."

Roving Jack bowed gracefully and sprang down the gangway, the loud hurrahs ringing in his ears.

Upon retiring to his bed, he fell into a deep and happy sleep, just as the gun of the "Intrepid" boomed over the waters announcing to the Fleet that the day had broke.

CHAPTER XLIII.

THE FORGED LETTER.

THE wind had blown from the eastward for ten whole days, and the fleet, which lay off Harwich, was prevented from going to sea.

The "Avenger" was lying at the harbour's mouth, waiting for the first chance to get away, that she might drop down to Portsmouth previous to her leaving the British coast.

The crew of the vessel were not allowed to go on shore in order that they might be ready to put to sea the moment the wind would chop round in their favour.

"Hal," said our hero, to his favourite companion, as arm in arm they paced the quarter-deck, "I am sorry that I have failed in my purpose of saving Jack Sheppard and Tom King from the doom that certainly awaits them."

"Who knows but that Sheppard may have been prevented from joining you ?" returned Hal. "Perhaps he is already in custody."

"No, for he has sent me this letter in reply to my offer," returned our hero. "Read it, Hal."

His friend took the letter and examined it.

"Short, pithy, and to the purpose," he said, laughing ; "but there is a tone of insolence that I should scarcely have expected from one to whom you have acted so kindly."

"Nor I," rejoined our hero ; "but what would you have from a thief and a cut-throat ? Still I am surprised, and rather disappointed, Hal," said Roving Jack ; "there was something in the fellow that pleased me ; and as he saved my life, I should have been glad to have had an opportunity of rendering him a good service."

"But, captain !"

"Well ?"

"This is a most villanous scrawl."

"It is, indeed," laughed our hero, taking the letter. "Scarcely visible."

"Yes," continued Hal, thoughtfully, "and though one would certainly not expect anything very brilliant in the way of penmanship or composition from a person in his circumstances, yet the writing and the style are certainly worse than I should have looked for."

"What follows then ?"

"Jack Sheppard, as it appeared at his examination before his last committal to prison, has received some schooling, and was apprenticed to a respectable tradesman."

"That is true."

"Don't you think, captain, that it is just possible that this letter may be a forgery ?"

"Ha !"

Roving Jack took the letter.

He scanned it anxiously.

"Have you ever seen Sheppard's writing ?" asked Hal.

"I have," returned our hero, quickly.

"And does this resemble it ?"

"Let me see. Sheppard wrote down his address. I have it among my papers."

Roving Jack drew forth his letter-case.

After a brief search he pulled out the paper in question.

He started.

The paper was stained with a *spot of blood !*

SIMON SMUT'S DREAM.

"Strange!" he said, musingly.

"Permit me," said Hal, taking the papers.

He closely compared the two writings.

"It is plain that this letter is a forgery," he said, in a tone of conviction.

"You are right, Hal; the thing is evident."

They exchanged looks of mutual surprise.

"But who can be the forger?" asked our hero.

"Wild, perhaps."

"No, this is not the thief-taker's writing, of which I have several specimens," returned our hero.

"Perhaps it is a ruse played by some of the poor rogue's evil associates, in order to prevent him from leaving his present course of life, and from joining us."

"It is not unlikely."

"Blueskin, perhaps, has played this scoundrelly trick."

"He is, of course, quite capable of doing anything brutal or treacherous," answered our hero; "yet I do not think he was the author of this."

"Why not?"

"Because Sheppard had quarrelled with him, and told me himself that he would let none of his companions know of his determination to leave London."

"But the young desperado has many mistresses, they say."

"Yes; two especially, Edgeworth Bess and Poll Maggot."

"Then you may depend upon this, they are at the bottom of this business; it is not likely they will be willing to lose their dupe, who is such a source of profit to them."

"But they must have kidnapped him," said our hero, "or why did he not meet at Portsmouth, according to our arrangement?"

"It is a strange business, but I will not leave England till I have fathomed its mystery."

"Look, captain, young Ben Atherstone has arrived."

As Hal spoke, the pretty, fair-haired boy, who has before been mentioned as a special favourite of our hero, came over the side and walked aft.

He touched his hat and smiled joyously.

"Come aboard, sir," said he.

Roving Jack seized his hand and shook it warmly. The three then descended the after hatchway, and entered the state cabin.

Meantime a strange event took place in the hold of the vessel.

A number of the seamen were, under the direction of old Clem Cleats, the boatswain, Mr. Junk, the purser, O'Kasey, the Irish mate, engaged in stowing away a number of casks, tea-chests, and the like ship's lumber.

Old Clem Cleats, despite his good-natured face, was rather inclined to bluster in the true seaman-like fashion.

O'Kasey, as we have seen, was a hot-headed, hot-blooded Irishman, and a very highly-spiced specimen of his peppery race.

Mr. Junk was a stout, small-eyed, moon-faced fellow, with a bald head, and ruby-tipped nose; he was "a man of few words," as he often declared, but, as brevity is said to be the soul of wit, he felt convinced that his lack of fluency in conversation was a proof of the possession of superior intelligence.

"Now, then, you block-headed, baboon-behaved, lady-fingered, lazy sons of guns, haul in, will ye? Look alive, be smart, ye lubbers, for its a'most eight bells, and we shall be wanted on deck," roared old Clem, in his ostensibly fierce, abusive, yet really hearty and rousing style. "Heave ho, my hearties; here, out of the way, you swab; but—why—how—dam'me, what's this?"

And old Clem stood for a moment in a state—as his shipmates after described it—of "flounderin' flabbergastration."

He had been attempting to heave along a large cask, which he found uncommonly weighty, when suddenly he was startled by a rattling noise that resounded from within it.

O'Kasey burst into a roar of alarm.

"And bedad the pork's alive, though dead and pickled; and, bi the holy poker, did ye ever see the like o' sich a blatherin' noise? Och, messmates, do but observe it; whir-r-r, clatter, clatter; and what the divil does it mane?"

It was certainly surprising.

The hold rang with a metallic clatter.

"Mr. Junk, sir, what is it?" gasped old Clem, grasping the purser's arm.

"The devil!" returned Junk, sententiously.

"Let me out! O lor, let me out!" cried the muffled voice.

There was a general shout of fright.

"Stave in the head of that barrel!" roared Mr. Junk.

Nobody seemed to like taking upon himself the execution of this order.

Old Clem, however, seized a spar, and was about to bring it down with a crash upon the cask.

To the utter dismay of all present, up popped a black, grimy imp from the barrel, with a shovel in one hand and a brush in the other, which he clattered together, making a most dismal row.

"The devil! the devil!" yelled the sailors, dispersing on all hands.

"Devil or not," shouted old Clem, upheaving the heavy spar, "I'll see if I can't shiver his ugly figure-head!"

"Hold off, old Neptune!" cried the imp, with an expressive gesture, performed by placing the tip of his thumb on the tip of his nose, and the out-spreading of his fingers.

Old Clem twisted the heavy timber in the air.

"What are you, you black-phizzed lubber?" he shouted, in a tone of dismay and rage.

"Never mind vhot I am," returned the imp, winking his eye.

He leaped out of the cask.

He squatted on his hams, like a Turk or a tailor.

"Never mind vhot I am; necessity has no lors, and though I'm perlite inclined, this is no time for ceremony. Be good enough to bring me somethin' to heat, for I'm as hungry as a vild dog of the vilderness."

"What brought you here, you rascal?"

"Vhot brought me? Vhy, this yere wessel, to be sure," chuckled the chummy, for the imp was no other than our old friend Simon Smut.

"And what do you want?"

"To see the capt'in."

"You shall see the bo'swain's mate, you scamp, and be introduced to him at the grating, where he'll entertain you with the tricks of his nine-tailed cat," roared old Clem, in a towering passion. "Seize the owdacious rascal."

Poor Simon would have fared roughly at the hands of the rugged tars, had not he found a protector in Ben Bouncer, who at this moment came down into the hold.

"Help! save me, noble capt'in! I throws myself on your royal hospitality. It's all through my devotion to yer patriotic honour as I've got into this yere black scrape."

"Why, who the devil is this?"

"Don't know, yer honour," returned Clem, touching his cap; "we found him in the pork tub."

"And very nigh pickled," added Sim, ruefully.

"Oh! I remember the fellow. Come, sirrah, you are the same idiot that volunteered to join our crew of pirate-hunters, are you not?"

"Heigho! here's a vorld! There every pure-minded patriot inspired vith a noble zeal for the good of his feller-creeturs is treated like a higeot."

"Well, this insane act reminds me of something I once heard told by Uncle Major Bouncer about a similar madcap, who, being determined to join the army on the march, stowed himself in the mouth of a cannon, where he fell so fast asleep that he did not wake till the gun was fired, projecting him against the walls of a fort, and nearly dashing his brains out. I remember another circumstance——"

"Werry good, Mr. Bouncer," interrupted the boatswain, impatiently. "But, in the meanwhile, what shall we do with the lubber? Shall we pitch him overboard?"

"Come, sirrah, I will leave you in the hands of the captain," said Ben Bouncer.

"Only bring me face to face vith that hero," cried Simon, eagerly, "and I vill plead my own cause vith such moving eloquence as vould move the heart of a wampire. Lead on, sir; I follers yer."

Much to the surprise of the crew, Sim Smut, through the mediation of Ben Bouncer, who had taken a fancy to him, received a full pardon and was permitted to remain on board and take his place among the other men.

Proud and elated, though rather sea-sick, Sim Smut mounted on the deck and stumbled about in the rocking vessel in a state of joyous excitement.

As he was walking forward to the forecastle a sailor touched his arm.

Turning round he perceived a tall, gauky, red-haired, cast-eyed person, whose chin was beardless, though he was by no means a tender juvenile.

Sim recoiled and stared at the sailor with a look of dismay.

The sailor, as he passed, uttered low twice in the chummy's affrighted ear,—

"Poll Potts!"

Sim staggered back, yelled, and fainted.

CHAPTER XLIV.

A TOUGH ARGUMENT BETWEEN PETER MOPER AND BOB STAY.

ONE evening the crew were taking their grog below.

One or two acquaintances had been admitted on board, and by way of keeping up the hilarity of the evening, Tom Taffrail, a smart young seaman, was called upon for a song.

But Peter Moper, another of the crew, and a very melancholy-looking fellow, rose up and protested against any singing.

"Avast," said he; "the wind blows pretty stiff just now, and singing may increase it."

"Belay, belay!" cried Tom Taffrail, "let's have none of your superstitious palaver now, old Peter; we never try to pass a merry hour or two but what you attempt to throw a wet blanket over us."

"A song, a song!" roared some twenty voices.

Tom Taffrail struck up, well aided by a powerful chorus:—

Blue Peter at the mast-head flying,
Warns us to set sail again;
The pirate bold our threats defying,
Scorning fear still ploughs the main.

But if once our guns should reach him,
Then his mettle shall be tried;
Grappled close we'll quickly teach him,
Britons will not be defied!

Tom Taffrail gave this in the true sailor's style.

He met with due applause from his hearers.

But Peter Moper sat with his arms folded, and although all his messmates were full of merriment, he scorned to join it.

"You sing about Blue Peter," said he, "but I am afraid it will be a long time before you see him flying at the mast-head."

"What ails you now, friend Peter?" asked Bob Stay, a sturdy and jolly-faced old tar; "what new maggot has got into your head?"

"It's no use gibing and jeering in that way, Master Stay," replied Peter Moper. "I positively tell you we shall have no luck in this voyage."

"Give yer reasons, old shiver-the-mizen."

"Why here we have been at anchor in these roads for ten days, and here we are likely to remain, for the wind seems determined to set right in our teeth."

"Boo! it will chop round to-morrow."

"Don't ye remember when we were going to weigh from Portsmouth, there were two cursed crows or ravens hovered over the vessel and pitched upon our topsail yards; that was a bad omen, you'll allow."

"Well, there may be summut in that."

"Summut in? Why, blow me, shipmates, although we fired blank cartridges at them, they would not come down till Tom Taffrail pitched them down with a charge of small shot."

"But, friend Peter," said Bob Stay, "I'm afraid you give way too much to these superstitious fancies; we have met with no ill fortune since we set sail, except, to be sure, that we have got wind-bound before we have cleared the British coast; but that's not a misfortune, it's more a matter of accident."

"Not a misfortune!" exclaimed Peter Moper. "I think it is. Accidents are misfortunes, ain't they? What the devil's the difference between them? If you break your neck by accident, that's a misfortune, ain't it? If you get shipwrecked, and lose all you have on board, that's a misfortune, ain't it? So now, Mister Wiseacre, I should like to know the difference between accident and misfortune?"

"Why, a great deal," replied Bob. "A man may find a sum of money by accident—that's no misfortune, is it? A rich relation may die by accident, and leave one a fortune—that's no misfortune, is it?"

"Stop there, bring to, Master Stay; you upset your own tactics there."

"How so, my hearty?"

"I grant that the accident is no misfortune to him that gets the property; but you don't mean to say that the accident is no misfortune to the person that is killed by it?"

"But, hark ye, shipmate—"

"No, no, Mister Stay; if you attempt to sail on that tack you are sure to go to leeward. I ain't superstitious; but although you and the rest of the crew may sneer at it, be assured that there are omens and forewarnings of what is about to happen: as, for instance, recollect the very day that we were preparing to sail, did not that old tom-cat scratch under his left ear, just before we left the George and Dragon? and when I said it foreboded ill luck, you all laughed at me."

"Pish!"

"Well, but wasn't I right? For poor Tom Jigger, who had carried too much sail aloft (i.e. got drunk), lost his bearing as he was stepping aboard, pitched into the water, and was drowned; that was an accident, and you'll allow that to be a misfortune."

"Granted, messmate; but blow me hard if I can see what puss a scratching under his left ear has to do with it."

"Avast; don't you remember when the owners in London paid Jack Gray, the boatswain's mate, with a cheque and because we were in a hurry, he held it to the fire to dry; and didn't I say, 'Jack Gray, you should never dry writing by the fire, because it's unlucky?' but I was right, for Jack Gray had the tails of his Flushing coat cut off, and pockets, cheques, money and all were grabbed by some land pirate, as he was on his way to the bankers, and there he went full sail down Cornhill, like a vessel that had lost her mizen; and that was an accident and a misfortune too, or the devil's in it!"

Bob Stay gave up the argument.

He declared Peter to be incorrigible, and therefore left him to pursue his own course.

Their visitors took leave and went ashore.

The night watch was set.

Peter Moper retired to his hammock, to ponder on future untoward events.

Deep silence reigned throughout the vessel.

Mr. Simon Smut retired to rest.

He found no slight difficulty in getting into his hammock.

He made several desperate bounds, and suffered some severe falls.

At length he found himself swinging in his strange bed.

The creaking of timbers, the dull plash of the billows bowling along the side of the vessel, the heaving and rocking motion, the grim-looking deck with its lantern glimmering at one end, its low beams arching overhead, its rows of hammock-swathed sleepers that looked like so many mummies hung up in a vault; altogether poor Simon felt somewhat excited and uncomfortable.

Every now and then the ship would give a pitch and roll, and poor Simon was in danger of being thrown out of his hammock.

At length, however, sick, sore, and outworn with fatigue, he fell into a profound slumber.

His dreams have been portrayed by our artist's pencil with more graphic power than our pen can command.

However, we shall hear some account of his first night aboard from the lips of the adventurous chummy himself.

CHAPTER XLV.

GONZALVO DE MERIDA, THE BUCCANEER.

AFTER a prosperous voyage, the good ship "Avenger" was safely moored off the shores of South America, not far from the great sea town of Rio de Janiero.

Our hero's first encounter with pirates was his adventure with Gonzalvo de Merida, a most notorious buccaneer, who, with twenty daring associates, ravaged the seas.

The most tempting rewards were offered for his capture, either dead or alive.

Hitherto all attempts had proved fruitless.

He was no common depredator.

He was descended from a noble family.

His youthful days, however, had been improperly spent.

He had associated with designing young cavaliers, who frequented the gaming-table, and planted the seed of his future misfortunes.

He had been affianced to a lady of great beauty, and their union was shortly to take place.

He had, however, squandered away so much money, and so encumbered his estate by gaming and extravagance, that he found his finances fell so short of what had been anticipated by the lady's parents that he felt ashamed to meet them until he had, in some degree, repaired his fallen fortune.

In consequence, their union had been from time to time delayed, until at last the day was irrevocably fixed, and no excuse was left for further delay.

He consulted with his companions what was best to be done.

The result of their conference was that one more attempt should be made at the gaming-table.

But not on the uncertain chance by which their former play had been guided.

Loaded dice were now to be used, and other desperate means resorted to.

Fortune at this time seemed to favour him.

He left the gaming house with a heavy sum of money.

He was overjoyed at his good fortune, and in-wardly chuckled at the unfortunate dupes he had plundered.

The day of his marriage approached.

He now felt none of those terrors or fears of exposure, which, but a few days since, had threatened him.

He purchased a splendid equipage.

His mansion was furnished like a palace.

He now seemed to defy the further frowns of fortune.

Never once did he listen to the voice of conscience, which told him that he had purchased riches and grandeur by treacherous and dishonest means.

The day at length arrived.

Gonzalvo de Merida, arrayed in costly habiliments, entered his carriage.

It rolled on swiftly, and reached the mansion of Inez.

The servants attended at the door of the carriage.

The morning was beautifully serene.

He determined on taking a circuit through the garden instead of entering the house at once.

He had already advanced down an avenue, thickly planted with trees.

A man suddenly started from behind a statue and stood before him.

His cloak was raised so high as nearly to cover his face.

"Senor," said the stranger, "before you enter the mansion, I must have a few words with you."

"You!" exclaimed Gonzalvo; "a perfect stranger! What can be your motive?"

"I'm no stranger; but your accomplice in villany!" replied the intruder, as he uncovered his face.

"Juan de Astorga!" exclaimed Gonzalvo.

"The same," answered Juan.

"Speak quickly, Juan," said Gonzalvo. "What can occasion this interruption? Be brief, for my absence at such a moment may cause suspicion and ruin my expectations."

"Thus, then, it is," said Juan. "Fortune has not been so propitious to me as yourself. Not satisfied with the sums I gained on the night we played with loaded dice, I went once more to the gaming-table; but the demon had deserted me. I had by mistake taken proper dice instead of loaded ones. Not being aware of the error I had committed, I staked heavily; I lost every throw, and left the gaming-table without a single sequin to help myself. I rushed into the street almost frantic; I knew not where to fly for succour, until I casually heard a party talking of your intended marriage. This reminded me of you, and I come to ask your aid."

Gonzalvo was surprised and chagrined.

"What would you have me do?" said he. "You, who can fool away a fortune in a few hours, would find the trifling aid that I could afford of little benefit."

"Trifling aid!" exclaimed Juan, as he cast a furious look on Gonzalvo. "Do you think I come to supplicate like a poor beggar? No, in this respect I command! Either give me a part of your ill-gotten wealth this instant, or ere another hour passes your greatness shall crumble into mere nothingness!"

"What mean you?" exclaimed Gonzalvo.

"To confess my participation in the last gambling affair, when we played with loaded dice," replied Juan; "to expose you, and——"

"Hush!" exclaimed Gonzalvo. "Not so loud! Here is my purse; it is full of reals; take it and quickly leave me. If we are seen together it may be the ruin of us both."

Voices were heard.

Juan, not wishing to be seen in his present disordered state, quitted Gonzalvo, saying—

"I leave you now, but we shall shortly meet again."

The voices sounded nearer.

Several servants who had been in quest of Gonzalvo approached.

They informed him that he was waited for at the mansion.

He followed them, and was conducted into the presence of Donna Inez and her father, surrounded by many noble guests, before whom the marriage ceremony was performed.

CHAPTER XLVI.

PETER MOPER'S PROPHECY.

THE "Avenger" lay off Rio de Janeiro two days longer, when the wind veered round to the north-west, and she put to sea.

A tide took them through the Sweyn, and they came to anchor for a short time off a picturesque island.

Next morning the wind was again favourable, and the "Avenger" cut through the water gaily.

The crew were congratulating themselves on the favourable weather which they now experienced, when they observed Peter Moper coming slowly towards them, with his usual countenance.

"Well, Peter, how fare you, old chap?" asked Clem Cleats. "Fine breeze of wind right aft; canvas well filled, going at the rate of ten knots; soon overhaul the pirates, eh?"

"I wish we may," replied Peter, with his usual doubtful look, "I wish we may; but I fear the wind won't last long in that quarter."

"What, more omens?" cried his messmates, with a general leer.

"Yes, more omens," reiterated Peter, with a look of rebuke. "That cussed cargo of pigs will spoil all. If the captain couldn't dine without pork at his table, why couldn't he have it ready killed? Pigs, at the best of times, are not lucky. Now, only look at that ugly porker with his nose pointed right ahead. What do you suppose he is looking at so intently?"

"By my shoul I can't tell," said O'Kasey.

"Ah, you ignorant lubber, I thought so," replied Peter. "He's looking at the wind, to be sure; he sees it plain enough—wind right ahead. We shall have it slap in our teeth before two hours are over."

The crew laughed at Peter's prophecy; but it was not quite such a hearty laugh as was the general custom.

That pigs see the wind was not altogether disbelieved, and that the pig's snout was pointed right ahead was beyond a doubt.

Hour after hour succeeded, but the wind still kept aft.

Evening came, wind still favourable.

Peter and several others went below to get their grog.

O'Kasey, who smarted under Peter's rebuke, couldn't forbear having a fling at him.

"Where's the wind now?" roared O'Kasey, with a laugh, and a mischievous glance of the eye.

"In the north," replied Peter, drily.

"And the pig's nose is to the south!" exclaimed Pat. "Blood and turf, it's impossible, man! How can the pig keep his nose to the south, and see the wind from the north—unless, to be sure, he might squint a trifle?"

Peter looked mysterious, and, with a solemn countenance, disdainfully eyed Pat O'Kasey, as he said,

"What can you expect from an Irishman but a blunder? Now, to show you you have no more brains than our stern-post, I'll just explain matters a little. I have been at sea many years, and have always paid strict attention to signs of changes of the weather, and such like; and that a pig sees the wind is more than all your philosophers and astrology chaps can deny. This pig of ours, as you all know, pointed due south, and we should have had the wind from that quarter in less than two hours had it not been for a scheme which fortunately entered my head at the moment."

"And what scheme was that?"

"Why," said Peter, "I lifted the pig in my arms, and turned him right round with his nose to the north'ard."

Pat and the crew burst into a loud fit of laughter.

"Ay, ay, laugh away," cried Peter, with a sneer, "but depend upon it, if it hadn't been for this expedient we should have been blown back a hundred miles by day-break. And you, Master Pat O'Kasey, you're a pretty lubber to go to attempt to overhaul my grammatics and my larning, a'nt you? What a pretty mess you made of it when our vessel was new-rigged, and we were so pestered with company that our brave young captain was obliged to excuse himself from allowing any more strangers aboard till we got out of the harbour; a pretty bull you made of it then, sure enough."

"The devil a bit of bull was there about it, Mister Peter," said Pat; "but I gave a clane, dacent, off-hand answer to a plain question, as my messmates here shall decide. Our ship lay alongside the pier; all the crew were on shore, except the captain, myself, and the mate. The captain and mate were down below, overhauling a chart, and I remained on deck to give answers to any inquiries. Presently there comes a great big gentleman, with his head as thickly powdered as if Katty Maloney had emptied her flour-tub over him. 'I want to come on board, and see the ship,' says he. 'You can't do that thing just now,' says I. 'And why not?' says he. 'Because there's nobody aboard but the captain, and he's just gone ashore,' says I. Now where's the bull in that, messmates?"

A roar of laughter followed, and the crew promised themselves a good cargo of mirth as long as they could set Peter and the Irishman foul of each other.

St. Iago was now but a few miles distant, and they brought up in order to take on board two military officers who wished to accompany the captain, to whom they were related.

They shortly set sail again.

The wind was blowing a stiff breeze from N.N.E.; Peter was at the helm; they were running through a narrow channel, sounding, and Peter knew that extreme attention was necessary on account of the number of shoals which were close to them.

Hal Hetherington was standing near the binnacle carelessly looking round, while he was whistling "Rule Britannia."

Peter looked at him once or twice with a countenance somewhat tinged with dissatisfaction, till, not able to contain himself any longer, he turned to him, saying,

"Don't whistle, if you please, sir."

"Not whistle!" ejaculated Hal. "My good fellow, what harm can there be in whistling?"

"Perhaps a great deal just now, sir," replied Peter.

"That is odd," observed the officer. "You must be a very extraordinary being; not two hours since you were whistling yourself."

"Ay, that may be," replied Peter; "but we had no wind at that time, but now we have got more than we want."

"What!" said the officer, "has whistling any influence over the wind?"

"Most undoubtedly," replied Peter, with a grave and somewhat consequential gesture. "*Never whistle when it blows hard;* but whenever you are becalmed, *you may whistle for a wind if you like.*"

The officer smiled, turned on his heel, and went down to the cabin, leaving Peter to deal with the rising wind in what manner he might think most proper.

CHAPTER XLVII.

CONTINUATION OF GONZALVO'S HISTORY.

THE noble guests at the mansion of Donna Inez partook of a splendid banquet after the marriage ceremony, and it was late ere the festivities of the evening concluded.

The new-married pair entered Gonzalvo's carriage, and returned to his mansion.

The next morning Inez's father visited them, and put Gonzalvo into possession of the fortune which he had promised to bestow on the marriage of his daughter.

About a month after that period, one evening, when Gonzalvo was about to retire for the night, a servant entered, and informed him that a stranger, who declined to give his name, desired to see him instantly.

Gonzalvo turned pale.

The hour was late.

Could it be another of the gamblers come to exact further aid?

He knew not what to think.

At first he thought of refusing to see him; but a moment's reflection told him that would be an act of cowardice, and this was a moment when nothing but bold measures would suit.

He descended to an apartment adjoining the hall.

He entered.

Juan was seated there.

Gonzalvo gazed at him with surprise.

"What now?" said he. "Did I not give you the aid you required? Why would you trouble me further?"

"Signor Gonzalvo," replied Juan, with a kind of ceremonious sneer, "I do not understand you; I had expected you would have given a more friendly welcome to one so deeply interested in your fortune; but as you appear impatient, I will at once explain the cause of my visit. You cannot have forgotten the success which attended us at the gaming-table, when you made use of the loaded dice? We laughed heartily at the dupes whom we had defrauded, and little dreamed that we should be discovered."

"Discovered!" ejaculated Gonzalvo.

"Ay, discovered," rejoined Juan. "You look agitated—your countenance turns pale; but you need not fear at present; your safety depends upon your own conduct. Now mark me—it has been discovered that you were the person who introduced the loaded dice, and this very evening you would have had a visit from some of those unfortunates who were plundered. I could not, however, help feeling for your situation: I called to mind that you had just become united to a young and amiable wife, while I had neither wife nor children to sympathize at any misfortune which might befall me; I, therefore, made up my mind to become a victim to friendship, and save you from disgrace: I denied that you had any knowledge of the dice being loaded; and, with a great deal of humility, and apparent sorrow, have confessed that I was the guilty person."

"Generous friend," exclaimed Gonzalvo, "such a noble sacrifice shall not go unrewarded."

"I don't intend to go unrewarded," replied Juan, significantly. "And that is the occasion of my present visit. In order to save time, I have drawn up a paper—all you have to do is to sign it, and our business is settled at once."

"What is the purport of this paper?" inquired Gonzalvo.

"It simply acknowledges certain obligations due to me, in consideration of which you agree to assign half your present estate to me."

"Madman!" exclaimed Gonzalvo, furiously. "Sooner would I beg my bread from door to door, rather be condemned to the galleys, than stoop to such conditions!"

"Don't be in a passion, Signor Gonzalvo," replied Juan. "I am cool, you perceive. You do not choose to sign the paper—well, you shall have your wish, and, therefore, I will use my interest to have you sent to the galleys. Good evening, Signor. I shall not trouble you with another visit. There are twelve more of our associates in villany that would be glad to see you. I will give them your address; perhaps they will meet with better success than I have done; at any rate, it will be worth a trial."

Juan advanced towards the door.

"Hold! miscreant!" exclaimed Gonzalvo, as he drew forth his sword. "Think not I will suffer you to escape my vengeance. Your life is in my power, and this moment——"

"Hush, hush! Signor Gonzalvo," said Juan. "Keep your temper as I do. Your sword is certainly a sharp argument, but I have two friends at hand, the sound of whose voice will ring your funeral knell."

With these words, he drew forth a brace of pistols and pointed them at Gonzalvo.

The two desperadoes gazed on each other.

It was a picture after nature.

It was two tigers measuring the strength of each other's power.

Each stood on the defensive.

At length Juan broke silence.

"Gonzalvo," said he, "you see I am too cautious to place my life in jeopardy. I know you well; and I feel assured you are not apt to be over particular as to the method of silencing friends who know too much of your affairs. Sign that paper, else this instant I will denounce you to the alcaide. For myself I care not, I would even ascend the scaffold, provided I should have you for a companion. I bear about me a letter addressed to Alvarez, detailing all the mal-practices of which we have been guilty: he would, of course, take immediate measures for your apprehension, for you are well aware that he is not friendly towards you, since you have been his successful rival in having gained the hand and fortune of Donna Inez."

"Leave me, leave me!" exclaimed Gonzalvo. "Another time we will arrange this matter."

"No time like the present," replied Juan. "I cannot depart without that paper. Your signature, signor, your signature. Time grows short; choose, therefore, between the alternatives—either accede to my demand, or be for ever disgraced."

" May all the direst plagues that ever cursed the earth await on thee, thou devil!" exclaimed Gonzalvo, as he took up the pen.

"Your signature," again exclaimed Juan, as he pointed to the paper with a demoniac grin, "or your own servants shall be the first to learn the true character of the master whom they serve."

Gonzalvo, trembling with frenzied agitation, hastily signed the paper, then started up, and advancing towards the door, exclaimed,

"Wretch, begone, and never let me see you more!"

"Signor, you shall have your wish," replied Juan, as he cooly folded up the paper. "Should I at any future time want the aid of your purse, I will not come myself, I will send Alvarez—my friend Alvarez—Alvarez, your rival."

With these words he rushed into the street and instantly disappeared.

Gonzalvo sent all the servants to rest, and rushing into his private chamber, loaded a brace of pistols, and throwing his cloak over his shoulders, quitted the mansion by a door which opened to the garden at the back, by which means he hoped to overtake Juan and wreak his vengeance on him.

From the moment he had been compelled to sign the paper, he had come to a resolution that Juan should not live to reap the benefits of it.

Gonzalvo was fully aware of the danger that attended his murderous project. He knew the power which the relatives of Juan possessed in Spain, as well as the danger of embroiling himself with his old associates, and he therefore determined to sacrifice his victim secretly.

Juan had also acted with some discretion, or at least with a determination that Gonzalvo should not escape if he assassinated him, for he had given a letter to his servant with strict orders to present it to Alvarez should he not return home at midnight.

The contents of this letter would state that if he should not see him within an hour, he might conclude he had been assassinated by Gonzalvo.

It was near midnight when Gonzalvo reached the strada.

He listened for awhile, all was quiet; he proceeded a little further—he paused—a footstep was heard at some little distance; he retired behind the pillar of a portico near at hand; the footsteps approached—it was Juan.

"Perish, most execrable villain!" exclaimed Gonzalvo, as he fired the pistol at his head.

Juan reeled and fell.

Gonzalvo instantly tore open his vest, and triumphantly plucked from thence the paper which Juan had that evening forced him to sign.

The report of the pistol had alarmed some of the inhabitants, and Gonzalvo, knowing that his safety depended on his reaching home before his absence could be noticed, snatched up the pistol and hurried away.

He reached the garden gate, through which he passed unobserved, proceeded to the chamber, replaced his cloak and pistols, and retired to his room without any of the servants being aware that he had been from home.

Juan having failed to return home at midnight, his servant delivered the letter to Alvarez.

Two hours had passed, and accordingly, he, with a party of friends, set out in search of him.

They observed several people gathered round a wounded man.

They approached, and, to their surprise and horror, beheld the corpse of Juan.

They loudly exclaimed against Gonzalvo, whom they designated as his murderer.

One man among them, who had the appearance of a mariner, had picked up the pistol which lay near the body, and hearing the name of Gonzalvo, seemed to recognise it.

"Gonzalvo!" exclaimed he. "Surely I know that name."

At the instant Alvarez and his party would have proceeded in a body to Gonzalvo's house, but were restrained by the mariner.

"Don't be too hasty," said he; "this affair seems to be wrapt in mystery, and it may be difficult to fix the charge of murder on Gonzalvo. I know him; let me go to him alone, and I shall, perhaps, be able to elicit enough to criminate him."

Alvarez and his friends agreed to this, and Ovieda (that was the mariner's name) arrived at the mansion of Gonzalvo next morning, and, with some difficulty, obtained an interview. When Gonzalvo entered the chamber, his countenance was pale and haggard, his step faltered, and his eye glanced keenly but fearfully on Ovieda.

"Friend Gonzalvo," said the mariner, "you do not seem to recollect me. Have you quite forgotten your old acquaintance, Ovieda?"

Gonzalvo drew back in horror.

"Nay," continued Ovieda; "you have nothing to fear from me. I trouble myself little about land affairs now. It is full ten years since I have been on terra firma. I have made the sea my residence; I have as fine a vessel as ever stemmed the wave, and I mean to live and die in her. But my time is short; I must be on board again before night. I have come to warn you of danger, and to teach you how to avoid it."

He paused, and looked round.

"Are we alone? Are there any listeners?"

"No," replied Gonzalvo; "speak low, and no one can overhear you."

"Listen, then," said Ovieda; "Juan has been murdered, and suspicion points at you."

"At me?" exclaimed Gonzalvo, in agitation. "My servants can bear witness that I did not leave the house the whole evening."

"I dare say they will," rejoined Ovieda; "but there is one circumstance which you will find it difficult to get over. This pistol, which has been recently discharged, and which laid near the body of the murdered man, bears a handsome silver plate, on which your name is engraved."

Gonzalvo stood motionless.

Ovieda had, indeed, spoken truly; for at the moment he took the papers from the open vest of Juan, his pistols fell out, and, the night being dark, he had by mistake, taken one of Juan's pistols, and left his own in its stead.

"Signor," said Ovieda, "you see I know the whole of the matter, and I am the only one who can fix the murder on you. Come, I will not be unreasonable. I don't want to see you mount the scaffold through my means, nor can I suffer such a golden opportunity as this to escape. You are rich. Share your purse with me, as I have formerly done with you, and for the present, I will conceal you from your enemies. Alvarez would give his head and ears to be master of the evidence which I possess. He would gladly agree to give ten thousand piastres to bring you to the scaffold. Now, I will *save* you from it for that sum. But time passes quickly! Put on your cloak and hat, and accompany me to my lodging; and, in the interim, I will make inquiries whether Juan still lives, as also whether he has declared the name of his assassin."

Gonzalvo hastily threw his cloak over him, and followed Ovieda to his lodging by the sea-shore.

The artful Ovieda cared not a straw if Gonzalvo and the whole of his associates swung together on one gibbet, so that he was the gainer by it; and now he saw a chance of turning this to double profit.

He sought out Alverez, and told him that he had obtained sufficient evidence to criminate Gonzalvo; but that he would not breathe a sentence of it until he could disburse five thousand piastres.

Alvarez was astonished at the demand, and refused to accede.

"Fool," said he to Ovieda, "do you forget that I have nothing more to do than to get some Alguazils and go and seize on the assassin, and bring him to justice?"

"True," replied Ovieda; "but *where* will you go to look for him?"

"Where but at his own house!" replied Alvarez. Ovieda smiled.

"Tut, tut, signor," said he, "no man will wait while the halter comes to him. Gonzalvo is too good a judge to remain at home until the officers go to fetch him."

"Where, then, must I seek him?" inquired Alvarez.

"Wherever you please," replied Ovieda, with a sarcastic grin; "but when you can pay liberally for the information, send for me, and I may tell you."

So saying, Ovieda quitted Alvarez.

He was enraged at his obstinacy, and from that moment resolved to compass his destruction. He therefore, returned to practise on the credulity of Gonzalvo. Juan had died within a few minutes after he had been shot, without uttering a sentence; but Ovieda kept that a secret from Gonzalvo, in order to suit his own purposes.

"Bad news," exclaimed he, as he entered the apartment where Gonzalvo was anxiously awaiting his arrival, "Juan still lives, and has accused you of attempting his murder. The magistrates are at this moment taking his depositions, because the physicians declare he cannot survive four-and-twenty hours. You will not be safe here twelve hours longer; at nightfall, therefore, you must take the advantage of darkness, and remove to a place of greater safety. But it will be necessary to have money; I have but little on shore. You had better, therefore, give me an authority to receive some before it is too late; for, in less than an hour, Alvarez, with the Alguazils, will go to take possession of your effects."

"He shall not survive that hour," exclaimed Gonzalvo.

He seized Ovieda's pistols, and rushed into the street, and, covering his face with his cloak, hastened towards his mansion, which he entered by the garden-door.

He listened a moment.

He heard the voice of Inez; she was beseeching them not to take her from the house.

He heard a voice in reply; the words were—

"Strive to forget the assassin Gonzalvo, and become mine."

It was the voice of Alvarez.

Gonzalvo instantly broke open the chamber-door—Alvarez was kneeling to Inez, declaring his passion—an instant more, and he ceased to live.

The ball from Gonzalvo's pistol had entered his heart, and he fell lifeless.

The report of the pistol alarmed the servants; Gonzalvo, fearing even the presence of his own domestics, threw up the window, and, leaping into the garden, was instantly out of sight.

The father of Inez had been informed of the malpractices of Gonzalvo, and had arrived at the mansion with a party of Alguazils, intending to seize him; but he was too late. Gonzalvo was nowhere to be found.

Ovieda had never lost sight of the main chance, and, in the hurry and bustle, had managed to get into the house, and laid his hand upon whatever was valuable that he could hide under his cloak.

He had managed to secure a casket of jewels, and two bags containing some thousands of piastres, with which he got clear off.

He stopped to rest his load when he reached a sequestered spot, thickly planted on each side.

Suddenly he heard a rustling among the foliage behind him.

A man darted forth.

It was Gonzalvo!

Surprise possessed the features of both.

"Where the devil did you spring from?" inquired Ovieda.

Gonzalvo agitated, exclaimed—

"I have been obliged to fly from my own house; it is filled with enemies. What am I now?—a proscribed murderer. My property seized; my estate confiscated, and a price set on my head. What land will now give me shelter?"

"No land at all," rejoined Ovieda. "You must give up your *land* freaks, and take to the *water*. It's better to run the chance of being *drowned* than being *hanged*. You are not quite a beggar yet,

however; but you may thank my intrepidity for that. Look! here is a casket of jewels worth more than a trifle; here's a couple of bags of piastres, and cursed heavy I found them, too; and here are some bank papers, made payable to you—wanting nothing but your signature. They are good in any part of Spain, therefore we must give them a good spread of canvas, and get them passed at some distant port before the news of your disaster gets known abroad. I've a devilish clever fellow on board that does our exchange business."

Gonzalvo listened to Ovieda with a vacant stare, and hardly seemed to notice what he said, for the events of the last two days had confounded him.

"Come, friend Gonzalvo," continued Ovieda, "night is drawing on, and I must get aboard soon; so make up your mind. You are no longer safe in Spain; matters are now too bad to be worse, therefore, cheer up, and make the best of a bad bargain. I am master of as fine a little vessel as ever doubled the coast of Spain. Come with me; your fortunes shall be mine. We'll join partnership. Give me your gold, and you keep the money that shall be paid for your bank bills. That's fair and even on both sides. Come on board with me, and you shall live a free and a merry life; and, if you don't like our ways, why you can return on shore to be hanged if you prefer it."

Gonzalvo raised his clenched hand, and emphatically vowed eternal enmity to his fellow-men.

"There's my hand upon it," exclaimed he, as he grasped Ovieda's outstretched hand. "I am yours: do with me as you will."

"That's well spoken," said Ovieda. "Now give me a helping hand with these bags. Our boat lies just beyond yon rock, and not half a mile hence: we'll soon be on board our little vessel. You can just see the tops of her masts peeping over that promontory, as much as to say, 'Come along; I'm waiting for you.' The moon will be up in two hours, and, as darkness is more convenient for my business, I shall take the liberty of leaving *terra firma* a couple of leagues astern of us before the moon is up."

They lifted up the bags of gold and jewels, entered the boat, and were soon on board the vessel.

They weighed anchor instantly, and, when they had sailed about two leagues from the shore Gonzalvo beheld several additions to the crew, which appeared to consist of all nations, and when Ovieda came on deck, after a short absence, his dress was materially altered. He wore a large fur cap, with a death's head on its front, a huge cutlass, and four pistols.

All merchandise was lowered into the hold, and in their place appeared small carronades.

The men also were busy in arming themselves.

Mulattos—blacks—all seemed to form a commonwealth.

Gonzalvo seemed at a loss to guess the cause of this metamorphosis, when Ovieda, observing his surprise, thus accosted him :—

"Friend Gonzalvo—for so I must now term you—your surprise is but natural. You thought us a merchant or trading vessel. No such thing: we are a set of free fellows, and we don't mind making free with any valuable cargo that falls in our way. We are pretty well known, for we have kicked up some brisk freaks among the merchant traders, and our name has got into vogue. You have, doubtless, heard of the daring pirate Rebino! Well! I am he! Now you know the whole of the matter. If you don't like to remain on board, we'll put you ashore the first time we touch land. If you consent to remain, you shall rank equal with me."

Gonzalvo resolved to remain on board, and, abjuring all thoughts of ever rejoining society, made up his mind to live and die a pirate.

CHAPTER XLVIII.

THE PIRATE SHIP DISABLED BY THE "AVENGER" —GONZALVO BLOWS UP THE SHIP TO AVOID CAPTURE.

THE British ship "Avenger" left St. Iago, and was soon on the broad Atlantic.

One day, about 2 P.M., the man on the look-out gave notice of a vessel ahead, under a press of canvas, and from the description, Roving Jack supposed her to be the pirate with Gonzalvo on board.

She came boldly on, with Spanish colours flying at her mast-head.

"If she is a pirate," exclaimed Roving Jack, "she has the impudence of the devil. Keep your ports closed; I think she mistakes us for a merchantman."

The strange sail approached, lowered her Spanish colours, and hoisted a red flag, with a sword and death's head.

She was a capital sailer, and sailed completely round the British cruiser.

"D——n her impudence !" said our hero, hotly. "Up with your ports, and give her pepper."

But the pepper came too late.

She flew before the wind as swift as an arrow, and the British ship lost her for that day.

"There," said Peter, "did you ever see such an evasive little devil as that in your life ?"

"Why, as to that matter, Master Peter," replied Junk, "I don't exactly know the true bearing of that 'ere word '*vasive*, as you calls it."

"Och, bother !" exclaimed Pat O'Kasey; "sure, and everybody knows what evasive means."

"Hush, hush !" interrupted Peter, "don't let's have any more blunders. How can an Irishman explain a word as is only to be found in the most larned dictionaries ?"

"And sure, Mister Peter, will you be after telling me I don't know the meaning of evasive ?" cried Pat. "Now, messmates, only listen awhile, and I'll tell you how nately I handled that word evasive.

"We had just got all our new rigging complete, and our sails were all unbent, and we lay at anchor in the roads, and the captain determined to sail next morning. Our beautiful new canvas looked so neat and clean from the shore, that boats full of fine gentlemen and ladies were coming on board every hour to see the ship. Och, and didn't I take care to hand the sweet creatures aboard genteelly ? Och sure, I was as busy as the devil in a high wind. Five o'clock came, and the captain said he must have no more visitors aboard, else we should not be ready to sail in the morning, as it hindered the men from their work. And sure, as I looked towards the shore, I saw another boat full of ladies coming off. So the captain says to me, 'Paddy O'Kasey,' says he, 'if those ladies come alongside, and want to see the ship, you must give them an *evasive answer*, and get rid of them as well as you can: and I'll go down below and wait till they're gone.' And sure enough he went below, and then the boat full of ladies came alongside, and they asked for the captain, and I gave them an evasive answer, and they went away with it a devilish deal quicker than they came; and the captain popped up his head, and said, 'Pat, are they gone ?' 'Yes, they are, your honour,' says I. 'What did they say ?' says he. 'They ax'd for your honour,' says I; 'but I gave them an evasive answer.' 'What did you tell them ?' said the captain. 'I said your honour had gone.' 'Gone where ?' says he. 'Gone to blazus,' says I, 'and you may go after him, if you plaise.' Now, wasn't that an evasive answer, Mister Peter ?"

"Well," said Peter, "after that, I think, you may shut you mouth, for you'll never beat that as long as you live."

"Sail a-head," called a voice above.

Roving Jack took his glass.

"It's the same vessel again," said he. "We'll

try for her this time, boys. The breeze is steady, and getting pretty stiff. We shall get her within range presently."

The breeze increased to a gale.

The "Avenger" spread her canvas kindly to it, and she ran ten knots.

The pirate was on a tack; but as soon as she went about, the "Avenger" gave her a broadside, which made her rather groggy.

But she picked up well.

The "Avenger" tacked, and gave her another broadside.

Her topmast went down, and there suddenly appeared great confusion on board of her.

The "Avenger" gained upon her.

The pirate was disabled, and seemed to make no way.

"There's some mischief among them," said the Pirate-hunter.

And he was right, as the sequel will show.

The shot fired from the "Avenger" had caused sad havoc.

Ovieda had been mortally wounded.

He was lifted on to a sail-cloth.

He beckoned Gonzalvo to approach, and bid the crew leave them for a few moments.

"Friend Gonzalvo," said he, "my time is come, and a short hour will close my career in this world. Our vessel is crippled, and cannot escape from her pursuers. On either side death is certain. Yet I cannot bear the thoughts of my brave crew being strung up to the yard-arm like so many rabbits. You are a bold man, and have courted death like a hero since you have been on shipboard. It now remains for you to achieve one more act of bravery to save us from disgrace. Hark ye! Our powder magazine is well stored. Your hand may accomplish the deed, and the pirate's crew will die as they have lived—like bold and desperate spirits."

Gonzalvo grasped his hand.

"By h—l, I'll do it!" he exclaimed, as he grasped the lantern.

Another shot struck Ovieda, and his lifeless body rolled on the deck.

The pirates, driven to desperation, flew to their guns once more.

The British ship rapidly gained on them.

A vivid light was seen on board the pirate's ship.

Gonzalvo had kept his promise.

He had set the ship on fire!

A cry of horror was heard among the lawless crew.

A minute elapsed.

A tremendous explosion took place; and when the smoke cleared away not a vestige remained of the pirate's vessel or his daring crew!

CHAPTER XLIX.

JACK SHEPPARD MAKES AN EXCHANGE WITH ISAACS THE JEW.

ISAACS the Jew, the clothes vendor, lived in a dirty, narrow court, near Ratcliff Highway.

Thither Jack Sheppard betook himself.

It must be remembered that the housebreaker was splendidly dressed.

He had adorned himself in his richest finery to do honour to the parting banquet given to him by his mistresses.

But he was unarmed.

He walked with his eyes moodily fixed upon the ground.

His heart was gnawed by regret, scorn, despair and anxiety.

He thought of the past, and shuddered.

The present had nothing to give him satisfaction.

His friend, his sweetheart, for whom he would have laid down his life—those few whom he had never wronged, those few whom he had cherished and served—as he thought of Jonathan Wild he almost loved him, in comparison with those dear ones who had betrayed him.

The thief-taker was a palpable villain, his enemy sworn; they had exchanged threats, they had felt all the defiant pride of mutual hostility; but "there, where he garnered up his heart," his friend, his sweetheart, to be deceived by them!

He arrived at the door of the shop.

The Jew stood on the threshold.

He was a little, weazened, hideous-looking fellow, dressed in a long gabardine of brown serge; his hair was long, red and shaggy; his lips curled with a treacherous leer; his deep-set, cunning black eyes had a false and subtle gleam, and his oily, sneakish voice was very repelling.

He cast a quick glance upon Jack Sheppard.

"Shtrike me! itsh Captainsh Sheppard!" he said, with an obsequious cringing, rubbing his sallow hands.

"Dam'me, what do ye mean, ye jibbering ape?" muttered Sheppard, fiercely, gripping his arm. "Is mine a name to be proclaimed in the market-place?"

"I peg your pardonsh, my tear poysh," said the Jew in a whisper; "come into de shopsh."

Jack Sheppard followed him down a step into a large, but low-roofed room, with shelves all round the walls, on which were piled suits of clothes of every material and variety.

The Jew looked quickly at the robber.

His sharp eyes detected at once that the latter was unarmed.

Jack Sheppard's sword had been abstracted from the sheath, which still depended from his side.

The robber at once fathomed the meaning of the old Jew's look.

He thrust his hands into his ample pockets, and pretended to grip a pair of pistols.

The old Jew hopped off a step or two.

"Vell, my fine captainsh, in vot vay can I sherve you?" asked the Jew.

"Are we safe here?" asked Sheppard.

"Shafe!" gasped the Jew.

"Aye, safe from intrusion?"

"Intrushion! Are you in troublesh, noble captainsh? are you purshued?" rejoined the Jew, in some alarm.

"I am always pursued," returned Jack, grimly; "sometimes I get taken, but always escape."

"Come dish vay, my noble captainsh," said the Jew.

He led the robber into a dark and dingy back room.

"And now, quick," said Sheppard, "for I have no time to lose."

"Vot can I do to sherve you, captainsh?"

"I want to exchange these clothes for a disguise."

The Jew's eyes glistened.

He knew that Jack Sheppard was liberal in his payments.

"Vot short of dishguish ish to be, my nabsh?"

"The dress of a poor labourer."

"Shtrike me, but that will come expenshive!" returned the old rascal, gravely, shaking his head and passing his hands up and down his knees,

"Expensive! A dress of the poorest sort will best serve my turn."

"Vhy, you shee, captainsh," rejoined the old Jew, with a leer, "your appearansh ish sho dish-tinguished that itsh almosht impoashible to make you look like a chaw-baconsh; if you ish not vell dishguished you vill be recognished at vonsh."

"Well, you shall have the clothes I wear, which you see are superfine, in exchange for a good disguise of any sort."

"Ve vill shee vot can be done, Mishter Sheppard."

The robber threw off his clothes and dressed himself in a rough suit of the poorest materials supplied him by the old Hebrew.

"By the shtaff of Jacobsh, it ish perfect!" cried the old rascal, with a chuckle of exultation. "Your own mother vould not know you, captainsh."

"Thus I throw off the coil," cried Jack Sheppard, flinging the richly laced and brocaded suit he had discarded across the room, "as the serpent sheds his skin. I have done with the past."

For a moment he stood pondering deeply. His mind reverted to Edgeworth Bess, Poll Maggot, and Blueskin.

He stamped his foot and exclaimed bitterly—

"Curse them! I should like to have borne away with me some kind remembrance of them; but, after all," he continued, inwardly, "what an un-grateful villain I have been to my indulgent old master, the carpenter; to my generous benefactor, Kneebone. What right have I to complain of in-gratitude in others, who have been myself such a thankless scoundrel? Wild! that villain! he lured me, as the fiend would tempt the soul of his victim, to destruction—he praised my villanies, called my ruffianly violence, courage; my priggish cunning, discretion; my vile deeds of street-robbery and house-breaking, acts of heroism! O, how he must have laughed in his sleeve at the mad, fond fool who could be deceived by such paltry sham! And now he has betrayed me and hunts me to the death! Hurrah for my new career! Welcome all its hardships; I will fly the cursed land, and breathe the breath of the fresh sea; and even yet I may fall in with the pirate-hunter—Roving Jack!"

"Holy Abramsh!" chuckled the Jew, "you are fery much dishturbed, captainsh; vot ish de matter? Shack Sheppard ish not de poy to tremble and quake and frownsh ish prows and knash ish teeth pecaush de shoulder-clappersh ish down—dere ish shum pretty blowen, shum dimber vench in de casesh. Ish Edgevorth Bess de cruel fair?"

"Stash your clatter," growled Sheppard. "And, now, harkye, old Isaacs; of course you know there is a reward offered for me?"

"Five hundred poundsh?"

"Yes; but you will not dare to betray me—ha?"

"Not for five thoushand, gallant captainsh."

"No, for that will spoil your trade."

"Dat ish true."

"I have been a good customer."

"A va-ry goot cushtomer, prave captainsh; I hope dat I shall not losesh your patronage."

"If you are faithful you shall be handsomely rewarded. You see this coat and these jewels? They are valuable, are they not?"

"Dat all dependsh vhere you cot them, captainsh," returned the old fence, leering. "De shtuff is goot enough, but the clothesh must pe altered, and the jewelsh re-set, and all thish silver procade mush be made into white proth (melted). Where did you get thish prave shuit vich becomesh your hanshome figure sho mosh petter than the disguish vich you have put on?"

"Never fear, old mousetrap; I bought them, and paid for them, and now I'll tell you what I want in exchange."

"Not mosh. I hope you won't expect too mosh; I am always too liberal in pisness," whined the Jew. "I have almost ruint myshelf."

"Body and breeches! let's have no haggling!" cried Jack, impatiently, "time is precious. Give me ten guineas and a brace of barkers, and I will be content. Refuse me——"

"I vill not refush you nothing in reashon, captainsh," returned the Jew, with glistening eyes; "although I shall losesh py dish pargain, I vill not refush you nothing."

"Shell out then."

The fence placed the money in the robber's hands.

He then went into a little room at the back of the shop, and after a few moments returned with a case of pistols in his hand.

"Are they fed?" asked Sheppard, taking them from the box, and examining the primings.

"Dey ish loaded to de muzzle," returned the old fence; "dey pelonged to poor Captainsh Hall."

Jack tried them with the ramrod, and then thrust them into his pocket.

"And now I am off," said Jack. "Mark ye, old Isaacs, five hundred pounds is a good round sum—but who would sell his life for twice as much?—if you betray me, there are those who will take care that you do not escape the punishment of treachery."

The old fence, with cringing air and oily tones, protested everlasting friendship and fidelity to his old customer.

Jack took a hasty farewell, and rushed out of the shop.

It was growing dusk, and as Jack stepped quickly along he encountered a grave and decent-looking old gentleman, dressed in a brown coat with brass buttons, black stockings, and clogged shoes.

He tried to avoid this passenger, but he stood in his way, and gazed intently upon his face.

Seeing that he could not avoid his scrutiny Jack Sheppard resolved to put a bold face on the matter, and, touching his ragged cap, addressed him in a changed voice.

"Ax pardon, yer honour, but could yer help a poor lad on the road? Travelled all day, zur, and ain't had a morsel of food; can't get no work."

The kind-looking old gentleman looked at him searchingly.

"It is strange," he said, "how much you resemble an old apprentice of mine."

"And who might he be, yer honour?"

"I will not offend you, friend, by mentioning his name," returned the other, with a sigh, "but, though he went wrong, he was, as a boy, a bright, clever, good-humoured fellow, and I was very fond of him. However, take this, and may you soon find honest employment."

"Amen, master," groaned Sheppard, with a pang of genuine contrition.

"What is your trade?"

"I was a carpenter."

"Indeed!" said the old gentleman, with a look of surprise, "then, perhaps, I can serve you. I am a fellow craftsman; my name is Owen Wood; I live in Wych Street. If you will call on me, I will see what can be done. Good evening, friend."

"God bless yer honour," returned Jack, with unwonted earnestness.

They parted, and the robber walked on with a heavy heart.

CHAPTER L.

THE TREACHERY OF OLD ISAACS THE JEW CLOTHESMAN.

No sooner had Jack Sheppard left the shop of the old fence than the latter threw on his hat, and, shambling to the door, looked down the street after him.

"Dere he goesh," chuckled the rascal, rubbing his hands with great satisfaction. "He tinks I vonldn't risk my life for five hundred poundsh; vhy, I would shell my shoul for half that shum! Hi! Benjamin! vhere are you, you shon of a tog? here, be quick, you fillain!"

A ragged, cunning-looking Jew boy came growling up a stair which descended to the kitchen below.

"Vot do yer vant now?" he grumbled, stretching his arms, and yawning.

"Come here, Ben, my shon," cried the elder, trembling with eagerness, and dragging the boy to the door. "Look there."

"Vell, vot am I to look at?"

"Shtrike me! are you plindsh?"

"No; my eyes is vide open."

"To you shee that fellow there? Look, he ish shpeaking to de old shentleman in de prown coatsh?"

"Who ish he?"

"He'sh nopody elsh but Shack Sheppard—he! he!"

"Vhot him as broke out of the shtone jug?"

"The fery shame, Benji tear."

"There's a reward offered for him, ain't there?"

"Yesh; five hundred poundsh."

"Oh, my eyesh! Ash he peen here?"

"Yesh! he as jusht left."

"But vhy didn't ye call in the runners?"

"Vhy, shmother me, do you tink dat it vould have peen prudent to enrage the fillain? He vould have cut my throat."

"And vhat did he vant vith you, father?"

"Vhy, you shee, Benji, my shon," returned the old Jew, laying his finger on his large hooked nose, and winking, "he vonted shome feathersh to fly vith; he ish going to eshcape from Englant, and he vos vithout moneysh, sho he left thesh fine clothesh in exchange for the ragged old shuit he vearsh now."

"But ish he armed?"

"Yesh, my shon; sho you mush pe fery careful."

"Vhat arms does he carry—barkers?"

"A pair of brads I showld him."

"Vhy, you old, fool, vhat did you do that for?"

The old fence giggled, and rubbed his lank, skinny hands.

"They vosh loaded, too, Benji."

"The devil they vos!" cried the Jew boy, aghast.

"Yesh, put I took coot care to shtop de fents vith pits of vire, my darling."

"Ho! ho! you're a deep 'un."

"Put look, my prave Benji, de old shentleman ish leafing him. You mush tog his stepsh, find vhere he goesh to, and vhere he putsh up for the night, and then you can run off to Pow Street and fetch Mr. Qvilt Arnold and hish men to arresht the rascal."

"All's bob, guv'nor," returned the Jew boy; "but mind, I goesh reg'lars in the reward."

"You shall have five poundsh, my poy."

"Five devils! Ve go halves, guv'nor, mind that."

And so saying, Benjamin took to his heels, and raced down the street, for Jack Sheppard had now turned the corner.

CHAPTER LI.

JACK SHEPPARD RESOLVES TO GO TO SEA—TRACKED BY THE JEW BOY—THE OLD TAR—BARABBAS MAKES A PROPOSAL—JONATHAN WILD'S PLOT TO CARRY OFF VIOLET—THE INTERRUPTION—BLUESKIN'S WARNING—THE ATTACK—FLIGHT OF JACK SHEPPARD.

MEANWHILE the unconscious victim of this treacherous plot walked onwards till he came to one of the back streets near St. Katherine's Docks.

He turned down this vile, dirty, and narrow thoroughfare.

He reached the door of a low public-house called the "The Three Ravens."

The windows were open, and exhaled a villanous compound of vile smells—the aroma of fried fish, steaming punch, tar, and tobacco smoke.

A terrible noise sounded from within, gruff laughter mingled with high oaths, the pattering of feet as of people dancing, and the squeaking of fiddle strings.

Upon the door-post were several placards, advertisements for able-bodied seamen to join various ships now lying in dock, but outward bound for many different ports.

Jack stood for some moments regarding these posters with an anxious look when a fine, rough-looking old sailor came to his side, and clapped him on the shoulder.

"What cheer, my hearty," he asked, in a deep, hearty voice, "are ye looking for a berth?"

"Yes, mate," returned Sheppard, starting, and grasping the pistols in his pocket; "I want to join some outward-bound ship."

"Are ye a seaman?" asked the old tar.

"No; unfortunately I am but a land lubber, never served abroad in my life," answered Sheppard.

"Ha! you don't say so, and such a likely young sapling, too," returned the old sailor, regarding him with a favourable eye. "Well, my hearty, it's never too late to mend, eh?"

"I hope not," returned Sheppard, sighing.

"Heave to, then. I like the cut of your jib, my cheery," laughed the sailor, "and I'll see what I can do for ye. I'm second mate of the brig 'Mermaid,' as purty a craft as ever hoisted the blue peter. So let us get into the caboose, and talk the matter over a glass of grog. I think I can find ye a place on our ship's books."

The two men entered the tap-room together.

It was crowded by a number of sailors and their friends, noisily carousing.

The old sailor led the way to the chimney corner, and seated himself.

He motioned Jack Sheppard to take a chair by his side.

They called for a glass of grog, and lighted their pipes.

Jack Sheppard looked round him.

He started, and rose to his feet.

A strong, broad-built, but dwarfish seaman had taken his station at the door.

In an instant Jack Sheppard recognized the dwarf Barabbas.

The sea-urchin nodded to him, and leered hideously.

The robber frowned.

He turned one sily towards the fire.

"And so, my hearty, you want to go to sea? Run away from home, eh? Do ye follow any trade?"

"Yes; I'm a carpenter."

"Say you so? Then that's all ataunto; for why? Poor Billy Ducks, our carpenter's mate, died on our last voyage, and you may have a chance o' stepping into his shoes. I'll speak to the skipper about it."

"Thank'ee, master," returned Jack, with a smile; "and now, if you'll tell me when and where to meet you again, I'll walk my chalks, for I must just bid my mother and friends good-bye, and then I shall be ready to go aboard whenever you want me."

"Hulloa! my hearty! what do ye mean? Don't heave anchor till the grog's out, I want to have a word with ye."

But Jack had risen, and was looking around him with an uncomfortable air.

At the end of the room, clustered apart at a separate table, sat a knot of swarthy, evil-looking ruffians, dressed in blue jackets and bucket-boots, and wearing scarlet caps, talking in hoarse whispers, while they puffed dense clouds of tobacco-smoke and drank deep.

He knew that they belonged to the crew of Wirth Wolfgang, the pirate, and conscious that he had been recognized, and that the ruffians, who, from time to time, cast curious glances at him, were in league with Jonathan Wild, he felt anxious to get out of the place.

"You are very kind, sir, I'm sure," said Jack, uneasily; "but as I promised my friends that I would return in half an hour, I will beg leave to depart at once. Shall I meet you again here, or elsewhere?"

"Well, my cheery, if you are determined to get under-weigh I won't detain ye," returned the seaman. "I think you may consider it settled that you can join our ship's company. A word from me will suffice with the skipper. Meet me here to-morrow morning at six bells, and I will take you aboard, for the 'Mermaid' is undergoing repairs, and you may be useful."

"I will not fail, yer honour. Good night."

"Good night, my hearty."

Jack walked towards the door.

Barabbas had left his post, and had joined the party of pirates, whom we have described as sitting apart from the rest of the company.

He was conversing with a tall, broad-built, bushy-bearded fellow, better dressed than the rest, and, to all appearance, one of the officers of the 'Raven.'

Upon seeing Sheppard slip to the door, he advanced towards him, followed by the man, the pirate to whom he had been talking.

"Messmate, ahoy," he cried, catching Jack by the arm, and laughing an eldritch laugh. "Don't ye know me?"

"Aye, once seen you can never be forgotten," said Jack, recoiling from the deformed with a shudder of abhorrence.

"You flatter me," rejoined the dwarf, grinning. "But, hark ye, messmate, we have something to propose to ye. You remember this gentleman, Mynheer Hans Trinkgelt, our first lieutenant?"

"Haw! haw!" laughed the Dutchman. "How goes it, muntmeister? It iz a very long time zat ve have not seen you; ze herr captain often zpeak of you; ve laugh often at your vondervoll escapes from——"

"Hush!" cried Jack, in alarm.

"Ass! be quiet," muttered Barabbas, fiercely. "Don't you see that you endanger our friend by such allusions?"

"Haw, dat's vehr true," returned the Dutchman, with a stupid stare. "I ask your pardon, muntmeister."

"Follow me; I want a word with you," said the dwarf.

Jack, however, drew back reluctantly.

But Barabbas gripped his wrist with a tight grasp, and dragged him out of the room.

Jack was overwhelmed with astonishment at the amazing strength of the hideous-looking little monster.

Barabbas hauled him along to another room.

Hans Trinkgelt followed.

When they had entered, Barabbas relinquished his grip on Jack's wrist, and locked the door.

"What does this mean?" asked Sheppard, suspiciously. "If treachery is intended, do not think you'll catch me unprepared."

He half drew the pistols from his pocket.

Barabbas laughed long and loud.

"Treachery? No, dam'me Master Sheppard, we leave that precious quality to you land-lubbers; aboard, all hands must work as one—without unity there's no safety at sea. I've got a proposal to make to you; you've run astern with a heavier craft, eh, and must steer clear?"

"You allude to Wild, I suppose?" said Sheppard.

"Aye, it was he who clapped you into rumbo?"

"Yes."

"Well, my brave, I'll put you in the way of making yourself secure as a ship in dock, and, more than that, I'll show you how you may wreak your vengeance on the old coney-catcher."

"How?"

"Why, 'tis easy."

"Yes," returned Jack Sheppard, savagely, "I know it is easy, and it shall not be left undone; I will kill him before I leave England."

"To be launched from Tyburn port," chuckled Barabbas; "besides, my hearty, old Nightshade, who pretends to read the stars as easily as a seaman can box the compass, has prophesied that old Jonathan shall hang."

"Then the conjuror lies," returned Sheppard, "for he shall die by this hand. I'll cut his throat——"

"No, but he shall have his throat slit by another —that's on the books," laughed Barabbas: "aye, and he shall hang too; so you may rest easy on that score of vengeance, except that I can put you up to a trick for plaguing him most confoundedly."

"How?"

"First, you must join our crew."

"What! and become a bloody pirate? Never!"

"Pirate! pish! He who robs is a robber; he who cuts throats is a cut-throat. What is your king's man when he boards an enemy's vessel but a murderer and thief?"

"In the service of one's country——"

"In the service of one's—self! Bah! you are a baby! Does the soldier or the sailor ask whether the cause he fights for is a just one? Not he! He fights for 'duty,' that is, bread and cheese and bubble."

"Bubble!"

"Aye, 'bubble reputation,' a blood bubble very often; moreover, the tiger preys on the fawn, the eagle swoops on the dove—'tis ever the mastery

of strength over weakness all the world through.
Hurrah! say I, for the

'Good old plan,
That he should take who hath the power,
And he should keep who can.'

Pirate, quotha? Ho, ho! This hand, shipmate,
has often been crimsoned with human blood; but
why should I care more for the life of vile and
cruel man, or false and wanton woman, than the
butcher in his reeking shambles does for the innocent lamb he slaughters?"

"You are a monster."

"Right; but why I know not; it was not my fault
that I am

'Deformed, unfinished, sent before my time
Into this breathing world;'

but, since it is so, I say with King Dick,

'And therefore, since I cannot prove a lover,
To entertain these fair well-spoken days,
I am determined to be a villain!'"

"But this is nothing to the purpose!"

Jack Sheppard drew back, and stared with awe
upon the chuckling fiend before him.

"Haw! haw!" laughed Hans Trinkgelt, "Mynheer
Barabbas iz von ztrange vellow, he zink too moch
ov his oglinez."

"I am reminded of it often enough," growled the
dwarf; "but let us come to the clinch. Will you
join our crew, Jack Sheppard?"

"I'd rather serve as recruit in the devil's army,"
returned Jack.

"But listen, my hearty: you hate Jonathan
Wild, and would not be sorry for the chance of
serving him a shrewd turn; well, I'll show you
how you may do it."

"I listen; but be quick, for I am in haste."

"Well, then, you remember the saucy kestrel
that bearded us in the cave at the Foamy Reef?"

"What, Roving Jack?" asked Sheppard, with a
start.

"The same; he is now Sir John Warbold, the
pirate-hunter. I hate him, and I never allow my
hate to remain unsated, and I want you to assist
me in carrying out my plot for vengeance. You
may make your own fortune at the same time."

"But what has all this to do with Jonathan
Wild?"

"You shall hear; the unconscionable villain
intends to carry off Violet Tremaine."

"And who is she?"

"The foster-sister of Roving Jack, and the
heiress to immense riches," returned the dwarf. "I
want you to marry her!"

"I?"

"You!"

"The devil!"

"That's just it; she might as well marry the
devil, of course. He, he! ho, ho! What will the
mighty pirate-hunter say when he hears that his
sister and ward has married Jack Sheppard, the
cracksman! Jack Sheppard, the felon! Jack Sheppard, the prison-breaker!"

"Wouldn't your vengeance be more complete if
you were to marry her yourself?" sneered Jack,
with a look of aversion.

"I can't, my boy."

"Why not, as well as I?" laughed Jack. "I
should think the lady's consent will not be expected in either case."

"I'll tell you why," returned the dwarf, sighing
deeply; "my heart is engaged elsewhere."

Both the robber and the other pirate laughed
immoderately at this speech.

A demoniac gleam flashed in the dwarf's red eye,
but he joined in the laugh.

"Ho, ho! he, he! Why should not I play the
gay gallant—the bold lover with the rest? I mean
to carry off Nell Peveril; but to business. Werth
Wolfgang's schooner sails for Scarborough to-
morrow; the Owlet's Roost will be attacked by
night; Violet and Nell will be carried on board
the 'Raven,' where a fleet parson will be ready to
tie the nuptial knot."

"Bah! such a marriage would never stand."

"But the shame of it will; and you're a smart
fellow, Jack, the lady may take a fancy to you, and
by the influence of her friends may save your neck,
for though you are condemned, you have never
committed the crime of murder."

"Give me time and you shall have an answer."

"Time? Why, the ship sails to-morrow, and we
have but a few hours left in which to carry out our
plan for bilking old Jonathan. Come, your answer."

But ere Jack Sheppard could reply, they were
interrupted by a loud knocking at the door.

"Open the jigger, here; quick, quick, or it will
be too late," cried a gruff voice from without.

All started, and drew their pistols.

"Who's there?" asked Jack.

"It's I, Jack, your pal—Blueskin."

Jack Sheppard threw open the door.

Blueskin rushed in.

His dark face was deepened like a purple hue.

He threw himself into a chair in a state of exhaustion, and wiped the perspiration from his
forehead.

The pirates and the housebreaker looked at him
with astonishment.

At last he recovered his breath sufficiently to
speak.

"Fly, Jack!" he cried, "you are pursued; Quilt
Arnold, Mendez, and a whole posse of the traps are
on your track; the hunt is as hot as h—. Get off
by the back entrance, or you'll be nabbed as sure
as Newgate!"

As if to confirm this assertion quick, heavy footsteps were heard in the passage.

Jack darted to the window.

He sprang out.

He reckoned not the height.

He lighted on his feet, however; but he felt
stunned, and reeled giddily.

Recovering himself he sped to the wall.

Over he scrambled.

He rushed up the street.

Meanwhile Quilt Arnold, the Jew Mendez, and
a large number of the Bow Street runners burst
into the room.

Blueskin, however, was gone.

He had rushed after Jack; but, less hasty than
his confederate, he had dropped from the window
by clutching the sill with his hands.

Barabbas made a sign to Hans Trinkgelt.

The Dutchman grinned, and seating himself at
a table drew a bottle and glass towards him, and
pretended to have been drinking.

The moment after Quilt Arnold had bashed in
the door, and entered the room, Barabbas ran to
his side.

He whispered something in Quilt's ear.

"Ha!" cried the thief-taker, "you have the pass-
word right enough; and now I recognise you, you
belong to Wirth Wolfgang's crew."

"Aye," returned the dwarf, in an under tone.
"What's in the wind, my hearty? Surely the
governor has not played us false?"

"False? No! but we are in search of Jack
Sheppard."

"Jack Sheppard?"

"Yes; he is concealed in this room."

"Belay, my hearty. What do you want with him?"

"I have a warrant to apprehend him."

"Then you must give chase at once, for he is gone from hence," returned Barabbas, clapping him on the shoulder; "but first tell me, are you acting under the orders of Mr. Wild?"

"Yes; see, this is his signature. He has commanded us to take Jack Sheppard, dead or alive, and we must obey."

"In that case I will assist you," said Barabbas, with well-affected eagerness; "and mind you let the great man know that we had a share in the capture of the rascal, for there's a heavy reward offered for him I hear."

"But where is he?"

"Not here. He left about ten minutes before your arrival."

"And why the devil did you let him escape?"

"Avast, Master Quilt, how the devil were we to know that the governor wanted him to be taken? I always understood that Jack Sheppard was one of Mr. Wild's lieges, in fact, his right-hand man."

"No; they've quarrelled, and the governor has sworn to hang Jack, and he'll do it, sure as fate."

"Why, dam'me, now, we've lost a good chance of winning the governor's approbation," chuckled the dwarf; "but, come, we must hoist sail, and give chase at once, or it will be too late."

"Which way has he gone?"

"To a caboose near the docks," rejoined the dwarf; "I think they call it the 'Blind Beggar.' Isn't that the sign, Hans Trinkgelt?"

"Yaw, dat is right; de 'Blind Beggars,' yaw, yaw!" grunted the Dutchman.

"This way, then, my hearties," screamed the dwarf, waving his hat. "I'll pilot you safe, never fear, and you may lay your life that Jack Sheppard will sleep to-night in Newgate."

With this he rushed out into the street, closely followed by the officers, as also by a jeering rabble of blackguards, and led them in a direction exactly opposite to that which Jack had taken.

CHAPTER LII.

CAPTURE OF JACK SHEPPARD AND BLUESKIN.

BUT Jack Sheppard was not destined to escape so easily.

He scrambled over the wall, and, reaching the street, ran off at a great rate in the direction of Holborn.

He turned to look if Blueskin were following.

That worthy was descried toiling along in the rear.

He hobbled painfully, and seemed to be suffering from a wound.

"Hulloa, my pal, are you hurt?" asked Jack Sheppard, running to his partner, and supporting him by the arm.

"That cursed dog!" groaned Blueskin. "Just as I was scrambling over the wall, an infernal brute of a mastiff set his fangs in my calf, and dragged me down again."

"What did you do?"

"I drew my chiver across his throat," growled the robber, savagely; "but not before his cursed baying had alarmed the landlord, who, with his ostlers, came rushing after me; however, I let out right and left, and floored my assailants, scrambled over the wall, and here I am."

"We must get back to Hind's," said Jack, moodily. "And yet I am half inclined to give myself up, for I am sick of this cursed life, to be hunted like a beast by these cursed hell-hounds, who thirst for my blood; to be betrayed by my own pals. A nice trick you have played me, Joe."

"Cheer up, captain," cried the elder robber. "I did all for the best. It warn't possible that I could let you go. And pretty Bess, lord love her eyes! she was frantic at the very thought of separation; and arter all, captain, you might have got nailed by the pirates, and been made to walk the plank, or swung off at the yard-arm, not to mention the perils of the winds and the waves. Here you are free, and may queer the nubbing cheat in defiance of fifty Jonathan Wilds."

"That remains to be seen," laughed a deep, ferocious voice, and a powerful man sprang out from the shadow of the wall.

"Talk of the devil, and he's sure to appear," growled Blueskin, pulling out a pistol.

Dashing Sheppard aside, Jonathan Wild sprang upon Blueskin, and felled him to the earth by a blow from his heavy bludgeon.

Jack Sheppard drew his pistols, and aimed them at Wild's head.

"Devil! I have you at last!" he cried, with a shout of triumph. "But this act of cutting off such a monster from the face of the earth—I have more than atoned for my worst crimes."

He drew the trigger.

The pistols flashed in the pan.

He looked in amaze at the weapons.

"The cursed Jew has betrayed me!"

Jonathan Wild laughed fiendishly.

"Is Jack as good as his master now?" he said, drawing an immense horse-pistol from his belt, and clapping the muzzle to Sheppard's head.

"Surrender, Jack," he said. "If you attempt resistance, I will lame you, and you shall go to the gallows on crutches."

Jack growled a terrible oath.

He leaped upon the thief-taker, and hurled him backwards against the wall.

This pistol exploded.

The bullet grazed Jack's cheek.

A terrible struggle ensued.

Although Jonathan Wild was far more powerful than the slim and even delicate-looking youth, who had rendered himself so notorious by his daring and subtlety, the chances were in Jack's favour, for he was as lithe as an eel; but just as, extricating himself from the thief-taker's grasp, he bounded away, his foot caught against the insensible body of Blueskin, and fell prone.

Jonathan Wild instantly pounced upon him, and, setting his foot upon his breast, gave a long low whistle.

A throng of runners came rushing to the spot, and Jack and Blueskin were both secured.

CHAPTER LIII.

THE CAPTURE OF JACK SHEPPARD—THE MOB— THE ATTEMPTED RESCUE — THE MILITARY CALLED OUT—THE FLIGHT AND RE-CAPTURE.

JACK SHEPPARD was hunted, and dragged swiftly along by his exultant captors.

He cast savage glances on either side, and he gnashed his teeth in bitter rage as he beheld the fiendish smile of malice that lit up the villanous face of the treacherous and brutal Wild.

But resistance was hopeless.

His wrists were fast locked in the handcuffs, and

a rope had been passed between his arms, lashing them close to his side.

Quilt Arnold walked on one side, sword in hand, the old Jew on the other, holding a pistol to the prisoner's head.

Jonathan Wild led the van, continually turning round to taunt his victim.

The rear was brought up by a number of well-armed, stern-looking constables.

As for Blueskin, he was a passive object, being still insensible from the blow he had received from Wild's bludgeon.

"You thought you would escape me, eh, Jack?" cried the chief thief-taker, rubbing his hands and leering with spiteful satisfaction. "When did you know me to fail in my purpose? You must be mad. I offered you a chance of reconciliation; you refused it, and it is now too late. I said I would hang you, Jack, and you will find that I will not be worse than my word."

"To catch is not to keep," sneered Jack. "I have escaped you more than once, and what has been done before may be done again."

"Thank ye, Jack, for the timely reminder," returned Wild, in the same sneering vein. "I will take precious good care that you shall be properly accommodated on this occasion. If you escape me this time I will forgive you."

Jack Sheppard laughed scornfully.

"Mark this, you villain, your career of treachery and scoundrelism will not endure much longer; I will discover all your black trickery to the authorities, and though I may not escape the halter, I shall die with the satisfaction that vengeance has overtaken you at last."

Jonathan Wild scowled darkly.

"Dog! do you dare to threaten me?" he growled, grasping his bludgeon.

At this point of their route they came upon a wide and frequented thoroughfare.

The news spread like wildfire that the redoubtable Jack Sheppard, the housebreaker, had been recaptured by the city marshal.

A great mob gathered around the prisoners and their captors.

Some of the bystanders, probably persons who had suffered from the depredations of Sheppard, Blueskin, and their gang, cheered the officers of the law, and congratulated them on having caught the escaped robbers.

Others, principally roughs of the roughest order, cursed and abused the constables, and uttered cries of encouragement and sympathy to the prisoners.

Not a few of the more violent seemed inclined to attempt a rescue.

They hustled the constables, and more than once made a rush, as if to separate them from their prisoners.

The officers, however, stuck staunchly to their duty, and laid about them vigorously with their truncheons and pistol butts.

Jonathan Wild, losing his temper, furiously charged the crowd.

He was greeted by yells, groans, and hisses.

Every moment increased the danger that there would be a general riot.

The counter cheers and abuse of angry men, the shrieks of terrified women, and the not unfrequent smashing of window panes, struck by the stones and other missiles that were flying about like hail, betokened the dangerous mood of the excited mob.

Jack Sheppard's piercing black eyes roamed round on all sides, seeking for a chance of escape.

But Wild, Quilt Arnold, and Mendez took good care not to suffer him to advance or recede a step.

They kept a firm hold of his collar.

Presently, by the pushing of the crowd, Wild and Sheppard were forced to the top of some doorsteps, whence they could be seen by all in the crowd.

Upon their sudden appearance in their elevated position, the turbulent roughs set up a shout of cheering and laughter.

"Hear me, good people," cried the prisoner, in a loud voice. "Listen to the words of a condemned man; hear my true charge against this bloody-minded, treasonous approver by my side—Jonathan Wild!"

"Hear him! hear him! Listen to plummy Jack Sheppard! Hurrah!" shouted the mob.

"Let's rescue him, Bill; he's the kiddiest diver on the pad," growled one ruffian to another.

"Aye, the pink of dimber dambers," laughed his companion. "I should like to knock that old coney-catcher on the sconce. It 'd be a Chris'en deed, Bob. Let's have a shy at it."

"And poor old Joe Blueskin's lumbered, too," cried a little pickpocket, standing on tip toe to overlook the crowd.

"Keep together, pals," growled a savage-looking fellow, who, he might be safely guessed, was by profession a foot-pad or burglar. "Let's get up a rump, and trip the infernal blood-hounds."

The crowd pressed so closely round the officers and their prisoners that there was no possibility of advancing or retreating.

"Hear me, good people; hear me but a few words. I make no attempt to escape; but give me a chance of denouncing the blackest villain that ever battened on a trade in human blood!"

"Silence, dog!" roared Wild.

He upheaved his bludgeon.

It fell with a terrible crash upon the brow of the prisoner.

Jack Sheppard reeled backwards, and fell half-stunned against a door-post.

Recovering his footing, he re-appeared, his pale face streaming with blood.

He held up his fettered hands and glared on Wild with a look of rage and disdain.

"Shame, shame!" cried some milder voices in the crowd.

"Shame to strike the poor lad, who is pinioned and can't defend himself," screamed women's voices.

"A rescue! a rescue!" roared the roughs. "Clubs! clubs! down with the harming beaks!"

A furious rush was now made upon the constables.

The hubbub and uproar were tremendous.

But the indomitable Jonathan, well backed by his satellites, opposed a stout resistance.

Suddenly the shrill fanfarre of a bugle was heard in the distance.

Then came the trampling of horses' feet, and the clanking of sabres.

A sudden cry arose in the crowd.

"The red coats!"

At this alarm, a panic broke out amongst the crowd, who scampered off in all directions.

Drums beating and bugles sounding, a troop of mounted soldiers were now seen filing down the street.

Jonathan Wild, who was panting from his late exertions, and displayed some marks of rough handling—one of his eyes being blackened and his lip gashed by a flint, looked towards the advancing soldiers with a triumphant leer.

"Bring him along, Quilt Arnold," he growled,

triumphantly ; " the devil, himself, shall not snatch him from my hands."

The thief-takers obeyed this mandate, and hauled Jack Sheppard along roughly.

Upon turning the next street, they found that part of the crowd which had been dispersed by the arrival of the soldiers, had re-collected.

This throng of roughs—for it consisted exclusively of thieves, blackguards, and vagrants of the lowest grade—followed the officers and their prisoners in sullen silence.

They seemed to be awed by the nearness of the military, who were slowly parading the streets behind them, and driving off the stragglers.

Suddenly there stepped from the thickest part of the crowd a dashing-looking gentleman, whose distinguished air and fashionable attire stood forth in striking contrast with the rough garb of the other persons in the crowd.

He passed close to Jack Sheppard.

The latter started, winced and turned his head.

He had felt a keen steel edge lancing his arm.

The attention of Jonathan Wild and his assistants had been divided by some obstruction—a passing coach or wain, which had brought them to a halt.

In an instant, however, Sheppard had recognised the man who had pricked his arm with a clasp which he was hurriedly concealing.

They exchanged one significant smile, and the man passed on.

It was Tom King!

Jack Sheppard had not advanced many steps before he felt the rope which had bound his arms slipping loosely round him.

Tom King had severed the cord with his knife.

A moment after, Jack had slipped one of his thin, supple hands through his handcuffs.

He stood unbound, and with his arms at liberty.

"So I have at ye!" he roared.

Leaping on Jonathan Wild, he clutched him by the throat, and bashed his head against the wall.

He then hurled him off.

Jonathan Wild stumbled, and rolled over on his back.

Quilt Arnold and old Mendez immediately sprang upon him.

Hitting out with his left hand, from which the broken handcuff still dangled, he struck Quilt a violent blow on the face, which knocked him heels over head.

Then with his right hand he seized the old Jew by the beard, and having nearly shaken his head off whirled him off and bounded away.

Of course all this passed in much less time than has been occupied in the narration.

Away he darted, the crowd making way for him, and encouraging him by their shouts and laughter.

The fugitive took the middle of the road.

Jonathan Wild and his men had now drawn their whingers.

They cut their way through the yelling, blaspheming, but now shrinking crowd.

At last they had forced their way into the clear part of the road.

Jack was discerned flying along like a hunted hare.

The Bow Street runners hotly pursued.

"Arrest! arrest!" they shouted, breathlessly. "Stop him! stop thief! knock him down! 'tis Jack Sheppard!"

Jack, however, was too fleet for them.

He distanced them, and turning the corner of the street, was too exhausted to proceed without stopping to recover his breath.

Panting and sweltering with perspiration, he leaned against the wall, and pressed his hand to his palpitating heart.

Nearer and nearer came the shouts of his pursuers.

Jack started like a hunted stag at the yelp of the hounds.

He braced his nerves for a fresh start.

He had not run many steps, however, before he was brought to a standstill by a formidable barrier.

It consisted of the levelled carbines of a file of soldiers who suddenly entered the street from a narrow archway.

He turned.

In vain, Jonathan and the rest were close upon him.

"Halt!" shouted an officer. "Surrender! If you stir a step I will order my men to fire upon you."

Jack Sheppard stamped his foot with rage and despair.

He folded his arms, and sullenly submitted to be again handcuffed by the grinning Hebrew.

Jonathan Wild said nothing ; in fact he was too short of breath to speak, but he fixed his eyes upon his now passive captive with the venomous gaze of a rattle-snake.

A file of soldiers on either side, the constables in front and rear, bound and manacled, the unhappy and misguided youth was marched off to a neighbouring round-house, where he was to be confined till the morning, when the warrant could be made out for his re-committal to Newgate.

CHAPTER LIV.

STILL A PRISONER — THE MILITARY ESCORT — THE TAUNTING FRIEND—DESPAIR OF EDGEWORTH BESS—HER ARREST—JACK'S IMPORTANT WAGER—THE ROUND-HOUSE.

JACK SHEPPARD was not destined to reach his prison-house without further adventure. Up Drury Lane, through the rookeries that constitue Seven Dials, the daring felon was conducted by his janitors

St. Giles's Round-House was already in sight. It was at that time, a square building, forming a sort of postern, and situated on one side of St. Giles's churchyard, having the church and churchyard in its rear, with a street in front. As the cavalcade passed along by the railings of the churchyard, a girl of about eighteen darted from the door of a high, dingy, squalid-looking house.

She was exquisitely pretty, and somewhat showily dressed, though her long fair hair was unbound and streamed in heavy tresses.

Upon seeing the prisoner, she uttered a piercing shriek.

Jack repelled her with a cold look.

Again she uttered a piteous scream, and reckless of the danger she ran of being kicked by the startled horses, she rushed through the guards and constables and flung her arms about Sheppard's neck.

"Oh, Jack! Jack!" she sobbed. "What is this? A prisoner, in the hands of this dreadful man? Oh, I will go with you ; I will die with you!"

"Ah, Bess," sighed her lover, "this is your work! But for you, I should now be serving my country and escaping my enemies. You have destroyed me —you, Bess, whom I loved, and for whose sake I have given up home, friends, peace, honesty, and life itself! This is the hardest to bear of all my sorrows and sufferings!"

"Forgive me, dear, dear Jack," sobbed the girl, as she tenderly kissed his pallid cheek. "I did not think of this. I could not bear to be parted from you. Oh, pray forgive me!"

"It is fate!" he sighed deeply. "It is not your fault; kiss me, wench. There, there; don't cry so, you unman me, and this villain exults in my pain. Leave me, Bess—good bye."

But the girl refused to quit her hold of him, and remained with her pretty head bowed on his breast and sobbing in the most heart-breaking manner.

"Why, lass, cheer up, now," said Sheppard, soothingly, "and I'll promise that I'll be with you soon; no prison shall hold me from you; keep up a brave heart, my pretty Bess."

Jonathan Wild, who had looked on with a malignant sneer, now rudely seized the girl by the arm, dragged her off, and shook her roughly.

"Ha, ha! you huzzy! so the decoy has brought you into the trap, ha?" he growled, with a brutal oath. "Come, you must to Bridewell, madam."

Edgeworth Bess clasped her hands and shrieked for mercy.

Jack Sheppard struggled with the constables, who held him back.

His cheeks flamed scarlet, and his eyes blazed with fury.

"Hell-hound!" he gasped; "release the girl, or by all that's holy you shall bitterly rue this day's work."

Jonathan Wild laughed heartily at the impotent wrath of his prisoner.

"And who shall be your dread avenger?" sneered the thief-taker.

"My name-sake—Roving Jack!" cried Sheppard, fiercely. "Aye, you may scoff my prophesy; but I feel within me a firm assurance that you will not survive me many months, and that you will be brought to the halter by Roving Jack!"

"Away with him!" growled Wild. "Quilt Arnold, you must sleep to-night in the round-house. Woe to ye, sirrah, if you do not keep good watch over your prisoner. As for this jade, she shall be carried at once to Bridewell—drag her away."

Edgeworth Bess once more uttered a pealing shriek and threw herself upon her lover's breast.

"Save me, Jack! save me!" she gasped.

Sheppard was silent with rage and despair.

The old Jew, Mendez, and several of the watchmen, dragged her away.

Jack Sheppard was led to the door of the round-house, which was immediately opened by the parish beadle.

Jack Sheppard was passed in, and locked up in a sort of cage at the back of the apartment.

Edgeworth Bess, who was still within a little distance of the round-house, when she saw the door closed upon her unfortunate lover, whom she, herself, had so shamefully betrayed, uttered one piercing scream, and fainted in the arms of the watchmen.

CHAPTER LV.

EDGEWORTH BESS RELEASED FROM THE CONSTABLES BY TOM KING.

"COME, my tear, ton't be sho fiolent," cried old Mendez, winding his arms round the waist of Edgeworth Bess, who recovered her senses after a short time, and struggled hard to get away; "nopody shall hurt youah, my tear, I vill take care of thatsh; put you musht go qvietlish. You know vot ish my ordersh; shtrike me funnish, but it ish not my vault, you know; pe quiet, then, and I vill do vot I can to get you out of your troublesh."

The old Hebrew spoke in fawning tones of endearment, detestable to the hearer.

Bess, finding resistance useless, gave up her attempts at escaping.

Still she sobbed bitterly as she walked on.

Mendez and the watchman still kept hold on her wrists.

The old Jew continued whispering soft things in the distracted ear of the luckless girl.

He pressed her hand, and even attempted to kiss her.

"My tear Edgevorth Bess, you have a friendsh in me ash vill die for you," he murmured with fervour. "Ah! I am not very youngsh, dat ish troo; but vot then? Holy Abramsh! a man ish not old at my age, I vill pe sho kind to yoush."

"Oh! you old monster!" sobbed Bess. "If you are so fond of me, why don't you let me go?"

"O! no!—no!—no!" chuckled Mendez, stroking his red beard and chuckling. "You are a pird too purty to be let out of the cage. I must keep you fast, my dimber dell, and if you don't like me, and vill shtill snub me, and treat me bad, vhy then, my tear, vhot can I do put leave you to your fate, and to the mershy of the law."

"O do pray let me go!" cried Bess, again bursting into a passion of tears.

"No; dat vould never do, my tear. Come along like a good girl, and pe quiet."

"Hulloa, Mister Abraham," cried the watchman, "this arn't the way to talk to sich a baggage as is a disgrace to her seck. Bring her along."

And uttering a savage threat, the watchman dragged her roughly by the arm.

They were now passing through a poor neighbourhood; but at back of the houses, which fronted another street—on one side was a wide open space where some buildings had been pulled down to make way for some new structure—a hospital or a prison—this space was skirted by a long low wall.

As the constables hauled along the sobbing girl, they were suddenly startled by a loud halloo from behind the wall.

They turned to see from whom the cry came.

A dashing fellow, mounted on a splendid white horse, leaped over the wall, and levelling a pistol at the old Jew's head, called out in a voice of thunder,

"Stand, you vagabonds! Release that girl, or I will fire!"

The watchman relinquished his grasp, and crouched trembling against the wall.

Tom King—for it was he—now galloped his horse to the side of Mendez, and seizing the old scamp by the bushy, red beard, hurled him aside.

"Your hand, Bess," he cried. "Spring. So!—so!—now for a rough ride. I am pursued by Wild, Quilt Arnold, and a dozen of the traps. Hold fast, and away!"

He shook the rein.

He dashed down a street.

Windows flew up.

Heads were popped out.

Men and women rushed to the doors.

Passengers halted, and stared at the reckless rider.

Children scattered in all directions to avoid being crushed under the horse's hoofs.

A donkey cart, driven by a loutish costermonger, stopped the way.

Tom King made nothing of this obstacle.

He encouraged his splendid horse by a cheering word, and lightly tapped her glossy flank with the riding whip.

The animal made a bound.

She cleared cart, donkey, and driver, and rattled in at a tremendous rate.

CHAPTER LVI.

A WILD RIDE — THE ROADSIDE INN — BARNEY WARNS TOM KING OF HIS DANGER—EDGEWORTH BESS CONCEALED.

EDGEWORTH BESS felt sick and dizzy.

Houses, shops, vehicles, faces swam past her in a swift, gliding panorama.

They crossed Holborn.

They dashed up Gray's Inn Lane.

They reached the highroad to Islington.

Tom King now slackened his pace.

Reaching the door of an old inn, the highwayman drew rein.

A ostler came rushing out.

The white mare was breathless, she trembled in every limb, and her mouth and neck were flecked with foam.

The ostler took the horse's head.

"Hulloa, Barney, is it you?" asked Tom, with a smile, as he wiped the perspiration from his flushed brow.

"Yes, it's me, captain," returned the fellow, grinning.

"What news?"

"Nothing bad."

"Ha!"

"Why, this is pretty Edgeworth Bess," said Barney.

"Yes; we've had a sharp ride; bring me a tankard of nut-brown."

"Shall I help the lady to dismount?"

"No, no; bring me something to drink; we must be off at once."

"Better not take the girl with you," said the ostler.

"Why not?"

"You'll find her an incumbrance."

"It will not matter, we are not far from Black Mary's, where we can have a rest."

"You'll never reach it, captain."

"Not reach it?"

"No."

"Why not?"

"Because the road is lined with scouts on the look out for you."

"Phew! how do you know that?"

"And, what's more, Black Mary's hovel is garrisoned by a company of the Bow Street runners."

"Is this truth, sirrah?"

"Aye, or I'm a liar."

"How do you know?"

"I saw them start for the hovel; there was Dan Shotbolt the dubsman, and Quilt Arnold."

"Who else?"

"There were four-and-twenty of them in all; they divided into two parties, and took separate ways."

"Did they stop here?"

"Yes."

"How long since?"

"Not half an hour ago.'

"Did they search the house?"

"In every hole and corner."

"And what said Nat Springald, the landlord?"

"He told them you had not been here."

"What did they say to that?"

"They abused him and threatened him in choice Billingsgate."

"Did he hold staunch?"

"No, captain; but I'm your friend."

"Did the villain offer to betray me?"

"Worse."

"Ha!"

"He promised to lay a trap for you."

"The false hound!"

"I thought I'd put you on your guard for old acquaintance sake."

"You're a brave fellow; take this—no, here's one heavier."

And he threw him a purse.

Barney caught it deftly, tossed it to try its weight, and with a radiant grin slipped it into his pocket.

"And where is Nat?"

"Not here, or I should not be talking at my ease, I'll warrant ye."

"Tut, tut, you fool—an answer."

"Well, then, if you must know ——"

"Quick, you blockhead."

"I hardly like to tell ye ——"

"Why not?"

"It might get me into a scrape."

"Swift, you may depend on my discretion."

"I will, captain; only ——"

"Curse you for a fool, speak quickly."

"A still tongue, they say ——"

"Perhaps this will open your lips."

And he tossed the fellow another purse.

"Ha, ha! the oil of palm works wonders," chuckled the ostler; "but I'm running a great risk in giving you this warning, for old Jonathan has vowed black vengeance against any one who shall help you off."

The ostler looked anxiously up and down the road.

"Stay a moment," he said.

He ran into the house.

Tom King waited impatiently for his return.

After a few moments he came back.

"There was an old pedlar here," he whispered, "sitting by the window."

"And what of him?"

"I didn't like the looks of him; he's some spy—some harming cheat, I take it."

"Where is he now?"

"Gone."

"Whither?"

"That's more than I can tell."

"Well, what about Nat Springald?"

"He is gone on to the 'Merry Haymakers.'"

"The devil! I had appointed to meet Dick Turpin there."

"I've made that all right, captain."

"How?"

"I've sent him warning."

"By whom?"

"Oh, a trusty messenger."

"His name?"

"Gregory."

"Ha! one of our gang. Good! you are a trump, Barney. And, now, say where is Wild?"

"Hard behind you, with another squad of the shoulder-clappers."

"Why the devil didn't you tell me that before?"

"You didn't give me time."

"Well, what's to be done?"

"Pretty Bess must dismount."

"But, she will be taken."

"I'll take care for that."

"She must be concealed."

"Yes."

"Here?"

"Where else?"

"But, can I trust you?"

"You needn't unless you please."

"What midsummer madness is this? While we are bandying words the bloodhounds are getting nearer."

"Exactly so."

"Well, what do you say, Bess? Shall I leave you in this fellow's charge?"

"Oh, yes," returned the girl. "Save yourself; you are in worse danger than I am. If this man will hide me away till night I will give him all the money and trinkets I have about me."

"No, no; he is already well paid," returned Tom King.

He sprang off the horse.

He assisted Bess to dismount.

She seemed faint and exhausted.

The highwayman gallantly imprinted a kiss upon her panting lips.

"Never fear, my dimber dell; you will be safe with Barney. But where is the cover in which we must hide away the pretty bird?"

Barney replied to this question by pointing to a hay-loft at the end of the stable-yard.

"Lead on; we'll follow," said the highwayman.

He conducted them to the end of the yard.

The hay-loft stood on one side.

The entrance was in the wall that faced the orchard at the back of the premises.

The door was reached by a ladder.

Tom King gallantly handed the lady up the steps.

He followed.

The place was a spacious loft, containing horse-harness, bundles of hay and straw, and stacks of corn.

"Now," said Barney, dragging along several trusses, "I will make you a snug nest in this corner, where you must lie close till I come to let you out."

He arranged the bundles of hay as a sort of screen, behind which Bess crouched down.

"Old Wild himself will scarcely ferret her out now," chuckled Barney. "But I must take away the ladder."

"Courage, Bess," said Tom King, smiling at her over the heap of hay and straw. "You must not be scared if you hear the tramp of the runners in the yard; the setters will not come here, my pretty partridge."

"No, captain, leave me alone to put them in the wrong track."

"And now we must leave you. Good-bye, dimber Bessie."

"Good-bye, brave Captain King."

The men laughed, and waved their hands to the fair fugitive.

They then descended the ladder.

Barney removed it.

He stowed it away in the coach-house.

They returned to the door of the inn.

Upon seeing her master the beautiful white mare pawed the ground, and whinnied affectionately.

Tom King patted her sleek neck.

"Quick, Barney," said the highwayman. "A handful of oats for Lightfoot, and a tankard of ale for myself."

The ostler soon furnished both.

Tom King took a deep pull.

"Hurrah for the road!" laughed Tom. "Som

times I feel defiant, and care not for the world's scorn and hate."

"Why, captain, I should think so," chuckled the ostler. "I often think of taking to the high pad myself. Who would not be such a spruce highwayman as you are?"

"He who would exchange conditions with me or with any robber in the world must be a fool indeed," sighed Tom. "But avaunt, the blue-devils! I must think of nothing now but how to save my neck."

The ostler fed the mare with a handful of corn, patting her glossy sides, and murmuring his admiration of her beauty.

The highwayman sprang into the saddle.

"Ta—ta, Barney, my buck, I shall not forget this good turn," he said, laughing. "When I make a good purchase you shall go share's in the swag."

"Thanks, captain," returned the fellow.

He finished off the ale, and then turned with a startled air.

"Hark!" he cried, holding up his finger. "The sound of horses' hoofs!"

"Aye, captain, 'tis Wild and his posse."

"They are close behind."

"They have just turned into the lane; they will sight you in a moment."

"I must be off, then, though, dam'me, I should like to have a pop at them."

"For heaven's sake don't let 'em see you, captain; not here, at least," cried the ostler, in great dismay. "They would kill me for this. Off!"

"Good-bye, lad," returned Tom, merrily.

He shook the rein, and galloped off, waving his hat.

"Harkaway, captain," cried Barney, turning his head from side to side, to see if the runners were in sight; he frantically waved his hands, urging the robber to make all speed.

Tom King disappeared round a turning in the road.

Barney drew a deep sigh of relief.

For a moment he stood bewildered.

"Yes: I have it."

With this exclamation, he ran off as hard as he could to meet the officers.

Upon turning a lane he perceived them galloping towards him in a cloud of dust.

CHAPTER LVII.

HOW BARNEY MET WITH HIS MATCH IN JONATHAN WILD—THE FARMER—THE PURSE IDENTIFIED—BARNEY ARRESTED—THE BLOW—THE PURSUIT.

BARNEY'S cap flew off.

Without stopping to pick it up he dashed on.

He stopped in the middle of the road.

"Halt! halt!" he shouted.

Then he leaned against a milestone, as if spent with running.

The next instant Wild and his men surrounded him.

The party consisted of a dozen Bow Street runners, accompanied by a fine, hale, old gentleman, apparently a farmer, who rode a handsome nag with pistols in his holsters.

"I have seen him, gentlemen," panted Barney; "he has just passed."

"Who has passed, fellow?" cried Wild, fixing a nce on the man's face.

"Why, Tom King, sir," returned the ostler, quailing beneath Wild's stern glances.

"Hurrah!" shouted the farmer. "Which road did he take, friend?"

"He went that way, sir," replied Barney, pointing to a road that crossed the lane.

"Then we have missed him,' cried the farmer. "Let us turn our horses, gentlemen, and give him chase."

But Wild remained silent.

He kept his fierce, gray eyes steadily fixed upon Barney.

"He took that road, eh?" he asked, in a ferocious tone.

"A—yes, sir," gasped the ostler.

"And yet you were at your master's house attending to his customers, how could you tell which road he took?"

"Why, sir, if—if you won't frighten me, and browbeat me, I'll explain," mumbled Barney.

"Speak, sirrah!" growled Wild. "If I find that you have played any foul tricks, you shall suffer for it, if there's not another rogue left unhung in England."

"I don't want to deceive ye, Mr. Wild," mumbled Barney. "I'll explain all. He came to the house."

"And why did you not arrest him? Remember, I know well enough that you are acquainted with the villain."

"Yes, sir," returned the ostler, quickly; "I do know him by sight."

"Then why did you not seize him?"

"Seize him? 'Fore heaven, Mr. Wild, how could I do that? The rascal was armed to the teeth, and there was no one at hand to assist me."

"The fellow's story seems probable enough, Mr. Wild," rejoined the farmer. "Surely he can have no motive to wish to screen the scoundrel."

"We will see," said Wild, grimly.

He got off his horse.

"Seize him and search his pockets," said the thief-taker, sternly.

Barney turned pale as death.

He slipped his hands into his pockets, and drew out something, which he attempted to throw away.

He was detected, however.

The officers caught his hands.

They found a purse in each.

Barney trembled violently, uttered a cry of fright, and dropped on his knees.

Wild, with a satanic leer, took one of the purses, and handed it to the farmer.

"Do you identify that article, Mr. Oakley?" asked the thief-taker.

"By George! you were right after all, Mr. Wild," returned the farmer, in surprise; "the scamp must, indeed, be in league with the highwayman, for this is my property. I was stopped last night by a villain on a white horse, masked, and close wrapped in a riding cloak."

"Tom King."

"Yes, I believe so; for, as I hear, he does ride a white horse, and infests this neighbourhood."

"And what else did he take from you?"

"My watch and seals, a silver snuff-box, a brooch and a pocket book containing bank notes to the amount of fifty pounds."

"Hold the dog fast," chuckled Wild, addressing his attendants. "What else have you found upon him?"

"Nothing, Mr. Wild, but this key, a pipe, some beans and a ballad."

"Let me look at the ballad."

The man handed it to his superior.

It was vilely printed, and was entitled, "The Good Man over the Water."

Wild leered.

"A Jacobite doggrel," he said. "Here's a pretty rascal; not content with being in league with robbers, and sharing the gains of felony, he must dabble in high treason."

"I bought the song of an old pedlar, sir, that rested at the tavern," pleaded Barney. "I have not even read it."

"No one can doubt the veracity of such a trustworthy person as yourself, Mr. Barney," returned Wild, sarcastically, as he put the paper into his pocket.

"There was one odd circumstance I forgot to mention in connection with this robbery," continued the farmer; "my sister-in-law and her maid were on the road when I was stopped by this highwayman, they were riding in a chaise about half a mile in advance of me; I afterwards learned that a man, mounted on a white horse, passed them, that he raised his hat, but made no attempt to molest them."

"That confirms the suspicion that attaches to Tom King," said Wild, "for he never robs women; and hence he is known on the road as 'the gentleman's highwayman.'"

"Ha, ha!" laughed the farmer; "well, 'twas a dashing knave, and since I have recovered my property I'll leave it to others to bring him to the gallows—I bear him no further malice."

"Nonsense," returned Wild, sternly; "you have a duty to perform which you owe to society, and I tell you, sir, you must not shirk it; besides, you are subpœnaed, and bound to prosecute."

"In that case, for heaven's sake let us lose no time in apprehending the villain,' said the farmer, "for I am unwilling to lose more time than is needful in the case."

"Be patient, sir," returned Wild, "the villain shall be lodged in gaol before morning."

"Let us push on then," said the farmer.

"As for this fellow," continued the thief-taker, grinning maliciously, "he is, upon evidence, an accomplice of the thief, and must take the consequence."

"No, no, Mr. Wild," cried Barney, in great trepidation, "I can swear ——"

"Anything to save your own neck from the halter, sirrah."

"Hear me, Mr. Wild," cried Barney, clutching his arm, frantic with terror, "I will lead you to a spot where you can take the robber."

"We do not require your assistance," returned the thief-taker; "my plans are so well laid that I have no doubt he is already in custody."

"Do but hearken, sir; don't be too hard upon a poor lad," urged Barney; "he offered me the money just to bait his horse and supply him with a glass of ale. I had no hand in the robbery, knew nothing of it—it was a sore temptation. I assure you I had no intention to defeat the ends of justice."

"Liar!" savagely growled the thief-taker.

With the loaded butt of his heavy riding-whip he stretched Barney senseless at his feet.

"Mr. Wild, this is needless violence," exclaimed the farmer, with great indignation.

"Violence be ——," growled Wild, brutally; "you don't know these fellows, sir."

He remounted his horse.

"Here, Barnesdale," he cried, to one of the men.

"Yes, sir."

"Clap the darbies on this rascal, and, with Thrapstone there, carry him to the tavern and hold him in charge till we return with the other prisoner."

"Very good, Mr. Wild."

"And now to horse, the rest of you."

"Which road shall we take?" asked the farmer.

"There is a short cut across the fields," returned Wild. "You are a hunter, sir, and well mounted, and will not mind a little rough riding."

"I shall enjoy it," returned the farmer.

Barney was handcuffed, thrown across the back of the horse, which was led off to the tavern.

"You mustn't be too hard upon that poor devil," said the farmer, pointing after the ostler with his whip; "we are all liable to temptation, and it could hardly be expected that the poor rogue should refuse a purse of gold to be earned on such easy terms."

"Mind your own business, sir, and I will attend to mine," replied the thief-taker, roughly.

The farmer coloured with anger.

"Zounds! sir!" he cried, testily. "You may be a good officer; but I must tell you that I think you a confounded unmannerly fellow."

"How so? The scoundrel has forfeited his life to the law, of which I am the servant," returned the thief-taker, sternly. "He shall swing, if there's not another rogue left unhung in England."

Then he turned to his followers.

"Are you all ready for the start?"

"Yes, sir," responded the men, respectfully.

"Then forward, gentlemen," returned the thief-taker, cracking his whip.

The horses gallantly leaped the fence, and the next moment were skimming like swallows across the broad fallow land.

CHAPTER LVIII.

THE PURSUIT — TOM KING GIVES WAY TO REMORSE.

TOM KING, meanwhile, had galloped his horse to a turning in the road where there was a high bank, thickset with trees, and surmounted by a tall hedgerow.

Here he dismounted.

He tethered the horse to the branch of a tree.

Then he took a pistol from each holster, and thrust them into his belt.

He took off his laced hat lest the glitter of its gilt brocade should betray him.

He clambered up the bank.

Screened from the road by the trees, he crouched down.

His post being elevated above the surrounding country, which consisted of flat fields and meadows, he peered through the bush.

His view ranging across the wide field, he could see all that was passing in the lane on the other side of it.

"Will the dog betray me?" he muttered, as Barney stopped the pursuers. "If so, what will become of pretty Bess? I was a fool to trust him."

In a state of great excitement, he watched what followed.

"Humph! that's the farmer I stopped last night," he thought. "The chase will be a hot one."

He saw Wild and some others dismount.

He breathed a curse as he noted the ostler's eager gestures.

But seeing that the man was pointing in an opposite direction to that which he had taken, he felt re-assured.

"Ha! then he's jannock, after all!" he exclaimed.

Then he saw the man seized by the officers.

He breathed hard with excitement.

The purses were produced.

"The game's up!" muttered the highwayman. "That fellow is true steel to the backbone. I wish I had Dick here, and but a couple of the others, and we fain would wrest him from the bloodhounds; and yet that Turpin is such a graceless brute that I don't believe he'd stir a finger to serve his best friend in distress."

Wild's furious gesticulations now commanded his attention.

"That villain!" he hissed, boiling with rage, "that devil, who buys his victims body and soul only to bring them to destruction! Ha! if he were within pistol shot, dam'me, I think I'd have a crack at him now."

So saying, he took aim through the bushes.

Then, as if convinced of the utter futility of attempting to reach his mark from such a distance, he lowered the weapon.

"Pshaw! it's no use," he cried, impatiently; "it would only make matters worse for the poor beggar Barney, and Bess, too. I fear it will go hard with her."

At this moment Wild felled the ostler to the ground.

"Phew! It's getting too hot for me," thought Tom: "I must put Lightfoot on her mettle."

He descended the bank.

He untethered his horse from the tree.

Mounting, he shook the rein, and dashed away.

He cast a hurried glance behind him.

The road was clear.

Drawing the rein, he allowed his horse to fall into a quick trot.

SIMON SMUT AT THE MAST-HEAD.

The landscape swam around him, in all its moonlit beauty of hill and vale.

Dark woods slumbered on the hills' sides; clear, bubbling streams leapt along in the moonshine; the golden corn waved in the fresh night breeze; the interlacing branches of trees whispered over his head.

The sylvan scene was calm and restful.

The road was lonely; but the solitude was peace, it was the loneliness of the "pathless woods," where man communes humbly with his Maker, and drinks in deeply the strong life of nature and repose—the peace so cruelly contrasted by the deadly apathy of sleeping, fever-dreamed cities, where crowded men pass away a trance-like interval between successive days of toil and sorrow.

There were the stithy, ear-piercing sounds of night, the boom of the flying beetle, the chirrup of the grasshopper revelling in the wet sward, the hoot of the owl in the woods.

Tom King looked upwards.

Over his head the glorious host of stars spangled forth in unclouded splendour.

The moon sailed along through the deep blue ocean of space, silvering the fleecy clouds and bathing the still landscape with her bright, cold beams.

Tom King, delighted by the quiet beauty of the

scene, walked his horse gently down a fairy glen, and looked about him with a sense of calm enjoyment.

But this peaceful feeling did not last long.

Soon the furies of remorse roused from their slumber and tore his heart.

He sighed, and then, as if to drive away care, he began to sing some wild highwayman's song.

He had a remarkably fine voice, and the dim words echoed back its notes right merrily.

After awhile he changed the tune to a soft and tender melody—he gasped and bit his lip till it bled.

"Agnes!" he muttered, hoarsely. "But why should I think of her? Oh, I have been a miserable wretch! I might have laughed at the scorn of those who spurned me in my ruin, poor gnats of an hour's sunshine! I might have died! But now it is too late; to the last day I shall be branded as a common thief, a highway robber!"

Lashed by the raging demons in his heart, he urged on his gallant horse.

He muttered fiercely, and shook his fist as at some imaginary foe.

Then again he drew the rein.

"Pah! I am mad!" he cried, in a harsh voice. "'What's done cannot be undone.' No. 'Consider it not so deeply.' I will not. Damn the world and all its belongings! Hurrah for the road!"

Tom King's despair found utterance in speech.

He almost shouted in his vehemence.

But conscious Nature alone heard the bitter, despairing cry of his heart.

"Why did I not turn soldier?" he muttered. "Good sooth, I am no coward; I am reckless of danger from my boyhood upwards. I am no mongrel-bred ruff, but descended of an honourable family; and, zounds, was there nothing for it but to turn thief?"

He groaned.

After a time he resumed his soliloquy in a musing tone.

"I wonder, now, with such thoughts and convictions, I can lead the life I do. But, there! hunger is a cruel tyrant, passion a seductive mistress, and man is a chameleon that takes the colour of the objects that he cleaves to. Out of my brain, maddening thoughts! leave me at peace for one hour."

Tom King spurred his horse savagely.

Then, relenting of such thoughtless cruelty, as the galled beast curvetted and dashed desperately onwards, he stroked her mane, with murmured caresses.

Faint and afar, wafted by the night wind, the sound of horses' hoofs was borne to his ear.

He caught the sound.

His thought was of Jonathan Wild.

Fury raged in his bosom.

"That infernal cacodemon shall not take me!" he exclaimed, aloud, clutching his pistol-butts. "If I could kill him I should be satisfied."

He drew rein, and listened.

The trampling of hoofs was now plainly heard, and the sound came louder and nearer.

"I will hide behind the trees and fire on him as he passes!"

The daring fellow had almost determined to carry out this purpose.

At imminent risk of being recaptured he slackened his pace.

Louder and louder sounded the trampling of the hoofs.

Shouts were borne faintly through the wood.

"I might fail," thought the highwayman. "I will take some other opportunity of glutting my vengeance."

He shook the rein and urged the mare to the top of her speed.

The aspect of the country now changed. A long range of wooded hills skirted the horizon, from which lower elevations spread out in all directions.

The road through the forest was, for the distance of nearly a mile, as straight and clear as a park avenue.

And, worse than all, a steep hill was before him.

But recklessly he plunged forward, and bravely his gallant courser breasted the steep ascent.

CHAPTER LIX.

THE FRUITLESS PURSUIT OF TOM KING.

STRAINING every muscle, the highwayman's gallant steed went toiling up the slope.

"Tallyho! yoicks! tallyho!"

The shout, as of a fox-hunter cheering the hounds, caused Tom King to turn in the saddle.

He beheld his pursuers sweeping along in a cloud far down in the vale below, and then pass up the side of the hill.

"Dam'me," laughed Tom King, "there is almost as much fun and excitement in being hunted as in hunting. I'll warrant now, a cunning old fox when he bilks the whole pack feels a pleasure that almost repays him for the peril."

"Yoicks! There he is! Hold on you vagabond!" roared the hearty farmer, waving his whip. "Harkaway, you dog! we'll overtake ye."

"Tally—ho—ho!" responded Tom, at the top of his voice. "Harkaway, harkaway! Come on, you snail-footed laggards. Come on, you draymen—ha! ha!"

And off he swept through the whistling wind as swift as a carrier pigeon.

Over the brow of the hill.

Down, right down at a fearful pace he rushes.

Still maintaining the same headlong pace he rattles along the road, level in this part for about a mile.

Again he casts a look behind him.

The old fox-hunter, outstripping the rest, comes bounding down the hill-side, making the old woods ring with his cheery shout.

Then one by one the other riders come bobbing over the summit of the hill.

The road winds.

"Forward, forward, my bonnie lass!" cries Tom, patting his noble steed. "Harkaway, my beauty! if I can but find some by-road or bridle-path we'll soon give these yelping ban-dogs the go-by."

"A highwayman! a highwayman! Stop thief! Stop him!" roared the pursuers.

Off flies Lightfoot like a speeding arrow.

Soon she has distanced her pursuers.

The shouts come fitfully, but even more faintly, in the breeze.

The man-hunters are lost to view by reason of the windings of the road and the intricacies of the forest.

Tom King looks on either hand.

On each side, the road is walled by steep, high banks.

Tom King has some thoughts of plunging into the wood.

But the trees are so thickly set, and their trunks

so intermingled with brush and furze, that progress would be rendered impossible.

Still the gallant and enduring animal, though hard-breathed, and lathered with foam, bears on her course.

At some distance ahead, two rugged lanes branch out of the road.

Tom King spurs hard to reach one of them.

Which shall he take, the right or the left?

There is not much time allowed him for deliberation.

He plunges up the narrow pathway on his left.

He turns and leaps his horse over a high thicket.

" Down, lass, down," he murmurs.

The sagacious animal crouches on her knees.

Tom King takes off his hat.

He flings his black, scarlet-lined riding cloak over his gaudy dress, completely concealing himself, and bends low down in the saddle.

He peers through the bushes.

Nearer come the shouts and the loud rattle of hoofs.

At last a voice shouts,

" Halt !"

It was the stern voice of the thief-taker which uttered this mandate.

The fugitive can hear the hard breathing of the half-exhausted riders, and the panting of their horses.

" We are at fault," said the farmer.

" He must have taken one of these roads," rejoined a constable.

" Aye, but which ?" said the farmer.

" This one to the left," returned the man. " Here are fresh hoof-prints in the mire."

" Well, friend ; but I should think the rogue knows the country too well for that," returned the farmer. " This lane leads only to the premises of a farm-house."

" Is that so ?" asked Wild.

" Yes. Don't you see the smoke from the chimneys, Mr. Wild ?"

" Yes, but we lose time."

" What do you propose, then ?"

" We will divide into three parties," rejoined the thief-taker. " You, Mr. Oakley, shall take the lane to the right, accompanied by six men ; I, with three others, will ride up this bridle-path ; Barnesdale, and the remaining two, shall sentinel the road, in case the rogue should emerge from any opening in the woods."

" A capital arrangement," said the farmer. " But we may lose each other."

" To prevent that," said Wild, " it must be arranged that whichever of the three party shall first sight the vagabond, shall fire one shot as a signal for the others to join them ; if they secure him let two shots be fired."

" A good plan."

" And now, gentlemen, let us separate. Barnesdale, keep a sharp watch along the road in each direction. Now, Mr. Oakley, you that way, me this."

" Bravo !" laughed the farmer. " And I'll lay ten guineas to one that I shall be the first to capture the dog. Is it a wager ?"

" Done !" said Wild. " Ride hard, gentlemen."

They parted.

Tom King kept well concealed by the bushes.

His inclination to try one shot at his ancient enemy was so great that he had much ado to curb his impatience.

Grasping their long, heavy pistols in their hands,

Jonathan Wild and his two satellites rode up the lane.

They carefully scanned the bushes on either side.

They passed.

A turning in the lane concealed them from view.

Tom King spoke to his horse, and patted her neck.

She rose on her legs.

The highwayman was about to leap her over the hedge.

He changed his thought instantly.

The road was watched by sentinels !

Again he caused the sagacious animal to crouch down.

He listened eagerly.

He could hear the watchers in the road shouting to each other.

" Zounds ! look yonder, Barnesdale," cried one of them, laughing, " that farmer is a rare old buck. See, he is riding a race with the others, and has gained a couple of lengths of them."

" Ha ! ha ! the old cove rides well," rejoined the other. " Now they're on his flanks—now he's away ! Egad ! sir, he's well mounted."

" See ! they reach the other road."

" Perhaps they sight the chase."

" No ; or they would fire a shot."

" Look ! look !' cried his companion, excited. " The farmer has well nigh knocked down that old clodhopper."

" Ha ! ha ! ha !"

" Silence ! while we are watching that old fool we are not keeping a proper look-out in the road."

" If Jonathan Wild misses his man, he'll raise the devil with his storming."

The men separated.

At this moment from the far end of the lane in which he was hiding, Tom King heard the baying of dogs, and the clanking of a gate closing to.

Then came the rapid patter of hoofs.

Jonathan Wild and his party growled their disappointment at having failed in their purpose.

They stopped their horses just by the spot where the highwayman lay concealed.

An old countryman came limping into the lane.

" Ho ! there ! you fellow !" shouted Jonathan Wild.

" At yer honour's sarvice, zur," returned the countryman, a little taken aback at this rough salute.

He took off his hat, and stared stupidly at the thief-taker.

" Have you met a party of horsemen riding at full speed ?" asked Wild.

" Aye, zure I has, yer honour," returned the countryman. " They be purzuin' of a gemman as were ridin' like mad."

" The scoundrels !" roared Jonathan. " Have they dared to disobey me ? I commanded them to fire a shot when they sighted the thief."

" It's Mr. Oakley's doings, sir," rejoined one of the men. " He is bound to win his wager."

" Curse his impudence and interference !" growled the thief-taker.

Then again he addressed the countryman.

" Was the man they were pursuing much in advance of them."

" Gad zo, zur ; he were indeed, and ridin' az the devil were behind him, as by token he nearly knocked I into the ditch."

" Which way have they gone ?"

"Down the lane, zur, into the Glenthorpe road."

" Forward !" shouted Jonathan.

Away they dashed.

The old countryman toddled up the lane towards the farm-house.

" Barnesdale, there !" shouted Jonathan, when he and the rest had reached the road. " Tom King has taken the other way, and that cursed Oakley and his party are in full cry. Spur hard for your lives !"

" Aye, aye, Mr. Wild," laughed Barnesdale. " Let's be in at the death for the credit of our office. Harkaway !"

The sound of their horses' hoofs was heard receding.

" Ha ! ha ! ha !" laughed the highwayman, " I begin to have faith in the gipsy dell's palmestry. I was *not* born to be hanged. Why, it was the farmer himself—my purchase—that they were pursuing. Now, dam'me, this beats cockfighting !"

He once more leaped his horse over the bush.

The next moment he was scouring along the road.

The morning broke.

Grey streaks illumined the east, and the stars faded out.

Tom King's noble horse began to show tokens of her exhaustion.

She hung her head and travelled painfully.

The highwayman cast a rapid glance around him.

He saw no signs of pursuit.

He therefore entered a little coppice by the road-side, and flinging himself from the saddle, unbitted the horse, and suffered it to graze and rest itself.

The sun had now risen, and the birds welcomed the returning day with loud and jubilant song.

The highwayman, reckless of danger and out-worn by fatigue, threw himself down upon a ferny bank, and fell into a profound slumber.

CHAPTER LX.

THE GIPSY GIRL WARNS TOM KING TO FLY—THE CHASE RESUMED WITHOUT SUCCESS.

TOM KING had slept he knew not how long, for he was quite outworn with weariness.

He started from his sleep roused by the pressure of a soft hand on his shoulder.

A gipsy girl, dark-skinned, but beautiful in form and feature, crouched beside him.

She clutched her red cloak about her, and pressed her finger on her lip.

" Hush !" she said, in an eager whisper. " The bloodhounds are on your track !"

" What, you, Jael, my dimber Roumany mort !" laughed the highwayman, catching her by the hand and passing his arm around her waist. " Now, by the light of those lustrous orbs, thine eyes, I care not if all the hosts of the Philistines be upon me, so I can enjoy the bliss of your presence for five minutes ! Sit down, my peerless Egyptian ; there'll be time to run when the pack is in full cry."

The gipsy girl smiled, blushed, and struggled to disengage herself from his embrace.

" You are mad !" she exclaimed.

" Ha, ha ! Why should I fear, my fair sybil ? Have you not prophesied that I shall not make my exit from this world in the manner so customary among the spruce gentlemen of my honourable order ? I lead a charmed life ; why should I now ' despair my charm ?' "

" Nay, then," said the girl, rising, and tearing herself away from his embrace, " since you mock me for my pains, I will leave you to your fate."

" Well, but what's amiss ?"

" Wild and his men are on your track."

" Is that all ? They have hunted me since yesterday morning," returned the highwayman, laughing.

" But they are here !" cried the gipsy girl, eagerly. " They have entered the wood, and, unless you mount and fly at once, you will be taken."

" Let them come," rejoined King, moodily, folding his arms and re-seating himself on the bank. " Why should I try to escape my deserved fate ? If any other but that infernal Wild were the leader of my pursuers, I think I should give myself up in the despair of my heart. Oh, bitter folly ! Yet who was so gay, so kindly disposed, as Tom King ? I tell ye, Jael, that I don't care one jot for the wrong I have done the world, against which I am justly embittered—at least, I mean *my* world. But what galls me is, that I cannot respect myself ; and by rushing to a sudden and violent death I cannot retrieve the past !"

" But you can by living an honest and a brave life !" returned the gipsy girl, with fervour.

" Too late," returned the robber, shaking his head. " If it had not been for that cursed affair of Kate Dulcimer, I might now be serving honourably under the flag of Roving Jack."

The trampling of horses' hoofs was now heard ringing through the bowery glades of the forest.

" Fly !" cried Jael, clasping her hands.

The highwayman's face darkened with ferocity.

" The cursed ban-dogs !" he growled. " I will turn at bay, and let that infernal thief-taker look to himself !"

As he spoke he drew his pistols and cocked them.

" No, no, Tom !" cried the gipsy girl, imploringly. " Save yourself, for my sake, Tom."

Tom King looked at her gloomily.

" And, if I were dead, Jael, is there one who would regret me ?"

The girl threw her arms about him, and sobbed on his breast.

" I should kill myself," she murmured. " You have been so kind to me. When I was poor and friendless you lent me a helping hand, and you have always been so honourable. Oh, there is yet time to make amends for the past. You can flee this country ; I will go with you ; I will be your slave. But do not linger a moment—away !"

Tom kissed her tenderly.

" For your sake, then," he said, with a smile, " I will mount and ride to Tottenham, where I shall meet Dick Turpin."

" Oh, avoid that ruffian," she exclaimed, vehemently. " He will be your ruin—he will be the cause of your death. I have read the lines in his palm, and I foresee that he is destined to kill his best friend ; and I read in yours that——"

Tom King interrupted with a light laugh.

" ' How shall my reckless life have end ?'
' You shall die by the hand of a trusty friend,'
Quoth she—quoth she."

" Let me kiss you for that prophecy, my dimber lass."

" But, hark !" cried the girl, holding up her finger.

" Hark, hark ! the watch-dogs bark !"

laughed Tom King

He once more pressed the blushing girl to his heart.

Then he remounted.

"Farewell, my peerless Egyptian," he laughed, as he gallantly waved his laced hat. "They must ride swift to overtake me."

"Away! away!" cried the girl.

At this moment a throng of the Bow Street runners burst forth from the wood, and came rushing towards the spot where the highwayman still lingered.

Jonathan Wild and the farmer were the leaders of this party.

"Give me law!" shouted Tom King. "A start of a dozen lengths, and then catch me who can!"

The farmer laughed.

Jonathan Wild thundered an oath, and fired a shot at the desperate outlaw.

Jael screamed.

"Off, my lass," cried Tom to the gipsy girl. "These villains may illtreat you."

"No, that they shan't," cried the farmer. "Off, you vagabond; we'll ride you down before you get out of the forest."

"Don't halloo till you're out of the wood!" laughed Tom. "Come on, you sluggards! Tally ho!"

And away he rushed at a reckless pace.

Enraged at having missed his aim, Jonathan Wild dashed his pistol to the earth.

He spurred on.

As he passed Jael he lashed viciously at her with his whip.

She cowered down, however, and avoided the blow.

Away flew Lightfoot, now refreshed and full of mettle.

Away sped the others in hot chase.

The farmer, the best mounted of the party, forged ahead.

The farmer drew a pistol from his holster.

Still he seemed loth to fire.

Tom King, who had turned in the saddle, and had also drawn a pistol, perceived this.

He replaced the weapon.

He laughed, and, waving his hat, cheered the old hunter.

Still onwards he sped.

The boughs rustled past.

The farmer kept close on his flanks.

Soon he was close alongside.

"You have a pocket-book of mine," panted the farmer, "containing notes for fifty pounds. Yield it up, you dog!"

"I will to you," laughed Tom King, throwing the book on the ground. "Pick it up."

"I'll see you hanged first!" roared the farmer, dashing on to the chase, regardless of all but overtaking his man.

Jonathan Wild was third in the race.

For many yards the old farmer and the highwayman rode side by side.

Oakley attempted to catch the robber's rein.

Tom King clubbed his pistol.

"Hold off!" he shouted. "I don't want to harm you."

Lightfoot sprang desperately onwards.

The farmer's noble horse began to show signs of exhaustion.

Tom King had now a fair lead.

Away and away he darted, leaping over every obstacle that impeded his rush.

Over meadow, through copse, and along the rustling corn-crofts, the hunted and the hunters swept madly on.

Tom King led them a wild chase.

He leaped hedge, ditch, and brook.

At some distance from the wood there was a village, through which the road passed, and the highwayman galloped towards it.

As he passed under the banks on either side the road, a shout was heard, and a number of men were seen running along beneath the trees.

They consisted of country labourers and Quilt Arnold's party of Bow Street runners.

Tom King entered the village.

He dashed up the main street.

A party of tipplers gathered at the door of the principal inn, laughed and cheered the dashing-looking fellow as he flew past the porch.

There was a little bridge that crossed the brook, and over it Tom rattled at a furious gallop.

Beyond was an orchard, through which the Bow Street runners were hurrying, shaking the fruit-laden boughs as they rushed under them, and bringing the ripe apples hailing down.

Quilt Arnold clambered over the wall, and discharged his carbine at the highwayman.

The bullet passed through his flowing hair.

At the same moment, Tom King being close-pressed by Barnesdale, turned and fired at him.

The officer was hit in the shoulder.

He uttered a dismal yell, tossed up his arms, and rolled out of the saddle.

Infuriated by the injury done to their comrade, the runners growled fierce oaths, fired their pistols in a volley, and spurred hard to overtake the fugitive.

But Lightfoot bore on gallantly.

The old farmer, whose face looked as red as the sun through a November fog, kept up a desperate pace.

Tom King, however, gained ground slowly and surely, and about noon had left his pursuers far behind him.

He turned into a narrow, rugged lane, and followed its windings till he reached a lonely dingle.

Here he drew rein.

His horse panted and quivered, hung her beautiful head, and showed every sign of extreme distress.

The highwayman dismounted.

For an instant he stood hat in hand, a triumphant smile lighting up his manly face, inwardly chuckling over his escape.

Then he turned his glance upon his splendid courser, which had borne him so bravely through the perilous day.

He patted her neck, and spoke soothingly to her.

She leaned her head on his shoulder, and caressed his cheek.

Tom King led her into the bush.

She walked very lamely.

Not many steps had she proceeded before she staggered, and, sinking on the earth, stretched her fine but strong limbs, threw back her moulded neck, and panted with exhaustion.

Tom looked at her with pride and affection.

He left her.

Wearily retracing his steps, for he was stiff and tired after his long and furious ride, Tom came to a stile half way down the lane.

He clambered over it, and, crossing a meadow, entered a corn field, and filled his pockets with grain.

Returning to the side of his exhausted steed, he fed her with the corn.

The beautiful creature turned her eloquent eyes

upon her master with a look of fondness, and nibbled the grain from his hand, though, seemingly, rather to please him than to satisfy herself, for she was too much exhausted to care for food.

Tom King rose, and, clasping his hands behind him, paced moodily about, absorbed in his bitter reflections.

All at once he started with a feeling of strange foreboding—a sense of the presence of something evil—an impulse which madly urged him to flight.

He turned.

A man emerged from the trees.

Tom clapped his hand on his sword.

"Why, Tom, don't you know me, my hero?" laughed a gruff voice.

"What, Dick?" cried the highwayman, with a smile.

"Aye, comrade," returned Turpin, for it was he. "Ha, ha, ha! You rode at a spanking pace through the village. I was at the window of the 'Seven Bells' when you passed. You have winged old Barnesdale; I helped to carry him into the inn."

"The devil you did!"

"Aye, for I had pulled a butcher's smock over my riding-coat."

"But where was Jonathan?"

"He roared like a mad bull, called for another horse, and started alone in pursuit of you."

"Is he on the track?" asked Tom, quickly.

"No, worse luck," growled Turpin. "But I have laid an ambush for him."

"Bravo!"

"That's a glorious mare of yours, Tom," laughed Turpin. "I will make a match with you if you like."

"Done! What's the odds?"

"Well, I'll lay six to one on Black Bess."

"And will lose," returned Tom.

"That remains to be seen," returned Dick. "But come, Tom, Bush and Fielder are bivouacking in the forest with some of the Roumanies of Red Ishmael's gang. Shall we join them?"

"Aye, comrade," returned Tom; "my rough ride has sharpened my appetite, and I am tired out. Let us be going."

CHAPTER LXI.

JACK SHEPPARD AND BLUESKIN ESCAPE FROM THE ROUND-HOUSE.

JACK SHEPPARD and Blueskin were confined in separate but adjoining cells.

The elder robber was recovering from his state of insensibility when borne into the round-house.

He breathed deeply, and, by the orders of Jonathan Wild, drops of strong spirits had been poured upon his lips.

He was locked in the cage or cell.

For some time during his imprisonment, Jack Sheppard kept huddled in a heap, with his arms folded, a prey to remorse and despair.

At length he roused himself.

His first thought was of escape.

His hands were fettered, and his feet shackled.

He felt in his breast.

A knife was cunningly concealed under his waistcoat.

This he drew forth.

With it he set to work, and, after some labour, contrived to remove his handcuffs.

He crawled to the wall.

He knocked softly.

"Joe!"

No answer.

"Hulloa! what are you calling for, young gallows-bird?" shouted the rough voice of the beadle.

"All right, old covey," laughed Sheppard, "I was only talking in my sleep."

"You'd better sleep without talking, my nab," growled the beadle, "or I'll spoil your dreams, I'll warrant ye."

Jack Sheppard made some jeering reply.

Then he abandoned himself to despondency.

The chamber, at the back of which the cages or cells were built, was crowded by a large posse of constables and watchmen.

At length, Jack's impatience of restraint overmastered every other feeling.

Once more he crawled to the side of his cage, and gave a tap, at the same time singing at the top of his voice some flash song.

He listened attentively.

After a moment he was rewarded by hearing a sort of grunt, and a gruff voice growled,

"I'm fly, captain."

"All's bowman, Joe," whispered Sheppard. "We'll give the dubsman leg-bail. I have escaped from St. Giles's round-house once before, and it shall go hard but I'll do the trick again."

"Bravo, captain!" returned Sheppard.

"Have you slipped the darbies?"

"Yes; are you in ruffles?"

"Rather," returned Blueskin, dolefully clanking his chain; "but hist!"

The beadle came to the door of the cells, opened the gratings, and peeped in.

Jack Sheppard immediately clapped his hands together, leading the gaoler to suppose that he was yet handcuffed.

The man then turned away.

Then the sounds of clinking cans, and the drawing up of chairs to a table was heard by the prisoners.

"Let's have a game at all fours, Mr. Guffin," said Shotbolt, the gaoler, addressing the beadle.

"Aye, we can make up a hand. There's you and I and Mr. Snatcher, and we can play dummy."

"No, there's no need to do that," said another voice, "I'll play with you."

"Ha! that's well said," returned the beadle. "Mr. Wild's man, Mr. Marks, gentlemen," he continued, introducing the speaker to the rest of the company, "a worthy and responsible man."

"Come, sit down, then, and let us pitch for partners."

Jack Sheppard had not been idle during this conversation.

He had employed himself in working with his knife at the lock of his shackles.

He contrived to disengage one leg.

Not, however, without hurting himself very much.

He took off his neckerchief.

He bound his fetters close to his legs.

"Mark ho!" he whispered.

"I'm down," returned Blueskin.

"Listen, Joe."

"With all my ears, captain."

"Here's a crack in the wooden partition."

"Yes; have you a file, my pal?"

"No, worse luck; there were three in the padding of my best coat, but I swopped that with the infernal old peach of a Jew."

"That's bad."

"But here's a knife."

"Hey! push it through the crevice, my pal."

Jack Sheppard complied with this request.

"And now, Joe, let's get up a roaring stave to drown the noise."

"I twig; strike up, my noble."

And blending their voices, and shouting with all their power of lungs, the two robbers bawled out the following delectable ballad:—

> "Of Robin Hood, that outlaw good,
> Our forest songs may tell;
> A gentle thief, he once was chief,
> And bore from all the bell.
> While Gilderoy was Scotland's joy;
> But all must yield, I ween, the field
> To gallant Claude Duval."

"Silence, you noisy scoundrels!" roared the beadle, thumping at the doors of the cells.

"All right, governor," laughed Jack; "you are enjoying yourselves, why shouldn't we?"

"Why not, dam'me," responded Blueskin; "never mind old St. Giles. Pipe up, lad! Chorus, my plummy Jack!

> "Oh, rare Duval! Oh, bold Duval!
> To rifle was his plan;
> Both young and old, of love and gold—
> The ladies' highwayman."

"Ha, ha, ha!"

"Silence, you villains! Have you no respect for my place?" spluttered the beadle, in great wrath.

The robbers replied only by a burst of derisive laughter, and continued roaring at the top of their voices all manner of doggrel snatches:

> "The round-house, the round-house,
> The jolly St. Giles's round-house."

Seeing that remonstrance was useless the beadle uttered a tremendous volley of abuse and condign threats, and returned to the card-table.

Meanwhile, Jack had whispered to Blueskin to return him the clasp-knife.

That ruffian obeyed and passed it back through the crevice.

Jack then mounted a stool.

He set to work at the ceiling.

He placed his mattress beneath to receive without noise whatever fell.

Soon he had removed sufficient lath and plaster to lay bare a large patch of the beams and flooring above.

Blueskin seconded his confederate's exertions by dancing about his cell, clanking his fetters, and yelling like a red Indian.

Jack had now succeeded in making an opening in the floor above.

He clambered up into the top room.

The round-house consisted of two stories.

The room into which Jack had thus forced an entrance was a square chamber.

The light was admitted through a small loop-hole, with an iron grating not large enough to admit of any one forcing their bodies through it.

The only furniture in the room was an old feather-bed, with a dirty blanket on a crazy truckle, and a high-backed, leather-bottomed chair, in which there was a jug with some water.

Jack Sheppard had now cast off his hopelessness, and was now all animation, all buoyancy, and braced his mind to a desperate attempt to escape with his partner.

His energies, his senses all hurried to his aid.

One eagle glance below, above, around the room, and his resolution was taken—his plan was laid.

It would have been easy for him to have removed a plank of the flooring, and penetrated through the ceiling to Blueskin's cell below.

But for some time he was almost afraid to venture such a bold stroke.

However, Blueskin kept up the same racket as before, dancing about in his clanking fetters, and taunting Sheppard with being chicken-hearted, and calling upon him to join chorus in his ribald songs.

The goalers and the watchmen were not very orderly in their conduct, for they added to the noise by their loud recriminations as they brawled over their cards.

This determined Jack to venture boldly.

He soon had torn up a couple of planks.

He thrust his head through the aperture.

He whispered a few hurried words to Blueskin.

"All's bob, my kiddy," chuckled the robber.

Then he shouted,

"Well, Jack! if you are in the sulks, and won't join me in a lively stave, I suppose I must give you up and go to sleep in disgust. Good night! my ben cove."

With this he stretched himself upon the bed and began to snore as if he had dropped asleep.

The quarrel between the gamesters at the card table now grew fiercer and louder.

Now was the time.

Sheppard helped his partner up through the aperture he had made in the floor.

Then, once more, he looked about him with a quick, comprehending glance.

The walls were massive.

To have made a hole through them would have occupied too much time.

The roof presented the best point of attack.

His first step was with his clasp knife to cut a stretcher or bar from the back of the chair.

One end of this he formed into a sharp point.

He mounted the chair, and commenced proceedings.

With the sharp point of the bar he soon managed to loosen a considerable quantity of lime and mortar.

He then dislodged several of the laths, and began to remove the tiles by poking at them with his bar.

He had made in this manner a very formidable orifice, when, unfortunately, one of the tiles rolling off the roof, which was rather slanting, fell on the head of a worthy clergyman who was passing, in deep meditation.

Turning sharply round and looking up in the confusion of his ideas, occasioned by the concussion on his cranium, he began to bellow out,

"Fire! murder! robbery!"

The alarm was distinctly heard by Jack.

He was aware that, to avoid immediate detection, he had not a minute to lose.

He made a plunge through the aperture which he had effected through the rafters.

With a sort of harlequin's leap he gained the roof.

Blueskin followed as nimbly as he could.

This was not managed, however, without removing a great quantity of tiles and rubbish.

It was nine o'clock in the evening.

The cries of the reverend clergyman, who happened to be Mr. Topping, the rector of St. Giles, soon brought a great mob around him.

A thousand questions were asked in a breath.

"What is it?"

"Where is it?"

"Who is it?"

"Murder! fire! thieves!" answered the reverend gentleman.

"Where? where?"

"There—there! the prisoners are escaping!"

"Where? where?" demanded a myriad of voices.

Jack saw that, to make his escape, he must create a diversion.

Mr. Guffin, the beadle, with the gaolers and constables, had now joined the group outside.

Mustering all his strength, and aided by Blueskin, Jack, holding on by the coping stone, pulled up a great part of the roof, and immediately dashed it down on to the heads of the astonished and affrighted mob below.

Then, sliding down a considerable way by a leaden pipe affixed to the back part of the building, he cautiously dropped into the neighbouring churchyard.

He looked quickly round for Blueskin.

His partner in guilt and adventure stood beside him.

"Oh, Jack!" groaned the dark-faced ruffian; "my leg! I have been bitten to the bone by that cursed mastiff. What shall I do? I shall be nabbed. Can't I hide here?"

"Yes—yes, for awhile," cried Jack, quickly. "This will do."

There was an unfinished grave at hand, covered with planks.

Sheppard tore away the wood, and Blueskin sprang into the earth.

Then Jack made his way over the church wall on one side.

Mr. Guffin, and the rest, armed with pistols and blunderbuses, had proceeded upstairs.

Jack Sheppard now joined the mob, most of whom were half blinded with dust.

He greatly added to their mystification, and his own diversion, by hallooing out—

"There he goes! I see him! That's his head below the chimney! No, it's only a tom cat, ah! There he is! escaping down that street. Stop him! stop him!"

The mob immediately gave chase at full speed.

While they made their way down one street, he, very safely and coolly, walked off down another.

CHAPTER LXII.

THE ABDUCTION OF VIOLET TREMAINE AND NELLIE PEVERIL.

WIRTH WOLFGANG'S schooner, the "Raven," lay off our hero's native village, Scarborough.

Is was a dull and misty day; the filmy fog rested like a thin cloud upon the unruffled bosom of the sea.

Wirth Wolfgang paced the deck.

His step betrayed impatience, and from time to time he leaned upon the bulwarks and listened to the lapping of the waves along her taut sides.

At length was heard the dip of oars.

"A boat alongside, mynheer," said a seaman, touching his hat.

A faint smile broke on the Dutchman's stolid face.

"Yaw," he grumbled. "It is Barabbas."

The look-out hailed the boat.

The cry was responded to by the dwarf, who in a few moments clambered over the side.

"You are welcome, Barabbas," said the Dutchman, speaking in his own language. "I began to fear that something bad had happened."

"All's well, mynheer," returned the dwarf, with a laugh. "To-night we will carry off our fair prizes—the old tower is as quiet as the Reef in a calm—and this mist favours our purpose."

"I wish it were done, Barabbas, for all that," returned Wirth Wolfgang. "I promised Jonathan Wild that I would sail for London to-night."

"And you can well keep your promise, mynheer," answered the dwarf; "for I shall carry off my lovely Nell at once. I have reconnoitred the Owlet's Roost; Sir John's mother is away in London, and Violet and my lass are alone in the old house."

"How many men will you want, Barabbas?"

"Twenty, mynheer; we can man two boats, and I will go ashore as soon as you please."

"Good!" returned the pirate captain. "But no violence."

"We shall overawe the household by our numbers, and violence will not be necessary," returned the dwarf.

"I will summon the men at once," rejoined Wirth Wolfgang.

He gave a prompt command to the boatswain.

The men mustered on deck.

Twenty were selected.

The boats were manned.

Barabbas took command of the party.

The boats were lowered.

The party pulled ashore.

They kept under the shadow of the overhanging cliffs.

They reached a little green before the Owlet's Roost by clambering the heights and following a rugged pathway.

The fog was denser than ever.

The grave old tower loomed darkly through the mist.

"Now, messmates," said Barabbas, "I will give ye a few words of advice. In the first place, we are on a service of a delicate nature, and one that must be carried out with tact and discretion; in the second, you must act promptly and with decision, for Mr. Wild is not the sort of person that it is safe to trifle with; you heard, too, what Mynheer Wolfgang commanded, that there should be no violence used, and that you should abstain from plunder."

"Aye, aye!" laughed the seamen.

"And you will remember that Nell Peveril is my prize. Whoever dares so much as to speak to her, makes he my foe!"

THE ENCAMPMENT IN THE WOOD.

As Barabbas finished speaking, there was a low murmur of dissent.

Some few of the seamen had seen, others had heard, of Nell Peveril's matchless beauty; and there was not a man of the party but would have sold his soul for such a prize.

"Who dares so much as speak to her, makes me his foe!" repeated Barabbas.

The murmur was hushed in an instant.

None cared to brave the dwarf's revenge.

"And," continued he, "Miss Violet Tremaine is to be used as gently as possible; such are my orders, and I will be obeyed."

"And the plunder — the valuables !" asked a voice.

"Mynheer Woolfgang has commanded that you should abstain from plunder. Forward !"

They crept forward—one behind another, winding their way upwards.

A man, a mile or two out at sea, would have said that a huge serpent was wriggling up towards the "Owlet's Roost," had he seen them moving on in Indian file.

At length they stood within ten yards of the old tower.

All was silent as the grave.

Not a light was visible.

"Hist !" said Barabbas in low tones ; "wait a few moments."

And he crept forward to reconnoitre.

Round—completely round, the old house he crawled with stealthy steps.

Not a leaf rustled, not a branch cracked beneath his noiseless tread.

The back of the "Owlet's Roost" seemed as silent as the forest. Not a soul seemed stirring.

Barabbas rejoined his men so silently, that they perceived him not till he was in their midst.

He then divided them into three parties.

One party of six was to remain where they were ; another party of six were to guard the doors and see that no one escaped, while the others were to accompany Barabbas into the house.

These arrangements being made, each party took up its proper position, and the dwarf tried the front door.

It was securely fastened.

He moved round to the side entrance and found that secured also.

"Nothing remains but to scale one of the windows," said he. "Hunt about for a ladder, my men ; but be careful to make no noise."

The men dispersed to hunt among the out-buildings for this necessary article, while Barabbas stood, with folded arms, gazing at the stout walls that stood between him and his treasure.

Let us now take a peep at the interior of the "Owlet's Roost."

Nell Peveril had retired to rest, but could not sleep.

Restlessly she tossed from side to side, seeking in vain for the slumber that refused to visit her eyes.

At length she stepped from her couch and approached the window.

She almost uttered a scream as she gazed out, for there, in the open space, were groups of men conversing in whispers.

The fog had partly rolled off seaward, and by the dim light she could see that they were armed.

What should armed men do at the Owlet's Roost at that hour of the night ?

They could be after no good.

She securely fastened the window and then hastened to the adjoining apartment, where slept Violet Tremaine.

The foster sister of our hero lay in a calm, deep sleep, the sleep of youthful health and innocence.

To awaken her was but the work of a moment. With a sigh the sleeper opened her eyes to find her friend standing by the bedside.

"Why, what brings you here ?" she asked.

"Hist ! there is danger."

"Where ? From whom ?"

"I know not. But there are armed men outside, and I feel certain that mischief is intended."

"Oh, that he were here, then we might laugh at danger," sighed Violet.

"As he is not, we must protect ourselves in the best way we can. Luckily the servants have arms. They must be aroused."

The bold girl was gliding away to alarm the household, when the voice of Violet stopped her.

"Do not leave me, dear Nell. I fear they may break into my chamber."

"Pshaw ! I have fastened the window, they cannot enter. Dress yourself, and I will return in a few moments."

Violet sprang from her bed and hastily assumed her garments, while her fair and bold friend glided from room to room to alarm the domestics.

This was soon done. The men servants armed themselves and began to barricade the doors with heavy pieces of furniture.

Then a loud, piercing scream was heard.

It proceeded from Violet's apartments.

Nell Peveril hastened thither, with a pistol in her hand that she had snatched from one of the men.

By the dim light a human face was seen peering through the window.

It was the dwarf, Barabbas.

The brave girl levelled her weapon and pulled the trigger.

There was a loud yell and a fearful oath. When the smoke cleared away that fiendish face was no longer seen.

CHAPTER LXIII.

TOM KING AND DICK TURPIN—THE GIPSY CAMP—
HORSES ON THE ROAD—CATCHING A TARTAR.

IT was some little time before Tom King could persuade his beautiful steed to arise and continue the journey.

The lovely creature was sorely fatigued, and though the highwayman longed to be away, he would not for the world use any severity to his favourite.

The gentle animal turned her lustrous eyes towards him in such a beseeching manner, that Tom felt almost inclined to leave her to rest and continue his journey on foot.

"Come, Tom," said Dick Turpin ; "time flies, and we must fly with it. Rouse up that beast of yours and let us be going."

"Lightfoot is no ordinary animal, nor has she undergone an ordinary journey. Stay a few moments ; she will be on her feet directly."

The gallant highwayman knelt by the side of his steed, caressed her, and spoke in encouraging tones.

At length she responded, and shaking her head, arose to her feet.

Tom threw the reins over the pommel of the saddle.

"Lead on, Dick."

"Follow me, Tom ; I know the road."

For some few minutes they walked in silence. Tom King thought too much of his horse to enter into any conversation.

Lightfoot followed him quietly, though occasionally testifying her affection by rubbing her nose against his shoulder.

There was no need to lead her ; whither her master went she would follow.

"How many of these sons of Egypt are there in the wood ?" he asked at length.

"A good dozen. Some of the rarest black-eyed wenches you ever saw."

Tom thought of the gipsy girl who had warned him against his friend, and wondered if she were among the number.

But he said nothing, for Jael's words had made an impression on his mind, and he began to speculate on the probability of the prophecy being fulfilled.

But gloomy thoughts passed away, as with joy he saw his favourite steed improve her pace at each step. The stiffness seemed to pass away from her limbs, the proud head was once more held erect, the step became free and light.

The slight rest and the food had done her good; nor was the beautiful animal ungrateful for the kindness.

"But, where is your steed, Dick? Where is Bonny Black Bess?"

"Safely concealed in a thicket close by."

"It's a splendid horse."

"Aye! Far better than your's."

"We will try to-morrow. Lightfoot is in no fit state for racing to-night."

"With all my heart."

"And where shall the course be?"

"The high road."

"How long the distance?"

"From milestone to milestone."

"Good! then our wager remains unaltered. There is a milestone by the Seven Bells,—that shall be our starting place, if you like."

"Very well. But the traps?"

"They will never think of looking for us at their own head quarters."

By this time the friends had arrived at the thicket where Turpin had concealed his steed, and a first-rate hiding-place it was.

The friends then mounted, and gently walked their steeds towards the dell where the gipsies were encamped.

A lurid glow over the tops of the forest bushes pointed out the spot, even had there been no other signs of their presence.

But there were other signs.

There were rough shaggy horses, and half-starved donkeys picking up their evening meal.

Above all these were shouts of laughter, as well as angry curses from the gipsies themselves, whose forms were hidden by the bushes amongst which they had encamped.

As the two highwaymen approached the camp, these sounds were hushed, and a rough voice called out—

"Who rides through the forest by night—friends or foes?"

"That's Red Ishmael's voice, I'll wager any money," said Turpin.

"You are right," replied Tom King. "Our Roumany friend has not the most musical voice, nor should I choose him as one of a party of glee singers."

"Ha—ha—ha!" laughed Turpin. "Ishmael loves the rattle of cudgels or the jingle of a good fat purse taken from a lonely traveller, far better than any of your silly glees or sonnets to the moon. But he is a brave and trusty ally."

The voice of the gipsy leader was again heard pealing through the dark aisles of the forest.

"Speak, travellers; show whether you come for good or evil. If friends, come on and welcome—if foes, turn aside or prepare for a stout combat."

"We are friends, as you should know," replied the clear, cheery voice of Tom King.

"Friends, Ishmael," said Turpin; "so stow your patter and swing the soup-kettle over the fire. I am as hungry as any fox-hunter."

"Come on, friends," replied the same voice. "But, if treachery is intended, beware."

The two friends rode forward into the light of the fire around which the gipsies were grouped, and dismounted from their horses.

Tom King perceived in an instant that his fair friend Jael was of the number, and, by an adroit movement, managed to place himself by her side.

A sinister scowl on Dick Turpin's brow showed that he did not approve of this arrangement, but, for the present, he said nothing. He had intended to captivate the fair Egyptian himself, and was sorely offended to see that she seemed in no way displeased with the advances of his dashing comrade.

"I would my bullet were in his heart," he muttered between his teeth as he gazed on them.

The wish was prophetic.

Who does not know the fate of the gallant and accomplished Tom King?

"You see, my charmer, I am still alive," said Tom, stealthily passing his arm round the waist of the blushing girl. "Neither friend nor foe has harmed me, and the officers have had a chase for nothing."

"I am glad to hear it. But I am sure you are in danger from him."

And she pointed towards Turpin.

"Pshaw! he is a good fellow, though at times apt to be rough both with tongue and hand. You must not look upon him as a murderer because his brow is black and wears a scowl."

"I care not for the look of his brow, but your life is in his hands."

"Then, my life is tolerably secure. But, tell me, my lovely lass, did that cowardly scoundrel, Wild, hurt you?"

"No."

"He struck at you?"

"He did; but I avoided the blow."

"The rascal! If I had him here he should have a good score from my thong, and not lightly laid on. Let him beware how he crosses my path."

At that instant Red Ishmael made a signal for silence, and every tongue was instantly hushed.

"I hear a sound of horses' hoofs upon the high road. Be in readiness, my lads; maybe the officers are coming back," said Ishmael.

"Coming back! What, have they been here?" asked Tom King.

"They have; on the look-out for a flying highwayman."

"Was Jonathan Wild of the party?"

"He was; curses on his black heart and ugly visage!"

"And Quilt Arnold?"

"Was not with them."

"Hist!" said Turpin, holding up a finger.

Silence again prevailed.

"I hear another sound besides that of horses' hoofs. Those horses drag a carriage behind them."

He sprang to his feet.

"Come, Tom ; we will give account of this vehicle whatever it may be."

"I am with you, my lad."

And he sang,

> "Oh ! with heart so light, and hand so free,
> A life on the road is the life for me.
> Hurrah ! hurrah !"

"Oh, stay," whispered Jael. "Why rush into unknown dangers when you have so recently escaped ?"

"Dangers? Why, my lovely lass, I never in my life saw a danger that could stop me. Nay, leave go my coat, and I will bring you back some fine trinket."

"How far is it, and which is the nearest path to this highway?" asked Turpin, as he sprang to the back of his coal-black steed.

"Five hundred yards ; the path lies straight before you."

Turpin at once put his horse in motion, and Tom King followed.

Ere they had proceeded half the distance between the gipsy camp and the high-road, the two were side by side.

"Take care of your pistols, Dick," said Tom, laughingly slapping his companion on the shoulder.

"What do you mean ?"

"Why, they have a habit of going off at a moment's notice, and I have no wish to see any one the billet of a bullet this evening."

"Then let them beware."

"You are savage, Dick."

"Only when thwarted."

"But put yourself in the same position. Would you not fight for your gold ?"

Turpin answered not, but in a moody manner toyed with the handles of his weapons, showing by his manner that he was not inclined to be baulked should a rich booty be in his way.

"What, moody man ! Come, you'll never win a fair lady's love unless you drive black care from your brow," said Tom King, urging his horse forward and taking the lead.

"Laugh away, Tom. No doubt the gipsy girl has put you in a laughing mood. I saw you whispering and the tender way in which you squeezed her hand."

"Ha, ha, ha ! Why she saved my life, and I think I ought to be grateful."

"Is that how you show your gratitude ?"

"How do you mean ?"

"By making love."

"Ho, ho ! You are jealous, Master Turpin ; never mind, my boy, all's fair in love and war, and really it would be exciting to have a rival."

"So, so ! But we are not far from the road, I should fancy."

"We must be close to it. Quietly, lass."

The last exclamation was addressed to Lightfoot, whose ears were erected and who uttered a half-suppressed neigh.

They were by the roadside at length.

A clump of thick bushes sheltered them from observation, though they could see up and down the highway.

A carriage, drawn by two horses, was approaching from the village at a very leisurely pace.

A postilion had charge of the horses, while a man, Tom King supposed to be a servant, sat on the front of the vehicle.

The windows of the coach were drawn up, so that it was impossible to tell how many people occupied the interior, or of what sex they were.

"Forward, Dick ; you see to the driver and the servant, I'll answer for the rest."

The two men spurred their horses out into the road.

"Stand !" cried Turpin, in a loud voice, presenting a pistol at the driver's head.

The man took no heed.

"Stand ! or I'll send a bullet through your brain !"

The horses were pulled up on their haunches, while Turpin sat on his steed immediately before them.

Tom King rode up to the carriage, and opened the door.

A glance at the inmates, and he swerved aside just in time to escape from a bullet that hissed past his cheek.

At the same moment a second pistol was heard, and the dashing highwayman beheld the servant fall from the box of the coach, shot through the heart by Turpin.

"Damnation ! they are officers !" roared the latter.

"Quilt Arnold is inside," said Tom King, as he found himself by his companion.

Turpin turned in his saddle, and with another loud oath discharged his second pistol into the body of the vehicle.

"A wasted shot," exclaimed King, as he beheld four men emerge from the coach with each a pistol presented at him or his companion.

CHAPTER LXIV.

SIMON SMUT IS SENT ALOFT, AND FALLS OVERBOARD.

"OFFICER of the deck—ahoy there !" cried our hero, as he stepped upon deck from his cabin late in the afternoon.

"Aye, aye, sir," exclaimed the officer, coming forward and touching his cap.

"Send a man up to the mast-head to clear away the halyard ; it has caught between the top-gallant cross-trees and the mast."

Roving Jack's eye had seen the slight irregularity, and he hastened to remove it at once.

"Aye, aye, sir ! Any other orders ?"

The young commander walked aft to the binnacle, and cast his eye upon the compass.

"Keep her head half a point more to starboard. Steady man—so !"

"Starboard it is, sir !"

"And call me as soon as you catch sight of a single rag of strange canvas."

So saying he retired once more to his own quarters.

The lieutenant then cast his eye around for some man to send aloft.

Simon Smut was the only one who happened to be disengaged.

"Here, you sir."

"'Ullo, mister, vat's yer good pleasure?"

"Is that the way you speak to your officers, you long-legged, lubberly son of a salt-junk cask!"

"My father were a 'spectibel member o' s'ciety——" commenced Simon, when a stinging blow from a notted cord cut short his explanations.

"Up with you, rascal, up to the mast-head, and clear away the halyard! Begone! and if I don't keelhaul you when you come down, may I be water-logged and sunk to Davy Jones! Up with you!"

The lieutenant flourished his instrument of punishment with such show of violence that Simon was glad to escape—up the rigging or anywhere to avoid the wordy passion of his officer.

Now, Simon, as our readers are pretty well aware, had a great genius for shirking any kind of work.

Hitherto he had studiously kept from going aloft—at least, only to a little height, and that for his own amusement.

He would have swarmed up a chimney twice the height of the ship's main-mast without fear, and joyfully have uttered his cry of triumph on reaching the top.

But, to ascend to the giddy height he was now ordered, made him tremble, and he stopped.

"Go on, sir!" roared the imperious voice of the officer. "No loitering."

Poor Simon crept on and on.

The wind was blowing freshly; there was a heavy swell on the bosom of the ocean, and the good ship rolled from side to side.

At length, he reached the mast-head, and commenced his task.

But neither his awkwardness nor his timidity had escaped notice.

Two tars on deck had just completed their task of stowing away shot in the racks, and were determined to have some sport.

"My eye, Bill! See that lubber there go up the top-m'st like the bear goes up the greasy pole at the Tower."*

Bill cocked his eye aloft, and spurted a mouthful of tobacco juice over the bulwarks.

"Let's have a game with the lubberly young dog," said he. "Come along."

The two active sailors were not half the time it had taken Simon Smut in journeying to the same altitude.

They each took an end and placed themselves astride the spar immediately below Simon.

Upon this spar would be his first resting place when he came down.

Simon was not long.

He slid down the mast gently.

He was just congratulating himself on the completion of the most dangerous portion of his task, when he felt himself jerked about in a very strange manner.

* Some years ago a collection of wild beasts was kept at the Tower of London. The Zoological Gardens were not then in existence.

He could not have believed that the wind and sea would have produced such an eccentric action on the mast and rigging.

He looked to the right hand.

He looked to the left hand!

There, on each side of him, sat a grinning sailor, astride the yard, jumping up and down on a rough see-saw principle, which greatly discomposed Simon's nerves.

"Stop, will yer?" he cried, clinging to the mast in desperation. "Hit joggles a feller?"

The sailors laughed, and continued to "joggle" him more violently than before.

"Carn't yer leave hoff when a cove axes? I shall fall, I know! Ho! vot a fall is there, my countrymen!"

"Stick to it, my lad—lash yourself to the mast! You'll do well for a storm-signal," said the sailor called Bill.

"They'll think we've got the blue peter flying at the main," said the other.

"My name is Norval—I mean Simon, and I haint got no acquaintance with yer blue Peters, nor hany other coloured natives."

"Ha, ha, ha!" laughed both the sailors, and at the sound the lieutenant's watchful eye was directed towards them.

"Ahoy, there! Come down on deck."

The two able-bodied seamen rapidly obeyed the command, and stood before the officer.

"No skylarking," said he. "To your work!"

The men touched their hats, and stepped forward.

But they cast an eye aloft, as did the officer, to see what had become of their lubberly companion, Simon Smut.

He was nowhere to be seen, though a dull, heavy plunge in the water told them plainly enough that he had fallen overboard.

The ship was at once hove to; but, ere the boats could be lowered, the light suddenly faded. A dark cloud had passed before the setting sun.

Some old spars, tubs, and other articles were thrown overboard, in the hope that he might be able to reach one of them, and all that night they cruised to and fro as near the spot as possible.

But when morning came Simon Smut was not to be seen.

His fate remained in uncertainty.

Had he met with a sudden death, and gone straight to the depths of the sea, had some huge monster swallowed him, or had he been drifted away by the tide?

No one could tell.

Report was duly made, and the words "Lost at sea," written opposite his name in the ship's books.

Some one or two were sorry; they had felt kindly disposed towards the romantic chimney-sweep, and looked upon him as a kind of pet dog.

But Simon Smut was not drowned.

Perhaps his destiny might be more closely connected with a rope; but that must be seen hereafter.

A pickle-tub that had been thrown overboard came near him as he struggled with the waves; he seized it, and was saved.

All through the night the angry ocean hurried him forward; and just as day began to break he found his feet strike against the sandy beach of a little green island.

He was almost exhausted with cold and fatigue, but managed to land.

His first care was to look out a nook sheltered from the wind but open to the beams of the morning sun, and having at length selected such a spot, he threw himself at full length upon the ground, exclaiming,

"I'm blest! 'Ere's a rummy go!"

CHAPTER LXV.

SIMON SMUT FINDS A WIFE—AND LIES IN STATE.

How long Simon Smut slept he knew not, but when he awoke the sun was high in the heaven.

His damp clothes had thoroughly dried on the uppermost side, though his back, which had lain upon the earth, was still damp.

He got up and stood with his back to the sun, to warm his unbaked side.

Presently he began to feel hungry.

The question was how to procure food.

He looked at the dashing, glittering ocean, and thought of the fried fish of his youthful days.

He cast an eye upon the green hills in the centre of the island, and a blessed vision of "baked taters all 'ot" rose in his mind.

"There must surely be something to eat here," he thought.

Another thought struck him, namely, that it would be advisable to look and see.

He rose, and walked into the wood.

No sound met his ear, save the chirping song of hundreds of birds, and the screaming of grey, green, and red parrots.

Simon thought of eggs.

He looked up into the trees in hopes of meeting with a nest.

During all this time he had never thought of throwing a stick at any of the feathered inhabitants of the grove.

But as no nests were visible, he caught up a heavy branch, and threw it with all his force into a bush where several species of birds were sitting.

He almost screamed with joy as he saw one of them fall down into the bush.

He ran and picked it up.

Then two disagreeable questions presented themselves to his mind.

Was the bird good for food?

How was he to cook it?

Simon Smut had never eaten raw meat, nor had he yet arrived at that stage of hunger when things which, in other moments, would be loathsome, become the choicest dainties.

He held his prize in his hand, and walked slowly onwards.

A rustling sound in the bushes excited his alarm.

He looked round.

Through the green foliage he could just see a dusky form.

Simon started in alarm.

He was among savages.

They might be cannibals. It was most probable they were, and so, perhaps, he would form them a dainty meal.

He stopped a moment to consider, while drops of cold perspiration stood upon his brow.

How should he escape? Should he fly towards the sea coast, or rush into the thickest part of the wood? A thought convinced him that escape would be impossible.

Simon Smut's acquaintance with literature embraced some wonderful accounts of the sagacity of the Indians of North America, and their skill in following the trail of man or beast.

All savage races, in his opinion, possessed the same keen instinct.

He walked on slowly, his hair on end, and every nerve of his body in a tremble.

He walked on and on, until at length he entered a kind of ravine, with high rocks on both sides.

Had he known that he was entering a *cul-de-sac*, or passage from which there was no escape save by retreating, he would have gone any other road.

But he fancied that he would find a hiding place, and so kept on.

Presently the forest ceased, and the bottom of the ravine became free from woodland.

Simon Smut walked on a few steps, then stopped as suddenly as though he had been stung by a serpent.

There, right before him, was a hut or wigwam of sugar-loaf shape, constructed of bark, and grotesquely painted.

To turn to the rightabout was the work of an instant, and again he stopped short.

There, right before him, in the very path by which he had come, was a tall savage, nearly black, with plume of feathers on head, and gorgeous striped blanket for dress.

"Oh! mercy! mercy Mr. Injen. I ain't done nothink wrong I 'ope!" cried the frightened Simon throwing himself upon his knees.

"Burracompoochery—kickery, kookery boo!" replied the native of the sunny island.

"No, please don't. I ain't good cooked, I know. The taste of the soot is in me, and all the water in the sea won't wash it out."

"Comery longerabong."

The savage approached and beckoned, when, to his surprise, Simon perceived that he had been addressing himself to one of the native *ladies*.

The painted warrior was a painted woman, with a black child behind her back.

Never while in the highest glories of his former profession had Simon been so black as that naked urchin.

"She might have put him a shirt on," thought Simon, whose ideas of modesty were somewhat shocked.

The woman beckoned in a more imperious manner than before.

"I'm going to be cooked," thought Simon, as with lingering footsteps, he followed his black guide.

She conducted him towards the wigwam, and bade him enter.

The hut was empty; but there was a bow, a quiver full of arrows, a spear for catching fish, and a shield.

But the warrior to whom these arms belonged was not to be seen.

The black lady motioned Simon to sit, and, then, with a tremendous box on the ears, sent her interesting and naked progeny outside.

"Don't 'urt the poor boy, as he ain't got no shirt on," said Simon.

The black woman grinned and began to stir up the embers of the fire.

She then pointed to a large box which stood at the very back of the hut, and made signs that he should take something out of it.

Simon Smut opened the box, and looked in.

Oh! wonder of wonders!

There was the pride, the emblem of his sooty profession.

There was the round-headed brush, the different lengths of handle, and the screws by which they should be fastened together.

The lengths were neatly fastened in a bundle by two new leather straps, and the whole apparatus appeared never to have been used.

Simon almost screamed with joy, and at once commenced putting the machine together, while the Indian woman really yelled with terror, as the white youth caused, what she fancied, a very tall tree to grow with surprising rapidity.

But Simon suddenly shook his head with a most melancholy air, as he reflected that on the island there were no chimneys to sweep.

The handsome new apparatus was useless.

He heaved a deep sigh, and slowly began to restore it to its place.

Other tools of his trade were there. A bran new scraper lay by the side of an unused hand-brush. The chest had evidently belonged to some speculative emigrant sweep who desired to carry the sooty profession into other lands.

The black woman, during this time, had boiled some fish, and now motioned Simon to come and eat.

He did so.

The fish was fresh, and Simon made a very hearty supper. Supper, he found, it must be, for the sun was already declining.

Nearly four and twenty hours had passed since he fell from the summit of the high and giddy mast; the ship was not in sight. No doubt his companions had given him up as lost—drowned.

He changed his dress; threw himself on the couch of the defunct Indian warrior—for the lady had by signs made him understand that she was a widow—and slept soundly.

The next morning he commenced a totally new course of life.

No more work—no more drudgery—no more climbing of crooked flues, or scraping of tarry masts. He found that he had a black wife, whose duty was to wait on her white lord and master—to cook his meals and to attend to his every want.

And a very pleasant style of life he found it, with only one drawback.

In the midst of all his pleasure the remembrance of Poll Potts would occasionally intrude, and then the dream of happiness would be marred.

The third day of his stay on the island he laid himself down upon the soft turf before his wigwam to indulge in a nap.

The hot sun poured down through an opening in the trees upon his face, scorching him with its fiery rays.

Though thus inconvenienced, he was loth to change his position.

A bright idea struck him.

He commanded his *wife* to bring out the sweeping apparatus.

The lady obeyed, though with very evident fear and trembling.

Simon hoisted it until it shaded his face like an umbrella, and then once more laid himself down to sleep.

His black lady-love posted herself near at hand to keep watch over the white master of her heart; and the black piccaninny——

Well, the youngster amused himself by tickling the nose of his step-father with a slender stick.

"Drat them muskeeters! Carn't yer keep 'em avay from a cove's nose?" exclaimed Simon.

Suddenly the woman held up her finger to enjoin silence, and, motioning him to lie perfectly still, crawled into the adjacent thicket as noiselessly as a cat after its prey.

CHAPTER LXVI.

THE PURSUIT—JACK SHEPPARD IN A CRITICAL POSITION.

BEFORE Jack Sheppard had gone very far he began to grow reckless, and resolved to return to the scene of his late incarceration to see or hear if possible how Blueskin had fared.

Mr. Gnffin, the beadle, and the mob had gone off at full speed along what is now known as Oxford street, so that there was no fear of unning against them.

The churchyard was wholly deserted, for no one dreamed that the rogues would venture back to their prison.

After looking very carefully round, Jack clambered over into the churchyard.

That was as silent and deserted as the street.

Had any one seen him they would have fancied him some ghoul or evil spirit, making its noiseless way amongst the tombs.

He reached the new-made grave where he had left Blueskin concealed.

Kneeling upon the earth he peered down into the recesses of the tomb.

"Hist! old pal! Blueskin! Where in the devil's name are you?" he whispered.

There was no response.

The grave was silent.

"Have they nabbed him, I wonder?" thought Jack, as he strained his eyeballs to catch a sight of his companion's figure.

He gently lowered himself into the grave, which he found was quite empty.

Blueskin had departed.

But which way, and for what reason?

"I must seek him," muttered Jack. "He would be almost certain to go to the ken."

Jack crept out of the grave as quietly and cautiously as he had crept into it.

Over the high boundary wall of the churchyard and into the street.

As he did so he saw a man emerge from the shadow of a doorway and advance towards him.

Neither dress nor figure were those of Blueskin.

Jack quickened his pace.

The stranger did the same.

"It must be a Bow Street runner," thought Jack, and his walk became a run.

The stranger ran also, and with such dexterity that he gained upon Sheppard.

The thief strained every nerve.

He sighed heavily as he glanced over his shoulder.

Each step lessened the distance between him and his pursuer.

The stranger was joined by a second man and then by a third.

Through lane, court, and alley Jack Sheppard fled; through scenes of squalid poverty with which he was well acquainted, and past dark nooks where vice-begotten wealth was hoarded up in obscure buildings.

"I must brick them," thought Jack, as he heard the footsteps of his pertinacious followers close behind.

He turned suddenly and crossed Drury Lane, hastening down a narrow street which led out of that thoroughfare.

A door stood open close by.

Jack entered, and, without stopping, fled swiftly up the dark stair-case.

In some of the rooms were heard sounds of rude mirth and revelry; in others the cries of misery and woe.

But neither roysterer nor mourner saw or heard Jack.

He gained the top of the staircase.

One pursuer was heard ascending.

To escape he must get out on the roof, but how could that be done?

A door was before him, and opening it he found himself in a low garret.

There was a window, however, and by it Jack determined to escape.

He squeezed himself through it, and stood upon the tiles.

"I have escaped," he thought.

But at that moment a loud shout was heard below, and looking down Jack saw that he was discovered.

The garret window, too, showed a sorry sight, for the pursuer was creeping through it, though but slowly.

"I must run, and take my chance of finding another window open through which I can descend," muttered Sheppard.

He mounted to the very ridge or highest part of the roof, and with nimble footsteps ran swiftly forward.

Those below, while they abhored the crimes of which he had been guilty, could but admire the daring and agility of his attempt to escape.

Scores of curious eyes were turned up to gaze upon him, but he heeded them not.

Suddenly he stopped, and his heart was filled with terror.

A few yards before him the row of buildings abruptly terminated.

There was no means of escape save by retracing his steps and passing his pursuer.

THE LADIES' DIVERSION.

THE dwarf Barabbas was not mortally, or even dangerously, wounded by the pistol Miss Peveril fired at him.

The bullet grazed his cheek—searing it as a hot iron would have done—and, after carrying away the lobe of his ear, did no further injury.

The wound caused him some pain; and the stunted being vowed that he would be revenged upon the daring girl whose hand had fired the shot.

For some few minutes he cursed, swore, and behaved like a madman.

His men drew him behind the shelter of a clump of laurel bushes.

"Hell's furies seize her! he shouted. "Her hand has drawn my blood—her back shall feel the weight of my vengeance."

"This comes o' larking with the gals," muttered an old sea dog, who stood at hand.

"You, too! curses on you! You laugh at my mishaps; perhaps you will not laugh when your shoulders are torn by the cat."

"Stow your blarney, mister," was the response. "All hands was piped for skylarking when we got into the boats. The cat's claws are cut."

This answer only added to the dwarf's rage.

The men held him, or he would have attacked the old sailor with his sword. On being prevented from using his weapon, he again cursed and swore—a proceeding which had not the least effect upon the minds of his hearers.

However, in a little time he began to see the folly of his behaviour.

"We must see about doing something," said he. "The house seems to be alarmed."

He was quite right. Lights were seen moving from window to window, and the stern, deep voices of men were heard above the clamour of the frightened women.

The men-servants in the "Owlet's Roost" had loaded their pistols and muskets; the doors and windows were barricaded, and the place put in as strong a state of defence as possible.

Brave Ellen Peveril commanded, directed, and, by her courageous bearing, animated every heart.

Violet Tremaine endeavoured to follow the example of her friend, but the imitation was a decided failure.

The pirates were now seen advancing from the shelter of the bushes.

They came on towards the door, which it seemed they were determined to force open, or scale the low window immediately over it.

The doorway was a narrow one, so that only two men could be placed in it to check the entrance of the pirates.

Loopholes had been cut, and from these projected the muzzles of two muskets.

"When you have fired, make way for others," whispered Nell, as she surveyed the arrangements.

The servants nodded, and in breathless anxiety awaited the approach of the pirates.

The attacking force had advanced half way to the house, on the clear open space between it and the bushes.

The brave girl gave the word,

"Fire !"

A cloud of smoke floated before their eyes, and the rattle of the muskets seemed echoed by a volley from the pirates.

Then the voice of Barabbas was heard urging on his men, who continued to press forward.

They were rather surprised, though, to be greeted by a second discharge from the building.

They halted, and fired in return.

As the garrison could not fire more than three or four shots at each volley, the dwarf imagined their force to be much smaller than it really was. But he could not understand the quickness of their fire.

The constant flashes and bullets from the door held his men in check, and the dwarf began to see that, in order to insure the success of his enterprise, it would be necessary to take other steps.

He called upon his men to spread themselves out in a semi-circle in front of the building, which they did, and thus kept up a continuous fire upon the building.

But, in this position, they were exposed to the fire of more muskets from the Owlet's Roost than before, and Barabbas found that he had a strong and very determined enemy to contend with.

In fact, had the dwarf anticipated so stout a resistance, he would hardly have been persuaded to undertake the task.

It was now very dark, for the moon had reassumed her veil of fog to hide the sight of such foul deeds from her chaste face.

The only light shed upon the scene was from the momentary flashing of muskets and pistols.

Barabbas left his men to continue the attack, and, under cover of the sulphurous canopy of smoke, crawled up to the door.

He examined it again, and soon saw that there would be very little chance of forcing an entrance.

But it struck him that he might plant a party on each side of the doorway in such a position that they would not be exposed to the bullets of the defenders of the house.

He hastily crawled back, and, directing them to continue their fire, took with him six men.

Three he posted on each side of the door, with directions to fire through the planks or through the loopholes which had been cut by those inside.

The advantage of this manoeuvre was soon evident.

The balls of the pirates inflicted some severe wounds on those inside, and even the heroic Nell Peveril herself did not escape without receiving a bullet through her tresses, which did no other damage than to sever a lock from her head.

"Retreat ! retreat !" she cried, but she herself was the last to leave the doorway.

They retired into the house, and kept up a fire from the windows.

But even this style of warfare did not continue long.

Barabbas had discovered that the door and the wooden porch were very dry and ancient, and another method of forcing an entrance suggested itself.

He gave directions to some of his men, who hastened to the outhouses, and returned with bundles of straw and faggots of wood in their arms.

"We are lost !" thought Violet, as from an upper window she watched the movements of her foes.

She hastened to her friend and companion, who had also seen the threatened danger.

"What can we do now, dearest Nell ?" she asked. "Those fearful men will set the place on fire."

"We must endeavour to hold out until help comes from the town ; they must have heard the noise of the firing by this time."

"But it is a long distance, and the wind blows from the town."

Nell was silent.

The wind had indeed begun to freshen, but, unluckily for her hopes, it blew, as Violet had said, from the direction in which the town was situated.

"Then we must trust in Providence," she replied.

The faggots and the straw were piled around the door and the wooden porch or verandah before it; a twinkling flame was seen, which each moment became larger and larger.

The fire began to curl round the two wooden pillars that supported the verandah, till at length the whole structure was in flames.

This was of course a great advantage to the pirates, and a disadvantage to those inside.

"Ha! ha!" laughed Barrabas. "See how the flames light up the windows! you can see where to aim your bullets now, my lads!"

His crew of ruffians poured in another volley, with a loud shout.

One of the men in the Owlet's Roost was struck in the forehead by a bullet, and fell down a corpse.

Another received a pistol shot in his shoulder.

In the meantime the house began to fill with smoke, which accumulated in dense clouds in the front rooms; so, by Nell's advice, they retreated to the basement of the building.

"What shall we do now?" said a groom, looking towards the two ladies for an answer.

"We must wait and see what their next move will be. They have set the entrance on fire, but that is all the damage they can do at present. The barricade in the entrance-hall will not be touched by the flames, and will keep them at bay for some time."

"Hark! they are trying the door again," said Violet.

"They may batter down the door itself with long poles, but they cannot enter until the fire has in a great measure burnt itself out."

In a minute or two there was a great crash.

The pillars that had supported the verandah had given way, and it was now blazing fiercely in a large heap before the door.

The pirates now left off firing, and it was very difficult to tell what their intentions were.

One part of the brave little garrison kept watch over the side entrance, in expectation of an attack in that quarter.

But no further attack was made either on door or window.

Half an hour of anxiety and suspense thus passed away.

CHAPTER LXVII.

BARABBAS'S ATTACK ON THE OWLETS' ROOST.

In vain did Nell Peveril and the servants at the Owlet's Roost endeavour to discover some signs of the enemy's presence or some clue to his plans.

One or two of them gave it as their opinion that the pirates, frustrated in their endeavours to force

an entrance, had retired to their boats, and gone away.

But Nell Peveril knew the dwarf better than to believe that.

All that she could do was to send one of the servants up to the roof, to look out and discover their motions.

Violet Tremaine and the others kept below, that they might be out of danger.

"Good heaven! what a dreadful night this has been!" exclaimed Violet. "How many hours is it to daylight, do you think?"

"Two hours, at the very least. But the fate of this house and its inmates will be decided ere then, I fancy."

"Heaven protect us! But see—are they not coming?"

"Where?" asked Nell.

"Here, on the lawn."

Nell looked out, and indistinctly saw a group of men advancing.

In a minute she could distinguish their forms more clearly.

"Yes, you are right! They are carrying ladders! They divide into different parties—they intend to attack us in several places at once!"

Then she drew herself back from the window and clutched her pistol.

"We must fight hard, now!"

The servants divided themselves at the windows facing the lawn, which had before been sheltered by the verandah.

"Shall we fire now?—shall we fire now?" they asked.

"No; do not fire till the muzzles of your pistols are at their hearts. They cannot mount more than two at a time at each window."

The ladders were fixed, and the pirates with a loud cheer, began to ascend.

Violet Tremaine was even persuaded to fire one pistol as she stood trembling, and supported by her stronger-minded companion.

The two men fell back from the ladder, and Nell gave a cry of exultation.

"We shall conquer yet," she cried.

At the same moment her weapons were wrenched from her grasp, and she found herself struggling in the hands of a couple of ruffianly-looking rascals.

A scream of terror from the lips of Violet Tremaine arrested her attention, and half turning her head, she saw that her gentle friend had also been seized.

The author of all this mischief was at hand, exulting in the terror and misery he had caused.

The dwarf gloried in the success of his enterprise.

"Help! help!" screamed Violet.

"Yes, my beauty, you shall have help when you get to your lover," cried Barabbas.

"Release me, ruffians! Help! Oh! heaven! have pity on me!"

"Ha! ha! it is fine music to hear you cry for help. And you, my beautiful Nell, have you nothing to say?"

Nell made no answer; but after a brief struggle resigned herself to captivity.

"You are mine now. Mine body and soul!" he continued. "A rare prize!"

The brave girl made no reply.

She was already meditating how to escape from the hands of her captors.

But at present she was too well guarded.

She looked around.

The merciless pirates were cutting down the survivors, and appropriating to themselves anything of value that caught their eyes.

The party, headed by Barabbas, had entered the doorway, while the attention of the defenders was drawn to the attack on the windows.

They had found no one to stop their way, and the rude barrier of furniture was speedily overcome.

Passing up the staircase, the dwarf had entered room after room, until he discovered that in which the two girls had stationed themselves.

He gave his men orders to make no noise till they had secured their prey.

They advanced silently.

The result is already known to our readers.

The girls were conducted into a room, and guarded by half-a-dozen of the ruffianly crew.

Barabbas himself remained in the apartment.

"Why have you committed this dastardly deed?" asked Violet.

"Why? Ha! ha! ha! For a good reason."

"Be quiet, dear Violet," said Nell, for the first time breaking silence.

For a few moments there was silence.

"Then you won't ask any more questions?" said the dwarf. "Ha! ha! I will give you some rare news, then, without your asking. Rare news! Glorious news!"

And he laughed malignantly, while a gleam of triumph distorted his features.

"What news? What mean you?" asked Violet.

"Rare news! A rare husband!"

"A husband? You rave, man!"

"I rave? So will you when you meet the bridegroom."

"And who may this rare bridegroom be?" asked Violet, forcing a smile to her pallid face.

"A rare husband! Jack Sheppard, the housebreaker!"

CHAPTER LXVIII.

SIMON SMUT IS DISTURBED BY PIRATES.

WHEN Simon Smut's black beauty left him so suddenly, it was not without good cause.

The lady's education had been a good one, and although she could neither play the piano nor paint on velvet, she could follow a trail through the wood, and tell the footstep of a human being from that of a wild animal.

Simon, however, thought not of danger.

That he, Chuquisaca (that was the woman's name), and the black infant should be disturbed or molested was a thing he never dreamed of.

The thought of a fourth party finding his way to the island never entered Simon's head.

He saw his black wife crawl away.

"Going to catch a bird or somethink, I suppose," thought he.

The young darkie had vanished also.

"It's a blessing that 'ere kid have avaunted and quitted my sight," he continued. "I can't stand his games, and shall have to whop him if he ain't civil."

Simon then closed his eyes.

His noonday nap had been disturbed, and he was determined to take advantage of the momentary silence to conclude his forty winks.

But he had scarcely closed his eyes when he opened them again.

He opened his mouth, too, and stared around with a look of surprise.

He bounded to his feet.

A loud, piercing scream came pealing through the aisles of the forest.

Simon knew the tones.

"What's the matter with that 'ere woman?" he exclaimed.

There was silence for a moment.

"Fell down and hurt herself, I suppose. I hope that kid has broke his neck, too."

Then came the shrill cry again, and, following it, the hoarse laughter of men.

Simon began to grow frightened.

What might those sounds portend?

Was it a party of savage Indians who would torture him to death, and then pick his bones?

Or was it a band of still more savage white men, who would kill him by slow degrees by the most fiendish cruelty that bloodthirsty ingenuity could devise?

Simon had heard fearful tales of the rovers of the sea—how they were wont to bury their plunder on little islands, and kill every one who approached the hiding-place.

He turned to fly. But whither should he go?

On which side was the danger?

He stared with all the force of his eyes into the bushes.

Not a living thing was to be seen.

Hist!

A light step is heard approaching, making its way through the bushes.

Another, and yet another.

They came from different quarters.

"Good Heavens! I am surrounded by the murdering ruffians!" exclaimed Simon, as he wrung his hands despairingly.

"I must make a move, though," he continued, still speaking to himself, and without any more consideration, he began to dash through the bushes at the greatest speed of which he was capable.

Yells and shouts sounded behind him; but the noisy cries only increased the rapidity of his flight.

He cast but one glance over his shoulder.

The sight struck terror to his heart.

Six or seven stalwart men, whose dress and appearance left no room to doubt their piratical profession, were in full chase.

Some of them had pistols in their hands; the others had their belts stuck full of weapons.

Of various nations were they, too.

There was the theatrically-dressed Spaniard, the sturdy, rough-clad Saxon, and the half-naked negro.

Simon sped onwards.

The shore was in view, where the sparkling, foaming waves came dashing up over the pebbly beach.

But there was a dark-looking object there which he had not seen in the morning.

It was a boat, and, at the sight, Simon's spirits revived.

He was fully fifty yards before his pursuers.

Could he succeed in reaching the boat and pushing it off, he might be saved.

The pirates evidently perceived his intentions, and resolved, if possible, to prevent him from carrying them into practice.

Shots were heard, and bullets whistled close past Simon's ear.

But though horribly scared, the ex-sweep never, for one moment, relaxed his pace.

He ran headlong against the boat, pushed her by main force into the water, and, with two awkward strokes of the oars, placed himself beyond the reach of his foes.

The pirates stopped upon the beach, and began to reload the weapons they had discharged.

"They mean to shoot me. I shall be killed after all!" the unhappy youth groaned, as he watched these warlike preparations.

He applied himself vigorously to the oars, although unaccustomed to the task.

Bang! went a musket.

The bullet crashed through the stern of the boat, knocking splinters up into Simon's eyes.

In his fright he dropped the oars and fell into the bottom of the boat.

Other weapons were discharged, and, although the bullets did not touch Simon, they whizzed by his head in such a style as to make him feel very uncomfortable.

Then they ceased firing after a few minutes, and the fugitive ventured to raise his head.

To his horror he saw that one of the Spaniards had stripped and was wading into the water with the evident intention of swimming after the boat.

On came the man; he was out of his depth, and swimming vigorously.

Suddenly he uttered a loud shriek, and threw up his arms.

Then there was a short struggle; the water became red and foamy.

Those who heard the cry and saw the bloodstained wave, knew that he had been seized and devoured by a shark.

This catastrophe was in Simon's favour.

None of the pirates seemed inclined to follow the example of their daring but luckless comrade.

The boat in which Simon was gradually drifted further and further from the shore; the bullets occasionally fired after him dropped into the sea some yards astern.

He was saved from the hands of his bloodthirsty pursuers.

Then came a new source of alarm.

Drifting out to sea in an open boat without sail or oars!

When would he reach land again?

What unknown coast would he be cast upon?

Or would he fall a prey to the grim destroyer—hunger, and leave his bones to be picked by sea birds?

With despair in his heart, he arose, and began to look about him.

Hurrah! hurrah!

After all starvation might for a time be averted, for there, in the boat, was a small cask containing water, a package of biscuit, and some pieces of salt pork.

Simon's courage began to revive, the more as he also discovered a rusty cutlas and a few carpenter's tools.

In fact, from the furniture of the boat, it appeared as though the pirates had mutinied against their comrades. and had been sent adrift to shift for themselves in the best way they could.

So Simon began to be of better cheer, and thought that he was not so badly off after all.

Poor fellow! His had been a rough life—few comforts, and many hard blows and buffets from the world.

He little knew the hardships he had still to undergo.

The boat drifted on and on until the island he had left behind appeared only a dim indistinct mass on the horizon.

The sun began to sink, and from its position in the sky, Simon began to be of opinion that he was floating in a south-westerly direction.

Night came on, the moon and stars were hidden from sight, and Simon laid himself down in the bottom of the boat to sleep.

CHAPTER LXIX.

SIMON SMUT ON THE OCEAN IN AN OPEN BOAT.

THE day had fully dawned, and the sun was high in the heavens, when Simon awoke from his sleep.

He sat up, swallowed some biscuit and water, and then looked around him.

The boat seemed to be drifting on towards land. There was a low sandy island right before him.

Simon little cared what that land might be, so that he could set foot upon its shores. He was most heartily tired of the ocean, and wished that he had never trusted himself upon its smiling, treacherous surface.

At length the bows of the boat grated upon the sand, and Simon leaped ashore.

He hauled the boat up a little way so that the waves might not carry it out to sea, and then sat down upon the sand.

For nearly an hour he thus sat in deep and melancholy reverie, till the scorching heat of a tropical sun, pouring down upon his head, roused him to a sense of his situation.

Simon began to turn his thoughts upon his present position, and to what would be the measures most advisable to take.

He hauled his boat a little further up on the beach (luckily the craft was not a very heavy one), and fastened the painter to the old cutlass, which he fixed in the sand up to the hilt.

He then proceeded to survey the island, or rather sand-bank on which fortune had thrown him.

It appeared to be about half a mile long, and rather more than a quarter of a mile broad.

There was not a vestige of any kind of vegetation to be seen, neither tree nor bush, nor even a blade of grass.

It seemed as though at high tide the sea dashed nearly over the island.

In the centre there was a high mound washed up by the waves, and, as the tide was still rising, Simon resolved to remove his quarters to this spot.

He carried up the water-cask, the biscuit-bag, the tools, and the pieces of pork.

Then he applied all his strength to the task of dragging up the boat; but he could not make much progress.

All he could do was to lift forward alternately the bows and the stern of the boat, and so make a very slow way forward.

At length, however, he accomplished his task, and, sorely fatigued, laid himself down to rest.

But the sun was too hot, so he had to arrange a shelter in the best way he could.

Necessity is the mother of invention, and although Simon Smut had not been, in his early days, remarkable for any great genius, yet the troublous times he had passed through had done much to quicken his wit.

Simon exerted all his muscles, and overturned the boat.

Then, with his hands, he scooped the loose sand away on one side, so that there was a kind of cavern formed, having the boat for its roof.

Simon crept in, and was sheltered from the rays of the sun, though he panted for breath.

As the day advanced, the sky began to assume a gloomy weird appearance.

Huge blocks of clouds, dark and threatening, were piled up along the horizon, behind which arose a substratum of yellowish-looking vapour, as though a London fog had gone out to sea.

Overhead and towards the south the sky was of a dull, fierce, red colour.

There was no wind perceptible, though the cloud-bank came nearer and nearer.

But presently a dull, continuous noise was heard, like the distant roaring of a mighty steam-engine.

The waves on the horizon began to be capped with white-crested foam.

Then came a slight wind—more—still more—wind and clouds came on together.

Each successive gust was stronger than the last, as the gale gathered strength.

"There is a storm coming, and no mistake," muttered Simon, as he watched the coming tempest.

As he spoke, the sulphurous vapour, that underlined the chain of dark clouds, suddenly glared with light.

The electric spark quivered through the air, throwing the heavy cloud-bank beneath into strong and startling relief, giving them the appearance of monster rocks, cliffs, and castles.

Then over the vast ocean came the distant sullen roar of the grand thunder.

For a moment the wind hushed itself, and a dead calm reigned around the little island.

Afar off rolled along, in one foamy line, a huge tidal wave, that seemed to be rushing onward in swift haste to swallow up the island, and the desolate human being on it.

Like the black angel of death is swept along, terrible in its strength and power, turning the ocean into a perfect maelstrom of seething, foamy billows.

Flocks of sea-birds came shrieking and whirling through the air as they fled from the coming gale.

A cloud of mingled sand and spray flew upwards till Simon was completely blinded, and was compelled to crouch down in his shelter to avoid the violence of the blast.

In a few minutes he was wet through to the skin.

The heavy spray and the rain beat into his little hovel in torrents.

In fact, had there not been danger of his being carried out to sea, Simon would have sooner withstood the violence of the storm.

The lightning flashed, the thunder rattled, the waves roared, the wind howled.

The combined elements kept up such a turmoil about poor Simon's ear, that he almost fancied the day of doom was come.

He tried to repeat a prayer he had heard on the only occasion he went to a Sunday school.

In vain.

He could neither remember the words nor the substance of the petition.

He thought the wind was growing less violent, and ventured to put his head out of his hut.

The sea was running literally in waves mountains high, for their crests even over-topped the rising ground on which he had taken refuge.

But what was that sight that greeted his eyes—a sight that suggested some renewed hopes of safety? Hopes that, alas! were doomed soon to be dashed to pieces.

"A sail! a sail!" he shouted, fancying almost that he was at the mast-head.

His feeble voice was lost in the roar of the storm; and the ship drifted on.

Her masts were seen to topple over one after another; bodies were seen dashing about in the midst of the tangled web of canvas that floated by the ship's side.

Loud cries for help were heard; cries that Simon was unable to answer, though he had in his heart a desire to succour those who were so sorely distressed.

At the top of the bursting waves of the eternal ocean leaps the frail and yielding bark. The hearts of its crew are congealed as to ice by the feelings of awe and terror inspired by their intense fear.

The racing waves come running up the sandy beach, and on them are spars, casks, splinters of timbers, and corpses.

Simon threw himself on his knees, and gazed earnestly, as though his own life depended on the safety of those doomed souls.

The stern seamen on board take off their hats, their jackets, and their shoes, as they prepare for a struggle with the terrible element which had brought them to such a perilous position.

The fierce blast whirls their long locks over their faces, and compels them to fix their feet firmly to the slippery rigging.

The storm raves around them, and their hearts are filled with all the deep, solemn feelings of men whose last hour is at hand. They feel the majesty of the wild glare and the fierce rush of the lightning, as it proclaims the omnipotence of the great Deity whose word rules the elements.

Crash! crash! crash!

The timbers of the ship part from each other, and louder even than the peal of the thunder or the roar of the storm, comes the long, wild death shriek of those doomed souls.

The waves beat over the spot where a gallant ship had been, but now there was nothing to be seen but fragments of wood, strips of torn sails, and bunches of green seaweed. A few dark human forms were seen struggling with the waves.

Simon shouted and waved his hat, in the hope that some poor fellow might make his way up the hillock, and be saved.

But, as he shouted and gazed, one wave, higher than any of the rest, came rolling up with tenfold greater violence than any of the others.

It bore on its crest some of the scattered atoms of the ship that had been, and a fragment of timber struck Simon on the forehead.

Stunned by the fearful violence of the blow, he fell to the earth, while the storm sung a loud chorus of triumph at its victory.

CHAPTER LXX.

THE ABDUCTION OF VIOLET TREMAINE AND NELL PEVEREL—THE PURSUIT.

THE shock upon Violet Tremaine's nerves was so great when Barabbas announced that Jack Sheppard was intended for her bridegroom, that she could scarcely keep her senses.

She knew well that she was in the power of lawless ruffians, who would not hesitate to employ force to accomplish any scheme they might have on hand.

Misery, degradation, and woe stared her full in the face.

"Ha! ha! my beauty!—how like you the news?" asked the dwarf, as his malignant eyes gloated on her distress.

The tones of his hateful voice recalled Violet to herself. She assumed a dignity and loftiness of bearing that would well have graced a queen.

"You threaten more than you can perform, dwarf; I shall never be united with that scoundrel whose name you have mentioned."

"Indeed, my lovely miss!—we shall see about that. And your fair companion, does she know the fate in store for her?"

"I neither know nor care," replied Nell Peveril, who treated Barabbas with the utmost contempt.

As she spoke she turned her back upon the dwarf.

"It is well! You treat me with scorn now—but a time will come, my fair lady, when you will bitterly repent your rash conduct."

"I hold a different opinion."

"You are mine. There are Fleet parsons to be procured, who will soon give me a husband's authority over you."

"My word is required to such a bargain, as well as yours, idiot!"

"And there are tortures that will soon wring that word out of you. Provoke me not too far, Nell. I love you—love you most dearly; and mine I swear you shall be, though heaven and hell combine to prevent our union."

To this speech the brave girl made no answer. She folded her arms, and in silence awaited her fate.

From all quarters the pirates began to pour into the room, laden with plunder of every description. Some had dresses, some had jewels, some had curtains and hangings, some pictures, some articles stolen from the butler's pantry; while not a few had paid a visit to the cellar, as the black necks of bottles were seen protruding from their pockets.

"Come, my lads, come," said Barabbas; "we must see about going. The noise we have been compelled to make, I should fancy, has alarmed the town."

"And if the noise hasn't, I should guess the light of the fire has scared up some of them from their beds."

"March, then, my boys; our enterprise is crowned with success."

One after another the sun-burnt, swarthy ruffians passed out of the doorway, kicking the corpses of the slain servants as they walked along.

When they were all on the lawn, Nell Peveril looked anxiously around through the dark night, to see if she could catch a glimpse of any one coming to her aid.

Far, far away she fancied she could hear the echoing footsteps of galloping horses.

"Courage, dearest; help is coming," she whispered to Violet, who was almost dead with terror.

"I fear it will be too late," replied Violet. "These ruffians will have hurried us off ere help can reach us, and then we are lost, unless we can leave some clue to the path our captors take."

"That is easily done."

"Silence, there. Gag those women," cried Barabbas, in stern tones.

Violet uttered a loud scream, and so did Nell.

The next moment they were both rudely seized, thick wrappers were passed round their heads, the ends were pushed into their mouths, and all power of speech was thus denied the poor girls.

But Nell Peveril's presence of mind did not desert her.

If the sounds she heard were those of friends coming to the rescue, she was determined they should have a clue by which to follow.

She gently passed one hand into the pocket of her dress, and drawing from it a letter, began tearing it to shreds. These shreds she strewed upon the ground at intervals, as they passed along towards the beach.

For she judged that they were making their way to the shore from the steep and slippery descent down which they were dragged.

The path became so steep, that the dwarf at length removed the wrappers from their eyes, in order that they might walk down with the greater safety.

Violet cast her eyes upwards.

A deep red glare tinged the horizon.

She sighed, and the salt tears began to fall from her eyes; for she knew that her ruffianly captors had set the Owlet's Roost on fire. Her home, the scene where so many joyous hours had passed, was doomed to fall a prey to man's wanton spirit of destruction.

Nell Peveril also saw the light, and though she felt a pang of regret at the thought that the rare old building was doomed, yet another thought gained the upper hand in her mind.

Those red flames would light friends on the path to the rescue.

Inspired by the thought she dropped still more fragments of paper on the path.

The action was seen by Barabbas.

"Ha, traitress! you shall suffer for this!" he shrieked. "Hasten, men, hasten, or we shall be followed!"

"Too late! too late! We are rescued! See, villain, the avengers are at hand!"

She pointed upwards to the path they had descended.

The dwarf's eye followed; and he could plainly see the forms of many men following in pursuit.

The pirates ran; half dragging, half carrying the helpless girls.

The Dwarf raved, swore, and threatened dire vengeance should his schemes be thwarted.

They gained the pebbly beach.

Those behind shouted—

"Stop, there! Ahoy! Halt, villains, or you shall all be hanged without mercy! Surrender, rascals!"

As all these cries met his ear the Dwarf laughed aloud.

His boats were close at hand.

He leaped into one.

Violet and Nell were placed in it; the men scrambled in, and, with their oars, pushed off.

The pursuers came down just in time to see the pirates fairly afloat.

There was a hurried consultation amongst them.

"Fire on them! Shoot the rascals! Send a shower of bullets after the rascals!"

Such were the sounds heard; but there was one that advised differently.

"Hold! hold! don't fire. Miss Tremaine is in the boat. She has been carried off by them!"

The warning came too late.

The flash of fire-arms was succeeded by the hiss of bullets.

One man in the boat fell dead, and his warm blood splashed upon Violet's pallid cheek.

Then arose a loud shout from the enraged commander of the boats.

"Fools! idiots!" shouted Barabbas. "You have slain those you came to save."

"Villains!" pealed back a loud, manly voice from the shore. "Your sins have caused their deaths, and your vile bodies shall pay the penalty."

Then another voice was heard, in more cheerful tones, crying out,

"This way, friends. Here is a boat. We can pursue the ruffians."

Barabbas heard the boat pushed off, and he urged his men to strain every nerve.

THE MEETING IN THE CHURCHYARD.

CHAPTER LXXI.

THE MEETING AT THE "PEACOCK."—OUT OF LUCK—PLANS FOR ROBBERY.

DICK TURPIN and Tom King met by appointment at the "Peacock," a famous old tavern at Islington.

Tom King looked rather dull and disheartened.

"Hillo, my noble !" cried Turpin, slapping his confederate on the shoulder. "What makes you look so gloomy ?"

"Cause enough, Dick," returned the other robber, with a smile ; "my spirits may be gaged by this thermometer ; they rise and fall with its contents."

As he spoke he laid a scantily lined purse on the table.

"Hey ! Then, dam'me, Tom, we're both in the same case," rejoined Dick Turpin, shrugging his shoulders. "How shall we replenish our exchequer ?"

"I suppose we must resort to the old means," returned Tom, with a sigh of disgust and impatience.

"Aye, truly, my gallant knight of St. Nicholas' returned Dick Turpin. "We are liege lords of the high toby, and must levy fresh contributions."

"Well, be it so," returned Tom, moodily. "It is useless to struggle with one's fate ; all my comfort is that it has been predicted that it will end soon and suddenly, a prophesy in which I have great faith."

"You are always brooding over that gipsy wench's prophesy," rejoined Dick.

"It affords me some sort of consolation," returned Tom, shaking his head. "However, as the funds are so low, we must look out for another purchase."

"Aye, my noble," laughed Dick; "we must take the road."

"Where are our comrades?"

"Fielder sent me word that he and the rest would start to-night on an expedition to St. Albans."

"Ha! what was the gist of it?"

"To stop some carriers on their way to London with a load of valuable silks and stuffs, and some bags of money."

"But there will be an armed escort with such a cavalcade."

"I suppose so."

"Then there'll be a battle royal?"

"Most likely."

"Then why are we not there?"

"I should have joined the adventurous party," returned Dick Turpin, "but the messenger that brought me the tidings arrived too late for my purpose."

"Humph! their force will be too small; they will fail," said Tom King.

"Let's hope for better luck."

"Meanwhile, what must we do to refill our empty coffers?"

"I'll tell you, Tom."

"Hist! we may be observed."

"I'll see to that."

Dick Turpin rose.

He walked to the door.

Having assured himself that they were safe from intrusion and eavesdropping, he returned to the side of his confederate.

"All's well," he said, reseating himself.

"And now, Tom, do you mark me?"

"Most attentively."

"You know Sir Maurice Lacy?"

"Aye, one of the bloods; a friend of Sir Ranulph Gayton, with whom I had the honour of crossing swords?"

"The same."

"Well, and what of him?"

"He will be here soon."

"What follows?"

"A train of lackeys, with his coach, in which his mother rides alone in her way to the family mansion at Hertford."

"And you propose that we should stop her ladyship's coach, and relieve her of her valuables?"

"I think it might be done."

"Yes, by the whole band; but it would be madness in us to try such a venture alone."

"Well, Tom, if you are primed for it, so am I."

"I'll risk all chances."

"So will not I."

"'A soldier, and afraid!'"

"Neither one nor t'other," laughed Tom; "but you know my principles."

"Principles!—fiddlesticks!"

"May be; but they are fiddlesticks that I'll use as I please. You must dance to my tunes, or I'll not play to you."

"What the devil is the matter now? Principles! What principles, comrade, can interfere with such a good purchase?"

"Hark ye, Dick—you know what they call me on the road?"

"Roaring Tom, the toby gloak—eh?"

"I am so called by the base vulgar; but to the 'elite,' the 'upper ten,' the 'beau monde,' the 'haute ton,' I am designated 'The Gentleman Highwayman.'"

Dick Turpin laughed heartily.

"What then, my noble? What has that to do with your fine principles?"

"Why, simply this—that I will not rob the ladies of anything but their hearts, or their kisses," replied Tom.

"Then you refuse to join me in this adventure?"

"Most decidedly."

"Then curse you for a fool! You are as full of crotchets and caprices as a boarding-school miss," growled Dick Turpin.

"Don't be angry, captain," laughed his confederate. "Necessity's a hard master, and we are all his slaves; and though I won't rob the mother, the son is fair game. If you will tackle the old lady, that's your own affair; leave me to manage Sir Maurice."

"Done!" laughed Dick Turpin. "Though I go alone, and have to outface half a score of well-armed fellows, I'll do the trick by stratagem, if not by force."

"And I will manage the young rake-hell," laughed Tom.

Then he frowned blackly.

"There will be one thing to reconcile me to this business," he said. "His father ruined me. It was he who led me to the gambling-house, like a lamb to the slaughter; but I will have my vengeance upon the son, I'll warrant ye."

"Hark ye, then, I'll go at once," said Dick Turpin, rising and advancing towards the door. "Where shall we meet in the morning, Tom?"

"If all's bob, I'll see you at Brantford."

"Right, my hero," returned the highwayman. "Black Bess is stabled here; I will mount, and ride on towards Ware, and so ben darkmans."

He tightened his belt, examined the priming of his pistols, and, waving his whip, stalked out of the apartment.

———

CHAPTER LXXII.

THE HIGHWAYMEN TAKE THE ROAD — THE OSTLER — THE CREDULOUS FARMER — GHOST STORIES — DICK PLAYS A TRICK ON THE RUSTIC — FAIRY MUSIC — BORROWING FIFTEEN GUINEAS—THE FARMER'S RAGE.

DICK TURPIN called for his horse.

The ostlers brought her out of the stable.

They loudly expressed their admiration of the noble creature's beauty and breed.

Dick vaulted into the saddle.

The men looked at his manly form, as he sat erect and firm in his saddle, and almost forgot the ugliness of his freckled, red-whiskered face, as their experienced eyes approved of his gallant bearing, for the rascal was certainly a splendid rider.

He just touched the horse's side with the whip, and she set off at a graceful canter.

At the corner of the high road Dick Turpin stopped.

He looked behind him.

A large and stylish cavalcade, consisting of a huge, cumbrous coach and a party of horsemen, some of them apparently gentlemen of rank, the others servants, appeared riding towards the "Peacock."

They were laughing and conversing gaily.

"I wonder how Tom will succeed with this purchase," muttered the highwayman, thoughtfully. "But I may well leave him to it, he's a dashing dog, and more at home with the gentry than I am. I hate palavering; give me the high road or a plant, as a mill-ken—a house-breaking job."

He rode on.

It was a bright, moonlight night.

The air was frosty.

The sky was spangled with stars, that glittered through the clear blue ether with intense brilliance.

The wood was comparatively deserted.

At long intervals, however, a strong party of travellers, banding together for mutual protection, would pass by.

They were too powerfully armed, and too numerous and determined-looking, to give the highwayman any encouragement for attacking them.

Sometimes a string of heavy waggons and carriers' carts, guarded by mounted men, would rattle by, but, as yet, Dick Turpin had met with no object at all suitable to his purpose.

After riding about three or four miles up the road, the highwayman halted at the door of a low and ill-looking hostel.

A fellow, dressed in a smock frock, came running out to meet him.

He made a peculiar sign.

Dick Turpin bent down his ear : the man pointed over his shoulder to the house, and whispered something hurriedly.

The robber smiled.

"I know the old chawbacon," he said, leaping from his horse.

"Aye, zure, capt'in ; it be old varmer Gosling, one o' the most credulous chaps aj ever were skeared in a dark lane by a crooked tree or a zign-post ; he be now listenin' to a most horrible ghost ztory as our parish clerk is tellin'. He's got a bag of gowld under his saddle, for he be goin' to market at Ware to buy zome beasts."

"Then, dam'me, I'll be his porter," returned the robber, laughing. "But bring us a glass of nut-brown, Luke, and put it down to my score ; I'll give ye a guinea for it when I come back."

The man grinned.

He entered the tavern.

Dick Turpin crept to the window.

He peeped in through the red curtains.

Beside the fire sat a fat old farmer, with a shock of silvery hair and a very red face, listening aghast to some tale of terror narrated by a little pale-faced, weasened old crony, dressed in a seedy suit of black.

The highwayman drew back, chuckling and rubbing his hands.

"Mark, ho !" he muttered. "A rare fat pigeon just ready for plucking." -

The ostler now brought out a glass of foaming ale.

Dick Turpin tossed it off.

"And what's to be done wi' the foine black mare, capt'in ?" asked the man.

"You must take charge of her, Luke, till I come back," replied Dick Turpin.

"Very good, zur, I'll ztow her away in one o' the ztables."

"But you won't play me false—ha ?"

"Loard, capt'in, arn't I zarved ye many a time avore ?" returned the rustic.

"Yes ; well and faithfully," replied the robber. "Look that you do so in this case."

"Fear now't, capt'in."

"Does the farmer ride alone ?"

"Aye, zure he do, zir."

"And when will he get on the road ?"

"Zo zoon as Muster Stretcher has done vinishing his lyin' ghost ztories."

"Then I'll push on," said the robber, laughing, "and waylay him on the road."

"Gad zooks ! do zo, capt'in," chuckled the ostler. "But doan'tee vorget the promus you've made I about the gowld guinea."

"You shall have two if I succeed, my boy," replied Turpin ; "and so look well to the mare."

"You may depend on me vor that, zur."

With this the fellow cautiously led the horse through the gate of the stable-yard.

Dick Turpin then removed his spurs and put them in his pocket.

He concealed his whip.

He wrapped his cloak tightly round him.

He strode on.

Walking as fast as he could he had in a short time placed a good long distance between himself and the old tavern.

At length he seated himself upon a mile-stone, and, folding his arms, began to cogitate upon his further proceedings.

A droll plan suggested itself to his mind.

He burst into a hearty fit of laughter.

"Ha ! ha !" he exclaimed aloud, in his glee. "That will do !"

At this moment he caught the distant click of a horse's hoofs.

It was a wild and solitary spot where he was resting.

He rose and walked for some distance down the road in the direction from which he heard the horseman advancing.

The old farmer now appeared trotting carefully along on a chestnut horse.

Dick Turpin crept to the bank.

Just as the farmer turned the bend in the road the highwayman threw himself down upon the bank, and placed his ear close to the ground.

He made no attempt to hide himself.

However, he turned his face towards the hedge.

He was choking with inward laughter.

Farmer Gosling rode up.

He at once caught sight of the robber.

He drew up his horse.

"Hulloa ! hulloa !" he shouted. "What's the matter, friend, are ye ill ? Have you been attacked by footpads ? They say that scoundrel, Dick Turpin, infests this neighbourhood. What is it? what is it ?"

Turpin did not answer.

He preserved the same attitude, crouching on the ground with his ear pressed close against the bank.

"Blame the fellow, is he dead ?" cried the farmer, lustily.

Still no answer.

"Dead drunk, mayhap. Well, it's no concern of mine," grunted the farmer.

He shook the rein, and spoke to his horse.

Suddenly Dick Turpin raised his head.

He held up his finger.

"Hist !" he exclaimed, mysteriously.

Once more he bobbed down his head.

He seemed listening with strained attention.

"Dash my wig ! what does all this mean ?" roared the farmer.

Dick Turpin once more looked up.

He shook his head solemnly.

Then he again pressed his ear against the earth.

"Blood an' 'ouns, man, what the deuce are you listening to ?" shouted the farmer.

"Ah, sir," said Dick, assuming an air of great mystery, "I wouldn't have believed—no, not if a bishop had sworn to it."

"Believe what ?" cried the farmer.

"No ; I would not have believed it," cried Dick,

stamping his foot emphatically. "No, not on the affidavit of an *arch*bishop."

"What wouldn't you believe?"

"This, sir," returned Dick, shrugging his shoulders.

Again he stooped down and listened.

"This! This what?" cried the farmer, whose impatience and curiosity were excited to the highest pitch.

"And yet, how can one doubt the evidence of one's own senses?" murmured Dick, thoughtfully.

"Are you drunk or mad?" cried the farmer, in amazement.

"Drunk I am not—mad I may be," returned Dick; "but tell me, sir, and tell me truly, do you not hear it yourself?"

"Hear what?"

"Do you really not hear it?"

"Gads my life! fellow! you make me as mad as yourself!" cried the farmer, in a towering rage.

"But hark!—hark!"

"Powder and blazes! I hear nothing."

"Nothing at all, sir?"

"The hooting of the owls—the babbling of yonder brook."

"Nothing else?"

"Ugh! what else should I hear?"

"Oh! the heavenly music! The crash of a thousand aerial harps!" sighed Dick Turpin.

"When did you escape from Bedlam?"

"And yet," continued Dick, thoughtfully, and without noticing this rude interruption, "I have often heard of them. One sensible man, the clerk of this parish, has vouched for the truth of such stories, and he is a shrewd, trustworthy man, a person whose veracity it would be a sin to doubt."

"I know the man, sir," cried the farmer, eagerly. "Mr. Stretcher, you mean? I quite concur in your opinion of him. What stories do you mean, sir?"

"About the fairies."

"Fairies—pish!"

"I have often 'pished' such tales myself, sir," rejoined Dick; "but I hear such melodious harmony of fairy music, that it is enough to charm me to sit here for ever and a day."

"Fudge!"

"Well, sir, I don't blame you for doubting a statement so extraordinary; but if you care to be convinced, you have but to dismount and hear for yourself."

Now the worthy farmer was one of the most credulous beings in the world, and found it impossible to resist his impulse of curiosity.

Accordingly he hurriedly scrambled from the saddle.

Dick still sat on the bank, and waved his hands with a languishing air of insane ecstasy.

The rascal acted his part so well that the poor farmer was completely taken in.

"Here, here, hold my horse, friend—she's such a bolter."

Nothing loth, Dick seized the rein.

"Now, now—where is it?"

"There, sir, there—t'other side o' the milestone."

"Here?"

"Yes."

"I don't hear it."

"Not the right place, sir. I'll show you."

"No, no—keep at the horse's head, man!" cried the farmer, hastily, "or she'll be off like a shot. Now, where is this music?"

"Just where you are, sir?"

The farmer took off his hat.

He laid his ear against the bank.

"Why, you rascal, I hear nothing!" he cried, indignantly.

"Try the left ear, sir."

The farmer moved to the other side.

His face was now turned away from the robber.

No sooner did Dick Turpin perceive this than he vaulted into the saddle.

With a loud laugh, he dashed away.

The farmer, instantly comprehending the trick that had been played him, sprang to his feet.

Uttering a roar of indignation, he started in pursuit.

Dick turned in the saddle.

"Do you hear the fairy music now?" he laughed, derisively.

He took the bag of gold from the saddlebow, and chinked it in his hands.

"The devil's in it if that is not magic music, and from the earth, too," he chuckled.

Then away he darted.

Panting and foaming with passion, the old farmer kept up the chase.

He had not run far, however, before he began to experience the effects of the unwonted exertion.

He was fain to fling himself down upon the bank and dry the perspiration from his heated brow.

Meanwhile Dick Turpin urged on the steed.

He was now within sight of the town.

He got off the horse.

Another scheme occurring to him, he let the animal trot on as before.

The innkeeper came rushing from the house.

"Why, bless my heart!" he cried, in utter astonishment, "here's farmer Gosling's horse returned without a rider!"

But Dick was ready for the occasion.

He stepped quickly up to the innkeeper.

"Your pardon, sir," he said, lifting his hat; "Are you the landlord of this tavern?"

"Aye, friend, what is your will?"

"You are surprised, no doubt, to see the horse return without his master?"

"Well, it's an odd thing, certainly."

"Well, sir, I must explain to you that I am a friend of Mr. Gosling's, who has met with some friends on the road, with whom he is going to the next village to engage in play. Not wishing to open his bag of money, which contains a certain sum, the amount he will require for marketing to-morrow, he has sent me to request you to lend him the small matter of fifteen guineas to make his game, and to keep his horse in pledge in the mean time until he returns in the evening."

"Ay, ay," returned the innkeeper, "a hundred guineas if he wants them."

With this he entered the house, and brought forth the money.

His liberality did not stop here.

He made Dick drink a glass of punch on the threshold, for the highwayman excused himself from entering the house, saying that he was bound to return on the instant.

Dick took a hasty leave.

The landlord once more went indoors.

The ostler stood at Dick's side.

His eyes glistened.

The robber put five guineas into his hand, and called for his horse.

Luke led him to the stable.

Dick Turpin mounted.

The ostler let him out by a back way.

Exulting at his success, the robber took the road to Islington.

An hour elapsed.

The landlord sat in the parlour, surrounded by his guests, smoking and drinking.

An hour or so passed.

At length the parlour door was burst open.

Puffing and blowing, farmer Gosling rushed in.

All rose in surprise.

"Why, my dear Mr. Gosling, what has happened?" he cried.

"Hath a fellow passed with my horse?"

"She's safe in the stable, sir."

"Where?"

"Why, here!"

"The devil!"

"Yes; but what need you have troubled yourself to send the horse as a pledge for such a trifle as fifteen guineas and so put yourself to the trouble of coming this cold night on foot?"

"Pledge!" gasped the farmer, "fifteen guineas!"

"Yes; I gave them to the man. He told me you had sent him."

"The villain!"

"Hey! what?" stammered the landlord. "Was not all right?"

"No!" roared the farmer. "The scoundrel was a highwayman."

"A highwayman!"

"Yes, and has robbed me of a bag containing three hundred guineas!"

The consternation caused by this announcement may well be conceived.

"Hang the dog! but it's some comfort he brought back the nag," growled the farmer, "but the rogue has made me pay three hundred guineas for hearing one tune of the fairies."

CHAPTER LXXIII.

DICK TURPIN'S FURTHER ADVENTURES — THE JEWELLER — A CUNNING TRICK — THE SNUFF-BOX — FOX HUNTING — THE RUSE — KINDNESS ILL-REWARDED — HOW TOM KING WOUNDED SIR MAURICE LACY — TURPIN'S ESCAPE.

AFTER this adventure Dick Turpin rode on towards London.

But after awhile, fearing pursuit, he made a detour through the country and reached Brantford at daybreak.

As yet he had not encountered Lady Lacy's coach, and concluded that she and her retinue had put up for the night at the "Peacock."

As he rode up the streets of the little country town the tradesfolks were opening their shops.

Amongst others he passed was a jeweller and goldsmith's.

The trader was counting a large sum of money.

Dick Turpin's eyes sparkled thievishly.

His first impulse was to rush in and pistol the poor fellow, and then seize his glittering treasures.

But the noise of fire-arms would cause an alarm.

No time was to be lost.

What could be done in this emergency?

He had a sword.

But there might be a scuffle.

He got off his horse.

He sauntered along the pavement, pondering for an expedient.

His invention, stimulated by his avarice, hit upon a plot.

He took out his snuff-box.

He emptied the contents into his hand.

Then slinking to the door he peered in.

The man was so busily absorbed in counting the money that he did not notice him.

But the robber's step on the floor caused him to lift his eye.

In an instant the villain dashed the handful of snuff into the luckless goldsmith's face.

The man yelled and danced with pain and raved with fury.

Dick Turpin deftly swept the money into his ample pockets.

He secured about fifty pounds.

Then, before the tortured goldsmith could prevent him, he rushed out of the door, and springing upon his bonnie Black Bess, scoured away.

"Hurrah for the road!" laughed the reckless outlaw, waving his whip. "How long would it have taken to earn so much blunt by honest means as I have secured to-night at one haul!"

His exultation, however, was somewhat checked when his eye fell upon the body of some gentleman of his craft swinging from a gibbet at the cross-roads.

He bit his lip and frowned.

Then he uttered a sullen, defiant laugh, and, according to a custom prevalent among the knights of the snaffle, saluted his defunct brother courteously as he passed.

He galloped on towards London.

As he was riding apace his ear suddenly caught the sound of carriage wheels.

He turned his horse's head and trotted to the bank side and got under cover of some bushes.

The sound of the carriage wheels grew louder and came nearer.

Dick could also distinguish the sound of horses' feet.

"Oh, if Tom, and Bush, Rose, Fielder, and Gregory were here to back me, wouldn't I clip the wings of these court butterflies?" muttered the robber; "but, curse it, this is too high a game for me to play single-handed."

While he was considering by what means he could effect his designs for plunder, his attention was attracted by a loud and cheery shout ringing across the fields and meadows, and the loud baying of a pack of hounds.

Presently a fox came rushing through the hedge, and shot across the road.

Poor Reynard showed every sign of distress; his reddish fur was ruffled, his bushy tail drooped, his long, red tongue hung from between his fangs.

"Tally-ho!" cried Dick Turpin, with sparkling eyes and the eager zest of a hunter.

The fox doubled, and, slinking back through the hedge, cunningly ran along the inner side of the hedge, baffling the pack that came pouring in a ruck over the long furrows of the ploughed glebe, and bursting through the bushes.

Turpin, unable to resist the temptation offered by the scene—for he considered fox-hunting the most delightful pastime in the world—cheered on the dogs.

They were at fault, and scattering up and down the road, expressed their impatience by incessant, deep-mouthed bayings.

At last they recovered the scent, and led on by two or three cunning old hounds, forced their way through the hedge, and were soon in full cry after the four-footed felon they were chasing.

The tantivies of the hunters' bugles rang merrily on the frosty air.

Turpin leaped his horse over the hedge.

He took a rapid glance around him, and across the country.

Down the white and winding road, on one hand, he perceived the coach and the party of cavaliers gaily rattling along.

Before him a scattered bevy of huntsmen came madly tearing along.

A sudden thought occurred to the robber, a plan by which he felt certain that he could make at least something in the way of booty.

The villain was well accomplished in his nefarious trade, being not only a brutal, unscrupulous highwayman and burglar, but also a skilful pickpocket.

The carriage and cavalcade were swiftly advancing, but had not yet appeared in sight, being still hidden behind the bend in the road.

Dick Turpin leaped back over the hedge.

Of course the gallant animal cleared it like an arrow.

But the robber had conceived a treacherous plan for robbing the cavalcade.

He dismounted.

Then he caused the beautiful black mare to lie down upon her side.

The splendid and sagacious creature was as docile as a dog.

Dick took her head in his hands, and laid it in such a position, and so arranged her whole body as to give her the appearance of having slipped down the bank, and rolled over in the road.

Then he tore his coat in the briars, tumbled over in the dust, lay down, and thrusting one foot through the stirrup, tossed away his hat and whip, and stretched himself out as if he had been stunned by a heavy fall.

The cavalcade now turned the angle in the road.

Several of the gentlemen who were riding in advance of the carriage, upon seeing the fallen horseman, uttered a shout.

They came dashing up.

"One of the huntsmen, Sir Ranulph; he has had a bad fall," said a gentleman.

"Aye, the poor fellow is killed, I think," returned Sir Ranulph Gayton.

"A splendid horse, too," said another.

"And the hedge is not high."

"No, but the bank is steep."

"It was this deep rut in the road that did the business."

"This day has been one of mischance," returned Sir Ranulph. "Our friend, Sir Maurice, is pinked by that ruffling blade who cheated us at cards——"

"That fellow was a highwayman, no doubt."

"Tom King, for a thousand!"

"And now," continued Sir Ranulph, "we find our way blocked by a dead man."

While these remarks were passing, Dick Turpin kept his eyes closed and his ears open, and affected to be quite insensible.

"What shall we do with him?"

"We cannot put him into the carriage, for Sir Maurice is there with Lady Eleanor Lacy. How far are we from the next village?"

"Four miles, at least, Sir Ranulph."

"At all events let us attend to the poor fellow."

The gentlemen, most of whom had dismounted, with the assistance of the servants, raised the prostrate man and bore him to the bank.

They then tried to get the horse upon her legs.

But the sagacious and faithful creature turned her eyes upon her master.

He made no sign, and she understood his wishes.

She resisted all their efforts to get her to stand on her feet.

"She is lamed for ever and must be destroyed," said Sir Ranulph, in a tone of regret.

"But let us see to her unfortunate master."

"Bring the flask of strong waters."

"And some water from the brook yonder."

"Loosen his cravat."

While these directions were being complied with, Dick Turpin slightly moved and uttered a deep groan.

Sir Ranulph bent over him and bathed his temples with his dainty laced handkerchief, which had been soaked in the water.

While he was being tended so kindly, the artful and graceless villain was not idle.

Quite unperceived by any of the bystanders, he contrived, with great dexterity, to relieve Sir Ranulph and two other of the Samaritans of their purses and watches.

He was particularly attracted by several large and valuable brilliants that glittered in the gentlemen's cravats.

He was, however, afraid to meddle with these jewels, lest they should at once be missed, either by the owners or the bystanders.

At length, after having been nearly strangled by the brandy which was poured down his throat, he thought it time to decamp, especially as one old gentleman who stood by was fumbling in his pocket to find his snuff-box, which the robber had abstracted.

He therefore moved his hand to his eyes and gazed wildly about him.

"Bravo!" cried the gentlemen, "he recovers; he is perhaps not much hurt after all."

They raised him up.

While doing so they were repaid for their kindness by the loss of the contents of their pockets.

"That cursed hedge," groaned the highwayman. "Thanks, gentlemen; a rascally trick of my companion's to leave me in this plight. Is the horse injured?"

"Ruined, I fear."

"Ha! I would as lief my own neck had been broken. Help me up, gentlemen—my leg is crushed, but, thank my stars, no bones are broken. Let me have a look at the poor mare."

With great difficulty, the gentlemen raised him in their arms.

"How did this happen?" asked one.

"Why, we were in full-cry after the fox, when I leaped my horse over the hedge. She took the leap gallantly, but stumbled at that infernal rut."

"I told you so, Sir Ranulph," rejoined one of the gentlemen.

"Can you stand?" asked another, addressing the robber.

"I think so," replied Dick, limping away towards his horse.

"We would offer you a seat in the carriage," said Sir Ranulph, "but it is occupied by Sir Maurice Lacy, who, besides being robbed, has been wellnigh murdered by a ruffian."

"Robbed—murdered!" repeated Turpin, in well-feigned surprise. "What, on the high road?"

"No, sir, but at the Peacock, a tavern at Islington."

"Was he alone, then?"

"No, our party halted there. We encountered a handsome, dashing-looking fellow, whose appearance was so distinguished, and his conversation so entertaining, that we suffered ourselves to be led on to play cards with him. At first he lost, but soon his luck changed, and amongst us he won five hundred guineas!"

"Five hundred guineas!" cried Turpin; then he added, mentally, "A rare night's work, though mine is the better purchase. But I must not holloa till I'm out of the wood."

"But, as we were shuffling the cards for the last time, continued Sir Ranulph, my friend Sir Maurice detected foul play. Swords were drawn, and in an instant Sir Maurice was run through the shoulder by the villain."

"Whom, of course, you immediately killed?"

"No such luck, sir," returned Sir Ranulph, with much chagrin. "I was not in the room when the gaming took place, but I entered just as the scoundrel was assailed by my friends. He fought his way to the door, and made a thrust at me as he passed ; and now I remember his face, which I saw but for an instant, I recognise in him the same villain that stopped my coach and fought with me some months ago."

"And his name, sir ?"

"Tom King."

"What ! the famous robber—the 'Gentleman's Highwayman ?'"

"The gentleman's devil !" growled Sir Ranulph.

"You may well say that, sir," returned Dick, seriously. "He is said to belong to the gang of that rascal, Dick Turpin."

"The same."

"Gentlemen, it is fortunate for you that he was alone. Had the rest of the gang been with him, you would have stood a chance of being robbed."

"I wish we could meet the ruffians !"

"That Turpin is a daring dog. But let me see to my poor horse."

Turpin walked to the side of Black Bess.

He caressed and encouraged her with soothing words.

After some time she struggled to her feet.

She stood trembling with excitement and anxiety, her head resting on her master's shoulder.

The gentlemen praised her in unmeasured terms.

"A noble creature ! If you felt disposed to part with her, I would purchase her at any price," said Sir Ranulph.

"The wealth of England would not buy her," returned the robber, with unaffected sincerity.

"Do you think you can manage to remount ?" said another, kindly.

"I will try," returned Turpin.

He placed his foot in the stirrup, and sprang into the saddle.

"'Twas rather an ugly fall," he said, with a smile ; "but I find I am little the worse for it."

"So it seems from the manner in which you sit your horse," said Ranulph.

"Gentlemen, in bidding you farewell, I must heartily thank you for the kind assistance you have rendered me," said Dick Turpin, raising his hat ; "I trust we shall meet again, and I wish you good night, and a safe journey."

The gentlemen returned his salute, and Dick Turpin dashed off at a rattling place.

He rode on for several miles without slackening his pace, but finally dropped into a quick canter, and made the woods ring with his exultant laughter.

He tossed up his hat in the glee of his heart, and then, with trembling fingers, he eagerly rummaged his pockets of their store of rustling bank notes, and richly glowing guineas, which he counted with great satisfaction.

CHAPTER LXXIV.

TOM KING'S STRANGE ADVENTURE—HIS HORSE TAMED—THE DREARY WALK THROUGH THE FOREST — THE WALTHAM BLACKS — DEER STEALERS CAROUSING — A NIGHT OF JOLLITY.

WE must now return to Tom King.

It is needless to recount his adventures of the Peacock tavern, for they have already been briefly but sufficiently referred to by Sir Ranulph Gayton.

When he had been detected in his cheating tricks at the card table, and been furiously set upon by the enraged gamesters, he fought his way to the door.

As he passed out he encountered Sir Ranulph Gayton.

They crossed swords.

In an instant Tom King disarmed his antagonist and bounded from the house.

His horse was waiting in the stable yard.

In a moment he had mounted, and was tearing along the road.

The young nobles speedily followed him, tumbling into their saddles, and giving hot chase.

Dick Turpin hastened on.

His beautiful white courser was in fine condition, and the hard road rattled under her flying feet, and the landscape on either hand swam dizzily past him.

The pursuers followed hard, most of them being splendidly mounted.

Tom King's escape appeared very problematical. Nothing recking, however, the daring scoundrel from time to time turned in the saddle, waving his hat, and urging his pursuers to come on.

But he found this diversion somewhat dangerous. Several pistol shots were fired at him.

More than once the speeding bullets passed close by his head, and crackled into the boughs of the low, sweeping trees.

"A highwayman ! a highwayman ! Tom King ! Stop him ! stop the villain !"

A sturdy fellow, a farm labourer, attempted to stop the mad career of the rushing steed.

He had cause to repent of his officiousness.

A downright blow from Tom's heavily loaded whip stretched him along the ground, senseless.

Onwards and onwards the robber urged his brave steed.

His progress was suddenly arrested by the appearance of a large number of well-mounted travellers, swiftly advancing towards him.

He turned.

Springing boldly over a high thicket and a wide, deep ditch, or ha-ha, he scoured across a gentleman's park.

He was forced to give up all idea of keeping his appointment with Dick Turpin.

He changed his course, and by a long detour, and at an easier pace, for he had outrun his pursuers and completely outwitted them, he made his way into the high road, which, crossing the borders of the two counties, brought him into Essex.

He finally arrived near Waltham, and here he was forced to get off his horse and lead her painfully along.

The sky had by this time become overcast with clouds, and the road was wild, dark and desolate, and penetrated through the heart of a wide, dense forest.

His horse, too, had got a stone in her foot, and progressed slowly.

Tom found himself much perplexed as to the right road to take.

He had lost his way.

Passing along a narrow path through the forest, he found himself emerging into the very road he had quitted before.

He muttered an impatient oath.

He looked up and down the road.

All was dark.

He continued his way.

The poor horse limped painfully and panted with anguish.

Tom broke a stick of dry wood from a tree.

Striking a light with his steel and tinder, he set fire to the branch.

Examining the horse's hoofs he found that a sharp flint had pierced one of them.

He tried to extract it.

His endeavours were fruitless.

Obliged to abandon the attempt, he dashed out the light, and once more led, or rather dragged along the poor horse through the gloomy woods.

All at once he perceived a dim light glancing through the wet leaves.

At first he took it for a wold-fire, or a glimmering Will-o'-the-wisp.

Watching it steadily, however, he soon perceived that it was stationary.

"Some cottage," he thought, "I can, perhaps, get there something to apply to my poor nag's foot."

He led his horse on.

After walking for some distance, he came in sight of the house.

It was large but low, being but one story high.

A rickety sign-post stood before the door, and swayed backwards and forwards in the wind, threatening every moment to topple over.

Tom King paused for a moment to gaze at the lone and weird-looking place.

The windows of a large upper chamber were ablaze with light and the sounds of loud laughter and revelry resounded from within.

Tom King was not a little surprised at what he heard and saw considering the solitude of the place, and its distance from the high road, and from any town or village.

"Come," said he, as a sudden impression forced itself upon his mind, "this may not turn out so bad, after all. 'Tis a party of fellow chips, comrades of the high pad, perhaps, or a party of deerstealers carousing; at all events, I'll put a bold face on the matter."

He stepped to the door, and hammered at it lustily with his riding whip.

"House ho!" he hallooed. "Open locks. A friend calls. House! house!"

There was a sudden hush.

So still was all within, that the loud ticking of an old case clock could be distinctly heard.

"Ha! ha!" laughed the highwayman. "'Tis as I thought, the rogues take me for a Bow Street runner."

Again he knocked loudly.

He got no answer.

He tried the door.

It was fastened from within.

"Phew!" he muttered. "'Tis a queer drum, and the lads within are over cautious."

> " ' O, I'm a tip-top toby gloak,
>   Tantarrara, tantarrarara,
>   With hand of steel, and heart of oak,
>   Tantarrara, tantarrarara.
>   I wrest what I will,
>   With a diver's skill,
>   From those rummy blokes as labour,
>   Sing tantarrara, rogues all, rogues all !' "

He paused.

A footstep.

"Who's there?"

"A friend, my roaring boys. Open, and let me in."

"Beware! I am armed!"

"So am I."

"What do you want?"

"What the devil should I want at an ale-house but a night's shelter and bait for myself and my horse?"

"The house is closed."

"So I perceive; but it can be opened, I take it."

"Who are you?"

"A friend."

"Give the word."

"I give it you; I am a friend, dam'me!"

"What's your name?"

"Jonathan Wild."

"Wild!"

"But none the less welcome in honest company, I trust."

"Are you alone?"

"No."

"Who is with you?"

"My horse."

"And you are Wild?"

"Dam'me, no; but I'm getting 'wild' enough at this infernal delay. Let me in, and be hanged to you."

"There's another inn a mile on."

"But a bird in hand is worth two in a bush."

"I can't admit you."

"Then I must admit myself."

"Take care; if you force the door I'll blow your brains out!"

"Blow away, my boy; I'm one of the right sort, I tell you. All's bowman, my noble."

"Stand clear, then; I will take a peep at you from the window."

"And a pop at me at the same time."

"No, fair and square; but I must see you."

"So, then, I am one of those phenomena that must be seen to be believed, eh? Look sharp, then. I am ready to face you if you'll only countenance me."

At this moment a window was thrown open, and a head thrust out.

Tom King looked up.

He started in great astonishment.

The face was black, and, surmounted with a powdered wig, looked the more comical.

"Who's there?" cried the black man.

"A stranger, your majesty," returned the landlord.

"Majesty!" repeated Tom King, "Zounds! but here's an adventure! So I'm to be presented to royalty—Satanic majesty, I should judge, from the royal phiz, or that hilarious potentate Old King Cole, perhaps."

"What fellow are you?" cried the man at the window.

"Your fellow, indeed!" laughed the robber, "for mine host says you are a king, and I am a 'king' too!"

"A king! What king?"

"King Thomas, otherwise Tom King."

"What! Tom King, the highwayman?"

"If I answered 'Yes,' what would you do—betray me?"

"Not I, forsooth—you shall be made welcome to our royal company."

"What monarch are you?"

"Oronoko, king of the blacks," laughed the other. Then he called down the stair—

"All right, Parvin, he's jannock—let him in."

A burst of laughter and a loud hum of conversation now succeeded to restraint and silence.

"I have it now," thought Tom, "I have fallen in with the Waltham Blacks, a crew of whimsical merry fellows, that are so mad as to run any hazards for a haunch of venison or spending a jolly evening. For my part, I always took the stories I heard of them for fables—'Gad, but I relish this adventure!"

The drawing of bolts and the falling of a heavy bar told Tom King that the door was being opened at the black's order.

The next moment it swung back, and revealed the landlord, who stood in the opening, pistol in hand.

"Come in, my night-bird," he said. "We don't often admit travellers; but since you seem to be one of the right sort, enter and welcome."

"But how about my horse?" said Tom. "The poor nag has got a flint in its foot, and is both tired and hungry."

"I'll see to your horse," returned Parvin; "and the beast shan't suffer in my hands. But if you like to come to the stables with me you can."

"My beast is always my first care," said Tom. "So if you'll put up that pop-gun and lay hold of the bridle, I'll follow you."

The man put away his pistol, and taking the bridle, led the animal round to the stables, which were situated at the back of the house.

Here, by the light of a lantern and with the aid of a knife, the flint was removed from the animal's foot.

It was fastened up to the manger, rubbed down with a wisp of straw, given a feed of corn and a bed, and then Parvin turned to Tom.

"Now, my hearty," he said, "your horse will be all right and comfortable, and you'll know where to find it if you want the beast in a hurry. So we won't keep his majesty and his jolly subjects waiting any longer, but back to the house."

Closing the stable door, Parvin preceded Tom King to the inn, and into a large room, where they were greeted by loud shouts of welcome from several voices.

A large party of well-dressed fellows were assembled.

They were all disguised, with blackened faces, and wore black gloves.

Tom King was formally introduced to a man more disguised than the rest, sitting at the head of the table, who was styled Prince Oronoko, King of the Blacks.

The highwayman was received very graciously, and placed on the right hand of the sable monarch.

The supper consisted of eighteen dishes of venison, in various shapes.

Roasted, boiled, with broth, hashed collops, umbel pies, and a large haunch in the centre, larded.

The table at which the roysterers sat was very large, and exclusive of Tom King, twenty-one sat down to supper.

Each had also a bottle of claret.

The man of the house and his wife sat at the lower end of the table.

A few of them had good musical voices.

The evening was spent with as great jollity as by the rakes at the "King's Arms," or the "City Apprentices" at Sadler's Wells.

About two the company broke up.

All of them assured Tom King that, upon any Thursday evening, they would be happy to see him at supper.

They also did him the honour to inform him of the rules by which their society was regulated.

The Black Prince informed him that their government was monarchical.

He stated that when they went upon any expedition, he had an absolute command.

But in times of peace, and at the table, he condescended to live familiarly with his subjects, as friends.

That no person was admitted into their association until he was twice drunk.

This precaution was taken that they might be fully acquainted with his temper.

When it was agreed that a brother should be admitted, he must provide himself with a good horse, a brace of pistols, and a gun to lie on the saddle bow.

Then he is sworn upon the horns over the chimney.

Thus is he constituted a member.

When all had departed, Tom King was shown to a little chamber, where he threw himself, more than half intoxicated, upon the bed, and placing his firearms close within his reach, having carefully barricaded the door, he sank into a long, dreamless slumber.

In the morning he rose early.

Having breakfasted, he called for his horse.

He mounted, and drank a stirrup cup with the landlord.

He presented the hostess with four guineas.

He then dashed off, and with a merry laugh, prosecuted his journey to London.

CHAPTER LXXV.

WHAT BEFEL OUR HERO ON BOARD THE PIRATE' CRUISER THE "SAN SALVADOR"—THE TYPHOON OR HURRICANE OF THE EASTERN SEAS.

THE "San Salvador," after her last encounter with the "Avenger," in order to escape from entire destruction, proceeded in the direction of the Eastern Seas.

In the contest her commander, Barabbas, had, by desperate means, contrived to still keep Violet Tremaine and Ellen Peveril his prisoners.

The dwarf had been also fortunate in securing Roving Jack, whose temerity in the action (by endeavouring, single-handed, to cope with the pirate) had ended in his detention and capture.

While skimming the waters one moonlight night. Barabbas, unseen, listened to a conversation (the first that had been permitted) between our hero and his well-beloved.

He essayed no remark upon that which was passing before him, nor did he indulge in his usual taunts and sneers.

"Let me look upon thee once again, that I may assure myself that it is no dream," said the young girl, pressing the pirate-hunter to her bosom. "No, it is indeed John Warbold, the adoration of my soul."

"Yes, Violet, 'tis I," replied the youth, "who can scarce believe I am the recipient of so much happiness. Let me also gaze upon you, that I may ascertain that I dream not."

Passing his hand gently through her tresses waved by the ocean wind, he continued,

"Smile upon me, dear one, as you smiled on our first protestation; cast upon me, perchance for the last time, those beautiful eyes, full of tenderness as on the day I learnt the secret of thy soul."

The maiden's heart was too full to answer.

It was her lover's voice.

She caught the sound, and started as the roe at the hunter's approach, and leapt once more into his arms.

"This moment of pleasure," cried the enraptured Jack, "amply repays the hours of torture I have suffered since I have been a prisoner in this charnelhouse and ship of death. Is it not so?"

"Yes, solicitude, sorrow, fear, are all forgotten."

"But how my Spanish gaoler came to my dungeon with your missive. How my hand trembled as I opened the letter he gave me. I pressed it with transport to my lips, and kissed it a thousand times; my tears bathed it, and though agony and despair rent my heart, I hastened, intoxicated with joy and breathless with delight, to your side."

"Let us be seated; I on this old sea-chest, and you——"

"At your feet, as I should be at this mysterious and nocturnal rendezvous," added our hero, in his usual gallant manner.

Resting on the rude oaken couch, after a pause. Violet exclaimed,

"Jack, you will hardly credit that which I shall tell you, for, despite my chagrin and remorse, a joy ineffable and pure at this moment seizes me and effaces every trace of peril or sorrow."

Suddenly the features of the maiden became overcast; the soft and happy smile vanished, and as the sunshine of spring is followed by the falling rain-drop, the ray that beamed in her laughing eye was obscured with a tear.

"Why, why is this, dear Violet?" said Jack, in astonishment. "To what am I to attribute this weeping?"

"A cruel destiny seems to hang over your condition and mine, and seems likely to pursue us from the cradle to the grave."

"What do you mean?"

"That the miscreant who commands this ship, impatient of your blood, has doomed you to death before to-morrow's sunset"

"Though your words strike upon my heart like a hammer of iron, I shall not shrink when my time comes," exclaimed our hero, boldly. "Life's cable, I feared, was nearly run out with me, for I could not expect much mercy at the hands of the buccaneers, against whom I have ever waged the war of extermination."

"My heart will break, Jack, for the sun which frowns upon you to me also wears a threatening aspect."

"Fear not, dear Violet, Providence that watches over the sparrow will care for you, and Heaven will be your protector when I am gone."

Musing, Jack Warbold arose from his recumbent position, and walked fretfully across the deck.

This scene, as the reader has been informed, had been witnessed by Barabbas; but he had remained unnoticed by the speakers, the last of whom came back to his mistress after he had taken a few turns.

"Violet," he muttered, "at noon endeavour to be near the ship's companion, for that is about the time I shall arrive. Await me at this spot, I beg, where you must remain concealed, and in silence."

"Why this mystery?"

"Rely on me—the only course that remains——"

"Is that of——"

"Flight—instant flight."

"Dare you——"

"Nay, Violet, reassure thyself; something tells me I shall succeed in the enterprise I am about to undertake."

"But Ellen Peveril."

"Shall be a partner in our escape."

"Hush!"

Heavy footsteps were heard advancing.

Violet Tremaine heard all this with a cheek now crimsoned with expectation, now blanched with apprehensive fears.

Leading her gently aside, affection, love, happiness inspiring his theme, our hero sought to paint the bliss that should be theirs in his intended project.

*　　*　　*　　*　　*

With the sun rose the daring crew of the pirate barque the "San Salvador."

The motley throng were gathered apparently from every corner of the earth, and were composed of all nations.

There were Lascars, Ethiops, and Chinese, English, French, the Italian and Spaniard. All were bedecked in costume agreeable to their taste, mostly romantic, but in all cases picturesque.

Barabbas, their stunted leader, was dressed as a sea-captain of the period of our tale, save that, in lieu of the received cocked-hat, he affected a broad, black "sombrero," ornamented with a silver band and tassels of that metal.

Rotaldo, his lieutenant and second in command, by birth a Spaniard, was similarly attired, and, like his senior, eschewed the headgear usually worn, and substituted in its place a scarlet velvet cap, highly, if not to say, richly decorated.

"We have every prospect of typhoon, skipper," said Rotaldo, who had been watching the barometer. "Not only the glass, but the weather also threatens us."

"Then it behoves us to make all snug and square," growled Barabbas. "Send down topgallant yards and small sails in the twinkling of a marling-spike, and we shall be out of it in a minute."

There were unmistakeable signs of that seaman's dread, the typhoon, a tempestuous hurricane peculiar to the Chinese and adjacent latitudes.

The sea was smooth, but the wild moaning of the wind gave notice of the approaching storm.

The white haze that had sprung up like a phantom round the devoted ship gathered fast, and grew thicker and thicker.

The men were turned up, everything of weight sent below, and the guns secured.

Suddenly, with the speed of lightning, came a blast of wind, which careened the ship, passed over, and in an instant she righted as before.

A few moments' suspense, and a second gust follows the first; then another and another, fiercer and fiercer still.

The sea, although tranquil now, appeared milk-white and of a death-like hue, as the typhoon, or hurricane, swept along in its impetuous and headlong career.

It burst upon the vessel.

The "San Salvador" bowed down to it to her gunwale, and there remained.

In a quarter of an hour the tempest had passed over, and the stout timbers of the corsair were relieved.

But, with the commotion, the ocean had risen in surging billows, and a gale blew fast and strong.

An hour elapsed, and the tyrannous blast again assumed its dominion.

It came more furious and wilder than on its previous appearance.

The waves rolled mountains high.

The pitiless rain in torrents descended.

The frail barque was on her beam ends, and there remained till the conflicting elements had hurried onward, to sweep destruction on the far-off region, but leaving behind them a boiling, raging, and tumultuous sea.

For a third time the typhoon returned, and all was of a murky, dismal gloom.

It seemed as if some heavy fog had been hurled by the angry wind.

Nothing was to be seen but the white and seething foam, scarcely discernible at the distance of half the cable's length when it was lost in a long, gray mist.

The storm stay-sail yielded to the force of the hurricane, and was rent into a thousand pieces, while the storm, which had gradually come on, at length assumed a fury too powerful for pen to describe.

This continued till twelve o'clock at night when all on board were awakened by a shock.

The thickness of the night prevented the pirates from seeing where they were, but throwing the lead over the side they found they were lying on shore on a sand-bank.

There was not more than fourteen feet of water on the deepest side; they were broadside on, and a strong current pressing them further up the shoal.

The current run like a mill race, and at each roll of the wave they were swept further onward.

The anchor that now was let go to prevent the vessel being carried on parted at the shank, and compelled the mariners to provide themselves with another.

Nothing could be done till daybreak, and with impatience the desperadoes awaited till the morning.

As the rising sun gilded the eastern horizon the mist cleared up, and the adventurous men found themselves more deeply embedded than ever in the sand-bank.

A small portion was observed above the water, and around this the water ran with greater impetuosity.

About three miles from the scene of this disaster were a cluster of small islands bearing tropical foliage, but without the appearance of inhabitants.

"I fear, skipper," observed Rotaldo, to Barabbas, "that we have little chance in this dilemma. Even if we lighten our vessel, heaped with golden spoil, we shall be dragged forward, and it seems m-possible to me to lay an anchor against the force of this current."

"Belay, belay your jawing tackle," retorted Barabbas. "Soft words won't fill an empty stomach, and we must try——"

"I see," interrupted the lieutenant, "that you yourself confess that our situation is anything but satisfactory."

The captain muttered a sort of growl between his teeth, then immediately sent all hands aft.

The order was obeyed.

The crew came aft.

On each countenance was depicted gloom and desperation.

"My lads," said Barabbas, "why are you disheartened?"

"We are doomed," seemed to be the general reply.

"Psha!" continued the deformed skipper, "the loss of a ship does not involve that of her crew—nor does it follow that the 'San Salvador' is to be lost, although she may be in great danger, as she is at present. What fear should we have? The water is smooth as a lady's palm—we have plenty of time upon our hands—we can make a raft and take to our boats.

"It never blows among these islands.

"We have land close under our lee.

"Let us try what we can do with our trusty galiot.

"Should we fail," concluded Barabbas, "despite all consequences, we must look to ourselves."

The pirates acquiesced in the remarks of their commander, and one and all went to work willingly.

The water casks were started.

The men began to work the pumps, and everything that could be spared hastily disappeared to lighten the ship.

Notwithstanding the efforts of the toiling crew, they found their anchor still dragged with the strength of the current and bad holding ground, that they went further on the bank.

Night came on before they quitted their labour—then a fresh breeze sprung up and created a swell.

This occasioned the ship to beat on the hard sand, and thus she continued until the next morning.

At daylight the men resumed their work at the pumps, but after a time pumped up only sand.

This told them that a plank had started, and that their endeavours were futile.

"Messmates," shouted Barabbas, as the discovery was made, "since fortune frowns upon us, let us do that which ever gains her smiles—courage ever finds favour in her eyes, and difficulties give way to enterprise and resolution. We must desert the ship and construct a raft, as I have already hinted to you. Let it be provisioned and used for those who cannot be taken into the boats."

These words had scarcely escaped the lips of Barabbas, when the yards were lowered, the topsails struck, and the raft commenced, under the lee of the "San Salvador," where the strong current flowing vigorously was checked.

In a few hours the raft was completed.

Water and provisions were then safely stowed on board.

Here, in the centre, a secure and dry place was made up for the reception of their prisoners, Jack Warbold, Violet Tremaine, and Ellen Peveril.

Violet being kept apart from the others, for what purpose the reader has yet to learn.

The fearless rovers next provided themselves with spare rope, sails, and everything that could prove useful as rigging in case of their being forced to go on shore.

Muskets and ammunition also formed no mean part of their cargo, and intended to be used as emergency required.

All being ready, before trusting their raft to the foaming waters, Barabbas addressed his followers—

"My brave companions, there is yet one thing we have neglected; in the hold of the forsaken barque is a fabulous amount of specie taken from the Spanish trader, who had the temerity to dispute our will. Noble blood has earned it, and noble blood shall preserve it! Let each, therefore, take his share, and deposit it in safety near the magazine."

The pirates then, for the first time, went down into the hold of their vessel, and handed out casks of dollars.

These were broke open, and they helped themselves.

This action was attended with no serious bloodshed, though the men quarrelled with each other as each cask was opened for its first possession.

At last every man had obtained as much as he could carry, and placed his spoil in the appointed depôt.

The boatswain then gave the word as the captives were lowered down, and took their station.

The courage of Roving Jack never for one instant failed him, as he gave a defiant look at the pirate captain and his lawless band.

The former of the last mentioned parties had noted well what appeared to him an important matter, and being aware that as the water and provisions were expended there would be no occasion to tow so heavy a mass, he constructed it in two parts.

These parts were separated, and might easily be severed.

Thus by these means the boats would have less to tow as circumstances would enable them to part with one of them.

On the given signal the boats took the raft in tow.

It was cast off from the vessel, and away went the pirates, pulling with all their strength to avoid being stranded upon that part of the shoal which appeared above water.

This, as the reader may suppose, was a considerable danger they had to encounter, and one which they very narrowly escaped.

———

CHAPTER LXXVI.

THE RAFT—THE STRUGGLE FOR LIFE—VIOLET TREMAINE CAST ADRIFT.

THERE were ninety souls in all.

The four boats were filled, the remainder continued on the raft.

The raft, being well built and full of timber, floated high out of the water, which was now again smooth.

It had been agreed upon that Barabbas should take command of the raft, while the boats should be under the control of his lieutenant—Rotaldo the Spaniard.

At the time they quitted the ship, both leaders were on the raft in order to consult with respect to the direction of the current, and the most advisable course to pursue.

After a deliberation, these men found that they were drifting towards the coast of New Guinea.

At that time its inhabitants were known to be cowardly, hostile, and treacherous.

And Barabbas decided on waiting for events, and see what might occur.

In the meantime the boat pulled to the westward, while the current set them fast in a southerly direction.

A new danger now threatened the mariners.

They discovered that a proa, filled with armed and hostile natives, was sweeping after them from one of the islands to the windward.

The proa, having reconnoitered her antagonist, commenced firing from a small piece of cannon on her bows.

The enemy advanced nearer, and her fire became destructive, while the pirates were without an opportunity of returning it.

Barabbas ordered the boats.

He and Rotaldo were now stationed to attack the natives as the only chance of escape.

The raft was accordingly cut, and the boats pulled away.

The voice of Jack Warbold, who had been allowed to volunteer in the party, was heard by his fellow captives.

His sword was seen to flash through the air.

A moment afterwards he plunged into the sea, and swam to the raft.

The men in the boats, anxious to preserve the money which they had secretly drawn from the magazine, agreed among themselves to pull away, and leave the raft to its fate.

The natives, imagining that in taking to their boats the pirates had some further motive, instead of firing as hitherto at the raft, gave chase to the fugitives.

Thus were those who expected to escape, and who had deserted their companions, deservedly punished, while those who anticipated danger and death from such a desertion, discovered it had really saved them from such a fate.

Those remaining on the raft amounted to about twenty.

Provisions on board they had sufficient for three or four weeks.

Of water they were very short, not having more than enough for three days at the usual allowance.

This article it was agreed should be so served out as to extend the supply to eight days.

When again under sail it was debated, as the raft was in two parts, whether it would not be better to cast off the smaller one.

This proposition was rejected, and they scudded on as usual.

On the fourth day they sighted land.

The difficulty under which they now laid was having no grapnel or anchor to the raft.

Our hero, who, since the departure of Barabbas and Rotaldo, who had gone with the others in the boats, had so ingratiated himself with the remainder of the disaffected as to be in a measure their leader and adviser, thus addressed his companions in the pressing necessity :—

" Messmates, if you have still confidence in yourselves, I think I have struck upon a plan that will surmount the difficulty that opposes us. There still remains a large amount of specie in the magazine. and what I propose is this, that each man should take his quantity of dollars, which being sewn up separately in canvas bags, to denote the share, should be sunk——"

" What, throw our treasure into the sea!" was the general exclamation.

" No; the weight of the coin (being attached to the ropes by which they will be lowered and raised) will enable us to hold the raft against the current for one night, and at daybreak we have every chance of reaching the shore which rises to our view."

" I, for one, refuse to act as you say," replied a swarthy pirate named Francisco, and who seemed elected as spokesman of the party, " I would as soon encounter the perils of the deep as invest my gold in such a madly adventurous scheme. Let us rather trust to the mercy of the waves, for if the current continues we shall be washed ashore by morning."

" Fools ! worshippers of Mammon !" exclaimed Jack, " who sell your souls for dross, rather than risk your money you would sooner part with life by the most miserable death ! "

Again and again Jack Warbold argued with his followers, but in every instance without success.

Violet Tremaine and Ellen Peveril, since the boats had quitted the raft, were allowed their liberty, and, like the partner of their captivity, were no longer prisoners.

Ellen proved a valuable adviser to her friend, and a comfort to the hero of our tale in his present misfortunes.

" Cheer up," she would say, " we shall yet build our cottage under the shade of yon cocoa-nut trees," indicating the afar off land, " and pass a portion, if not the remainder, of our days in peace. For who, indeed, is there who will find us in these desolate and untrodden regions?"

As night closed in the hapless people neared the land, but, the breeze dying away, they were swept back by the current.

The pirates now rose, and, in spite of the endeavours of Jack Warbold, rolled into the sea all the provisions and stores.

They kept back one cask of spirits and the remaining stock of water.

Francisco, who had hitherto seemingly befriended our hero and the females, now assumed the leadership of the band.

These he ordered to the upper end of the raft, and he sat down with them himself.

Each exhibited gloomy threatening looks, as all became engaged in close consultation.

These proceedings Jack Warbold noticed with a feeling of considerable anxiety.

He advanced towards the conclave and again urged them to anchor with their money.

He urged in vain, for they peremptorily ordered him from their presence.

Dejected at their refusal he returned to the after part of the raft, upon which he had erected a secure retreat for Violet and Ellen.

He leant on it in deep thought and melancholy, for he imagined that its occupants were wrapt in the arms of peaceful slumber.

" What distracts you ?"

" The folly, guilt and avarice of these fearful men," was our hero's reply to Violet's question. " They will die rather than risk their hateful money."

The quivering lip of Violet proclaimed the struggle she underwent to repress her almost uncontrollable indignation. Skilled, however, in the mastery of her emotions, she repressed it.

" They have the means," continued Jack, " of saving themselves and us, and they will not. There is weight enough in bullion on the fore part of the raft to hang a dozen floating masses such as this, and yet they refuse my entreaties."

" Cursed love of gold, it makes men fools, madmen, aye, villains !"

" We have now but two days' water, doled as it is drop by drop."

Violet gave an involuntary shudder.

"Look yonder at the storm-tossed crew; look at their emaciated, broken-down, wasted forms, and yet see how they cling to money, which probably they will never have occasion for, even if they gain land."

"You are suffering, Jack, from privation," said Violet, mildly; "but I have been careful; as I thought this would come, I have saved both water and biscuit. I have here four bottles; drink some, it will relieve you."

Jack Warbold swallowed the contents of the cup, rendered more exquisite to his arid throat than the most delicious wine, for the excitement of the day had pressed heavily on him.

"Thanks, dearest Violet; thanks; I feel better now. Good heaven! are there such fools as to value the dross of metal above one drop of water in a time of misery and suffering like this?"

The evening closed in as before.

The stars shone brightly.

But there was no moon.

At midnight our hero was called, and went to relieve a man from the steerage of the raft.

Usually the pirates had lain about in every direction, on this occasion the majority of them remained forward.

Jack at the helm was communicating with his own thoughts when a sound arrested his attention.

He could distinctly hear the smothered noise of a scuffle, and the stifled voice of Ellen Peveril crying out for help, and calling his name.

Quitting the helm, the daring youth seized his cutlass and hurried to the spot.

Ellen was bound to a spar, and her oppressors securing her.

Quick as the lightning's flash our hero cut his way to the fainting woman, but was himself seized by the dastards who had surprised him from behind.

"Let go the ropes!" was the cry of those who held him, and in a few seconds Jack Warbold, with seared eyeballs, beheld the after part of the raft with Violet Tremaine upon it drift from the one on which he stood.

"For mercy sake save her!" shrieked Jack, struggling in vain to disengage himself from the grasp that held him back. "Monsters! you are murdering her before my very eyes!"

Violet, overcome by terror for the moment, became motionless as a statue; suddenly, as if waking from a dream, she stretched out her arm as if to invoke succour.

It was in vain.

The loving and beloved were separated more than a cable length.

Jack made one last desperate struggle, but, as one stricken by palsy, fell down senseless, and without reason.

CHAPTER LXXVII.

ALONE WITH DEATH—THE WIDE WASTE OF WATERS—AT THE MERCY OF THE WAVE—THE SHRIEK FOR HELP WHERE NO HELP CAN COME.

WHAT power is sufficient to portray the feelings of the fond and doating Violet?

Bewildered and maddened, she beheld the raft fade imperceptibly from her view.

Recovering from her swoon, she cried—

"Who's there?"

No answer.

"Who's here?" she exclaimed, in a louder voice, then gathering her scattered senses she called to mind the incidents of the past hour.

"Alone, alone, on the wide waste of waters! Heaven have mercy on an erring soul! To thy care let Violet, the wretched Violet, commit herself."

With these last words the poor deserted girl sunk down on the edge of the raft, and fell over on her side, with her long hair floating on the passing wave.

After remaining in a state of torpor for some hours the sun glared fiercely upon her.

The golden rays dazzling her eyes, she at length opened them.

"Ah! me! where am I?" she cried, in despair, as she cast her glassy orbs on the vast expanse before her.

A sudden shriek, more piercing than the battling elements, escapes the lips of the castaway.

Yes; there it lay, black, fierce, and bloodthirsty, waiting for its prey.

She was not mistaken.

Motionless by her side drifted an enormous and rapacious shark.

Its white teeth glared in its open mouth, fleeced with foam, and its eyes assumed an orange tinge.

At that moment they gleamed in the dark with a blue phosphorescence imparting to them a kind of wolfish lustre, and veiling their real hue.

Recoiling a few steps after she had started up, she turned round and beheld the raft vacant.

'Twas now that the horrid truth flash conviction to her very soul.

"Oh! Jack! Jack!" she cried, "you are gone for ever. I thought it was only a dream; I recollect all now. Yes all—all!"

Here Violet sank down upon her cot, which had been placed in the centre of the raft, and remained absorbed in grief for some time.

The demand for water at length became imperious.

She rose up, seized one of the bottles and drank.

"Yet, why should I drink?" cried the frantic girl. "Why preserve life?"

She looked around the horizon.

There was sky and water, nothing more.

"Is this the death I am to die?" she continued. "The cruel death—to linger here till water be expended, and then to await, under a burning sun, while my vitals are parched within."

The thought was madness.

"Nevertheless, be it so.

"Fate, I dare thee to the worst. We can die but once, and without him what care I to live?"

After a pause, Violet again spoke.

"But may I not see him once more? Yes, I may, who knows? Then welcome life. I'll nurse thee for that bare hope."

Bare indeed, with naught to feed upon.

"Let me see, it is still here."

As violet uttered the sentence, she looked at her belt and perceived her dagger was still in it.

"Well, I will live since death is at my command, and husband life for my brave lover's sake."

Here Violet threw herself on her resting place that she might forget everything.

She did.

For, from that morning till the noon of the next day, she remained in a state of torpor. When she arose she was faint, and again desolation was before her, for Heaven and ocean alone met her gaze.

"Oh! this solitude is horrible," she murmured; "death would be a release; but, no, I must live for him who holds my heart."

Violet refreshed herself with water and a few pieces of biscuit, and folded her arms across her breast.

Anon, black and heavy clouds span the canopy of Heaven.

Lightning darted through the firmament, disclosing more fully the frail raft to the vacant eye of Violet.

The thunder's majestic peal resounded in the vault above, while terrific flashes cast their glare from every quarter.

The breeze rose up fresh, and the limpid waves washed the feet of the outcast.

"This pleases me better than the withering calm heat; it arouses me from my hideous stupor."

As Violet uttered the words she cast her eyes upward and gazed on the forked flame till her vision became lost.

"This is as it should be," she exclaimed; "bolts of Heaven strike me as ye list—waves wash me off and bury me in a briny tomb. I care not."

Then, pointing to the dagger that hung suspended from her girdle, she continued—

"This little steel can do as much.

"Death, I fear not. I laugh at, and defy thee.

"There is no hope.

"I mount my funeral bier.

"I wait the will of destiny."

Violet regained the secure space which our hero had fitted up for her in the centre of the raft.

She threw herself down upon her pallet and closed her eyes.

The thunder and lightning was followed by a drenching tropical rain, which ceased not till the morrow morning's daylight.

The wind continued fresh, but, as the sky became clear, the sun broke forth.

Violet was motionless; her garments wet, and she shivered in every limb.

As the day advanced the heat of the sun affected her exhausted frame.

Her brain wandered.

She saw around her verdant meadows—fields waving ocean-like with golden corn.

In every direction the cocoa-nut was rocked and tossed by the wind.

Her imagination then pictured to her distorted fancy that—

She saw Jack Warbold in the distance hastening to her.

She held out her arms.

Strove to get up and meet him.

Her limbs refused their office.

She called—she screamed; then sunk terror-stricken and exhausted.

CHAPTER LXXVIII.

THE STRATAGEM—HOW ROVING JACK AVENGED HIMSELF ON THE PIRATES OF THE RAFT—ONCE MORE ON LAND.

WE must now return to Roving Jack and follow his strange destiny.

It was not until the dawn of day he opened his eyes.

Ellen Peveril was kneeling by his side.

His mind was distraught and pictured to his fancy a scene of dread calamity.

At last it rushed upon him, and he buried his face in his hands.

"Be comforted, Jack," said the brave woman; "let us put our trust in Providence, and we may reach the shore to-day. Once on land, we will find means to escape these ruffians, and go in search of Violet."

"Oh, what a cruel death will be hers!" muttered our hero. "She will waste away beneath a scorching sun, without one drop of water to moisten her parched and burning throat—at the mercy of the storm, drifting about in the wind and wave alone, with none to hear her death-shriek or close her eyes!"

Ellen Peveril offered consolation again and again, but her efforts to restore the companion of her misfortune were in vain; suddenly, after a few minutes' reflection, he started up.

"Ellen, I am myself again!" he exclaimed. "I am tranquil, calm now; but it is the calm that presages the tempest. Listen: Violet will be avenged!"

*   *   *   *

It was a lovely night; the silver moon danced on the waters, and the sea was unruffled by an air which moved not on the heavens.

Here, on a raft, were twenty desperadoes, ready for murder, combat, and spoil, but rendered powerless by the poison Roving Jack had mingled with the water they had drank.

Each of the party, feeling in their delirium that treachery had been practised, watched the other, not knowing upon whom to lay the odium.

Our hero feigned to suffer as the rest, and hinted that, for sake of gain, one of their number must have administered to his companions some pernicious drug, and that, on reaching land, that was not then far distant, he could give an antidote which would defeat the purpose of the dastard and traitor who had attempted the life of one and all.

Staggering, as if under the influence of the deadly draught, he, with apparent difficulty, took the helm, taking care that Ellen Peveril should be by his side, to whom he might entrust it in case of need.

The stifled groans of some of the expiring pirates soon told that the poison they had taken was performing its duty, and that the moment of vengeance was drawing near.

The knowledge of this bore Jack up as he felt the keen edge of his cutlass, impatient for the time when retribution should arrive.

At length he gave a signal to Ellen Peveril, which was promptly obeyed.

Suddenly she let go the halyards of the yard, and the sail fell upon their dying enemies in such a manner as to entangle them.

As the sail and yard fell clattering down, the work of death commenced.

There was no parley—no suspense—and each man met his fate.

The voice of Jack alone was heard, and his reeking blade was soon bathed in gore.

Revenge nerved his arm, and it stayed not while one remained who had sacrificed the beloved Violet.

As may be imagined, the sail falling on the crew enervated by the noxious drug they had taken, fell an easy prey to their destroyer, Roving Jack, who was thus enabled to perform his task of blood with little or no difficulty.

Some fell where they stood.

Others reeled back, and were buried in the green waters of the ocean.

Whilst most were pierced as they floundered under the fallen canvas.

In a few minutes the carnage was completed.

The pirate-hunter stood against the mast to recover his breath.

"Violet, thou art avenged!" exclaimed he, after

a pause ; " but what are these paltry lives compared to thine ? Should I——"

The thought that his revenge was satiated again choked his utterance, and he could say no more.

Averting his face from the gaze of Ellen Peveril, he wept bitterly.

As the morning broke the breeze sprung up, and the two survivors on the raft shared out the unpolluted water that they had secreted for their own use.

Neither Jack Warbold nor Ellen Peveril felt the pangs of hunger, but the water revived their spirits.

The rising breeze now freshened, and in two hours the wanderers expected to reach the shore they had sighted.

In this they were disappointed, the step of the mast giving way to the force of the wind and causing the sail to fall upon the raft.

This occasioned great delay.

The wind again subsided.

And they were left within about a mile from the looming beach.

Tired, and worn out by his feelings, Jack Warbold fell asleep, leaving the faithful Ellen by his side at the helm.

He slept soundly.

He dreamed of Violet.

He thought he slumbered under a grove of cocoa-nuts in a sweet sleep.

That she smiled and murmured his name, when he was awakened by a struggle that was taking place near the spot upon which he reclined.

A gleaming knife was at his throat, and Ellen was overpowered by a pirate who, not having partaken of the poisoned water, had secreted himself in order to avenge his comrades' death.

Startled to his senses, he threw up the arm that was about to strike with death his fainting companion, and a terrific struggle for life took place between the antagonists.

Anticipating the attack, the pirate, measuring the short intervening distance, stood on his guard.

His sword was firmly set between his teeth, and his two pistols with magical abruptness appeared in his grasp.

He fired, but his opponent, with the rapidity of lightning, threw himself to the ground, and rose again when the danger had past.

Thus foiled, the pirate stood before his foe like a wild beast caught in a hunter's trap.

He was foaming, furious, and breathless, and evidently dismayed.

He looked the very serpent, and the malignant scowl of his small and snaky eye gave singular force to the resemblance of that hideous reptile.

Roving Jack, his generous enemy, gave him time to recover from the surprise his dexterity had caused, and met his stern defiance.

Now was witnessed a conflict unparalleled for intense and eager thirst of blood.

It was truly the death grapple of the lion and the serpent.

The swords of the combatants flashed fire at every stroke, and seemed unrivalled for quickness, each being so skilled that their weapons seemed to play with a motion rapid and incessant as to parry and thrust at the same instant.

The encounter was for some time continued with unabated fierceness, when the weapon of our hero snapped at the hilt.

At that moment he would have assuredly perished had not Ellen Peveril, who had recovered from the swoon into which she had fallen, thrown herself before him.

The sword of the pirate was hastily descending on her devoted head, when Jack seized his wrist. The steel flew from his grasp as he received a mortal wound from the broken blade of his intrepid and youthful adversary.

Our hero gazed awhile in solemn and impressive silence on the man he had destroyed.

His broad forehead darkened with deep thought, and his eyes saddened with painful recollections of the beloved girl whose untimely fate he had so well avenged.

Soon, however, his noble eye brightened, and a fervent look of piety, joy, and resignation was written on his features.

Once more left to themselves on the raft, Jack Warbold and Ellen Peveril, to their surprise, discovered that during the contest they had gained the shore, so long looked at with anxiety and suspense.

The spars were jerked by the running swell, and rubbed against each other as the grounded raft rose and sunk to the waves breaking on the beach.

As the surf was trifling, the landing was secured without difficulty.

The beach was shelving and composed of firm white sand, interspersed with various brilliant coloured shells, and the white fragments and bones of animals forced out of the element to die.

The island, like those of the latitude, was covered with a thick wood of cocoa-nut trees, whose tops waved to the breeze or bowed to the blast.

This produced a shade and freshness delightful to the castaways, who had so long suffered from the effects of a torrid climate.

Jack no sooner reached the land than he run down to the furthest point in order to look for the portion of the raft which held Violet.

It was nowhere to be seen, and Ellen Peveril, aware that the worst paroxysms were past and that there was no danger of her companion throwing his life away, followed leisurely on his footsteps.

" Gone, for ever gone !" exclaimed Jack.

" Not so ; the same Providence which has been our preserver, will, I feel assured, assist Violet.

" It is impossible she can have perished among so many islands.

" Most of which are inhabited ; and a woman will be sure of kind treatment."

"I wish I could think so," was the ejaculation of Jack Warbold.

" A slight reflection may convince you it is the wisdom of the Omnipotent that she should be separated from you.

THE ESCAPE.—*See next Number.*

"Not only from you," continued Ellen, "but from so many lawless companions, whose united force, had we not resorted to stratagem, we could not have resisted."

"True."

"Do you think that after any sojourn on this island, the pirates would have permitted you to remain in quiet possession of the maiden?"

"No."

"They would respect no law, social or moral; and Violet, by their apparent brutality, has been miraculously saved from ill treatment, shame, and death."

"Ellen Peveril, you have been my guardian angel, and now your words bring comfort to my afflicted heart."

"But we will not be idle."

"No; we will make a raft and follow in her trail, for I will not give up the hope of finding her, though I travel the wide, wide world."

"Be it so, if you wish; I will follow your fortunes."

"But let us now return to the raft, seek the refreshment we so much need, and after that, dear Ellen, we shall consider the plan we had best pursue."

With this both went to the spot where the raft had been beached.

The articles which had been saved had not been landed; these were shortly carried on shore.

Jack Warbold, aided by Ellen, then collected the carpenter's tools, the best arms, and all the ammunition.

The possession of the latter they deemed would give them an advantage in case of necessity.

They then dragged on shore some sail and small

spars, all of which they carried up to a cluster of cocoa-nut trees about a hundred yards from the beach.

In half an hour they had erected a strong tent, which screened Jack Warbold as he buried the ammunition in a heap of dry sand.

He then, for their immediate wants, cut down with an axe a small cocoa-nut tree in full bearing.

This could supply that which they now required, namely, water or drink.

Evening closed in as Ellen had thrown herself down on the spare sails, and fallen asleep.

Profiting by the opportunity, Jack set out to explore the island upon which they had been thrown.

It turned out to be a small one, not exceeding three miles, and at no one part more than five hundred yards across.

Water there was none, unless it was to be obtained by digging for it, and, as it will be seen, the young cocoa-nuts prevented absolute necessity.

On his return the moon was bright above him, and the sky spangled with glittering stars.

It was a night for contemplation, communion, and adoration of the deity.

As he entered the tent, he found Ellen still sleeping, and in a few moments was reposing at her feet.

His dreams were of Violet.

He thought he saw her fair form issue from the waters.

Another instant she had climbed up the raft, and seated herself next to him.

Suddenly the hated chuckle of a deadly foe fell upon his ears, and her for whom he would have died a thousand times, gone from his side.

The storm came on, and once more he beheld her battling with the waves.

Jack tried to join her but some hidden power held him down.

Violet waved her hand, and said,

" We shall meet again, Jack ; yes, once more on this earth we shall meet again.

*   *   *   *   *

The sun was high in the heavens, and scorching in his heat as Jack rose from his rude couch, and awakened Ellen.

He was pensive and sad during the morning meal ruminating on his fearful dream, which, with all its terrors, had afforded him consolation.

" We shall meet again, were her words," exclaimed he. " The vision spoke truly ; providence, I thank thee."

In half an hour the pirate-hunter hoisted his sail and, with Ellen Peveril, quitted the island.

Need it be asked in what direction he steered ?

In the quarter where he had last seen the raft with the isolated and well-beloved Violet Tremaine.

CHAPTER LXXIX.

VIOLET FINDS SHELTER IN THE INDIAN'S HUT—
THE OBI WOMAN, OR SORCERESS—BY WHAT
MEANS VIOLET TREMAINE REACHED THE ISLAND
OF TIDORE—AN UNEXPECTED VISITOR.

WHEN Violet again became conscious she discovered herself lying on palmetto leaves in a small hut.

Where was she, and what had occurred during her delirium, let the reader learn.

The raft upon which she had been found after tossing about for two days was driven on the eastern coast of Papua, better known as New Guinea, a settlement in the Indian Archipelago.

She had been discovered by the natives who chanced to be on the beach bartering with some of the people of Tidore.

Tidore being one of the Moluccas, or adjacent Spice Islands.

At first they began to deprive her of her outer clothing, although they perceived that she was not dead.

In doing this they discovered on her a diamond of great value, which had attracted the attention of one of the savages.

Failing in his endeavour to remove the jewel, he had recourse to his blunt knife, with which he commenced sawing at her finger.

At the command of an old Obi woman, or sorceress, the barbarian desisted as his knife was about to lacerate the flesh.

On this the Papuan carried Violet into her hut.

Here she lay between life and death for many days.

She was carefully attended, but required little, except the moistening of her parched lips with water and the brushing off of the mosquitoes and flies.

When Violet opened her eyes she beheld her deliverer standing by her bedside.

She was a woman of large size, very corpulent, and almost unwieldy.

Her hair, which was dark, and woolly in its texture, was partly plaited and partly frizzled.

The dress she wore consisted of a scarlet robe, and an ornamented cloth encircle l her waist, while a scarf of yellow silk depended from her shoulders.

A few silver rings and a necklace of mother-o'-pearl adorned the person of this singular mortal, whose teeth, jet black from the use of the betel nut, and whole appearance excited disgust in the breast of the wretched castaway.

She addressed Violet, but her words were unintelligible.

The sufferer, exhausted with the slight effort she had made to answer, fell back again upon her couch and once more closed her eyes as if in death.

But if the nurse was odious in semblance, she was kind in disposition.

By her attention and care Violet imperceptibly recovered, and, in three weeks, was able to crawl out of the hut and enjoy the evening breeze.

The natives of the island would at times surround her, but from fear of the Obi woman treated her with respect.

Their crisp locks were, like those of her whom they held in terror, frizzled or plaited, and in most cases powdered white with chunam.

A few palmetto leaves round the waist and descending to the knee, was their only attire.

Rings through the nose and ears, and the feathers of the bird of paradise, were worn in every case by these wild children of nature ; but the tongue in which they spoke was a stranger to their captive.

Violet felt grateful for life.

Beneath the leafy trees' shade she sat, and watched the swift peroguas as they skimmed the bright blue waters.

But her thoughts were elsewhere ; they were on the bold pirate-hunter.

Two months passed away, and Violet remained beneath the roof-tree of the Obi woman.

On their last morning, the people of Tidore returned to the land on which she had found shelter.

The captain on board the arriving vessel bore a warrant with him.

This order commanded him to bring the female

who had been cast ashore to his ship, and repay those who had taken charge of her.

This officer, speaking Portuguese, made signs to the Englishwoman, who was unacquainted with his language, that she must accompany him, and prepare to leave her present home for one prepared for her at Tidore.

Any change was preferable to staying where she was, and Violet followed her new companions to float along the smooth seas.

The next day they gained the place of their destination, and she was led up to the Portuguese fortress.

The curiosity of those who were stationed at that stupendous stronghold were at once roused.

This was not to be wondered at, since the history of her escape, given by the natives, appeared nothing short of miraculous in the eyes of the spectators.

From the commandant to the slave, every one was waiting to receive her.

Her beauty, her form, her grace, astonished each beholder.

The commandant addressed her, when she gave this explanation to his questioning.

She was by birth an Englishwoman, and had been abducted from her home by the nefarious artifices of a notorious band of pirates, against whom her lover had ever waged war.

In following in her pursuit, he had unfortunately been taken prisoner by his enemies, who, immediately on his capture, found means of escaping from the ship he had commanded, and which was then engaging them.

She then recounted the treachery of the daring adventurers with regard to the raft upon which she had been found, and her subsequent entire separation from the buccaneers.

At the end of the narrative, she was informed by the commandant of the colony, that she would, after so much suffering and misery, find a retreat on its shores, and that its inhabitants, remarkable for their hospitality, would be sure to give her a cordial welcome.

That everything should be done to make her happy during her residence in the island.

And that, in a short period, they expected a vessel that on its return would land the fair Violet on her native soil.—

England, the home of the happy, the brave, and the free.

After the interview, Violet was escorted by a guard to the Portuguese fortress.

Here arrived, the attendants conducted her to the chamber allotted to her use.

Of this chamber it is necessary to speak.

It was Gothic in design.

Massive in structure.

It was antiquely furnished, and richly carpeted, while the arms of the royal house of Portugal were suspended from every corner.

Over the enormous mantel-piece was a remarkable portrait.

This picture represented a religious votaress in a loose sable robe holding a rosary and missal in her hand, and her head concealed by the wimple.

As Violet entered the gloomy apartment, it became so dark that it was found necessary to illuminate the great lamp that was suspended from the centre of the roof.

Scarcely had this been accomplished when a terrific storm came on.

Vivid flashes of lightning dazzled and blinded the gaze.

Heaven's artillery, majestic and appalling, broke overhead.

Suddenly a peal louder than ever rumbled through the illumined firmament, followed by a crash as if the vast building had been struck by a thunderbolt.

At that moment the picture that surmounted the mantel-piece fell, disclosing an aperture, from which a flight of steps descended to the floor of the apartment.

Down from this recess came a tall personage, attired in the dark habiliments of a monk.

He issued forth, or rather glided towards the terrified inmates of the chamber.

His face was cadaverous, livid his lips, and his black eye seemed to flash with fire.

But his countenance was hid from view by the ample folds of his drawn hood.

His garments, mouldering and faded, contributed greatly to his spectre-like appearance.

The two negresses appointed to attend upon Violet startled at the sight they witnessed, and ran away, leaving their mistress alone in the presence of the mysterious visitor.

On a sudden, as if by magic, the gloom disappeared, and a silvery light shed over the scene.

The moon had broken through the thick, black clouds, and illumed, as bright as day, the region around.

With the light the dark figure became more visible to the excited maiden.

"Why do you thus trouble me, unhappy vision?" she cried, faintly. "Leave me, I conjure you. I feel I have not long to live, and would die in peace."

"Daughter," replied the monk, "thou art young, fair, and it is not yet thine appointed hour of death."

"Ha!"

"My intention is not to trouble but to serve thee. Thou hast enemies abroad."

Amazed and startled at the strange encounter, Violet trembled in every limb.

"Take this phial. Drink, and thy strength will return to thee."

"How do I know you are not an emissary of the foes of whom you have spoken?"

At this remark the monk raised the liquid he had produced to his own lips in order to show that his assertion was in accordance with truth, when Violet took the little vessel from his hand, and with assurance drained the contents, saying,

"I will drink, and fear nothing."

The moment she had swallowed the potent draught, she became restored, and recovered her wonted vigour.

"Now, daughter," exclaimed the monk, "I will avert the danger that threatens. Let not thy courage fail thee, for that which I shall tell will require thy utmost fortitude to withstand."

"What can this mean?"

"Hast thou followed up the precepts which thou hast been taught? Has thou reverenced the sublime mystery which has been unfolded to thee?"

"I have done my best, father."

"Hast thou called upon the Holy Virgin, and upon the saints, those intercessors for mortals erring like thyself?"

"Father, you speak enigmatically. Tell me, I pray you, why you put these questions to me?"

"I will answer you," replied the monk. "You will shortly be arrested by the holy inquisition."

"On what charge?" exclaimed Violet, after a pause, for the sudden intelligence had, for the moment, seemed to deprive her of the power of speech. "There must be some grave error, and how is it possible that I who have reached your shores but a few hours can be deemed guilty or accused of a crime ?"

"I grieve to say that there are men in the land who maintain that they have discovered upon you the implements of sorcery. And magic in a Catholic country is visited on its professors with penalties of the highest degree."

"But what can have induced these men to make so false a declaration ?"

"They observed, on your first landing among them, that you wore around your neck the secret token by which the enchantress is distinguished."

"Surely the trifling gift of a poor Obi woman is no proof that the wearer professes occult arts ?".

"No ; but the fact with the superstitious ever excites suspicion. This is not the only cause of premises. Your miraculous escape from death upon the raft is supposed to be due to supernatural agency. You must deliver up those who assisted at the ceremony, and bring them forward, or your life will be forfeited and the stake prepared for you."

Violet threw herself down on a couch in the corner of the room, and passed her hands over her forehead.

"Burnt alive !" she exclaimed, "and these are Christians ! 'Tis a cruel death ; but what is ordained must be, and the deity that permits, gives power to his creatures to submit with resignation to his will."

Musing, she continued,

"God of my fathers, give me also strength against these wicked beings, and enable me to bear all. It is my destiny, and I cannot save myself."

"But another may do so," replied the monk, archly. "Listen. When first I saw thee, 'twas not the fashion of thy face and form—though, from the hand of heaven, thou wert rich in beauty—that riveted my heart, but thy womanhood, which hath such firm devotion in her love, that made me covet thine."

"Nay, holy father, such thoughts as those are impious in your breast, since a sacred vow destines you to a life of celibacy."

"I feel such vows are offensive in the sight of heaven, and that to gain possession of thy heart I would freely hazard the torments of the damned."

"The request you demand, should I accord in your scruples, I can never grant."

"Say not so. A single word from thee may change the tenor of my life, and the man that has been good and virtuous become wicked and depraved."

"There is an inseparable barrier between us."

"The proverb will tell you that the transgressor writes with sand, the victim of transgression with marble. My love is stamped in an impressible material ; but my hate may be engraved in adamant. In a word, will you deign to listen to my protestations ?"

"I cannot. I am betrothed to another."

"Then my rival will perish, and his mistress is his executioner."

"Your words have some hidden signification."

"Attend to those which I am about to utter, and you will learn if they have or otherwise," replied the monk.

"What am I to understand from this ?"

The monk continued—

"Truth, they say, is stranger than fiction, and what are all the tales of wild romance to the one I now relate ? On the self-same day your raft reached the hospitable land that gave you welcome, another reached it, but at many miles distant. The frail frame bore on its timbers two human beings, travel-worn and exhausted."

"Gracious powers ! should it be——"

"These wanderers met a fate worse than that they had braved on the angry waves. They fell into the hands of those whom of all others they would have avoided—the daring buccaneers, from whom they had so lately escaped."

"The monsters have murdered them."

"No ; their punishment was reserved for a mature consideration. In the power of his enemies the more robust was tried, found guilty, and left to die. But how ? A consultation was held, to devise a plan by which the wretched captive could suffer the greatest amount of lingering torment previous to dissolution. He was condemned to suffer the pangs of fire by having his right hand consumed in flame ; his lacerated flesh to be anointed with molten lead, while his body, writhing beneath the agonies of his torture, was to be torn asunder by the united exertions of eight powerful horses. The name of this miserable wretch I at length discover ; it is John Warbold, the pirate-hunter. His life is in your hands ; say, will you save him ; will you save yourself ?"

It would be impossible to picture the agony of mind Violet Tremaine suffered during the above terrible recital. She was pale, breathless, and intensely moved. She felt as if reason was forsaking her, and but for her superhuman efforts, such a crisis would have occurred.

But her failing senses warned her that hers and her lover's welfare depended on her mental balance, and she strove to maintain it. She succeeded, and, with indescribable terror, after a pause, exclaimed,

"You say, mysterious man, that it is in my power to work out preservation. Let your finger point out the road, and I will take it, though the fiends of hell beset the path."

"The means are easy."

"Name them."

"Love me with a love unfettered by the marriage chain."

At that moment Violet endeavoured to pray, but her tongue clove to the roof of her mouth.

The monk dropped the cowl that had hitherto disguised his features. They were those of the hideous and deformed pirate, Barabbas !

CHAPTER LXXX.

THE PIRATES' STRONGHOLD.

ON the north-western extremity of the island of Tidore was the gorge of Magalheans, a dangerous defile leading from nutmeg groves bearing the same name.

The region, unlike the neighbouring country, clothed with tropical verdure and vegetation, was precipitous and almost inaccessible through its barren rocks.

On the steepest escarpment, two hundred feet above the valley beneath, towered a pile of stone-work, the remains of an oriental palace.

This building dilated to gigantic proportions against the sky.

Within its crumbling walls were now settled a horde of desperate men, for the pirates had converted this stronghold into a dwelling, from which they from time to time issued to follow their nefarious calling.

Beneath the rendezvous were a series of dungeons, where the lawless men stowed away their illgotten riches or secured their prisoners till a ransom was sent for their release.

In one of these vaults the dull light of a brazen

cresset imperfectly illumed the noxious cell and disclosed the figures of two captives.

The one, on a pallet of straw, appeared a young mariner, being dressed in the habiliments of those connected with a seafaring life.

His countenance was pale, and though his slumber was calm, it was not evidently the sleep induced by nature's best nurse.

The other was reposing on a similar couch. He appeared the more youthful of the two, but was attired in a garb corresponding with his companion.

In age this boy could scarcely have been more than eighteen, perhaps not so much, as his slight though exquisitely symmetrical form, slender even to effeminacy, denoted immaturity.

The flaxen tresses and pale blue eyes of either of the youths would have proclaimed him as one of a more northern clime, while the daring spirit peculiar to the features of the seamen of England told at once they were natives of that country.

In the first named the reader may recognise our hero, Roving Jack.

In the second, under the guise of manhood, the faithful and devoted Ellen Peveril.

The dark night was succeeded by a bright morning, as the sun which glimmered from a narrow loophole gave evidence.

Betimes Ellen awoke and rose from her bed and stood watching her companion; suddenly he started up as if from a dream, to behold her bending over him.

"Yes, I remember all now, and 'twas no dream!" he exclaimed, fitfully. "We are once more in the hands of the accursed pirates, who will not hesitate at once to sacrifice us."

"Providence, Jack, which has hitherto been our protector, will not, I feel assured, desert us in this dire extremity," replied the disguised maiden. "Depend upon it your messmate, for such our enemies take me to be, will find means to encompass them yet. Take courage."

"For myself I want not courage, Ellen; but for you, for Violet, a fearful foreboding portends that evil will surely come."

"If it is so decreed, let it come. I and Violet have long been prepared for the worst, and, in spite of your seeming indifference, Jack, so have you."

Ellen spoke these words with a calmness that at once astonished and delighted him to whom they were addressed.

"But the sufferings that——"

"Those suffer least who have the most fortitude to bear up against them. I am but a woman, weak and frail in body; but I possess that within me which, I trust, will not make you feel ashamed of Ellen Peveril. No, Jack, you shall have no wailing, no lamentation, no despair from my lips. If I can console you I will. If I can assist you I will; but, come what may, if I cannot serve I will at least die for you."

"Your presence in misfortune unnerves me."

"It should not. It should add to your resolution. Let fate do its worst."

"Depend upon it, Ellen Peveril, that will be ere long."

"I am not so sure of that; succour ofttimes comes from men and sources that we little expected. Listen: While you have been sleeping, I have been thinking; by the lantern's dull glimmer, I have explored every nook and corner of this loathsome prison, and have discovered an outlet that may afford us the means of escape."

Roving Jack started to his feet at the happy thought, and requesting his companion to lead him to the spot she had spoken of, followed on her footsteps.

Both proceeded to the back of the dungeon, when Nelly, removing the iron bar that fastened the door, disclosed a passage.

This passage was void of every ray of light, and left its occupants in total darkness.

In the emergency Jack took the lead.

Finding himself deprived of light in the manner we have described, and placed in a very uncertain situation, he proceeded to descend some narrow, broken stairs at the end of the gloomy road with all the caution in his power, and still attended by his faithful friend.

But with all his care he could not avoid making a false step, which brought him down the last four or five steps too hastily to preserve his equilibrium.

Arrived at the bottom he stumbled over a bundle of something soft.

The living mass stirred, and uttered a groan.

This again deranged our hero's descent, and he floundered forward, and finally fell upon his hands and knees on the floor of a damp and stone-paved dungeon.

When Roving Jack had recovered himself, his first demand was to know over whom he had fallen.

"I was a man a month since," answered a hollow and broken voice.

"And what is he now, then," said the startled mariner, "that he thinks fit to lie upon the lowest step of the stairs clewed up like a coil of unspun hemp?"

"What is he now?" returned the same voice. "He is a wretched trunk, from which the branches have been lopped away, and which cares not how soon it is hewn up with the axe, and cast as billets into the furnace."

"Friend, I am sorry for you; but stay. Are we to be friends?"

"You are a sailor——"

"A sailor? And how do you know in this cursed dark cavern that I am so?"

"Because your voice is familiar to my ear, and I know you to be he whom men call the Pirate Hunter."

This intelligence somewhat staggered our hero, who, veiling his emotion, changed the conversation by asking the forlorn inmate of the place what food he had in it.

"Bread and water once a day," was the reply.

"Let me taste your loaf, friend," said Jack, "since it appears we are likely to become comrades in this abominable pit."

"The loaf and jar of water," answered the other prisoner, "stand in the corner, two steps to your right hand; take them and welcome; with earthly food I have well-nigh done."

The party advised did not await a second invitation, for since his late capture he had not broken his fast.

Groping out the provisions, he began to munch at the stale black oaten loaf with as much heartiness as a keen appetite alone can supply.

While Jack's teeth kept time with his tongue, he speedily finished the rude meal which the benevolence or indifference of his companion in misfortune had abandoned to his voracity.

When this task was accomplished, he began anew to question his fellow captive.

"It seems, friend, by what you have asserted, that I am not unknown to you. Such a confidence should be reciprocal—pray what may your name be?"

"It will avail you little to know," replied the more taciturn prisoner.

"Speak freely, in order that I may judge of such a matter," replied our hero, with a slight abruptness.

"Well, then, Tomaz Sebastien is my name; I was called also the 'Tiger of the Sea.'"

"If I am not mistaken, you were the pirate I chased in company with your friend the deeply execrated Barabbas?"

"Yes; I was his best friend—I am now his worst foe."

"Wherefore?"

"He was the leader of the band who, two months since, surprised the castle of a Spanish grandee on the neighbouring coast.

"It was richly stored, and avarice tempted the pirate to possess the wealth report gave out it contained.

"We, the daring rovers of the main, ascended the cliffs on which the structure stood by ladders of sapling, drawn up by an accomplice who had sought the service of its master.

"The eagle screamed around us as we hung 'twixt heaven and earth.

"The tide and wave roared against the rock and dashed asunder our brave skiff, yet the heart of no man failed him—in the morning there was blood and ashes where there had been peace and joyance at sunset."

"I have heard of this matter," interrupted Roving Jack.

"During the attack an intrepid youth had possessed himself of a diamond necklace, which Barabbas demanded as his share of the booty, a request that was refused by him who held the spoil. Exasperated, the pirate chieftain drew his knife.

"And the boy fell lifeless from its murderous blow."

"That boy," continued Sebastien, "was my son, and I vowed revenge. It is a vow that I will never break."

"It may be so, for I must confess that revenge is a sweet morsel; but, before you attempt to carry out your purpose, be careful that he is rendered harmless. I know the monster before to day, and should he suspect you he may change the manner of your execution from simple hanging to breaking your limbs on the wheel with the coulter of a plough, or putting you to death otherwise by torture."

"He does suspect me, and, for that reason, has confined me a prisoner in this living tomb, for he will never again permit me to quit it with life."

"Your hate still endures?"

"Yes, and will endure for ever; dearer to me was the child that fell by the hand of the base Barabbas than the five sons who are mouldering in earth, or are preyed upon by the fowls of the air."

There was a brief pause, then the aged pirate continued his narrative, in a tone of strong emotion.

"Yes, my sons, blood of my blood, bone of my bone, they are all dead. Why should I wish to survive them? The old trunk will feel less the rending up of its roots than it has felt the lopping off of its branches; but my favourite offspring must be avenged. The old eagle must stoop on a foe. I will purchase, for my boy's sake, life and freedom, by discovering his assassin to his direst enemies."

"You may attain your end more easily," said a third voice, mingling in the conference, "by entrusting your secret to me."

All pirates are superstitious.

Tomaz Sebastien was no exception to the rule.

"The arch enemy of mankind is among us!" he cried, springing to his feet.

His manacles and chains clattered as he rose, while he drew himself as far as they permitted from the quarter whence the voice appeared to proceed.

His fear in some degree communicated astonishment to our hero, who, likewise, turned his face to the same spot.

"There is no cause for alarm," said the voice that had been heard before; "though I come strangely among you, I am a mortal like yourselves, and my assistance may avail you in your present strait, if you are not too proud to be counselled."

While the new-comer thus spoke, he withdrew the shade of a dark lantern, by whose feeble glimmer Roving Jack could only discern that the speaker who had thus mysteriously united himself to their fellowship was a young man, and habited in the costume of one of the company of his own ship "The Avenger."

CHAPTER LXXXI.

THE PIRATES' DUNGEON—HOW ROVING JACK AND ELLEN PEVERIL CONTRIVED TO GET OUT OF THE SAME.

THE first glance of our hero was at the feet of the stranger.

But he saw neither the cloven foot which the ancient legends assign to the foul fiend, nor the horse's hoof by which his satanic majesty is distinguished in central Europe.

On a closer scrutiny he was delighted to find that the supernatural intruder was no other than Ellen Peveril, who still maintained her disguise as a young English mariner.

"So, Jack," she cried, in a lively manner, "you took me for an evil spirit, and supposed I passed to you through the keyhole of yonder door, which, by-the-bye, I have made secure to prevent any interruption during our discourse."

"Ellen," answered the Pirate-hunter, "you are a brave girl, and deserve the laurels of a hero for the part you have taken in our dangerous enterprise; but, tell me what discovery you have made, for, by the bright beaming of your eye, I can readily learn that some adventure has befallen you."

"I shall not reserve my secret," she cried.

The remaining captive, either in suspicion or disdain, paid no attention to the conversation that had taken place between his fellow-prisoners.

"Are you aware that death awaits us?" said Ellen, addressing Sebastien; "and that to-morrow you will leave this dreary place for the gibbet."

"Those who are dearest to me," replied he, "have trod that path before me."

"Then you would do nothing to shun following them."

The pirate writhed in his chains before answering—

"I would do much," he at length exclaimed; "not for my own life, but for the sacred vow I have taken to have Rotaldo's life."

"Rotaldo?"

"Yes; he who commands this stronghold in the absence of our chief Barabbas. Even this morning it was my purpose to have stabbed him to the heart, but at the sound of footsteps, my hand forsook the dagger, and the hour of revenge had passed away."

"Good; I see I may trust you. But it is getting late, and we have much on our hands. I doubt not you will do anything for your liberty."

"Anything but forego my revenge."

"Its hour is at hand!" was the exclamation of a fresh voice that seemed to issue from the same quarter in which Ellen Peveril had made her mysterious appearance.

As before, Roving Jack, and the no less surprised Sebastien, turned to encounter a party of whose presence they had been unaware until now.

He appeared a stalwart man, and dressed in a costume combining the attire of a Malay and a Mahomedan.

His beard was so profuse that it literally seemed to cover his face, while the shade that covered his left eye, and the uncertain light of the dungeon, most effectually concealed his features from view.

"Who is this man?" exclaimed Jack, raising a bar of iron ready to strike him down in the event of an unsatisfactory answer.

"A friend, as his deeds will show," returned Ellen.

"How do you know that?" was the exclamation of our hero, who still, with his unweildy weapon, stood in an attitude at once of defence and attack.

"I encountered him as you quitted my side, and he might have betrayed me had he so desired; but, in the place of molestation, he offered to protect me, while the wrongs he has suffered at the hands of these pirates, has made them his enemies as well as your own."

"How are you named, and what is your occupation or calling?"

"I bear the name, senor, of Juan Velasquez. I am a native of Mangola, one of the Moluccas, and at the present time act as warden to the keep now tenanted by the pirates, who hold the neighbouring seas in awe."

"But you yourself are one of this merciless band."

"Alas, senor, man cannot control his destiny."

"Why have you come hither?"

"To make proposals that will prove of service both to you and myself."

"What if I scorn the friendship of a banditto and outlaw."

"You can have no hesitation when the guerdon is to be life and liberty.

"Is such our paction?"

"Upon the word of a Christian man," replied the pirate.

"Your frail promise," said Jack, "is an insecure alliance as our lives rest on it."

At this moment the murmur of voices and the clattering of steel told the listeners that the passage which they had traversed in entering was now filled with armed men.

The total darkness which still prevailed therein prevented them from immediately discovering the door of the dungeon in which the prisoners were confined, and which they, as already stated, had fortunately fastened with its strong, ponderous and iron bar.

As the pirate received this intelligence, he rushed to remove the same, when he found himself seized from behind, and held firmly, and rendered powerless by the grasp of Roving Jack.

His hirsute mask was now withdrawn, and the features of the suspected pirate, Rotaldo, exposed to view.

The attack of our hero was so sudden and unexpected, that he easily prostrated his adversary on the floor of the dungeon.

He held him down while his right hand was pressed heavily on the captive's throat.

He was ready to strangle him on the slightest attempt to call for assistance.

"Treacherous hound!" exclaimed Jack; "it is now my turn to lay down the terms of capitulation."

"Granted."

"If you list to show me the private way by which you entered the dungeon, you will escape death."

"I will do as you desire," stammered out Rotaldo, grasping with difficulty for breath.

"I have another condition to make; you must become my *locum tenens*, or substitute, in this infernal den."

Jack maintained his gripe upon the ruffian's throat, compressing it a little, while he asked questions, and relaxing it so far as to give him power of answering them.

During the above proceedings Ellen Peveril had stationed herself near the door of the apartment.

She was armed with the dagger that had been taken from Rotaldo, and stood ready to pierce the first intruder who should endeavour to force an entrance through it.

"Where is the secret passage into this dungeon?" demanded the vanquisher of the vanquished.

"Hold up the lantern to the corner of your right-hand; you will there discern the iron which covers the spring," replied the latter.

"So far, so good."

Here Roving Jack resigned Rotaldo to the keeping of Sebastien.

"Do as you see me do," he exclaimed; "clap your hand thus on the weasand of this buccaneer. If he offer to struggle or cry out, fail not to squeeze him doughtily, that is, till he swoon; there is no great matter, seeing he designed your gullet and mine to harder usage."

"If he offer speech or struggle," returned Sebastien, "he dies by my hand."

"That is right, man; very spirited—a thorough going friend that understands a hint is worth a million."

A notice from Ellen Peveril now warned our hero that the pirates had retired, but would immediately come back with numbers to attack them. On this Roving Jack pressed the spring by which the secret door flew open.

So well were its hinges polished and oiled that it made not the slightest noise in revolving.

The opposite side of the door was secured by very strong bolts and bars.

Besides these hung one or two keys, designed apparently to undo fetterlocks.

A spiral staircase, ascending up through the thickness of the castle, landed on the lantern tower.

"Let us now labour for your liberation, friend Sebastien," cried Jack.

To examine his chain was our hero's first occupation.

It was undone by means of one of the keys which hung behind the private door.

The silken cord with which Rotaldo had been bound was with some difficulty removed by him.

Unseen and cautiously he advanced to Ellen Peveril.

A hissing laugh proclaimed his freedom.

In a moment the ruffian twined himself around her person, and stifled her cry of alarm.

The maiden felt herself sinking.

The hot breath was upon her face.

And a horrible mouth approached her throat.

She experienced a sudden and sharp thrilling pain.

Her senses failed her, and she could not utter a word.

The monster, having no other weapon, had sought to fix his teeth upon her neck, but in doing so had fell a motionless mass.

The manacles Roving Jack had taken from Sebastien had stunned the vampire.

He then bore the fainting maiden up the steps, and landed with his burden on the platform of the lantern tower of which we have just spoken.

At the moment, the pirates, with an increased force, again arrived at the door of the dungeon.

This had been so firmly secured that it defied their utmost endeavours to force it.

Execrations, deep and loud, were uttered by the disappointed rovers.

After mounting the flight of stairs with Ellen, Roving Jack reached their top.

A narrow opening cheered his progress.

Passing this, by means of a trap-door, he came at once upon the summit of the column.

What was his surprise, we may say delight, to find a coil of rope.

It was fixed to the iron framework that enclosed the elevation of the lantern tower.

The tower was upwards of two hundred feet from the ground, and was used by the pirates in stowing away their spoil or contraband merchandize.

Here the means of escape at once presented itself to our hero.

Depositing Ellen, who had now recovered, in a place of safety, he first tried the durability of the rope.

He found it was of sufficient strength to sustain his weight.

It was of more than sufficient length to enable him to reach the distant earth beneath his feet.

Quick as thought he threw the cord over the edge of the structure.

He advanced to the brink to see if it had fallen to the ground.

With an exclamation of joy he exclaimed,

"We are once more free!"

Ellen shuddered at the perilous position, and sought him to avail himself of the flight offered, but requested that she might remain.

"Go, go," she cried, "but I have not the courage to face this danger. Go, I beseech you!"

"What, and leave you here to fall into the hands of the pursuers? Never!"

"Heed me not," continued the terrified Ellen; "I have my means of escape likewise."

With these words the maiden pointed to the dagger at her side.

"What is my life to yours?"

"By Heaven!" cried our hero, frantically, "if you do not obey me, I will fling myself into the abyss below, and become a prey to the vultures of the region!"

So saying, the speaker advanced to the precipitous edge of the tower as if to put his threat into immediate execution.

"Hold! I will do as you desire, and may God give me strength in this fearful venture!"

Ellen Peveril, at the instigation of our hero, grasped the rope, which he had fastened with a firm knot to the iron rail above their heads.

With one bound she leaped fearlessly from the parapet.

Jack looked over the dizzy height.

For a moment the rope on which the maiden hung vibrated with a shock.

As she found herself swerving to and fro in mid-air she could scarcely repress a scream.

Her brain reeled as she gazed downward.

What a frightful space was between her and the valley beneath!

Her head involuntarily sank over her shoulder.

Her eyes closed.

But as she knew her safety depended on her own powers of tenacity, she ever firmly clutched the quivering cord.

The rope continued its oscillations.

The gripe of Ellen continued unrelaxing.

Her peril appeared imminent.

Soon her situation was more perilous than ever.

A shout, or rather shriek, had resounded in the region hard by!

A body of men in military uniform had witnessed the daring attempt at liberation.

They had seen Ellen launch herself from the lofty lantern tower.

Though these men were foes, being pirates in the disguise of the Garda Costa, or military preventive service, as if by mutual consent, they suspended hostilities.

It was a feat of such hair-breadth risk that all gave her up for lost.

But when she had descended all evinced an admiration of the daring adventuress.

One of their number, during the exploit, with a dastardly disposition, had raised his musket, but the coward was kept at bay by the poised pistol of Roving Jack.

Ellen having gained the ground, our hero next attempted to escape by the same means as his companion.

The rope whirled round and round, but the intrepid youth, contriving amidst the gyrations to insert the point of his foot in the walled column of the tower, gained his equilibrium and pursued his perilous descent.

Looking upward he beheld the malignant and exulting features of Rotaldo.

It is needless to state he had discovered the mode of escape adopted by the prisoners.

In an instant he resolved on the only revenge in his power.

His gestures, ferocious and savage, indicated that he would exercise his utmost ingenuity to cause fear and torture to his flying enemy.

Before he attempted to cut the rope he shook it with all his force.

This jerked it convulsively first on the right then on the left.

Finding he could not dislodge his brave foe, he had recourse to another expedient.

Taking firmly hold of the iron bar of the lantern roof above him, with great exertion he pulled the rope up several feet.

Uttering a hideous and unearthly yell he let it suddenly drop.

JONATHAN WILD ATTEMPTS TO ARREST PAUL PEVERILL.—*See next Number.*

Though greatly shaken, our hero maintained his grasp.

Finding him rapidly making his descent, the brutal Rotaldo, muttering curses between his teeth, proceeded to saw with vigour the frail cord.

Roving Jack gazed upwards, then cast his eyes to the ground beneath.

He was still more than one hundred feet from it.

"Ho, ho," bellowed the pirate; "not so fast, my young spark, not so fast. You shall reach your destination without further efforts of your own—aye, and somewhat quicker too——"

"That fate shall be your own, miscreant!" shrieked a voice, in close proximity.

There was a struggle, and Rotaldo rolled heavily over the edge of the column, which he grasped with a tenacity of desperation and despair.

His glowing eyeballs glared on his assailant.

It was the liberated Tomaz Sebastien.

His deadly foe, Sebastien, after the encounter in the dungeon, had been watching Rotaldo.

He perceived that he had been stunned and not disabled.

Profiting by the darkness of the place, he had concealed himself, thinking most likely when the pirate had recovered himself he would attempt to do further mischief.

A precaution wisely taken, as the present circumstance shows.

Rotaldo still hung to the stonework, and would

not release his hold, although he had received a tremendous blow from his enemy with a bar of iron.

His energy seemed to rise with the emergency, for the next moment he had actually risen to the flooring of the tower.

"Spare me!" he groaned, while the blood from the wound in his head nearly choked him. "Spare me, and I will make reparation."

"Repentance comes too late when the deed is done," cried Sebastien, bitterly.

With this remark, Sebastien searched for his knife, intending to disengage his enemy's hand by severing it at the wrist.

Not finding it he had again recourse to the iron bar.

This time, instead of striking at the head of Rotaldo, he began to beat his fingers as he was holding the iron framework of the tower to support himself.

The means were effectual, for, by smashing the bones of the hand, the pirate was forced to relinquish his hold, and was precipitated headlong off the eminence.

Being a bulky man his great weight accelerated his fall.

He descended head foremost.

His skull came in contact with the sharp edge of the iron lantern.

The projection shattered it at once, and his brains bespattered his victorious antagonist.

Just as his huge frame reached the ground, our hero, Roving Jack, had alighted near the spot in safety.

CHAPTER LXXXII.

TOUCHES UPON A SCENE IN WHICH ROVING JACK PLAYS A PROMINENT PART — THE ORDEAL BY FIRE.

WE must now draw the attention of the reader to a small bamboo cottage, situated some few miles distant from the spot of the late adventure.

The country seat was delightfully embosomed in a forest of trees.

The vegetation was luxuriant and refreshing from its vivid green.

The light colour of the house, being opposed to the dark foliage, offered a strong, but at the same time an agreeable contrast.

In one of its chambers, till lately, there was a single occupant.

Of this party we can only say:—

That any one who commanded a sufficient knowledge of the world could perceive, on encountering him, that they had a very dangerous person to deal with, and that it behoved them to be careful how they proceeded in a mutual transaction.

He was apparently a man rather advanced in years, with a pair of very broad shoulders—so broad, indeed, that few possessed their equal.

The muscular limbs and burly frame could, at first, hardly be supposed to belong to such a stunted individual as he who called them master.

Considering he was decidedly below the average height, his squareness of figure, aided by a loose coat of brown cloth, edged with silver, reaching half-way down his legs, made him look almost as broad as he was long.

A slight noise attracted his attention, and he started.

He had been so occupied with his thoughts that he had not heard the sound of approaching footsteps.

On turning round to the spot from whence this sound proceeded, he faced a young man.

This visitor was dressed in a sort of semi-military attire, and wore high riding boots.

He was at once recognised by the owner of the house as a courier.

He immediately advanced to the new comer, and his manner assumed that of grace, ease, and affability.

The courier then handed a letter to him.

He, with the utmost determination, perused the superscription, then darted his piercing eye at his companion.

Whether it was that he perceived his uneasiness, or that his quick perception of character detected some imposition that was likely to be practised on him, is immaterial.

Suffice his observer noticed his countenance change and his demeanour alter to a frigid coolness.

"You are lately arrived in this country," said he.

"Just arrived, sir."

"By what ship?"

"'La Belle Susanne,' now riding in the offing."

"That is not an English vessel."

"No, a French frigate carrying despatches to the Portuguese governor of this island; we sailed from the port of Marseilles six months since."

"In a foreign service, how comes it that you convey English letters?"

"The letter you have in your hand was entrusted to my keeping by an individual who begged that I would deliver it to you privately; having well paid me for the confidence, I, in duty bound, have acted as he desired me."

"How did you discover my retreat?"

"From the information I received from the same party who gave me your letter."

"What sort of a man was he?"

"Middle-aged person, of moderate height; by his dress I took him to be an Englishman."

"But his appearance——"

"Was somewhat vulgar, while his aspect was very shrewd."

"He wore a hanger by his side?"

"Yes; and bore marks of having had a good many desperate engagements, for his face was covered with cuts and scars."

"Good," exclaimed the questioner; "your statements are in accordance with facts, that I can no longer doubt you, and my previous suspicions are removed."

Though the weather was extremely hot there was a small fire burning in the grate of the apartment in which the speakers were standing.

He who held the letter placed it before the smouldering flame.

His object was soon apparent.

For certain lines of writing traced in invisible ink appeared at the instant.

These eagerly scanned, he hurried to his escretoire.

Penning a few lines, he proceeded to enclose them in a cover.

This cover he secured firmly with a small mass of black wax.

His hand almost imperceptibly trembled as he affixed the seal.

The writer of this epistle was the daring buccaneer —Barabbas!

The paper bore the address—

"JONATHAN WILD,

"Newgate.

"London."

We must now follow on the footsteps of Violet Tremaine.

The unhappy girl was experiencing a sad fate.

Accused of sorcery, she had been arraigned.

The Holy Inquisition, crediting the idle belief and evidence of the superstitious settlers of the Island of Tidore, had deemed her guilty of such a crime.

She had been tried, condemned, and sentenced to death!

A fearful death, too—death by the pains of fire!

The morrow was to end all Violet's hopes and fears.

All her suspense would cease, all her misery terminate.

Although her situation was appalling, she slept until her last sleep in this world was disturbed by the unbarring and unlocking of the door of her cell.

The head gaoler made his appearance with a light.

Violet aroused, started from her couch.

She had been dreaming of love and happiness—but awoke to grief and sad reality.

The gaoler then desired her to put on a dress that he carried on his arm; it was of black serge with broad white stripes.

Two hours passed, and the gaoler again entered the cell.

He now summoned her to follow him.

She was led into a large hall.

In this dimly-lighted spacious apartment she was furnished with a wax candle, which she was ordered to hold in her hand.

After this another dress, called the "Sanbenitos," was put over the poor girl.

This garment had flames painted upon it—a terrible signification of the penalty she was about to undergo.

So motionless and terror-stricken was the victim, during the proceeding, that one might have imagined her to have been suddenly petrified.

Anon there was an agony of doubt,—an agony worse than that of death.

A poignant anguish followed the semi-stupefaction; and it was frightful to perceive the convulsive tremor of Violet.

Heavy drops of perspiration mantled on her brow.

She shrank aghast; and all was horror, dread and fear!

As the sun rose, the great bell of the Cathedral tolled, and the high altar was hung with black-cloth, lighted up with thousands of tapers.

The mournful procession, leading the prisoner to execution, in half an hour left her dungeon.

Violet headed the train.

She was bare-headed and bare-footed.

The banner of the Dominican was raised above her head, while the monks of that order followed, arranging themselves in two lines.

In this manner they arrived at the funereal pile.

All was over now, save the last and most tragical scene of the drama.

The stake was set up on a raised stone platform, in an open square, in the centre of the city.

The balconies of the buildings being thronged with ladies and cavaliers in their gayest attire, and the surrounding space filled by the rabble, all of whom seemed in the highest excitement, and anxiously to await the fearful ordeal they were about to witness.

The executioners, who had been sitting on, or standing by the piles of wood and faggots, awaiting their victim, now stirred at her approach.

Violet could not walk.

She was supported by the hooded familiars.

These myrmidons of tyranny and superstition carried her to the stake.

When they put her opposite to the horrible instrument of death, her courage appeared to revive.

She walked boldly up, folded her arms, and leant against it.

The masked executioners now commenced their sanguinary duty.

Chains were passed round the body of Violet.

The wood and faggots piled around her.

She waved her hand indignantly as a monk approached.

"Unhappy woman!" he exclaimed. "Had you followed my counsel this would not have happened."

Receiving no answer, he continued,

"Now it is too late; but not too late to save your soul."

Violet involuntarily shuddered as the monk whispered in her ear.

She gave a scream, and muttered firmly the word—

"Never!"

"Why this obstinacy? Why this hardness of heart? You are still silent."

"If I am so," replied she, "it is to show that the flame that will shortly consume my wretched body has less terror in my eyes than——"

"Remember, it is the eleventh hour—the twelfth has not yet arrived."

"I shall welcome its coming."

"I implore—I conjure you at least take this load of guilt from my heart."

"Leave me."

"There is but a minute left."

"And the minute is mine own."

"Will nothing move thee?"

"Try me," replied Violet, firmly, "try me, cruel man. If you gain but one word from me, call me craven—I am but woman; but I dare you—defy you."

"Unhappy woman!"

"Say rather unhappy priest, for my suffering will soon cease, while you must still endure the torments of the damned. I leave you to your conscience, if conscience you still retain; nor would I change this cruel death for the pangs which Barabbas will undergo in his future life."

The monk, who, as the reader may have surmised, was the disguised pirate.

Fearing disclosure and treachery on the part of Violet, the wily Barabbas made no remark to her denunciation, but hastily seized a torch held by one of the familiars, and proceeded to kindle the faggots heaped around the stake.

His murderous hand was arrested.

A wild and joyous shout of triumph resounded in the air.

And the whole neighbourhood was in the hands of a determined band of horseman.

One of their number was more daring than the rest.

Despite the tremendous opposition he encountered he contrived to reach the spot where Violet was bound to the stake.

Another moment, and he would have been too late.

He only arrived just in time to strike down Barabbas as he was on the point of setting the pyre of sacrifice in a blaze.

This horseman was our hero, Roving Jack!

———

CHAPTER LXXXIII.

THE DESPERATE FLIGHT OF ROVING JACK WITH
VIOLET TREMAINE—OUR HERO'S ADVENTURE
AT THE POSADO OR PORTUGUESE WINE HOUSE
—HOW IT TURNED OUT AND WHAT CAME OF IT.

ACROSS the back of his bounding courser, Roving
Jack flung the almost lifeless body of the rescued
Violet Tremaine.

Fleet as the wind he rushed from the spot.

The scene of his triumph and his woe.

His desperate flight was attended by a brave
band of Papuans (the natives of the island), who,
crushed by the oppression of their rulers, had aided
in his daring enterprise.

Following these in pursuit were the military and
Portuguese authorities.

The whole country was now alarmed by the cries
and by the tramp of horses.

Men from every point rushed into the road to
seize the foremost fugitive, Roving Jack, who bore
the senseless Violet ever in his arms.

His fierce looks, furious steed, and the impetus
with which he pressed onward, quailed those who
had the temerity to offer to stop his headlong
career.

His blood spins through his veins, and mounts to
his brain, as he and his peerless burden skim the
earth.

Glade, waste, and woodland are past, and appear
and vanish as in a vision.

The horse and rider are driven forward.

The flints sparkle beneath the goaded beast's
hoofs.

Roving Jack, having far out-distanced his foes,
now turned to welcome his friends—the brave
natives whose succour had so materially contributed to crown his efforts to save Violet with success.

They were nowhere to be seen.

They could never have deserted him in this
moment of peril.

He must have mistaken the road leading to their
encampment in the forest.

In turning his steed's head to pursue his hazardous journey the animal stumbled, and injured its
leg.

"Cursed chance," exclaimed our hero. "Could
anything be more unfortunate? The horse is so
disabled that he cannot stir an inch, and to proceed
on foot is certain destruction. What can I do to
save her now?" he continued, despairingly looking
upon Violet. "There is but one course; I must
resort once more to stratagem, and heaven grant I
may succeed in circumventing those who are still
pursuing us."

Not far distant from the spot upon which Roving
Jack was standing, he perceived a solitary dwelling.

It appeared lonely and unoccupied.

But on a second glance he found he was mistaken.

The grape branch hanging over the door, proclaiming it to be a "posado," or Portuguese wine-
house.

He now hesitated whether he should enter it or
not.

The appearance of Violet, who had partially
recovered, determined him on adopting the former
course.

In a few minutes he arrived at the isolated
tenement.

The aspect of the place did not much please our
hero.

For all the windows were closed with shutters
except one.

An old bay casement fronting the unfrequented
road.

He again looked at Violet, hesitating whether it
would be safe to trust her in this strange abode,
when a man issued from its door.

He was the ostensible landlord.

A peculiar sensation came over Roving Jack, as
he met his face.

Some confused ideas came across his mind that
he had seen it before.

When and where for the life of him he could not
tell.

However, there was no help for him now.

Violet was sinking from fatigue and want of
food.

And he must trust to chance whether he had
acted with prudence in confiding her to the
mysterious character this landlord appeared to be.

He was taciturn in disposition.

Ugly in appearance.

And had he been tall, herculean in proportion.

After a pause he ventured to speak.

"A nasty day for a journey of pleasure, senor."

"It is not one of pleasure."

"Business, perhaps?"

"No—necessity. We have been attacked by a
party of hostile natives, who sprung out upon us
from the neighbouring forest."

"You were obliged to fly?"

"Yes," returned Roving Jack, "and must get you
to afford us food, shelter, and protection, till you
can send for further assistance."

The landlord, feigning to believe the tale our
hero had invented, ushered him and Violet into the
house for entertainment.

His sinister smile and malignant grin showed
that he had calculated upon some advantage from
his guests, and that he meant to take the earliest
opportunity of profiting by it.

Violet and Jack were then conducted into a dingy
room.

The closed shutters of which were opened on
their entrance.

Here they ordered some omelettes and wine, and
sat down to wait for them.

While noticing the melancholy aspect of the
chamber, Jack could not help also noticing that his
host would every now and then return to the room
and open a cupboard.

Of course he concluded that he was engaged thus
while preparing the meal.

His appearance and disappearance was always
attended with a furtive glance.

After this proceeding the mysterious man would
open the outer door of the dwelling, go out, and
remain standing, as if in expectation of somebody.

These things considered, at length Roving Jack
took it into his head that the landlord meant foul
play.

In such an emergency, how could he act?

To desert Violet was out of the question.

To risk his own life would be at once to sacrifice
Violet's.

While engrossed with these reflections, the landlord appeared for the last time.

He bore in his hand two plates, containing the
omelettes.

These he put on the table, without the ceremony
of laying a cloth.

He next proceeded to produce some bread from a
dirty tray that had remained under a dirty cloth at
the further end of the room.

"Senor," said he, "did not order what wine he
would like, so I have acted on my own responsibility
and brought red.

"That will do," said Jack, coolly, as the landlord drew a bottle from his pocket.

Violet and our hero were now left alone to enjoy their repast.

They knew they must eat to support nature, so set to work energetically.

Jack had placed his lips to a tumbler of wine, when an inconceivable sentiment caused him to place it down again on the table untasted.

It was a suspicion.

Driven with the force of the speeding arrow into the very recesses of his soul.

The thought aroused him as a pistol-shot.

The wine had been drugged—thank heaven he had drunk none of it.

At this moment the eyes of the landlord peered into the apartment. He closed the door, which he fastened on the outside with the bolt.

Roving Jack felt his heart throb with intense force as he contemplated that he was now a prisoner.

After a pause of fearful anxiety, a second door opened and shut with a heavy slamming.

It was that leading to the open road, along which retreating footsteps were heard. They were the footsteps of the crafty landlord, hastening to give information that he had taken the fugitives.

Before our hero had time to utter a word, or reflect upon the desperate peril in which he was placed, a sound was emitted of a trap-door opening with a hollow clangour beneath his feet.

The floor receded, the macinery having been suddenly turned, and a figure emerged from the dark recess.

To describe the effect produced upon Roving Jack by what he now saw were impossible.

He passed his hand across his brow.

He gazed upon the object before him in doubt and amazement.

In an underbreath, and with a look as if life depended on the inquiry, he exclaimed—

"It is—?"

"Tomaz Sebastien!"

"I can scarcely believe my senses. How is it possible that you can have discovered us?"

"This is no time for explanation," replied Sebastien. "It is sufficient that I was retaken by the pirates, confined here, and have found means to escape."

The sudden appearance of Sebastien had again thrown the enervated Violet into a delirium.

Exhausted nature had deprived her of all power.

And her helpless condition would impede the fugitives in the premeditated flight.

Come what might, an effort must be made to save her in this dire extremity.

"The first thing we must do is to secure the door, which is fastened on the outside."

With the words Jack began to collect the lumber and furniture of the room, which he intended to form as a barrier to the entrance.

He had scarcely commenced his labours when they were arrested by Sebastien.

"Stop, friend," he cried; "I have thought of a better and a surer plan, and one that will involve our enemies in one common ruin."

"What do you propose?"

"Let my deeds, and not my words, answer the question."

Sebastien at once commenced carrying out the plan he had devised.

Drawing a small crowbar from the wall at his side, he commenced raising the boards that formed a flooring to the apartment.

In a few moments a tremendous gulf appeared at his feet, and entirely facing the door by which their pursuers must enter. Having finished his task with the same coolness with which he had performed it, he remarked to his companion—

"This chasm is wide enough to receive twice their number."

"Your device is ingenious," answered Roving Jack, "but I fear it will do us little service. When our enemies return, they will, like ourselves, perceive the abyss and find means to pass it without danger."

"That we must prevent."

"How?"

"By simply closing yonder shutters. The total darkness that then reigns will prevent their seeing the pit that is dug for them, and they will unsuspectingly fall into it."

"True, I had not thought of that."

"At all events, if such a catastrophe does not take place, it will at least give us more time to reach the 'Black Valley.'"

"Arrived there—?"

"We are near the margin of the island, off which lies the French frigate, 'La Belle Susanne.'"

"We can hail her."

"And they dare not refuse to shelter us. A treaty with your country compels them to give us aid, support and protection."

Gladsome with this intelligence our hero caught Violet in his arms, and hastily passed with her through the trap-door by which Tomaz Sebastien had gained admittance in the first instance.

Closing the shutters and leaving the chamber where he had been of such service to its occupants, Tomaz Sebastien followed in their steps just as a body of armed men were entering the house to search for them.

* * * * *

After traversing a series of tortuous and subterranean passages, Roving Jack, with the others, reached the egress abutting on the "Black Valley."

This locality seemed as if hewn by God's hand out of solid rock.

The path rolled its way through a mighty chasm of cliffs several hundred feet high.

The one side presented enormous masses, and the other recesses, as if the great stone girdle had been rent by a convulsion.

The plain was overspread with prodigious fragments of rocks.

Some of them were smooth and bare.

Some contained soil and verdure in their fissures.

These were crowned with shrubs and trees.

The eye commanded a long stretching vista, seemingly closed, and shut up at both extremities of the valley by coalescing rocks.

Roving Jack and Tomaz Sebastien proceeded through the gloomy region with as much speed as the precarious state of Violet would allow them.

They had nearly reached its confines when they came upon a semicircular ledge.

Up to it there led a short flight of steps.

Over it waved the canopy of a tall, graceful birch tree.

Here they sat, for their exertion had been too great to be long endured.

After a pause our hero addressed the partner of his toil.

"Tomaz Sebastien, I am greatly your debtor," said he.

"On the contrary, I consider myself bound to you; for though I have been a bad man, I am a conscientious one."

"You opened my prison doors."

"Have you not done the same by me: but for

you I should have been still pining in a dungeon."

"I see, you think me a friend, and I will prove myself one."

"You promise more than you will be able to perform. This world has no longer pleasures for a runagate like myself."

"I have wealth."

"Wealth cannot purchase happiness."

"But it bestows comfort."

"Humph! you talk like a boy, as you are. I tell you I shall never know peace of mind more," said Sebastien, moodily.

"I am not so confident of that. In England I have more power than you imagine. I bear a title which my ancestors won for me at the sword's point in fighting the battles of their native country. If you reject my friendship and consolation, you will, at least, acknowledge my generosity which shall provide for your latest days."

"Young man," replied the other, with feeling; "I am not insensible to the nobleness of your heart, nor ungrateful for your kind intentions towards an aged man. But Tomaz Sebastien cannot accept your proffer, he is of too proud a stock to receive your offer, and unwilling to become a pauper on another's bounty."

Just then a large stone fell from the top of the cliff.

A loud voice was heard.

The watchful Sebastien descried the danger, and this was the warning.

Forthwith he rose, and beckoned his companions to follow him.

There were paths dangerous to the unpractised feet.

These paths along the ledges of the rock, led up to several caves and places of concealment.

In an instant not a living creature was visible in the valley.

The fugitives were hidden, or nearly so, in the recesses of the dell.

The gleaming torches of the pursuers now hurried to and fro, as if seeking every corner of the wild region.

Presently across it runs a wild shout of triumph.

A prisoner is taken.

On the green sward, upon the summit of these precipices, they have discovered Tomaz Sebastien.

A party of soldiers, of the Portuguese guard, are upon him.

He is questioned, but answers not.

"Why are you making signals?"

"To whom?"

"And for what purpose?"

One, more daring than the rest, dragged Tomaz to the edge of the cliff, and addressed his comrades in the vale below.

"See, we have caught the aider and abettor in his own net. A lighted quick match bound between his fingers, will soon make him tell the whereabouts of the heretics flying from justice."

"A noble prize."

"If the caitiff refuse to open his lips, fling him over on the jagged points of the cliff."

Sooner said than done." In the next moment the would-be executioner lies in the valley, an inert and blood-stained carcass, while his assailant Tomaz Sebastien, had vanished like a shadow.

He was mixing with the tall green broom and bushes, making, unseen, his way to the shore.

"Satan has saved his servant!" cried Barabbas.

The pirate still wore the disguise of a monk, and appeared heading the soldiers of the inquisition.

"Follow me," he continued, addressing them. I know my way into the bed of the valley, and

the steps up to the tiger's cave. 'Tis there the impious heretics have taken refuge. The hunt is up—we will be in at the death."

The soldiers, following their leader, dashed down a less precipitous part of the wooded banks. They hurried into the depths of the vale.

They reached the spot upon which but lately the fugitives had stood.

All was silent and solitary.

Not a soul was to be seen.

"Here is a bible, dropped by one of them," cried a soldier.

"Give it to me."

The name of Violet Tremaine was stamped upon the cover.

Barabbas read the words as the book was handed to him.

"Soldiers, our prisoners are near us. Search strictly, and they must be taken!"

As the pirate spoke these words, he dashed the holy volume from him, and spun it away into a pool.

The men, on an order given, began to climb up the rocks.

They were strangers, and knew not those which protected the valley.

Their united weight caused nature's water-gate to give way.

A noise came upon their ears like distant thunder.

The ascensionist became irresolute, then appalled.

A slight current of air, as if propelled, came sweeping forward.

It whispered along the sweetbriar and the broom.

It came deepening, gushing, roaring on, and shook the surrounding precipice as if by an earthquake.

"Heaven be merciful! What is this?"

The words issue from a hundred mouths, intermingled with screams of terror and the shrieks of death.

Now came forth a sound like that of many myriad chariots rolling on their iron axles.

It was the torrent burst up among the moorlands.

It was the ocean, mighty and awful in its power, that was at hand.

Then it came.

Tumbling through the broken barrier into the "Black Valley."

In a moment it was filled with one mass of gurgling waves.

Huge agitated clouds of foam rode on the surface of the blood-red waters.

An army might have been swept away by that flood.

Barabbas and his myrmidons perished in a moment.

High up in the cliffs, far above the sweep of destruction, were three persons—Roving Jack and the companions of his desperate flight.

CHAPTER LXXXIV.

A YEAR ELAPSES—ROVING JACK ONCE MORE IN MERRY ENGLAND—DICK TURPIN IN A NEW CHARACTER—SHARKS ALONG SHORE.

A YEAR has elapsed.

And the scene of our story is laid once more in merry England.

It is in the country, a rustic spot near Chatham, in Kent.

On the roadside stands an old-fashioned house.

The sign betokened it to be one of entertainment.

While a notice that good accommodation for man and beast might be obtained within gave further evidence, if any doubt might have existed on the point.

At the period of our story, the rude bench and table that stood in front of the dwelling for the use of the passers by who might require refreshment, was now filled with the guests.

They had arrived from the town of Deal by the waggon.

The waggon standing hard by in order that the horses might take a feed of corn and drink from the trough of the "Travellers' Rest," the sign by which the inn was distinguished.

The good people who had stopped to bait the beasts that carried them had not forgot to perform a similar office for themselves.

Each was engaged in an occupation agreeable to his own taste.

Some were drinking.

Some were eating.

But all were singing.

At the end of the last song, for the passengers were about to depart, the burthen was repeated by two voices in the waggon.

This caused a general laugh.

Why should such a simple incident do so?

When we are left alone with the landlord of the hostel and the waggoner we will tell the reader.

In a few moments all the travellers paid their reckoning, each one having arrived at his journey's end, and the parties mentioned found they were by themselves.

"That's a frolicsome young sailor lad you have with you, Giles," said the landlord, addressing the waggoner, who bore such a name.

"Yes, he be."

"He and his companion seem to be on excellent terms with each other, even with regard to mocking our merriment."

"Yes, after your good dinner, measter, and a stiff sarving out of grog, as the sailor calls it, they both turned into my waggon for a snooze, where they still are."

"Where did the seaman pick up this new-found friend?"

"Why, he overtook him about a mile from your house."

"Humph—I guessed as much—I know him—that is, I don't exactly know him—I only think that it may be as well to put the sailor on his guard, for I have a suspicion——"

"But he hasn't, measter, bless yer, he be so free-hearted, honest, and open 'imself; besides, the Jack tar have taken such a moighty fancy to t'other chap, that he won't suffer un to pay a penny for nothing."

"I hope he mayn't repent it."

"Well, I don't noa."

"How far is the sailor going with you?"

"All the way to Barnet."

Further conversation was now stopped by a peculiar intonation, intended no doubt for singing.

The vociferous harmony proceeded from the waggon, the straw of which began to move.

Beneath it peered the jovial and weather-beaten face of the sailor to whom we have alluded.

Suddenly a young man in the garb of a seaman started from under the straw, and with a gravity attendant sometimes on intoxication commenced dancing a hornpipe, much to the surprise of the horses of the waggon, who appeared to be entirely unaccustomed to such a performance in their vehicle.

After the saltation the mariner jumped out of the waggon, and insisted upon shaking hands with the landlord, and offering him a friendly greeting.

His gripe might be compared to the clasp of a smith's vice, his hug to that of a Norwegian bear.

The waggoner had to undergo a similar ordeal, to whom the sailor addressed the following words:—

"Well, skipper—or rather coxswain, seeing as how you hold the helm—when are we about to set sail?"

"Sail, measter? I be'ant got none."

"Shiver my timbers! I mean, when do we weigh anchor, and bear to windward?"

"Well, somehow or other, I don't think the wind will get up to-day."

"My eyes, what a grampus!—can't understand a seaman's lingo. When do we make for Barnet, I ask?"

"Oh, ah! as soon as yer likes—and the sooner the better."

"Then bring to, and pipe all hands, for I've a fancy for getting under weigh myself."

The waggoner cracked his whip, and the willing team answered its summons.

"Belay there, belay; I want a word with my messmate afore you tack and tack—Roger, ahoy Roger!"

Roger answered the summons.

He issued forth as his late companion had done.

He was enveloped in straw, and appeared very drunk.

With some difficulty the young seaman assisted him to descend from the waggon in which until now he had been sleeping.

"Steady, steady, my lad," said he. "Belay, and I'll steer you. Avast, avast, you're more sheets in the wind than I am. Eh, I say, hilloa there—skipper—landlord—what will you take, eh?"

Roger was not so drunk as he seemed, for he had scarcely reached the ground than his staggering left him, and with apparent friendship responded to his friend's late request.

"Don't be so free with your money," he said; "'tis true, you are new among friends; but, beware, you might be imposed upon."

"And will, if you remain with him," thought the landlord.

"To be sure you can afford to be a little free," simpered Roger, fawningly, "for you are not destitute, eh?"

"Destitute."

The sailor gave his pocket a slap, and made the money in it jingle, as he uttered the word—

"Destitute! No. Did you hear that golden tongue give you an answer. Plenty of shot in the locker. So, landlord, freshen-hawse, d'ye hear."

"Aye, a cool pot of porter," said Roger.

"That's cool of you that havn't to pay for it," replied the landlord.

"He pay! No, I shall, you lubber; I order it. Nay, I'm no shark to swallow the bait and then shake myself off the hook—

"I shall pay for all," said the seaman; "here's enough," he continued, "to settle for a hogshead of porter, and a purser's bread-bag of tobacco; so slip the painter, and sarve out."

The landlord and waggoner who had witnessed the altercation, exchanged looks and shook their heads.

There was more in the action than met the eye.

The former then entered his tavern to execute the order he had received.

The latter busied himself in the waggon, and with his team.

Roger and his dupe were no sooner left alone

than the former eyed the well-filled pocket of the sailor, which he had so unwarily indicated.

"My good friend, take care of your money," said the cunning observer, "you sailors are so unmindful; you've doubtless got more. You should put it —— ah, by-the-bye, where do you keep it?"

"What's that to you?" was the quick answer of the questioned.

"Me?—I asked for your own sake."

"That's all?"

"I should be destitute of gratitude if I didn't feel concerned for you."

"You don't say so!"

"You are bound for the north road—so am I."

"And so you told me before, and advised me to bear you company in the craft."

With the word "craft," the speaker pointed at the waggon, now drawn to the road side.

"To be sure.

"Having money about you, 'tis less dangerous than travelling in coaches.

"Besides, they often meet with accidents.

"Umph! Been long from sea?"

"Just paid off from the 'Albemarle,' Captain Oakheart—as brave a commander as ever hoisted blue bunting; and I'm his coxswain.

"Many a yarn I could spin about him!

"We were boys together in the same ship.

"But now we are paid off, he's gone to sling his hammock in the old castle in which he was born."

"And you?" inquired the other.

"Am bound for my father's roof. He's a Hertfordshire farmer, and had bad crops lately; I must overhaul the accounts, and new rig the poor old soul."

"A dutiful and affectionate son! You'll be rewarded."

Roger now placed his finger in close proximity to the sailor's money, and continued speaking—

"So this is for him, eh? Do be careful of it. Now I know it's for a worthy man I feel so interested in its safety."

"Lor', really; do you, now?"

"Oh, put it away carefully."

"Bless you, stupid head, so I have; d'ye see this black silk handkerchief round my neck?"

"Any of it there?" said Roger, with an eagerness that might have aroused distrust in a less ingenuous disposition than the poor sailor possessed.

"Just a sea store for present use."

"Well, now, that is careful. I see you've tied it with a knot—a tight knot too. How ——"

"Trust me, I know where to find my stuff. All in front."

The young seaman placed his hand upon a fob, as much as to say that that receptacle held his money.

"All in front," he continued. "I ain't looking behind me at every step, like a monkey in search of his tail."

At this point of the conversation, Boniface, the landlord, came from his house, bearing in his hand a foaming tankard of porter.

Whether the inviting beverage had any effect or not on the waggoner, the deponent saith not; but the sailor found that stolid individual standing by his side at its appearance.

"Well, really you sailors are such worthy people," said Roger, as he observed the drink being brought.

"No wonder the girls in every port fall in love with you."

"I believe they do, and remain true too as long as you can treat them. I shall never forget my first coming on shore. I was a young 'un then."

"I see, quite innocent. Fell in love at first sight."

"Yes, over head and ears with one, Poll Maggot," continued the seaman. "Such a craft. We were at a dance at the back of the Wapping.

"'Ma'am,' said I, 'will you take a step with me?'

"I'd just spliced my arm to her waist, and was about to fire a salute, when a decent chap with a red coat and Jack-boots steers in between us, and says,

"'Mister Sailor, I loves that young woman, and neither you nor any other man shall kiss her.'"

"What presumption!" chimed in Roger.

"I believe you, indeed. Oh! it was side out for a bend in no time. Well, he was a decent chap, and stripped like a good 'un; but not put together as I was, all ribs and tucks like a tinker's donkey, but made up of arms and legs like a superannuated spider."

"Well, you made all sail at him."

"Yes, and should have run him down if the liquor I'd drank hadn't puzzled my eye. He waited till I was within hail, then bobbed a one side."

"You had a good way on you?"

"And ran end on to the store-room bulkhead? Down went a whole barrow-load of pewter, and the landlady set up as great a row as a hundred sea-gulls after a piece of pork."

"What was the conclusion?"

"I don't know, but the end of it was I found myself rolled up in the straw the next morning in a place they call the 'lock-up,' and locked up I was, and accused of being one Jack Sheppard, being found in company with a lass that called herself his wife."

During the recital the seaman had drank rather lustily, while, on the other hand, his companion, unseen, had evaded every draught offered to him.

The pot was now drained to the bottom, and the sailor cried loudly for more.

"Here, landlord, serve out again," said the liberal tar, handing the mug to the party addressed.

"Not a drop more you get here, my lad. Good day, and take care of yourself."

Boniface having delivered himself of this speech, walked quietly into his house, leaving his guest in a pleasing state both of doubt and astonishment at the conscientious scruples of the honest innkeeper.

DICK TURPIN'S ATTACK ON THE TRAVELLER.

CHAPTER LXXXV.

THE THEFT IN THE WAGGON.

No sooner had the landlord entered his house than Roger gave his companion a knowing wink.

"If he won't supply us," said he, "I think I know a party that can."

The speaker drew a bottle from his pocket.

"Look here, we shan't run aground, it's real Jamaica."

The only answer the sailor made to the remark was by taking the bottle produced into his hand and swallowing a portion of its contents.

After a second draught, he pronounced it to be excellent rum.

"I can't help thinking of your adventure in Wapping," said Roger; "it only shows you what scrapes these women lead us into."

"Avast, there, avast," replied the seaman, "not a word against the fair sex. That yarn I spun you was the folly of a boy; I thought I loved then, but now——"

"Eh, caught again?"

"Aye, messmate, and brought to by the tightest frigate that ever skimmed the earth's ocean."

"What's her name?"

"Nelly."

"Is she pretty?"

"I believe you; you never saw so much bone and flesh put so well together."

"I think I see her now."

"And when she sees me there'll be a salute; she'll fling herself into my arms—not with a sister's embrace, no, but with a true woman's coil, when her arms are firm and her heart warm."

"Yours will be a happy meeting."

"Yes, we've been spliced and not seen each other for a year or two now, poor thing! she thinks I'm dead. I got into a scrimmage with some piratical sharks, and it was reported I'd gone to Davy Jones."

The waggoner, now growing somewhat impatient, advanced to the travellers.

"Measters, the team be ready; we must be off."

"Not till we drink Nelly's health."

With these words Roger pretended to take a strong pull at the bottle, and then began to stagger as if suffering from the influence of its effect.

"Bless her," he hiccuped, "bless the pretty Nelly—the darling Nelly!"

"Holloa, I say!" exclaimed the mariner, "what right have you to bless my wife?"

"I can't help it, it's my weakness," said Roger, stumbling, and finally allowing himself to sprawl upon the ground.

"Why, he's nine sheets in the wind. Steady, messmate; let me steer you into the cabin."

While the noble-hearted seaman was assisting the falling man, the latter clung to his black handkerchief, as if for support, and secretly managed to cut it from his neck.

With difficulty, Roger was at last placed on his feet.

"Now, then, messmate, another tack, and you're in your berth."

"I shan't go without Nelly," replied the individual addressed, assuming an air of drunken obstinacy.

"Come, come, man, port your helm and turn in."

Suddenly altering his demeanour, Roger exclaimed, as if in gratitude for the favour he was receiving,

"Thank ye—bless you—lending a helping hand to a poor devil that can't help himself. Oh! it's noble—it's virtuous—it's worthy!"

"Here, crowd all sail," said the sailor, to the waggoner standing at his side.

After some considerable exertion, the two men succeeded in lifting Roger into the waggon.

But not until that worthy had contrived to make himself master of all the money the seaman possessed.

"There, he's safe enough now," said he, panting after his arduous task, and leaning his back against the waggon to take breath.

"How terribly drunk he be, to be sure," cried Giles, the waggoner, as he emulated his companion in wiping the perspiration from his forehead.

"He could no more help himself than new-born babe put on his breeches; I was obliged to lift him right in, and now I'll have a turn in myself," said the mariner, about to mount the vehicle.

His ascent was interrupted by the landlord, Boniface, who at the moment made his appearance with his bill.

While the waggon horses' bells were heard to jingle, as if to indicate their readiness to depart.

"As you will pay all," said Boniface, addressing the sailor; "why here's your bill."

"How much?"

"Seven and ninepence."

"Say eight shillings, and give the change to the Dollymop."

"Where's your friend?"

The sailor smiled, and pointed to his head at the question.

"Mum," said he; "Roger has shifted ballast, top heavy, and turned in."

Boniface took the hint, looked into the waggon, and then laughed.

"Let's see, landlord, what do you make the reckoning."

The sum was repeated.

"Then I may as well pay out and settle scores."

The sailor, with the words, began to feel for the handkerchief which had been abstracted.

While doing so he continued to speak.

"How suddenly my messmate went off, didn't he? Well, it serves him right; he tried once or twice to-day to make me drunk; and now he's spooney himself, while I am steady as—aye, where's my handkerchief?"

"Why, what's the matter?"

"Which of you have done this?"

"Done what?" replied his companions, in surprise.

"My handkerchief's gone."

"What the one I seed thee tie the money in?" said the waggoner.

His placid and simple mien received an impression of further amazement, when the following accusation was brought against him.

"Yes, you swab, and now you've stolen it."

"Aye, what! stolen—I," replied the now stupefied Giles; "well, I never heerd the loikes of that."

"But you shan't touch my other store, for that's sacred, and it would take a cleverer fellow than you to——"

As the sailor turned to his pocket, he found that it had been cut off.

Desperation nerved his arm, as he seized the landlord and waggoner each by the throat, and dragged them forward.

"Villains," he exclaimed; "that has gone, too. The money that was to have saved him, who has been more than a father to me, from want; the gold that was to have gladdened the eyes of her whom I love better than life."

Suddenly the speaker relaxed his hold.

A tear stood in his eye.

A smile gleamed on his face.

"But no, you could not do so black a deed, you look like honest men, you did it but in jest to frighten me, and so you have. The last news I had from home was that my wife was in sickness, he whom I may call father failing; that little store was to give them bread in their adversity, to cheer their life in youth—in age; give me back that which will make them doat on me, keep famine from their cabin and give comfort to their cot."

Wiping away the trickling moisture from his cheeks, he continued,

"It was a cruel jest, but I forgive you."

"Young man," said the landlord in a voice of pity, "I am sorry, I feel for you. We have not taken your money, but I suspect who has."

"Tell me who you think it is and I'll clapper-claw him in the handling of a marlinspike."

"I fear your late companion has something more to do with this affair than we."

"Why the man was too insensible to——besides he lies sleeping in the waggon."

As if struck by a sudden impulse, the seaman advanced to it.

"I will know, I will be convinced."

He cried out for Roger.

There was no reply to the summons.

"I've been robbed, rouse man or I'll——"

The seaman now jumped into the vehicle.

He repeated his exclamation.

The obdurate Roger answered not, nor were there any signs of his presence.

"Oh! found the lubber, he's got under the straw of the craft."

The straw was parted but the thief was gone, leaving behind him a coat.

That coat contained a letter written in an almost illegible hand.

"The mystery is solved," said the sailor, as he perused the paper, "the robber is no other than ——"

"Who?"

"The notorious highwayman Richard Turpin."

"Turpin?"

"Yes, the letter also informs me of his whereabouts."

"Where is he to be found?"

"At the pirates' decoy house."

"Near Rotherhithe?"

"I'll be there to-night and beard him in his lair, though Beelzebub himself kept the larboard watch."

CHAPTER LXXXVI.

SHOWS THAT A WINDOW MAY BE USED FOR OTHER PURPOSES THAN ADMITTING LIGHT— JONATHAN WILD—THE PIRATE'S DECOY HOUSE —A LEAP FOR LIFE.

PAUL PEVERIL, for that was the name of the seaman spoken of in the last chapter, arrived in London after a hasty journey.

Of course, immediately on his arrival, he bent his footsteps to the pirate's decoy house at Rotherhithe.

It was a lone, dark-looking building on the banks of the Thames.

Its considerable size, architecture, and tall, twisted chimneys, showed that it had, at one time, been occupied by more wealthy tenants, and had been built in the days of "good Queen Bess."

It stood alone.

And as the path which abutted on the house was little frequented, the crafts which belonged to the owners were allowed to rest quietly in their moorings.

Paul knocked at the door of this mysterious abode.

Some minutes elapsed before his knock was answered.

Presently he heard a heavy tread along the passage.

This was succeeded by the rattling of a chain and bar, and the pulling back of a ponderous bolt.

When the entrance was thrown open, a muffled figure was exhibited holding a large horn lantern.

The glimmer of which was thrown full in the face of the intruder.

Unabashed, Paul enquired if Dick Turpin had arrived yet.

Being answered in the negative he then demanded whether he would be long.

The only reply he could obtain, was,

"What he wanted with the highwayman?"

On making a particular sign and uttering the pass-word, the man with the light ushered the seaman into an inner room, from which they ascended to the floor above.

As Paul followed his conductor along the passage, the boards of which being without carpet, it gave a hollow, ominous sound,

He could not help noticing the bare walls, staircase, and landing, festooned with cob-webs and destitute of covering as the passage.

Having entered a spacious oak chamber, with large lattice window, Paul was desired to take a seat.

The moment he had done so another person entered the room.

He appeared to be a middle-aged, middle-sized man.

And was dressed in a dark brown suit of the period.

He carried a ponderous sword by his side, which being wielded by the muscular arm of the strongly built body of its owner, must prove it a very formidable weapon in an affray.

"What is your business here?" said he, addressing Paul, abruptly.

"My business is with Dick Turpin," replied the seaman, putting on a look as defiant and fearless as his questioner.

"Indeed; then learn that Dick Turpin has no secrets from me; so again I ask, why you are come hither."

"Before I answer," said the seaman, "I must know the person in whom he places such a confidence."

"Humph, you seem a bold man to face the lion in his den without counting emergencies; so I will respond to your wish. You ask who I am; I will tell you."

This singular personage then seated himself and requested Paul to place his chair beside him.

Looking the seaman sternly in the face, he commenced speaking.

"I am the king of knaves," said he, "and establish an uncontrolled empire over all practitioners of crime.

"This is no light conquest, nor is its government easily maintained.

"Resolution, subtlety, severity, are required for my dominions.

"And these qualities I flatter myself I possess in an extraordinary degree.

"Professing to stand between the robber and the robbed, I plunder both parties."

"You are then——"

"Jonathan Wild, the renowned, and noted thief-taker."

Paul Peveril, taken by surprise at this intelligence, and knowing the character of his enemy, determined to act with caution.

He resolved on the artifice which will appear in the following conversation between himself and his nefarious associate.

"But to business, sir; I have told my history, now tell yours," said Wild.

"I am a seaman."

"Your dress indicates as much. What service?"

"I have been in both."

"Humph, what was your last vessel?"

"A king's ship."

"What post did you hold?"

"I was coxswain of the 'Albemarle,' man o' war."

"You are a deserter."

"Yes, obliged to strike my colours; cut and run, as you landsmen have it."

"Felony, I suppose?" asked Wild, coolly.

"Yes," replied Paul.

The blood imperceptibly mounted to his cheeks, as he stammered out the falsehood.

"Coming on shore" he continued "I fell in with one of your gang."

"Dick Turpin?"

"I told my tale, and he said he could aid me; that I was just the man you wanted, and gave me the pass into this house, where he promised to meet me."

" And he will be true to his appointment, or I am greatly mistaken in my man."

Wild rang a bell, and the man who had conducted Paul into the room made his appearance.

Wild ordered a can of grog to be made.

It was brought and partaken of.

But moderately on the part of the seaman, who, whenever he could, shirked the glass.

Under the genial influence of the liquor, Wild became more communicative.

" I say, friend," said he, " don't you think an active fellow like you (for I have learnt by your mouth you can put your hand to the helm) might make money enough of your own and be independent,"

" Well to tell you the truth, Mr. Wild, I never gave it a thought."

" Do so now."

Wild made the remark with some bluntness.

" You've been at sea some years."

" Yes."

" And you've not got coin enough to jingle on a tombstone."

" No, my messmates would tell you that the prize money is ever sifted with a gridiron."

" All that falls through goes to the officers.

" That which remains comes to the men."

" I tell you what," said Wild, " you are just the lad for me, and it's your own fault if you don't make your fortune."

" At least I'll try."

" You seem brave, quick, and intelligent ; if you will serve me, I will serve you, so let's have another glass, and see if we can't make a bargain."

After Wild had dispensed the fluid, he handed a glass to Paul, recommending him to wet his whistle.

The seaman acquiesced with a smile, being accompanied in the action by his companion.

A few remarks had passed between them relative to the matter last spoken of, when Wild rose from his chair.

He went to the corner of the room and opened a sliding panel.

In this Paul discovered a regular stand of arms, short cutlasses with baskets round their handles, pistols, tomahawks and other kinds of warlike weapons.

" This is the sort of rigging I require for the vessel which I wish you to steer," said the thief-taker.

If the seaman made no reply, his gesticulations served for one.

He gave a furtive glance.

Run his forefinger across his throat.

And then pointed downward.

" No, not exactly that" exclaimed Wild " no, not a pirate, but a little given to this."

Here the speaker indicated the small rum cask that had been placed on the table.

" Oh, I see" said the other in a whisper, " You mean smuggling."

" Right as a trivet, will you join me ?"

" Should I refuse——"

" You've a desperate man to deal with."

" Then I consent."

" I thought you would," interrupted Wild. " I liked you at first sight, and thought I saw some devil in your composition. Now listen, I am going to place myself in your power, but remember you are in mine.

" On running our last cargo," he continued, " we were opposed, the mate was killed, I fired and he was avenged."

" And you want me to fill his place, I suppose."

" Yes, now mark me, had you not consented to my terms, you would never have quitted this place since you have done so, you are free to depart."

Jonathan Wild pointed to the door through which Paul had to pass.

" Recollect, my reputation is in your hands ; seek to injure it, and my security must be your death."

The door now was widely opened by some one on the outside.

A sudden gust of wind issuing from the spacious staircase beyond, in a minute extinguished the lamp that was burning.

And the chamber was left in perfect darkness.

" Confound the wind," exclaimed Paul Peveril, " it has put out the light and left us floundering about like porpoises in a fog."

" There is a strange voice here, but one I have heard before."

As he uttered the words, the new comer entered the room.

" What is he doing here ?" continued he.

" Ratifying a compact ; he is about to become one of us."

" Indeed ! I think I know him."

" You don't know much harm of me," answered Paul Peveril.

" Nor much good," muttered the other to himself ; and then addressing Wild he continued, " This fellow may blow the gaff on us."

" He has engaged to the contrary," said Wild.

" I care not for him or his bond."

" So it seems.   Come hither ?"

While thus speaking Wild advanced to the closed shutters, which he opened with his own hand.

The beams of the moon brightly shining in the heavens above, disclosed everything as clear as the noonday.

The late visitor scanned the features of Paul Peveril with a strict scrutiny.

" Hum, a fine fellow," he exclaimed ; " it appears you know our purpose ; will you swear never to give evidence against us under any circumstances ?"

" No, I will not promise that."

At the moment Paul uttered these words, he in his turn looked into the face of the party who had last addressed him.

He was much altered and very differently attired, but for all that the shrewd seaman knew him again.

" 'Tis that piratical lubber Dick Turpin," Paul muttered to himself.

Another mishap now befel Paul Peveril.

He suddenly remembered that he in haste had forgot to provide himself with weapons, which his present emergency would almost of a necessity require.

He was alone armed with a clasp knife, which hung suspended from his waist belt.

" This, and courage, then," said he, " must stand my friends."

" You have heard the conditions," exclaimed Wild, " and you refuse to concede to them."

" I refuse to——"

" Enough ! your blood be on your own head."

Wild and his confederate cocked their pistols, and presented them at the head of their prisoner.

For such Paul now was, as the door had been securely fastened on him.

Looking at the poised weapons, he raised his hands, and spoke thus, with apparent indifference.

" Belay, belay ; hear me out ; don't be in such a hurry ; as far as concerns this unlawful trade you're engaged in, I will swear by heaven——"

Here the ruffians again raised their firearms.

"I will swear by heaven," continued the seaman, "never to give auy evidence against you."

"And what other evidence could you give?" returned Turpin, fiercely.

"None as yet."

"I say, my lad," said Wild; "I see you are a bit of a sea attorney, and that before half an hour your throat will not require a handkerchief; join us, or in five minutes you are a dead man."

"I fear he is not to be trusted."

"I, too, have my doubts; but he's just the man for us, if he were."

"I never made much of such fellows," said Turpin, while his pistol gave an ominous click with his finger. "Stand by, and we'll have an enemy less in a minute."

"Not now," replied the thief-taker to Turpin, as he caught the arm he had raised to fire.

"Are you mad?" said the latter, endeavouring to disengage himself. "I tell you if he lives he will betray us. He knows us both, I see he does; let go my arm!"

In the struggle that took place between the two confederates, the pistol of Turpin went off in the air.

Enraged by the accident, the highwayman, with intense malevolence, rushed upon Paul Peveril.

With the butt-end of the discharged weapon he aimed a deadly blow.

The fell intention was anticipated by the seaman, who, in the meantime, had drawn his knife.

This he used with such good effect as almost, apparently, to sever the left hand of his adversary at the wrist, and following up the cut with a desperate wound in his breast.

"Take that, villain!" cried Paul Peveril, in triumph, "for robbing me in the waggon."

"I told you, Wild, he knew us," cried Turpin, faint from loss of blood.

"Yes, scoundrels, I know you both, and fear you not, though death stares me in the face, and two murderers are at my throat; I see I must die; you may kill but you can never cow the British sailor."

Jonathan Wild had been so amazed at the intrepidity of the gallant defence and attack he had witnessed, that, for the moment, he stood like one paralyzed and powerless.

At length his wonder ceased, and unbridled passion worked its way.

The thief-taker used his weapon, but he failed to hit his mark.

Good fortune had again come to the rescue of the brave tar, the pistol of his dastardly foe only snapped in the pan.

Paul Peveril took advantage of the time used by Wild in repriming.

There was an old sea locker under the chamber window.

The lid of this the seaman wrenched off just as Turpin, weakened by his wound, attempted to seize him.

A tremendous blow from the board felled the highwayman like a stricken ox.

Wild, for a second time, pointed his pistol and fired.

And, for a second time, was disappointed in his aim.

The lid of the locker, held before Paul Peveril, had proved as armour; though the ball had split it into a dozen pieces, it had entirely shielded its bearer from any harm.

"Now, Dick," said the foiled thief-taker, addressing Turpin, who had partially recovered from his late injury, "brace yourself together for a few moments and we shall manage him; all hands upon his throat, throttle and through the window with him."

"The window!" cried the desperate seaman; "'tis my only chance; 'tis my last effort. God befriend and aid me."

With the quickness of the thought he sprang to the casement.

It was fastened.

This impediment did not intimidate the captive.

Springing upon the chest that stood beneath it, he with his clenched fist shattered the frame, which opened at the blow.

Jonathan Wild and Dick Turpin pounced upon him as kites butt upon a carcase.

Their efforts were futile, for Paul had thrown himself backwards into the river that was sluggishly meandering beneath the window that had so miraculously afforded him the means of escape.

CHAPTER LXXXVII.

TOM KING ON THE ROAD—THE HIGHWAYMEN'S RENDEZVOUS AT SHOOTER'S HILL—THE EXPECTED TRAVELLER—HOW THE PURSUED GAVE LEG-BAIL TO THE PURSUERS—A PHANTOM RIDE ACROSS BLACKHEATH.

LET us now mount the steed and accompany that *chevalier sans peur sans reproche*, Tom King the highwayman.

This eve he appears, as he ever does, the easiest and pleasantest chum going.

All know he is the handsomest man about town, and the best fellow on the road.

While his "stand and deliver" is sure to arrest attention and produce an effect at once commanding and irresistible.

Look at his symmetrical figure cased in a suit of green velvet set off with silver, ruffles and lace.

His pistols in his holsters.

His mask on his face.

Is he not the envy of the men, the adoration of the women, from the village damsel to the highborn duchess?

He is as superior to the banditti of other countries, as the hardy seamen of England are to her worst foes.

But we digress, we are pursuing our journey with the illustrious personage of whom we have made the above remarks.

Animated by a kindred enthusiasm, we ascend the steep hill with glorious Tom King.

With him we dash through the bustling village.

Sweep over the desolate heath.

And plunge into the eddying stream, without pause—without hindrance—without fatigue.

The main road of Kent is reached, and we arrive at Shooter's Hill.

How beautiful the silent country and valley at its foot appear illumed by the star-spangled canopy of heaven

All peace around, slumber, we might almost say death, for with the exception of the solitary horseman there is no sign of life to be seen.

"By the mother that bore me," said he, "my pals have disappointed me, and I shall have to undertake the job alone; no matter, I must make the best of a bad bargain and land the swag myself; the prize is too tempting for me to allow it to slip through my fingers without a tussle. Let me see, how goes the enemy?"

With the words, Tom King pulled out a ponderous

gold "yack and onions," otherwise an enormous watch with its appendage of seals.

"Ten; the cull won't arrive for half an hour, in the mean, the sluggards may pull foot and come up with me."

So saying, the highwayman dismounted and fastened his horse to a tree.

After this he himself paced backwards and forward beneath the wide-spreading branches of some neighbouring oaks.

Fretfully he hummed in his measured step the uasn chaunt,

"On the high toby spice flash the muzzle."

A ditty much in vogue at that period with the fraternity of whom Tom King was so illustrious a member.

He next bethought him of a new means of whiling away a few tedious moments.

Flint, steel, and tinder were in the pouch of the Knight of the Post.

And a short pipe was at hand.

"Divine tobacco," he mused, "I'll try thy balmy comfort to allay the restlessness that this adventure causes me."

Within a few seconds there was a stream of vapour exhaling from his lips.

And tracking its still and murky course through the surrounding air.

Suddenly the stillness of the night was broken by the clatter of horses' hoofs.

In an instant Tom King vaulted into his saddle.

He discovers from the summit of the hill a body of riders

These riders are making its ascent.

Ever cautious, ever wary, the highwayman observes their approach with distrust.

Anon, a shrill whistle rings along the imperfectly shaded roadway.

The signal is returned.

A short time elapses, and a voice, in close proximity, shouts out the somewhat mysterious sentence—

"Old Oliver whiddles."*

Tom King recognised his pals, and lustily returned their greeting.

"Nante palaver; I'll ride by his glim to the chase."

As he uttered this jargon, he found Fielder and Rose, two roadsters, by his side.

They were attired in that garb highwaymen were wont to affect.

And in each case armed, booted, and spurred.

"You are late, my rum culls," continued Tom King. "I should have guessed you had padded the hoof from London instead of namussing† on the spanking prads‡ that carry you."

"The beaks nearly pinched us in a boozing ken in the Borough. To avoid such an unpleasantness, we have taken a longer route."

"Oli compoli," laughed Tom King, "since you've queered the rum coves, we can at once to business."

"Yes, business afore pleasure," answered a husky voice.

It was that of one of the party who had continuously stopped at every public-house on the road down, "to moisten his clay."

We quote the words of the party alluded to.

"What, Joe, is that you? How glad I am to see you after so long an absence! You ought to have

sent us a lock of your hair in a paper parcel to let us know you were in the land of the living."

"Stow your patter, Tom," said Blueskin; "mayhap I hadn't the chance, seeing that the county crop was wisiting the wicinity in which I'd pitched my tent."

"I see—knucks in quod. How have you and Jonathan Wild come together again? I thought, since your late quarrel, you had sworn to do for him?"

Blueskin gave an unmistakable gesture, and concluded the remark by stating that—

"There are sometimes wheels within wheels."

Tom King gave a nod as much as to say that he entirely coincided with such an opinion.

"I saw the governor to-day, and have made it all right."

"And Jack Sheppard?"

"Oh, he's as scarce as ever; he'll never return to serve Jonathan Wild. Mark me, he and the captain will never more be pals; since that affair of Violet Tremaine's, they've sworn to do for each other."

"Where is he?"

"How should I know?" replied Blueskin, with a cunning leer. "All I do know, is that he's got off clean and free, and has given leg bail to the darbies as was waiting for him in Newgate."

"I'm glad of it; Jack's a noble fellow, and I should be sorry to see him spring from the ladder."

"He'll never do that without ample vengeance at the hands of Joe Blueskin."

"Come, Tom, it's time to stash this gab; the pigeon must be ready for plucking," said Fielder.

"True," answered the highwayman, "Blueskin, after this little matter's settled, I must talk over another to you; for the present, 'mum's' the word."

"Are you sure," said Fielder, addressing Tom King, "that you can depend upon your information that this gallant comes on to London to-night?"

"Sure? why, didn't I tell you that I learnt all from the dimber dell Flash Nance, and that she tipped old Blowbellows the farrier, who was shoeing his nag, a guinea to physic the animal, and delay him a day longer, in order that I might search for you and Nat Rose?"

"Who are ever ready and willing to collar the 'mopusses.'"

"Yes, yes," continued the gentleman of the road, "I'm sure enough, and, by my reckoning, he will pass this secluded spot in two minutes, so no more, look to your barkers, and at once to ambush."

Either elevated by the drink of which he appeared so freely to have partaken, or excited by the golden prospect presented to his view, Blueskin gave, somewhat boisterously, the following stave—

"Believe me, there is not a game, my brave boys,
To compare with the game of high-toby;
No rapture can equal the highwayman's joys,
To blue devils and such give the go-by."

"Hold your screeching, do, owl, or you'll scare the prey; see, he's coming up the hill at a glorious pace, 'tis a beautiful beast he rides. Out of sight, Joe, if you hope to share his gold and shun the halter."

"That's personal, Tom Fielder," replied the worthy addressed, who evidently, more than ever, was labouring under the effects of intoxication, "I shall demand an apology on the instant."

"Apology be ——"

The expletive had not passed the lips of Fielder when his assailant was on him.

"Out knife!" exclaimed Blueskin ferociously, as he rapidly advanced.

---

* Oliver means the moon. To whiddle is to blab.
† Namussing—travelling. ‡ Prads—horses.

A kick in the ribs from Fielder sent him rolling into the ditch hard by, where he comfortably slept till morning revealed to him his singularly strange resting-place.

"'Tis better as it is," said Tom King, as he witnessed the issue of the struggle; "strong waters might have made Joe troublesome, and we want no quarrelling now.

"Nat Rose and myself," continued the speaker, "will draw up in yonder nook close; Tom Fielder, you take your stand here, in the shade of this elm; thus this gallant of high degree will stand between us before he is aware that we are waiting to pay our respects to him."

Each took up the position allotted to him.

The expected traveller was soon within bowshot of the highwaymen, who awaited his coming.

Boldly he urged on his homeward journey, mounted on a swift and fiery courser.

Suddenly it received a check, and reared up on its haunches, for the hand of a stranger had seized the bridle.

The rider was almost thrown backwards, but being a good horseman, managed to keep in the saddle.

"Friend or foe?" he cried, placing his disengaged hand on his pistol.

"That entirely depends upon yourself," replied Fielder, still holding the horse's head.

"Your words are an enigma—what do you require of me?"

"Your money—or your life."

"I will part with neither but with a desperate struggle, as you may find to your cost. I am on an errand of importance, and cannot part with my money."

"We must have it!" said the other highwaymen, issuing from their concealment.

"Be ruled by me, good sir," remarked Tom King, with courteousness and affability, "concede, I beg, to our wishes; we merely require your purse, watch, and that diamond ring that sparkles so brightly in the moonshine on your finger."

"I tell you once and for all that I will never yield them while I breathe," exclaimed the traveller, defiantly; "there are three on your side; I am alone, still I defy you."

"You are a brave man," said Tom King, "and I regret to put your courage to the test, but stern necessity compels me and my comrades to take toll."

"Beware how you attempt your purpose. I am armed, and I promise to shoot him through the head who advances to rob me. Who is bold enough to be that one?"

Not another word passed.

There was a flash, and a leaden bullet leaped from the tube through the air, and embedded itself in a neighbouring oak.

The traveller had dexterously evaded the shot of the highwayman, who, to his chagrin, found he had missed his aim.

The report of the pistol again startled the affrighted steed, and it plunged forward as if it had received a powerful electric shock.

The sudden action of the animal caused him to snap the bridle which Fielder still held in his hand, and his master was free to depart.

This he did, taking advantage of the momentary amazement of the highwaymen, who had been witnesses of the late maladventure.

With the swiftness of the wind the uncontrolled horse and its rider dashed on a wild and reckless career.

Leaving their pursuers far behind.

The pace of the goaded beast might be termed truly terrific.

The road is straightforward, and success seems to crown its triumph.

The eyes of the steed are dilated, and sparkle like globes of dazzling light.

While the nostrils, expanded, snorted forth a volume of smoke emitted, as it were, from some hidden fire.

Shot after shot is fired after the flying fugitive.

The bullets whistle through the air within an inch of their mark.

Fleetly speed the highwaymen, but fleeter still the traveller.

The pursuers are outwitted.

And the pursued vanished as a phantom.

This point of the story now brings us to an extensive moor, fringed by distant woodland and picturesque country.

It is called Blackheath.

The reader must bear in mind that this spot, so familiar to the holiday folks, in former days bore a very different aspect from that which it enjoys in the present.

It was then only a very wide waste, surrounded by bogs, and in many parts almost a morass.

In this unfrequented region the traveller and his horse had arrived.

He had far out-distanced his followers.

And now slackened the speed of the jaded animal that bore him.

He had scarcely advanced three hundred paces on the desolate road when the mist arising from the oozy earth enveloped the path in a thin, but heavy fog.

In a short time after he had become involved in the dim cloud, he noticed that another horseman was making his way towards him.

He was apparently coming from an opposite direction to that by which he had himself come.

At the distance he could not discern the features of the rider.

But his figure was so far discernible.

And the traveller at once recognised that it was one of the party who had so lately assailed him.

His first impulse was to shoot the man at once.

His second consideration to reserve his fire, and await contingences.

Mounted on a good charger, the highwayman was soon near his side.

Neither riders essayed to speak.

Each kept apart on either side of the turf that edged the roadway.

The traveller held on his course.

The highwayman did the same.

The former fancied in the imperfect light that he discovered in the lineaments of his companion a resemblance to one he had met before.

Superstitious awe at length aroused him from the sluggish stupor into which he had fallen.

He put spurs to his horse.

And galloped onwards.

The moment he did so a bullet grazed his saddle.

Exasperated, and staggered, the traveller returned the shot.

With what effect, let the next chapter show.

CHAPTER LXXXVIII.

THE OLD BELL INN AT BERMONDSEY—JACK SHEPPARD OFFICIATES AS OSTLER, AND IN WHAT WAY HE ACTED WHILE ENGAGED IN THAT CAPACITY—OLD FRIENDS MEET—THE RECOGNITION — A PLAN TO ROB AND MURDER A WEALTHY GUEST.

THE "Bell" Inn was one of the old-fashioned hostelries, and, affording entertainment for travellers, was well supplied with every comfort and accommodation to those who staid to refresh or lodge beneath its roof.

It stood at the extremity of that locality, re-nowned for its produce of leather, called Bermondsey.

And was approached eastward by an ancient stone bridge over a small stream bearing the name of the "Mill Pond."

Being situate on the lower road into Kent, from which county it was distant some mile and a half, it was much frequented by carriers and others, who found a suitable convenience for their cattle in its extensive stabling.

In the inn yard was now stationed an individual with whom our readers have been before acquainted.

This individual, though in strict disguise, still maintained his habitual mien.

There was his intelligent face, fine hazel eye, and clear olive complexion.

His effrontery, his mental energy and resolution, were unchanged.

While his forehead, lofty and broad, exhibited the same sleek, shining black hair as usual, which, being closely cropped to admit of his occasionally wearing a wig, gave ever a singular appearance and bullet shape to his head.

Jack Sheppard—it is his portrait we have drawn —was now engaged as ostler, under the name of Joshua, at the inn we have commented upon.

He had assumed this character with success, in order to defy the detection of Jonathan Wild, with whom the daring cracksman had lately quarrelled.

As he busied himself in his new capacity, he sang, anything but inharmoniously, the following racy and plastic ballad :—

> " When tame fools are sleeping,
> From clouds the moon's creeping,
> We knights of the road mount our horses and fly
> O'er common and heath,
> Well armed to the teeth,
> We bid all to stand, with ' Deliver or die! '
>
> " To our doxies back creeping
> While for cash fools are weeping,
> We freely delight and the yellow boys fly,
> We forget, in each glass,
> And the smile of each lass,
> That we one day must swing for—' Deliver or die! '"

"Marry, come up! a pretty melody, and well tuned," said a soft voice, whispering in Jack's ear, after he had ended, somewhat abruptly, his song.

He turned, and discovered Edgeworth Bess standing by his side.

Her face, like a mixture of lilies and roses, beamed with delight on her paramour.

Her charms at this moment were capable of triumphing over the heart of a prince.

It is not to be wondered at, then, that beauty, wit, and admirable grace found favour in the eyes of the renowned Jack.

THE FIGHT WITH THE HORSE.

And that perfections seldom found united in one person should invent stratagems that had ever fail d to part the constant couple.

"Not she for whom the Lapithides took arms,
Nor Sparta's Queen could boast such heavenly charms."

Following the fortunes of her lover, Edgeworth Bess had taken service in the same house that had given him shelter.

While he acted as ostler, she undertook the duties of chamber-maid in the inn.

This was a plan adopted in order that Jack Sheppard might carry out the deception he was practising, and which was intended to be of essential service to the hero of our tale in its attainment.

"Ah! my dimber dell, it's you, is it?" exclaimed

Jack, as he perceived Edgeworth Bess. "How do these new quarters suit you?"

"Right well, sweetheart," she replied. "I am never so happy as when near you."

"And yet you have given me cause to doubt you. Bess; where woman most loves she most ha es, and you would not be the first tempted either by gold or revenge."

"If I have ever injured you by thought or deed, may Heaven pardon me. I have sworn to dedicate my future life to your service. If I have unwittingly been the cause of your reckless career and folly, grant me your pardon for the devotion I shall bestow on you."

"To doubt once, Bess, is to suspect for ever."

" You wrong me by such a thought. Turn from the temptress, error; repulse her when she would entice you in. Shut your ears to her soft, persuasions and burst the chains she has cast around you."

"Let time prove if I have rightly construed, woman."

"Still unkind; but I can forgive you from my heart. Jack Sheppard shall never rue the day he trusted Edgeworth Bess."

"Hush! hush! girl, not so loud. The very walls in this place have ears, and on the slightest hint we shall have Jonathan's men on our scent."

With the remark, Jack Sheppard looked carefully around to see if they had been observed.

Satisfying himself on the point, he continued,

"Now, Bess," said he, "I am going to prove the sincerity of your words."

"I will hold with you to the last, Jack."

"Call me Joshua, the name by which I am known here since our mutual escape from the myrmidons of the thief-taker. Listen, I am going to entrust you with a secret."

"A secret?"

"Yes, to day has arrived a new mistress to the inn."

"I have not seen her yet."

"So much the better, she might recognise you though she has failed to recognize me."

"Ah! you know her?"

"Yes. And she knows me. When we are better acquainted she may prove our friend."

"Her name——"

"Is Nelly Peveril. From her I may gain tidings of Sir John Warbold."

"Better known as Roving Jack."

"He has promised to do much for me, and I expect——"

A loud knocking at the outer door interrupted Jack Sheppard, and summoned him to the gateway.

Opening the ponderous doors of the fore-court leading to the inn, he encountered the guest who had demanded admittance.

It was the traveller whose adventure with the highwaymen we have related in the previous chapter.

On approaching him, he appeared a young man of well-proportioned figure.

He was at once symmetrical, handsome, and vigorous.

While his features glowed with health and manly beauty, it could also be observed they were tinged by exposure to a foreign sun.

Proud of his waving ringlets, he allowed nature's ornament to fall carelessly over his shoulders.

Being dressed in riding attire, his general outline was revealed to great advantage.

Looking hard at Jack Sheppard, the newly-arrived horseman failed to recognise him in his disguise.

A similar state of things happened to his opponent, both being unaware that they were known to each other.

"I give you a good evening, friend," said the rider; "I am a belated traveller, and seeing your inn on the way, have called to obtain accommodation and refreshment until morning."

"You couldn't have acted more wisely, my master," replied Jack Sheppard; "the Bell Tavern is the best one between this and Dover, and our larder will supply you to a nicety."

"I'm glad to hear it; let it at once bestow a meal on me, and I will pay for the best it affords."

"Sharp set, eh?"

"Yes, my journey and its results have made me as hungry as a wolf."

Without saying another word, Jack Sheppard, in his capacity of ostler, led the horse into the stable.

Its owner followed quickly on his heels.

No groom could have bestowed more attention on the animal committed to his charge than did the cracksman.

This gave satisfaction to the traveller, who dropped a crown into his palm.

He then advanced, and caressed his horse, apostrophizing,

"Thanks to thy unwrung withers, I am safe at last—thy vigour seemed inexhaustible—thy muscle, bone, and sinew as bending iron in the fearful race."

The horse pricked its ears, and uttered a low neigh, as much as to indicate that he had only done his duty in the ordeal through which they had passed.

"Noble fellow," said the traveller, contemplating still the steed; "this is not the first time you have brought your master off in the hour of need; but he will not be ungrateful. Thy old age shall be cared for, and thy pure blood ne'er be disgraced as a hack on the road."

Turning to Jack Sheppard, the speaker continued,

"Corn and water; I must see my nag well bestowed before I refresh myself."

"They are faithful creatures, good sir; and if your mistress is as true to you as your horse, you may defy all the Philistines that ever wove a hempen cravat."

Jack Sheppard having attended to the directions given to him by the traveller, that party left him again by himself.

"That gallant," said he, "must have had a hard ride, if I may judge from his fiery, hot, and jaded beast. I wonder if he has met with any of the gang on his journey; if so, he has given them the double, and blown their cattle."

In a few minutes the traveller again returned to the stable.

He seemed in haste and nervously excited. This emotion ceased when he learnt that his suspicions were groundless, as the lines following these will show.

"Friend," said he, "help me to search the stable."

"You have lost something?"

"I trust not, for I can never replace the papers that——"

"Since it is of such value," said Jack Sheppard, "we will look into every nook and corner, if you suspect it to be left here."

With a horn lantern he commenced a strict examination of the stable, but was stopped in his labour by the traveller, who had proceeded to dislodge some straw that lay near one of the mangers.

"Thank heaven, I have found it," said he, raising a saddle-bag, which he had taken from its place of concealment; "this contains a treasure I would not part with for the wealth of India—the right and title of her I love."

"It seems heavy."

"Yes; the rogues who waylaid me in my journey hither missed a good booty; a thousand marks in gold is not an every-day prize.

"But," continued he, "pointing to the pistols that garnished his belt, "they should have bought them dearly, as the contents of these snappers should have convinced them."

"Shall I carry it in for you, sir?" asked Jack Sheppard, as he ogled the saddle-bag with a peculiar leer.

"No, my good fellow, this receptacle and I will

never part company till what it contains has passed into the hands of their just owner.· Look to my horse—he deserves all your care—and I will repay it, if you will give a little extra service on him."

For a second time the traveller left the stable, leaving as before Jack Sheppard its only human occupant.

"A thousand marks!" said he, "that would be worth risking life for. I should be a man, if I had only half the money."

Here he seemed lost in reverie, and alike insensible of every object around him.

Sitting with both his hands clasped on his knees, he rested on the same for their support, and continued musing.

Suddenly his face became more fully revealed—animated and earnest—and his deportment changed to boldness mingled with a reckless air.

"I'll do it!" he exclaimed.

As Jack Sheppard uttered the words, another person peeped in at the door and cautiously entered the stable.

His footfall was so light as not to attract the notice of his companion.

He advanced towards the horse that had lately borne the traveller, and with the same silent step as hitherto.

Closely regarding the quadruped, he exclaimed,

"I'm right; that's the very horse—I'll be sworn to it! To think that I should track him all the way here, and then——"

At this moment the stranger met the gaze of Jack Sheppard.

"Ah, the ostler!" he continued; "then, 'ben darkmans,' help me out of this dilemma."

Obscurity reigned in an instant.

The sickly flame of a candle stuck in a sconce against the stable wall had been extinguished by the intruder, who at once and immediately found himself in the grasp of an adversary.

His rushing was as quick and unexpected as that of the Indian who dashes on his foe.

Jack Sheppard, as most are aware, was a man of great personal strength, square-set, slightly bandy, with a frame like the "god of strength," Hercules.

His assault was energetic, and the struggle desperate.

Though his rival was of slighter proportion, and considerably taller, his superiority in this respect availed him little, and at length he declared himself vanquished.

Each panted for breath.

After a pause, Jack addressed the assailed with a contemptuous retort.

"Holloa, friend, what's your business here?"

"Business? Oh, I only come for pleasure. Strolling about; just looked in and saw——"

"Saw what?" exclaimed Jack, with impatience.

"'Tis he, I'll swear," answered the other, joyfully, recognising the voice that addressed him.

"Why don't you speak, you say you saw——"

"One of the prettiest rascals in his Majesty's dominions, if he hadn't deserted the trade of a gentleman to take up that of a sorry wielder of curry combs and brooms of birch, and doffing his cap and crying 'God save you, sir,' for a paltry groat, to travellers, instead of boldly bidding them to stand and deliver on the king's highway."

Jack Sheppard relighted the candle, placed it in the horn lantern, and held it up to the stranger's face.

"You seem to know me: for my own safety I must know you. Who the devil is the man?"

"No devil at all, Jack; only one of his favorite sons, who has been sent here by his special favour to——"

"As I live, Tom King!"

"Yes," replied Tom King, for he, indeed, it was, once better known by the sobriquet of the "Gentleman Highwayman," and, if fame belie him not, the master of three mistresses and as many nags.

"Tom, you were the model of infidelity."

"Aye, and that's a failing the fair sex can never overlook; one of the Dalilahs, in a fit of jealousy, peached, and, but for my prad, should have taken my leap from the ladder."

"Tom, you'll never ride backwards up Holborn Hill."

"So my pretty little gipsy tells me. I'm to meet King Death by the hand of a friend; there's some comfort in that reflection. But come, we've more weighty matters to think of than the casting of nativities. I guess the reason I have found you in this queer slum."

"I shall come out of it with flying colours soon, Tom. I am only waiting my time to send Jonathan on all fours and fit him for the surgeon's knife. I only want——"

"What?"

"A little ready rhino."

"You shall soon have a cheque on my bankers."

Tom King pointed to the traveller's horse significantly as he made his last observation.

"Eh! you don't mean?" said Jack Sheppard, starting, and taken by surprise at the cool way in which his comrade had hinted his amicable intentions.

"Where are the saddle-bags?"

"The what—the saddle-bags? Um!—that's singular—they are the very things I've been thinking of for the last half-hour. What do you know about them?"

"I—I know all about them," said Tom King, with his usual imperturbable freedom from passion, "they contain a thousand golden marks; it is they that have drawn me to your rendezvous."

"The devil doubt you!"

"You have an indistinct notion, Jack, of that social law called 'meum et tuum.'"

"Fortunately, I have got over such ridiculous scruples."

"Good, then the money must be ours."

"Aye, but how?"

"Easy enough."

"I'm at a non-plus."

"The owner of the coin sleeps here to-night."

"And goes at daylight in the morning——"

"He must never go."

The significant glance and peculiar sang froid of Tom King, as he uttered these words, staggered, for the nonce, his more susceptible confederate, who soon, however, recovered his equanimity.

"Our prey once mounted on that horse," continued the "gentleman highwayman," indicating the traveller's horse, which now eyed the ruffians, "and fairly off, may defy Satan and and all his imps to stop him."

"I see you intend to find means to delay his journey."

"Precisely so. I've a plan in my head."

"What is it?"

"These stables are at a convenient distance from the house."

"Well."

"Nobody will be stirring at the early hour you say he starts. 'Tis then we must strike the blow."

Jack Sheppard's livid cheek now took a more ghastly hue.

This, Tom King quickly observed.

He fancied that compunction, or a dread of the anticipated assassination, had unnerved his accomplice, so flew to that resource which ever stimulates crime.

"Come," said he, "let us go into the house and talk this matter over a beaker of brandy; it will give fire to our blood, courage to our hearts; depend upon it the potent liquid has often carried the boast into execution."

"Yes, and it has many crimes to answer for, the present among others; but, there, the compact is made and I mean to fulfil it, Jack Sheppard's a man of his word."

"Let Tom King hear the one to gainsay it. I'll now go into the house."

"Do so, and I'll follow you."

Left alone, Jack Sheppard paced to and fro for some time, as if lost in deep and painful reflection; at length he aroused and thus communed with himself—

"Now, if I would be honest, the devil won't let me; first he throws in the way temptation in the shape of a lump of gold (what a weight it is!) then he sends his instrument, in the person of my old pal, Tom King, and yet have I not sworn to— Psha, it's the old story—

"'The devil was sick,
The devil a monk would be,
The devil got well,
The devil a monk was he.'"

A slight rustling of straw now was heard at the extremity of the stable.

"Treachery or an eaves-dropper. Let their life pay the forfeit of their folly," said the robber, dashing to the spot from whence the sound proceeded.

To his astonishment, Jack Sheppard encountered Edgeworth Bess!

CHAPTER LXXXIX.

THE DEATH-STRUGGLE IN THE STABLE—WHAT DISCOVERY JACK SHEPPARD MADE AFTER THE DARK DEED—AND HOW HE PROFITED BY THE SAME.

MORNING arrives after a long, dread night is passed.

The rising sun shines brightly on the wooded landscape that stretches from the vale of Bermondsey to the smiling hills of Kent and Surrey.

And disperses the white mists hanging over the marshy grounds that lie adjacent to the locality.

All nature is speedily aroused by the beneficent sun-light.

Why does it settle on one spot more than all others?

Would it peer into a chamber of death?

Would it know what is passing there?

Would its slanting beams, shooting through a narrow crevice of a stable, reveal the marble countenances of two men engaged in an act of murder?

Will it frown upon their crime, or regard it with a lenient eye?

Let time show.

At day-break, Jack Sheppard and his associate, Tom King, found themselves listening at the stable door.

They awaited their victim in solemn silence; and neither uttered a word, or ventured the slightest remark.

There was something so terrible in the moment, by anticipated assassination, that the stern hearts of the robbers seemed as it were to chill with horror.

The faces of both were blanched to the whiteness of death.

The moments pass tediously.

Still not a breath is drawn.

Suspense gives way to feverish anxiety.

At length a footstep gave warning that the dark deed must soon be accomplished.

"Hush, I hear him," said Jack Sheppard. "He is coming! to your post—away."

Quick as the thoughts were uttered, Tom King obeyed the order.

And sprang to a hiding-place at the extremity of the stable.

He had hardly secreted himself in his refuge, when the intended victim of robbery and murder was seen coming across the long wooden gallery that surrounded the inn-yard.

He slowly descended the stairs leading from the same.

He bore with him his saddle-bag, and advanced to the spot where Jack Sheppard was waiting for him.

Refreshed by a placid slumber, he looked more than ever the picture of health, vigour, and manliness.

His open countenance, and beaming eye of fire, might have curbed a less stout heart than that of the pretended ostler.

"Good morrow, friend," said he, addressing that person. "How the dawn gladdens all that gleams around it. I envy not the sluggard who prefers his bed to the sight such a morning as this gives"

"Aye, sir, you speak truly," said his treacherous companion. "Could the sun pierce through the shutters he might now, perchance, behold the gambler dreaming that his luck had deserted him."

"The drunkard fevered by excess of wine."

"The courtezan terrified by fancies that her beauty has faded and her fascinations fled."

"But we are moralizing, while time most precious to me is flying."

"Where's the horse?" continued the traveller. "I thought you told me last night that he should be saddled and ready. Bring him out, my good fellow; I have not a moment to lose."

"You must please to bring him out yourself, worthy sir," replied Jack Sheppard, with rather a sulky air. "The devil's in the horse, I think; he let me saddle him, but not an inch would he stir when I wanted to bring him from the stable, and I had no fancy to have my brains kicked out, for he reared up with such violence that I was glad to escape his fury."

"Ha, ha, ha! that doesn't say much for your honesty, friend," replied the traveller, laughing. "My steed has an uncommon aversion to rogues. I'm afraid you stinted him of his corn last night."

The traveller now entered the stable.

He was followed thither by Jack Sheppard.

Unsuspectingly, he patted his horse, as the noble steed seemed to greet his welcome with sorrow.

And, had he been spared time, he might have read in the eloquence of his sagacious eye a warning more certain than that which mortal tongue could have uttered.

He was indeed a noble beast.

Every point was perfect, and his skin sleek and smooth as velvet.

While the winged Pegasus could hardly have excelled him for speed or strength.

No sooner had the master advanced to this faithful creature than Tom King snatched the saddle-bag that hung upon his arm.

So sudden was the theft that the robbed man, for the moment, could scarcely believe the evidence of his eyes.

However, recovering immediately from his astonishment, he put his hands to his belt for his pistols.

These had been secretly abstracted by the cunning ostler.

As in most cases where danger or terror assail a man and deprive him of such presence of mind as a desperate case requires, did heedlessness attack the incautious traveller.

Had he called for assistance, he might have saved his life.

Depending on his own prowess, he appeared to forfeit it.

Finding himself without weapons, he climbed to the window from which King was escaping, and was about to seize him as he was passing through it, when another impediment crossed his path.

This obstruction came in the shape of Jack Sheppard.

Undaunted, the brave man grappled his new antagonist.

His skill, strength, or dexterity gained him an advantage.

At the moment of his triumph, a stream of blood flowed through the stable, and the crimson tide saturated the straw on every side.

Tom King had stabbed him from behind, and he fell gore-stained and inert, with a dull thud.

"Heavens! Tom," cried Jack Sheppard, "I'm afraid you have slain him."

"I hope not; the blow I gave was to disable, not to kill. Let the world say what they will of Tom King, they shall never brand him as a murderer."

"I know, Tom, that your soul revolts at bloodshed, and that if the stranger dies by your hand, he falls by mischance, not malice."

"Believe me, Jack," replied Tom King, "although my life has been a reckless one, I never till now have spilt blood, save in honourable defence."

"Nor I, Tom; I've ever pledged myself to such a course, and Jack Sheppard and Tom King are not the men to violate an oath."

"We may be thieves, but we are men of our word."

"Well," continued Tom King, after a pause, "what is done can't be undone, and we must endeavour to make reparation for this deed by future atonement."

The robbers now knelt by the side of the traveller, in order to ascertain whether his wound was really fatal.

Tom King only saw one object.

A rigid figure stretched upon the earth.

There the victim lay placidly, with the smile of death stamped upon his face.

Tom King turned away, but he *must* look again.

The sight fascinated him.

The dark hair, unloosed and wandering over the shoulders of the assassinated man, contrasted strongly with the marble whiteness of his skin.

Yes, there he lay—cold and motionless.

Cut off in the morning of life.

In his bloom—in his manhood.

Tom King again knelt down by the corpse, and clasped its icy hand.

His heart told him that the stain of Cain was on his brow.

That his crime had destroyed a fellow creature, and brought him to an untimely end.

There was madness in the thought.

His remorseful ejaculations made his guilty companion shake with terror.

But his grief was too violent to last long.

Suddenly he became calmer and composed.

He rose from his kneeling posture, and assumed one of almost indifference.

He paused for a moment.

Then spoke with a solemnity profound and impressive.

"Jack, mark well my words; I have a presentiment that the crime which lies now heavy on our souls will prove neither the basest nor the blackest —that we shall not be the miserable wretched outcasts, condemned of heaven and mankind—but that even good may come of the offence that has brought this unfortunate man to an untimely grave."

Thus exhorted, Jack Sheppard and his accomplice raised the lifeless form of the murdered traveller.

Time was speeding on, and they had not the opportunity of burying the body.

"What is to be done?"

Jack Sheppard had made his preparations.

At the rear of the stable was an old house and ruined mansion.

A most miserable neglected place it was, and nearly overgrown with long rank grass and wild weeds.

Desolation seemed complete.

The glass was removed from all the window panes.

Some of the walls had been pulled down, and the bricks and plaster were scattered about on every side.

All the lower entrances were closely barred with rusty iron.

And appeared not to have been disturbed for years.

To render further seclusion and mystery to the dilapidated building, it had the reputation of being haunted and the residence of a supernatural tenant.

Affording such security and concealment, to this spot the highwaymen conveyed their inanimate burden, which was deposited till evening in one of the cellars of the crumbling structure.

Carefully ascertaining that they had not been observed, they returned to the stable of the "Bell" inn.

Treading with noiseless step they soon reached it.

Despite their caution a new obstacle presented itself.

As they came to the door of the stable a dog on the other side of the wall began to bark violently.

Jack Sheppard was equal to the emergency, knowing the character of the watchful and ferocious hound.

"I'll manage him," he said, "till I can get you off clear."

A familiar utterance of his name silenced the animal for the moment, but he again began to give signs of a further outcry.

In the meantine the robber had possessed himself of some prepared meat.

This he tossed to the violater of peace, who uttered a low growl and was heard no more.

"Where is the saddle-bag?" said Tom King, when they were once more quiet and had re-entered the stable.

"Here," said Jack Shepherd, taking it from the blood-soaked straw, "I have it; 'tis bought with a man's life. How it seems to burn my hands."

"This is not the time for sentiment, though I can imagine your feelings, Jack, by my own. Repentance never comes too late, and we shall make ample amends before the noose is tied."

Tom King smiled as he made this remark, but his smile was more harrowing even than his former rigid mien.

"The first thing that must be looked to is the horse," he continued.

"You must dispose of him," returned Jack. "I must remain at the inn."

"True; my road lies for Barnet," said King, "and I can readily sell him at the fair."

"But the plunder?"

"We must share at once, and then I'll be off with the animal before any one is stirring from the inn."

The spoil was divided, and Tom King mounted for his journey.

A figure crossed him as he was coming out of the stable, and disappeared none could tell whither.

"Were I superstitious I could have sworn," said he, "that Jonathan Wild had stood in my path; but that is impossible since I know at this moment he is a hundred miles off. Pshaw! had it been so, what need have I to fear him on the 'mibbing cheat.'

"'The Tyburn Tree
Has no terrors for me.'

Let better men swing. I'm at liberty."

Dashing along at a swift pace the highwayman bid his friend adieu, and shaped his course northward.

Jack Sheppard returned to the stable in order to remove every evidence of their crime.

He had buried in a deep hole the straw stained with the blood of the murdered traveller.

He then cleansed the stable of the same with a plenteous supply of water.

He next thought of what he could do with the saddle-bag, which still remained in his possession.

To burn it would excite suspicion.

To hide the same in the manger would be dangerous and more than probable lead to detection.

The old well in the ruined house!

It was never used by the ghost-fearing neighbourhood, and was forty fathoms deep!

That would offer an assured and safe place of concealment.

While hurrying to deposit the saddle-bag in the unfrequented well, curiosity unaccountably prevailed upon Jack Sheppard to open it again.

In doing so there was a compartment in the traveller's pouch that had escaped notice on its first hurried observation by the excited highwaymen.

This receptacle contained writing on parchment.

Jack Sheppard drew forth the scroll.

He was about to replace it when curiosity prompted him to read the characters inscribed upon it.

The name of Violet Tremaine and her secret were at once revealed to him, while the crest of the family of Warbold fully authenticated its contents.

Jack Sheppard started at the intelligence as if he had seen an apparition.

He was completely overpowered.

His chest heaved violently.

His lips were apart, but no breath seemed to issue from them.

At length he aroused from his lethargy.

"Heaven could never have permitted such a calamity!" he cried. "I would have risked a thousand lives rather than have sacrificed his—my most generous enemy, my best friend! That traveller's garb could never have concealed the Pirate-hunter from my eyes! A feeling of the deepest gratitude would have warded the blow aimed at his breast. I'll not believe it; Roving Jack could never die at the hands of Jack Sheppard!"

*   *   *   *   *

In the struggling starlight a masked figure was seen passing to the ruined mansion in which the highwayman had secreted the body of their victim.

It was a night well fitted for a mysterious enterprise.

Calm, dark, and profoundly still.

The strange visitor passed beneath the thick trees that shaded the road.

And the gloom in this spot was almost impenetrable.

He then kept on the grass, so that no noise should be made by the sound of his measured footstep.

As he neared the house he halted.

No one was watching, and he entered.

No sooner had he done so than he placed the spade he carried in his hand against the passage wall, and commenced lighting a dark-lantern.

A gust of wind nearly extinguished it, and the noise of the creaking casements added to his fears, or rather, apprehensions.

Listening at the door to hear that all was still he closed it and proceeded to the cellar.

Shouldering his spade this strange personage descended to commence his task.

Surprised at the emptiness of the cellar his alarm was instantly excited.

He searched every part, but what he sought was nowhere to be seen.

For a few minutes he stood transfixed with wonder.

At length it found vent in a sudden exclamation.

He rushed to the door for the intention of summoning aid.

But reflection forced itself upon him, and checked the action.

None must know the strange adventure.

None must repeat the story of death.

What is that which now attracts the eye of the bewildered man?

A faintness seized him as he picked up a hastily scribbled note.

A note written with human blood!

Some pointed instrument furnishing a pen.

A cypher, forming the superscription, told that the letter was addressed to himself.

With difficulty he made out the following words:—

"You are spared the pangs of remorse. I was wounded, but not mortally. I have escaped the death your confederate's knife intended for me. I am alone to blame. I should have revealed myself sooner; now a worse fate, I fear, menaces me. I am again in the power of Jonathan Wild, and—"

Here the writer broke off, evidently having been surprised during the writing of the communication.

"I will save, or die with him."

As the speaker uttered these words, the mask that he wore fell from his face, and revealed the features and convulsive efforts of Jack Sheppard.

———

CHAPTER XC.

SHOWS HOW THE HORSE OF ROVING JACK WAS DISPOSED OF BY THE ASSASSIN AT BARNET FAIR.

A PLACE, some eleven miles north-west of London, called Barnet, is the scene of great festivity at the present time.

The reason will soon be apparent when the reader shall have glanced over the few following lines.

The old town received in the days of the second Henry, the adjunct of Chipping, which signified that it was privileged to hold within its limits a large cattle market, or, in modern parlance, " a horse fair."

That ancient institution is being carried out with great efficacy and much mirth.

There are pens, coops, and stabling of the old-fashioned style.

With shows, booths, and stalls of the new ; for the place boasts the attractions of pleasure as well as business.

Punch and Judy faces the couper and magsman, as the antiquated Richardson's stage opposes the horses tied up, or led about for sale. Farmers, graziers, and horsey men, busy themselves about bargains.

While their spouses or daughters patronize the peripatetic drama or chronicle their " little drops and eat nuts of gingerbread."

In the open space alloted for the sale of cattle, there was seated, or rather lounged, a slender, elegant-looking young man.

With a dark, languid eye, sallow complexion, and features wearing that pensive expression peculiar to dissipation.

Habited in a light summer riding-dress, he, in manner and appearance, had all the air of a perfect gentleman.

Beside him, stood a graceful animal, whose breeding seemed as that of his master—to be of the first water.

In a word, it was difficult to say which was the most attractive object, the horse or the horse dealer.

For it was in this character Tom King had hoped to dispose of the only evidence of his late crime—the traveller's steed.

While in this position, a troop of farmers halted before him.

They had donned their best attire, and had strolled through the fair either to make purchases or participate in its enjoyments.

They were a formidable band, ruddy with health and ready to stand by each other if occasion required, for the trickery of the fraternity who ever attend races and cattle markets rendered such an union necessary.

The foremost of the party, having satisfied his curiosity, allowed his followers now to proceed, and leave him alone with the highwayman, who could see at a glance that he was likely to meet with a purchaser of his horse.

" By gums !" quoth the farmer to himself, " that be a main pretty nag, every point parfect, and a ' moral' of strength and speed. I mun ha' a talk wi' that chap about 'un."

" That be a foine beast on your, measter," continued the farmer, addressing Tom King.

" Yes," replied he, " thorough bred, and boasts blood in every bright and branching vein."

After the eulogium, Tom King repeated the well-known lines—

> "While with neck like a rainbow
> Erecting his crest,
> Pampered, prancing, and pleased,
> His head touching his breast,
> Scarcely snuffing the air,
> He's so proud and elate
> As the racer pure blooded,
> Who starts for the plate."

The farmer further examined the horse, and then demanded its price.

" Forty guineas."

Tom King then expatiated upon the animal's birth, parentage, and appearance."

There was no redundency of flesh.

His nerve and sinew were palpable through the veined limbs.

" Look at the proudly-arched neck—the glowing eye-ball—the flowing mane.

" Pace tremendous — action graceful — temper gentle."

Carried away by such attractions, the farmer struck his hand into Tom King's, and, by such a proceeding, concluded the bargain and sale of the horse.

Tom King at once gave it up to one of the farmer's men, who led it out of the place, whilst its new master proceeded to take out a canvas bag to pay Tom King the sum agreed upon.

" Come, farmer," said the highwayman, " we mustn't part over our transaction with dry lips. The doors of yonder tavern are open ; let us seal it by a glass in its comfortable parlour."

In a short time the parties mentioned above found themselves in the interior of the " Falcon Inn," which was adjacent.

The scene presented one of bustle and animation.

The tables were covered with refection, liquid and solid.

And the benches with hungry and thirsty guests.

The latter exhibiting every shade of character.

There were horse-jockies, exquisites, and country bumpkins.

Carriers, cattle-dealers, and a motley crew, whose tanned skins and tawdry habiliments proclaimed them at once to be of a gipsy tribe.

The wall resounded with the clatter of the trencher and pewter flagon.

The air reeked with the fumes of tobacco.

The equally savoury exhalation of cooked meat pervaded the apartment.

Tom King and the farmer speedily took their seats in the comfortable hostelrie.

Here they discussed each a rummer of punch.

" Heard the news ?" said a guest, at a neighbouring table.

" Well, friend," replied Tom King, " that admits of some consideration before I answer you. I have read the Gazette this morning on my journey down."

" Ah ! 'taint in that," said the other, with the air of a man who received intelligence with the mark " private and confidential."

" Well, then," continued the highwayman, " it is more than probable that I am ignorant of the facts I presume you are about to mention."

" Oh ! it'll all come out," argued the inflexible guest.

" Indeed !"

" I shouldn't at all be surprised if they are not already taken."

" 'Zounds ! mon !" shouted the farmer, who had gradually lost his patience during the late unconnected conference, " tell us what thee know'st without philandering like a broken harrow. Out wi' it at once what hast heard."

" Oh ! it's a most awful tragedy."

" Dang it, then, keep thee chops shut," muttered the farmer. " I can't abear tragedies, ever since I seed in Lunnon the young Roskins act Macbeth."

" But Jonathan Wild will soon pop upon 'em ; he's the fellow to nose out a secret."

Tom King started ; but in a moment recovered his wonted coolness.

" Did I understand you," continued he, " that the noted thief-taker——"

" Is down here, and looking for the perpetrators of the crime."

" You speak of crime. What crime ?"

" That of murder. 'Tis said that a traveller on a

homeward journey from Kent has been waylaid and assassinated."

"What are the authorities about?" interrupted Tom King, with affected warmth. "Why do they allow the roads to be infested by bands of desperadoes who plunder whosoever they meet?"

"No man's life is safe."

"Government must look to it."

"Look at that fellow, Tom King."

"Aye; with a composure that puts a hermit to blush, 'tis said, he smashes screens, pockets dimmocks, and charms away fawnies in prime twig."

"You be talking of Tom King!" chimed in the farmer. "Ecod! that be the very chap as robbed me on the great north road. He met I, as may be now, at tavern—'Three Cranes.' Kegworth Old Town.

"While I were taking a sup, I towd him where I always kept my money, in a riding-box, under the seat of my chaise. Moind ye, I thowght he were some gentle folk, or the loikes, he had such taking ways.

"Well, we parted arter all sorts of cautions on his part, seeing as I had taken a little more liquor than usual, and he feared I might fall in wi' bad company.

"Which, faicks, I did.

"For, on the road hoam, who should I meet but a smartish spark, not unlike un as I'd seen at the 'Three Cranes.' I could a sworn it 'ud been the same only, drat it! he wore a masking.

"'Your money,' says he.

"'I ain't none in my pocket,' says I.

"'I knows it,' says he; 'but you've got some——'

"'Where?'

"'In the riding-box, on yur right hand side.'

"With that th is same spark unseats me, and helps hisself to a bag of coppers that I had ta'en in change of the county bank.

"Lucky I'd seen double, and put by accident all my gold into box on the left."

"And this was your adventure with Tom King?"

"Yes, so I larnt was the name of the rascal arter the affair."

"Now you call it to my remembrance, I recollect that——"

"You recollect—why, you dinna mean to say that——"

"Come, come, no aspersions, if you please; this gentleman is a highly respectable member of society, and I can vouch for his character."

We must now call attention to the individual who made this remark.

His appearance was anything but a guarantee for his assertion, for Blueskin had, snake-like, cast his skin, and encased himself in a new toggery and disguise to carry out a certain scheme best known at present to himself.

Some traces remained, but not a vestige of the original tobyman.

Blueskin's own mother wouldn't have known her offspring.

The alteration was not to be attributed entirely to a change of costume.

But more probably to a contest—we may say fight—which had taken place between himself and three police officers.

And in which he had come off victorious, though he bore such evidences of a slashing "fracas"

Cheek, nose, and lip were woefully swollen, each trespassing on the other's precincts.

His right lamp (that is, his eye) was furnished with a suit of mourning, while his left luxuriated in a black patch.

Blueskin's grinders, or teeth, seemed to have shared in the honours of that combat, if we may judge by certain apertures in the pearly row, one of which is taken possession of by a short pipe.

But dismissing further description, we proceed to matters more urgent.

In defending his companion, Blueskin had other objects in view.

His peeper, though shaded, had spotted the farmer's gold.

It was the purchase money for the horse he had bought of Tom King.

It was still in the canvas bag, which rested for security under the countryman's elbow.

Watching his opportunity, the robber made a sign to his confederate to attract the farmer's notice, while he could lay hands upon his coin.

A significant glance from Tom King intimated that the venture must not be made.

Whether Blueskin misunderstood the token, or that temptation had overcome obedience, he paid little attention to it.

For as a party of morris dancers stationed themselves beneath the window, and caused the farmer for the moment to get up to observe them, Blueskin snatched up his money, and was out of sight in an instant.

As may be supposed the whole assemblage literally stood aghast at the sudden, unexpected, and impudent theft.

For a few seconds not a soul could utter a word.

All were breathless, stupefied, and amazed.

The farmer at length aroused from his evident emotion.

Seizing the arm of Tom King, he held it fast just as that individual was about to move off.

"Not so fast, my young blood," said the enraged dupe. "You stir not out o' this house till thee can'st give some proper account of theeself and—"

"Hang it man," replied Tom King, with consummate effrontery, that threw his assailant and the surrounding crowd at once off their guard, "what do you mean?"

"I mean that you have made yourself the tool of the scoundrel who has robbed me, and that you are a partner in his tricks and dishonest practices."

"Really, my good fellow, your conduct astonishes me as much as that of the fellow who so unceremoniously has decamped with the cash. Did I not take into consideration that the extraordinary proceeding of which we have all been witnesses, has for the moment affected your usual perspicuity, I should certainly deem you as one labouring under insanity."

The composure of Tom King while making these remarks, now more than ever found him favour in the eyes of the spectator of the curious scene.

"Moighty fine—moighty fine." continued the farmer; "but thee can'st not get over me by such palavering—he cawed thee friend—and birds of a feather flock together."

NELL PEVERIL BAULKS QUILT ARNOLD.

"I can assure you, my good friends," cried Tom King, "that I never in my life saw the villain."

"He a' got my money."

"Your money—your money—come I like that," replied Tom King, in retortion. "Why do you hold me if you thought he'd got *your money?*"

"Aye—why—why?" said fifty voices, anxious for an explanation, which the dander-headed farmer seemed unable to give.

"Good people," said Tom King. "this is an old trick of the hoary-headed reprobate."

The farmer was able to open his mouth "'tis true," but too bewildered to speak or deny the highwayman's assertion, who continued in accents of disdain, mingled with some show of pity.

"It won't do, old man," he said. "I'm not going to be choused out of my money in this manner. I dare say you know where the amount you pretended to pay me for my horse is gone to, and I shan't lose sight of you till I've got it back again, so I tell you plainly."

At length the farmer recovered from his utter astonishment and managed to stammer out the following words, but cautiously endeavouring to effect something like a reconciliation—

"Whoy, what the dickens dost take me for, mun! Dost think I be one of the foine Lunnon sharpers, as come down to foire to trick honest volk out o' their brass?"

"Your horse!"

"Why, dash my wig, I could buy your horse and you ten times over, for all your fine laced jacket, and Dutch talk; my name's Peveril.

"Dick Peveril, o' Seven Elms Farm, three miles from St. Albans.

"There's plenty there as will answer for me; just step o'er there to me; and though I'se been done loike, I'll pay thee the money once more, as becomes an honest English yeoman."

"Stop, stop!" said a voice; "I'm not so sure, farmer, that you will have occasion to do so."

The voice was that of no other than the guest who had addressed Tom King on his entrance into the tavern, and who, during the preceding events, had remained as a silent observer.

"I may be considered wrong," said he; "but there's such tricks played now-a-days, that the fair trader is never sure that he is not dealing with a rogue."

"This is unpardonable," said Tom King. "Dare you, fellow, to insinuate that I am playing falsely?"

"We shall see," was the curt reply. "I now call upon every one present to aid me, if such an assistance is required, and woe to him who refuses to grant it."

The demeanour of the speaker was so authoritative, that it seemed to electrify all that heard him.

"You have told me," he continued, addressing Farmer Peveril, "that some time since you were robbed on the great North road by a highwayman; look into the face of the man who stands before you, and see, on a strict scrutiny, if you cannot recognise the features of the thief."

Farmer Peveril did as he was told.

He peered into Tom King's face.

Scratched his head.

And then violently slapped his knee with the palm of his hand.

"Odds, bodikens! sure enow, 'tis he."

"Yes, 'tis Tom King," said the highwayman, with all the calmness incidental to himself; "and now to confront my approver."

Turning to the man who had denounced him he continued,

"Jonathan Wild, I am not sorry we have met thus, for good (that you little anticipate) may come of it. Despite your disguise, I was aware of your presence the moment you first addressed me.

"I betrayed no emotion.

"I gave you no cause for suspicion.

"But can truthfully assure you had my snappers be n primed, you would have been worms' meat half an hour ago."

These words had scarcely escaped the lips of the highwayman, when two men appeared from the crowd.

They were Quilt Arnold, and the Jew, Mendez.

"Just in the nick of time," exclaimed the thief-taker. "Tom King, you are my prisoner."

"Not first without a struggle for it."

The last speaker seized a chair, and put himself in an attitude of defence.

The arms of the Jew clasped him from behind; but the Israelite received a tremendous back fall which literally stunned and laid him senseless on the floor.

Taking advantage of the embarrassment, Jonathan Wild and his satellite closed with Tom King, and succeeded in slipping a pair of handcuffs over his wrist.

There was a malignant smile on the countenance of the exulting villain as he addressed the captured man.

"Tom King, this is your last venture—a lodging in the stone jug and bread and water, will satisfy your wants while you live. The assizes are on next week, and your little trouble will soon be over."

"Jonathan Wild," exclaimed the highwayman, contemptuously, "I scorn, I defy you!"

"Defy, aye?"

"Yes, defy you. I shall never swing from the tripple tree of Tyburn."

"It is written, written, signed, decreed by the hand of fate!"

"We must all bend to destiny."

CHAPTER XCI.

THE MYSTERY OF THE BLUE CHAMBER—WALLS HAVE EARS — A DESPERATE RESOLVE — THE CRUCIBLE OF MOLTEN LEAD—FATALITY.

EDGEWORTH BESS sat silently in the Old Bell Tavern on the eve of the day on which the assassination of the traveller had taken place.

She was gazing upon the dying embers of a wood fire, that had been piled up between the brazen dogs on the brick hearth.

Why dost thou sigh, sweet maiden? Art thou not happy?

She never knew happiness till she had met with one who now scorned her.

Dost thou love no longer?

No; hate, a deadly hate has turned a confiding heart, and pierced it with the pangs of jealousy.

Suddenly she rose from her sitting posture, and advanced to the door of the apartment, in which she had remained for the last half-hour buried in deep thought.

Thoughts of vengeance.

As she glided along the room, her face grew lividly pale.

And her eyes were fixed with a strange and snake-like glistening.

"Faithless one," she cried, "I can never bear a rival; so far I am safe. Since you have warned me, the meddlesome jade can do me little harm if I nip her project in the bud. She is now closeted with Jack Sheppard. This looks like mischief. I must find out what she is about to propose to him.

"They are in the blue chamber, but the door is locked.

"No matter, they will find it difficult to keep their secrets from Edgeworth Bess."

Walls have ears, girl. Walls have ears.

"I must dispose of this matter at once."

So saying, the jealous woman hastily flew to the apartment which her inconstant lover and his fair companion were supposed to be occupying.

She arrived and stationed herself at the door.

Listening attentively, she could hear nothing, yet she felt assured they were within.

She now went into the adjoining room, and proceeded to unlock the door of a small cupboard near the fire-place.

Stepping into the recess, Edgeworth Bess, with great caution, unbolted a second door and passed through it.

She now was actually in the very chamber she had wished to enter, but concealed from view by a thin board which formed the part of a bookcase.

A crack in the wood enabled the observer to have a command of the room.

And allowed the conversation going on therein to reach her.

The two persons she expected to find were there.

They were at no great distance from the spot upon which she stood.

Jack Sheppard was talking earnestly, while Ellen

Peveril was listening to his narration with breathless anxiety.

At the very first words Edgeworth Bess was overwhelmed.

They were words of love!

Unrequited affection caused a deadly rancour to settle in her bosom, and under its baneful influence she fainted.

In her delirium she could not distinctly hear all.

Jack Sheppard spoke with vehemence and rapidity, Ellen low and pensively.

Though her rival had failed to learn the close of the discourse, not a syllable was lost upon Ellen Peveril, who, at its conclusion, threw her arms around her companion's neck and bathed his breast with tears.

Edgeworth Bess retained sufficient consciousness not to make known her presence.

At the climax she breathed hard and watched with the deepest anxiety the fond embrace of her lover and the maiden.

There was a brief pause, and the indignant paramour of Jack Seppard felt as if she had been stretched upon the rack.

She was a woman of great nerve, and did not underrate the danger with which she was about to surround herself.

She confronted it boldly, and by so doing its appalling proportions seemed to diminish.

"Woe upon both of us!" she cried.

At the same moment she stole secretly from her hiding-place, and hurried to accomplish a vengeance for her slighted love.

*　　*　　*　　*　　*

Ellen Peveril had retired early to rest.

Sleep is was not, for she lay awake long after her usual hour for slumber.

She could not dismiss the tidings she had learned from Jack Sheppard.

Nor the impression it had made upon her brain.

At last she fell asleep.

But it was only to wake soon from a wild and troubled dream.

She thought that she saw a female by the fitful glimmering of the dying fire in the grate!

That her eyes wore a livid hue and fixed themselves on her own.

Fascinated, she could not move the hideous glance.

Her face kept growing paler and paler.

Her gaze grew brighter and brighter, and more and more terrible.

Sick at heart, Ellen Peveril then felt a reeling in her brain and choaking in her throat.

Still she could not turn from the phantom.

The long black ringlets of hair that hung about this shadowy figure's neck and shoulders seemed of a sudden, and yet slowly, to become instinct with life.

One by one they uncurled themselves, some moving their heads to and fro, others writhing as in agony up and down.

In a word, their contortions resembled those of leeches in a vase, seeking to fix their bodies, but failing in every attempt.

Anon, these hideous creatures, arching and stretching themselves out, twisted round the neck of the sleeper.

So tightly, that they appeared ready to strangle her.

In alarm and agony she woke, and found the counterpart of the spectre standing by her bedside.

It was Edgeworth Bess!

She had heard of this woman, of witches, and their cunning, and now began to hold that she who looked upon her so strangely was one in real earnest.

Ellen Peveril slept no more that night.

Suspecting that her attendant, from some cause that she could not divine, had taken a dislike to her, she conceived a design to try her sincerity, and determined upon carrying it into immediate execution.

Although the dreamer had started into thorough wakefulness, she pretended to be still asleep, in order to watch the actions of her suspected companion.

She first advanced to the bed, and finding that Ellen Peveril lay still, commenced her fearful task.

The demeanour of Edgeworth Bess caused her intended victim to thrill with horror, and her heart to beat thick.

Her hair was loose, and hung straggling about her neck.

As she passed the foot of the couch the light from a lamp that was burning on a table fell through her locks upon her face, and Ellen saw the very figure pictured in her vision.

She saw, too, that the terrible woman held in one hand a small knife.

Slowly and stilly, like a sepulchral spirit, she glided on.

But away from the spot upon which the supposed sleeper reposed.

Going to the place where she had hung her dress up, she took the same down and ripped open one of its sleeves.

She took something out, and went to the hearth, where she fanned the nearly extinguished fire to a flame.

Having laid the knife, and whatever else she held in her hand, beside the lamp upon the table, she appeared searching for something about the hearth.

At last she was heard to mutter—

"Not here! How foolish—heedless of me. I must go and fetch it from below."

Edgeworth Bess moved towards the door.

The heart of Ellen Peveril beat high within her.

The moment her enemy should be gone she could leap from the bed and rush past her down the stairs and fly from the house.

For, strangely, she felt to be in it would be more dreadful than to be in her most dreaded presence.

Edgeworth Bess suddenly stopped as she came to the door.

Laid hold of the latch, but did not raise it.

She continued then to speak, in a low and almost inaudible murmur—

"Not here! Perhaps it was for some good end that I forgot it. Shall I give them one trial more?"

The words seemed to stifle the afflicted woman.

She sighed and sobbed.

Not loudly, indeed, but as if her heart were cracking.

"One trial more," she continued, in a paroxysm of despair. "I dare not give it thee, dear Jack. Dear still, though lost to me for ever."

Edgeworth Bess still lingered in the room, and, as if suddenly calling to mind something that had slipped her memory, exclaimed,

"Yes, I had forgotten; 'tis here, I hid it for security."

With these words she hurried, still without noise, to a stool near the fire.

She raised the cushion, and from under it took a small ladle of iron.

Poising the leaden weight she had taken from

her garment she put it gently in the hollow of the vessel.

Then knelt upon one knee and set it upon the fire.

In a minute she turned her face towards the bed and then raised it up.

Ellen saw, though her features were frightfully writhen with bad passions, that there were tears in her eyes that bespoke an inward struggle.

She rose, notwithstanding, and whispered,

"Now! No flinching."

And walked up to the bed with the ladle containing molten, bubbling lead in her right hand.

Just as she brought this forward to pour the deadly distilment into the ear of her victim she started up.

With an outcry Ellen seized her arm.

"Shameless assassin!" she cried, "I have caught you in the trap which you set for me. Tremble, for a terrible retribution will avenge me."

Edgeworth Bess did not scream or even start, but stared at her rival with a malicious smile.

With a strong effort she freed her wrist.

And flung the ladle and its murderous contents into the fire.

After a pause nature gave way under violent emotion.

The baffled and conscience-stricken woman sank upon the couch, hiding her face in her ice-cold hands.

The alarm had scarcely been given when the door of the chamber opened, and Jack Sheppard presented himself.

He was wrapped in a laced cloak, which he threw off on his advance into the room.

Since the discovery of a secret, of which the reader will be made acquainted shortly, there was a marked change in his character.

His demeanour was so much refined and improved that he could scarcely be recognised as the same person.

His paramour, at the sound of his voice (for he had spoken on entering) turned rapidly round, though her back had hitherto been away from him.

She fixed her glazing eye upon his, and uttering a piercing scream of anguish, fell into his arms.

That look, that shriek, Jack Sheppard never forgot till his dying day.

"Jack, condemn, scorn me, if you will, but at least have pity on an erring woman.

"If blighted hope has driven me to a desperate deed, let a pure affection blot out the crime which heaven in its wisdom has frustrated. Though this guilt has been spared my soul, can guilt be greater than mine? Can I hope for pardon?"

"All are pardoned," replied Ellen, mildly, "if they make atonement for the wrongs they have committed."

"Your words, your kind-hearted looks afford me consolation," exclaimed Edgeworth Bess, "and I feel I shall overcome the unhallowed passion that consumed me.

"One word," she continued, "if I dare utter it—the past—"

"Is forgiven, forgotten."

"How can I thank you for so much goodness; yet disappointed love will turn a spirit; ofttimes that is glorious in purity, and envy, malice, and remorse abide in a heart that once was free from guile."

Jack Sheppard, who had hitherto remained silent, being unacquainted with the terrible scene that had been enacted during the last half-hour, now came forward.

"What Bess," said he, "have you been jealous of this maiden?

"You have little cause, as you will own when I tell you she can never be mine.

"The dying pirate, Barabbas, has made a full confession.

"Ellen Peveril in infancy was torn from her family.

"A family wealthy and noble, of which I possess the proofs.

"But, stranger still, the family is my own, and I will assert the rights of which she has been so long deprived with all the authority a brother possesses."

A shudder ran through the frame of Edgeworth Bess, as she listened to the disclosure.

A tear stood in her eye as she regarded her lover.

Unable to control her emotion she threw herself into her outstretched arms.

"Ellen Peveril, thy sister!" she exclaimed. "I see it all now. What a fearful escape! Had I known that ere my vile scheme had been devised—"

Grief choked her utterance.

She gazed for a moment in silence.

Then, unable to control her emotion, threw herself into the outstretched arms of Jack Sheppard.

CHAPTER XCII.

THE "SEVEN ELMS"—TIDINGS FROM THE SEA—LOVE AND LOVE'S TOKEN—THE PURSUIT OF THE UNKNOWN—HE FINDS SHELTER IN THE FARMHOUSE—THE SECRET CABINET.

BENEATH two tall trees, whose boughs completely overshadowed the roof, stood a dwelling, called the "Seven Elms."

A plain but substantial old English farm-house.

Seated on a bench under the foliage sat the owner, already introduced to the reader as Richard Peveril.

"Old Dick Peveril," as he usually termed the individual in question when on exceedingly good terms with himself.

With a tankard of ale by his side and a very long pipe in his mouth, he was puffing time and sorrow away.

The smoker, placid and calm, looked, under the influence of the balmy weed, the very picture of benevolence, contentment, and good-heartedness.

The hand of time had marked him by increased corpulence and decreased vision, while a scantier breathing told that he was travelling onwards to the goal we must all reach.

Still the regular habits of a country life imparted a glow to his somewhat wrinkled cheek, and gave him all the appearance of a hale, hearty and temperate man.

Though temperate, there were all the evidences of plenty around him.

Cornfields and haystacks enclosed his homestead on all sides.

Poultry crowded the yard, cattle the stalls, horses the stable, while the farm servants seemed busied in its various occupations.

A young wayfarer pursued his journey along the rural road that led to the cosy retreat.

Towards dusk he arrived at its door, and gave the owner a vociferous greeting in the words—

"Ship ahoy! Bouse all taut, skipper, and run up signals!"

Hearing the approach of the stranger, the farmer turned to look at him.

The imperfect light of the evening prevented the

former from distinguishing either the form or the features of the latter.

"I needn't ask whether Farmer Peveril be in the way, since I find him lying at anchor near his own gate."

"Right, man ; I be he, at your sarvice."

"You don't remember me—can't make out the figure head?" observed the new comer, with a smile.

"Well, I can't say as how I do," answered the farmer, a little perplexed by the incident. "The voice seems familiar loike to me—but I be getting a little deaf, and my eyes doan't sarve their measter quite so well as they did fifty year sin'."

"Never mind, old salt," replied the other; "you'll recollect me by-and-bye. I bring you despatches from an old friend."

"At that word, old Dick Peveril never yet closed his doors, no matter whether he be gentle or simple, rich or poor ; follow me."

The farmer led the way into the house.

Then up a broad and bannistered flight of stairs leading to a commodious parlour.

Arrived here, the guest was requested to seat himself and partake of the good cheer that at once graced the table in the shape of a cold sirloin of beef, York ham, cold fowl, with every condiment and adjunct required for the dishes.

The room was furnished in the old-fashioned style, plentifully supplied with valuable china, japanned cabinets, and a curious carved cupboard in one of the corners, the shelves of which exposed to view numberless big-bellied bottles containing spirituous liquors of all grades and denominations.

This showed that, though the former had a character for abstemiousness, he could enjoy life's comforts, in his own way, with a keen zest.

After the meal, he sat down, once more, to his pipe.

His new companion soon followed such a laudable example.

In a few minutes, the region around emitted the redolence of tobacco mingled with the perfume of punch, a bowl of which had, during the interval, been introduced to the parties enjoying themselves.

After a pause, the guest broke silence.

He was a young man of rather prepossessing appearance, and, as he had already acquainted his hospitable entertainer, a seaman in the Royal Navy.

"Once more on the green earth," he merrily shouted out, " I feel like a ship dancing through the spray, steering for the haven of joy."

"Ah," replied the farmer, reservedly, and stopping to relight his pipe with some ceremony, "that's a haven you sailors don't often moor in."

"The devil we don't. How do you make that out, friend Peveril ?"

"Why, your's be such a loife of ups and downs, hardships and dangers, that, I take it, you bean't gotten time to think on happiness."

"Lor' love your silly, good heart, you don't know the bliss that crowns a tar's troubles. Whenever I steer for my lass's arms, and find myself chained within 'em, I wouldn't change coats with the first lord of the admiralty. Her very name brings tears into my eyes, and I feel I could hug every craft that shows a woman's flag at her fore. A sailor not know happiness, do you say ? What cheers him in the dreary watch ? What sustains him in the dark, wild waves of the storm ? What nerves him in the battle and hour of death, but the blessed thought—unequalled by any earthly bliss—that he may be spared to return to wife, children, and friends."

"Well, measter, I be but a plain-spoken man, and, I dare say, for them as likes it, the life of a sailor has its charms."

"Talking of charms, farmer, mayhaps you didn't know one tight little frigate as lives somewhere about this quarter ?"

"Well," he answered, with a look of profound solidity, "I don't think you'll find any one of that name in our parish, and I've been overseer sin.—"

"No, bless your innocence, that isn't her name."

"I thought not."

"Her name is—"

"Yes."

"No, 'taint that.

"Dang it, man, then, what is it ?"

"Ha, ha ! I've got it — she's called Ellen Peveril."

"Why, you dinna mean to say that—"

"She's my wife."

The farmer, for the moment, seemed transfixed with astonishment.

"What, dad, don't you know me ?" said the sailor, advancing towards him, and warmly shaking his hand. "I'm Paul—Paul Peveril. Have years and foreign travel so changed me, that you don't know your own son ?"

"God bless thee, boy !" ejaculated the father, rubbing his eyes. "I hope I'm not dreaming ! No, it be he, sure enough. Eh, let me embrace thee, for I were sore afraid I had to see thee no more !"

To describe the questions and congratulations that now ensued, or to relate the particulars of the extravagant joy of the honest farmer, would be altogether superfluous.

Still, we may make allusions to the following facts :

First, he hugged his son to his breast, and with such warmth, that, had he been anything but the individual he was, all the breath would have been squeezed out of his body.

His second performance was a caper about the room, in which he must have stood unrivalled, had he presented it for public competition.

The third and last fantastic action of the excited parent was to get rid of a red nightcap, which he generally wore in his domestic duties, and insert it between the bars of an iron grate, now filled with what cooks call a roasting fire.

The unusual excitement of the respected and elderly individual having, in the end, subsided, "from natural causes," as a jury would say, Paul proceeded to inquire after "his dearly beloved Nelly."

"Well, lad, I be sorry that she bean't here to meet thee," said the farmer ; "but a letter arrived a few days sin calling her to Lunnon."

"At a place they call ' Bell inn,' at—"

"Drat it ! I a' forgotten the crackjaw name on the place ; but that bean't here nor there, seeing as how I've received a second letter, stating I moight expect her home again this evening."

"If she don't arrive, I shall set sail for London, without waiting for orders."

"Well, lad, as thee wishes. We can talk matter o'er in morning."

"Morning ! I must start to-night. Do you think I can sling in my hammock without seeing her whom I love better than all the world ?"

"Go thee ways, lad—go thee ways ; but you shan'na' walk sixteen mile when I've got one o' the best nags a mon ever put his leg over. I bought un at Barnet fair, where they took I for a soft un —faix, I were nearly ta'en in though."

As the farmer spoke there was a gentle tap at the door.

"Who's there?"

A gentle voice replied,

"'Tis Nelly."

At the sight of Paul, every vestige of colour left her cheek, and she flung her arms round his neck in an instant.

"Husband, dear husband," she screamed, "we meet again, and the hope deferred that has borne me up through so many difficulties at last is realized."

"Yes, Nelly," said Paul, "like you, I put my faith in true affection—when the blast shrieked and howled through the rigging, and the faces of messmates grew pale with fear. I have thought of you, and an angel whispered hope and comfort in my ear.

"When the word was passed for action, the thought of thee has seemed to turn the bullets from my breast.

"When I crept to my hammock with the blood of the foe on my hand, I have called upon my angel wife, and mingled Nelly's name with my prayers to the Great Commander.

"Do you remember this locket?" said the seaman, taking it, attached to a black riband, from his neck; "'twas your gift on our last meeting. I have never parted with it night or day for one instant, since I received it from your hands."

Just then there was a noise of hasty footsteps without.

Ellen tottered to the entrance of the room, but ere she could reach it her strength utterly failed her, and she sank upon a chair.

"What ails you?" her husband cried, springing towards her.

"A sudden faintness—it will pass off soon."

Another instant the door flew open, and a man, enveloped in the ample folds of a cloak, rushed in.

"Ellen, 'tis as I suspected," he exclaimed, "our pursuers are upon our track. You must afford me concealment, or I shall be arrested."

"Arrested!" cried the others, who were now more startled than they had been at the abrupt appearance of the intruder.

"Yes, but I will set him free."

Ellen seemed to regain her strength while uttering these words, as suddenly as she had lost it.

"Stay, wench," replied the farmer, "let's look afore we leap. Dost know what art doing?—to harbour a malefactor be against all rule and license."

"This is no time for explanation, farmer," replied Ellen Peveril, "moments are more precious than jewels. You shall know all when the danger is past; confide in me."

"Aye, lass," replied the seaman, "I never yet doubted thee, nor will I now. How can we serve this stranger?"

"By giving him concealment for a few short hours."

"If that be thee desire, Nell, thee wish will shortly be gratified. Listen; there be nooks and corners in this old building, now standing for two centuries, that would puzzle old Beelzebub and all his imps to find out; this be one of them."

The farmer had no sooner spoken than he advanced to one of the japanned closets standing in the room and opened the door of the same.

This closet was larger than the others, and reached to the ceiling.

Carefully removing the shelves within it he then proceeded to touch a spring concealed in the carving of the cabinet.

The instant he did so the back part receded, and disclosed a passage constructed in the wall sufficient to hold a man.

"This will be close quarters," said the stranger, "but I have been put to greater straits than this in my time, and can easily accommodate myself to circumstances."

"Thee hast not come yet to our hiding-place."

The speaker then touched a second spring, as ingeniously contrived as the first, when an aperture, apparently blocked up by stone-work, was exposed to view.

Within was a chamber garnished with necessary appendages.

"In this apartment thee must lie secreted," continued the farmer; "we will victual it, and thou canst hold fortress against enemy for a week."

"Before a seventh of that time I trust to be far out of harm's way."

The stranger then entered the assured retreat, which was without delay at once closed upon him.

Many anxious thoughts passed through the breast of Ellen.

She knelt and prayed to avert the threatened calamity.

Comforted, she arose, and, with a smiling face, exclaimed,

"Now I am fully prepared to meet our foes."

"Foes? What dost mean, wench?" asked the farmer. "Surely a pretty face like thine can have none such."

"The companion of my flight," replied Ellen, "has incurred the enmity of the noted thief-taker, Jonathan Wild."

"Jonathan Wild!" exclaimed Paul; "avast, lass, do you expect him here?"

"Every minute."

"So much the better. He and I have scores to settle; and it strikes me forcibly that he'll be the wrong side of the purser's book. I'll cut and run. Belay, don't believe I'm going to turn tail upon the privateering swab. But as he uses hot shot, I'll betake me to ambush, in order to return him his own fire."

With these words Paul Peveril left the apartment.

CHAPTER XCIII.

THE ARRIVAL OF THE OFFICERS AT THE FOUR LANES' END—A SEARCH FOR THE FUGITIVE—HOW JONATHAN WILD DISCOVERED THE DEVICE AND HOW AGAIN HE WAS THWARTED—THE THIEF-TAKER'S METHOD OF ENFORCING COMPLIANCE TO HIS WILL.

ONE of old Peveril's labourers was returning to his cottage late in the evening.

He had arrived at a place called the Four Lanes' End, an open space, about two miles distant from the farm at which he worked.

Whistling from want of thought, and pursuing his way homewards, he was suddenly roused by the trampling of horses.

Looking to the spot from whence the sound seemed to proceed, he distinguished a body of horsemen advancing at a rapid trot.

Their number, as far as he could guess by a hasty glance, was ten or twelve persons.

At first he took them to be a troop of mounted soldiers, for one and all of the party were formidably armed.

Their dress, however, upon a closer inspection, forbade any such persuasion of mind.

They were all powerful men, headed by a leader

who, if not more powerful than his followers, had certainly the appearance of being more determined.

He looked more merciless than ever, and as ferocious as disappointment could make him

He still wore his ponderous hanger by his side, with which (to use his own words) he could cleave his enemy to the chine.

The leader was, in fact, Jonathan Wild the noted thief-taker; his companions or comrades, the officers attendant upon justice.

Wild shouted to the rustic he had met.

Then halted his men.

The former, who had evinced some suspicion of the riders, would have taken to his heels.

But fearing to disobey a personage so potent as he who hailed him, he attended to the summons.

Jonathan Wild put a few brief and authoritative questions, and was satisfied with the answers he received to them.

Then, pointing with his finger in the direction of the "Seven Elms Farm," rode forward to it with the others who accompanied him.

Jonathan Wild made no advance to the owner of the farm, whom he found standing at his door, but bade him come down to the bridle road, in which, for the present, he remained.

"Let me see," said the thief-taker, "you and I have met before; your name is—"

"Dick Peveril, old Dick Peveril, aged sixty-six, born at Little Heath, near Hertford; have lived in the county all my life, till twelve acres of deuced—"

"Stop, stop, farmer, this is not the information I require; I am flying at higher game. You have doubtless heard of the notorious Jack Sheppard?"

"Sure, sure, mon; who hasn't heard o' the daring blade? But what's up wi' 'im, now?"

"Have you not heard?"

"Heerd what?"

"That he has again escaped from the hands of justice?"

"As, 'tis said, that the prison's not built that can hold 'im."

"Listen, farmer, and take my warning; there are whispers that you are well affected to this malefactor."

"Volks will talk."

"Take heed that you give him no shelter, or you will find little mercy from the authorities, or Jonathan Wild."

"Hast thee done?"

"No, another duty remains with me."

"Indeed, what be that?"

"I must make a strict examination of your house and premises."

"What for?"

"Merely to ascertain if report be true, and whether the fugitive is really concealed within them."

So saying, the thief-taker gave orders for his men to dismount.

One of their number led the horses to the stables in the rear of the farm.

And, without asking permission, supplied them with fodder standing in the neighbouring racks.

A sentinel was placed at each door, and none were allowed to leave the house.

Springing from his saddle, Jonathan Wild was the last to enter it, and proceeded to the very room occupied lately by the guests.

Here he ordered refreshment for himself and followers, and examined the labourers and servants on the farm.

Neither of these being entrusted with their master's secret, could give any information satisfactory to the new-comers.

The last questioned was the farmer himself.

Jonathan Wild prayed him to be seated, and, by assuming an air of affability and concession, hoped to worm out the truth from the simple-minded yeoman.

"Your daughter is well favoured, farmer," said he, commencing his insidious attack.

"Well, measter, for the matter o' that, she be pretty fair, I may say a comely wench."

"She has been married."

"Yes, but till lately has—"

The farmer stopped in his remark. and cast down his eyes, as if hesitating whether he was compromising himself; then, turning the conversation, continued,

"Mayhap, you would like a cup of wine wi' your cold collation. I'll go and broach a cask."

"Not now. I will take a glass of your stoutest ale shortly, but matters of more import engross our thoughts now."

At this juncture one of Wild's band came into the room, whispered in his ear, and then retired.

"Farmer," continued the thief-taker, "I see it is painful for both of us to equivocate; therefore, let each of us make a clean breast of it. To show you I act with sincerity, I will speak first."

Peveril merely answered the following observations by looks of surprise.

"Are you aware that you are giving shelter to one accused, and more than probably guilty, of murder?

"You start—well you may. My story is briefly this:

"A short time since a gentleman arrived from abroad.

"He brought with him a favourite horse, the faithful companion of his travels.

"On his arrival in London, he put up at a certain tavern, bearing the sign of the 'Bell Inn,' and located in the suburb of Bermondsey.

"He entered the building with a large sum of money—which he intended for a particular purpose—and never left it.

"From that day to this he has never been heard of, but within the last few minutes his horse has been found in your stable.

"I may be wrong in suspecting you of connivance, but my public duty compels me to sift the affair to the bottom."

At the conclusion of the discourse, the farmer raised his hands to heaven, and appeared buried in deep reflection.

"It can never be," he muttered to himself—"she would never give shelter to an assassin and thief beneath her father's roof."

"I have succeeded," cried Jonathan Wild; "thy tongue, thy looks, betray thee, old man. Go and fetch your keys—I will have every part of the house searched, and every hidden recess opened to me."

"There are no such places, that I know of," said the farmer, trembling between doubt and fear.

"Thou liest!" continued the ruffian, fiercely. "Refuse to show them, and heated iron to thy feet shall extort the secret."

His companion bowed, but was in such a state of trepidation as to be unable to offer any remark.

"I will begin my search with this chamber," said Jonathan Wild.

He glanced around the room, and peered into every crevice during his scrutiny.

But nothing could the crafty man discover by the course he had adopted.

The farmer breathed more freely, and began to think all danger was over, when he saw that the careful examination of the apartment had not awakened suspicion.

But his fears returned, as he beheld the thief-taker fix his eyes on the huge closet that concealed the fugitive.

His agitated looks did not escape the notice of Jonathan Wild, who feigned not to perceive them.

The hint was sufficient, and he acted on it.

"I think I have forgot to look into yonder closet, farmer," he observed significantly; "my opinion is that it possesses a false back—if so, hammer and hatchet, I'll borrow thy friendly assistance."

These implements were produced at his order, and his own men bringing them, commenced to execute a further search, by staving in the boarding behind the case.

A single blow of the iron shivered the frail wood-work, and exposed to view the passage to the fugitive's chamber, which was still concealed by the masonry that masked it.

Jonathan Wild, usually an adept at discovery, was now altogether amazed at the emptiness of the aperture.

It had evidently contained a captive, but he was put to his wits' end to make out how he could possibly have escaped from the same.

Suddenly, something shining on the floor of the cell attracted his attention.

He picked it up, then gave way to one of those fits of laughter which may be supposed to emanate from the arch-enemy of mankind.

"Our prisoner cannot be far off," said he, "since he has so lately left us a memento of his absence."

With these words, the thief-taker held up the article he had found.

It was a portion of the spur worn by Jack Sheppard in his journey to goad his horse.

"The fugitive cannot have left the house, then?"

"No one has passed the doors."

"I shall not trouble myself to investigate this matter further, but at once bring it to a positive conclusion."

Jonathan new turned to the farmer, who during the previous scene appeared to hesitate how he should act in the emergency.

"Old man," he exclaimed, "it is evident the caged bird has not flown away altogether; though for the moment I am foiled, I am not vanquished."

"Proceed," replied the other, with firmness.

"You will save me some vexation and yourself much misery, if you concede to that which I am about to ask you."

Peveril was silent.

"Mark me, you must produce the man who has taken refuge here, or suffer severely for your foolish obstinacy."

"When I think of Ellen's entreaty," groaned the farmer.

Though he had muttered these words to himself and between his teeth, they were heard by the thief-taker.

"Your own tongue convicts you," said he. "I had my doubts till this moment, now the truth has come out. Deliver up——"

"That I'll never do."

While the farmer uttered these words, Ellen, who had been listening unobserved, advanced and confronted Jonathan Wild.

The moment he saw her a plan flashed across his savage mind.

She should help him to discover the man he sought.

She should be the executioner of him whom she had tried to save.

Clothing his countenance with a sardonic smile, he advanced to and addressed the woman who stood before him.

"Damsel, my last appeal is made to you, and I trust it may not be made in vain.

"I hope you will spare me the necessity of enforcing compliance.

"Refuse to inform me of this robber's hiding-place, and I shall be compelled to fire the house, that he may perish in a death of agony amidst its blazing ruins."

"Heed not what he says, girl," cried the farmer, indignant with passion; "cruel and bloodthirsty though he be, I cannot believe he can put such a diabolical threat into execution."

"You mistake your man!" exclaimed the thief-taker, with intense malignity. "Mark me again, Richard Peveril (since you say that is your name), you will soon discover your error. In the exercise of my public duty, I ever bear a warrant signed and sealed by the Chancellor of England.

"This document gives me power to act with refractory criminals or their abettors as I deem expedient.

"Should a thrust from my hanger, or a bullet deprive either of life, in a case of necessity, I am held harmless, and no law in the land can reach me."

"I have no doubt that Jonathan Wild," replied the farmer, sarcastically, "would for a moment, in malice, hesitate to commit murder, then cloak the crime with the authority he has abused."

"That taunt you will pay for dearly, old man."

Jonathan Wild turned to his followers, and thus addressed them:—

"Gather together all the wood, straw, and combustible material you can lay your hands on; pile them in heaps around this building, and ignite the mass.

"We must roast out the fox, since he refuses to leave his covert by any other means. Quick! kindle the flame at once."

"Oh, no, no, no! I implore you spare him!" cried Ellen, frantically throwing herself at the knees of the thief-taker.

"I cannot listen to your prayers," said he. "You have refused my entreaty, I must refuse yours."

"You dare not do this cruel deed."

"Dare not," laughed the monster. "You have yet to learn the iron will of Jonathan Wild. Yes, there is one way to move me, and that is——"

Before he could finish the sentence, the stone entrance to the secret chamber fell back, and the concealed stranger stood before him.

For the moment paralyzed, he stood without motion.

The next he laughed exultingly.

"So I have found the man I wanted. Jack Sheppard, you are my prisoner."

Jack, who had thrown off the cloak that had hitherto disguised him, now stood before Jonathan Wild defiantly.

His sister started up, flew into his arms, and buried her face in his bosom.

He yielded to uncontrollable emotion.

And seemed alike fearless, and unconscious of the danger that menaced him.

"I have betrayed you," said Ellen, grief almost stilling her accent.

"No, no, you are blameless. I overheard all that has passed, and the dastardly determination of my bitter foe; base as he is, I could hardly credit that he would carry it out."

FIRE! FIRE!—SEE NO. 28.

"But you found that had you not come forth I should have been as good as my word.

"The farm would have been in flames.

"And fire and faggot, instead of a halter at Tyburn, been the instrument of death."

"To save such a calamity, I have issued from my retreat; but I tell you to your teeth, Jonathan Wild, that the rope is not yet spun that shall hang Jack Sheppard."

"You will yield?"

"Never with life."

As he was about to draw his pistol, Ellen clasped her brother in her embrace.

"If he die, let me die too," she exclaimed.

The action of the terrified woman insured the destruction of the bewildered man.

His situation of embarrassment gave an advantage to the thief-taker, who, aided by his followers, disarmed him in an instant.

Ellen staggered, fainted, and fell on the floor.

"Now, then," said Wild, "to horse and away," after he had firmly secured his prisoner.

Struck with a sudden idea, the old farmer, as if by magic, altered his demeanour from one of sadness to one of gladness, and he arrested the departure.

"I were thinking, Measter Wild, that thee'll never get to Lunnon this night."

"Perhaps not, but I hope to hear St. Sepulchre's bell strike the fourth hour of morning."

"Then I can tell thee that thou'lt be deceived for once in thee life."

Smiling, Peveril continued.

"Thou'lt never reach Newgate by the time."

"Indeed; I should like to see who will prevent me."

"A power stronger than thee and I possess. Dinna yer struggle wi' it; or yer'll come off second best, mun."

"You are prevaricating, farmer; I see you are hinting at danger. Speak freely. What do you mean?"

"Well, then, that the storm that is now about to burst over us will render the road impassable, and that you and your prisoner may chance perish in a flood."

"If you are speaking truly, 'twould be as well to delay our journey."

"Do as thee wilt," said Peveril, with a cunning leer. "only recollect that I warned ye."

With the words, he raised the inanimate Ellen, and consigned her to the keeping of an aged female domestic, who bore her carefully from the room.

Jonathan Wild paced abstractedly to and fro.

Ever and anon he glanced at Jack Sheppard, and narrowly observed the farmer.

The latter gave neither sign nor token by his countenance of the stratagem he had formed in his head for the release of the captive.

After a pause, he addressed him.

"I can rely upon the information you have given me?"

"It is strictly correct," answered the old man. "Ask any of the neighbours, and they will tell thee that after rain the valley be inundated, and that to cross it, even by day, is perilous to horseman or traveller on foot."

"Then my mind's made up; I'll pass the night at the farm, where you must find means of disposing of the man I have taken in custody."

"I can readily do so. Adjoining the house is a temporary stronghold, used in days gone by for purposes of security; its windows are grated, its doors secured by bolts, bars, and locks."

"This is fortunate," cried the thief-taker; "within its walls I'll bestow the prisoner."

At a signal from their leader, the whole party at once proceeded to the fabric that the farmer pointed out to them.

It appeared evidently to have formed at one time a place of duresse or dungeon, most probably during the Commonwealth or the wars of the Roses.

Its fitness and strength at any rate justified such a conclusion,

As the officers and their prisoner arrived at the old building, the latter was in the midst of the circle, who carried each a loaded pistol in his hand.

He was not bound, but deprived of every means of resisting his keepers.

He looked somewhat depressed, but cast a defiant glance upon them.

Jonathan Wild, before entering the porch, made an examination of the so-called "fortress."

It was all that he could desire.

It had an outlet to a neighbouring churchyard.

It possessed but few windows, all at a considerable altitude from the ground, and guarded, as also was its single door, by bars and strong ironwork.

The interior was then surveyed by the thief-taker, and found to answer his purpose in every respect, as far as security and attempt at escape were concerned.

Jack Sheppard had scarcely been conducted into this prison when a distant sound disturbed his gaolers.

Their principal issued from the gate to learn the cause of interruption.

To his surprise he perceived a horseman making a descent down a steep embankment a little to the left of the spot upon which he was standing.

The horse plunged, and fell down the declivity, dragging its rider with him, entangled in the stirrup.

The termination of the event could not be ascertained by the observer, as everything at the bottom of the valley was screened from view by intervening brushwood and clusters of overhanging foliage.

Jonathan Wild despatched messengers to the scene of the disaster. What came of it we reserve for the next chapter.

————

CHAPTER XCIV.

SHOWS WHAT TOOK PLACE IN THE CHURCHYARD AND ITS IMMEDIATE VICINITY.

THE men soon returned who had been sent out to learn how the horseman had fared in his late perilous descent.

As luck would have it, he had escaped with a few scratches.

Jonathan Wild was somewhat taken by surprise at the further intelligence he received.

"The man is not seriously hurt, you say?" enquired the thief-taker of the assistants.

"No," said one, who turned out to be Quilt Arnold, "there are no bones broken, and his wounds, such as they are, will heal before morning."

"He's a lucky fellow," said Wild, "that he has suffered no mischief; for, I take it, in these outlandish parts, he'd get very little attendance from a surgeon."

Quilt Arnold drew the speaker aside after a pause, and addressed him in a low tone.

"You are wanted," said he.

Wild started.

"Hush!—be cautious, or you will rouse suspicion."

"Who the devil can it be?"

"You have named the party rightly. It is the devil, and no one else, for he alone can frighten you. But now he came up and whispered in my ear the pass-word of our community, 'and bid your master, Jonathan Wild, come to me without delay. 'Tis a matter that concerns him nearly. Tell him within the hour to meet me in the ruined church hard by. If he refuse within the hour he will rue his negligence.' With this he vanished like a spectre. I fear he intends some evil towards you."

"Nothing more likely."

"You won't go, of course?"

"Of course I shall; it may be necessary to have a knowledge of his purpose."

"But danger——"

"I defy. Jonathan Wild fears neither man nor devil."

"You speak truly; for till now I could scarce believe it."

* * * * * *

To an old monastic structure, whither he had been directed, Jonathan Wild bent his footsteps.

The old church seemed despoiled and desecrated, and abandoned to the ravages of decay and time.

Its roof and walls, crumbling and ivy-covered, rendered it even more picturesque than in its pristine days of glory.

Brier and weed usurped the pavement, and moss-grown were the monuments and marble tombs.

The only object varying from the scene of peace was the figure of the thief-taker, whose steel scabbard clanked ominously, as he trod the hollow aisles.

Suddenly he came upon the person he was seeking.

He was seated with the utmost composure in one of the unoccupied niches in the body of the sacred building.

The costume of this individual was quaint and singular, while his movements were grave, imperturbable, and deliberate.

His dress consisted of a jerkin and breeches of brown frieze, highly ornamented with round small brass buttons; the latter garment, being exceedingly full at the seat, and tight at the knees, proclaimed him to be one of the natives of the Netherlands or Holland.

Red hose, high boots, and a steeple hat completed his attire.

The Dutchman also possessed other particularities, such as a weather-beaten, red, and broad face, eyes small and twinkling, and a beard and head of hair, both of which were bushy and stubborn.

His sole occupation appeared to be that of smoking, if we may judge from the manner in which he contemplated the vapour emitted from his kindled pipe.

Jonathan Wild in an instant recognised in the phlegmatic personage his old companion in crime Wirth Wolfgang.

Neither spoke, but the former beckoned to the Dutchman to follow him, and proceeded until he came to the entrance porch.

Having glided through it, both men were in the open graveyard attached to the old church.

Had they not been deeply engrossed in their own thoughts, they would have observed a figure creep stealthily along the outer wall, spring over it, and make his way cautiously to the ancient fabric.

Having come to a halt, Jonathan Wild inquired,

"What brings you here, Wirth?"

After several whiffs the individual addressed took the pipe from his mouth, and in a rather mysterious and husky voice, replied,

"Muntmeester, a leetle pusiness ant a leetle pleasure."

"Do you bring good or evil tidings?"

"Perhaps bad, perhaps goot—cela dépénd—wot you call in English, as you like."

"Hang it, Wirth, let's have no Dutch lingo, but speak out. What do you want?"

This was so grave a question, that the party of whom it was demanded continued under its contemplation more stolid than ever, and finally coughed, and shook his head in that manner in which a Hollander only can perform those operations.

"What do you want?" repeated Wild.

"Mein vriend, I want vot you vouldn't pay me some very long time ago."

"I tell you that you have no proof that——"

"Haven't I! and perhaps I haven't got no broof of someting else what you hafe done, which will sent you a long way at the expense of Jean Bull—hein."

"Do you think I'm a fool?"

"No, but I thinks you are a rogue. Listen, Mynheer Wild, I hafe got you letters safe, and other broofs what you know not."

"I must manœuvre with this fellow."

"Come, come, I wants de money," said Wirth Wolfgang, tapping the ashes out of his pipe on an adjacent tombstone; "'tis dwo hundred and vivty pound. Pay me, Muntmeester, or I shall be obliged to go t'oder vay to work to make you."

Seeming to consent for the nonce to the Dutch-man's demand, Jonathan Wild, masking his design with a countenance of deceit, addressed his associate—

"I was but jesting with you, Wirth Wolfgang. You shall be paid, and fully paid. As an earnest of my word take this ring on my finger; its value is worth half the amount of the sum I am indebted to you."

"Very goot. I will take it as security."

"And you will not refuse to serve me in a little matter I have on hand?"

"Vill you pay me vell? I can't afford to do vicket things so cheap as I did vonce. I've got a new master since we last met, and he is a tyrant."

"A master?" replied Wild, eagerly. "Who is he?"

"Mien conscience," said Wirth, striking his breast.

At this remark the thief-taker gave a loud laugh.

"You laugh. Many volks laugh at vot they do not onderstand; that is de case with you, Mynheer Wild, when I talk of conscience."

"Well, well, since I have agreed to your terms, I trust we are to be better friends."

"Stop; you let me see in mien hand de two hondred and vivty pounds vot you owe me, and I swear by all my hopes of habbiness in dis vorld and de next to make you von present."

"A present?"

"Don't be in a hurry, mein yonker, I will put into your hand that teufel's imp, Roving Jack."

Positively stunned by the information, Jonathan Wild for the moment stood petrified, and in distrust looked fixedly at the Dutchman as if he would penetrate the very depths of his soul.

Recovering his self-possession, he uttered, with a sudden vehemence—

"Can it be possible that the grave can give up the dead!"

"He escaped from de ruins where Jack Sheppard lay his body."

"Yes, and——"

"Make for de river to get a boat."

"You were cruising and saw him hail you?"

"Ja, ja; just so. I was set in de stern of mien shallop, when I heard de voice of some one concealed among de reeds dat grow along de water's edge."

The Dutchman paused, and then resumed—

"I pull towards de bank, and there I find von man; he was pale, trembling, and covered of blood. I know his face, and say to myself, 'this, if I mistake not, will bring me some gelt.' He was too faint and sick to notice me; and got into my boat for shelter and protection."

"Shelter and protection!" cried Wild, with a hideous grin. "The fool had better trusted himself in the den of a lion. Well, how have you disposed of him?"

"I will tell you when I shall have filled mien hooker."

The gentleman appealed to went through the mysterious ceremonial peculiar to himself of filling the bowl of his pipe, and with an equally grave solemnity of lighting the same with a piece of German tinder.

Having buried himself in a profundity of smoke and sober speculation, Wirth Wolfgang proceeded with his discourse.

"Donder und blitzen! when dis, what you call, Roving Jack, got into my boats, he was so weak from de loss of de blood he fell down, and swooned quite away, having no more sense than if he had taken a cask of brandewyn. 'Dat is better nor good,' thought I, as I clap my old sea-cloak over him dat no von might not see de kinchen with one little eye."

"You took him down the Thames," interrupted Wild.

"Yah!" replied Wirth. "You are better nor a witch. When we came to the haunted hulk——"

"Lying off the marshes near Erith?"

"Very goot! some of my prave poys were on board her."

"Stowing away contraband merchandise, and waiting for the tide?"

"We soon get yong Teufleskin on board, and confined him in de hold."

"With rats and total darkness for his companions."

"And he von't got rid of them," said the Dutchman smiling maliciously, "onless de varmint take it into their head to gnaw through the iron band that binds him to the rotting vessel."

"Mynheer Wolfgang," replied Jonathan Wild, delighted, "this capture to me is worth a king's ransom. Roving Jack, I have ascertained, carried about his person papers that——"

"Yah! and those paper I mean to keep as mien guarantee."

"What! would you mistrust your old friend?"

"I trust nobody. Don't you, Mynheer Vild, or you may chance to die of that unpleashant complaint de hempen fever."

"You have known me so long——"

"So long," replied the Dutchman, drily, "that I mean to keep you where I've got you—under mein thumb."

"Name your price."

"I will name mein price when the vork is done."

"I may expect to see you then——"

"Three days hence."

"Where?"

"At your own house in de Old Bailey."

Jonathan Wild and Wolfgang then each took their separate roads, the latter chuckling at the power he maintained over his late companion, and forming a resolution to use it to his advantage.

The wily plotters had scarcely quitted the spot upon which they had held their conference when the figure of a man was seen to rise like a phantom from behind one of the tombstones in its immediate vicinity.

It was Paul Peveril.

He had heard all that had passed, and had determined on means to defeat the black design.

*   *   *   *   *

We must now revert to Jack Sheppard.

The reader will bear in mind that we left him a captive in the stronghold, attended by the myrmidons of his implacable enemy, Jonathan Wild.

Jack Sheppard disposed of his gaolers, who proceeded to betake themselves to certain creature comforts in the shape of various strong waters, sent them in a well-filled hamper.

The heavy door of the temporary dungeon was at once locked on the inside.

Firstly, with a view to prevent a possibility of escape on the part of the prisoner.

Secondly, that all chance of sudden intrusion might be prevented.

Benches were then drawn together round the fire, and the contents of the basket displayed and called into requisition.

Whether the savoury dishes that the farmer had supplied them with at his dwelling were provocative of thirst or not is immaterial, suffice that the liquors were considerably diminished in quantity in a very short period.

Bottle after bottle was emptied almost as soon as the cork was drawn.

As a matter of course, the proceeding unloosed the tongues of the drinkers.

They began to laugh, talk, and lastly shout.

"This will never suit, Mr. Wild," said Quilt Arnold, who appeared the soberest of the number; "we must comport ourselves less boisterously, and, if you have no objection, I will volunteer an old song."

Uproarious applause followed this suggestion.

Order was restored, pipes re-lighted, and Quilt Arnold commenced—

> "Did you ever hear the like,
>   Or ever hear the same,
> Of the five women barbers
>   That lived in Drury Lane?
> The first a bold Virago,
>   Her name was Cut-purse Moll,
> As Joan of France or English Nell,
>   Was fair and stout withal.
> The next Nan Hide, who won the hearts
>   Of gentles great and small,
> With syren smiles entrapped false Monk
>   The Duke of Albemarle.
> Of Mulsack's wife, of Edgeworth Bess,
>   Poll Maggot, too, I ween,
> You would not find the like of such
>   To hoax or shave you clean."

Before the song was finished, the whole of the party, with the exception of the singer, had dropped asleep in an inebriated and helpless condition.

It was now long past midnight.

The torches which illumined the vast apartment were nearly exhausted.

And the vapour which arose from their flickering flame obscured, in a great measure, the moving of a large wooden panel at the further end of the chamber.

Quilt Arnold started, as he perceived an aperture in the wall.

He tried to rouse his companions, but failed.

All being, as already stated, stupefied with drink.

The light, struggling through the mist, now revealed a figure advancing from the recess to the only one capable of noticing it.

Quilt Arnold for a few moments steadily regarded the object before him.

It was motionless, spectre-like and silent.

"'Tis the foul fiend."

These words were uttered by the terrified man as though he was overtaken by superstitious apprehensions.

With this again he was about to endeavour to seek assistance from the drowsy band when he discovered in the supposed phantom the person of Ellen Peveril.

Jack Sheppard, who had burst from his bonds, now sprang forward, leaped through the opened panel, and was out of sight in a moment, while the liberator held her pistol, loaded to the muzzle, at the head of the astounded gaoler.

"One word, one gesture, and your life is forfeited. Attempt to give an alarm, and I can only die; but, at the same time, remember, you will die with me."

Quilt Arnold, overcome, moved not a limb, save in terror.

Ellen poised her weapon with a firm hand and unerring aim.

"I carry arms," she continued, "for protection and not to shed blood but in my own defence. Choose, then, shall I kill you as a dog, or will you allow me to defend the passage till your prisoner is beyond reach of danger?"

"I promise not to give alarm till an hour has passed over our heads."

"I require your oath to——"

"I swear to keep my word."

"Enough; in the time you have given Jack Sheppard he will make good speed, and you will not again catch him use whip and spur as you may."

With the words Ellen Peveril passed through the panel from the apartment.

She had hardly shut it when Jonathan Wild was heard returning from his interview with Wirth Wolfgang, and knocking for admittance at the barred-up door.

CHAPTER XCV.

THE HAUNTED HULK—THE PHANTOM SKIPPER AND HIS DROWNED CREW—ROVING JACK'S COMPACT WITH "VANDERDECKEN, OR THE FLYING DUTCHMAN," AND HOW HE GOT OUT OF THE HOLD.

On the bosom of the lordly Thames, in about three fathom of water, unmindful of the spring cable, which hung down as a rope which had fallen overboard, there lay motionless as death the hulk of a sunken vessel.

She was of gigantic proportions, and would challenge the admiration of all who could appreciate the pristine merits of her build.

So beautiful had been the construction of this mighty ship, that, floating on the waves, one could have imagined her a created being of the ocean, and fashioned by the divine architect, rather than a simple specimen of the skill of man.

A dismantled deck and broken masts were now all that remained of her imposing and elegant model between the meeting of the firmament and horizon, her vast body being buried in the waters of the flowing stream.

Her occasional impediment to the traffic of the river would have caused her removal, but that superstition, common to the age, forbade such a course with regard to the "haunted hulk."

She had been one of the privateers in the service of Holland during a war with that country and our own, nearly a century previous to our story.

Forcing her passage from the Medway to the Thames, she had foundered at the spot where she ever remained.

And universal consent had stamped it as impiety to raise her from the supposed altar of retribution.

To add still more to the bigoted notions of our ancestors, the craft bore the ominous name of the far-famed and dreaded "Vanderdecken, or Flying Dutchman."

We must now go on board, and be further surprised.

Instead of a small vessel of ninety tons, as she appeared from the water's edge, we discover that she is upwards of two hundred.

Her breadth of beam is enormous.

And those spars that once appeared so light and commanding in grandeur, of unexpected dimensions, though falling fast into decay.

Her decks of fir-planks, without the least spring or rise, are wasting and water-soaked.

While her ropes of Manilla, metal stanchions, and bright boarding pikes perish in the desolation that rankles in the wreck.

Everything seems but as a remembrance of the past, and corrodes with the action of the river under which it is emerged, or festers from the corruption of the damp, dark, fetid atmosphere the rotting timber engenders.

In the hold of this gloomy vessel is a youth.

He wears a pair of loose sailor's trousers, the rest of his body is naked.

Though his countenance is handsome and intelligent, it wears now a mournful and sad impression.

And truly so, for Roving Jack, the character we have described, is once more in the hands of his bitterest enemies.

Without hopes, without food, and with death.

Forlorn, he exclaimed,

"Yet, why should I murmur, if my life is to be taken by the fiat of heaven, that deals with us as it thinks fit? Not a sparrow falls to the ground without *His* knowledge, and it is for *Him* to save or sacrifice. I am but the creature of *His* will, and I must bend to the command of One whose ways are inscrutable."

At one time he would call to mind all that had passed and acknowledge it was too true.

At another he would persuade himself that his senses had been worked up in a moment of excitement, and that the whole event was an illusion.

While in this—we might almost say supernatural—state, betwixt sleeping and waking, an extraordinary scene was pictured to his view, as in a vision.

Suddenly, the fastenings of one of the port-holes were removed, and the gushing waters, as if by magic, stayed their course and flowed past instead of into the vessel.

When the shutters descended, they unfolded a light so vivid as almost to dazzle the eyesight of the beholder.

This very light of brilliant day overthrew the resolution of Roving Jack more than the previous gloom and darkness by which he had been surrounded.

Presently he became aware of the presence of a man who had glided like a phantom through the stream into the hold in which he was imprisoned.

He was habited in a green, old-fashioned dress of the Dutch style, with enormously full breeches, each garment being covered profusely with white sugar-loaf buttons.

High boots encased his legs, while a conical black hat and red feather formed his head-gear.

His whole appearance was unearthly and ghostlike.

His face that of a corpse.

"Advance!" said the spectre, welcoming Roving Jack with a melancholy smile.

"There is a sepulchral tone in your language which chills me as the thrilling blast of winter," replied the pirate hunter.

His blood curdled when he felt no mortal hand grasped his own.

"The ember-like light of your eye," he continued, tremblingly, "fills my soul with horror, as does that of the snake, which fascinates to destroy. Let me fly from thee."

"To what? To poverty and despair?" exclaimed the spectre.

"If I boast not of riches still I possess them."

"No; they are confiscated—passed into other hands, and owned by the powers of darkness."

"Ah! am I to be deprived of my just rights and titles?" asked Jack, in surprise and dismay.

"I am forbid to reveal secrets, but can offer a remedy for your misery. Because I pity your forlorn condition, you liken me to a serpent."

"Forgive me, I——"

"Are you content to confide in me?"

"I am."

" Have you the courage to dive into the mysteries of this haunted ship, where, spellbound (for the crimes of her master and his pirate crew), she lies as in the moment of destruction, her men torpid and insensible as rocks of granite, her coffers filled with gold."

A deep rate zeal now inspired Roving Jack, and roused within him a strange feeling of curiosity.

An excitement which conducted to hope was better than a nothingness worse than death.

And he felt that he was fulfiling an awful doom or working out his own destiny.

" I would see all—learn all——"

At that moment the moon was on a level with the waters.

And the secret of the necromantic vessel could become visible to human eyes.

"To enable you to avert any danger that may threaten you in the ordeal, accept this talisman," said the spectre.

With these words, the figure placed in the hands of Roving Jack a charmed harpoon.

It was encrusted with the rust of ages.

And a potent safeguard to those who might dare to intrude into the supernatural retreat.

For an instant all became again profoundly dark, and a strain of music, plaintive and soft, was heard.

Through a thin vapour then could be discerned this picture for the reader's inspection.

Rocks and waters rose and discovered the half-buried hull of the " Vanderdecken," in mid-ocean.

Her ropes were green with sea-weed, her timbers much decayed, and her windows and lanterns of painted glass broken.

Her crew laid about on the sand as if in the last convulsions of the drowned.

Bales of merchandize, chests of gold, spoil and plunder of every description scattered themselves around.

Roving Jack surveyed this scene with awe and wonder.

The more so, when shuddering, the spectre bid him again advance to gaze upon a coffer he had opened, filled with gold.

"Art thou cold? Here are beams will warm thee."

" Gold ?"

" Uncounted. This inexhaustible wealth may be thine ; but first hear my story.

" Many years ago, in the olden time, 'Vanderdecken,' the pirate, and his devil crew, were the terror of every sea.

" Never passed a day that these decks were not crimsoned with blood enforced by violence.

" At length the bright star of destiny set ; tempest, wreck and mutiny ensued, and I was dragged from my cabin and manacled in this very hold.

" As I lay in my prison, fettered, loudly descended to my ear the drunken sounds of mockery and defiance.

" The rage of superhuman force possessed me.

" I burst asunder my iron bonds, and reaching the port-hole of this devoted vessel, snapped in twain as a thread the cable that held it fast.

" In furiously dashed the booming waters.

" With every roar the ship descended—deeper and deeper down.

" I cared not for myself ; to die avenged was all that Vanderdecken craved.

" For the act, I and my crew, for a certain period, are doomed to visit earth, and suffer torments for the crimes we are compelled to commit thereon.

" Hark ! The land bell strikes ; the moon sets. Witness, but fear not ; thou art innocent, and from thy untainted breast the curses of the dead men will flow harmless back as sea foam from a rock of iron."

While the spectral helmsman yet spoke the moon sank below the level of the waters, changing them to cerulean, then deep blue.

The old lanterns one by one then lit dimly up with a dull, lurid, red glare.

The clock struck, and the withering carcases of the doomed crew became animated and made alive.

Silently as death they formed into small parties, as if meditating a mutiny, of which Vanderdecken was the object.

They soon advanced on all sides, and attacked their phantom skipper.

They stabbed him.

They flashed their fire-arms at him.

The flames were of crimson, but no sound prevailed, and the victim defied the death blows dealt him.

Suddenly the murderous band are hushed into stillness.

An unknown and human voice trespasses on their unhallowed rites.

Roving Jack saw no more, for the intense darkness of his dungeon again assumed dominion.

Had he dreamed, or was it a fearful reality ?

Through the flickering beams emitted by the opening above him he again saw the vision.

The glassy eye of Vanderdecken was turned to the bright glance of a mortal.

And the pirate and his crew had changed their mouldering garbs and grisly forms for those of beings endowed with life.

He turned his head from the fearful scene he had witnessed.

He swooned, and fell heavily on the dungeon floor.

On his recovery, Wirth Wolfgang and his followers were standing by his side.

" Ya—ya ! He ish not dead yet !" exclaimed the Dutchman. " Hist ! Mein Kinchin, we haf brought you something for to haf eat."

" No, no ; keep it yourself," replied Jack, faintly ; " you have more need of it than I. A burning fever is consuming me, and, unless some aid arrives by chance, I feel I have not many hours to live."

" While dere is life dere is hope, so say you Inglis."

" For me, none. Abandon hope all ye who enter here."

Jack maintained a sullen silence for some time, then again spoke.

" You will, at least, tell me your reason for bringing me here, since you see me so entirely at your mercy. Common humanity should not offer a refusal to my request."

" I can accord it, mein yong vriend, since you are beyond de reach ov all earthy power."

" Speak ! Tell me !"

" You can call to mind, mynheer, no doubt, that your life was attempted on de night you staid at de old ' Bell Inn ?' "

" I am aware only that a knife gleamed before me, and I fell covered with blood. I remember nothing else."

" Nothing of the ruined house to which you was taken after you had received vot was supposed your death-wound ?"

" I have strange recollections of a dark abode—of a hasty flight—of a rescue by a boat ; but all wild and dreamy. I can picture nothing distinctly till

I awoke in this fearful place. Tell me, I entreat, how I came here ?"

"I found you faint—almost dying on the banks of de river, some two miles from de place vhere you had escaped. To prevent discovery, I have brought you hither."

"Why you have done so I do not yet quite understand."

"There be two reasons why Roving Jack should be 'on boad der 'Vanderdecken,' " said the Dutchman.

"The first ?"

"It is safety."

"The second ?"

"Mein own advantage. Act fairly with me," continued Wolfgang, and, perchance, the fiend who rules my destiny may allow me to act fairly by you."

"What are your conditions ?"

"Those which are in your power to grant."

"Name them."

"I require the papers which reinstates Violet Tremaine in ——"

"It is impossible for me to ratify our compact, since those papers are fallen into the hands of those by whom I was so murderously attacked. Jack Sheppard and Tom King——".

"Very goot, they will not long remain here, for Jack Sheppard vill mount the ladder, ere he is a month older."

The voice that had startled Roving Jack in his delirium, and dispersed the phantoms, was now again heard resounding through the cavities of the sunken vessel.

Roving Jack had no difficulty in recognising the voice as it came near to him, and rose clear and distinct above the din of the ebbing waters and creaking chains around him.

"There it comes. Put your helm hard aport ! Down with it, man ! Luff, and shake the wind out of her sails, or over she goes clean and for ever !"

The words had hardly escaped the lips of Paul Peveril (who owned the voice heard in the first instance) than that individual appeared at the open hatchway, and looked down into the hold, taking a somewhat lengthened observation of its several occupants.

One of the pirates, more venturesome than the rest, attempted to ascend the steps, bolt through the scuttle, and thereby gain the deck.

Paul Peveril, with his shoulder of mutton fist, gave him a very unceremonious rebuff, and down he dropped again.

"You don't seem to be in a very snug berth, skipper," said the sailor, to the astonished Wirth Wolfgang, whose head of hair he described as long enough for the coxswain of old Admiral Benbow's barge.

"Are you hard up on a clench here," he continued, "and never a knife to cut the seizings ? Just out with your top-lights and look ahead."

Recovering from his surprise, the Dutchman answered drily,

"De sentinel never leave his post ontil he is reliefed."

"Right, mynheer ; that's king's ship discipline all the world over ; so we'll pass signals from our own timbers."

"What ship ?"

"You have heard of Vanderdecken ?"

"What the 'Flying Dutchman,' who fires hot shot, and gives no quarter ? I met him in latitude 18°. latitude N. 1 forget the longitude. You might as well try to eat peas with a pitchfork as weather him. You don't mean to say you sail in that devil's

craft ? If you do, you are hooked to a man, flounder as you will."

"Messmates," said the foremost of the pirates, "I have no wish to steer for execution dock, or dangle in chains on the Thames margin at St. Clement's reach. This intruder is a spy, and to save our own necks, we must slit his weasand."

"Belay, belay. I'm here on no privateering commission, but bear a flag of truce at my fore."

"Why have you sought us ?"

"To save you from a dance upon nothing at the yard-arm. I have a proposition to make you, though you are such a lubberly, infarnal, damned set of swabs."

At the words, twenty knives gleamed in the air.

And the buccaneers prepared to take summary vengeance on the intrepid seaman.

"Haul taut, and heave to," he cried, waving his enemies back, "till I have given orders to clear decks for action."

"Firstly, skipper, to you I must address my words.".

Wolfgang advanced to the speaker.

"You have a prisoner on board."

"What tongue has disclosed this ?"

"Your own."

"Where ?"

"In the grave-yard, near St. Albans."

"Ah, seaman, you have betrayed yourself, not me."

"What do you mean ?"

"You should have kept your secret."

"How so ?"

"By revealing it you have sealed the doom of him you came to save."

Paul tried to speak, but could not.

"You know too much for my safety. You and he must both perish."

Scarcely had these words been uttered, when the rattling of musketry ran through every crevice of the hold of the hulk.

Not a single pirate, save one, lived to tell the mysterious death they had met with.

This one was the skipper.

Wirth Wolfgang was nowhere to be seen.

The fate of the crew, and how they fell, is reserved for the following chapter.

CHAPTER XCVI.

SHOWS HOW DICK TURPIN ROBBED A LEARNED DIVINE, AND HOW HE CAME OFF SECOND-BEST IN THE ADVENTURE.

THAT night the bosom of the Thames received thirty dead bodies.

They were those of the pirates of the haunted hulk.

Hulk no longer, for gunpowder placed between the crumbling decks had worked a final destruction.

Her heavy iron guns vanished away, her beams and timbers separated in air, then slowly sank in water.

The remnants of the hull that floated on the surface of the river being the only emblem of the once dreaded pirate ship, the "Vanderdecken."

The stratagem that destroyed the crew may be told in a few lines.

Paul Peveril, aware of the imprisonment and prison-house of Roving Jack, had solicited from government the aid of a body of marines, to assist him in the daring enterprise of subduing the pirate band in their own citadel—the haunted hulk.

The trap was completely set, and four boats moved silently with muffled oars on the Thames to the scene of action.

Each boat was manned by twelve hands, and each hand furnished with twelve rounds of ball cartridge, with a further store if necessity required it.

Arrived at the vessel, it was environed on all sides by the assailing party.

With stillness of death they ascended the wreck, and posted themselves in various portions of the same.

More especially in the compartment adjoining the hold, where they could command their deadly aim at their unsuspecting enemy, and behind which they could raise a formidable barricade.

The success of the project need not be told, since, with a single exception, the ocean banditti perished on that fatal night.

* * * *

Heavily along the road which crosses Enfield Chase, rumbles a carriage.

One of those carriages of the early Georgian era.

Massive in decoration, ponderous in construction.

The vehicle is occupied by a personage equally portly and portentous.

The Very Reverend Doctor Ephraim Spintext, a high church dignitary.

The exalted individual has many fat livings.

And possesses, by virtue of his holy office, vast and broad ecclesiastical domains.

Though a minister of the gospel, he is not averse to rational recreation or enjoyment when it comes in the shape of dinner parties, good cheer and old port.

He is now returning from a participation of the second, and drowsy under the influence of the third.

In short, the learned doctor has had what may be aptly termed a skinful of wine, and is asleep in his carriage.

While in a pleasing dream of tithings, benefices, and preferment, his ear is assailed by the inharmonious words,

"Stand and deliver!"

Suddenly starting from his dream, the first object that meets the eye of the divine is a loaded pistol, peering gracefully through the window of the vehicle that carries him.

Again the ominous sentence, "Stand and deliver!" is repeated, with a command that his money may quickly change hands.

The proud parson now found that he was in the power of a highwayman, one of those minions of the moon who consider objectionable a nay to their answer.

The Very Reverend Doctor Ephraim Spintext was a man who was endowed with a considerable share of confidence, and began to lay about him.

Not with carnal weapons (he was a man of peace), but with more potent instruments of defence, namely, texts of scripture.

He commenced his cudgeling of the bold robber with the eighth commandment—

"Thou shalt not steal."

Finding his adversary was about to parry the thrust, and act upon the offence, he followed up his attack with greater vigour by asserting,

"And, furthermore, Solomon, who was surely a very wise man, speaketh in this manner, 'Rob not the poor, because he is poor.'"

Dick Turpin, who was really the party addressed, before easing the old cull of his swag, determined to finish the cant in his own strain.

To attain such an end, the highwayman rubbed up his memory, and treated his antagonist with some scraps from the holy writ.

"'Verily, thou vessel of wrath,'" said Dick Turpin, assuming the air of the devout, "'if thou hadst regardest the divine precepts as thou oughtest to have done, thou wouldest not have wrested them to such an abominable and wicked sense as thou hast done.'"

"Friend, if I have taken tithe, it hath been but my godly possession. The prophet saith the labourer is worthy of his hire, and if I——"

"Thou should'st have been content in sack-cloth and ashes, whilst thou wert wallowing in filthy lucre," said the highwayman.

"Why, thou vile robber, dost thou aggravate my misfortunes, and attempt to extenuate thine own horrid crimes?"

"No aspersions on my profession, I beg, sir," replied Turpin, "for Solomon's words, which you have just quoted, are also these, 'Despise not a thief.'

"But, it is of little purpose to dispute," continued the speaker; "my time is precious, as I have to wait upon a rich dowager before morning, and the substance of what I have to say is included in a few words."

"Which are——"

"I require your cash, ring, and gold hunting-watch."

"I cannot consent, friend, to such a request."

"May I never be brought to the crap,* then," returned Turpin, "if I don't send your reverence out of the world, to your old master, the devil, in an instant."

The terrible words had their desired effect.

The minister was mumchance,† and nodded assent.

Thirty broad pieces of gold soon found themselves in the highwayman's pouch, who, with a polite bow and a smile, bid his dupe "good-night," and they parted.

Dick Turpin had not proceeded far on his road when he suddenly pulled up Black Bess, the mare upon which he was seated.

"Now I come to think of it," he said, "I've done wrong in letting off such a rich ecclesiastic as his reverence, Doctor Ephrahim Spintext, in such an easy manner. As he has come a long distance it is evident that he has more gold on his person than in his purse. I mustn't have done with him yet."

Coolly again taking out his "bull-dogs" (a pair of pistols), he put spurs to his animal and rode after the carriage he had lately stopped.

He had not proceeded in its pursuit three minutes when he perceived that it had stopped before an old country ale-house, called the "King Harry."

The occupant had descended to seek its shelter while the vehicle was, by his orders, to continue its journey onwards.

This proceeding puzzled the highwayman, who could not make out why his dignity could possibly condescend to rub its greatness against the oaken tables of such a humble place of entertainment.

"I must do it," said Turpin. "But how to get at the parson, since he knows me, without exciting suspicion? 'Tis too good a prize to let slip, and yet I don't see my way clear how I can do the trick."

Casting up in his mind the pros and cons, he at length seemed to have hit upon a plan by which he could effect his desired purpose of again robbing the reverend gentleman.

---

* Crap—gallows. † Mumchance—silent.

THE ATTACK ON THE "HARRY THE EIGHTH.'—*See page 219.*

"Impudence must befriend me," said he; "though I begin to have some qualms."

Riding leisurely to the door of the tavern, the highwayman dismounted and entered it.

Ensconced in the snug parlour he encountered the object of his search.

He was engaged, for his mightiness, in a somewhat *lowly* occupation.

Yes, the *eminent* divine was discussing the merits of bread and cheese.

The staff of life and its accessory being in companionship with a quart of lusty ale.

"Good doctor," said Turpin, with an assurance that staggered the party addressed, and in an instant recognised the features of the man who had so recently robbed him.

"This audacity surpasses belief!" muttered the divine to himself, at the same time evincing symptoms of being anything but comfortable in his present society.

"It's plaguily dark," continued the imperturbable highwayman; "and the road, I consider, would at this hour be dangerous to travel."

"I have very good reasons," replied the other, drily, "for coinciding in such an undeniable opinion."

"Your voice, worthy sir, is familiar to me—we have met before."

Turpin, unabashed, treated his companion to a stare full in the face.

"Your assertion, as was your previous remark, is strictly correct; to my cost, I have reasons for acknowledging the 'great' fact."

"Ah, yes, I remember *you.*"

"And I (by a peculiar antithesis, if I may be permitted to use the word) shall never forget you. You were kind enough to oblige me with forty pounds——"

"In gold, for which I have no receipt at present."

"We never give them in the City in business transactions."

"I suppose it is deemed unnecessary when the amount is certain to be repaid in full."

"Doctor Ephraim Spintext, for that I learn is your name," said Turpin, "there is a little matter standing between us that may as well be settled on the nail, and as it concerns only ourselves, if you have no objection we will hold our conference with closed doors."

With this Turpin doubly locked up the apartment, and placed the key in his coat pocket, at the same time remarking—

"Fairly trapped—caught like a woodcock in its own springe."

The sensitive organs of the divine, as may be imagined, were necessarily excited by the proceedings of the highwayman, who after them unceremoniously slapped him on the shoulder.

"As your reverence was kind enough to conform to my wishes on our first meeting," said he, "I trust I shall find a similar complaisance on our second."

"May I ask what your demand in this instance may be?"

"A very simple one, my dear sir—the loan of your cloak."

"I find it will be useless for me any longer to dissemble," said Spintext, firmly ; "your intentions are too apparent for me not to perceive them. Ruffian, you have already robbed me, and now, with unparalleled effrontery, make a further demand upon my purse."

"I trust you will not compel me to resort to ulterior means."

"This assumed indifference on your part, fellow, is both offensive and useless," said Spintext, "therefore you must learn my determination at once, and without reserve. I positively refuse to yield another penny, and I——"

"I see I shall have to make short work of you, doctor, and stick by my old friends—friends that never fail me."

With these words, Turpin drew a brace of pistols from his pocket, and placed them on the table at which he and the doctor were seated.

"Now, no flinching," continued the highwayman ; "dub up the garment I require, or I'll pay your reverence off as Paul did the Ephesians."

The courage of Spintext, at the sight of the loaded pistols, resembled that of Bob Acres—it oozed out at his fingers' ends ; but his mind assumed a more tranquil state as, with a sigh, he delivered up his cloak.

"I have ever boasted," said Spintext, "that I would never be robbed by a single highwayman."

"And you find that such a boast was void," sneered Turpin, who commenced searching the habiliment he held in his hand.

"On the contrary," said Spintext, "I should not have resigned my cloak had I not seen you had a confederate."

"A confederate?"

"Yes—the man who now stands at your elbow."

The "ruse" succeeded.

The moment Turpin turned to regard the supposed intruder, Spintext whipped up his pistols, and exclaimed——"

"You may see with half an eye how matters now

stand, rascal ; make your peace with heaven, for you haven't two minutes to live"

"Thank you for the information," said Turpin, scarcely recovering from his surprise at the late turn of events ; "but I shall never fall by a blue-plum." *

"Advance a step, villain," said the divine, presenting both the weapons, "and I send a brace of bullets into your head."

"Do you take me for a green-horn?"

"This is bravado ; but you will find out your mistake, for I shall think no more of shooting you than I would of snuffing the candle which stands upon this table."

"Be it so ; I'll take my chance."

"You're an amusing rascal, and I am willing to spare your life on one condition."

"You are vamping up some scheme to further betray me."

"Is life nothing?"

"What are your proposals?"

"Those which, in honour, you should agree to."

"Name them."

"Return me the amount you have robbed me of, and depart in peace."

"Suppose I say—no."

"Why, then I fire."

"Fire and be d——d."

Spintext obeyed the blustering injunction.

He fired—not at Dick Turpin, but through the window.

The highwayman now remained in a state of passive stupefaction, gazing vacantly to understand the motives of his generous associate.

Suddenly the parson's wig was removed, and supplanted by a sleek, glossy, black head of hair, closely cropped, and his features changed from a sanctified to a rollicking air.

"What, didn't you know me?" said the individual, proceeding to disrobe himself, and appear in his own person. "I gave you more credit for discernment, and could not have believed that the dashing Dick Turpin, the high spice toby gloak, and terror of the road, could have been so easily outwitted."

"I must readily admit," said the party addressed, laughing, and recovering from his surprise, "that you are the last person in the world I should suspect of ' taking holy orders.' "

Before closing the chapter and continuing our story, we must remark that so cleverly had the disguise been effected that the most sapient, astute, or cunning would never have recognised in the Very Reverend Doctor Ephraim Spintext, the renowned, daring, and dexterous robber—Jack Sheppard !

CHAPTER XCVII.

JONATHAN WILD IN PURSUIT—THE ARRIVAL OF THE OFFICERS AT THE " KING HARRY " ON THE ENFIELD ROAD—DICK TURPIN AFFORDS JACK SHEPPARD MEANS OF ESCAPE.

WHILE Jack Sheppard and Dick Turpin were yet within the walls of the " King Harry," a party of horsemen drove up furiously to the door of the same.

A presentiment of danger at once occurred to the first-named as he hurried to the window to ascertain if his previous suspicions were correct.

The casements were fastened and barred, but he

---

* Blue-plum—bullet.

could easily overhear the conversation that was taking place outside the house.

"We've got him now," said a voice, which Jack Sheppard at once recognized as that of Jonathan Wild. "The description given by Doctor Spintext's servants of the robber so exactly tallies with the man we want, that no doubt remains that he is within or near this building."

"Don't be too precipitate, Mr. Wild, or the bird may yet take wing, and give us the go-by."

"You are right, Quilt Arnold. Caution is but necessary and requisite. Jack Sheppard is a ticklish customer, and has as many expedients as a cat has lives."

"Yes, he's a devil of a fellow; but if we keep our eyes open now, I think we shall 'land' him."

"I think it devilish hard if we can't manage him amongst us," said Wild, dismounting.

An example followed by his attendants, one and all of whom descended from their steaming horses.

"He's a desperate character we have to deal with," continued the thief-taker, "the hardest I have ever met, if I may except Sally Wells, that was lagged for shoplifting. The jade, in a bout, attacked me with a carving knife, and when I had disarmed her, bit off a couple of fingers from my left hand."

"But, now we come to business," said Wild, as if he had formed a sudden resolution. "In the first place, are your weapons in working order?"

"Primed and loaded," was the general reply.

"And your blades?"

"Sharp as razors," was again responded.

"Good. With firm hearts and steady hands surround the house, while I and Mendez enter it. On the slightest attempt of its inmates to leave, fire, and bring them down, no matter if you shoot the Lord Mayor of London."

The orders given were strictly obeyed.

The "Harry the Eighth" became as a beleaguered fortress, and Jonathan Wild, accompanied by his Jewish satellite, passed its threshold.

While Jack Sheppard had been occupied in watching his pursuers at the window, Dick Turpin had been deeply and equally engaged in another part of the room; stealthily drawing a red phial from a secret pocket in his coat, he mingled the contents with those of a flask he held in his hand.

"Dam'me, Dick, the flunkies have peached,* and I shall be taken if you don't stand my friend," shouted Jack Sheppard, in desperation. "Give me your snappers, I'll flip† one or two of them before I give up my worthless life."

"Hang it, Jack, never say die," said Turpin, pettishly. "What's the use of winging the pigeon to fall by the swoop of the hawk? Don't be in too great a fluster, and I warrant me I'll put the Philistines off their scent."

"But how am I to escape? Every door and window by this time is guarded."

"Never mind; don't make use of 'em," said Turpin, jocosely.

"But how am I to get out of the house?"

"Very easily."

"There is no time for fooling, Dick," replied Jack Sheppard, "when my neck may be stretched before I'm many days older."

"I quite agree with you. Hanging is not a subject for jesting," continued the still composed Turpin. "Take a drop of this; 'twill give you courage."

* To peach - to give information.
† To flip—to kill or wound.

There was a peculiar and sinister look about Dick Turpin as he uttered this remark and handed some brandy to his companion, who seemed to be too much occupied to notice his expression of countenance.

Jack Sheppard mechanically pressed the liquid to his lips, and gulped the contents of the vessel at a draught.

As he was returning it, Abraham Mendez, as if by magic, popped his head in at the door of the apartment, favouring its occupants with a sardonic grin.

His head was the only portion of his body permitted to enter, for the next moment he was flung heavily downstairs, carrying in his fall the portly personage of the landlord and Jonathan Wild, both of whom were following on the Israelite's footsteps.

Jack Sheppard, taking advantage of the prostrate trio, leaped over them, and gained the entrance of the inn.

As he emerged from the door, he was grasped tightly by an unexpected hand.

Looking up, he beheld one of his late goalers.

There was no delay, no hesitation on the part of the highwayman.

A blow from his pistol made his enemy bite the dust.

Leaving the inert mass, with the blood literally gushing from the wound, Jack Sheppard commenced running in direction of the field where a horse was waiting to receive him.

His danger was not yet passed.

At the outcry, Jonathan Wild and his men hastened to the spot from whence the sound proceeded, while another difficulty presented itself in the path of the pursued robber.

Though the late terrible encounter was but the work of a few seconds, it gave an advantage to those following in pursuit.

Threading the field, unprotected by bush or hollow, the fugitive was now a fair mark.

Ten weapons were raised, ten discharged.

The deadly missiles passed swiftly by, but failed, providentially, to reach or hit him.

He is still far in advance, but his race is nearly run.

Arriving at the tree under which Black Bess was tethered, Jack Sheppard sank at her feet, and an extraordinary sensation overpowered him.

His head felt light upon his shoulder, accompanied by vertigo, or dizziness.

His hands and feet were cold, though his exertion had been excessive, while every object around him swelled to a gigantic size.

Though in this strange state, he remained perfectly conscious, but at the same time imperfectly able to control action, thought, or words.

He fancied he saw a figure standing by his side, staring down, and staring at him.

His confused ideas seemed to recognise the form of Dick Turpin.

He was watching, with a grim smile, the efforts of Jack Sheppard to raise himself, without any motion to assist him.

The stupefied highwayman felt, as his sight grew dimmer and dimmer, for a sealed packet.

The man at his side made a sudden dash at it, but as suddenly checked himself.

The suspicion of treachery now entered his head.

The horrible idea did not daunt Jack Sheppard, but seemed to give a new impetus to his exertions.

"I must resist this drowsiness," he cried. "I must leave this spot while I have yet the power.

"Now, or never.

"Voices assail my ears, but it is not too late.

"They are upon me.

"I will not sleep. I will act, and force my muscles to their task."

By a superhuman effort, the speaker sprang to his feet, and was about to vault into the saddle, when his associate, Dick Turpin, flung him again to the ground.

His eyes glistened like a meteor, and glared blood-red.

His aspect was that of savage ferocity, and sudden resolution.

"Treacherous coward," exclaimed the prostrate man, "this is your work. To fall by a foe is man's common lot, to fall by a friend his direst fate. "I see it all now," he continued, "the brandy you gave me was drugged, that I might the more easily be vanquished. But I shall defy you yet; and, mark my words, Dick Turpin will live to rue the day he betrayed Jack Sheppard."

With these words, the speaker fell backwards, and, for a few moments, remained motionless, as if deprived of sense.

A hand was discovered stirring close about him, and forcing a passage to his bosom, where the coveted papers were concealed.

Presently, through the medium of his senses, Jack Sheppard could see the robber in front of him carefully select and put aside certain of the documents he had so foully possessed himself of.

Then he heard the sound of footsteps and the trampling of horses.

Jack Sheppard once more endeavoured to cast aside the langour which spread over him, and finally struggled into a sitting posture.

Here he recognised a man who had joined his late nefarious companion.

That man was the renowned and noted thief-taker, *Jonathan Wild!*

"The papers are ours!" exclaimed Turpin. "I have kept my word, Jonathan Wild. Now where is Roving Jack and the right to the estate?"

CHAPTER XCVIII.

THE CELEBRATED ESCAPE OF JACK SHEPPARD FROM THE OLD PRISON, MOORFIELDS.

AFTER his capture, Jack Sheppard was conducted to a dungeon in the old prison in Moorfields, at that time deemed the strongest place of "duresse" in the kingdom.

His daring deeds, on the highway and as a housebreaker, had rendered his name such a terror to the community, that the authorities had considered, on confining him in the strong keep, they could most effectually secure his person, and at the same time prevent any attempt at those escapes which he had effected with apparent ease from other gaols.

His cell was in a casement.

The fore part of the same was six feet wide and ten feet long, divided by a party wall.

In the inner wall were two doors, and the third at the entrance to the casement itself.

The window in the thick brickwork was so situated that though he had light, he could see neither sky nor living object.

Within and without this window were gratings of iron.

Chains were fixed to his ancles on the one end, and at the other to a ring, which was incorporated into the wall.

Another ring encompassed his body; from this hung a chain fixed into a bar, at the end of which was a handcuff.

It is here necessary to state that the old prison of Moorfields had originally been erected by the kings of former days for the purpose of incarcerating state offenders, hence its formidable character and aspect.

As a state prison it resembled very much in appearance some gigantic stronghold of a fortified garrison. It bristled with cannon, and was guarded night and day.

Ever having a detachment of the Royal Grenadiers stationed at the tower within its precincts, it was approached only by a drawbridge over a broad moat.

This drawbridge, again, was lowered only at certain periods of the day.

The moat surrounded the massive and gloomy pile, which was octagonal in shape, and composed of solid masonry.

The gates and doors within the building were ponderous, secured with iron, and apparently impregnable; the narrow windows were all covered with double bars; whilst every point and opening were strongly protected by spikes, sharpened rods, and chevaux-de-frise.

A wooden gallery, reached by two flights of steps, extended along the summit of the exterior wall, which bordered on the ditch forty feet above the bottom.

This terrace was constantly filled by sentinels, whom the officers visited every half-hour.

To any one who had the least notion of this fortress—its discipline, and the means taken to retain its inmates when once confined—the mere idea of escaping from it would appear the effect of insanity, and would inspire nothing but pity for the man so devoid of sense as dare to conceive it.

But the courage and boldness of the intrepid Jack Sheppard were raised by these obstacles, and he resolved to overthrow them or perish in the attempt.

Left to himself, the highwayman considered his situation in the worst point of view, and determined either on flight or death.

His detention became insupportable to his impatient temper.

Nothing seemed to him that might not be undertaken; and he began to deliberate how he must accomplish his purpose.

His first endeavour was to free himself of his chains.

In this he succeeded by forcing his right hand through the handcuffs. though the blood trickled from his nails in the effort.

His attempts on the left were long ineffectual.

Obtaining a brick from the grate, he went to work on the rivet.

It was negligently closed, and it at length yielded to his labour.

The chain was fastened to the rim round his body by a hook, one end of which was not inserted in the rim.

Thus, by setting his foot against the wall, he had strength so far to bend the hook back and open it as to force out the link of the chain.

The remaining difficulty was the chain that attached his feet to the wall.

The links of this chain he took, doubled, twisted and wrenched.

At length, by a desperate effort, springing forcibly up, Jack Sheppard succeeded in snapping off two links, and once more stood an erect, free, and almost unfettered man.

Thus fortunate, and able to move about with facility, he hastened to the doors of his dungeon.

These were doubled, and formed of stout oak.

Without, was an open space or front cell, containing a window, and likewise shut by double doors.

Jack Sheppard seeing the clinching of the nails by which the lock was fastened, conceived at once that no very large piece of wood need be cut.

His conjecture turned out in the end to be correct.

Setting to work vigorously with a knife he had secreted, he cut through the wood to find its thickness.

It proved to be only an inch.

Possessed of this knowledge, he found it was now possible to open all four entrances.

This would be a labour of some hours.

He might be disturbed before its completion.

Hope revived in his bosom, and he deferred his project till the following night.

To prevent detection it was now necessary to replace his fetters.

Groping about, the link that had flown off was found and hid.

Jack Sheppard, as in the case of the knife, had hitherto had the good fortune to escape examination, as the possibility of ridding himself of his bonds was in no wise suspected.

He now tied together the separated links ; but when he again tried to force his had into the ring, it was so swelled, that every effort to replace it was fruitless.

The whole night was employed upon the rivet, but in vain.

Noon was the hour of visitation, and danger and preservative caution obliged him to attempt forcing his hand into the handcuff.

After excruciating torture, he effected this necessity.

Everything had the appearance of order, and the warders entered and examined the dungeon.

After their departure, Jack Sheppard found it impossible to again free his right hand while it continued swelled.

He therefore remained quiet for several days.

On the forth night he was so far recovered as to be able to disencumber himself of his irons.

Taking his knife, he began his labour.

In half an hour the first of the double doors flew open.

The next was a very different task.

The lock was soon cut round, but it opened outwards.

Therefore, no other means were left but to cut the whole away above the bar that crossed it.

By incessant and incredible labour, this was done as the sweat dropped or literally flowed from the body of the captive, and his lacerated fingers were clotted with his own warm blood.

But he beheld the road to freedom before him. At the bright vista, his hopes grew stronger, and his efforts were redoubled.

The first of the next double doors was then attacked, which, turning inward, was as soon conquered as the previous one.

The fourth was now gained ; but had to be cut away as the second had been.

His strength here began to fail him. Both hands were raw.

Resting awhile. he began again, and made a cut a foot long. Suddenly the knife snapped, and the broken blade fell to the ground.

"Cursed chance," exclaimed the captive, "this is the end of all my hopes."

Dispirited, mad with pain, and wet with blood, Jack Sheppard returned to his cell.

As he laid on its rude pallet, his soul sighed again for freedom, and the bright beams of liberty again shone upon his path.

Reclining, he devised a plan that would forestall every obstacle, and anticipated measures by which he could overcome them all.

The first was to climb the chimney, in spite of its many bars and gratings.

These he managed to remove by using the iron leg of his flap table.

The iron he pointed by rubbing the metal on the floor.

This most painful and troublesome of his labours he accomplished ; though, in reaching the top of the chimney, he was entirely covered, and almost choked with the soot.

Not having the means of placing guards on his knees and elbows, they were so excoriated that the blood ran down on his legs and hands.

The roof gained, Jack Sheppard looked over the parapet, and found that he had to make a descent of at least sixty feet, while the cord which he had taken from his bedding amounted to but half the required length.

Consequently, he would have a very heavy fall.

The attempt was too hazardous, as from the great altitude he might be disabled, and of a necessity once more become a prisoner.

He groped his way for some distance in the hope of finding a portion of the building on which he could alight with more safety.

At length he came to the spot facing the governor's garden.

The night was extremely dark and cold, the snow heavily descending, while ever and anon the flash of some distant light from the building would disclose to his view the arms and accoutrements of the sentinels who paced their rounds on the boarded rampart, glistening and vanishing in the momentary blaze.

Arrived at the point above-named, Jack Sheppard discovered in close contiguity a tree of considerable size.

This tree, at a glance, he conceived would break his fall, and allow him to reach the ground in safety.

As quick as the thought, he lowered his rope and descended to the full tension.

Balancing himself with the cord on a stone projection, he gave a sudden leap into the tree.

Its branches received him, and by their means also he was enabled to descend into the garden beneath.

Crossing the paths he arrived shortly at the exterior wall.

Beneath the shelter of the wooden gallery at the summit, he went to work steadily to remove some of the stone-work to form an egress.

This he accomplished with a pointed iron bar he had removed from the chimney by which he had escaped.

He contrived to remove the granite blocks one by one, and in the end, succeeded in making a hole sufficiently wide to creep through.

This undertaking was completed in a very short time, for the chief of the rounds, provided with lights, inspected the spot every hour, and concealment would be impossible.

As Jack Sheppard passed into the aperture, he felt the road to freedom was now open.

To his dismay he found that he had a moat to cross, and another stone barrier to pierce.

The water was six feet broad and four deep at

this point, and a vigorous frost setting in, it was filled with floating ice.

Undaunted by fatigue, and benumbed by the cold, he remained in the moat, until he had succeeded in forcing a second passage through the wall, lying on its margin at the further side.

At the sight he gave way to transport, and was moved to tears.

As he sprang through the last opening, the watch came round with their lanterns, and from the gallery above, cast their lights upon the fugitive.

Just as the clock struck the fifth hour of morning, Jack Sheppard was on the high road.

The prison guns fired, and all was bustle and commotion behind him, sounding alarms to follow in his pursuit.

CHAPTER XCIX.

THE MEETING OF THE ROBBER-BAND IN HORNSEY WOOD ON MIDWINTER NIGHT—TRAVELLERS IN THE SNOW—THE CROSS OF GOLD—JACK SHEPPARD'S INTERFERENCE AND STRANGE INTERVIEW WITH VIOLET TREMAINE.

IT was towards the close of the eventful day spoken of in our last chapter that a company of highwaymen were seen to secret themselves in the intricacies of Hornsey Wood.

Their object in doing so was to waylay several rich travellers who were expected to pass that way on their road to London.

As the desolate country and wild region were clad in snow, each of the band was nestling in the warm fur cloak that covered him, and the whole of the men were stationed round a fire composed of wood gathered from the dismantled trees surrounding them.

Impatient of delay, the robbers had placed themselves in a position which commanded a view of the open road.

All were supplied with flasks of brandy, and seemed to drink deeply to the success of the expedition for which they were thus assembled.

"It is strange," said Tom Fielder, "that we have heard no news of the runaway."

"Captain Sheppard has good reasons for keeping out of sight," replied Blueskin; "he's not the man to desert his pals when there's danger threatening them, or business to be done."

"Well, Blueskin," said Nat Rose, "I know you've a sneaking kindness for Jack, and would always have a good word for him, if he gave you a ride backwards down Holborn Hill; but still I must say that his absence in the present instance is very unsatisfactory, and——"

"Stop, stop," interrupted Blueskin; "mayhap he don't know of the 'lay,' seeing as how he only slipped the darbies at Moorfields this blessed morning."

"Oh, bless ye, Edgeworth Bess has put him up to it; she's concealed at old Ishmael's, as he knows, and he wouldn't be an hour out of limbo without paying her a visit. In a word, Blueskin," continued the highwayman, "I have, for some time, had my doubts as to Captain Sheppard, and my suspicions aroused respecting his inattention to the interests of our fraternity."

"Captain Sheppard has lost his wonted courage ever since he formed a friendship with that fellow 'Roving Jack,'" said Fielder. "Plunder, which used to be his aim, he now shrinks from and, as I'm a freebooter, I think he would hardly dare to rob a hen-roost, if he had no eggs for breakfast."

"You are right, Tom Fielder!" exclaimed another of the gang, "for, as I am treasurer to this ere respectable society of toll collectors, I knows that the mopusses are uncommon scarce of late, and that my official office has become, in parliamentary language, a sinekoor (sinecure). Not a copper have I had in charge for the last six hours," continued the individual, "and, therefore, as I hate idleness, I begin to think of quitting this law'ess life, and return once again to flue-faking." *

"A marvellous good resolution, my pippin," muttered Blueskin, the lieutenant of the party. "But, remember, Master Simon Smut, that as you've only entered our society lately, we must have no shirking, no sheering off to the enemy, no traitors."

"Lor bless yer, Mr. Blueskin," replied Simon. "Though my spirit for adventure has led me into many difficulties, I don't think any one can accuse me of snitching.† I respects myself too much for that; besides, didn't I swear——"

"Yes, most roundly, when you were collared the last time we were crib-cracking." ‡

"No, I don't mean that sort of wulgar expression, I mean that I've taken a sacrament oath to be faithful and true to the lads of the 'high toby.'"

"Yes," replied Blueskin, coolly; "but the chances are, my queer cull, that you would forget your oath for the sake of the reward that has been so liberally offered by the government for the apprehension of one and all of us."

"Do you doubt my honour, Mr. Blueskin?"

"Honour?"

"Yes; I've always heerd about honour among thieves, and I wish to make myself agreeable to the company I keeps."

"None of your soft sawder, I tell you plainly, young soot-bag; that, as you have thought fit to enter into our hazardous service, so you must remain in it until——"

"Yes, how long?"

"Until death or Tyburn Tree shall relieve you from all further obligation."

While Blueskin was yet speaking, the lights of a distant carriage were seen, and its dark outline visible in the snow-covered roadway.

Fielder and Rose were directed to give an account of the travellers, to bring them to the robber's rendezvous, when they might, at their leisure, ease their pockets.

Immediately upon the order given, the two highwaymen hurried away.

In a few minutes a piercing shriek was heard and before Blueskin had time to ascertain from whence it proceeded, Fielder and Rose returned.

They bore with them a female.

The richness of her attire and nobility of her mein proclaimed her as one of the wealthy class who dwelt in London.

On perceiving her, Blueskin assumed a humble deportment.

He took off his hat, and approaching with much seeming diffidence, exclaimed,

"I ask your pardon, fair lady, for interrupting you in your journey; but as we are poor, take pity on us and bestow your alms."

"What would you?" demanded the terrified Violet Tremaine, for such was the name of the prisoner who had fallen into the hands of this fierce banditti.

"We would possess ourselves of whatever valuables you may have about you. For instance," continued

---

* Flue-faking—chimney-sweeping.
† Snitching—betraying.
‡ Crib-cracking—breaking into a house.

Blueskin, "now, here is a diamond necklace, and on your fingers are rings, sufficient to satisfy the most rapacious robber that ever cried 'Stand and deliver' to a noble damsel."

"Take them, they are yours," cried Violet Tremane, "and now suffer me to pass without further interruption."

"I cannot suffer you to part thus," replied Blueskin. "Consider, we have scarcely met, and besides, my comrades may not be satisfied that you have given up all you possess."

"You have everything of value."

"Not so ; this cross of gold and ring," exclaimed the robber, catching the arm of Violet, and eying the ornament that hung suspended from her neck.

"Nay !" replied firmly the weeping lady, "that you shall never have. Deprive me of the cross," she continued, "and life itself would be comparatively worthless."

"That's hard, too," growled Blueskin ; "but you must consider our necessities, fair lady ; we really must have it."

So saying, the robber, without further ceremony, unclasped and gave the golden cross into the hands of the treasurer—Simon Smut.

That worthy, having ogled the ornament with a peculiar glance, placed the same into the thieves' strong box—his breeches pocket.

"Oh, in mercy, take not that !" exclaimed the anxious Violet. "Let me but have that memento, and all the wealth I possess shall be at your disposal."

At that moment, attracted by the cries of the lady, a man had advanced to the spot.

It was Jack Sheppard.

His rich highwaymen's habiliments were travel-soiled and dirty, and his whole appearance was that of one who had suffered much from fatigue and great exhaustion.

Suddenly bursting in upon his lawless companions, he levelled a pistol at the head of the foremost who had advanced towards Violet Tremaine.

"He rushes on death who moves a step forward !" exclaimed Jack Sheppard.

The action had been so unexpected, that the whole party seemed one and all to be overcome by surprise.

Violet Tremaine was the first to recover.

She uttered a scream as she recognized the features of the highwayman.

He started at the summons, and encountered her glance.

Jack Sheppard conjectured little who was before him, for Violet had retained her veil during her interview with the banditti, and consequently had remained unrecognised by them.

With that quickness of perception which at once supplies information on emergency, he felt that the lady before him was in danger.

Dignified, and without betraying any emotion, he compelled his confederates at once to retire, which they did, with little grace and less satisfaction.

Jack Sheppard, nevertheless, retained his composure, and abided the issue of events with his arms folded on his breast.

After a pause, when alone, Violet Tremaine spoke, and addressed Jack Sheppard.

"You, sir, who appear to possess the power to enforce your commands, I thank you from my heart. Your followers," she continued, "have stripped me of all, and without a murmur have I yielded to them ; but that cross, of little value to others, is to me inestimable, 'tis the hope of my life, the only link to a destiny most cherished, yet most sad. Let the relic be restored to me, I implore you."

"You appear to be anxious for the bauble of which you have been robbed?" returned Jack Sheppard, coldly.

"More so than you can believe," answered Violet, with emotion. "You seem young ; your heart has not had time to harden, so listen to me. If the being you ought to love most in this wide world were lost to you—a father, a mother, a child—and you had alone this proof to recognise this being, say, would you not cling to retain the treasure?"

"With my best heart blood," replied Jack Sheppard, "and my life is already forfeited for an attempt of the same sort last night ; the token shall at once be given back to you."

With these words Jack Sheppard summoned Simon Smut to his side.

Taking the cross from the startled treasurer with a stern and stedfast gaze, he returned it to the anxious lady.

"A thousand thanks," she exclaimed ; "this generous action merits a reward and —"

"Since you consider yourself, madam, obliged to me," replied the highwayman, "I offer you the means of discharging the debt due to Jack Sheppard."

"Jack Sheppard, the man who——"

"Has restored you your cross. I would ask you to justify the poor outcast, as far as may be, in that society to which you are returning ; to tell the great ones of the land that you have made acquaintance with the execrated Jack Sheppard, and that you could receive him without blushing even in your own mansion."

"Your words, like your actions, are not those of a robber, like one brought up by chance, devoted to crime, perhaps even by the authors of his being," exclaimed Violet, still preserving the incognito.

"I am as chance left me," sighed Jack Sheppard, thoughtfully.

"Yet, would you live in arms against society?"

"Say, rather, why should I do otherwise? What boon should I ask of society—a name which it has refused me from my birth, a family which has doubtlessly rejected me as a disgrace? Society has treated me as a foe." continued Jack Sheppard. "Are we not even? A son of a felon, its laws have made war against me ; destitute I have made war against the laws."

"Hatred for hatred !"

"If ever I returned to its bosom it will be to combat it with greater advantage. 'Tis hard, I grant, to be hanged, but harder still to die of hunger."

"You renounce, then, all human probity?"

"Our probity is in sharing, yours in accumulating. It is very easy for the rich to be just and submit to laws which they have instituted for themselves against the poor," continued Jack Sheppard. "Those who roll in revenues and eat from plates of gold know not the toil that sometimes furnishes an honest meal. What is to be done, then, in a society which robs because you are poor? You must rob to become rich ; you must rebel openly, and obey only instinct, like us knights of the road."

Violet shuddered at the callousness with which the highwayman spoke.

"The life of a senator," he cried, "is less brave but more secure. Virtue and crime have been long only words. To kill a man is an act of itself, neither good nor evil, but which becomes, according to language, a murder or a victory."

"To take money on the highway," said Jack

Sheppard, in conclusion, "as I do, is a theft; but to impose an unjust tax on the people, and squander away the public wealth, is perfectly just and justifiable."

"You are jesting; this is unseeming levity," answered Violet.

"I do not jest, my good lady," exclaimed the robber. "Rogues you know must live; pilferers will be pilferers, whether upon the road, or in more dignified stations."

On a signal from Jack Sheppard, the carriage of Violet Tremaine drew up to the spot upon which she was standing.

"But your horses are ready," said he, pointing to the animals pawing the ground, as if anxious for their mistress's reception into the vehicle they were drawing. "You are at liberty to depart, madam, whenever it shall please you."

"Before I go, receive from my hand this ring."

Jack Sheppard received the gift from Violet Tremaine, while a low bow on his part seemed to give a tacit and speedy assent to her wishes.

"If," she continued, "I am not greatly mistaken, you will, ere long, quit your lawless life, and, should the bandage fall from your eyes, and repentance enter your soul, present that ring at the gate of the Royal Palace, and whatever your danger, whatever your situation, aid will come to you."

"I shall remember your kind offer, lady fair, and I trust, ere long, to be able to put them to the test."

With the words, Jack Sheppard led Violet Tremaine to her carriage, and, having seen her safely seated, he waited, apparently in deep reflection, till the vehicle was far out of sight.

CHAPTER C.

JACK SHEPPARD QUITS THE BAND—HIS ARRIVAL AT ST. JOHN'S GATE—THE FAITHFUL CHAMBERMAID—THE STRANGER IN THE NEXT ROOM—HOW THE INTENDED VICTIM FOILED AND DENOUNCED THE ASSASSIN.

JACK SHEPPARD once more returned to his comrades.

He was both surprised and enraged at beholding the coldness and hauteur with which he was received by them.

"Why, how now, Blueskin," he exclaimed, angrily, "you look out of temper."

"Then do I look as I feel, captain," replied the party addressed, with a brow scowling with rage and disappointment.

"Well, your anger matters but little," replied Jack Sheppard, "for we are now about to part—perhaps for ever."

Not more suddenly does the falcon turn at the call of her master than did Blueskin start at the words his comrade had uttered.

He peered into his face as if to seek some further confirmation as he stammered out,

"You don't mean that, Jack, do you?"

"Aye, but I do," replied the highwayman, "or in other words, I am about to turn honest. I shall abandon you and the band."

"By heaven, I thought so!" exclaimed Tom Fielder, ferociously.

As he spoke, he drew a clasped knife from his belt. Stealthily he crept towards Jack Sheppard.

In another moment the deadly weapon had been plunged in his breast but for Blueskin.

The latter arrested the blow, and whispered in the ruffian's ear.

"Hold, Fielder, this must not be, nor dare to stain your blade in the blood of him who has been so long the favoured of our gallant fraternity!

Nay! look not so fiercely," continued he, "or you dangle from the mare with three legs * in a jiffey."

Turning towards Jack Sheppard, Blueskin addressed him—

"And so you would turn honest, eh? 'Psha, you are clean gone mad to a certainty."

"Yes," replied Jack Sheppard, calmly, "I shall hasten to London and seek that fortune chance may throw in my way."

"Now, if I could not blow out my brains with the pistol I hold in my hand," muttered the faithful tobyman.

"Nay, I know you will not do that, Blueskin, because—"

"Because what?"

"Because you love me, man."

"That's true," replied Blueskin, hastily, "and no gammon. I've shared your perils like a man, and I'll follow you to the world's end like a dog. Now tell me Jack," he continued, "why are you about to quit the honorable profession in which you have embarked."

"I shall not quit it," answered the highwayman. "I shall be a robber still, but on a broader scale. The harm is not in thieving, man, but in the means employed. The fraudulent bankrupt stalks abroad often when the honest debtor rots in gaol.

"If you work against the law as we do," said Jack Sheppard, in continuation. "You gain little, and work in the dark; but come, clear up this cloud, Blueskin, look better tempered. We have known each other long—very long."

"Yes, captain, many's the crib we've cracked together when pale Oliver has put on his night-cap."

"Well, those days are over, we must shake hands and say good bye, unless, indeed, you will go with me. What say you, old friend?"

"No," answered Blueskin, doggedly, "the road is the best home for the brave, and I should cut a sorry figure in genteel society, where

'The priest calls the lawyer a cheat,
    While the lawyer be-knaves the divine,
And the statesman, because he's so great,
    Thinks his trade is as honest as mine.'

No, Jack, I can't be honest if I would. I was born to be a prig, and man can't control his destiny."

Both Jack Sheppard and Blueskin remained silent for a moment.

After the pause the latter was the first to speak.

"Well, for old acquaintance, captain, I won't send you into the world without something in your pocket; take this purse."

It was one that had been taken from Violet Tremaine, and appeared well filled.

"Take it," continued Blueskin, forcing the money on his unwilling companion, "for it may be a long time before you get the first proceeds of your new trade, 'honesty.'"

"Blueskin," said Jack Sheppard, "since you will take no refusal, I will accept the sum as a loan only; but mark you, it will be repaid, and with compound interest, too."

"As you like, boy, as you like. I know your proud spirit before to-day. But remember," continued the old robber, moved to tears, "these arms—my cabin will be ever ready to receive you when you have discovered the infidelity of the world."

"And remember you, Joe, that whatever be my fate—whatever befal me, you will hold the chief place in Jack Sheppard's heart."

With these words the highwayman tore himself from the embrace that Blueskin had offered him.

Mounting a horse, he rode rapidly away, and shaped his course in the direction of London.

---

* Dangle from the mare with three legs—to hang.

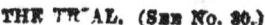

THE TRIAL. (See No. 30.)

As Jack Sheppard departed, his quondam associates gazed after him. All, save Fielder, evinced a silent sorrow. With him the feeling was very different. He had long entertained a feeling of jealousy towards his noble comrade, and now affected a belief that his motives in leaving the band were merely for the purpose of betraying it.

Secretly following Jack Sheppard to London, he put up at the "St. John's Gate," Clerkenwell Green, in which inn his intended victim had taken up his quarters for the night.

Here Fielder resolved to abide until an opportunity should offer when he might slay Jack Sheppard, and claim the large reward that had been offered for his apprehension.

While the highwayman was engaged in the stable looking after his horse, Fielder entered the house by another door.

Here he engaged a bed-room, where he purposed to remain till his plan was ripe for execution.

While buried in his black and gloomy reflections, his notice was attracted by the sound of voices in the adjoining apartment; and, as if fate favoured his design, the voices were those of his enemy, Jack Sheppard, and Millicent Hunt, the chambermaid of the time-honoured hostelry.

"Well, my pretty lass," said Jack Sheppard, favouring her with a kiss, "I'll warrant me, the old 'St. John's Gate,' unless it has lost its character, still keeps a good larder."

"Yes, so please you, gentle sir," replied Millicent, smirking, and apparently by no means displeased with the chaste salute she had received from the jovial guest; "we have meat, fish, and fowl, in galore, ready for the saucepan or spit."

"My keen appetite won't allow me, damsel, to wait for cooking. Have you no cold viands? I can make shift with a venison pie and a rasher of bacon."

"You must be a wizard, good gentleman; for that is one of the dishes that are now in the pantry."

"Then let me have it without delay, my charming abigail, for my journey has put a keen edge to my teeth."

Millicent at once departed to fulfil the order, which had been enhanced by a further one for a tankard of ale.

She shortly reappeared, spread a cloth of snow-white linen on the little table, and placed the pie and its adjuncts before the guest.

Jack Sheppard sat down, ate heartily, and drank lustily, stopping every now and then, in the course of his meal, to compliment his fair attendant, who, nothing loth, received the regard very graciously.

After the meal, as Jack Sheppard was gazing

round the room, his eye rested on a door in the apartment he had not hitherto observed.

Seeing it was one of communication he inquired where it led to.

"Oh, that door is seldom used," replied Millicent. "It conducts into another room, I believe; I have never passed through it, as it is always kept locked."

"To another room, you say," mused the highwayman. "Is it inhabited?"

"It is," replied Millicent; "but the partition is solid and the door thick, so that you need not fear interruption."

Satisfied with this answer, Jack Sheppard once more assumed a mien of good humour.

To cheer his spirits he requested his attendant to bring him a beaker of brandy, and slily slipped a half-crown into her hand for her assiduity.

As Millicent retired, the highwayman casually glanced at the purse he had taken out of his pocket to reward her.

He saw amongst the money it contained a scrap of paper.

Curiosity prompted him to unfold it.

It was a letter, written by the hand of the pirate-hunter, and addressed to Violet Tremaine.

"How had it come into his possession? It must have been taken by Blueskin from the carriage they had stopped at Hornsey Wood. It's occupant, then, must have been no other than—"

His contemplations were suddenly put a stop to by the appearance of Millicent, who bore on her face evident symptoms of alarm.

"Don't be afraid, good sir," she exclaimed, "as my apprehensions for your safety may be entirely groundless; still, to tell you the truth, if you have money about you, you can't be too cautious; there is no knowing who comes in or goes out of these inns, and since I've made inquiries about the man in the next room—"

"A man," interrupted Jack Sheppard, starting to his feet.

"Yes," answered Millicent, "and I've just understood that he busied himself very much about you and your affairs."

"How so?"

He only arrived while you were engaged in the stable, and, I am told, selected the room adjoining your own, and asked many very strange questions."

"This is singular. What sort of a man is this mysterious individual?"

"I have not seen him, but they say he is very ugly and not at all like you."

Jack Sheppard kissed away the compliment.

Millicent curtsied and retired, leaving the complaisant highwayman full of doubts and fears as to who could be the stranger in the next chamber.

Resolved to know the worst, he looked through the keyhole, from which the key had been removed.

To his consternation, he beheld Fielder advancing stealthily towards the door.

He held a large knife or poignard in his hand.

Not a moment now was to be lost.

To give an alarm would be certain destruction; to attempt to escape impossible.

As rapidly executing as conceiving an idea, Jack Sheppard extinguished the lamp with which he was furnished.

He had hardly done so, when the door was thrust open.

Behind it swiftly, and without noise, the highwayman concealed himself.

Breathless, he beheld the dark figure of the intruder move slowly towards the bed.

By the embers of the fire he saw his bright steel gleam in the air, and then descend.

The assassin had raised his dagger, and plunged it, as he thought, into the heart of his former companion.

As a tiger springs from his lair did Jack Sheppard pounce upon his secret foe.

There was no time for parley, penitence or prayer.

Before he could utter a word, Fielder's own blade was buried in his breast, and the floor of the apartment bathed by his blood.

He struggled for some time in the agonies of death, but the ebbing tide of life choked all utterance.

Seizing the dying ruffian by the throat, the highwayman exclaimed, with bitter irony,

"Miscreant! traitor! you would have had my life. I have taken yours. A reward is offered for the hunted outlaw; you shall pass for him. I will fire my pistol at your very brow; and when Tom Fielder is no more than an unrecognisable corse, without form, feature, or life, then will I call him Jack Sheppard, and gain that prize for which you have bartered a life. I shall be worth three hundred guineas; you will be dust. Stir not—'tis in vain," said Jack Sheppard to the feeble wretch, who endeavoured to release himself from the tight grasp with which he was held. "You wanted my place in the band; you shall have it in chains on the gibbet by the king's highway."

"Say no more, but kill me outright," groaned Fielder, as if suffering from intense agony.

"Have your wish."

With these words, the highwayman fired full in the face of his guilty accomplice, and then denounced him to the crowd assembled as the notorious and proscribed robber, Jack Sheppard.

CHAPTER CI.

THE SMUGGLERS' HAUNT ON THE ESSEX MARSHES —A FEW INCIDENTS THAT OCCURRED TO JACK SHEPPARD WHILST AN INMATE OF THE SAME.

ON the night after his adventure at the "St. John's Gate Tavern," Jack Sheppard found himself treading the Essex marshes.

The reason why he had chosen this rude and unfrequented tract will soon be made apparent to the reader.

The bleak, barren waste, the highwayman was traversing on foot, was a broad region of bog, fen, and moor, presenting an unvaried surface for miles around.

It was the haunt of the bittern, the refuge of the plover, whose shrill evening cry echoed through the morass, and pierced the ear of the passing wayfarer in the stillness of night.

It was deep winter, and the gloomy landscape was rendered still more cheerless by the mantle of falling snow.

On the eastern extremity of this extensive plain stood a solitary and lone house, surrounded by a stone wall, broken into chasms partially filled with weeds, by which the place is overgrown, and having an entrance leading to the main road through a dilapidated portal, beneath which is an old iron gate, swinging upon its rusty hinges in the biting blast.

The occupant of the tenement was, in the present instance, the gipsy, Red Ishmael.

Ostensibly (for his habitation was on the margin of the Thames) he fulfilled the duties of ferryman.

But, in reality, he was the principal of a gang of smugglers.

These ever used the place as a rendezvous, and where they might, with security, stow away their contraband merchandise.

Jack Sheppard, in order to avoid the gaze of the curious, who might either recognise or betray him, thought it better to leave the high-road, and take that cut across the marsh, to the house where he could count upon shelter and concealment.

He had reached the gipsy's tenement within a hundred paces, when a distant sound struck upon his ear.

As he turned to note the spot from whence it proceeded, he beheld a horseman spurring in his direction, and riding at the top of his speed.

Apprehensive of being followed, he passed through a cleft in the outward walls, and entered the premises of his friend, the ferryman, Red Ishmael.

From the exterior of this dwelling let us glide into the interior.

An antiquated chamber, meanly, but comfortably furnished, with a glowing fire roaring up its broad chimney.

The two occupants of this apartment are seated over a supper table.

The one is Jael, the gipsy girl, the other Edgeworth Bess.

"Red Ishmael," exclaimed the latter. "makes his return from London rather late. Why, Jael, you have prepared supper an hour too soon."

"He will not be long before he is here." replied Jael, thoughtfully, as though engaged in some deep contemplation.

After a pause she continued,

"He knows I am too timid to remain in this house alone, and without protection after nightfall."

"What, Jael, you are surely not afraid of ghosts?"

"No; but that terrible Dick Turpin!"

"Another lover?"

"Yes, and a very troublesome one," interrupted Jael. "You know how I dislike him, yet he follows me about as if he were my shadow, and starts upon me at each turning of my path as if I had made some appointment with him."

"I cannot say, Jael, that I admire the man myself. His character is, too, to say the least of him, suspicious. The band all consider that he had some hand in the last capture of Jack Sheppard."

"Yes; but the brave fellow is once more at liberty, and, as you know, will come to see us as soon as he can do so with safety. Red Ishmael has promised to give him concealment till he can communicate with his friend, Roving Jack, who, you know, now has power with the government, or he never could have got a reprieve for the gentleman highwayman."

"Ah," speaking of Tom King, "does Turpin know of your regard for him?"

"To be sure he does," replied Jael, with a smile; "but he laughs at his rival and swears roundly that though he's an odd-tempered fellow, that the road doesn't boast a better man."

"I trust he may never be deceived."

"I suppose you have heard the prophecy respecting my love?"

"Yes. Tom King is to fall by the hand of his best friend. Mark my words, Turpin will be his assassin, if there's truth in palmistry."

"Your words bring to my mind a fearful dream I had last night, followed by one more appalling."

Edgeworth Bess then continued,

"Methought I was dead in my coffin, and Jack Sheppard married me in my shroud."

"How horrible!" said Jael, with an involuntary shudder.

"I think nothing of it," was the remark of Edgeworth Bess, "nor do I believe in omens. He who made us, and framed the universe, can punish or avert as his wisdom see fit."

Further conversation was stopped suddenly by the appearance of Red Ishmael.

The gipsy was enveloped in the ample folds of a cloak, embroidered with a "Maltese" cross on the shoulder, while a broad-leaved hat rested on his profuse head of air.

His demeanour betokened anxiety as Edgeworth Bess addressed him,

"Welcome, Ishmael, supper is waiting for you. Take your easy chair. What's the matter?" continued the speaker, gazing at the troubled man. "Why this unusual paleness? You surely are not well?"

"Yes, well—very well," he replied, seating himself at the table, endeavouring to change the point of discourse; "get me a mess of hot pottage. I have fasted long and have need of it."

Edgeworth Bess hastened to obey, and shortly set the required dish before Ishmael, who had muttered to himself in the meanwhile the words,

"How shall I reveal it to her!"

Though the sentence had been spoken in a low tone, it had fallen on the ear of the attendant woman, and riveted her suspicions.

"You do not eat, Ishmael," she cried, after a pause, watching narrowly his countenance.

"No; if I do it will choke me."

Marvelling more than ever at the strange words uttered by the gipsy, and reproaching herself for not questioning him sooner, Edgeworth Bess repaired her error by at once enquiring—

"What has happened?"

"Tell me first, wench, when did you hear from Jack Sheppard?"

"Yesterday. A faithful friend brought news of his escape from the old prison of Moorfields, and that I might expect him sooner or later at this welcome refuge."

"I fear, girl," said Ishmael, "such hopes are a vain delusion."

"A delusion?" answered the woman, somewhat indignantly. "Jack Sheppard is as true as his own blade, and would never utter a falsehood—most of all to Edgeworth Bess."

"I fear that which I heard is too true."

"To what is it you allude? Does it affect the man I love? Is he dead? Let me know it; I would rather bear the worst."

"Listen. The streets of London to-day have resounded with one cry."

"Name it."

"That the inanimate body of the notorious Jack Sheppard had been found, frightfully mutilated, in a chamber of the 'St. John's Gate Tavern' at Clerkenwell Green."

The hands of Edgeworth Bess were hardly raised to brush off the tears that were gathering in her eyes when she heard the well-known accents of her lover's voice.

She caught at the sound, and rushed to the window to which Jack Sheppard had climbed.

Disengaging himself from the trellis work that hung about the casement, he entered the room, and springing forward, caught the overjoyed maiden in his open arms.

The next moment she fixed her eyes as if under the fascination of some venomous reptile.

She could not move her glance from him who stood before her, though she trembled as she gazed, and lastly muttered forth—

"Who speaks?"

"I, your true love, Jack Sheppard."

"A phantom!"

"No, but a wretch that would shake off mortality rather than endure the persecutions I have this day suffered."

"Are you alive?" said Edgeworth Bess, still labouring under the effect of the delirium into which she had fallen.

"Yes, this hand—touch it, girl—was ever yours," said the highwayman, hanging affectionately over her; "the heart it leads to still pulsates for thee. Touch it, I say, or thrill it into death."

In a few moments Edgeworth Bess recovered, and Jack Sheppard gave a hasty account of his escape from prison and assassination.

Her fond greeting, her many questionings, and ultimate surprise may be better imagined than described.

"I am sorry to spoil a love meeting," said Ishmael, who had witnessed the scene with a spirit of good-humour, "but I think it is necessary that I should have a word to say in this matter."

"He is a friend."

"And welcome here. But I fear he cannot tarry long."

"Why so?"

"You may depend upon it that when Fielder is missed, your artifice will be discovered."

"Granted."

"The whereabouts of Edgeworth Bess are known to the band, and this, in all probability, will be the first place that will be searched."

"You are right, Ishmael," said Jack Sheppard. "I will put out to sea at once, for I have formed a project that I hope may end my days in happiness."

"It is impossible. My lugger can never make headway; for the hard frost of the last few days has covered the Thames with ice, and I myself passed over it to reach the opposite bank."

"What is to be done, then?"

"Nothing—till a thaw allows us to proceed on an outward voyage."

"Till that time?"

"I must give you shelter."

While Ishmael was speaking a loud knocking was heard at the outer door, and a clamour of many voices.

The intruders one and all appeared restless, impatient, and determined.

For they had no sooner summoned admittance into the house than they enforced it by bursting open the door.

Before Jack Sheppard could descend from the window footsteps were heard on the stairs.

Ishmael spoke not, but pointed to a very broad cedar chest that stood in the corner of the room.

The hint was sufficient; the highwayman was its occupant in less than a second, whilst Edgeworth Bess hastily concealed herself behind some hanging curtains that garnished the apartment.

So rapid had been these incidents that a minute had not elapsed since their commencement and the entrance of the man and his followers who had so unceremoniously broken into the house.

The leader of the party wore black crape over his face, as if for the purpose of disguise, and carried a burning torch in his hand, which, on coming into the room, he stuck in the floor near the fire.

Casting a glance round the room, he exclaimed, in a voice of thunder—

"Where's Jack Sheppard? We knows he's here, so deliver him up, if you'd save your neck from a halter."

"Jack Sheppard? He's not been with us, or——"

"You lie, dog; he has been traced to this hovel, and woe to all who give him shelter."

"You call me dog; that is not a name that Red Ishmael can answer to."

"Oh, I see, you have turned genteel; that cursed word has been a rock a-head. When I first knew you, you were a plain, toiling artisan; your wife a brisk sempstress; you were no sooner wed than she dinned that word 'genteel' in your ears; you robbed your master; you flirted on till you robbed again, and still you flirt on as near the gallows as may be."

"You seem to know me well," replied Red Ishmael; "but no better than I know you; you are—"

"Jonathan Wild," replied the other, revealing his features by moving the crape that covered them.

The gipsy started on seeing the thief-taker.

"Well," he continued, "what ails you? One would think you had encountered a wolf instead of a friend."

"A friend!"

Red Ishmael gave a sarcastic grin as he uttered the word.

"Yes; haven't we known each other for years? Haven't we tippled together till our tongues have wagged like bell-clappers, and our hearts become as warm as spiced ale? Did not we agree to rob your master's house. and didn't I blow the gaff upon you?"

"Villain!"

"Call me what you will, Red Ishmael; fortune has placed you in my power, and I were worse than an ingrate—a fool, not to avail myself of the advantage."

"I do not understand you."

"You will do so, presently; in a word, give up Jack Sheppard, or you may chance to find yourself under Tyburn tree, or with as many bullets in your body as there are spots in a deer-skin."

"You have had my answer," replied Red Ishmael, with firmness.

"Enough; and you shall shortly learn my determination. Secure him."

Jonathan Wild had no sooner uttered the words than his myrmidons darted upon Red Ishmael.

He offered no resistance, but treated them with a sardonic smile.

They first pinioned him, and passed strong cords around his body. These again were passed through a firm iron hook in the wall, which gave their prisoner no chance of moving more than a foot in any direction.

The gipsy made no remonstrance at these proceedings, but displayed self-restraint, and continued equally silent.

Jonathan Wild, having satisfied himself of the security of the captive, ordered his men to leave him to himself, and search the cellars beneath the building.

"I am told," said he, "leading from them is a communication to the river, and the runaway has hoped to avail himself of the secret passage; as we have not given him time for a light, he is, doubtless, in the intricacies of the same."

The thief-taker, having whispered a few inaudible words into the ears of his companions, they departed on the errand on which he had sent them.

Edgeworth Bess, watching her opportunity, glided out, and followed on the footsteps of the men who had quitted the apartment in which she had been concealed.

Silently descending the stairs, she saw them enter the place to which Jonathan Wild had directed them.

They were no sooner in the cellar than she secured the door upon them, and hastened to achieve her grand point.

"I must, if possible, prevent the use of fire-arms," she said, creeping stealthily back to her original hiding-place; "for the alarm will give a warning to the men I have so easily entrapped; but, should it be necessary, we must take our chance."

Jonathan Wild, in the mean time, had menaced his prisoner; failing to extort a confession from him by conciliatory means, he was determined to try the effect of coercive measures.

"Red Ishmael," he exclaimed, "the time was when you had no roof for your head to rest under o' nights; your curtains were the wild hawthorn hedge, your candle the pale glow-worm, and your pillow the moss-covered stone. Since you have thrived, and, by roguery, scraped together a few golden pieces—wrung from the idiots who have consulted your infamous conjurations and astrological cheats—you suppose that you can impose upon me. Mark me," continued the thief-taker, "I give you five minutes to consider whether you will obey me or not; refuse, and a terrible doom awaits you."

Jonathan Wild paced the room for a few moments. There was malice in his eye—revenge on his lip.

Suddenly he discovered, in the further part of the room, a heap of loose straw.

Drawing it aside, he came upon a barrel, on which was inscribed the word, "powder."

"Sure, hell itself has sent this cask and its contents to anticipate my purpose; nothing could be better."

With the passive demeanour of an anchorite the thief-taker took out a quantity of the powder, and coolly continued to lay a train across the room leading to the passage outside.

It was at this juncture that Jael, the gipsy girl, rushed to his side, and perceived his dreadful intention.

"Oh, heavens!" she exclaimed, "what would you do? Oh, let me warn you from perdition's brink."

"What would I do?" laughed Jonathan Wild, hoarsely; "can't you guess, girl, by this powder in my hand? blow this house and its contumacious tenant into atoms."

"You will not be so cruel," shrieked the terrified maiden.

"Cruel? pshaw! you are young; you have never felt the pleasurable pang of revenge."

"You will sacrifice us all."

"No; the innocent will not suffer for the guilty. You, myself, and companions will leave the house; he alone will remain."

Jonathan Wild with his last words indicated Red Ishmael, who bearded his adversary with a look as bold and defiant as his own. He had, however, made up his mind without calculating chances.

Suddenly the torch which lighted the apartment was covered by a woman's cloak.

The fire in the grate being extinguished, all was in total darkness.

Stamping with rage, Jonathan Wild exclaimed—

"A spy—a traitor; whoever he may be, he shall dearly rue his temerity."

Rushing from the room he encountered, at the door, Edgeworth Bess. In her hand she held a pistol at the staggered thief-taker.

"Monster!" she cried, while passion almost subdued her strength; "one step further at your peril."

Jonathan Wild started beneath the fierce woman's gaze, to which the moon through a window gave a pale blue light.

"Witch! how gained you entrance here, standing there like an accusing spirit in the beams of night?"

Overcoming his momentary superstition, the thief-taker continued—

"Who are you?"

"One you should know ere this. I am Edgeworth Bess."

"Ah! what is your purpose here?"

"To avert a deed of cruelty."

"Foiled!"

"No; you are the first to perish."

Anticipating an attack, Edgeworth Bess levelled her weapon. It hung fire, and she was foiled.

"Thank you, Bess; I hold a charmed life," exclaimed the thief-taker. "Let me give you a caution; before you use your snappers, just look to see if the flints are all safe."

He was preparing to cut the woman down with his hanger when his arms were clasped from behind.

Jack Sheppard had issued from the cedar chest in which he had hidden, and come to the rescue just as she had fallen senseless at the feet of her merciless enemy.

At this moment was heard an outcry from below. It was the voices of those imprisoned in the cellar, and who had discovered the trick practised on them.

Wild's shouts, mingled with those of his enraged attendants, arose loud and stunning. The region resounded with imprecations loud and deep.

There was no time for deliberation, for the officers were breaking through the impediment that encumbered their path.

Jack Sheppard dragged his struggling antagonist to the edge of the deep staircase, and precipitated him over the bannisters to the floor beneath.

His great weight accelerated his fall, and he descended head foremost.

Taking advantage of the senseless state in which the ruffian had alighted, Jack Sheppard's next object was to circumvent those who were now coming to his aid.

Bearing the fainting form of Edgeworth Bess into the chamber in which the late scenes had been enacted, he, with the assistance of Jael and the now liberated Ishmael, proceeded to barricade its door, the heavy cedar chest and cumbrous furniture forming a most efficient obstruction from within.

The fugitives had completed this task, descended by the window into the garden, and entered the wizard's shaft—of which we shall give a description in the next chapter—before their enemies were able to make the slightest progress with the difficulties that beset them.

CHAPTER CII.

JACK SHEPPARD'S PERILOUS PASSAGE OF THE FROZEN THAMES.

WHEN Jack Sheppard and the companions of his flight arrived in the garden of the Ferry House, his attention was attracted by Red Ishmael to a withered chesnut-tree that stood near them. It was large, solitary, and lightning-scathed, and named the "Wizard's Shaft." The reason why it was so called may be learned from the following lines :—

In the huge trunk of the tree was a secret door, distinctly visible from the print of a bloody hand impressed upon it.

Tradition had assigned a cause for this mysterious mark.

"In olden times, so the story goes," exclaimed Red Ishmael, addressing his friends, "a traveller, clinging to the spot, was murdered, and since that time 'tis said no one has been able to remove the stain of guilt."

With the words the speaker opened the entrance, and disclosed in the hollow of the tree a deep abyss—gloomy, wide, and descended by a deep staircase hewn out of stone.

This led to a passage under ground, which, opening some half mile further up, formed a secret entrance to the Thames, and was used by Ishmael and his smuggling band to land their unlawful cargoes.

The gipsy had more reasons than one for availing himself of this retreat. Besides concealment and security, it afforded further means of escape.

As the reader has been already informed, the continued and severe frost had really, in many places, made the Thames a highway for travellers on foot, while it had hemmed in its chilling embrace the craft that usually floated on its waters.

Near the spot indicated by Ishmael the ice was so thick that it would bear a burden of great weight; while, at the same time, it stretched itself across the river, thus giving a free passage from one bank to the other.

This was just the requirement of the fugitives; for, encamped on some neighbouring ground of the opposite shore, was the tribe of Red Ishmael. Once arrived at this rendezvous they might defy anything like pursuit.

It is unnecessary to follow Ishmael and his companions through the passages of the subterranean roadway, but come at once to its outlet on the river, for to this point they had arrived in safety, and the Thames at their feet with its broad expanse or sea of ice appeared as some dreary and impassable waste.

I's surface was broken and irregular, and covered with a thick clothing of recently fallen snow. Here and there were dark chasms or openings, through which unfrozen water had burst its bondage; while again in many parts were treacherous pitfalls dug for the unwary, the stream having partially thawed, and hiding its bosom only by a thin and fragile coating of ice.

Narrow paths, known only to the dwellers on the borders of the river, now intersected it in various places, and to attempt to cross the frigid path without a guide would be as perilous as an attempted passage of the trustless quicksand.

"As I suspected," cried Ishmael, "we have reached the river in safety; from this spot I can see smoke curling from the camp fires. Courage, and we shall reach them before our followers can escape from the house we have left behind."

"And yet," replied Edgeworth Bess, "it is a terrible alternative and fraught with so many unseen dangers."

"A stout heart, Bess, and all will go well with us," exclaimed Jack Sheppard. "Ishmael knows the perilous pass; trusting to his guidance and the guidance of heaven, we shall make a way over the frozen river as safe as its banks on which we are now standing."

"The moon has hid her head. Is it safe to make the venture in the dark? Shall we wait till morning?"

"If we wait till morning the venture will not be made at all, for our pursuers, aided by daylight, will discover our track."

"'Tis our only chance. Every moment is precious, and a grave in the river is better than a felon's grave in Newgate."

With these words the passage of ice-girt Thames was essayed by the fugitives.

The hazardous experiment might have inspired terror in stouter hearts, but its achievement gave them life and dispelled every fear.

In many parts the tract was soft, slabby, and pliant, that it seemed scarcely able to bear the weight of a water fowl.

As Ishmael and his followers hurried on the unsecure footing the quivering ice bent and groaned beneath their feet, leaving behind them rents, cracks, and chasms. While yet completing the dangerous journey new dangers beset them.

Behind them came loud shouts, and the tramp of many feet.

The warning was not unheeded, and told the fugitives that the pursuers had descried them, and were at hand.

"By hell, I see them!" exclaimed the leader, in a loud voice of triumph; "their figures are distinctly discernible in the snow."

"Where! where!" cried twenty voices.

"To the left," was the reply. "The rash fools are endeavouring to cross the ice."

"Cost what it may, they shall not escape me. Follow in their track, and they yet may be taken," thundered Jonathan Wild.

As the thief-taker spoke he descended the bank, and, with his attendants, made for the road his flying prisoners had taken.

Ishmael was now heard exhorting.

"Follow me, in Indian file," he said; "we have arrived at the wished-for goal, and a minute's caution will see us in safety, while our foes will perish in our footsteps. Do not swerve a hair's breadth from my track, or such a deviation would be fatal."

The gipsy was uttering the last word when a shriek of despair thrilled through his veins.

There was a floundering plunge, and three human beings were emerging from under the ice.

After a short struggle in the water came horrible and stifled cries.

It proceeded from the drowning men, and told the pursued that three had been destroyed in endeavouring to seize them.

"The poor creatures have sunk!" cried Jael. "What a fearful death!"

"Have care, girl, for yourself," replied Jack Sheppard, "or, like them, incautious, you may meet a similar fate."

"Quicken your pace," cried Ishmael, "our enemies have taken a fresh track, and may reach us before we reach the gipsy encampment at the 'Devil's Gap yonder.'"

At this moment a shot was fired.

It knocked off the hat of the gipsy without doing further damage.

The man who had fired, being in advance, fancied he had hit his mark, and announced his triumph exultingly to his companions.

The next moment, a ball from the pistol of Jack Sheppard numbered him with the dead.

"Waste no more powder and shot, Jack," exclaimed Ishmael; "they have diverged from the beaten road, and will perish to a man."

When Jack Sheppard and his companions had passed the river in safety, he stood in silence upon the bank.

As he listened to the advance of his pursuers, the prophecy of the gipsy was terribly verified.

The hapless party, fearful of the escape of the fugitives, had taken, as they supposed, a nearer cut to the shore.

The course they had taken was madly venturesome, and they were totally unacquainted with the dangers that beset the frozen river at almost every point.

As they were passing over it, suddenly, and without warning, the sides of a snow-bank became loosened, and were drawn from their edge.

The next instant, the whole sheet of ice broke with a wild roar into myriads of pieces.

The whole of the advancing party, in consternation and alarm, descended at once into the vast crevice.

Some made an effort to reach the brink of the cleft, but the weight of their bodies only further shattered it.

Some threw themselves upon a flat surface, but the screams and struggling of those in the waters destroyed the frail support; while others, benumbed and exhausted with fatigue, were sucked beneath the ice never to rise again.

As one by one became engulphed they implored assistance in most piteous terms.

Their agony was mocked and prayers wholly unheeded by the fierce Ishmael, and fiercer still, Jack Sheppard.

In a few appalling moments not one of the numerous victims flitted before their eyes, while the moon, throwing an earthly glitter over this part of broken river-ice, fully revealed their rigid figures, stretched in a ghastly shroud of water, and in death.

"We are triumphant," exclaimed Jack Sheppard. "Not one of our pursuers lives to tell this night's tale of horror."

"Heaven have mercy on them," said Jael. "May our souls be spared this terrible crime."

Averting her head from the dreadful scene, the gipsy girl uttered a prayer.

She was joined in the supplication earnestly by Edgeworth Bess.

"All is over, and our danger is passed."

With the words, the highwayman turned to lead onwards, and commenced the ascent of the bank.

"No, there is yet a miserable wretch left," rejoined Ishmael, looking behind him; "he is still battling with the stream, and likely to extricate himself."

"I see him. He is within pistol-shot."

Jack Sheppard raised his arm to fire.

Jael arrested it.

"Oh, no, spare him whom heaven appears to spare," she cried; "too many guilty and unhappy beings have been sacrificed already."

"As you will, Jael," answered Jack Sheppard, unwillingly replacing his weapon in his belt. "I trust no mischief will come of this clemency; and that the man snatched from death may not betray you in return for the obligation."

Little did Jack Sheppard know that the man saved was Jonathan Wild, the thief-taker.

Little did Jael know that the life she had pleaded for, was that of *   *   *   *

CHAPTER CIII.

THE THIEVES' CAVE IN THE OLD MINT, SOUTH-WARK.

THE Old Mint was situated in an obscure quarter of the Borough of Southwark.

It was skirted by a deep and broad kennel, called The Moat, which fell into the Thames near old London Bridge, and bordered by neglected gardens, running in the direction of St. George's Fields.

It was inhabited only by thieves, mendicants, gipsies, and the most nefarious characters.

These fled hither either for security or to escape the punishment due to their different crimes or offences.

Like the Alsatia of old, it gave refuge to the destitute and depraved, and offered sanctuary to the robber, pirate, or even murderer.

Its numerous ramifications, secret haunts, and mysterious outlets defied pursuit of the fugitive from justice, whose officers shrunk from entering the terrible precincts with the same sort of aversion as the traveller avoids the coiled embrace of the hideous serpent.

If one, with more temerity than his brotherhood, chanced to enter the purlieus, he must have been a sly fox indeed ever to come out of them again.

A mock monarch, called the "Master of the Mint," governed the disreputable locality.

This post, at the period of our story, was filled by one Baptist Kettleby.

He was supported in his authority by two other functionaries, bearing the titles of Lord High Chancellor of the Cadgers, and Privy Purse of the Canting Crew.

Joe Blueskin had accepted the latter office, with all its emoluments and perquisites, showing a balance of nothing on the debtor side of the account.

To the sanctum sanctorum we have described, Simon Smut had come as fast as his legs would carry him.

Plunging into many a puddle, dashing into many a blind alley, and meandering over broken pavements, he was forced to pause in hesitation.

The entangled intricacies of the narrow lanes and courts had so perplexed the murky individual that the maze at Hampton or Rosamond's Bower must have at once occurred to his oblivious mind.

"Devil take these ere cussed winding streets!" exclaimed Simon, panting for breath, "since the devil must have been the architect, and planned them arter the fork with which he picks up us blessed sinners. I don't see my way into or out of 'em clear any way. It seems to me," he continued, to himself, clapping his forefinger to the side of his nose, "that I've undertaken a wild goose chase, and that the only goose in the affair is my precious self."

Suddenly the speaker espied a long, narrow street, that had hitherto escaped his notice.

He at once darted down it.

It was sloping and unpaved, and became more and more soiled with mud the farther he proceeded down it.

Going towards a light, seemingly at the bottom of the thoroughfare, he encountered three individuals, the first being the Whip-Jack.

He was habited in his sailor's gear, consisting of a guernsey shirt and very dirty canvas trousers.

He appeared to be a cripple, and to have suffered mutilation, if the observer would take trouble to notice his lower limbs, which presented a complicated system of the wooden-leg institution.

The Whip-Jack addressed Simon Smut in Romany, pedlar's French, or idiomatic slang.

It was all one to the chummy, who knew not what to make of the singular reception, so imitated the gesture of the worthy accosting him for an answer to his question.

The second of the two now wriggled himself up to the stranger.

He was the Palliard of the vicinity.

Like his companion, the Whip-Jack, he was a cripple, but one of another species.

He appeared to have no legs at all, and was hopping about upon both hands, while he was seated in something resembling a bowl.

This deformed being gave vent to a greeting in some foreign lingo.

"And he must be a clever fellow," thought Simon, "if he understands it himself."

So, as no good came of this interview, he made up his mind to quicken his pace, and was about to decamp when the third party obstructed his path.

He was the Dummerar.

A board on his breast signified that his tongue had been cut out (while in imprisonment) by the Algerines.

Chummy, supposing correctly that the dumb cannot spead, and that his last saluter was less likely to express his intentions than the former two, bestowed a benevolent smile on his companions, and trudged off.

In a trice the Drummerar followed in his footsteps, accompanied by the clatter of the bowl of the Palliard, and the thump, thump of timber-toes of the Whip-Jack on the pavement.

All these in pursuit, and treading upon the heels of Simon Smut, opened a volley upon him at once.

He stopped his ears and made a run for it; but of no avail, for also ran the Whip-Jack, the Palliard, and the Dummerar.

The latter finding miraculously use of the tongue that had been cut out by the Algerines, and making the welkin ring with his shouts.

In a minute the denizens of the Mint were attracted to the running contest.

Their name was legion, which, as a ball of snow, gathered as it rolled.

The three pursuing fiends stuck to the fugitive as bird-lime to a twig.

No respite—no cessation—each pursues his way.

The Whip-Jack unbuckled his strap, shouldered his wooden legs, and leaped like the bounding roe from the hunter.

While the Palliard, standing bolt upright upon his feet, clapped his heavy bowl of wood upon poor Simon's head, and led him in darkness to a favourite rendezvous.

"Where am I?" cried the affrighted man.

"In the Thieves' Cave in the Mint," replied the Dummerar, with a fluency of speech very different from his previous muteness.

Simon Smut, relieved of his bandage, cast his eyes around him.

He was in the nefarious den above alluded to.

Here no honest man had ever penetrated; here unblushingly crime uncovered its guilt-stained visage.

Here no delegate of justice dare show his face, or, doing so, would pay a fearful penalty for his rashness.

It was the haunt of the highway robber and petty pilferer; the abode of vice, mendicity, and vagabondism.

Within its limits now appeared assembled gipsies, burglars, roadsters, and blackguards of every description, foreign as well as native.

The ranks of this body were further increased by the presence of "morts," "antem morts,"* "dells," "doxies," and their "coes."

Fires, around which stood motley groups, were blazing far and near.

All was bustle, uproar, and confusion, mingled with the coarse laughter of men, the shrill voices of women, and the smothered cry of neglected children.

Simon Smut, by the faint and flickering light of the fires, was enabled to notice the peculiarities of the place into which he had been ushered.

It appeared an immense apartment, worm-eaten, ruinous, and falling into decay.

The walls were perforated by sundry small windows; at least, they might have been windows had such recesses contained glass.

Above were sculptured several faces of odd loooking hags, who might be fancied as witches watching some nocturnal orgies.

In fact, the whole region appeared to the eyes of the spectator as some unknown world inhabited by creatures as fantastic and extraordinary as that world itself.

Simon Smut was still held by his three persecutors, and deafened by the bleating voices of the throng around, who, with one accord, shouted, "Lead the intruder to our monarch!"

From every quarter burst forth derisive cheers as he was conducted to the august presence of the "Master of the Mint."

Near the largest fire, upon a hogshead of no matter what, this potentate, Baptist Kettleby, was seated, arrayed in the mock insignia of royalty.

He presented a mirthful countenance, heightened by that artistic touch, "love of liquor."

His eye was sparkling, his cheek red, which, by the bye, as in a spirit of generosity, had imparted a similar hue to his nasal prominency, for the "Master of the Mint" had, in its true sense, a "very jolly nose."

His lips were also rubicund, moist by frequent potations, mellow as an autumn plum, and endued with a peculiar curl; this gave him the character of good humour, while it imparted also a sort of dignity in his official capacity.

He was reposing on his rude throne, smoking the calumet of peace, and quaffing his favourite tipple, dog-nose, when the offending Simon Smut was brought before him.

"What dirty varlet have we here?" asked Baptist Kettleby, assuming at once all the grandeur of mien of the "Great Mogul" or the Emperor of the Indies.

"Your highness, my lord," stammered forth Simon.

"Call me master or comrade, which you please, only make haste about it. What have you to say in your defence?"

"I don't half like them words; it puts me in mind of the big wigs. I went once among 'em."

"By the devil's hoof this is trifling," interrupted the now testy Baptist Kettleby; "your name?"

"Simon Smut."

"Then, Simon Smut, mark me," continued the Master of the Mint, "since thou art in my august presence I tell thee, as thy judge, thou hast entered our territories without being one of its subjects. Thou hast violated the privileges of our notable sanctuary, and unless thou art a prig, a cadger, or a vagrant, thou wilt—"

"I've the honour to be all them three individuals," replied Simon, hastily.

* Antem morts, or unmarried women.

BEARING HOME THE BODY.—*See No. 31.*

"Where are your testimonials ?"

"I ain't got none."

"Then let those who can speak to thy badness of character stand forth."

"Bless yer, I don't know not never a soul in this 'ere slum."

"Then," said the Master of the Mint, waxing wrath, "must thy body be fastened in a sack, passed through yonder window, and thrown into the Borough moat."

"My eyes, what treatment," replied Simon, who had recovered sufficient firmness to talk resolutely. "Now if any of you had come down to our crib at Cow Cross I should have axed you in."

After this announcement he continued—

"I should have fetched yer a pot o' heavy, a new buster and some Field Lane sasengers, and there ain't no better nowhere, say nothing of the max as is to follow."

"Give us your hand, old fellow, them's my sentiments ; your heart's in the right place, and I'll stand by you."

The party uttering these words had only just entered the circle of the august assemblage. He was received by some such an ovation as that offered to a crown prince by the inhabitants of a small German principality.

Before them was one of the luminaries of the great prigging world, Joe Blueskin, their privy purse, who had literally *fought* his way to greatness, and maintained his dignified position by his strong *right arm.*

Cheer after cheer welcomed his appearance ; clapping of hands and thunders of applause lasted for several moments.

Finally, Blueskin doffed his beaver, which he had withdrawn to acknowledge his favours, and the popular demonstration was hushed into nothingness by the stentorian voice of the Master of the Mint.

"Since thou wilt be sponsor for the varlet who has had the audacity to enter our realms without the types of authority," said Baptist Kettleby, addressing Blueskin, "it is necessary henceforward that he become one of us."

Simon Smut caught eagerly at the proposition.

"Thou consentest to enrol thyself, then ?" rejoined the Lord-Chancellor of the Cadgers, who now appeared in such a state of intoxication as to create doubts in the public mind whether he would be able to fulfil his duties as their legal functionary in the matter in hand.

"Unroll myself?" answered Simon. "In course I do."

"Thou acknowledgest thyself one of the crew?" interrupted the master of the Mint.

"One of the crew?"

"Echo not my words," he continued; "but tell me if thou art willing to become a subject of the kingdom of slang."

"Decidedly so."

"Good; then let us at once proceed to the inauguration."

A wild shout was raised by the whole assemblage, who placed Simon on an oaken table.

The principal, turning to the novitiate, with a dirty skin of parchment in hand, upon which were inscribed certain strange characters, commenced his harangue in a solemn voice—

"Kneel down, Simon Smut, and repeat the requirements of our fraternity."

He obeyed the mandate, while the Master of the Mint mounted on the table, and stood by his side.

"In the name of High Pads, Queer Gills, and Sarkmen, I swear to be true to this brotherhood. That I will obey the authority of those who reign in the region of scamp. That I will never peach, split, or blow the gaff on my pals on the mouching lay. And finally, I will serve truly, and interfere never with the rights of Crank, Cuffin, Dimber-Damber, or Olli Compolli, by which title his excellency the upright man is distinguished. In witness thereof, 'So help me Salamon!' the oath of our creed."

After repeating the abjuration Simon Smut received a smart thwack from the lath-sword of the Lord-Chancellor of the Cadgers, who performed his office with all due honour and drunken gravity.

"To be admitted into our fraternity," said the Master of the Mint, "thou must show thyself worthy of such an honour, therefore at once prove thy skill at picking a pocket."

On a given sign several vagabonds brought forward a portable gibbet, from this was suspended the stuffed figure of a man, the effigy being covered with as many bells as a drove of Castilian mules.

Baptist Kettleby pointed to a rickety stool placed under the above-named figure.

"Get upon that," he said.

The words were addressed by the Master of the Mint to Simon Smut, who the next moment mounted.

The stool quivered under his weight, but by oscillations frequent of arms and legs, he contrived to maintain his centre of gravity.

"I shall break my limbs," cried the equilibrating individual.

"Better them than thy neck beneath the 'wooden shroud.'"*

"What am I to do now?"

"What I shall tell thee."

"Proceed!"

"Stand on tiptoe that thou may'st reach the dummy under the halter."

"Consider it done."

"In the pocket of the same you will find a purse."

"What then?"

"See if thou canst filch it without making any of the bells speak."

"Should I succeed?"

"Thy freedom of the Mint is granted, and thou art an established, enfranchised, and complete vagabond."

"But, spite o' me, should the tinklers chatter?" exclaimed Simon.

"Why, then, my queer cull," chimed in Blueskin, "thou wilt be soundly thrashed within an inch of thy life.

"This wholesome chastisement will continue for a week, or so; or rather, to such times as thy proficiency in the craft of 'fly faking,' shall render it unnecessary.

"Then, and not until then, shall we call thee a comrade, and a worthy member of the community of the 'Island of Bermuda.'"*

"Come, quick, varlet, said the Master of the Mint, stamping his foot impatiently upon the barrel he had remounted, whose hollowness caused it to sound something like a big drum. "To thy task; recollect if I hear a single clapper, thy shoulders smart for it."

The motley crowd applauded the words of Baptist, and ranged themselves in a circle round the tristful tree.

Their pitiless laugh greeted Simon as he advanced, whilst the bells of the effigy, with their tolling tongs, seemed to him as so many serpents, ready to bite his tremulous hands as he came near them.

Suspecting, correctly, that there was no evasion of the ordeal for him, Simon went to work resolutely.

He crossed his left leg over his right.

This wouldn't do, so he changed the position of the right leg to the left.

That was better.

He raised himself on tiptoe, and, breathless, stretched out his arm to the effigy.

His finger, in safety, had reached the coveted pocket.

In another moment, the purse it contained would, in all human probability, have left its receptacle, but for an unforseen accident.

Simon was seen to totter; the stool upon which he stood was seen to totter; and the figure was seen, not only to totter, but literally to perform the evolutions concomitant with a song called "dancing mad," and give forth the stunning jingle of some thousand bells.

The mystery of the mal-adventure was soon made apparent.

The frail article of domestic furniture had dislocated a joint, or, rather, broken a leg, and thrown poor Simon off his balance.

Mechanically catching at the dangling dummy, he had of course come to the ground, and the impulsion of his body set the chimes ringing their ominous peal.

As he lay, like one dead, with his face towards the ground, he heard the coarse ribaldry and diabolical laughter of his persecutors.

Their mirth was not of long duration, for before it had scarcely commenced all were startled by a piercing shriek; it proceeded from the neighbouring street, which was extremely dark.

A wick, steeped in oil, and burning in an iron cage at its corner, enabled, however, an observer to distinguish three forms—a woman struggling in the grasp of two ruffians, who vainly endeavoured to stifle her cry of terror.

"Help! help! for heaven's sake!" screamed the unfortunate girl.

"Halt! scoundrels, and let the wench go," roared a horseman, in a voice of thunder.

He appeared suddenly, and dashed out of the gloom that surrounded him.

It was Tom King, the gentleman highwayman; he was armed cap-a-pie, and had his drawn sword in his hand.

One sweep of his weapon bore across his arm the struggling maiden like a silken scarf, the next laid her on his saddle, while her assailants, stupefied and awe-struck, were sprawling on the pavement some yards off.

Recovering from their surprise, they were again about to rush upon their enemy to regain their prey, when they found the horse and its burden had vanished as in air.

The crowd who had witnessed this scene from the windows of the thieves' cave now opened and made way for a bright and dazzling figure; it was the gipsy girl, Jael. She was accompanied by her preserver, the gallant Tom King.

CHAPTER CIV.

WHAT BROUGHT TOM KING TO THE MINT—HIS JOURNEY FROM HERTFORD — THE CRIPPLED HORSES—THE FARRIER AND THE FORGE—HOW THE TABLES WERE TURNED ON SHOTBOLT THE GAOLER.

WE must now anticipate the previous chapter, and account for the appearance of Tom King in the purlieus of the Mint.

It will be remembered we last left him in the hands of Jonathan Wild, arrested by that individual for a supposed complicity in the murder of the hero of our tale, "Roving Jack."

From circumstances which will be made apparent hereafter, his trial had been postponed, and he had remained since his committal in the county prison of Hertfordshire.

From this prison, however, after the lapse of a few weeks, he was removed, and conducted under a strong escort to London, where the gates of Newgate were to open and receive him.

While on his road hither the officers of justice and their prisoner met with a trifling incident which led to great results.

Having crossed the county's border, marked by a narrow and rushing stream, they entered Middlesex, and pursued their way along a lane.

It was shaded by trees, through which might be seen glimpses of picturesque and woodland scenery.

It was whilst travelling this sylvan glade that the leader of the party, Dan Shotbolt, noticed that his horse was lame, a similar misfortune happening to the rest of the party, for each, on examining the beast that bore him, discovered that the animal had lost a shoe.

This was a loss indeed, and it was impossible to proceed without its being remedied.

But unexpected assistance arrived, in the person of a gaping countryman, who, for the nonce, we must call Zekiel Gosling.

"Hulloa, Bumpkin," cried Shotbolt, addressing the yokel, who gave no answer to the summons but a vacant stare.

"Hark ye, fellow; if you don't take heed of my words," continued the gaoler, "you may get into trouble."

On hearing these words, the rustic became more communicative, and touched his forelock in token of obedience.

"I be only a zimple lad, loike," said he, "and don't mean thee any offence, measter."

"You know this place?"

"Ayes, every acre on it. I've helped to raise many a crop about here, 'cos I've four little children to keep, so, you sees, as I be only a poor ignoramus you munna——"

Shotbolt cut the conversation short by inquiring if there were a smithy in the neighbourhood.

"A what?" said the obtuse Zekiel.

"A smithy," replied the officer, with a little impatience.

"Well, I can't say as how I've ever seen one, and yet, in my time, I must ha'," scratching his head as if to drag out elucidation.

Zekiel, with perfect simplicity, asked in the end if the object required "was aloive."

"Fool, our horses are lamed, and we have need of a farrier, that they may be re-shod."

"Oh, if that be all thee wants," replied the complacent countryman, "I can readily be of service to thee. Follow me, and I will take thee to a forge hard by."

In a few minutes the whole party, verging from the main road, came upon a quaint building, in front of which was placed a broad signboard supported by uprights, bearing the words—

"ENOCH HAMMERBRASS,
"Farrier, Wheelwright, and Blacksmith."

Attached to the house was a shed and open, and exhibiting all the paraphernalia connected with the above trades, such as anvils, hammers, forges, and a gigantic pair of bellows.

"This be my uncle's," said Zekiel, pointing to the residence to which he had conducted the travellers; "and if any man in England can draw thee out of the quandary thee horses have fa'en into, I'll stake my loife it be Enoch Hammerbrass."

With these words, the speaker gave several hard raps at the shed-door.

There was no answer given to the loud knocking.

"My uncle," continued the same party, "must be taking a longer afternoon nap than usual, therefore, I warn ye that he will get up more savage than ever for being waked up."

"Who, in the name of the devil, is that kicking up this rumpus?" said a hoarse voice.

It was that of the farrier, Enoch Hammerbrass, whose head, encased in a red woollen night cap, now emerged from a top window of his dwelling.

"It be I——"

"I? Who's I?"

"Thee nephew, Zekiel Gosling. Come down. I mein ha' a word wi' ye."

"What do you want?"

"Here be some strangers that——"

"Strangers? Tell 'em to go to the devil, I'm asleep."

Enoch's head popped in, then out again at the salutation of Shotbolt, not unlike the child's puppet of Jack in the Box.

"Farrier, you must descend," cried the officer. "Our horses require your attention. We are servants of the state, so you will refuse to obey me at your peril."

The blacksmith, rather a shrewd-looking fellow, gave a significant nod, and intimated his attention to orders, by saying,

"State servant, eh? I'll be with you directly. I've been an old comrade in arms, and know what duty requires."

By the time all the party had dismounted, the farrier had issued from the house, and commenced deliberately lifting up the hoofs of their several steeds.

"They appear each to have lost a shoe," said

Enoch Hammerbrass, after he had completed his examination.

"Yes, and they must be replaced without delay, as we must reach London before night sets in."

"Give me time to light a fire, and I'll see what I can do for you. Zekiel, you must lend me a hand."

The farrier beckoned the party to his side.

With his aid the horses of the travellers were ranged in the shed, while their owners, with their prisoner, entered the house adjoining.

They were all hungry and thirsty, and sat down to some refreshment which was ordered to be provided for them.

Presently, the brisk glow of the forge fire lit up with its lurid glare the sinewy form and brawny arm of the blacksmith, who commenced his labour. Soon was heard his bellows blowing, and then the measured beat of his heavy sledge upon the anvil.

"Come, lad," said the farrier to his nephew, "while our customers are enjoying themselves, we may as well see if we can't finish the job we have on hand."

"I'll be with thee, nunkey," replied the attendant, tucking up his sleeves, and buckling to at the work to be accomplished.

"In the first place," said the farrier, "before we make a commencement, where is the prisoner, our old pal, Tom King?"

"Bound hard and fast in the garret."

"Then he's safe enough."

"Aye, safe enough if he only makes use of the knife and rope which we sent him under the crust of the pigeon pie."

"Good. Now bring out his nag, the fleetest of the number."

The farrier addressed the animal brought out.

"Wench, you shall have a good shod this time, I warrant thee."

While the attendant plied the bellows, his companion placed a glowing iron on the anvil, and fashioned a shoe.

"I should like to belabour all the enemies of the gentleman highwayman like this heated metal," he added, as he struck from it the burning sparks like chaff from a thrashing floor.

In a very short time, three of the horses were in a fit state to proceed on their journey; not so the remainder, who were crippled by the insertion of a nail in their foremost hoofs.

The three uninjured horses were now led round to the back of the shed. Those maimed being left tethered to the posts within it.

While this was going forward, the captive, Tom King, with the knife (that had been so ingeniously conveyed to him in the pie), managed to free himself from his hempen bonds.

This accomplished, with scared looks, and on tiptoe, he hurried to the window of his temporary prison.

He noiselessly opened it, and attached to its strong framework the rope that, with the knife, had been furnished him by the crafty farrier and his nephew.

Having thoroughly secured the cord, he mounted the sill, and prepared to descend by it to the ground.

A quick and continuous knocking at the door of the chamber he was quitting (and which entrance he had taken the precaution to fasten) told him that he must not hesitate for one moment in his flight.

Trusting to the frail means offered for escape, he came to the ground just as his gaolers espied him from the window through which he had passed.

"I ha' gotten him, measters," said the farrier, feigning to capture the runaway; "be quick down or he'll gi' me the weather gage yet, for he be mortal strong, and I canna hold 'un long."

Believing in the sincerity of the farrier, the others rushed to his rescue, giving Tom King a moment's parley with his cunning confederates.

"Where are the horses?" asked Tom King, springing forward with lightning swiftness.

"They are behind the shed, captain."

"How am I to get to them?"

"Pass through it; but be careful to shut the back door after you."

"While you——"

"Will be at your side before you can vault into the saddle."

"But if——"

"Stash patter; it's your only chance; see, the Philistines are upon us."

As the farrier spoke, Shotbolt and his men made their appearance.

Three bullets whizzed past Tom King as he leaped into the open shed, the door of which was slammed in the face of his adversaries, and barred from within.

"Come forth, Tom King," thundered Shotbolt; "you are trapped, and cannot escape us. Surrender, or, by the heaven above us, it will be the worse for you. Open the door, I say, or we will force it. If you continue obstinate, we will burn the building."

"Nay, measter," cried Zekiel, "you munna do that, for it be my opinion the chap inside are found a way to hide himsen elsewhere."

"We'll soon find that out."

With these words the officers, one and all, burst into the shed.

Their chagrin and baffled rage was apparent when they found it empty.

A door at the back had been opened, but shut as firmly as the front one, which was again closed upon them.

In a word, the officers, and not Tom King, were prisoners.

"We shall nab him yet," said Shotbolt, exultingly. "His horse, if he has one, must be jaded by our journey, and cannot carry him very far, while we shall get a relay at the next town; so mount, and once more be on the road."

The officers at this juncture discovered that their steeds had been tampered with, and that the nails embedded in their feet had stopped all possibility of pursuit.

"This artifice proves, comrades," exclaimed Shotbolt, "that we have been betrayed, and I more than ever suspect the farrier and his man."

"Whoy, mun, doan't thee guess who they be?" replied a voice in close proximity. "They be no other than Joe Blueskin and his pal Simon Smut in disguise."

From whence that voice proceeded, or who was the owner of the same, the listeners failed most egregiously to make out.

CHAPTER CV.

THE STOLEN INTERVIEW BETWEEN TOM KING AND JAEL ON BANKSIDE, AND WHAT FOLLOWED ON THE SAME—THE PATRICO OR PRIEST OF THE GIPSY TRIBE — LOVE, JEALOUSY, AND REVENGE—HOW THE RIVALS ENCOUNTERED EACH OTHER IN SAINT GEORGE'S FIELDS.

THE scene once more changes to the vicinity of the old Mint in Southwark.

The scene being the exterior of a picturesque and ancient tavern, situated on a spot, now, as then, known as Bankside.

On a rude bench, in front of the house, sat two young people alone, and apparently lovers.

The one was the figure of a gipsy maid, with jet black hair twisted in endless folds, garnished with golden beads and a scarlet kerchief.

Sparkling as the sunbeams was her dark and Oriental eye, while her costume, though of gaudy hue, was in exquisite taste with her exquisite person.

The other appeared a gallant of the day, without any pretension, and in possession of a remarkable handsome countenance.

This spark was the noted high toby gloak, Tom King; his companion, Jael, the damsel he had rescued on the previous night.

"Though it was dark, you recognised me, eh?" said Tom King, placing his arm round the neck of the gipsy maiden.

"Oh, yes, in an instant," she replied, with a smile, and a look of inexpressible kindness.

"How was it, then," resumed Tom King, "that you slipped away from me in such a hurry?"

The soft smile of the Sybil faded away, and her features became overcast.

"Why is this, dear girl?" said the highwayman, gazing upon her in astonishment; "you must, if you regard me, tell more of this affair."

Jael still continued silent.

"In your stead you left me with a strange-looking fellow, that report gives out is in league with that supernatural being the Flying Dutchman. What the devil could he want with you?"

"I don't know."

"Curse his impudence! A rascally vagrant to attempt to run away with a girl like a nobleman; but he dearly paid for it, my riding whip curried his rough hide most soundly."

"And yet," continued the highwayman, "can I wonder at his presumption when I take into consideration what a charming creature you are?"

Tom King's ordnance had suddenly taken fire at bright Egyptian eyes.

Jael first hung down her head at the remark.

Then gently raised it, disclosing a countenance glistening with pride and joy.

At that moment she was passing beautiful.

It was now that her admirer remarked a small cross that hung round her neck.

"What is that?" he asked.

"That is my secret," the girl answered, gravely.

"Then I should like to know what that secret is."

Without making any reply, the gipsy drew herself towards the roadway.

The nearer she approached it, the more slowly she moved.

An invisible loadstone seemed to attract her to the spot, and she burst into tears.

"To what am I to attribute this sadness?" said Tom King, evidently puzzled by the strange motives of Jael. "You are not going to leave me thus, I hope"

"There is an insurmountable barrier between us. We must not meet again, and if I might give you counsel, it would be to forget me."

It is unnecessary to detail what further passed between Tom King and his inamorata, and his surprise when he learnt her decision from her own lips.

It will be easily imagined how he entreated and protested; but all to no purpose. Jael was not to be moved by either vows or prayers.

She could not cease to love, yet she could never marry him.

Tom King knelt.

Jael and Jael alone was the sun that shone upon him.

He had striven to forget her; but in vain.

He now deplored his reckless life, and blamed himself for having wandered from the paths of honesty.

But he would reform—he wished to reform—he intended to reform.

A wife would change the dashing knight of the post into a simple and hard-plodding yeoman.

Jael should see how steady he would be in future.

He was tired of the road, and would quit it for a less hazardous life.

She might shake her head, but his declarations were true for all that.

It was nonsense to tell him of other women, Jael and none but Jael should be his bride.

By persisting in a refusal she would drive him to desperation.

There had been a spectator of the scene that had passed between Tom King and his fair companion.

Unobserved, he had watched them intently from an upper window of a neighbouring house.

This was no other than the patrico * or priest of the gipsy tribe, better known to our readers in his former character of Dick Turpin, the highwayman.

The voice of Jael had struck upon his ear, and he remained gazing upon her in an attitude of profound reverie.

At the casement he stood absorbed, grave, and without motion.

He was all thought, ear, and eye.

It was difficult to say what was the nature of his glance, or the fire that flashed from it.

It was a fixed gaze, yet a gaze full of disquiet and commotion.

From his profound and death-like repose of body there appeared no life about him but in his overstrained organs of vision.

From the moment he had perceived Jael, his deep gloom had become deeper still.

All at once he started up.

His whole frame shuddered as trees shaken by a gust of wind.

Darting from the window at which he had remained during the discourse of Jael and Tom King, he descended with a view to confront them in their stolen interview.

On his arrival at the spot where they had been standing, in place of the lovers he beheld another object which struck him almost as forcibly.

It was the Dutchman—Wirth Wolfgang.

The patrico advanced a few steps, stopped short, then looked stedfastly at him.

His look had nothing in it ironical or sarcastic.

It was a gaze, serious, piercing, calm.

After a pause he broke silence.

"If I am not greatly deceived, I am in the presence of Wirth Wolfgang?"

"Yah, mynheer, dat is right; I am he."

"How happens it that I find you in the Mint, after——"

"Stop, mein friend; let me gif you some goot advice. If you want to get on in de world, never trouble your head vith vhat don't consarnt you, and never ax imbertinent questions."

"Your advice is sound, Wirth, but ill-timed and out of place."

"Berhaps so; but I am hongry and dirsty, and

---

* History tells us that at one period of his career, Turpin was duly inaugurated as a patrico in a gipsy band; whether for the purposes of concealment or otherwise it is not made manifest.

must take de sounding of dis place to see how de gat jomp."

"Your wants will be readily supplied when you have answered my questions."

"Broceed, yah, nain spraicken. Not a vord—hold mine schnapps-lapper quiet like Bemgarten church-yard in vinter.'

"In the first place, tell me what has become of Jael? She was standing here just now, but has vanished like a phantom."

"Dat ish not so clear to me as you, mynheer."

"You are trifling with me, Wirth; it is impossible she could have left the spot without passing you. Come, tell me which road she has taken?"

"Sdop, I vant to speak. Did you say Jael?"

"Yes, the gipsy girl."

"She is a prave frau; do she love you?"

"No—but that is of no consequence."

"By de moder of mein fader! I know vhat vill make de kinchen love you dearly."

"Name it."

"Sdop again. You let me see in mine hant five hundred pounds, and I promise you shall make one present to de lady, in return for vhich she shall tank you kindly and love you for it. Dere, is it a bargain?"

"My hand upon it."

"Goot; to-morrow night, if you keep your vaith mit me, I shall be as goot as my vord. Meet me here, and——"

At this moment, the sound of a footfall being heard, the plotters separated, each taking a different road.

Wolfgang, looking after his retreating companion, who, with hasty steps, was making his way for the neighbouring Mint, muttered to himself,

"Der debil take you for von bad-hearted tief! I drust you so far as I can see you, mein friend. Yes, I haf got vot they call a rod in pickle for you dat shall dickle your doby, all zo as if you was squat down in a pot of poiling pitch mit notin' but your skin to cover you."

*   *   *   *

The celebrated tavern of the "Cross Shovels" stood at the eastern angle of the Mint.

Its principal room was very spacious, but very low.

Its floor was ever covered with tables, tankards, and guests, who were principally composed of gallants, topers, and profligate women.

It was now night, and the disreputable house, glaring with fire and candle, looked in the distance like a farrier's forge, compared with the heavy atmosphere that hung about its open door.

The sounds of drinking, swearing, and altercation, resounded within the tavern; from which might be discerned swarms of confused figures, engaged in such unprofitable occupations.

From the interior, let the reader wander to the exterior of this abode.

He will there find a man, walking to and fro, not unlike to a sentry before his box.

This man is watching all who enter or leave the place before which he is parading.

A muffled cloak conceals his features, and descending lowly, entirely disguises his person.

At length the tavern door, which had been suddenly closed, opened.

It was for this signal he appeared to be waiting.

Two of the roysterers who had been drinking, staggered out by the portal.

The gleam of light that escaped from it disclosed their faces.

The man wearing the cloak stationed himself in a dark recess, to observe and then to follow them.

"The bell of St. Mary's Overie has struck seven," said one of the tipplers; "this is the hour I have made an appointment with Jael."

"Donder and blixen," replied his associate, with an articulation anything but distinct. "Dese womens are no petter than a parcel of damaged goots; and take more trouble for one, dan I would give for the whole sex if you could tie them up in von betticoat."

"Why, friend," said the other, "it strikes me you are drunk, or, as you sailors say, three sheets in the wind."

"Yaw—yaw, that is very proper what you call goot," rejoined the addressed, reeling, and stumbling. "When the shoolp is loaded, you may scut mitout de ballast."

In the last speaker no doubt will be recognised Wirth Wolfgang.

And in his companion the illustrious and renowned Tom King.

The zigzag path into which these worthies were drawn was closely followed by him who was watching them, still enveloped in the ample folds of the mantle that covered him.

"In the name stingo and brandy wine, man," exclaimed Tom King, "try to keep your perpendicular, or I must leave you to your fate; time flies, I tell you, and I've an appointment at eight.'

The exhortation of the highwayman seemed to have anything but its effect on the Hollander, who shortly propped his body in propinquity with a wall, then descended with it heavily into a gutter.

The next moment the fallen individual was snoring in a "thorough bass," while Tom King uttered a curse, and away he went.

The man in the cloak followed him, leaving the Dutchman to sleep by himself under the canopy of heaven.

They had no sooner departed than the Dutchman became suddenly sober, rose from his slumbers, and bent his steps to a neighbouring hovel, in which Jonathan Wild was awaiting his arrival.

We will leave the thief-taker and Wirth Wolfgang in company, and follow on the footsteps of Tom King and his pursuer.

The highwayman had reached the bridle-way of Blackfriar's, leading to an open space of land designated as St. George's Fields.

While here, he perceived that some one was pursuing him.

Chancing to turn his eyes, he saw a shadow immediately behind him.

Tom King stopped; the figure stopped.

He walked on; the figure walked on also.

He felt some alarm at the discovery, but continued his journey.

Having arrived at the "Monk's Oak" (the spot upon which the Obelisk now stands), he once more looked around him.

The then lonely spot was absolutely deserted, and nothing was to be seen but the same dark figure which was approaching him with slow steps.

So slow that he had time sufficient to observe well his hat and cloak.

When within a few paces, the strange visitant paused, and remained motionless as a marble statue.

His eye was lit up by that vague glare which issues from that of a beast of prey in its darkened lair.

Tom King, who was brave and would have scorned a pair of snappers levelled at his head, literally trembled at the sight of the man before him, who seemed as one petrified.

He stood for some minutes in silence, hesitating

whether he should speak to (what appeared in his view) an apparition.

At length, by a forced laugh, he broke silence.

"If you are a robber, you had better seek game on the highway or elsewhere, for, by my faith, I have spent my last rap on the tavern table of the 'Cross Shovels,' and have not the ghost of a coin left in my pockets."

The hand of the figure darted from the cloak that was stretched over it, and grasping the highwayman, shouted in his ear—

"Tom King!"

"The devil!" cried the astonished knight of the road. "You know me?"

"Yes, and your errand across this unfrequented tract," replied the mysterious stranger, in a sepulchral tone. "You have, to-night, an assignation?"

"I have," answered Tom King, more amazed than ever.

"At the hour of eight?"

"Yes, and it now lacks one quarter to the appointed time."

"The rendezvous is the 'Dog and Duck,' in the vicinity?"

"Precisely so."

"You are to meet a comely damsel?"

"Aye, and one whose beauty far transcends the peerless charms of dames of high degree."

"Her name is——"

"Jael, the gipsy girl," said Tom King, gaily, having recovered his levity by degrees.

"'Tis false!"

"Hell and fury!" cried the highwayman, releasing himself from the gripe in which he was held, and menacing his opponent, who drily repeated his words.

"'Tis false!"

Choaked with rage at the second taunt, Tom King searched for a weapon.

"Man or fiend, I care not which," he exclaimed, "you must answer for this."

"When and where you please."

"I am satisfied. The place shall be this spot, the time shall be this very moment. The blood of one of us must make atonement for this insult."

The highwayman produced his pistol.

His antagonist neither flinched nor stirred; but addressed him in a tone tremulous and scornful.

"You forget you have an engagement, and that a fair maiden is waiting for you."

The simple words had their desired effect on Tom King.

His sudden burst of passion was allayed in an instant.

And the weapon he held in his hand dropped to his side.

"To-morrow you shall find me ready to cut your throat with a blade or pierce your breast with a bullet," continued the man of mystery; "but this evening I prefer that you should keep your appointment with the lady of your love."

Tom King assented to this proposition, at the same time remarking,

"Well, I give you credit for greater discernment than myself in this affair. Had you pinked me, I should have been compelled to disappoint Jael; as it is, I can keep my promise, and settle our little difference to-morrow as well as to-day."

"Go to your assignation," repeated the stranger, whose voice still trembled either from rage or fear.

"Upon my word, sir," stammered out the highwayman, with some embarrassment, "I must compliment you for your courtesy, and regret that I am beholden to run a sword perhaps through your gizzard."

"And why should you do so, when my weapon may have to perform a similar office for a spark as rakish as yourself?"

"I see, you are one after my own mould, a hearty cull, and——"

With the words, Tom King gave his forehead a significant tap.

"Bless me, I forget. I must have some, and yet I haven't a penny."

"If you require money, young sir," said the stranger, "I can lend you this."

The highwayman felt a hand slip a purse into his own.

He grasped the first warmly, then pocketed the second.

"On the faith of a toby gloak," he exclaimed, "you're a devilish good fellow. We ought to be friends not enemies."

"On one condition we may be so," resumed the unknown

"Name it."

"Prove that I am in error."

"That's, perhaps, more easily said than done."

"No; the means are at your disposal."

"Indeed! I am glad to hear it."

"You have only to conceal me in some nook from which I may learn whether the girl is really the same that I have imagined."

"To that I can consent without any hesitation," said Tom King, "so come along with me, and judge if I have spoken correctly or not."

CHAPTER CVI.

SOME SHORT ACCOUNT OF THE ONCE CELEBRATED "DOG AND DUCK," NEAR LAMBETH MARSH—WHAT TOOK PLACE WITHIN THE PRECINCTS OF THE SAME ON A CERTAIN NIGHT IN THE EARLY PART OF THE LAST CENTURY.

TOM KING and his mysterious companion left the "Monk's Oak" with hasty steps.

In a few minutes they arrived, through the open space adjacent, at a solitary tenement, rejoicing in the somewhat peculiar name of the "Dog and Duck."

It was an out-of-the-way place, and surrounded by a neglected woody bower. supposed to be the remains of an orchard belonging to a royal palace that was inhabited by Edward the Black Prince, at Kennington.

The "Dog and Duck" in the earlier part of the reign of George the Second, became, on account of its pleasant and open site, a place of public entertainment.

The old building alluded to in this story was then destroyed, and the mazy coppices attached converted into pleasure gardens.

It flourished for many years as a resort for pleasure-seekers, who, in the summer months, flocked to the favourite retreat.

After a period, however, of more than half a century, it lost its character and attractions, and became the haunt of the dissolute and depraved.

On account of crimes that were committed within its limits, it was found necessary at length to repress them, and entirely do away both with the house and grounds.

There is a stone in the wall of the modern Bethlehem, or Bedlam, which marks the spot where once raised its head the famous rendezvous, known as the "Dog and Duck," St. George's Fields, Southwark.

Tom King stopped before the low door of the house we have described.

Then kicked against it violently.

A light glimmered through its crevices, and it was opened, discovering an old woman holding a lamp in her hand.

The hag was dressed in coarse clothing, and bent almost double by age.

The interior of the hovel corresponded with her mean appearance.

The walls were of bare and crumbling plaster.

The fire-place was dismantled, and the ceiling, formed of decaying rafters, covered with cobwebs.

On the entrance of Tom King and his mysterious companion, the latter drew his cloak up to his eyes, as if for the purpose of concealment of his features.

After a few words had been spoken, the crone whispered in the ear of Tom King, and beckoned to him to follow her.

He complied, and ascended some stairs to the room above, the light disappearing with the highwayman and the old woman.

The companion of Tom King, being left by himself, groped about in the dark for some moments, then mounted to the door through which he had passed.

It was wide enough open to allow him to see all that was taking place in the adjoining apartment.

He trembled, and a cloud darkened his eye as he beheld the lovers.

They were alone, seated on a wooden coffer by the side of a lamp, the glare of which threw a strong light on their graceful forms, heightened by the beams of the moon couched on fleecy clouds, peering through the chamber window.

Jael was confused, flushed, palpitating, her gaze downcast, and her cheek crimson.

"Oh, you will not despise me, I hope," she said, without raising her eyes to the face of Tom King, radiant with delight. "I fear I am acting very wrong in this affair."

"Despise you, dear girl; why should I do so?" replied the highwayman, with his accustomed air of gallantry.

"For having accompanied you to this lonely dwelling."

"Pshaw! I can never despise you for such an act, though I must freely confess that I am angry."

"Angry!" exclaimed Jael, looking at the speaker in alarm.

"Yes, angry," he continued, "that you put so little faith in me as to suppose I brought you to this place for some other reason than your security and protection."

The gipsy girl was silent for a moment, and rose from her seat.

A sigh burst from her lips.

A tear stood in her eye.

"Pardon me," she sobbed, "if you believe me to doubt one whom I dearly love."

"No, my dear girl; it is for me to ask pardon," said Tom King, in transport, throwing his arm around the waist of Jael. "And do you love me?"

"Yes, with heart and soul," replied the maiden. "Could I do otherwise? You are kind, generous, handsome, and have saved my life; I—who am but a poor foundling."

Tom King led her again to her seat, and placed himself beside her, closer, aye, much closer, than before.

"Now, Jael," he said, "you must listen to me seriously."

"Indeed I shall do no such thing," she replied, coquettishly, "until you tell me whether you sincerely love me in return."

"Do I love you? Can you ask such a question? I love, and can never love any other but you," said Tom King, pressing Jael to his bosom.

She raised her eyes with a look of angelic happiness towards her lover's face, and faintly murmured—

"Assured of this I can freely die."

"Die! how you talk, girl; when two fond hearts unite 'tis the very time to live."

"I have a fearful presentiment that evil will come to one or both of us this very night."

"Pshaw! these are childish fancies! Don't alarm yourself about such trifles; haven't I told you how passionately I adore you? And, may I never see daylight again," continued Tom King, "if I don't make you and myself the happiest of mortals in Christendom."

As he spoke his eyes seemed to glisten more and more joyfully.

The stranger, with the eye of a hawk, had been watching all that had passed from the partly opened door.

He quivered, froze, and boiled, at the scene which met his gaze.

His face resembled that of a caged tiger unable to spring upon his prey.

His eye gleamed in the shaded corner in which he stood with a blue phosphorescence on its surface

"To deceive me now would break my heart," said Jael, still clinging to her lover. "Since I am thine what need I of parents? To me thou art father, mother, all, since I so well love thee and thou givest back my passion! When I am grown old, ugly," she continued, "shall I be still adored?"

"You will ever be the object of my affection."

"Then am I the happiest, the proudest of women!"

As she spoke Jael threw her arms around the neck of Tom King.

A sweet smile and eyes dim with tears were fixed on him; and he pressed his burning lips to those of the trembling maiden.

At that moment she beheld another face.

It was the convulsive, livid face of the stranger, who had sprung from the door with an upraised knife in his hand.

Jael was struck motionless by this terrible apparition.

She had not power to speak or scream, but fell senseless on the floor.

Turning to raise the fallen woman Tom King became aware of the presence of the party who had unwittingly caused the mal-adventure.

He had to all appearance overcome the extraordinary commotion that had taken place within him, and assumed an air at once placid and free from any approach to malignity or hatred.

"Why have you disobeyed my injunction," said Tom King, "and entered the apartment without a warning? Your folly has thrown the poor girl into a fainting fit from which I fear she will not shortly recover."

"That is unfortunate, truly," said the stranger, "for we shall not be able to carry her off, and I can already hear the trample of horses along the causeway."

"What do you mean?" said Tom King, who had now raised Jael from the floor into his arms. "I did not think to meet you thus; and I begin to suspect that you mean no other than foul play."

"Let the issue determine whether it be so or not. This is no time for parley. You will find I am no foe; I come to warn you. Jonathan Wild," continued the stranger, "has discovered your meeting place, and your life is beset."

THE BURGLARY.—(*See No. 32.*)

"Trust me, in time of need, my arm can keep my head."

"True, Tom King; but will not thy heart unnerve thy arm? See her dream of happiness, which the bright smile on her pallid cheek bespeaks, is even now upon him, who will, for ever, be torn from her fond embrace if he hesitates to follow me in this moment of peril."

"What would you have me do?"

"Fly, while there is yet time; the darkness of night cloaks the neighbouring heather; beneath its shadow you may chance to elude your pursuers."

"But Jael——"

"Shall be my care. I can afford her means of protection of which you are not aware. This ring, the signet of the patrico of her gipsy tribe, will shield her from any harm or persecution."

There was no time for further speech or hesitation, for, as the last words were uttered, a loud knocking was heard at the outer door, and admittance demanded in the king's name.

The stranger extinguished the light, and all was buried in darkness, while the highwayman made for the window, and descended into the garden.

His pursuers, who had burst into the room he had quitted, descried his flight, and fired several shots after him.

While crossing a plank he had thrown over a little stream at the rear of the premises, one took effect, and Tom King fell either dead or wounded.

The officers hastily reached the spot, and raised the fallen man, who gave no signs of life.

It was while engaged in this occupation that they discovered that the building they had so lately reached was on fire.

Whether this circumstance was the result of malice, accident, or design, none were able to answer.

In a moment smoke seemed to burst forth from every window, and the tenement being built of wood, was a sheet of flame.

A fierce glare was thrown upon the group below, and the whole region around bright as day at noon.

By the light two dark figures were seen emerging from the burning mass.

The one was a man, the other a fainting woman borne upon his shoulders.

CHAPTER CVII.

THE TRIAL OF TOM KING FOR THE MURDER OF ROVING JACK—HIS INNOCENCE PROCLAIMED.

A MONTH after the incidents related in the last chapter had occurred, Tom King, having recovered from the effects of his wound, was brought to his trial.

The appointed day was a raw one of the month of March, and as murky as one of those of November.

The passages and staircases of the Hall of Justice, dimly lighted by oil lamps, seemed to render them even more sombre than ever through the heavy atmosphere.

The court itself was in a crowded state, owing to the notoriety of the crime and its supposed perpetrator.

The jurors were already in waiting, as might be perceived through the cloud of fog and breath that hung about the densely-packed assemblage, while the black vapour, which hung also like a dark curtain on the outside of the great window, imparted an additional gloom to the exciting scene.

Presently there were several candles lighted here and there, which threw their rays on the heads of the clerks poring over piles of papers.

The anterior portion of the spacious chamber was occupied by the multitude.

Right and left were lawyers seated at tables, busily engaged with their various writings and documents, more or less connected with the case before them.

In a short time the sound of wheels were heard, and the voices of the mob gathered in the street.

It was the judge who had arrived.

He entered the court and took his seat, followed by an equally high legal functionary.

The buzz of the surrounding spectators was awfully hushed at this appearance.

As the bystanders imposed silence, the details incidental to a trial were then proceeded with, and the prisoner summoned to the tribunal.

Tom King advanced with calm dignity to the bar.

His dress was simple—even neglected—his long and light brown tresses flowed over his shoulders, and his countenance, pensive, sad, and expressive, seemed, for the moment, to disconcert even those who might be termed, not unjustly, his enemies.

The judge ordered the clerk to read the accusation.

The highwayman listened without evincing the slightest weakness.

He appeared to have forgotten that he was at all interested in the proceedings.

The judge then questioned him in the usual manner :—

"Your name? Your natal place? Have you a counsel?"

These interrogations having been satisfactorily replied to, he continued :—

"Prisoner at the bar, you are charged with the murder of one Sir John Warbold, better known to the world as 'Roving Jack.' Do you plead guilty or not guilty?"

Tom King spoke in a firm voice as follows :—

"My lord, before I plead I would wish you to listen to me. If you would ask, did I spill blood in anger, hate, or premeditation, I can answer, No. If you would ask whether, in an unguarded moment, I have fatally used a weapon in self-preservation, I must answer, Yes."

"This answer," said the judge, "goes far to condemn you; but the law of England should ever temper mercy with justice, and, in virtue of its powers, names————"

"Your clemency, my lord," replied Tom King, "will avail me little."

"The only chance of life you have left hangs by a slender thread."

"I have neither witness nor counsel."

"Prisoner, there has been a mysterious paper left on my table, but of so vague a purport that 'twere almost idle to read, yet it is my duty to give you every advantage that my duty yields."

With the words the judge produced the document he had spoken of, broke the seal, and read—

"Let justice for a space stay her hand. There is one who will appear ere sentence be pronounced and wake the conscience of the really guilty."

"No one has appeared," said the judge, after he had finished the perusal of the letter, "therefore let the evidence brought against the accused be submitted to the jury for their consideration."

An important witness was to be first under examination.

It was the noted Jonathan Wild.

He slowly ascended the witness-box.

It was observed that he appeared more than usually pale, and that he kept his eyes fixed on the ground, evidently with the intention of avoiding the gaze of the prisoner.

After a pause he made the following statement—

"On a certain day named in the depositions a gentleman, bearing the name of Sir John Warbold, arrived at an inn in the suburb of Bermondsey.

"He had valuable property and papers on his person which excited the cupidity of the landlord, who, with the assistance of the prisoner, as it afterwards appeared, determined to possess themselves of the same.

"Those papers, by a fortuitous circumstance, were found upon his accomplice, and have fallen into my hands, and I hope to bring forth sufficient evidence to prove that the arraigned man was accessory to if not the actual perpetrator of the murder."

Here Tom King, to whom such details were naturally painful, interrupted the witness, saying—

"Jonathan Wild, your malevolence will be your own destruction, but it will not be mine. Without further essay, I shall plead guilty to this charge, and acknowledge that the unfortunate gentleman, whose death I regret more than any here, fell by my hand."

At these words a silent tremor seized upon the whole assembly.

The judge from his seat exclaimed—

"What led you to commit this foul murder?"

"My lord, your pardon; Tom King is no assassin!"

"You already admit that you have slain a fellow creature; I can find no other term for such a crime."

"I am guiltless of intentional bloodshed."

"May I ask, then, who has induced you to perpetrate this act?"

"No one."

"The idea of such a deed must, at least, have been suggested by somebody."

"What is not self-conceived is badly executed."

The dignity with which the highwayman had uttered his words had elevated him to a position such as that which the Roman hero might be supposed to obtain from his fellow countrymen on his victorious return to his native land.

The entire audience were entranced with admiration.

At that moment Tom King seemed to be the judge of his judges.

His eye, like the lightning's flash, confounded his prosecutors, and proclaimed the energy of his soul.

All at once his face, which had hitherto preserved an unchangeable serenity, was agitated.

Emotion obscured his vision, and, in broken accents, he exclaimed—

"I recognise it! I recognise it!"

What had caused this remark?

Let the reader learn.

As Tom King was following the judge's eye and looking along the room, he saw a figure which rose above the judgment seat and advanced a few steps. Suddenly it stopped and looked round at the two members on the bench.

They appeared quite unconcerned, and were evidently not aware of the presence of the individual in question.

Tom King stood amazed, and watched the mysterious visitor intently, whose features being partly disclosed appeared to be of the colour of a bluish wax.

He remained motionless for a few seconds, and from the action of the head appeared merely to look down pensively upon the court below, and to take no notice of the prisoner, whose fixed and trembling gaze was upon him.

Almost without warning, this strange being vanished as some phantom, and passed through the large hall window as by some ethereal egress.

The examination of several other witnesses then proceeded.

Tom King heard their evidence with stoical calmness.

"I call upon you," resumed the judge, "what you have to say in answer."

The figure now for the second time appeared to the fevered imagination of the prisoner.

It seemed to him as if it was prevented by some hidden mystery from revealing itself to the people in the court, yet possessed the power to cover with darkness their thoughts.

A peculiar change came over the judge's face.

A tremulous motion seemed to pass through his frame, and his voice faltered as he repeated the words,

"What have you to say in answer?"

"My lord," replied Tom King, evincing extreme terror, "it is impossible for me to reply while that figure is glaring at me from yonder window."

As he spoke the eyes of the whole assemblage were at once directed to the spot indicated.

There was no one to be seen.

"Prisoner," said the judge, "your words are wild and incoherent. Why do you upraise your hands in frantic gesture?"

"Because I have seen some unnatural being—a restless spirit of the other world!"

This reply fell like a thunderbolt amidst the silence of the auditory, and terminated further interrogations on the part of the prosecution.

On the papers taken from the murdered man being produced in court, the jury, after the usual preliminaries, retired.

In ten minutes they gave in their verdict—

"GUILTY!"

The judge rose to address them.

"Gentlemen," said he, "since the accused has confessed his crime I have but a few words to utter and a painful duty to perform. May it please the court to maintain silence."

Every head was in a moment seen uncovered, while the president, in a low tone, demanded,

"The black cap."

The condemned prisoner seemed to be anxiously looking at the solemn scene.

But his dim eye no longer saw objects before him.

The clerk of the tribunal began writing, and then handed a long parchment to its president.

During the prevailing stillness a chilling voice pronounced these words,

"Prisoner: on such day as it shall please our lord the king, at the hour of noon, you shall be drawn in a tumbrel through the streets of London to the place of execution at Tyburn, where you will be hanged by the neck on the gallows until you are dead. Your property, if you have any, will be con-

fiscate to the crown, and your remains interred without consecrated ground.

"This is the sentence of the court, whose humble representative I am, for the crimes by you committed and murder done upon the body of Sir John Warbold, Baronet, and heaven have mercy on your soul."

"Oh, this is a dream," murmured Tom King, as he felt rough hands bearing him away.

It was now night.

The lights, having received no accession to their number, gave so faint a glare that objects a short distance off were scarcely discernible.

The face of the judge, by whose side stood a lamp, was alone to be distinguished.

Opposite to him, through the haze, and at the other extremity of the hall, he could perceive an undefined patch of black moving along the dark floor.

The figure advanced with a firm step, and ascended the witness-box.

Arrived here he spoke to the judge, who magisterially resumed the seat he had lately quitted.

The assemblage, pale and halting, greeted the new comer with a buzz of pleasure.

Without betraying the slightest emotion, he continued.

"My lord, since the condemned man has confessed the crime, it is time for me to speak, and in doing so will prevent this court from committing a legal murder."

"This assertion is most extraordinary," replied the judge; "it is incredulous that a man would wantonly accuse himself of a crime which would jeopardize his life, unless, indeed, his reason had left him. I suppose, witness, this is a plea you are about to offer in his defence?"

"Your lordship misunderstands me; I am not here to offer a subterfuge for crime, but to protect the innocent and confound the guilty."

"Am I to consider you as a witness or as an accomplice in this mysterious affair?" asked the judge.

"As a witness, one whose testimony you dare not doubt, and must readily admit that justice is at last enlightened."

The usual oath having been taken by the last speaker he cast his eyes around the hall, and fixed them intently on one spot.

It was that upon which Jonathan Wild was standing.

He had been looking on attentively, apparently without concern.

As the witness pointed to him he became violently agitated, the more so at his affrighted words—

"I challenge that man."

"My lord," stammered out Jonathan Wild, "the conduct of this stranger is so inexplicable, and his proceedings so irregular, that I begin to suspect he is in league with the prisoner for some sinister design.

"If you will allow me," continued the thief-taker, "to make inquiries, I have no doubt I shall be able to discover something respecting him."

"My lord, if you suffer Jonathan Wild to leave court for this one instant you will do so at your own peril."

The judge, perplexed, made no reply, leaving the witness to continue his discourse.

"I solemnly assert that he has in his possession papers which he has unfairly obtained; firstly, with the view of using them as evidence against the culprit at the bar, then turning them to his own advantage by taking possession of property, the owners of which he falsely believes are dead."

" These papers, then——"

" Are the title deeds of a lady of the name of Tremaine, in conjunction with those of the supposed victim of murder. They were concealed in a box which the pilferer has undoubtedly brought with him."

" My lord, this impeachment of my public character is most unjustifiable," said Jonathan Wild ; " I shall be able to prove that the documents in question were entrusted to my keeping."

" By whom ?"

" Sir John Warbold."

" 'Tis false ! for, villain, learn," said the witness, " that Sir John Warbold himself now confronts you, nor will he pause till he has brought you to a bar of justice to answer for the numerous crimes you have committed in the name of the authority you have so grossly abused."

At the sight of Roving Jack, the thief-taker writhed in the agony of passion and disappointment ; he stood bewildered and stupefied.

" What mockery is this ?" he muttered to himself. " I saw him fall with my own eyes. Can it be ? No, 'tis phantasy : the dead can never again revisit earth."

Tom King, who had hitherto lain apparently senseless on the floor, at the voice of our hero started.

The thought that he was innocent of bloodshed woke him up from his stupor like a pistol shot.

By a desperate effort he raised himself to the barrier before him, and beheld the man whom he deemed he had murdered standing by his side.

At the blest thought his blood boiled with delight.

His nerves seemed strung with newly-recovered vigour, and a thrill of joy rushed like lightning through his frame.

CHAPTER CVIII.

JONATHAN WILD'S HOUSE IN THE OLD BAILEY— THE CAPTIVE OF THE SUBTERRANEOUS VAULT— WITHOUT FIRE, AIR, OR LIGHT, AND WITH DEATH — A FRIEND IN NEED IS A FRIEND INDEED—THE STARTLING ESCAPE OF JAEL THE GIPSY GIRL.

JONATHAN WILD'S house was situated in the Old Bailey, and abutted on the walls on the great gaol of Newgate.

It was a massive building, resembling a fortress in appearance.

Being built upon a double basement there was almost as much of it under ground as above.

In the lower portion there were various subterraneous abodes, dark, mysterious, and mute.

They served either as a prison or sepulchre, sometimes both, and became more and more contracted the lower descent was made into the earth.

When once the miserable captive, who had given offence to the great thief taker, was buried in these dungeons there was no leaving them but for the gallows.

It was a farewell to hope, to life, to light, and the entombed, with one enormous complicated lock, was shut out from every object of the living world.

In one of the fetid vaults Jael, the gipsy girl, had been placed after her abduction.

There she was wrapped in darkness, and immured, as it were, alive.

Since her incarceration she had neither waked nor slumbered.

In the profound gloom that surrounded her she could not distinguish the night from the day.

A fearful dream from dread reality.

Her solitude was alone disturbed by the hollow clangour of a trap door.

This when opened admitted a hand which gave her food, but emitted no glimmer of light.

How long she had been an inmate of this horrid cell she could not tell as she could hear no bell or clock to denote the lingering flight of time.

At length, wearied by suspense, one day or night, she perceived a reddish glare suddenly enter through a crevice in the roof above her head.

Peering upward she next beheld the rusty hinges of the iron-barred door revolve and grate upon the iron framework.

From the aperture appeared a figure, bearing in its hand a shaded or dark lantern.

The intruder was covered by a black wrapper, while a hood or cowl of the same colour concealed his features.

For some moments Jael gazed on the spectral form.

The tenant of the vault and its mysterious visitor appeared as two statues, calm, immoveable, and death-like, for neither spoke.

After a pause, with doubt and fear, the gipsy girl broke silence.

" Who can you be ?"

" A friend."

The exclamation caused the captive to shake in every limb.

" Are you ready ? ' continued the same sepulchral voice.

" Ready ! Ready for what ?"

" To meet death."

" Yes ; I am fully prepared," cried the maiden, firmly. " Will it come soon ? '

" At the hour of noon to-morrow, twelve hours hence."

Jael's head sank upon her bosom ; but joy rather than sorrow was depicted on her countenance.

Raising once more her face, she murmured,

" The hours will pass heavily, but they will end."

The stranger fixed a hasty glance upon the speaker, but essayed no remark.

Suddenly he turned as if to scrutinize the dungeon.

" Without light, air, or fire ! 'tis a terrible fate !"

" Yes. God's meanest creatures are permitted to bask in the sun's rays, while the wretched Jael pines in unpenetrable and loathsome darkness."

After a pause, the stranger spoke,

" Do you know, girl, why you are a prisoner in this terrible dungeon ?"

" I dare not tell ! I dare not think !"

" What would you say if one were bold enough to bid defiance to your enemies—in spite of their threats to burst open your dungeon doors and unlock your fetters ?"

" I would bless, worship him for such sweet liberty."

" Enough, follow me."

With the words, the stranger took hold of the arm of Jael.

The poor girl was almost chilled to her vitals by his clammy touch.

" Oh, heavens !" she exclaimed, " 'tis the icy hand of the dead !"

Her fearful companion threw back his hood.

A sinister face that had so long haunted, met her gaze.

Its baneful apparition roused her from the stupor into which she had fallen.

She addressed the Patrico, Dick Turpin, for he it was, in apparent tremor.

"Wretch! not contented with the betrayal of thy friend, Tom King, you must needs seek to injure him further by the destruction of the woman whom he holds most dearly in his heart."

Emotion choked her utterance, and she sobbed convulsively.

Dick Turpin answered not, but eyed his victim as a hawk about to pounce with winged lightning upon his prey.

Both remained silent for some minutes.

"Listen!" at length said Turpin, recovering his composure. "Pity, rather than condemn me. If I have had recourse to cruel means to attain the haven of my hopes, blame me not, but the spirit which holds dominion over the passion. I have been a villain, miscreant, murderer, what ye will," he continued; "but my ardent nature failed to control my guilt. Thy beauteous image, Jael," frantically exclaimed Turpin, "has plunged me deeper and deeper into crime, and like the wretch perishing in the snow, thy love caused me to nestle in the fatal slumber."

Jael at these words bent with terror.

Her flowing tears ceased.

And she gazed with the vacant stare of an idiot.

The Patrico knelt on the dungeon floor, regarding the stupefied maiden with an eye of fire.

While a thick veil of oblivion seemed yet to pass over the inmates of the dungeon, Jonathan and his satellites entered by its secret-door.

The object of their visit did not seem apparent.

But they ranged themselves silently round the unconscious Jael.

No one had yet observed from the trap-door in the roof above them a strange-looking spectator who had been watching all that had passed during the last hour.

In an attitude motionless, he witnessed the scene that has passed his eyes.

In the very first moments of his mysterious appearance, he had, unnoticed, securely fastened to one of the cross beams of the ceiling a knotted rope, the end of which reached the stoned floor below.

All at once, on the entrance of the thief-taker and his followers, he sprang from his position, and seized the quivering cord.

With feet, knees, and hands, he glided down it like rain from a penthouse.

He ran up to two of the men, who were preventing Jael, who had swooned, from falling, and felled them with the blow of his enormous fists, like stricken oxen.

With the swiftness of thought, he seized the fainting girl in one arm as a child would a doll.

While the other enabled him to ascend the rope, bearing his burden upwards with the agility of a startled cat.

He arrived safely at the summit of the building before Jonathan Wild and the others, who literally stood aghast at the daring adventure, could recover from their surprise.

They were left in darkness, as the only light which remained in the apartment had been extinguished in the scuffle.

The shock brought Jael to her senses, and she recognised in her preserver the person of the Dutchman, Wirth Wolfgang.

On the tower of Newgate, to which he had conveyed the gipsy girl, he fancied, from its isolated position, she would be free from molestation, and that her pursuers would never imagine that he would have the temerity to place her so near the spot of her late persecution.

He had judged rightly, for the London criminal is more securely hid in the vast metropolis than on the distant shores of America and Australia.

CHAPTER CIX.

THE MYSTERY OF THE LEADS AND ROOF OF NEWGATE.

IT is now necessary to give some short description of Jael's refuge, and the means by which Wirth Wolfgang was enabled to convey her to this sanctuary.

It is, perhaps, almost needless to say that the ancient city of London was surrounded by walls, moats, and ramparts, and entered only by four principal gates, the fifth being added very early in the twelfth century.

This gate being more lately built than the others, and supported by two stupendous towers, was called "New-gate."

For fifteen score years it had been a place of duresse, when it was rebuilt by the renowned Sir Richard Whittington.

This and every successive structure retained its original name, and became eventually the common gaol of the county of Middlesex.

The building at the period of our story still retained one of the towers of the ancient gate at its south-east angle, and adjoining the prison chapel.

The tall column springing from the sombre mass of stone and iron of the prison at its feet, like some black arrow pierced the haze of horizon.

To this place, from the house of Jonathan Wild, there was a secret thoroughfare, which, by a fortuitous chance, the Dutchman has discovered, although such a knowledge was not imparted to the thief-taker, who, with his followers, was totally unacquainted with the existence of such a communication as that stated.

Let us now follow Wirth Wolfgang and the trembling Jael on their perilous passage.

After his recent affray, the Dutchman succeeded in reaching, with his charge, the open landing of Jonathan Wild's house.

With the stealth of the fox, he crept noiselessly up the broad stairs, and shortly arrived at an opening that led to the roof.

Without much difficulty he mounted it, and proceeded with caution along the tiles.

As he did so the iron-tongued monitor of the neighbouring church of St. Sepulchre proclaimed midnight.

The sky was obscured by a sombre clouding, and it was extremely dark.

Wirth Wolfgang had to feel his way.

A false step would have precipitated him from the dizzy height to the street below.

The venturesome climber gazed for a moment to ascertain if he were followed, and, having satisfied himself that his retreat had not been discovered, he stepped onward more boldly.

Having passed Wild's house, he reached an adjoining building, a story higher than its neighbour.

Groping about, to his joy the Dutchman discovered a ladder.

Ascending it, he passed through an open door.

He had now reached what was called the lower leads.

It was a flat surface covering the part of the

prison of Newgate contiguous to the principal gateway.

This spot was surrounded on all sides by walls at least fourteen feet in height.

It has been already stated the ancient tower of Newgate was at the south-east side, while the fugitive had issued out on the north.

To gain the wished-for point, then, he must still traverse a considerable portion of the roof of the main building.

Nothing daunted, he pushed onward in his direction; but his progress was arrested by a massive door.

This door was studded with spikes, and guarded by a bristling *chevaux de frize*.

Unable to force it, he mounted the door he had last passed through, placed his hands upon the wall encircling him, and drew himself up, Jael, the partner of his flight, being drawn up after him.

Both had now reached the highest elevation of Newgate.

From this position the prospect that appeared before the eye was indeed sublime.

The moon bursting from the ebon bonds rendered discernible surrounding objects.

First and foremost might be perceived the majestic dome of St. Paul's, hanging like some dark cloud from the heavens.

Beneath the foot of the solemn temple lay the city slumbering, one vast extent of spire and roof, pointed, countless, and crowded together like the ripples of an ebbing river.

Far off might be seen distant country, the heights of Kent and Surrey, the crowning woodlands of Highgate and the northern eminences.

Proceeding along the wall, Wirth and his companion soon reached the tower that was to offer them concealment.

*   *   *   *   *   *

On the eve of an eventful day, which had been spent in a useless search of the fugitives, Dick Turpin confusedly returned to the neighbourhood of Newgate.

On passing near the bounds of the prison he came upon the figure of a man, apparently travelling in haste and disguise, which riveted his attention.

He felt convinced that he had encountered him before, though the individual in question had scrupulously endeavoured to hide his features from the passers by; curiosity prompted him to follow in the direction he had taken.

The stranger, he observed, incessantly cast furtive glances around, as if to avoid the pursuit of some one.

He took a circuitous and tortuous route to his destination, which happened to be no other than the chapel of Newgate.

A sudden idea made the perspiration start from every pore of the Patrico Turpin.

Strange noises seemed to ring in his ears.

Extraordinary fancies took possession of his mind.

He saw neither houses, pavement, men, or women jostling against him in the public path, all of which were as one confused chaos of objects, blending each with the other.

The hair of his flesh stood up as he saw the man he had watched enter the chapel by a disused door.

Starting from his reverie, the patrico, with a silent footstep, advanced.

Pressing lightly against the panel, he found, to his surprise, that it opened.

The stranger in his haste had evidently forgotten to fasten the entrance after him.

Turpin now found himself in the sacred building.

The façade was dark.

The sky behind it glistened with stars.

The interior, solemn as a tomb, being impartially lighted by the crescent of the moon, which had not long been above the lofty horizon.

With a hurried pace he passed through the lonely aisle.

At the extremity he beheld a reddish glare behind a cluster of pillars.

He ran towards it as a star.

It was a small lamp burning, and must have recently been left in its position by the person he was following.

He took the lamp, which had been placed opposite the door of the Newgate Tower, which formed a portion of the chapel wall, and commenced an ascent of the staircase, winding through the venerable pile.

His light attracted the notice of the passers by, who from the roadway observed it mounting from window to window to the top of the column.

All at once he felt the cold night breeze upon his cheek, so knew at once that he had nearly reached its summit.

He cast his eye down between the iron framework of the tower, and for a time contemplated.

But to the casual observer he appeared neither thinking nor feeling, but as one passive in the hand of a demon.

While in this attitude a gust of wind extinguished his lamp, and at the same moment he saw something white above him.

A shade—a human form—a woman appeared through a veil of mist at the opposite angle of the tower.

He trembled with emotion as he gazed upon her.

He had scarcely the courage to look at the spot upon which she stood.

She came towards him slowly as he remained like one petrified.

He moved not, stirred not, while she advanced.

Suddenly she turned backward, and again entered the dark vault of the staircase from which she had emerged.

"'Tis Jael!" exclaimed Turpin. "She must not escape me a second time."

CHAPTER CX.

PREPARATIONS FOR AN OUTBREAK IN THE MINT — ARMING FOR ACTION—BLADES, MUSKETS, AND PIKES AT A PREMIUM AMONG THE MEN OF CANT—THE SILENT MARCH OF THE RABBLE THROUGH THE STREETS OF LONDON.

WE must again turn to the Thieves' Cave in the Mint.

It was now a monstrous hive where an incessant buzz was kept up night and day.

One evening in particular, had the peace authorities chanced to enter this resort, swarming with the children of vice, they would have remarked that there was a great tumult, and that the vagabonds or whatever other title may be applied to the inmates of this disreputable abode, were both drinking and swearing more lustily than usual.

In an open space without were sundry groups.

They were conversing in a subdued tone.

It was evident that some important enterprise

was planning, if not actually about to be undertaken.

Here and there were men and even women crouching, and whetting some rusty blade or other on the pavement.

Some were engaged in a temporary forge, the glow of whose fire cast a red glare on the characters that surrounded it.

The occupation of these individuals was the making of pikes, brown bills, and such offensive weapons.

While far and wide might be seen members of the motley crew priming or loading every description of fire-arm, from the old arquebuss to the modern musket.

From the conversation of the topers, that is to to say, of those drinking at the rude tables, it would be difficult to say what was the nature of the project.

They merely appeared to be in high spirits, and, between the legs of each might be seen some glittering weapon of steel.

Notwithstanding the confusion which reigned in this assemblage three principal groups crowded round three principal personages.

The reader has been acquainted with them heretofore.

Their names being—

Baptist Kettleby, Master of the Mint.

Simon Smut, the "locum tenens" of the Lord Chancellor of the Cadgers, who, being too drunk to fulfil any onerous office, had retired, not from office, but into a neighbouring coal box for the night.

And last, but not least, the high spice toby-gloak, Joe Blueskin, of immortal memory.

Amidst the din, which was something like that within a bell in a grand peal, was heard the voice of the last party mentioned.

"Come, coves of cant, arm yourselves; make haste, we shall start in an hour for Newgate."

The voice of a young warrior next rose above the uproar.

A rusty breast-plate guarded his panting bosom, and a perforated saucepan, in place of a helmet, protected his head.

This individual possessed a saucy, red snub nose, locks of light hair, rosy lips, and darting eyes.

The organs of vision having a slight tendency to obliquity, which might be ungenerously termed a squint.

He had a belt stuck stock-full of daggers, a long sword at his thigh, and a large jug in his hand, from which, ever and anon, he took "a lusty pull."

Every mouth around him was drinking, cheering and laughing.

"Gentlemen blackguards," he vociferated; "for I am now one of your fraternity, and I mean to extinguish myself."

"Hear, hear!" and roars of laughter from the opposition.

"No, I don't mean that exactly, 'cos I don't intend to put my light under a bushel in this ere noble cause. No! I repeat, with repetition, that if you will allow me, I will show you that this is to be a glorious day."

A gentleman with a black eye and a short pipe suggested the substitution of the word night, in the place of that of day.

"Well, a glorious night if you like," retorted the speaker, boiling with indignation, and bubbling with beer; "but that's neither here nor there, 'cos I'm a vagabond, and my name is Simon Smut."

"Bravo! bravo! the ayes have it."

"I could lay a wager not one o' you would turn back on the prigging lay."

"Not one, not one."

"Then, brothers, we are going on a rare expedition."

"We are valiant coveys."

"And going to break into Newgate to carry off poor Jael the gipsy girl in defiance of the bench of bishops and all the judges and thief-takers in the land.

"We'll lay siege to Jonathan Wild's house, and burn him like a rat in his hole.

"There'll be lots of plunder, and we shall do the trick in less time than an alderman takes to eat a basin of turtle soup."

The rest of Simon Smut's harangue was lost in the tumult and bursts of laughter that swelled around, and his eye swam in ecstacy as its final sentence was hailed with three separate, distinct, and tremendous cheers.

Then followed a moment of comparative quietude, during which Blueskin, as leader of the expedition, instructed his army of knaves in the order of battle.

While this was going forward the crew continued to arm themselves at the further end of the cave, where such whispers as these might be heard passing from one to the other.

"Poor Jael," said a gipsy, "she is our sister; we must release her."

"Is she still in the *Stone Jug?" asked a Jew-looking pedlar.

"Either there or in Wild's house, we don't know which; our spies have failed to make out how she has been conducted hither."

"I am only surprised," returned the other, "that we know thus much, seeing that she was clandestinely carried off after the fire at the 'Dog and Duck.'"

"We should never have made the discovery at all but for the Dutch skipper, Wirth Wolfgang," said the first speaker; "he had been in league with Jonathan Wild for some secret purpose on the the night in question, where by accident he learnt the plot. Following on the footsteps of the plotters he was a witness of the abduction and retreat of the gipsy maiden."

"My handicraft will be in requisition to-night," cried one of the smiths working at the forge, and taking notches out of a broad-sword.

"And mine too," replied another; "I've shod and sharpened three score of pike, and a dozen bills since morning."

"Yes," continued a third, "and, I warrant me, before long they will do their work, and many a one will be food for the crows."

"True; but first we must force the Poultry Compter's boys," interrupted a fourth, "and then we shall be strong enough to venture upon Newgate."

Blueskin, having giving his orders, next proceeded to gather and distribute arms during the singing of one of the peculiar songs of the lawless crew.

"When brave Duval to the crap was brought,
    At the 'Crown' he took his very last draught;
    He took the bowl, he drank and smiled,
    Saying, 'Your turn will come,' to Jonathan Wild.
        And so say we, so say we,
            Tra-la-la! tra-la-la!"

"Comrades," said Blueskin, "you know what hour it is?"

At the sound of his voice there was a hushed silence and quiet like the calm that presages the hurricane.

* Stone Jug, or Newgate.

"It lacks not quite a quar'er to the appointed time of starting," the highwayman continued; "I am told we shall meet the greatest rascal unhung in England as our first obstacle. So much the better. One reason more why we should take our sister, the charming Jael, out of his clutches."

"We shall get on swimmingly," said Blueskin, "for our surprise is unexpected."

"Jonathan and his men are mere hares, we are strong."

"The officers of the parliament will be finely taken in to morrow."

"They will go to the cage; but find the bird flown."

At that moment a distant bell struck.

Blueskin, as some enraged lion springing from his den, leapt on a rostrum.

He uttered one word.

It was shouted in a voice of thunder —

"Midnight!"

At the given signal the horde sprung in a torrent from their cave.

It had the effect of the sound "to horse!" upon a regiment in halt.

The rabble, armed with muskets, pikes, bludgeons, sledge hammers, and every conceivable description of offensive weapon stole stealthily to the appointed rendezvous.

There was no noise, no clanking of iron implements, no confusion; but all was order, discipline, and regular manœuvring.

The principals seemed to arrange and marshal their followers with a true spirit and perfect military precision.

The moon was obscured and the sky overcast as they commenced their march.

The Mint and its purlieus were quite dark, not a light was to be seen.

It was nevertheless filled with a multitude of both sexes, who talked in low tones together.

A vast buzz was to be heard, and the weapons glistening in the gloom.

Blueskin, at the entrance of the unknown quarter, mounted on a huge stone.

He cried aloud,

"Keep in ranks, ye men of cant. Remember, silence in passing through the streets. No torch is to be lit till we are in sight of Newgate. Onward!"

The immense multitude again divided into columns, taking different routes, and lessening in the distance.

In a few minutes the night watch fled panic-stricken before a long black procession crossing in silence old London Bridge, from which they descended, and passed through the winding and massive streets of the time-honoured city.

CHAPTER CXI.

WHAT WIRTH WOLFGANG ESPIED FROM THE LOFTY HEIGHT—THE BEACONS LIGHTED—AN UNEXPECTED INCIDENT — THE BEAM FALLS WITH A FEARFUL CRASH—SIMON SMUT AGAIN DISTINGUISHES HIMSELF—NEWGATE IN FLAMES.

ON the night of the late adventure, Wirth Wolfgang was struck with a singular restlessness, and could not sleep.

Being at the top of the Newgate Tower, his eye naturally passed over the city at his feet, and, in a fit of abstraction took a dreamy survey of the same.

The night, as we have already mentioned, was very dark.

London, at this period, was scarcely lighted at all.

Consequently, at a gloomy period, it presented to the eye, regarding it from an eminence, a confused aggregate of black masses, intersected here and there by the whitish curve of the Thames.

While Wirth's eye wandered over the haze, an unaccountable fear gained upon him.

During the day he had been upon his guard. He had observed several suspicious men furtively glance at Jael's asylum.

And he began to imagine whether her refuge had been discovered.

All at once, as he was scrutinising the city on the eastward side, he observed that it had an unusual appearance.

There was a motion at this point which undulated to the vision, not unlike the waves of a river.

The movement appeared advancing in the direction in which he was standing.

At last, notwithstanding the intense darkness, he could distinguish a column of heads and a crowd spreading itself in the valley below him.

He had a confused foreboding of mischief, and began to consider what course he had best pursue.

Ought he to awake Jael, who, at this critical moment, was sleeping, to assist her to escape from her concealment?

No; that would be to deliver her into a worse fate than death!

The streets were invested by an apparently excited mob, who would regard neither law, honour, nor social duty.

This assemblage seemed to increase every moment.

The noise they made was so slight, that all the windows and houses in the neighbourhood, notwithstanding their presence, remained shut up and closed.

Suddenly a light appeared.

It was the signal.

A torch had been kindled.

A second blazed on the right.

A third on the left.

"To your work, boys," shouted the stentorian voice of Blueskin, amidst the stillness of the night.

His words seemed to have a magical effect.

In an instant a myriad flaming brands shot up above the heads of the multitude, shaking their blaze in the dark region.

So suddenly and strange did these fires spring forth, that one might have imagined a scene of enchantment was taking place.

A long lurid streak fell upon the ghastly sea of faces, and revealed to Wirth Wolfgang a spectacle that made him lean against a post like a drunken man.

He distinctly saw a frightful rabble of men and women.

They were armed with scythes, pick-axes, pikes and brown-bills, who raised their glittering heads apparently in thousands.

Wirth Wolfgang, who had no idea till now of the presence of this human mass, erroneously conceived their object to be the destruction of the gaol by fire.

In that case Jael must of a necessity perish in the flames.

The door of the tower had been securely fastened by Turpin, who, the reader has been acquainted, had visited the spot clandestinely.

Wirth now possessed no means of communicating with this strange army.

It was now making evolutions.

Certain divisions were taking their stations about the vast building.

And the Dutchman roused himself to arrange his means of defence.

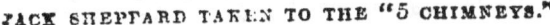

JACK SHEPPARD TAKEN TO THE "5 CHIMNEYS."

Blueskin, on his arrival, had put his troops in order before the gates of Newgate. Though he expected no great resistance within the prison, yet he resolved to preserve a defence (by facing about) in case of a sudden attack of the military, who would doubtless be summoned shortly after the outbreak. Accordingly (like a prudent general) he drew up his brigade for such an emergency. As soon as this manœuvre was completed, Blueskin called on his followers to aid him in the rescue of Jael. Unluckily, Wirth Wolfgang either could not hear these words, or misunderstood their signification. One of the lieutenants delivered his banner to the leader. Blueskin solemnly planted it between two paving stones. It was a pitchfork, on the prongs of which hung a bleeding lump of carrion. This done, he turned round and surveyed his brethren; their eyes glistened almost as much as their pikes. After a moment's pause he gave the word of onslaught.

Several separate parties of stout fellows with brawny limbs and the faces of blacksmiths, bounded from the ranks. They bore ponderous hammers, pincers and crowbars, in their horny hands or on their lusty shoulders. They made for each door of Newgate, and were at work in no time with their pincers and levers. The crowd looked on, while the doors, stout and stubborn, still held firm.

"They are tough and obstinate," said one.

"They will soon give to our blows," said another, making the air ring with the strokes of his ponderous sledge.

"Courage, comrades," shouted Blueskin, "I'll wager my head that you'll force an entrance, bear off Jael, and fire the infernal den before Jonathan Wild is fly to our game ——"

A tremendous crash interrupted the speaker. An enormous beam had fallen from the Newgate tower and crushed a dozen men belabouring its gate. The huge missile bounded on the stones of the street into which it had dropped with the noise of a piece of ordnance, breaking a score or two of legs among the crowd, who scampered off in every direction.

The uninjured blacksmiths, with terror, discontinued their work, and Blueskin himself treat d the deadly messenger with that polite greeting known as a respectful distance.

"Well, I've heard on things tumbling from the

sky," said Simon Smut, "but never could believe it without ocular demonstration. It strikes me forcibly as I've got it now."

Consternation and dismay had fallen on the spectators who had witnessed the late calamity.

For some minutes they stared upwards, more than ever astounded at the mystic appearance of the piece of timber.

"This is the devil's work," cried twenty voices.

"On the contrary," replied others, "the log appears to have been thrown to us from the skies."

"Hold your tongues, you fools; I know how this comes; but say no more about it till we've finished our business."

Though Blueskin made this observation, he was as much in the dark as his companions, and knew as little as they how to account for the fall of the beam.

Meanwhile nothing was to be seen on the Newgate tower, and the top of it was too high for the light of the torches to reach.

The ponderous lamp of wood lay across the pavement and roadway.

Nothing was heard save the groans of the wretches mangled beneath it.

The first shock over, Blueskin fancied he had discovered the author of the mischief.

His remarks appeared plausible to his associates.

"Depend upon it, friends," he exclaimed, "Jonathan Wild has recognized us, and intends defending the citadel; if so, we'll unearth the fox before he fancies he has safely secured himself."

The men of slang looked first at the tall column of the Newgate tower, jutting its head into the black heavens and then at the broad beam lying at its threshold.

Something had damped the courage of the fierce assailants.

"Once more to the attack, boys," shouted Blueskin.

Not a soul moved a foot or stirred a finger.

"What!" continued the robber, "are you frightened out of your wits by the little twig that has snapped over your heads?"

"No, 'taint exactly that, captain," replied the foremost man; "but the door is all clamped with bars and studded with iron. Our implements are of no use; the pincers fail to serve us."

"What do you require, then, to break it open?" asked Blueskin.

"We want a battering-ram."

"Here it is, then," replied the robber, indicating the fallen beam. "Jonathan Wild has kindly sent you one. Thank you, Jonathan," he added, making a mock obeisance to the Newgate Tower.

This piece of bravado on the part of Blueskin produced the desired effect.

By some two hundred vigorous arms the log was picked up like a feather, then dashed against the door the smiths were unable to force.

The door yielded not, though the cavities of the tall column were heard to groan under the terrific shock.

At the moment a pitiless torrent of stones was hailed down upon the invaders of the Sanctuary.

"This is no joke," cried the captain of the party; "the tower is shaking its balustrade upon us."

Blueskin was right; an enormous piece of the parapet had been dislodged and hurled down, cracking skulls in all directions.

Already heaps of killed and wounded lay bleeding at the feet of their comrades, who, nothing daunted, filled up the thinned ranks.

The beam continued to batter, but without avail; the door only groaned.

And still the stones came showering down.

It is almost unnecessary to tell that this unexpected resistance which so exasperated the crowd, proceeded from Wirth Wolfgang, at the top of the tower.

Presently the eyes of all were raised to this point.

They had descried, by the uncertain glimpses of the moon, which had partially shown herself for a few moments, the figure of the Dutchman.

"Is there no way of forcing that infernal door to reach him?" cried Blueskin, in a fit of desperation.

"Shall we give it up for a bad job?"

"Shall we leave Jael a captive still in the hands of the enemy?"

"Let us make one more trial."

"We shall never succeed."

"I don't know that," returned Blueskin. "Where's Simon Smut?"

"Killed, no doubt; he was at our first attack."

"More's the pity; he could have helped us in this fix."

"Captain," said a gipsy, addressing Blueskin, "he isn't killed, for I saw him sneaking away from us just now."

"S'death! the coward, to leave us in the lurch in the very nick of time! No! as I live, there he is, crawling up the pillar of the Newgate Tower."

There Simon Smut was, sure enough.

The brave lad had chosen an ingenious mode of reaching its summit.

The shaft of the column was here and there indented with angles and projections which furnished a ready means of ascent to one accustomed to climbing as Simon had been as a chimney sweep.

He mounted like a monkey up the jagged eminence.

Heels, toes, elbow and knees were each in requisition.

"Head, tail; back'ard and forrard," as he expressed himself, all went to work at once.

He seemed as quick, darting, and sure-footed as one of the antelope species.

Simon soon arrived at the balcony, and nimbly leaped upon it.

The cheering of the vast multitude attended this feat, who rent the air with their loud huzzas.

Simon Smut himself joined in the general shout.

But, all at once, the timorous youth was struck dumb with horror.

He perceived Wirth Wolfgang crouching behind him, while his eyes displayed two balls of fire.

Before he could utter a sound Wirth was upon him.

He caught hold of the poor nervous Simon.

Then pushed him with superhuman force from the pinnacle.

Quietly resting his two elbows on the stone-work, the Dutchman regarded his luckless antagonist in his descent.

It was not so perilous as anticipated.

There was a shriek, a splash, and nothing more.

Simon Smut had been hurled into a large tank of water that exposed itself on a neighbouring roof.

Of the circumstance the multitude beneath were unaware.

A cry of horror burst from ten thousand throats.

"Revenge and storm!" were the only words uttered.

Then followed prodigous yells, curses and imprecations, intermingled with all languages, dialects and accents.

The supposed terrible death of poor Simon Smut had rendered his companions mad with rage.

Fury and vengeance found ladders, and torches multiplied two-fold.

Wirth Wolfgang beheld the rabble preparing to mount the eminence upon which he had been standing from all sides.

Suddenly a flood of flame burst upon the scene of confusion, which, up to this moment, had been buried in darkness.

Newgate was burning!

In a few moments the whole city, to a considerable distance, was illumined by the flames.

The outline of its vast proportions projecting far above the neighbouring houses formed a gigantic patch of shadow amidst all the glare.

The whole vicinity was at once in a commotion.

The bells of the churches proclaimed the intelligence of fire.

The living mass in the streets were yelling, screaming and climbing.

Wirth Wolfgang, a parantly powerless against such a host, trembled for Jael.

Wringing his hands, he swooned from sheer despair.

———

CHAPTER CXII.

THE CONTINUATION OF THE RIOTS IN LONDON— ARRIVAL OF THE MILITARY—THE FIRING ON THE MOB FROM THE WINDOWS—HOW JAEL, THE GIPSY GIRL, GOT OUT OF NEWGATE, AND WHAT TOOK PLACE AFTER THAT EVENT.

WIRTH WOLFGANG did not long remain in his state of stupefaction.

His critical situation at once aroused him from his lethargy, and seemed to tell him that he must be up and doing.

The brave Dutchman, assailed on all sides, had lost, if not all courage, all hope; not of saving himself—he never once thought of that—but of saving Jael.

He ran in consternation round the gallery of the column.

It was on the point of being carried by the mob when their further ascent of the Newgate tower was abruptly stopped.

A tramp of horses was heard in full gallop, and making for the scene of action.

Presently a wide column of cavalry, riding at speed, and a long file of flambeaux, poured with a tremendous noise into the multitude.

They were headed by two leaders, Roving Jack and Tom King.

They had come to the rescue.

The affrighted spectators turned and faced about.

Wirth Wolfgang heard the din, saw the naked swords, and our hero at the head of the horsemen.

He observed the confusion of the rabble; the consternation of the stoutest, the alarm of the weakest.

At the sight of the unexpected succour he mustered strength and threw down the foremost of the assailants, who were already striding into the gallery.

The mob defended themselves with the courage of despair.

Taken in the flank and rear, with their backs towards Newgate, they were at once the besiegers and besieged

The conflict was terrible.

The soldiers gave no quarter.

Those of the rabble who escaped the point of the sword were cut down by the edge: being badly armed, those massacred foamed and bit.

Men, women, and children, darting at the horses, clung to them, like so many cats, with tooth and nail.

Some of the mob thrust their torches i to the faces of the slaughtering troops; some, being pulled from their horses, were literally stoned to death; while others shared a fate as fearful, being backed to pieces by the blunt blades of the enraged enemy.

One was conspicuous above the rest of his followers.

He was armed with a sharp scythe, attached to the end of a long pole.

With this formidable weapon he mowed at the horses' legs, and brought down more than a score of riders with the apparent ease of cutting a field of clover.

This individual was the prime mover of the enterprise, Joe Blueskin.

He appeared likely to exterminate the whole phalanx opposed to him, when a shot laid him prostrate.

The windows of the neighbouring houses had, during the terrible conflict, been thrown wide open.

The occupants, being of a wealthier class, took part in the affair, and bullets were showered from every story upon the rioters in the streets below.

The region was soon filled with a dense smoke from the gunpowder used, and streaked ever and anon with flashes of fire poured forth by the murderous fusillade of musketry.

The desperate multitude were at length discomfited. Their want of discipline and proper weapons had materially assisted in their overthrow.

It was a piteous sight to see them fleeing in all directions, wounded, scared and bleeding, leaving their dead comrades in heaps upon the pavement.

When Wirth Wolfgang, who had been busily engaged watching the progress of the terrible struggle from the leads of Newgate, witnessed the defeat of his supposed enemies, he gave way to a transport of joy.

" Prave poys!" he exclaimed, "you haf saved ma fraulein, de duivel. I had almosht fear for her at von time. Ja, Ja, Muntmeester; but if any unforseen accident had come to de youker, donder und blitzon, who shoult lay de fault on mein shoulders?"

With a quick step the Dutchman then hurried to the retreat of Jael, the access to which he had so gallantly defended.

His surprise—his terror—his dismay may be imagined on reaching her asylum to find it empty.

This circumstance we must explain. When the mob had commenced their attack upon Newgate, Jael, overcome by the powerful excitement she had suffered, had fallen into a slumber. Although her sleep was heavy she was soon aroused.

The incessant shouting and increased tumult awoke her before she had rested many minutes.

At first the superstitious fear of the gipsy assailed her. She fancied that some unhallowed beings were engaged either in mysterious rites, or in infernal battle.

Presently the truth was revealed to her, and she learnt that the conflicting host were desperate men and women struggling with frantic might.

Her terror here took a new form. Had her asylum been discovered by her enemies? Was it her life or liberty they sought? Had she to live or die?

Whilst wrapt in the burst of anguish, Jael heard a footstep approaching her; she looked up and observed a stranger. She could not distinguish his features for the person stood in the shade of the room, which had no light in it save the occasional glare cast from the flaming torches in the chasm below.

The party who had just entered the chamber addressed her by name. The voice appeared to be not unknown to her, and she gave a faint scream.

"You have nothing to fear," said the stranger, "you may trust in me."

"Who are you?"

"Your friend!"

"Your tokens?"

"I have two."

"And they are —— ?"

"Tom King and Wirth Wolfgang."

These names gave Jael fresh courage, for she knew that till now that the latter personage was alone aware of her refuge.

She surveyed her companion, as well as she could in the intermittent gleam, from head to foot.

She could only see a dark figure, muffled up in the ample folds of a cloak.

This apparition seemed to strike her as one dumb.

She would have avoided the stranger, but he would not suffer her to depart.

"Why, would you leave me at such a moment?" he exclaimed. "You must not tarry, but depart in haste."

The maiden still paused.

"My good girl," said the stranger, "why do you doubt my intentions? Since you force me to make the avowal I must tell you that you are in danger."

"From whom?"

"Jonathan Wild. He and the vile mob who are sacking the city will take your life."

"Impossible! I have never injured them."

"The flesh of the wolf requires the tooth of the dog."

"Can your words be true?"

"They are true. I am sent hither by Wirth Wolfgang, who is your friend. Only follow me, and in a few minutes you will be in safety; what is more, you will be in the arms of him you love."

"Then I can have no hesitation in accompanying you, for with him I can either live or face death as fate decrees."

Jael, satisfied with the stranger's fidelity, rapidly descended the stairs of the Newgate tower.

Following in his footsteps she passed through the chapel.

Though dark and solitary the lonely aisles reverberated with echoes from the uproar of the besieging rabble in the streets.

Arriving at a door leading out of the chapel the man in the cloak unlocked it with a key he drew from his pocket.

The gipsy and her companion were now in an open space at the rear of Jonathan Wild's house.

They avoided the residence, and came to a second door.

This was opened as the first, and disclosed a street.

It was entirely deserted, and, being at some distance from the tumult, was in a measure free from noise.

As the fugitives proceeded through several tortuous thoroughfares it seemed entirely to cease.

After a short time they came to a narrow street.

It was composed of very old houses with gable ends, and the upper portion of the tenements seemed to project half across the roadway.

A rude tablet of stone carved on the corner building bore the figures,

"A.D. 1517,"

to show the year in which the edifices were raised.

At the extremity of this street was an archway through which might be discernible a landing place leading to the Thames.

The breeze which followed the current of the water, shook the trees of the neighbouring churchyard, while its rustling was distinctly audible at the point in question.

Jael, descending to the margin of the river, descried its bosom streaked with light.

It was the reflection of the flames of Newgate, then burning.

Anon a dense cloud of smoke shut out the silvery moonlight, and men on distant roads seemed to travel in the shade.

The obscurity passed, the sky became tinged with a hue of blood red, as if the vast city was vomiting hidden blazes.

The scene on the banks of the Thames was now a sight to give a sense of the vanity of this world, and of all the wealth and glory of it.

The conflagration of Newgate and its surrounding neighbourhood mounted towards the heavens in an immense sheet of fire.

This proceeded furiously, and without restraint till at length the whole city appeared in flames

The shipping on the river, and the heaps of merchandize stored away upon its quays, were illumined as if by a glowing globe of light.

The atmosphere was as clear as when the summer sun shone, yet tinged with a lurid glare that might apostrophise the final day.

In a word, the man who could not have witnessed the spectacle could not have had a right apprehension of its grandeur and dreadfulness.

While Jael was contemplating the work of desolation, her companion had hailed a boat.

This individual had not observed, while he was standing under the pointed archway, two figures issue from its gloom to his side.

They were disreputable characters, bearing the names of Long Finger and Harold Bell-the-cat.

Both men were armed with stout staves.

"Save you, sir," said Long Finger, addressing the stranger, who had become suddenly aware of his presence.

"What do you want?" replied he, startled by the abrupt appearance of the robber, but maintaining his wonted resolution of character.

"What do I want!" echoed the other, with a sneer, "why I want everything."

"The deuce; your wants are many, friend," cried the stranger, "and I regret I have not the means of supplying them."

There was a pause.

The stranger remained still; so did his opponent, Long Finger.

At length, wearied by the tedious delay, the former requested the latter to stand aloof, that he, and the maiden with him, might proceed on their way.

"Stand aloof, eh?" sneered the party addressed. "egad 'tis well to talk of standing. I and my friend here," he continued, pointing to Harold, "are tired of standing."

"Yes, we are tired of standing—in the pillory," said the last-named worthy, who for the first time had broken silence during the interview.

"In the pillory, you say," continued the stranger; "perhaps you brought such a punishment on yourselves."

"If all who deserved it took the place we have just left," observed Harold, indignantly, "many dressed gallants would get a sore pelting; but this isn't the thing; do we do business or not?"

" That depends upon its nature ; tell me, what do you require ?"

" Charity."

" That's a sneaking mode of crying, 'stand and deliver.' "

" Well, bestow a trifle on us, sir gallant," resumed Harold ; " you have a close fist else."

" You'll find it close to your head if you don't move off."

Long Finger, ever restless and impatient, new put in his word.

" Come, come, submit quietly, and dub up your cash without further pa'aver ; this is a glorious land of liberty, and we mean to rob you."

" Or cut your throat !" interrupted Harold. " If you have any choice in the matter you will find us most accommodating."

At the end of this speech the speaker found himself opposed to the muzzle of a pistol.

The deadly weapon being well primed and loaded with ball.

The quick and steady hand that levelled it produced desirable results.

To use the language of the fraternity of the "betting world" Long Finger and his chum Harold Bell-the-Cat had " edged."

They were nowhere to be seen.

They had availed themselves of that convenience known as "Shanks's pony," and, like prudent generals, preferred retreat to defeat.

The party who had come to the rescue was no other than Simon Smut.

In the gloomy region which surrounded them neither Jael nor her companion could recognise their preserver ; while he, on the other hand, for a reason which in the end will be made apparent, had no wish that his " incognito " should be discovered.

It may, perhaps, seem strange to the reader that Simon Smut should appear thus *a propos*, and inconsistent that he should arrive so opportunely.

Let him bear in mind his antecedents; when the adventurous youth had been hurled by Wirth Wolfgang from the Newgate tower, and fell into the tank beneath, he, as a matter of course (urged by the immutable laws which govern human nature when surrounded by difficulty) tried to get out of the same with the utmost celerity.

His endeavours were successful, and panting and dripping wet from his emersion in the water, he at once laid himself out on the roof of Newgate " to dry." We quote Simon Smut's own words.

While intent in this peculiar position his eye suddenly rested on the fabric from which he had fallen.

It was then that his notice was attracted by two figures within it.

They were those of Jael and the hooded stranger.

Suspecting either mischief or treachery he had watched them closely, and participated in their flight with what good purpose events have shown.

" Friend," said the stranger, advancing to Simon Smut, who still remained unknown to him, " a friend in need, they say, is a friend truly ; you have rendered me a service worth a thousand fair speeches."

" Well, I can only say, master," answered the other, " you are welcome, and if your road lies westward I will bear you and yonder lady company beyond these precincts. Though the Alsatia of old, which stood in this neighbourhood, has ceased to exist, the present gentlemen of Whitefriars are always stirring with the owl and the bat, and you may meet members of the family before you reach home."

" I thank you for your courtesy," replied the stranger ; " but a boat awaits my signal at yonder stairs. But by what name shall I know my champion ?"

" You may call me John Jackson," said Simon, evasively ; " I'm 'prentice to a merchant here close by."

" A 'prentice and abroad ? Does your master give you license at such an hour ?"

Suddenly, fearing that his subterfuge would be discovered, the questioned stammered out—

" My back will taste of the stirrup leather, I dare say ; but I shan't grieve at that since my playing truant has brought me to your rescue, and that of the pretty maiden who bears you company."

Jael smiled, but maintained the silence she had evinced hitherto.

" Ecod, sir gallant," continued Simon Smut, " there was some good sword play at Bankside this evening ; I was there. Mahoud, the black bear, was baited ; he nipped asunder Ralph, the butcher's dog, and played the very devil among the other curs."

This redoubtable individual, having been cut short in further discourse, then received a piece of money from the stranger, and seemingly departed ; however, having some doubt of his intentions and sincerity, he determined not to lose sight of Jael till he had satisfied himself on the point.

He first observed that the unknown led her to a seat in an angle of the archway, then descended himself to the brink of the river, which a boat was nearing, impelled by two rowers.

" Rest on your oars," he cried to the men, " and be ready to receive your charge ; should fortune favour my hopes, Jael must be mine. Once in my power, she will soon be reconciled. My bright star is in the ascendant ; for see, the bird flies to the net "

With the words, the speaker beckoned to the gipsy girl.

She obeyed the summons, and at a sign, entered the skiff waiting for her, and hid in the shade of a decayed fence, composed of stakes, crossed with laths upon the water's edge.

" Haste, with what speed you may, to Percy House, Stangate !" said the stranger, giving orders to the boatmen. " We are expected to arrive there within half an hour."

From his hiding-place, Simon Smut distinctly saw the man in the cloak now take his seat in the stern of the vessel, while his attendants cut the rope which moored it, and pushed off from the shore with a long pole.

Having taken their stations, they plied their oars, and by the bright light of the terrific fire which still raged in the city, were observed to row towards the place to which they had been directed.

" With this intelligence to Tom King," said Simon Smut, darting from the corner in which he had found concealment, and running down the unfrequented streets like one labouring under insanity, " it will never do to let the little bird build her nest in the jaws of a crocodile !"

CHAPTER CXIII.

PEDLAR'S ACRE.

THE boat, bearing Jael and her companions, pursued its way rapidly up the river, and hugged the right or Surrey bank.

The gipsy girl, though she had trusted herself to the guidance of the unknown, seemed to watch his actions every now and then with a feeling of indescribable terror.

He was seated governing the helm like a spectre.

The cowl of his cloak was still down, and formed a kind of visor.

Every time he opened his arms to propel the rudder, his wide black sleeves gave him the appearance of some gigantic bird flapping its wings.

Since his departure from the shore, he had not uttered a syllable, or allowed a word to escape from his lips.

In fact, there had been no noise in the boat, than such as proceeded from the oars, blended with the dash of the water against the sides of the little vessel.

Suddenly it came abreast of a point of land jutting out into the river.

A shock apprised the occupants that it had reached the shore.

Though at a considerable distance from the tumult they had quitted, the appalling uproar was not deadened on their ears, and the blazing fires of the city shone as brightly as ever.

The unknown rose, stepped up to Jael, and offered his arm to assist her in landing

She refused the aid, and sprang without help from the boat.

She appeared so terrified as scarcely to know what she was doing or where she was going, and stood at length in a state of stupefaction.

When the gipsy girl came to herself she was alone on the river's strand with the unknown.

All at once a cold and clammy hand grasped her's.

Jael strove to speak, but her tongue clove to the roof of her mouth.

Her limbs trembled, her teeth chattered, and she became paler than the rays of the moon which fell upon her cheek.

The mysterious companion of the maiden still continued silent.

With a hasty step he began to move towards a solitary house some half mile off.

Jael, as she suffered herself to be irresistibly drawn along, had a vague feeling that fate was enforcing a decree.

She had lost all power, and followed the path mechanically.

The tract of land traversed was flat and marshy.

It was known by the name of "Pedlar's Acre," and situated on the banks of the Thames near old Lambeth.

The air was damp and unwholesome, for the swamp by which the region was surrounded had not been drained as in later times.

Having proceeded for some time, they came to a point where the road verged to the right, and seemed to bring them again nearer the river, and involved them in a thicker mist.

Jael looked around on all sides.

Not a soul was to be seen.

The lonely spot was absolutely deserted.

Meanwhile, the unknown dragged her along with the same silence and the same swiftness of foot.

She soon lost all recollection, and seemed to walk or proceed onwards as in a dream.

Suddenly she passed a lighted window, made an effort to resist, and cried,

"Help! help!"

The casement opened, the inmate of the chamber appeared at it with a lamp burning in his hand.

He muttered a few words, and then retired.

The gipsy girl felt the last glimmer of hope was destroyed.

Her companion spoke not.

He held her tightly in his grasp, and contemplated her emotion.

After a pause she mustered a little strength, and, in a broken voice, asked,

"Tell me, I beseech you, who and what you are?"

The unknown made no reply.

After a pause, he turned suddenly towards Jael.

As the man approached he raised his cowl

"Oh," stammered the maiden, petrified with horror, "my suspicions are confirmed. I know it must be he, and no other."

It was indeed the patrico.

"Listen to me, Jael,' said Turpin, and she shuddered at his fatal voice.

He continued, while his broken sentences betrayed the inward agitation experienced.

"Arrived at this secluded dwelling, I would speak with you.

"We can go no farther.

"Fate delivers us into each other's hands. If you still reject my suit, I dread to think of that which I shall be compelled to accomplish.

"The end will be terrible."

Having proceeded thus far, the speaker's voice became faint. He resumed after awhile ——

"Jael, turn not your bright eyes from my face, but hearken to my words, they are momentous. Girl, I love you; open not your lips; give me no answer if you despise my passion."

Jael was silent.

"Beware, girl,' exclaimed Turpin, in accents of desperation. "Nothing can be more true than my devotion; could your youth and fond imagination paint but one tithe part of the fierce hell which rages in my bosom—could you read the horrid conflict—you would not hesitate to assuage it at any hazard, at any cost."

Jael still answered not.

"There is a fire consuming my heart," continued the patrico, "night and day, day and night; does this claim no pity?"

"None!"

Turpin buried his face in his hands. Jael heard him for the first time weep. In a moment the paroxysm of grief was over, and the man, shaken by sobs, was as unpliant as marble.

"Jael," he cried, furiously, "since you will hate me for ever, I will take no compassion on you; tremble for your obstinacy."

"There is a fearful import in your words, Richard Turpin, and your eye glistens with anger."

"You see which way my revenge will point."

"Oh! man, let not rage or disappointed love urge you to commit a crime for which you may be sorry hereafter!"

"You plead for my rival; but mark me, you have signed his death-warrant."

"Monster! would you dare ——"

Turpin interrupted her with vehemence. "Tom King will die six hours hence if you refuse me."

Coldly folding his arms across his breast, he contemplated the horror-stricken Jael, and continued—

"Choose between us; shall Tom King live or hang?"

Jael stood motionless as a statue.

Her eye glared wildly as she muttered these words to herself—

"For him—for him—I must ——"

Her lips continued to move, but her tongue ceased to articulate any audible or distinct word.

She passed her hand slowly over her face and regarded her fingers wet with tears. The door of the house before which she was standing now opened, and a man came from it.

This man was Jonathan Wild.

At the sight of the thief-taker, Jael sank, and remained motionless upon the ground.

It is now necessary to describe the habitation before which the gipsy girl had fallen. It was called " Percy House," and stood at the ferry of Stangate, near the present site of Astley's Theatre.

Tradition had assigned it as the rendezvous of Guy Fawkes and the place where he and his fellow arch conspirators had stowed away the gunpowder intended to be used for the destruction of the King and Parliament of England on the 5th of November, 1605.

It was a mean-looking dwelling standing at a short distance from the river side, and its secluded situation and miserable aspect seldom induced any traveller to visit it.

On one side was a deep, muddy sluice communicating with the Thames.

On the other the ancient ferry established by the abbots of Westminster to pass from their monastery to the prelate's residence on the opposite shore.

Within, it possessed but slight accommodation, and only numbered four apartments.

One of the best of these was assigned to Jael, and to which, in a state of delirium, she was conducted by Jonathan Wild and Dick Turpin.

She remained unconscious for two hours.

In her retreat she was paid every attention that circumstances would permit.

At first she seemed rapidly sinking, and that the shock had been too much for her; but at length, having fallen into a placid slumber, she seemed to breathe more freely, and partially to recover her strength.

On awaking she discovered herself stretched upon a pallet.

Jonathan Wild was standing by.

They were alone.

As the maiden recognised the malicious man she strove to release herself by escaping from a window.

She writhed in despair, made many a bound of agony, but the thief-taker held her with seeming supernatural force.

His grip was as efficient as a ring of iron, and his sinister laugh rang in her ears, as he exclaimed,

" Not so fast, girl; we have had some difficulty in securing you, and cannot suffer you again to elude us."

" What harm have I done to you," replied Jael, " that you should thus persecute me ?"

" I am actuated, maiden, by the strongest incentive human nature knows—interest. I am represented to the world as a monster."

" You are a villain !"

" In that respect my character," coolly interrupted Jonathan Wild, " is not original, for so are many men."

" Without principles."

" Your pardon, I have principles, and such, girl, as might bear improvement. Morality, from the lips of a pretty woman, comes with a better grace than scandal."

" You possess no feeling."

" That thrust I parry, since I feel the insults you are heaping upon me."

" You spare neither man nor woman in your hate."

" Stop, girl," said Wild; " let me answer your accusation, then judge if I have cause to love them."

He continued his narration in the following words :—

" One of your sex once wronged me. That

which made me most what I am is a branded name.

" I am of illegitimate birth.

" My brother, and only one, was born in wedlock, and neir by law to wealth of which I should have been part possessor.

" One night, in poverty, I dared to knock at the rich man's door; he said he knew me not, and spurned me from his threshold.

" Sickness and hunger turned shortly my home to one of desolation, and changed my wife from a comely damsel to a shadowy spectre.

" A burning fever dried up her life blood and killed her.

" One solace yet remained—a girl, a babe, the perfect resemblance of the mother she had lost."

" Is she, too, dead ?" asked Jael, like the lamb in the fable.

" To me she is so," replied Jonathan Wild, as he began to laugh and gnash his teeth.

" You are one of the accursed tribe that stole her from my bosom; only think when the poor little one was asleep "

As the thief-taker thus spoke he took into his hand a chain suspended round his neck.

To the last link was attached the remnant of a broken cross.

He placed it fervently to his lips, and gazing upon it, murmured to himself—

" Memento of one beloved, let me press it to my heart ! Curiously cut, no portion but that which she wore could match with the badge of recognition !"

" Let me look at that crucifix ?" said Jael, shuddering.

" Gracious God !" she exclaimed, as she drew a similar one from her breast and discovered its form and devices.

On seeing the counterpart of his treasure Jonathan Wild uttered a stifled yell, staggered a few steps and fell.

He attempted to rise but could not.

He approached Jael on his hands and knees; seizing the ribband flowing loosely from her bosom, he compared the residue of the cross hanging to it with his own.

He joined them, and the jagged edges of the golden ornament matched with each other to a hair's breadth.

He sprang once more upon his feet.

His face beamed with celestial joy as he drew Jael to his arms.

Trembling in every joint, and with a voice that seemed to issue from his very bowels, he cried aloud—

" 'Tis my own child !"

" Are you really my father ?" responded Jael, as she felt horror mounting to the very roots of her hair at the avowal.

" Yes, girl, thy guilty and penitent father !" exclaimed Jonathan Wild. " Scorn him not, for he will live to make atonement for his past errors, and drag thee and himself from the abyss of crime into which he has plunged !"

Jael smiled in affection, and fastened her lips on his.

The conscience-stricken man stood absorbed in that fond embrace.

He gave no sign of life save a sigh from his oppressed bosom, and the tears which flowed from his eyes like a passing shower.

" Child, how I shall love you !" he at length cried out. " We will leave this country, where my name is so deeply execrated; in a foreign land we can be happy. I have money, property; it shall be bestowed on you. You shall no longer blush for me, for I will be good and virtuous. The well spring of my tears, which have oozed drop by drop for twenty winters and summers, are drying now."

At that moment the report of fire-arms was heard in the vicinity of the garden beneath the chamber.

Jael, with terror, threw herself into the arms of Jonathan Wild.

That night a party of armed men attacked the secluded dwelling, and attempted to carry off its fair inmate, with what success a future chapter will show [see illustration of No. 31].

CHAPTER CXIV.

DICK TURPIN'S FAMOUS RIDE FROM LONDON TO YORK.

DICK TURPIN, as the reader may imagine, had not left Jael with Jonathan Wild without some cogent reason.

He had been directed by the thief-taker to intercept "Roving Jack," who was now on a journey to Yorkshire to recover certain portions of his estate which lay in that county.

He was supposed to arrive at his destination by six on the following evening.

Dick, unaided by a relay of horses, to avoid suspicion, had undertaken to arrive at the place in question before him.

He had given Jonathan Wild his word that he would do it, and his mare "bonny Black Bess," would never suffer him to break it.

We will now leave Dick Turpin hurrying over the river marsh at "Pedlar's Acre," and conduct ourselves to the whereabouts of his rival, Tom King.

Simon Smut had informed the highwayman of the carrying off of Jael, and the place of her incarceration.

On receiving the intelligence, he had made his way to the river, and arrived at a small tavern at Queenhithe, over the door of which hung the sign of the "Crown and Sceptre."

He entered, and called for refreshment.

Having disposed of the same, he expressed his desire of crossing the river.

The obliging landlord observed that there was a waterman asleep on the parlour bench.

"Boat wanted!" aroused the drowsy sculler.

"Hulloa, my hearty; I'm ready for a spell," he cried, starting to his feet. "Where's the party?"

"There's the gentleman who requires you," replied the host, pointing to Tom King, who had gone down to the water-side.

"Where to, master?" said the waterman, following his fare, and touching his woollen cap.

"Stangate Ferry," answered the highwayman; "or the nearest point to Percy House, which stands near it."

"Come along, master; I know the place; we shall be there in a jiffey."

Moored to the steps, in front of the tavern Tom King had quitted, were several wherries.

They were dancing in the current, and, like the person they were about to receive, seemed uneasy in their position, and impatient of restraint.

Into one of these boats the waterman jumped, and, having assisted Tom King to a seat within it, immediately pushed from land.

The tide running down rapidly, they were carried at first towards "Old London Bridge."

In a short time the vessel was righted, and proceeded in the direction of St. Saviour's Church.

This passed, it came upon the old and ruinous prison called the Clink, standing near the old palace of Winchester, on the banks of the river.

Presently the Globe Theatre on Bankside was reached, above which floated its banner.

Adjoining this, was the old Bear Garden, whose savage inmates made themselves distinctly audible.

Paris Garden, at Christchurch, next came in view; beyond this was open country and marsh.

Arrived at this point, Tom King heard the sounds of horse's hoofs rattling along the shore, where the boat in which he was seated had stranded.

Thinking the rider might aid them in the difficulty, he hailed him.

This man made no reply, but continued to advance towards the spot from whence his summons had proceeded.

"What brings you here to-night?" said the new comer, narrowly watching the two individuals before him. "The time and place are so ill-chosen that, as a traveller, I must entertain doubts for your greeting."

"Your suspicions are groundless," returned King. "You see only two men on the horns of a dilemma; our boat is entangled in the weeds of the river, from which we are unable to extricate it. We are friends, and——"

"Friends, I must have stronger assurance than words for that."

"Upon my word, stranger," said Tom King, "if I cannot speak well of your courtesy, I must compliment you on your candour, and, certainly, a brazen front and oily tongue are great odds against honest anger."

"You may think you have me at 'vantage," replied the other, "but you are mistaken, for I know you and your purpose."

"Indeed!" said Tom King. "May I ask the name of him who seems but ill-disposed towards me?"

"No, but I can assure Tom King that all his fair prospects are darkness for ever.

"He goes to seek his mistress, but will find her not.

"She will wait his coming on the threshold.

"She will find him there—a stark and rigid corpse."

As he spoke, the horseman drew a pistol from his belt, and deliberately fired at Tom King.

The ball lodged in his breast, and he fell with a groan, lifeless.

"The prophecy is fulfilled! He was doomed to meet death at my hand, and at my hand he has met it," cried the assassin, who was no other than Dick Turpin.

The waterman, who had hitherto witnessed the scene between the two highwaymen in silence and wonder, at its termination boldly rushed forward.

He seized the bridle of the horse, and endeavoured to dismount Dick Turpin.

The latter put spurs to his animal, whose impetuosity at once overthrew its master's antagonist.

In an instant both man and beast were out of sight.

Anon, five men bore home the lifeless body of Tom King. (See Illustration of No. 30.)

We will here dedicate a page or two to Turpin's famous ride to York.

Passing preliminaries we conduct the reader to Windmill Hill, on the north-western side of the metropolis.

THE OLD HOME---(*See No.* 34)

From this point the highwayman is commencing his journey in pursuit of Roving Jack.

In a short time he reaches Hampstead, and dashes towards Highgate.

Arrived here, Crouch End and Hornsey toll-bar are soon passed, the spikes of the bar and a donkey-cart waiting at the closed gate being cleared apparently with ease by Black Bess and Turpin.

This incident caused great surprise to the proprietor of the petty vehicle, and much chagrin to the bilked collector, who suddenly aroused from his last forty winks.

The poor fellow, who had been dozing all the night, was not in the best humour to be thus ousted the first thing in the morning.

Skimming, like an eagle on the wing, the brave mare and her rider next entered Hertfordshire.

The limits of two counties left behind, they then entered merry Huntingdon, and in the fourth hour had accomplished sixty miles.

Lincolnshire, Rutlandshire, and Leicestershire are next reached and travelled through, and Notts gained.

The noble Black Bess, at this period, gave symptoms of distress, and for the second time on their journey the highwayman and his steed stayed to bait.

While resting at a road-side inn a traveller entered the room in which Turpin was ensconced.

As he did so, the heavens, which had been obscured by dark and lowering clouds, suddenly poured down a terrific shower of rain.

The atmosphere became so thick that nothing was discernible, save that which was made so by the vivid lightning that ever and anon darted before the eyes of the terrified spectators.

The forked fires were, in every instance, succeeded by a peal of thunder that seemed to shake the earth beneath it with a violent convulsion.

The appearance of the traveller in the chamber seemed somewhat sudden to Turpin.

In fact, he rather glided than walked as he proceeded.

His countenance, as far as could be discerned in the haze, was livid and cadaverous, while his garments, mouldering and much worn, gave him something of a ghost-like aspect.

Without returning the fixed glances of his fellow guest, or deigning to notice him, he pursued his way to the further end of the room, and took a seat.

Turpin, who had been engaged over a hasty meal, lost his appetite, and pondered on when and where he had met his mysterious companion.

He felt a curious presentiment that he had seen him before.

While yielding to doubt and fear, the highwayman determined to address the stranger.

He was about to do so when a dazzling flash seemed to blind him.

Having recovered the shock, he turned to the spot where the visitor was stationed, but found his chair unoccupied, while he himself had passed noiselessly away.

Dick Turpin, dumb-founded, hastily quitted the room for the stable of the inn, in quest of Black Bess.

Here the figure again presented itself.

The gloom at this spot was darker than ever, and, though in close proximity, he could not distinguish the features of the spectral intruder, who raised his hand menacingly on quitting, or, more properly speaking, vanishing from his sight.

Shaking off his apprehension, Turpin once more started for York.

As the bell of a distant church struck five on that eve the river Ouse was crossed.

He had now only nine miles to finish his journey, and an hour left from the given time of its completion.

Long before it the spires of York had broke upon his view, and he had arrived upon the city's boundaries.

The minster proclaimed six o' the night, when Black Bess tottered and fell.

The poor beast had been ridden to death !

As Turpin carelessly contemplated the quivering carcass, he exclaimed,

" I've done it, though ; I've killed the best mare in England."

Muttering, he continued,

" The eye of posterity will be upon us ; 200 miles in 10 hours, eh ! Winged Pegasus couldn't have kept our pace. The feat will immortalize horse and horseman, and children unborn will laud the deeds of Dick Turpin and bonny Black Bess ! "

The highwayman was roused from his reverie by the sudden appearance of a man, who seemed to issue from a tangled thicket adjacent.

He at once recognised that it was the same stranger encountered on his journey.

Seized with a peculiar sense of danger, Turpin fled swiftly from the presence of him he had reason to dread.

Having gone some distance he glanced behind, and, to his surprise, if not terror, beheld but too plainly that the pursuer was rapidly gaining upon him.

This caused the highwayman to renew his exertions.

Heedless of every impediment, he dashed madly on.

The other followed in the path like his shadow.

On the outskirts of the city of York was a solitary dwelling.

This Turpin had succeeded in reaching just as the one who was giving chase was within a few yards of it.

With a wild effort he rushed into the tenement, which appeared deserted.

Fastening the doors and shutters of the house, he congratulated himself on the protection offered.

To his dismay, he next found that he had left his weapons in the holster of the saddle of Black Bess.

And that in dire emergency was without arms.

His fears were then increased by a loud knocking at the door.

This at once told how intent his supposed enemy was upon the prey he had, for the moment, lost.

Presently the windows of the room were dashed in.

Dick Turpin gave himself up for lost, conceiving, and with some show of probability, that his persecutor was forcing an entrance there.

He was deceived.

All was soon quiet.

He listened.

No sound met his anxious and keen ear.

All seemed silence and security.

But, to assure himself of the latter, the highwayman took the precaution to examine the closets in the apartment, and, finally, the well staircase which led to the upper chambers of the house.

Scarcely, however, was the latter door opened than, awe-struck, Turpin beheld the man whom he had hoped to have avoided.

In the aperture frowned the gaunt form of the mysterious stranger.

He stood before Dick Turpin.

He was now holding a pistol in his hand.

His countenance was stern.

His look betrayed the vindictive feelings that struggled within him.

The glance that was cast seemed to strike the bold robber as a basilisk.

His stout frame shook.

His lips quivered, and he sank powerless.

On the ground he lay as one in a trance, devoid of sense, feeling, sight.

After a while he woke to consciousness.

The terrible figure had changed its character, and appeared to have assumed that of a Dutch captain.

Was this a dream ?

Or was it reality ?

The first fumes of fear having gradually dispersed, Dick Turpin rose to find that he was not invested by a spectre, but by a creature of flesh and blood, and that it was indeed Wirth Wolfgang who stood before him.

His terror, without being augmented, altered its form.

He now conceived a notion of the possibility that his flight had been discovered and followed up.

" You have discovered my retreat, then, Wirth ?" said Turpin, exhibiting a composure he was far from experiencing.

" Yaw, you may say dat," was the Hollander's reply.

" You bear letters of marque, eh, privateer ?"

" Nein, mynheer," answered Wolfgang ; then, turning the conversation, continued, " 'Tis a verre long time since we have greeted, goot friend, and yet I shoul' haf known you if we had for to meet on a proad plank on ze Atlantic."

The peculiar manner in which the last words had been spoken, caused Dick Turpin more than ever to regard his companion with a feeling of distrust.

Being determined at once to learn his intentions, he exclaimed,

" What brings you to this part of the country, Wirth ?"

" Vell, a leetle business and a leetle pleasure."

" Well, business first—it should, according to the maxim, precede pleasure."

" Dat ish goot ! Never take von reef in until you are in der channel. Listen : I haf had von dream last night."

" A dream ?"

" Yau ; and a very droublesome dream, too. I was spanking dro' de vaters in my yawl. Vhat do you think I see on de banks ?"

" I can't imagine."

" I see two men ; one pursued de oder. His eyes glared wildly, and dere was murder in his step."

" Murder ?" stammered out Turpin, glancing with intensity and suspicion at the utterance of the word.

" Yau, mynheer, dat ish drue," continued the

Dutchman. "His object was revenge, dire and deadly revenge. I witnessed then a scene of horror and darkness, such as froze up de current of mein blood. Dere was a flash, and der pistol ball leapt from de tube to de rival's heart !"

"You recognised the assassin ?"

"What you say ish right, mynheer. His face was dat of your own, Dick Turpin !"

"And the victim ?"

"Your best friend in dis world, de prave Tom King !"

"I am betrayed !"

"Tush, donder and blitzen ! You forget, muntmeester, dat all dis was only a dream."

For some moments Turpin remained motionless as a statue.

He then shook his head doubtingly, and muttered—

"Cursed chance, and I am without a weapon !"

After a pause, Wirth Wolfgang again raised his voice—

"Before I go on with my leetle matter of business, I will settle one of pleasure."

"What would you do ?"

"Mein duty. I have a warrant for your apprehension."

"Ah ! who has done this ?"

"Me, mien friend ; you don't remember me. I am your former accomplice, whose wife, like a tief as you are, you shtole from mein affection and left to perish far away !"

"Nay, recur not to the past," cried Turpin, imploringly ; "my interest."

"Your interest ?" laughed Wolfgang, bitterly. "Before I ask for it, answer me von plain question."

"Which is ?"

"To name de man who has destroyed and broken mein peace for ever."

"I have been to blame, certainly," returned the supplicant ; "I know it, and do not attempt to deny it."

"Vine words, vine words indeed, to a man you haf ruined," exclaimed the Dutch skipper ; "but death and hell ! why do I breach ? I mean to save Jean Ketch von trouble, and for fear you should shlip dro' his vingers, I may as vell tell you——"

The speaker paused, and then continued,

"Your hour has come, mynheer. You haf taken your last look of dis vorld."

As Wirth Wolfgang thus spoke, he cocked his pistol, and held it to the head of Dick Turpin.

The latter, seeing no hope of mercy, thought only of prolonging his existence, even though but for a few minutes.

Aid might arrive.

His cruel enemy might yet relent.

At any rate, some contingence might occur that would, perchance, save him.

"Hold !" he exclaimed, "this is a mean cutthroat sort of vengeance."

"I am wronged."

"Be it so. That is the reason why, if you possess the spark of honour, you should give me one of the weapons you hold in your hand."

"Indeed ! '

"We can then decide our difference by fair and noble means."

"Muntmeester, when you robbed me of mein happiness," replied Wirth Wolfgang, "you refused my challenge."

"I was a villain."

"Dat is goot. Dere is no denying dat. You haf deserved no petter of me than to die a dog's death by mein hand."

"You will give me a chance of my life ?"

"Ja—ye-es, dough it is but a poor von, for if I miss you, it will be the first time I haf ever missed my man. Here is your weapon."

With these words, the generous Dutchman now handed Dick Turpin a pistol.

As he turned his back to take his ground, his treacherous adversary fired at him.

The aim was a bad one, and Wirth Wolfgang rushed fiercely towards the coward, who threw himself on his knees, and implored for mercy.

"Why !" exclaimed the enraged skipper, "you surely cannot have de face to ask dat ?"

"Do not murder me."

"Ha ! ha !" exclaimed Mynheer, laughing in derision. "De daivel take me," he continued, "if I am not almosht ashamed to strike such a puling miscreant. You haf not de heart to die like von man, for die you must, and dat before de night ish many minutes older."

"Nay ; I meant you not unfairly," said the pleading robber, "the pistol went off unawares, on my honour—on my soul it did."

"Stop ! for dere is one hears you dat does not like liars. Don't swear away your precious soul, and you are so near for to die."

Wirth Wolfgang uttered the sentence with solemnity, and raised his finger the while towards heaven.

"Grant me but an hour," implored Turpin, in an abject voice.

"Not half an hour," vociferated his enemy, "not de fourth part of one. De stroke of seven is your death-knell."

Here the speaker pointed at the clock standing in the corner of the room.

Its hands showed that it wanted but five minutes to the fatal period.

Turpin still knelt and entreated to be spared.

But Wirth Wolfgang continued firm and obdurate.

"Make up you accounts wid God !" he cried. "Pray, pray ; I'll stand aside for de time."

"Is there no hope for me ?" sighed the trembling wretch. "No chance ? The seconds fly like lightning, and a thousand bells are ringing in my ears, as if Satan himself was pealing me a welcome into hell. I can think of nothing—speak of nothing but death," he continued. "Death ! I hear it in the roaring of the flames ! I see the ghastly form in the shadows on the wall."

Was there no escape ?

Yes. Turpin heard steps—the tramp of horses, too.

The sound seemed to come nearer and nearer.

At this instant the chamber clock struck the seventh hour.

The hour that was to seal the earthly career of Richard Turpin for ever.

Wirth Wolfgang approached him.

He cocked his pistol, and exclaimed,

"The last moment has arrived. Are you ready ?"

"Spare me, spare me !" cried the victim of his wrath, in mortal agony, and averting his face from the eyes that glared so terribly upon him.

Wirth, resolute in his purpose, seemed deaf to entreaty.

As the last stroke of the clock struck upon the ear, he discharged his weapon full at the head of Dick Turpin.

He fell to the earth heavily, a livid corse, first heaving a deep groan.

At that moment the outer door was forced open with a terrific crash.

CHAPTER CXV.

THE DEVIL'S PUNCH-BOWL POLL MAGGOT AND
HER GUESTS—HIGHWAYMEN VERSUS GAMBLERS
—HOW SIR MAURICE LACY PROFFERED ASSIST-
ANCE TO HIS FRIEND, AND THE MEANS BY

WHICH HE INTENDED TO CARRY OUT THE SAME.
TIME had rolled onward and some ten months had
elapsed since the supposed death of Dick Turpin,
when a party of men were discovered one night
seated in a tavern called "The Devil's Punch Bowl,"
which tavern was also dignified by the name of the
"House of Call" for highwaymen, for its frequenters were usually knights of the road, and
in the present instance its spacious parlour was
tenanted alone by that fraternity and professed
card sharpers.

Among the guests were two individuals already
known to our readers, Sir Ranulph Gayton and Sir
Maurice Lacy.

These men, of good birth, family, and education,
were now the associates of the most abandoned
characters.

What had wrought this change? That most
dangerous of all passions—play.

The destiny of the gambler, it has truly been
said, is inscribed on the gates of hell.

It makes the son ungrateful; the husband remorseless; the father the foe of his offspring.

But, dissertation apart, it is sufficient only for
our purpose to say that the parties mentioned had
fallen from their exalted station and become depraved, unscrupulous, and worthless.

The interior of the tavern already alluded to
presented a scene of animation and bustle. Its
walls resounded with laughter, and its tables were
covered with glasses and well-filled tankards.

The jovial crew of guests were enjoying themselves, each according to his own taste, and principally engaged in singing the following song:—

"Here's to the gallant cavalier
That braves the road in quest of gold;
Here's to the nymph each heart holds dear,
Ne'er to his love may she prove cold.
Let the rosy wine flow;
Let the toast go round,
And every heart shall bear a part
In pleasure's festive bound."

There was no one more conspicuous in the merry
assemblage than the fair hostess, Poll Maggot.

She was one of those women who seem to be
younger and more attractive as they grow older.

She had increased, it is true, in bulk, but her
admirers only considered her plumpness an improvement.

Her sleek tresses, her laughing eyes and smooth
brow, set, as it were, care, solicitude, and old Father
Time at a nonplus.

Her guests, regaling themselves after their song,
proposed the health of the mistress of the hostelry.
A proceeding that was carried out with all due
ceremony by the brawling company, accompanied
with lusty shouting and a thumping of the tables.

"I hope, my good sirs," said Poll Maggot, laughing, "that you do not expect me to return thanks
individually for the honour you have done me; if
so, I shall have to occupy your attention from this
time till to-morrow."

"You have only to speak and we are dumb-
founded, mine hostess," replied Sir Ranulph
Gayton.

The words of the speaker were somewhat thick
and husky, and evidently provoked by the deep
draughts of which he had partaken that evening.

"I will sum up what I have to say in a few

words, Sir Ranulph," said Poll Maggot, with a
smile, "it's only to thank you, one and all, for your
favours, and I must acknowledge that you, gentlemen of the road and town, have formed a merry
and gallant band in my house. Lone widow that I
am, since my last husband's sudden death at Tyburn,
I don't know what would become of me but for
your charitable visits."

One at the further end of the table now put in his
veto; it was the highwayman, Nat Rose.

"No more sighing about your husband, hostess,"
he said, "recollect sudden death is what we of the
"Post" are all subject to."

The general laugh of the company having subsided, Poll Maggot addressed one of their number
in particular.

"Well, let us change the discourse to one more
lively. By the way, Sir Ranulph Gayton, how goes
on your love affair with Violet Tremaine, she
that's betrothed to Sir John Warbold, whom I shall
never cease to call Roving Jack by name?"

"Faith! ill enough. Nothing can turn the
maiden's stubborn heart; however, no bird flies so
high that it may not be taken by the fowler some
day or other."

"You are right," said a voice, which had been
hitherto silent.

It was that of the celebrated gamester, Sir Maurice
Lacy.

"What if I lend you a hand," he continued, "to
wing the fair prey you are speaking of, Sir Ranulph
Gayton?"

"You, Sir Maurice Lacy? And I pray you tell
me how you can accomplish that in which I have
hitherto so signally failed?"

"The means are easy enough if I only   your
permission to put them in force."

"How will you set about it?"

"My intention is to ruin the lover of the fair
mistress, Violet Tremaine, at play."

"Have a care how you ruin people," interrupted
Poll Maggot; "recollect that my former paramour,
Jack Sheppard, who you treacherously gave into the
hands of justice, I hear is lurking about the town,
and threatens your life if chance permits that you
should meet him."

"There is no fear of that, Poll," answered Sir
Maurice, "Jack Sheppard is safely locked in
prison."

"Granted," exclaimed Poll Maggot, "yet you
may not be so secure as you fancy, for 'tis said, and
with some truth, that the prison is not built that
can hold gallant Jack Sheppard."

While this conversation was going forward most
of the company had finished their glasses, and now
began to call for a fresh supply.

"Hola, hostess!" cried one.

"More brandy, more brandy," vociferated another.

"To the cellar, Poll, or we must do the office for
ourselves," exclaimed the rest.

With such admonitions as these, the buxom
woman could do no other than attend to the surrounding clamour.

As she did so, we must return to our friends, the
dissolute baronets.

"Well," said Sir Ralph Gayton, addressing, and
coming forward to Sir Maurice Lacy, "you were
talking of serving me in the affair of Violet
Tremaine, for whom you know I have suddenly
taken a great passion."

"Yes," replied the other gentleman, "you have
been my friend, and I will prove yours. I have
scores to settle with this Roving Jack, and I shall
not be satisfied till I have witnessed his downfall.
Tutored by my instructions, since his accession to

wealth and fortune, he has become devoted to play."

"A gambler !"

"Yes; the seeds of this vice are now implanted in his heart, which brings in its train poverty, disgrace, and crime; his resort is ever the gaming house, where he has lost to me in the last four months half his estate."

"Can this be possible? I can scarcely credit what I hear."

"'Tis true, nevertheless," said Sir Maurice, superciliously; "but your good fortune and mine does not end here."

"I see; you are not content with what you have won already?"

"No; I am determined my vengeance shall be ample and complete. You see these dice?"

As he spoke Sir Maurice Lacy produced two cubes, apparently composed of solid ivory.

"These dice." he resumed, "are loaded; one single throw and Roving Jack is left without a penny."

"What a scoundrel!" ejaculated Sir Ranulph Gayton, in an underbreath, and with difficulty concealing his contempt.

"You don't seem satisfied," replied Sir Maurice, who had noticed the reserve of his companion.

"I am perfectly so," stammered out Sir Ranulph, assuming the usual composure; "I should be very ungrateful if I were otherwise, as you have discovered the time to me when I can subdue the lady."

"You know the old adage, 'When poverty peeps in at the door, love escapes by the window.'"

"I read comfort in your words, Sir Maurice. Violet Tremaine will yet be mine."

"I'll do the best to make her so," replied the villanous baronet, as he was about to replace the loaded dice; "and if I succeed not, may these false instruments be buried in my determined heart as firmly as I now grasp them in my determined hand."

"That is a strange wish," muttered Sir Ranulph, to himself; "but stranger still should such a wish be gratified; an unaccountable anxiety, a painful presentiment, weighs on my spirits, and stifles the joy that should spring up in my heart."

"So late! I have an appointment with my dupe," said Sir Maurice Lacy, looking at his watch.

"If so," replied his companion, "I will bear you company; a scheme has just entered my head that may serve us materially in our project. We will talk the matter over on our road."

The two gallants were taking their departure as Poll Maggot crossed over to them.

She curtsied lowly, and, with bewitching simplicity, accosted them, with what intention may be guessed from the following dialogue.

"Good day, good sirs," said the Amazonian beauty; "it cuts me sadly to separate, but haply you have about you some slight token of remembrance, some trifle of consolation for your absence."

While she was yet speaking she eyed archly a silver snuff-box from which one of the gentlemen was taking snuff.

"That's a neat box, Sir Maurice," she observed, with seeming disinterestedness.

"Pray accept it," he replied, for what other could a man do placed in such a perplexing situation?

"That would be robbing you," said the sly enchantress, at the same time taking care to secure the present, and place it safely in her pocket.

"Have you no word for me, Polly?" chimed in Sir Ranulph Gayton, pressing her hand in his own.

"I shall be jealous of my friend if he occupies all your smiles."

The speaker paid somewhat dearly for his complaisance.

His fervent grasp had betrayed the brilliant that adorned his finger.

We need not say who became the subsequent possessor of the same.

The ring fitted Poll Maggot marvellously well.

She did the donor the honour to wear it for his sake.

Sir Ranulph Gayton and Sir Maurice Lacy were followed from the "Devil's Punch-Bowl" by a third and unseen party.

Who and what he was the reader will learn in due time.

CHAPTER CXVI.

A NIGHT AT D'OSYNDARS—DEEDS IN THE DARK.

YOU would have seen on a certain stormy night, in a solitary house in the neighbourhood of the metropolis, a man in the prime of youth deeply engaged over a pack of cards.

The broad and lofty chamber in which he was seated was lighted by two candles.

These being burnt to their sockets showed how deeply he had been interested in his ardent occupation.

He followed with anxious looks his hazardous manipulation.

Ever and anon he suddenly stopped, as if to anticipate some unknown secret.

Full of despair, and violently agitated, he had continued for hours to deal and play with the cards before him.

At length, having accomplished his apparent object, flushed, nervous and powerfully excited, he exclaimed with enthusiasm,

"I have discovered it!"

Again and again he applied to his cards, and again and again with similar success.

"Yes," he joyfully continued, "nine, ten, knave, ace; that's it. The calculation proves perfectly correct. I have at length reduced it to a certainty. It is a manœuvre that might recover all—all that I have lost."

There was a pause—a hesitation.

"But, what says honour!" exclaimed the gamester; "I dare not think, for, if I succeed not, I am irretrievably ruined. Let me, for the last time, try the experiment."

As the cards were being shuffled by Roving Jack—for the reader has no doubt recognised in the above individual our hero—the voice of Violet Tremaine was heard in the lawn beneath him.

"Violet's voice!" he cried; "then it must be morning."

As he undrew the curtain of his chamber window the golden beams of dawn woke him to remorse.

Yes, it was broad, sunny, daylight.

All the long night he had not slept.

Over the talismanic tablets he had forgot the repose due to nature.

Fatal infatuation!

Soon there was a tap on the outside of the door, and a well-known and beloved name pronounced.

"Yes, Violet, tarry an instant while I put away the books."

Thus saying, our hero thrust the cards with which he had been playing into a table drawer.

While doing this he observed,

"She must not perceive the nature of my nocturnal studies—studies that give paleness to the cheek, anguish to the heart."

Sighing, the speaker put out the tell-tale candles, doffed his robe de chambre, and in morning dishabille, received his betrothed.

Violet Tremaine made her appearance with a freshly-gathered bouquet in her hand.

"Many happy returns, Sir John, of this day."

In surprise, he replied,

"This day, my birth day, dearest girl? I really had forgotton it—thanks for the sweet remembrance."

Planting a fervent kiss on the brow of Violet, our hero in return accepted the bunch of flowers she presented to him.

As he regarded the gift, he cast a glance askance at the giver.

"Pure emblem of yourself, I warrant me they come from—"

"From your own castle in Devonshire—near your native place—from the rustic bower where you and I have so often sat to contemplate the delights of a country life."

"Yes, Violet, they surpass the pleasures of the glittering town. Here, each joy has its heart ache—every sweet its bitter."

"Come, come," you are too severe," replied Violet. "Though I admire the country, like a swallow I would fly from it in winter."

She continued then to say,

"But I have a favour to ask of you, Sir John. This day you must at least be mine. I have planned a little fairy tale for the amusement of the company invited on your natal day."

This announcement seemed to confuse our hero, who, in haste, exclaimed,

"My dear Violet, what you ask of me is impossible. I have promised an engagement with—"

"Your near friend, Sir Maurice Lacy."

"Yes," replied the party addressed, who seemed somewhat abashed at the avowal.

"Really, of late, Sir John," cried Violet, not a little provoked, "your every thought seems his. He surely can spare you on this occasion, or I shall think him unkind."

"Spare me—by heaven, he must, he shall!" exclaimed our hero, petulantly. "Violet, you have bound affection's chain around my neck, and shall lead me where you will. I will break this worthless engagement. I must be from home—or—"

Here his notice was attracted at a voice behind him.

It was that of Sir Maurice Lacy.

He had stood at the open door of the apartment contemplating the lovers with a keen eye.

At his appearance, Violet at once excused herself and quitted his presence, leaving the gambler and his dupe alone.

"How, Sir John Warbold," remarked the former, "not at home to me?"

"I am at home to no one," replied the other, with acrimony. "I have promised myself this day to Violet."

"You forget, perhaps, that last night also you pledged yourself to me and two others to give us at the tables of D'Osyndars* our revenge this evening."

"Did I give my word?"

"Decidedly so. Recollect, too, you left off winner."

"Ha, ha! I—a trifling sum."

"Have you tried over the calculation by the cards as I instructed?" inquired Sir Maurice Lacy.

"All the night long I tried it," was our hero's answer.

* D'Osyndars. A noted gambling house of the last century.

"You succeeded?"

"Well."

"Then our losses are repaid."

"I wish it were with honour."

"Pshaw! we but plunder plunderers."

* * * * * *

We must now picture to the reader a view of the celebrated "hell," or gambling house, known as D'Osyndars.

It is night, and its spacious rooms are brilliantly lighted up.

Tables for cards and dice are set out at every corner.

Coffee is served as their occupants are sitting down to basset, or engaged in the exciting game of hazard.

Ever and anon delicious wines went round in flowing bumpers, a circumstance which contributed greatly to increase the spirits of the company—losers as well as winners.

On arriving at this den of iniquity our hero and Sir Maurice Lacy ascended the stairs and entered the room where hazard was always played, for it was agreed upon by the wily sharper that fortune, in the first instance, should be tempted at this game.

His victim, with "lucky dice" provided by his destroyer, turned to play.

In a few minutes he had swept a hundred pounds off the board.

"Did I not tell you how you would succeed?" whispered Sir Maurice. "Stake your all, and good fortune will still attend you."

Our hero obeyed the injunction.

The cubes rattled in the box and seemed as if by magic to fall precisely as he wished them to fall.

He was surprised at his run of luck.

He seemed to get back what money he pleased, and trembled with excitement to find himself in half an hour worth at least two thousand pounds.

His exulting look goaded now another adversary to play.

This adversary was no other than Sir Maurice Lacy himself.

Thinking that his supposed friend had some object in this, he unhesitatingly accepted the challenge.

He was somewhat piqued the next moment to find that the total amount of his gains had been named as the stake.

Abashed, confused, and not knowing what to make of the proposition, he was so placed that he could not but accede to it.

A sudden idea seemed to calm him when he remembered by what unfair means he had won his money.

"I have still the loaded dice," he muttered to himself; "the blind goddess will attend me in this venture."

"Come, Sir John," said his opponent, "as you still hold the box you may as well give the first throw."

"I have no choice," responded Roving Jack, "therefore let it be as you desire."

As he was about to throw, a sudden faintness seemed to seize him.

His sight grew dim, and his arm paralysed.

This gave his opponent the chance he had premeditated.

Nat Rose, the highwayman, who had now entered as his accomplice, seeing the embarrassment of our hero, took the opportunity as he put down the box of exchanging the dice in it.

After a minute the latter had recovered himself, and played with extreme caution.

"Seven's the main," he cried.

"A nick," exclaimed Sir Maurice, the victor.

Roving Jack staggered to see his evening's winnings vanish at a cast.

All eyes were upon him as he doubled the stakes.

Sir Maurice was willing, and they went on.

Four thousand pounds were placed on the table, and changed hands in a few moments.

Our hero was again vanquished.

There was another throw.

It was the last.

His estate against twenty thousand pounds.

Having reached this fearful climax, the pivot upon which turned his sole hope and fortune, Roving Jack seemed scarcely to move or breathe.

He grew pale, and beads of sweat gushed from his forehead of marble.

Notwithstanding the fixed gaze that greeted him on every side our hero rattled the box bravely, and threw the dice with apparent unconcern.

The next moment he was a beggar, for Sir Maurice Lacy rose from the table the winner, and in the supposed possession of £40,000.

His antagonist stood stupefied at his ill-success, but he bore his defeat better than might have been expected.

All at once he strode quickly across the room as if struck by some sudden idea, and faced the baronet quitting it.

He would gladly have avoided the meeting, but escape was impossible.

Roving Jack seized his arm and held it fast.

"Sir Maurice Lacy," he exclaimed, "I shall not allow you to quit this place until I have ascertained whether or not I have been swindled out of my property by trickery and dishonest practices."

"Such language ill becomes you, Sir John. Are you mad or drunk?"

"Neither, villain! cheat!"

"Cheat!" roared Sir Maurice. "Do you dare to insinuate that I have played unfairly in our late game?"

"You have used loaded dice, I am certain," replied Roving Jack; "I noticed the peculiar way in which you handled them. As you continued to win, my suspicions were confirmed that you were playing with the fell instruments by which you had tempted me."

"When you are calm," replied Sir Maurice, coldly, "I shall expect an apology for this undeserved insult."

"Produce the dice that you have used in proof it is one."

"I have them not; some one has abstracted the——"

Roving Jack gave vent to a disdainful laugh.

He released the grasp he had hitherto maintained of the baronet's arm.

And in bitter accents exclaimed,

"'Tis a subterfuge, and I shall not withdraw the charge I have brought against you."

"Boy you presume," returned the other, contemptuously.

"Boy that I am, you fear me—you fear to look the victim you would have robbed in the face—and since you heard me, I have but one resource. Sir Maurice Lacy, you are a coward and villain!"

With the words Roving Jack advanced suddenly on Sir Maurice Lacy, and struck him full in the face.

The baronet's pale cheek burnt crimson.

His dark eye flashed fire.

Putting his hand upon his sword, he exclaimed in wrath.

"A blow!—blood must answer that."

"When and where you please."

"To-morrow."

"At earliest dawn."

"With all my heart."

"The place of meeting?"

"Name it yourself."

"To me all places are alike," said Roving Jack. "Anywhere be it—say near the old Elm Tree, near the Abbey Yard, at Westminster, at the time appointed—it will be a retired spot."

"Agreed," rejoined Sir Maurice Lacy. "I shall be there at the hour. Master Nat Rose, you will do me the favour to act as second in this affair 'of honour?'"

"I shall reserve my choice of a friend," continued our hero. "Heaven knows the bankrupt may not need one."

While the scene was going forward, one of the servants of the establishment hurriedly entered the apartment.

His excited looks at once betrayed that something alarming had occurred.

"Escape, gentlemen, as well as you can! not a moment is to be lost!" cried the terrified man, "Jonathan Wild and his myrmidons are about to attack the house."

Dismay ran through the company present like wheaten straw in a glowing furnace.

Some made for the garden at the rear of the house.

The door of which being fastened, they proceeded at once to burst it open.

Others endeavoured to hide in some out-of-the-way corner till the danger was past, or to reach the trap door that opened on to the roof of the assailed mansion.

The rest crowded to a large oriel window that stood adjacent to them.

Before they, however, could pass through it, the thief-taker had entered the room.

"I arrest all present in the king's name," he thundered.

"It may be so," replied one of the party; "but though we are betrayed, we may not so easily be taken."

In an instant every light was extinguished.

And all was buried in extreme and total darkness.

The next moment a dreadful encounter took place.

Thirty swords were drawn, and flashed their fires in the gloom.

Yet none could tell who or what was his adversary.

Each man seemed bent upon his own safety, regardless of the fate of friend or foe.

Blood flowed like water by the slippery state of the flooring.

Imprecations and groans told that men every moment were dying.

Shots fired in each direction incessantly, and seldom failed to hit one of the closely-packed combatants.

One who fell beneath this murderous volley was our hero—Roving Jack!

CHAPTER CXVII.

THE MASKED BALL—THE BLACK DOMINO, AND THE FORGED LETTER—ROVING JACK ARRESTED—ST. JAMES' PARK IN THE OLDEN TIME—AN ESCAPED FELON—THE DESPERATE STRUGGLE BETWEEN JACK SHEPPARD AND HIS DENOUNCER—ARRIVAL OF THE NIGHT-WATCH.

THE mansion of Sir John Warbold was now one of great festivity.

Violet Tremaine, in honour of his natal day, had invited the gentry of the surrounding neighbourhood to a masked ball.

At nine o'clock the company began to arrive.

In a short time, every access to the house receiving the guests, and the spacious lawn in its front, became thronged with carriages and sedan chairs.

At each point, footmen and attendants were to be seen escorting parties to the revels, and bearing in their hands either tall canes or flambeaux.

Every variety of costume appeared to be assumed by the assemblage, who pushed forward into the gilded saloons, lighted by candelabra.

The spacious ball-room was soon crowded by these worthies, bedecked as merry monarchs, turbaned Turks, and Dutchmen; added to such fantastic characters as Punchinello, Harlequin, and Pierrot.

The female denizens enlivening the scene by their diamonds dazzling, and as so many Sultanas, Queens, or Dames of Court.

To give splendour and attraction to the fête, nothing had been neglected.

All the chambers were magnificently decorated, and parterres of the choicest flowers, upon which countless tapers shed their lustre, stretched themselves on whatever side the spectator turned.

The lively dances of the period were performed to the music of a powerful orchestra.

Performed bouquets were handed to each lady guest.

The delicious wines of France and Germany, and hot-house fruits, were dispensed at the various buffets.

Towards midnight the dancers, fatigued with their exertions, were regaled with a sumptuous supper.

It was a repast that might have vied with the Roman feasts of old, abounding with the most tempting dishes and delicacies of the season.

After this banquet, we must follow a domino, wearing a mask, who appeared to follow some one into an ante-chamber.

On reaching it, this same domino encountered the two bright eyes that had attracted him to the spot.

These individuals were the only occupants of the room they had entered.

The one was Sir Ranulph Gayton, the other Violet Tremaine.

The thick mantilla, fastened at the back of her head, and falling over her shoulders, concealed partially her features.

But enough was revealed to give evidence of her beauty.

She started at first, from the unexpected intrusion on her privacy, but resumed her composure on learning its import.

After an apology for his supposed transgression, the baronet continued,

"'Tis most extraordinary that our host has not yet arrived. I have carefully scrutinized every mask, but have failed to detect Sir John Warbold among their number."

"I grieve to hear you say so, Sir Ranulph," replied Violet, despondingly. "I am more surprised than you at his absence on such an occasion and at such a moment."

A neighbouring time-piece denoted the hour.

"Heavens!" continued the lady. "the clock strikes two, and yet he returns not. False one! he no longer loves me."

"Oh, say not that!" interrupted the baronet, fawningly. "Your intended has a faithful heart, though, perhaps——"

Violet, half offended, eyed the speaker, then spoke somewhat peevishly, as follows:

"Sir Ranulph Gayton, the word I uttered was not for the hearing of others—it was a thought that spoke. I have not betrayed myself."

"Nay, such coyness with me, Violet, is simply ridiculous," he replied. "Your admirer, Sir John, is my friend, and I am the guardian of all his secrets. But, come when he may," continued the indignant baronet, "I shall make it my business to reprove him for this neglect of you."

"Neglect of me! reprove him! you!" exclaimed Violet with haughtiness.

Sir Ranulph, disdaining to answer the censure, was about to throw himself at the fair one's feet, when such an action was suspended by the sudden appearance of an aged personage, rejoicing in the name of Old Adam.

He was one who had been in the service of the family from boyhood, and for half a century had acted as steward of its estate.

"Madam," said the faithful servant, in a tremulous voice, "I am afraid you are surrounded by difficulties, and come to see if I can be of any use."

The flush which had tinged her cheek during her interview with Sir Ranulph Gayton now gave way to a paleness resembling death.

With fearful anxiety, she enquired:

"What, in the name of mercy, has now happened?"

"A—an accident."

"An accident—to your master?"

"Yes, he has been wounded, but in no danger, as his hurt is but slight."

"Thank heaven!"

"The worst remains to be told," said the steward.

"Let me know, then," replied Violet, hastily and in great agitation.

"In a word, Sir John Warbold has been arrested."

"Arrested! Heavens! from what cause?"

"I fear debt, madam," replied the old man. "We have officers in the house; the plate, the furniture, the carriage are all seized upon."

"And no instructions—no letter from him in this dreadful extremity?"

"None, lady, that I can hear of."

"This is scarcely credible, Adam," replied Violet, almost frantic. "Go; make again inquiry: bring tidings where your master is, while I dismiss our guests. "No," she cried, suddenly stopping short; "they must not yet know the sad calamity. Adam, on the duty you owe this family, I charge you be silent on this affair; bribe the men to continue so, while I will mask an aching heart by smiles and blandishments to our visitors."

The aged man quitted the room to obey the injunctions of his mistress.

Violet, overcome by her direful position, for a moment lent upon a chair for support.

She was evidently taxing her failing strength to the uttermost.

Still her bright lustrous eye beamed with resolution.

As her glance wandered it suddenly fell upon Sir

AN INTERESTING CONVERSATION.

Ranulph Gayton, who had been unwittingly a witness of all that had passed.

In a great state of perturbation he approached Violet, and cried,

"I, of a necessity, know your present trouble."

"And yet you are here?"

While speaking, the maiden was observed to shudder.

"You faint."

"No," she replied, proudly, checking the steps advancing to her aid, "not I, indeed; but surely there is one who at such a moment might claim your sympathy."

"You allude to Sir John Warbold," interrupted the baronet. "I go to tender him my services—nay, my life, should he require the sacrifice."

Sir Ranulph turned to take his departure, but suddenly paused.

His progress was arrested by Nat Rose the highwayman, who held a note in his hand.

He greeted the persons he encountered, and pointed to the writing.

"A letter."

"For me?"

"If your name be Violet Tremaine, madam, yes."

She took the letter, broke the seal tremblingly, and exclaimed,

"'Tis his hand!"

She had not observed her companions, who seemed to understand each other, if one might judge from the looks that were exchanged between them.

While Violet was reading, Sir Ranulph was heard to mutter to Nat Rose,

"She doesn't detect the forgery."

"My sight grows dim," said Violet, endeavouring to peruse the lines upon the paper. "All seems to me confusion."

"Fortune crowns my wishes," whispered the baronet, to his companion.

Turning to the lady, he continued,

"Madam, if you will suffer me, I may be able to decipher this apparently strange letter."

"No, sir," she retorted, rousing her energies; "it is directed by him for me, and must be for my eye alone. Presently this foolish feeling will have floated past. I said so; I can read it now."

Once more taking up the paper, Violet commenced reading its contents:—

"DEAR VIOLET.—Do not let what has happened trouble you; all may speedily be remedied, perhaps, by yourself. How my lips only must disclose. I am at Lord Darnford's."

Sir Ranulph Gayton, affecting a pleasing surprise, exclaimed,

"At Lord Darnford's, eh? I know him well. Sir John Warbold could not have found a firmer friend."

Violet continued to read the letter, which ran as follows:—

"I am not arrested, but secreted. Do not reveal my place of concealment to any one but my tried friend - Sir Ranulph Gayton. Incaution might destroy me, caution save me! Come to me on this injunction. My confidant will escort you in safety. Every moment is an age.

"Yours, dear Violet,
"LOVING AND BELOVED."

"How proud I ought to feel of this honour," said Sir Ranulph, glancing slyly at Nat Rose.

"The request is very singular," said the lady.

"Yet very natural," replied the baronet, in a tone of forced calmness

"What can be his motive?"

"To urge, probably," he continued, "some assignment of property on your part, which is to become his on your marriage."

"It may be so," answered Violet, with hesitation. "Yet I cannot conceal my surprise that he should wish that this proceeding be carried on without the knowledge of his trusty steward."

"His letter enjoins such a course," replied the baronet; "therefore, you may depend upon it that Sir John has some good reason for advising you."

We will now leave Violet Tremaine hesitating between doubt and fear, and retire to a far distant spot.

It was night when a dark figure leaped over the moss-grown paling of St. James's old park.

The pleasaunce of former days bearing this name bore a very different aspect to that which the present one bears.

It was merely an undulating and open tract of land, covered with aged oaks and an elastic sward, and had more the appearance of some country wood than the beautiful English garden of modern times.

The individual who had entered this leafy wilderness in haste seemed as one avoiding a pursuit.

His dress consisted of grey cloth of the coarsest texture, and he wore a great iron ring on his leg.

His head, devoid of covering, was bound with a kerchief, while his shoes, broken and travel-soiled, seemed to be filled with blood from wounds in his feet.

He shivered, limped, and glared around him on all sides.

In a word, the man was an escaped felon, and no other than the notorious prison-breaker, Jack Sheppard.

A few minutes' rapid walking brought him to an eminence that formerly stood in the centre of the park.

From this point he seemed to contemplate the quietude of the scene around him bathed in the beams of the moon.

Through the broken vista of trees he discerned the tall chimneys and picturesque outline of the once-celebrated Buckingham House.

At his feet meandered a branch of the Thames, still preserved and known as the ornamental water.

"I have once more escaped my dungeon bars," exclaimed Jack Sheppard, musing, "and am again at freedom; unchained, I can raise my arm."

As he spoke, the fugitive from justice discovered still a broken fetter hanging from his wrist.

"I had forgot," he cried, "this link, rusted by a victim's tears, yet remains; the spots shall, in future, be those of blood, and Sir Maurice Lacy's, too, my cowardly denouncer."

At this moment a voice fell upon the ear of Jack Sheppard.

It chilled him like an ague.

It was that of the man of whom he had spoken.

Almost immediately after the alarm Sir Maurice Lacy was seen wending his way through the shrubby intricacies of the beaten pathway of the park.

He had not proceeded many paces when he observed some one approaching him.

The spot was lonely, and dotted with trees that threw their arched and interwoven branches across the chasm beneath.

Startled by the ominous and sudden appearance of a figure at such a time, Sir Maurice Lacy drew back and retraced his footsteps in order to take a more open and frequented road.

This was prevented, for, on suddenly turning, Jack Sheppard pounced upon him from behind.

The man thus arrested did not recognise his opponent, but knowing the neighbourhood was at night occasionally infested with footpads, naturally concluded his assailant to be one.

"Who are you, fellow?" said Sir Maurice, vainly endeavouring to release himself from the hold that was maintained of his person by him whom he addressed.

"If you want money," he continued, "I have none for such as you are."

"Money?" cried the other. "Money from you? I'd sooner receive the deadliest venom in my palm than gold at your hands!"

Sir Maurice knew the voice of Jack Sheppard the moment he spoke, and then pronounced his name aloud.

"Yes, I am Jack Sheppard," he replied; "he whom you betrayed, and who has contrived to snap the fetters that bound him."

"Impossible! Again escaped?"

"If you doubt my words, Sir Maurice, Mr. Austin, the turnkey of Newgate, will bear them out."

"You intend to murder me?"

"I don't consider it would be a crime to rid the world of such a rascal as you have proved yourself to be."

"You may, perhaps, find the task you have imposed upon yourself, Jack Sheppard, more difficult to accomplish than you anticipate."

"That may be."

"What would you say," continued Sir Maurice, "if I called the night-watch? I have but just passed them on their rounds."

Jack Sheppard exhibited the pendant chain on his arm, and exclaimed—

"Why, with this iron, if you attempted such a thing, I could strike you dead at my feet. But I am not a dark assassin," continued he. "Meet me, then, to-morrow, as man to man, and sword to sword opposed. You have only to promise this, and I promise to molest you no further."

"You have my word."

Several lights appeared at this moment among the neighbouring foliage.

They were the lanterns carried by the night-watch.

On perceiving them, Sir Maurice Lacy at once raised a cry, a cry that was answered as soon as given.

Jack Sheppard, at this act of treachery, with a malignant scowl at his enemy, exclaimed.

"Double traitor! have you so soon broken your promise?"

"An oath extorted, is no oath at all," retorted Sir Maurice Lacy.

With the words, he rushed upon Jack Sheppard, and drew his sword.

His enemy, observing his tactics, stepped nimbly back, and succeeded in disengaging himself from the grasp his adversary had fixed upon him.

The latter, foaming furious and breathless, though baffled, was not dismayed, and a second time advanced to the attack.

The conflict now between the contending parties was unparalleled for intense malignity and rancour on both sides.

The swordsman wielded his weapon with unabated fierceness; but it was shivered by the chain which guarded the arm of Jack Sheppard.

Despairing of success, and thirsting for revenge, Sir Maurice Lacy used his broken sword as a poignard.

In making a thrust with this, his foot caught in some upraised ground, and, fortunately for his opponent, he fell in the deadly attempt.

The latter, taking advantage of this incident, by a quick movement, was enabled to wrest the weapon from the prostrate man.

The next moment the blade descended heavily in the direction of his heart.

But the time of Sir Maurice was not yet come; the armour, which he ever wore beneath his dress, protected him from the insidious daggers of his secret enemies.

CHAPTER CXVIII.

THE FIVE CHIMNEYS OR THE PEST HOUSE IN TOTHILL FIELDS.

FINDING himself thwarted in his deadly intention, Jack Sheppard dropped the dagger from his palsied grasp, but he still maintained the hold of his treacherous adversary.

Sir Maurice now tried to release himself from the iron gripe that made him a prisoner.

The struggle was short but desperate.

Both men were powerfully built, energetic, and apparently well matched.

Suddenly, Jack Sheppard made a feint, and, by a well-directed manoeuvre, flung Sir Maurice Lacy from him.

He fell with a terrible crash, while his head, coming in contact with the trunk of an adjacent oak, rendered him incapable of offering any further resistance.

He raised his eyes for a moment, but his dancing vision could distinguish no object.

He was stunned, bleeding, senseless.

We will leave Sir Maurice in the custody of the night-watch, who shortly arrived at the place of the late encounter, and follow Jack Sheppard and the fortune that attended him.

As may be supposed, he quitted the scene of his late adventure with as much speed as possible.

He had not proceeded far in his rapid flight, when the booming of a distant gun rushed through the heavy air.

A second and a third answered the signal.

The firing apprised Jack Sheppard this his retreat was being made known, and that he must avoid the sentinels at the Park gates.

By a circuitous route, he arrived at the then pleasant village of Pimlico.

A very different place from the present princely suburb.

It, at the period of our story, contained but some few houses, two hostelries, celebrated for their Derby ales, and a bun-house but lately standing, near the Royal mews.

Passing through the unfrequented hamlet, he shortly arrived at a broad expanse of land, known to our ancestors as Tothill Fields.

This spot is now covered by the mansions of South Belgravia, and its adjacent neighbourhoods.

An angle, near Rochester Row, still marks the pound in which the stray cattle of the common were enclosed; Vincent Square and Warwick Street, its "Tourney Ground and Willow Walk;" and Douglas Place, the Pest House, in which were deposited the bodies of those dying of the dreadful Plague in 1665.

This tenement became, in after years, a strange dwelling-house or sanctuary for thieves, and may be remembered by some of our older readers as the "Five Chimneys," in the Vauxhall Bridge Road.

Its present occupant was a fence, in league with some of the most notorious malefactors and highwaymen of the day, to whom he ever gave shelter for a "consideration."

The quaint, Dutch-looking structure, was in a ruinous state; in some places unroofed, in others, without windows, shutters, or even doors.

The tenant, to keep up his ostensible character of dealer in old stores, the neglected garden surrounding his equally neglected dwelling was ever filled with rusty and incongruous fragments, such as blocks of stone, iron, and ponderous heaps of ship timber.

From this chaotic mass, and towering above it, might be seen, here and there, broken pillars, mast heads and bowsprits, and demolished statues, which, when seen in the moonlight, gave a sort of grotesque but at the same time terrible effect to the whole locality, and could inspire nothing but terror into the breast of any one who had the temerity to enter it.

It was late at night, when several persons issued from an obscure public-house on Thames bank, called the "Spread Eagle."

They shaped their course across Tothill Fields, and in direction of the tumble-down building alluded to.

By the uncertain glimpses of the moon, the appearance of the somewhat jovial party could not be clearly distinguished, but when she broke from her dark rack they were exhibited to no very great advantage to themselves.

They were of that description of character to which men, in open daylight, generally give what is called a "wide berth."

Crime and debauchery were stamped upon their features, resolution and remorselessness in their fierce and restless eyes.

In a word, they were a portion of a noted band of highwaymen.

Among their number was Blueskin, who addressed his conversation to one more than the rest of his comrades.

He was a tall, handsome man, dressed in riding costume, and named Slashing Nat Wetherby. He has already been introduced to our readers in the earlier chapters of this story.

He was the pal and boon companion of poor Tom King.

Well, Nat," said Blueskin, "so you've turned up at last. I thought I was never to see your face again."

"I came so suddenly upon you," replied he, smiling, "that I suppose you took me for a bailiff?"

"Not so bad as that, comrade, when I look at your hat and boots; you seem to be in prime twig, and to have been doing it in style of late."

"Yes, I am not only rejoiced to see you, but also to tell you that I am now one not unknown——"

"To the thief-takers?"

"No, to fame. I have quitted the road to turn gambler; I win with the dice what you extort with the pistol, and find I'm a considerable gainer by the bargain."

"Well, Nat, I don't like your trade so well as my own," added Blueskin, "but tastes differ. After all said and done, there's nothing like the game of high toby. Listen. For instance, we'll say the coach of my Lord Tom Noddy is leaving the town on the stroke of ten, and rumbles shortly on a country road.

"'Yes, if my eyes don't deceive me, there it comes.'

"'Comrades, are you prepared? Put on your masks and follow me. We must receive his lordship with all due dignity. Conceal yourselves in the hedge-side; courage and success attend us. Stop's the word as we drag forth the inmate of the carriage.'

"'Don't be alarmed, my lord, we merely require your watch, that diamond ring that adorns your finger, and your cash.'

"'My watch was too slow this morning,' cries the timorous noble, handing his ticker, fawney, and blunt.

"'It's going fast enough now,' replies the roadsman, pocketing the spoil, with all the assurance of a man who feels he has said a good thing; then, handing his dupe once more from the seat he has dislodged him, politely wishes him a brave good night, and sings—

"On the high spice toby, flash the muzzle,
Freely mounted, hand in rein,
Tyburn tree, be it my fortune,
If by Philistines I in ta'en,
Lilli bulero, ho!"

"Hush, Blueskin!" said Nat Wetherby. "If I am not mistaken there is game in view."

"Where?"

"Yonder," replied the first, pointing to a figure in the distance that had attracted his attention.

He was a little removed from the group that were noticing him, and enveloped in a "roquelaure," or antique cloak, evidently worn for the purposes of disguise.

On observing that Blueskin and his companions had become aware of his presence, he once diverged from the road they were taking, and with such haste, that in a few seconds he would have been out of sight.

One of the party, anticipating the escape of a rich booty, fired at the retreating stranger.

The shot told, and he fell to the ground, apparently wounded.

He uttered no cry, though his whole frame shook with powerful emotion.

"Hang it, Ned Bush," said Blueskin, addressing the man who had discharged the weapon; "why have you winged the pigeon before knowing whether the bird is worth plucking? Have you so soon forgotten my commands as your leader," continued he, "that blood shall not be spilt save in self-defence, or on extreme emergency?"

"Well, it seems I never do right in your way of thinking, Blueskin," replied Bush, sulkily. "I did all for the best. I saw we might let a chance slip through our fingers, and so——"

"Hurried to violence," added Blueskin. "This is not the first time I've had to reprove you."

"Perhaps my company isn't required by the band," answered Bush, more sullen than ever.

"I'll say no more, Ned," exclaimed Blueskin. "I don't want to quarrel with you, but, mark my words, obstinacy, and a morose temper, often bring men to ruin."

The highwaymen had now reached the spot upon which the stranger was lying.

There was no blood on his body, and he appeared rather to be in a stupor, than much hurt.

Blueskin's first action was to draw a brandy-flask from his pocket, and pour a portion of its contents down the throat of the prostrate man.

Strong spirit, for a moment, partially revived him, and he opened his eyes.

But the restorative soon again lost its power, and the patient once more lapsed into lethargy.

While in this state, stifling sounds issued from his bosom, as one struggling violently for respiration.

Blueskin now unmasked a lantern, which he had taken from one of his comrades, and peered into the face of the stranger.

He looked deadly pale; but the highwayman in a moment recognised his features.

"Well, there's the hand of fate in this," exclaimed Blueskin, in astonishment. "The very man of all others that I had hope to come across has, by a miracle, fallen into my hands."

"Who is he," inquired Nat Wetherby, advancing to the speaker, "in whom you seem to take such a lively interest?"

"You will know by and bye," answered Blueskin, extinguishing the light he held in his hand, and rendering discovery of his secret difficult by the immediate darkness. "Ask no questions at present, and your curiosity will be the sooner gratified. I've a reason for not disclosing the name of this mysterious personage. So take my hint for it that the thing's right, and let mum be the word."

No more passed between Blueskin and his companions.

On a given signal the body of the unknown was placed on their shoulders, and at once carried in the direction of the robber rendezvous at the Five Chimneys.

Preceded by Blueskin and Nat Wetherby, the cortege moved stealthily across the fields leading to their destination.

Arrived here they came to a halt.

The access to the lone tenement was afforded by a rude bridge composed of a couple of planks and a hand-rail, the construction having to pass over a weed-covered moat.

The premises here were of rather a strange description. The proprietor being a trader in illegal goods, placed such as might not lead to detection in this portion of them.

They consisted principally of ironwork of every shade, shape and character. There were rusty chains flung together in heaps; anvils, sledge hammers, and old ovens at every corner; while broken anchors, dismounted cannon, and such material were seen, turn which way you could.

The entrance to the main dwelling was ornamented with a massive arch, formed by huge upright and horizontal beams, from the centre of which hung a large, cracked, and crazy bell, for what purpose none could tell, as the worn-out metal vessel was devoid of a clapper.

Beyond this, through the open doorway, on the present occasion, might be seen the occupants of the house, grouped around the fire within.

They were a motley crew, and in appearance resembled those who had arrived.

The fresh breeze of night was blowing over the wide and adjacent extent of open country, as Blueskin and his companions entered the strange domicile described.

They were greeted on their arrival, and an inquisitive glanced at the body they bore with them.

The landlord of the tenement then addressed the highwayman.

"How's this, Blueskin? What have you brought here?"

"A body."

"Dead?"

"No."

"Drugged?"

"Can't say."

"Is it safe, think you?"

"Quite; I know the party."

"Ah! what's his name?"

"I must for the present withhold it."

"Strange," muttered the landlord, while a grim smile settled on his countenance; "but, however, you are accountable for your conduct, Blueskin, and I don't think I run much risk in trusting you."

"When Blueskin betrays a pal, or snitches upon an upright man," said the robber, "may he dance a Tyburn hornpipe on nothing before he's a month older; but as I've undertaken a job," he continued, "I suppose I must go on with it. I'll get you to lend me a hand, Shadrach."

These latter words were individually addressed to the landlord, who bore such a name.

"How can I serve you, Joe?" said Shadrach, vainly concealing the eager curiosity he experienced.

"By letting me have a dozing ken," replied Blueskin, "for our captive here."

With the words he indicated the body of the unknown, which had been stretched by his companions on the floor of the apartment, and entirely concealed by the wide roquelaure in which he had been covered.

The landlord shook his head, then reversed the action.

"Let me see," he observed, "there's the garret on the roof; it's only filled with lumber, and he'll sleep as quietly a'twixt the broken bottles as if he was on a feather-bed."

"Well, I'll make shift with that till morning," said Blueskin, "then you and I will talk this matter over a little further."

"Ain't there any clue by which I might guess?" interrupted Shadrach, still exhibiting an inquisitive feeling.

"None whatever; you will learn everything in good time. Till then, bear a hand with the glim, and light us with our guest to the chamber you have spoken of."

* * * * *

When the unknown woke from his slumber and delirium, as may be supposed, he was startled to find himself in his strange dormitory.

It was lit by the transient rays of the moon, fire or candle being neither within or about it.

This circumstance produced an odd effect on the various fantastic objects that literally choked up the chamber.

There seemed to be in the precinct every description of lumber, from the worm-eaten bird-cage to the service of Dresden china.

Compressed in admired disorder were antique vases, iron pans and jars of all sorts, crucibles, crucifixes, retorts, and kettles without number, while accoutrements, disused garments and rusty weapons were strewn about, and garnished in some instances with some broken statue wrought in bronze or some such metal.

From the chamber the spectator next turned his eye to its window.

His scattered idea and confused memory served not to recal the incidents of the past hour.

Something he remembered of a form that seemed to take pity on his wretchedness; but, beyond this, all was darkness and despair.

Into whose hands had he fallen?

Were they enemies or friends?

Was he to meet death at the assassin or the hangman's hands?

By the window shelving he discovered he was placed at the top of the house that had given him shelter, and that escape by that means would be attended with great risk and much danger.

From this point, however, he was able to distinguish its locality.

Before him was the broad common and the "Five Fields,"* over which a bright moonlight shed its lustre, and sent quivering its radiance in each dell and nook.

A few sounds arising from the banks of the river betokened only the passing craft, and the profound stillness that reigned abroad.

On the right, afar off, might be discerned the ancient pile called Lambeth Palace.

On the left, the venerable towers of the Abbey of Westminster stood out in bold relief from the mass of wood and vista of broken trees by which it appeared to be embowered.

While the prisoner was contemplating the above scene before him, and devising a scheme that had just come into his head by which he hoped to release himself from captivity, a footstep was heard approaching the chamber.

The door opened, and a man stood at the entrance.

He carried a horn lantern in his hand, which exposed his features.

Jack Sheppard (for it was he who had been imprisoned) recognised in a moment his friend Blueskin, who exclaimed,

"Welcome, captain. Jack Sheppard will find a safe retreat in the 'Five Chimneys.'"

CHAPTER CXIX.

ROVING JACK'S RETURN TO HIS HOME—A GAMBLER'S MEDITATIONS—THE FAITHFUL STEWARD AND THE INCOGNITO—HOW AND BY WHOM A DEBT OF GRATITUDE WAS PAID.

THE mansion of our hero, in which the masked ball had been held, was now a scene of death-like silence, compared with the clamour and laughter which had resounded within its walls an hour previous.

In a word the revels had ended.

The guests departed, and the fatigued lacqueys sought that repose which their overtasked powers required.

Roving Jack stood before the house.

He was alone, and appeared as some spectre, for his ghastly looks were calculated to appal him who chanced to behold the miserable man.

He seemed more dead than alive.

Hollow-eyed, haggard, and broken down.

He uttered a sharp cry, and hurried up the lawn to the portal.

He passed through the arched entrance and ascended the spiral staircase.

He paused here to take breath before entering his solitary chamber, from which glimmered a feeble light.

"At length I have reached home!" faltered Roving Jack. "Home, did I say? It is no longer mine. House, cash, plate, are in the hands of my creditors and the stern ministers of the law's decree. I have lost everything!" he sighed. "Heavens! into what a sink of iniquity has my

* The "Five Fields" are now covered by Eaton, Belgrave, and the neighbouring squares.

guilty passion plunged me ! When I think of the dice-box my brain is on fire, and I can feel my very nails eat into my flesh !

"At its rattle my blood is stagnant with intense anxiety, and the fall of the fatal cubes strike as a thunderbolt upon my heart."

Suddenly he became more composed, and tottered towards the door.

He reached it, stopped, and murmured forth—

"To-day my sorrows may end ; and by the bullet of the treacherous gambler, Sir Maurice Lacy, my body may be extinguished in the tomb. At dawn I meet him ; let me await, on my couch, with feverish excitement, the appointed hour."

On going into a chamber, Roving Jack confronted one who was patiently anticipating his return.

It was old Adam, the steward.

Roving Jack scarcely seemed to notice or thank the faithful domestic, who rose on his entrance.

He then drew a chair near the fire.

Seating himself, he remained for some minutes wrapt in meditation.

At last our hero spoke in a voice almost broke by emotion.

"Begone, Adam," he said. "Do not let me be disturbed on any pretence till noon to-morrow. I have much to do, and need repose."

The steward, without uttering a sentence, at once yielded to the imperious gesture that enjoined his departure.

Our hero, left to himself, was about to recline on a sofa in the apartment, when he perceived through the gloom—for light had been extinguished, save that from the dying fire in the grate—a female figure emerge from the door, and advance towards him ; it was the same who had been noticed that afternoon, standing pensively before the mansion. (See illustration to No. 33.)

The presence of the party at such a period must be explained.

She had been a guest at the ball, and, by retaining her masquerade attire and domino, still continued disguised.

Roving Jack was, therefore, unaware who or what his mysterious companion was.

"I have tidings to communicate to Sir John Warbold," said the domino.

"Not now—not now, my good lady," he cried. "I am unwell ; to-morrow I will with pleasure listen to you ; at present I am not equal to it."

"To-morrow may be too late," replied the mask, mysteriously.

"Is this woman a sorceress ?" thought our hero. "How can she know what has passed so far away ?"

"In the first place," continued the domino, "I must acquaint you that your release has been effected."

"Ah ! can it be possible ? Whose kind interference has——"

"No matter ; suffice that peace is restored, and that your house is free and clear again. Now let us, Sir John, speak of other debts."

"Not till I've settled this which appears to be a debt of gratitude," said Roving Jack.

He strode to and fro within the room, and his aspect had taken a great change.

Suddenly he turned on his heel, and addressed the fair incognito.

"This act of kindness, bestowed and unsought, must stand first in my thoughts. You must tell me, madam, who has paid this money."

"One who has wronged you, and finds it is never too late to remedy an injustice."

A sudden faintness seized Roving Jack ; but it passed off soon.

The domino continued with solemn earnestness.

"I implored him to save you, and he did not turn a deaf ear to my entreaties ; for the injuries he has inflicted on you, he has discharged your debts."

"What is the name of my benefactor ?"

"Jonathan Wild."

With the words the speaker glided hastily from the apartment.

The mask she wore fell from her face and disclosed the features of Jael, the daughter of Roving Jack's quondam enemy.

Our hero could not speak, but rushed towards the door in order to intercept the fugitive.

Ere he could reach it, she had passed from his sight, and fastened it on the outer side.

He was for some minutes lost in abstraction, when he was startled by footsteps, and the locked door opened.

In another moment old Adam entered the room, holding in his hand a letter.

"I should not have intruded on your privacy, Sir John," said the old steward, bowing, "but as this letter bears upon it the handwriting of Mistress Violet Tremaine, I thought I should do wrong in withholding it an instant."

"From Violet !" exclaimed our hero, in surprise. "Has she left the house ?"

"Yes, Sir John ; some hour or so since."

"With whom ?"

"Sir Ranulph Gayton."

Roving Jack made no reply ; but hastily snatched the note which old Adam had brought, and glanced over its contents as if with troubled foreboding.

"How wild and pale he looks," muttered the steward, observing the demeanour of his master.

The latter having perused the letter, sank into a chair.

He became lost in a deep and painful reflection.

At length arousing himself," he exclaimed,

"Would you believe it, Adam—she is false—she —Violet."

"False !"

"I—I am forsaken—deserted for another. Read, read, old man."

Giving the writing into the hand of the steward, Roving Jack continued speaking in deep dejection—

"Here I stand alone in the world a ruined, despised, and heartbroken man. Yet I deserve it all ; after the exposure that has taken place, I could not hope to remain the master of Violet's destiny. She has snatched herself from the abyss to which I was about to drag her."

Old Adam read the letter that had been handed to him, and muttered aloud its concluding sentence :—

" 'I withdraw both my hand and heart to resign them to one more worthy. Need I name—Sir Ranulph Gayton ?'

"I am doomed !"

"She, so mild," sighed the steward, contemplating Violet's letter, "seemingly so good to abandon you thus in tribulation. I cannot believe it ; there must be some cheat."

"Do not seek to palliate the offence, Adam," cried our hero, firmly, "my punishment is just— very just."

The wheels of a carriage were now heard approaching the mansion.

At the sound, Roving Jack sprang forward, and listened with intense interest.

His heart swelled almost to bursting at the idea that Violet, relenting, had again returned to him.

Old Adam hastened to ascertain the truth of this suspicion.

Suspense extended this moment to an age.

'Tis not her foot that treads with lighter bound than echo's own.

'Tis not her voice that sounds like music in the gloom, for the steward soon re-entered the apartment with a downcast look, and evidences of perturbation.

" A gentleman, who says he waits upon special business, has sent this card," and Roving Jack had no sooner received it than he exclaimed hurriedly,

" 'Tis my second ! I had forgot this duel."

Then, drawing himself up to his full length, proudly continued,

" He shall not wait for me, Adam. What is the hour ?"

" By the morning, six."

" Ah, so near the appointed time !"

" Are you going abroad so early, Sir John ?"

Our hero disregarded this remark, and continued thoughtfully,

" Well, nothing is left me but to die. In half an hour all will be over ; my heart will ache no longer. The grave has sweet oblivion for the wretched."

These dark mysterious words fell upon the ear of the old steward, who, though unbid, followed his master, who was now directing his steps to the Abbey yard at Westminster.

To this spot we must now take the reader.

What took place within its precincts will appear in the next chapter.

CHAPTER CXX.

THE OLD ABBEY OF WESTMINSTER—THE DUEL AT DAWN.

AT no time had the old Abbey at Westminster looked more beautiful than on the eventful dawn that was to decide in a duel the fate of our hero, Roving Jack.

It was a bright, clear summer's morning.

The beams of the coming day sparkled on the grey walls of the venerable structure.

And its two dark massive towers, with their slated penthouses piercing that beautiful specimen of architecture, the façade and the immense mullioned window.

Alike fell the rays on the statuary, sculpture and solemn grandeur of the building, imparting that tranquil effect ever produced by sunlight on the tombs of the dead.

The abbey formerly, as some may have heard, stood upon ground known as Thorney Island.

This tract was overgrown with weeds, trees, and environed by the water of the Thames.

Thus, the sacred structure could only be reached by a wooden bridge built over the stream that flowed around it.

At the present time this frail passage was crossed by an individual.

He regarded with caution every object around, and awaited silently and calmly the approach of some one who he seemed anxious to meet.

His eyes flashed with fire, as, in the distance, he beheld two men advancing towards him.

He welcomed them with a smile as cutting as a razor's edge, then hastened to conceal himself from their view.

In the centre of the Abbey yard, which he had now entered, stood a solitary oak.

Tradition gave out that it had been planted by the hands of Edward the Confessor himself (the founder of the Abbey), at a period of seven centuries antecedent.

Whether there was truth in this assertion we leave for the antiquary to decide.

Enough for our purpose that it was thoroughly decayed, and that three people could stand in its enormous and hollow trunk.

Jack Sheppard—for he was the individual we have spoken of—no sooner arrived at this tree than he concealed himself in its cavity.

It formed an excellent hiding-place, and from the gnarled and knotty opening could observe all that passed before him, without being seen himself.

Down the glade came presently the two persons he had been watching.

The one, Sir Maurice Lacy, was dressed in a heavy suit of dark velvet, and jack boots

He seemed more morose than usual.

The famished tiger in pursuit of blood seemed less ferocious than he.

Crafty and cruel withal was this baronet.

Not like the darting swallow which ruffles the lake, but the serpent which venoms the water.

His companion was attired similarly to himself ; but his air, manner, and looks differed in every respect, for Nat Rose the highwayman possessed that comfortable sort of assurance peculiar to the lower order of his fraternity.

He imitated the example of Sir Maurice Lacy ; but did not appear in the slightest degree to be disconcerted by the occasional rebuffs he met with at the hands of that party.

A cold reception neither surprised or mortified Nat Rose, while a warm one only produced a similar effect on this stoical knight of the post.

Sir Maurice Lacy and Nat Rose had placed themselves in the open mead, and exactly in front of the refuge of Jack Sheppard.

From this spot he overheard the following conversation that took place between them :—

" We are arrived before our opponent," observed the baronet.

" So much the better ; there will be time to talk over the matter on hand."

" You have provided means for our flight when our enemy, Roving Jack, has been disposed of ?"

" Yes. As luck would have it, after I left you, I fell in with a Dutch skipper."

" He has agreed——"

" To land us safely in Normandy for a consideration, where we can remain in safety till this affair is blown over."

" This man is to be trusted, you think ?"

" Yes, he is a staunch Catholic, and tells me he fought for King James at the Battle of the Boyne, so he will not betray us."

" You have told him, then, that we are partisans of the Pretender ?"

" I thought it the best course. The Jacobite party are too full of hope and confidence to trouble their heads about the peccadillos of their adherents."

" Yes, I think we may consider ourselves safe ; but now let us turn to the plan with respect to our victim," said Sir Maurice.

" It is thoroughly understood on my part," answered the highwayman.

" You have the pistols ?"

" Yes," replied Nat Rose, producing and laying them on a neighbouring tombstone.

" The one for your adversary," he added, " is merely primed with powder, the other——"

" Which I shall use ?" asked Sir Maurice Lacy.

" Contains two bullets."

At this juncture the Abbey clock commenced striking, and proclaimed the sixth hour of the morning.

The solemn chimes seemed as the knell of Roving Jack, who was now advancing to the death that menaced him.

His air was dejected as he paced the unfrequented region.

But his step was firm, and seemed to dim the lamp of memory.

A profound silence attended his approach to Sir Maurice Lacy, whose pale cheek took a livid hue as he gazed upon his enemy.

He drew not a breath, and evinced a transitory feeling of horror at the anticipated assassination.

"You are late, Sir John," remarked the baronet, who had recovered his composure, and treated the party he had addressed with a contemptuous smile.

"Yes, Sir Maurice," replied Roving Jack, with an equally scornful gesture. "Circumstances beyond my control have delayed me. Nevertheless, I am as anxious as yourself that the affair between us should proceed."

"I have demanded an apology from Sir John Warbold, for his aspersions on my character, and a retraction of the calumny he has uttered."

"I decline to give them, since I find, to my sorrow, that what I have stated is in accordance with the truth."

"If such is your determination," replied Sir Maurice Lacy, coolly, "I have but one course to adopt."

"And that is——"

"An appeal to weapons."

"Willingly. Where are the pistols?" exclaimed our hero. "Are they ready?"

"Yes, they are here."

With the words Nat repaired to the place where he deposited them.

There were four in number, and enclosed in a case fastened with a steel clasp, which he at once opened, saying—

"We have two pair."

"One, I trust, will serve," said Roving Jack, taking a weapon, its fellow being given to his adversary. "The shot," he continued.

"Must be decided by dice, if we are to fight like men of honour," said Sir Maurice Lacy.

He compressed his lips and seemed to smile as he spoke.

Nat Rose next handed some dice to our hero, with which he was to cast lots.

A significant glance passed between the former and his nefarious companion as Roving Jack shook the box and threw on a tombstone—

"Eleven!"

Sir Maurice followed in his turn, but threw only—

"Nine!"

Thus he lost the advantage over his hated antagonist.

"Fortune smiles upon you," said the baronet, sardonically, and bearing his defeat better than might be expected.

"Fortune has no smiles for me now, Sir Maurice Lacy," replied Roving Jack; "nor do I merit them. She poured her favours in my lap, but I have thrown them broadcast to the wind. And should your bullet dart through this aching heart, it will but rid the world of a broken gambler and a beggar!"

The addressed essayed no answer to this remark, while Nat Rose, in the meantime, had measured the ground.

He was to act as second to Sir Maurice Lacy, and had promised Roving Jack—who, for reasons unknown, had come unattended—any service that might be required in such a capacity.

In a few moments all the requisite preparations were made, and the combatants took up their separate positions.

They saluted each other, then poised the weapons with which they were armed.

The god of day had risen majestically in a cloudless sky to witness two men arrayed for a direful conflict.

The one thirsting for blood, the other in poignant anguish, betraying wrongs imposed.

The same sun which smiles on the blushing face of nature frowns at the assassin, and casts upon his marble countenance a shadow that is to wing his flight to perdition.

At the given signal Roving Jack raised his pistol.

The hazard of the die had given him the chance of firing first.

He fired—not at his adversary, but in the air.

Still, a fearful shriek followed the explosion, and Sir Maurice Lacy fell a corpse!

For a moment, at the unexpected catastrophe, our hero stood motionless.

His brain burned as a hot iron.

His heart seemed chilled by an ice-bolt.

Presently he advanced and gazed on the livid, green, convulsive face of his lifeless adversary.

"Wounded—dead!" he murmured, "impossible—quite impossible, unless some demon, plotting my soul's ruin, has turned back the bullet from its open direction."

Sir Maurice Lacy had met death at the hand of an unseen enemy.

It was that of Jack Sheppard.

He, who would have slain an innocent man, had fallen by the very instruments used to commit the murder.

The way by which the highwayman was able to achieve this undertaking is told in a few words.

As the reader may remember, he had overheard the treacherous plot that had been devised by our hero's enemies for his destruction.

Jack Sheppard, as soon as he became aware of it, contrived to emerge from the tree that afforded him concealment, and secrete himself behind the tomb upon which the fire-arms required for the encounter were remaining.

Stealthily as a cat, he crawled to the spot, and, while the preliminaries of the duel were being carried forward, raised himself to a level with the coveted slab.

Here he found pistol and powder, but no bullet.

Without one, the weapon would be of no avail.

A lucky thought; the dice.

Let them supply the place of the leaden messengers of vengeance.

The loaded cubes, therefore, which had ruined hundreds, brought also ruin on their owner, the stern, implacable, and remorseless Sir Maurice Lacy.

His wish had been gratified.

The false dice, which he prophecied would be buried next his heart, if he failed in his nefarious engagement, had fulfilled the omen, and lodged themselves deep, aye even deeper in his bosom, than the bullet with which he would have sacrificed his adversary.

Sir Maurice Lacy no sooner fell than Nat Rose found himself detained by a powerful grasp.

Leaping with agility from his covert, Jack Sheppard had pounced upon him like a kite upon a carcass.

The ruffian struggled manfully, and nearly succeeded in releasing himself.

Fortunately for his assailant, he stumbled over a tree at this instant.

ILL TIDINGS—*See next Number.*

As he lay on the ground, he discovered he had been wounded.

Whether by a weapon, or injury in the fall, he could not determine.

He only saw that blood was flowing freely from him.

Writhing with pain and vengeance, he vowed to take the life of him who approached.

At that moment, he felt a pressure at his throat, and was brought to surrender without further effort by a blow that descended upon his head.

"Our work is not yet done," said Jack Sheppard, addressing our hero, who had felled their antagonist by means of the butt-end of his pistol. "We must take him to the 'Five Chimneys.'"

"Why so?"

"He may be of service to us."

"In what way?"

"In more ways than one. First we must examine the ruffian's pockets and see if we can't glean anything from their contents. I saw Sir Maurice Lacy hand him some papers just before you came up," said Jack Sheppard.

"Then we will proceed to the search at once," rejoined our hero, stooping to carry out the proposition.

"No, not now," interrupted Jack Sheppard; "though it is still early, the road will soon be astir with passengers; therefore we have no time to throw away upon that which may be done hereafter with equal facility. Follow my directions, Sir John, and good may come of it, or I'm sorely mistaken."

"You must lend me some assistance," the speaker continued.

With the words, he placed the wounded man's legs over his own shoulders, and aided by Roving Jack, proceeded with his burden in the direction of the rendezvous he had named.

The capture of Nat Rose led to important results.

Having been conveyed in safety to the "Five Chimneys," he was here compelled to make confession of his late nefarious deed and its purport.

Amongst other information, Roving Jack learnt the place of Violet Tremaine's detention.

Armed with this knowledge, he determined to save her or perish in the attempt.

CHAPTER CXXI.

THE CAPTIVE'S ADVENTURE PICTURED IN A DREAM—THE DRUGGED GOBLET—POLL MAGGOT AND HER GUEST—UNDER WHAT PLEA VIOLET TREMAINE REFUSED TO SIGN THE MARRIAGE CONTRACT—THE PEN AND THE PISTOL.

WE must now revert to a chamber in the "Devil's Punch Bowl," in which the hostess, Poll Maggot, is busily engaged.

It is necessary for us, before we proceed further in our narration, to give some short description of this apartment.

Its walls were panelled with oak, and garnished here and there with crimson hangings.

The furniture consisted of large high-backed chairs, and a grotesquely carved table, near which stood an old-fashioned mirror, reflecting all the objects in its immediate neighbourhood.

At the nether end of the room, a heavy stone wrought mantle-piece projected itself from the wainscoting some feet.

Showing that the time had been when it sent its huge fires blazing up the huge chimney—puffing many a volume of smoke over the heads of the jovial guests who might have frequented the tavern on such occasions.

Poll Maggot having completed the task imposed upon her (to which we shall not allude at present) proceeded to open a curtain disclosing a small recess.

Within it appeared the sleeping figure of Violet Tremaine.

Suspended over her couch, a lamp threw a faint light upon her features, now deathly pale.

Though she slumbered camly, her repose seemed to be induced rather by some narcotic than natural fatigue.

This supposition would be correct, for the deep sleep which bound up the senses of Violet Tremaine was occasioned by the potent medicament that had been administered to her.

After a time she awoke, to find herself in the chamber we have described.

The stream of light descending from above first attracted her attention.

Starting, her gaze was then fixed on vacancy, if a mind distraught and filled with strange images can be called so.

In this musing attitude, and almost deprived by terror of consciousness, her confused memory pictured her late adventure.

By degrees she called to mind that the captor had borne her down a flight of steps, and that for a considerable distance along a gravel walk and lawn.

She remembered next, still as in a dream, being placed in a carriage, and driven with great swiftness through a park, commanding a view of tangled shrub and foliage.

The journey was so rapidly performed, that she expected the vehicle in which she was seated would be dashed every minute into pieces.

She fancied that she then shrieked for assistance, but that her cry was stifled by an unseen hand placed over her mouth.

Beyond this all was oblivion, darkness, for her mind wandered, and a torpor overpowered her.

While yet meditating, she was aroused by a gentle tap on the shoulder.

Violet raised her eyes, and her glance fell upon Poll Maggot.

The buxom hostess was beside, and supporting her from falling.

She held a large goblet filled with liquid to her lips, and compelled her to swallow a portion of it.

The stimulant revived Violet; but still it produced a strange excitement, against which she seemed vainly to struggle.

"Who are you?" at length she demanded of her present companion.

"I am the mistress of this house," answered Poll Maggot, blandly, "and in the confidence of Sir Ranulph Gayton."

"Sir Ranulph Gayton!" echoed Violet, suddenly recollecting the name.

Trembling from head to foot, she raised herself, and dashed aside her tresses, as if to gather her scattered senses.

"It must have been a dream," she exclaimed, in a low tone; then, addressing Poll Maggot, continued, "Sir Ranulph Gayton, you say, that is quite right; he said he would attend me to the house of Lord Darnford; then why am I here? Pray, let met me depart, or my friends will be alarmed."

"What, go, my lady?" replied Poll Maggot, laughing; "that would never do—no, no. You assure me you know Sir Ranulph Gayton," continued the hostess; "I can hardly credit it, since you wish me to disobey his order."

"His order—what order?"

"Why the baronet would murder me out right,' said Poll Maggot, "if I suffered you to depart."

"Indeed! but as I am my own mistress, I insist upon quitting this place."

"You cannot."

"How! am I, then, a prisoner?" cried Violet, in fresh alarm.

"I say not that; but the windows and doors of my house are barred."

"Gracious heaven! what a dreadful thought floats across my brain," muttered the terrified lady.

She had been entrapped, deceived, and betrayed.

The odious place of concealment must be some den of vice.

What is her doom?

To the last question Violet received the flippant answer of Poll Maggot, who explained away all doubt by stating that she believed Sir Ranulph Gayton to be a man of honour, and that he intended to marry the person whom he had so foully carried off.

"Yes, truly," continued the imperturbable hostess; "I heard him bid the lawyer draw up a license, to be ready on his return to the inn."

"Which will be——"

"Very shortly."

"Oh, woman," exclaimed Violet, imploringly, "you are of my own sex, and should take pity on me. I'll repay you in such terms that my life will scarcely requite the debt."

"Lady, what you ask of me is impossible," replied Poll Maggot. "I am so in the power of your admirer, that I dare not for the world offend him."

"Will not this tempt you?"

As Violet spoke, she drew from her wrist a valuable bracelet, and placed it in the hand of Poll Maggot.

"Jewels, I declare" said she, her eyes gloating upon the costly ornament. "Well, I never saw any thing so beautiful."

"Woman like, vanity is her besetting sin," murmured Violet to herself. "I shall succeed."

Perceiving the change that had taken place in the sentiments of Poll Maggot, and that the influence of wealth and power enslaved her fancy, the captive again addressed her.

"Would not, I say, such a gift as those gems," continued Violet, "induce you to have less terror of Sir Ranulph Gayton, and more consideration for me, his victim?"

"Why, yes," replied Poll Maggot, superciliously; still regarding the bracelet which she had fastened on her arm. "As you say—it is not creditable to Sir Ranulph to—how they glitter to be sure—these gems must be worth at least——"

"Many hundred pounds," said Violet. "They shall be yours, if you let me but escape from this terrible abode."

"I was about to remark," continued the hostess,

eyeing the present, "that these gems are the most brilliant I ever beheld—still my gratitude to Sir Ranulph ought—they'll be the very thing for my green velvet robe."

"Oh, trifle no longer with me, good woman," cried the impatient Violet, perplexed by the seeming indifference of her gaoler. "Tell me at once, do you consent to give me liberty, or——"

"At present I cannot help you," replied Poll Maggot; "but since you have been so generous, I will at least prevent your enemy from doing you the great injustice he premeditates; but I must and will set myself right. I have just thought of a scheme which I trust to carry out. You shall hear what it is in the morning."

"Why not tell it to me at once?"

"No, it would serve no purpose to mention my intention till I am able to realise it, and I have no doubt you will be surprised when I tell you that——"

Further conversation was put a stop to by the sound of footsteps.

Poll Maggot placed her finger to her lips, and murmured—

"Hush! Sir Ranulph Gayton is here."

She had scarcely uttered the words, when the individual named made an abrupt entrance into the chamber.

He was habited in a riding-dress, and was booted and spurred, and carrying pistols in his belt.

He stood in the door-way for an instant, as if to notice the looks of perplexity that betrayed themselves in the features of the two women who were before him.

They trembled beneath his gaze, for, although his demeanour was at all times blunt, and failed to impose respect, yet the energy corresponding to his character impressed, or rather commanded, a feeling of awe.

Having satisfied himself by a strict scrutiny, as it was supposed, that Violet Tremaine was still in good keeping, he advanced into the room.

"You have arrived opportunely, Sir Ranulph Gayton," said Poll Maggot, recovering her composure, and greeting the baronet with a curtsy.

"I rejoice to hear it," said he; "for I had shrewd suspicions that you were plotting against me, and that my company was not desired by either you or your gaol-bird yonder." With the words, Sir Ranulph inclined his head towards his prisoner.

"Now only to think," replied Poll Maggot, "how we are deceived in opinions which we form on various subjects; for instance, the lady here whom you supposed so ill-favoured to your suit, has, by my advice, become more compliant to your wishes."

"Indeed," said Sir Ranulph, with a sinister glance, "I do not doubt, Poll Maggot, the efficacy of your qualifications in love making, but I fancy some odd mistake has arisen in your present venture."

"Nothing of the kind, Sir Ranulph," rejoined the now somewhat indignant hostess; "you can have no idea of the effect I produced on the lady's heart when I pointed out your attractions, such as kindly disposition, superiority of birth, good temper and good looks."

"I am beholden to you, Poll," said Sir Ranulph, with a grim smile on his lip, which seemed to intimate that he was not quite inaccessible to flattery.

Having imposed silence on the intrusive attendant, who was about to speak further on the matter in hand, he next, by a significant gesture, bid her leave the room for awhile.

Poll Maggot did not answer the monition by words, but obeyed it slowly, and with dignity, for she was one of those persons who will not be hurried out of their own pace.

Looks were exchanged between the hostess and Violet which were thoroughly understood by the latter.

Sir Ranulph Gayton and his captive were now alone in the apartment.

The baronet dropped the riding mantle in which he was muffled, and, at the same time, fell on one knee.

"Gentle Violet," he exclaimed, "you will welcome back your bridegroom?"

The lady started back, but recovered herself in an instant, as one who recollected that she had a part of dignity to perform.

Sir Ranulph rose and continued speaking as he drew a packet from his vest.

"Yes, I shall, ere long, be the happiest of men."

Violet noticed this action on the part of her companion, upon whom she kept her looks fixed.

After a pause she observed,

"You address me in riddles, Sir Ranulph Gayton. Speak plainly that I may rightly hear, and duly understand you."

"In a word, then, you are my wife; for such this paper will confirm you soon. Love, you will sign it?"

"Before I do so," replied Violet, firmly, "I must be guided by my conscience; you must allow me at least some days for reflection."

"Impossible! I expect the priest here within the hour to join our hands."

Violet darted a convulsive glance on the speaker, and exclaimed,

"Sir Ranulph Gayton, since you have proceeded to this extremity, further disguise on my part is madness."

"Your determination, then, is——"

"To refuse consent to this impious union, and that my hands shall lay lifeless in their coffin rather than seal the engagement."

The baronet remained silent for a few moments as if struck by the remark, while Violet continued in a subdued tone, to appeal to him.

"You know, Sir Ranulph Gayton, that I am betrothed to another, to one you call friend; restore me once again to——"

"The man who was to wed you," interrupted the now hot and fiery baronet, "is a beggar, and his dwelling-place will shortly be a gaol; therefore, when a fool so lightly holds his love and fortune it is time for a wiser hand to seize them both."

With the words, Sir Ranulph Gayton dragged Violet towards the table and again insisted that she should sign the marriage contract which he had placed upon it.

"Release your grasp, ruffian!" exclaimed the struggling lady, vainly endeavouring to escape from her persecutor.

"Do you forget," she continued, "that I am a gentlewoman? You will have to answer gravely for this offence."

"Your threats are in vain," replied Sir Ranulph, still maintaining a firm hold of Violet's hand, "remember, if you refuse to ratify this compact, you will become my mistress in place of my wife."

The maiden made no reply to this insult and no longer resisted the party who had offered it.

Her stedfast glance fell upon him, and an almost imperceptible smile passed across her features.

Slowly advancing, she took up the marriage contract Sir Ranulph had alluded to.

Her eye quivered, and her hand slightly trembled as she scanned the writing on the parchment.

Having finished its perusal, she exclaimed, "You

tell me I must affix my name to this document, Sir
Ranulph Gayton."

The baronet acquiesced.

"To do so, I must have a pen." ·

"There are writing materials before you."

"I perceive them. I perceive, also, ——"

"What?"

"Pistols!" exclaimed Violet, "with which I swear
to fire upon the first man who attempts to hinder
my departure from this infamous house."

Before he was aware of it, Sir Ranulph found
himself opposed to a brace of pistols primed and
loaded to the mouth.

They were those he had inadvertently placed
upon the table at his entrance into the chamber.

CHAPTER CXXII.

MIDNIGHT VISITORS — THE FLIGHT OF VIOLET
TREMAINE FROM HER PERSECUTORS—A MASKED
LANTERN SOMETIMES OF ESSENTIAL SERVICE IN
THE DARK—THE OPEN PANEL AND THE SECRET
PASSAGE—JACK SHEPPARD ARRIVES MOST OP-
PORTUNELY — HIS DARING ESCAPE AFTER A
RESCUE.

THE triumph of Violet Tremaine was but short
lived.

It was soon evident to her enemy that the shock
had been too much for her, and that nature was
sinking fast.

Suddenly she became so faint that she could
scarcely move.

He cheek was deadly pale.

Her hand nerveless, allowing her to be easily
disarmed.

Sir Ranulph Gayton had no sooner got possession
of the weapons which had well nigh marred his
well-conceived plot, than he fired them both
through the window as a signal to his followers.

In answer to the summons, Poll Maggot was the
first to enter the chamber.

She was followed by two men wrapped in sable
cloaks.

These individuals were further disguised by hoods
fashioned like the cowl of a monk, drawn down
over their grim features.

The hostess then advanced a few paces and whispered some inaudible sentence in the ear of Sir
Ranulph Gayton.

He nodded his head in token of obedience, then
hastily quitted the chamber in company with his
confidant.

The baronet and Poll Maggot had no sooner left
Violet with her mysterious guardians than they
threw off the habiliments that concealed them and
appeared in their real characters of Jack Sheppard
and the hero of our tale.

As may be readily supposed, both had been admitted into the house by the connivance of its wily
mistress, who had accepted the bribe that Violet
had offered, anticipating one that she was to receive
from Roving Jack.

"I don't know how it is, Sir John," said Jack
Sheppard, in a low voice, "but I've a strange foreboding that ill will come of our adventure here to-
night."

"Surely, now that it is on the point of being
crowned with success, your heart don't fail you?"
replied our hero.

"No; but I'm afraid of treachery."

"Treachery, how so? You don't suppose Poll
Maggot is going to betray us?"

"No; but I can't help thinking that we are

trusting to a frail reed—a woman once jilted, takes
strange fancies into her head, and—"

"I have often thought that the fair sex would
be your ruin, Jack; depend upon it the man that
lavishes favours on all can trust none."

The attention of the speaker was now attracted
to Violet Tremaine.

She was still on the ground, but had raised herself to a sitting posture.

She appeared in silent contemplation with her
hand supporting her chin.

While a fixed and solemn glare, like one in
insanity, started from her eye.

Our hero addressed her, but she did not answer
him.

Terror it seemed had taken away the power of
utterance.

In a short time the reverie of Violet ended.

She heaved a heavy sigh, and gazed vacantly
around her.

In doing so, her eye rested on Jack Sheppard,
who had advanced in the place of our hero.

"Why am I disturbed at this late hour?" she
cried, wildly addressing the highwayman. "Why
am I aroused from quiet sleep and sunny dreams,
where thought flowed on as silver sheeted water
over sand of gold."

"I am a friend," answered Jack Sheppard,
kindly.

"A friend?"

"Yes; and am here to shelter you from a darkening storm, whose fury threatens to overwhelm
you."

"You are not what you seem."

"So it may appear, lady; but still you may trust
me. I come to offer you means of flight."

"I cannot accept them," replied Violet, wandering and abstracted. "I must not leave him—he
has enemies abroad'"

"Poor thing," said Jack Sheppard, "grief must
have brought this upon her."

Then resuming, he muttered in the ear of the
listener,

"If you do not fly with me, your life, entangled
as it is by circumstances, must be lost."

While Violet was yet hesitating, our hero had
arrived at her side.

The sudden effect produced by his appearance
was truly marvellous.

The maiden passed her hand across her brow,
and gazed upon him in amazement and doubt.

With a look as if her life depended on the question, she asked in an underbreath,

"Is it really you?"

"It is your beloved," said Roving Jack.

While uttering the words, he received Violet in
his arms.

Suddenly a momentary emotion was awakened
in his bosom, and regarding her features with a
feeling more akin to pity than to admiration, he
exclaimed,

"I had forgotten. You are no longer mine."

"No longer yours?" echoed Violet, not more
surprised at his words than his change of manner.

"Yes," continued Roving Jack, casting down his
eyes, as if to avert them from her gaze, "are you
not another's wife?"

"No—nor ever will."

"Hold—do not add falsehood to perfidy!"

"Heavens! can you believe me untrue?"

"You cannot, Violet, deny that, unmindful of
your sex and reputation, you quitted my roof at
night with Sir Ranulph Gayton."

"Why I did so was to seek you."

"To seek me?" rejoined Roving Jack, who began

to view Violet's conduct with increased astonishment.

"The man you have named," said she, "told me you were ruined—plunged in grief—and desired to see me. He gave me this letter," Violet continued, showing one. "You will observe, it is your writing."

Roving Jack took the paper into his hand, and rapidly glancing over its contents, then tore it into a thousand fragments.

"It is a forgery," he cried; "Violet, you have been betrayed, and I have wronged you."

A fond embrace—not words—accorded her lover's forgiveness, while he, in turn, regarded the maiden with deep commisseration.

"Sir Ranulph Gayton," he exclaimed, "is a villain of the blackest hue. I wish he and I were struggling upon some precipice, with only one step between us and eternity. Though the abyss of hell yawned at our feet, I'd plunge him into its eternal flames, merely to behold his agony as fire engulphs him in its tortures."

Jack Sheppard, who had been busily engaged during the late conversation between the lovers, now advanced.

The nature of his occupation will be soon made apparent.

"Now, Sir John," he cried, "I think I have arranged everything, and you and the lady can escape at once."

"Jack Sheppard, you are a faithful fellow," replied our hero; "and though I am most anxious for Violet's safety, I cannot, in honour, purchase her freedom at the risk of your life."

"No," added Violet; "you must accompany us in our flight, or I feel that we shall have selfishly sacrificed you."

"Compose yourselves," said the highwayman, endeavouring to reason his companions out of their apprehensions; "though I have work to do after your departure, I shall overtake you before you have proceeded a hundred paces on your journey. There is nothing to be alarmed at, since no one but the hostess knows of our retreat."

"That may be true," replied Violet; "but still the danger you run in remaining here after our absence must necessarily cause us uneasiness."

"There will be no danger if you leave the house without delay; moments are now getting precious, for the time allowed by Poll Maggot for detaining our enemies has nearly expired."

"Right, Jack," said our hero; "since you think our fears for you are groundless, we had better speed on our way."

The individuals who had been speaking now retired to the further end of the apartment in which they were standing.

Jack Sheppard proceeded here to draw aside the hanging covering the wall.

Behind them was an open panel, disclosing a secret passage running many hundred yards underground, and communicating with an out-building near the garden gate.

Our hero at once entered the refuge, while Violet Tremaine cautiously crept after him.

Without tarrying to observe Jack Sheppard, who watched his companions pass along the gloomy road, they proceeded hastily onward.

Having reached the basement floor by various descents, they at length came upon the subterranean way already spoken of.

It was arched overhead, but devoid of light.

Fortunately the fugitives had provided themselves with a masked lantern.

By the feeble radiance emitted from it, they discovered a door, apparently leading to some cell.

Our hero struck it with his hand.

Being of iron, it returned a hollow and dismal clangour.

Here we will leave the lovers awhile, and return to see how Jack Sheppard is occupying himself.

As the reader is aware, he had been left alone.

Sagacious, deep, and calm, he had ever overcome difficulties, and was now anticipating those which might beset his present venture.

"Let me see," said he; "the locksmith's daughter is a very good servant for children and fools, but of no service where resolution and strength are her master. Bolts, bars, and chains will give way in an instant," he continued, "so I must barricade the door if I would defy pursuit."

Suiting the action to the word Jack Sheppard at once moved some of the cumbrous furniture of the apartment to its entrance.

He had hardly commenced his labour when he heard footsteps on the staircase, and the voice of Sir Ranulph Gayton muttering imprecations and exclaiming that he had been betrayed.

Disappointed in carrying out his intended stratagem, the highwayman found that he must now trust to his heels for safety.

He sprang towards the egress through which his late companions had passed.

His astonishment and dismay can be conceived when he discovered that the opened panel had been closed and the spring was on the other side of the door.

"D——n!" cried Jack Sheppard. "There's no outlet that way, and I am a prisoner! But never say die, is my motto," he continued; "and it's strange if I can't find some means of getting out of the hands of these Philistines."

Undaunted and fearless, the brave highwayman seemed, in this as every other case, equal to its emergency.

His first precaution was to extinguish the lights of the apartment, so that his enemies were in total darkness.

Sir Ranulph Gayton was the first to enter and the first to speak.

He was armed to the teeth, and stood at the door on his guard that he might prevent any escape on the part of the prisoners by that means.

"Who speaks?" cried the baronet, in a voice of thunder, which sounded most ominously in the gloomy region. "Surrender yourselves quietly, and no harm will befal you. As you value your lives and safety you will not stir! Resistance will be useless; the chamber is hemmed in by followers on all sides!"

After each injunction Sir Ranulph Gayton paused, but received no answer to his mandates.

At length, sentinelling the entrance of the chamber, he advanced a few paces into it.

He listened attentively, but heard not the slightest sound.

"You may depend upon it, Sir Ranulph," cried one of his followers, "that our captives have taken refuge in some of the subterranean apartments with which it is said this old building abounds."

"If such places really exist," replied the baronet, "we must explore them; but I doubt if they can afford concealment, since their secret entrance is both unknown to them and us. They are still in this room, I feel assured; therefore let it be the first place that undergoes a strict search."

As he spoke a broad glare of light flashed from without, and several men arrived on the landing bearing torches.

Every object around them was now disclosed, and the chamber, hitherto dark, made light as day.

Great and deep was Sir Ranulph's mortification to find it empty; but he confidently reckoned on coming up with the runaways, the overturned furniture revealing that their absence had been but lately.

Midnight was tolling, and it became necessary to take some decisive step.

No further time was to be lost.

Sir Ranulph gave orders to his men to arm and follow him.

The order having been obeyed, he next posted them so as to surround the house and grounds attached to it, with a view to keep the fugitives within their precincts.

The wooded garden, in the rear of the premises, became one of the first points of attention.

Its intricacies were examined with additional precaution, but nothing was found lurking within them.

The weather had now begun to show itself favourable to the enterprise.

The dark clouds which had obscured the heavens gave way to the moon, which had forced herself through her ebon rack.

At this moment the whole party stood still.

One of their number, in the struggling rays, had seen a dark object issue from a chimney of the building they had quitted, and alight upon its roof.

"What can it be?" said Sir Ranulph, addressing the party who had given the intelligence.

"So far as I can judge, it is a man."

"Of what dress and appearance?"

A satisfactory answer having been given the baronet exclaimed, in exultation—

"'Tis Jack Sheppard! We have uncaged one bird, then; the others can't be far off."

Having uttered these words, the speaker called together his force, and disposed of them at points where the highwayman had been seen, and at which he would most likely attempt to descend.

They crept as near to the spot as they could, taking care not to lose each other's support.

As their comrade had averred, Jack Sheppard was seen making his way on the house top.

He was an adept at climbing, which seemed to him as a result of professional education and long experience.

He leapt from prominence to prominence with the light step and prowling sagacity of the hunter of the wilds.

Suddenly his progress was arrested by another individual who, without doubt, had descried his mode of escape.

Young, active, bold, and possessed of presence of mind, the highwayman turned to face his new enemy.

There was a desperate struggle, and one of the combatants went sheer down twenty feet.

He struck against a projection, which launched the wretched man outwards, and he fell with such force that his skull was crushed like an egg-shell.

"Who has fallen?" said Ranulph, vainly endeavouring to conceal his agitation at the late conflict.

"We can't tell," was the general reply, "the features are so disfigured."

"We shall soon discover," said the baronet, while a cry resounding through the air proclaimed that the fox who had been chased was now spared.

The proceedings of Jack Sheppard, to which the exclamation related, had been unfortunate.

He had no sooner overcome the antagonist, whom he hurled from the roof, than it was covered by twenty more to oppose him.

Their torches gleamed as so many furies urging his soul to perdition.

This determined band at once threw themselves upon the highwayman.

After a severe struggle he was thrown to the ground, two of the number being drawn forward by his strenuous exertions falling across him, yet, notwithstanding this advantage, Jack Sheppard hoped in the end to circumvent his pursuers.

Suddenly, by a superhuman effort, he sprang up, and dashed forward to the very extremity of the parapet that encircled the roof of the invested building.

The deed was so unexpected and desperate that assailant and assailed stood passive in each other's view.

The latter was the first to recover consciousness and activity.

The point upon which he stood was scarce wide enough for two persons to stand abreast, and being provided with a massive weapon in the shape of a broken rafter, could hold his position against a myriad of foes.

But these preparing to use fire-arms, such a resistance on the part of Jack Sheppard would have been madness.

Turning, he found the angle of the neighbouring house abutted within twelve feet of the spot upon which he was standing.

Quick as the thought he sprang towards it, though the chasm beneath was sixty feet.

Providence, who delights in those who dare, placed her sheltering wing over the adventurous highwayman.

He gained in safety the wished-for haven in defiance of the threats and menaces of his enemies, not one of whom had the temerity to follow his bold example.

Had those sentinels who witnessed this last adventure remained at their post instead of indulging in an idle curiosity or worse passions, they would doubtless have observed two individuals issue from an embowered retreat in the gardens attached to the tavern, yclept the "Devil's Punch-Bowl."

The one was a young lady of slight and sylph-like form, so delicately made, and so beautiful in countenance, that it seemed the earth on which she walked was too grossly massive a support for a creature so aërial.

Her eyes showed token of tears; but they were tears of joy.

While her colour was heightened by the flush of intense emotion.

The other was a youth of noble bearing, upon whose arm his companion bent, and like her he seemed to be avoiding observation by gliding beneath huge trees that skirted their path, and whose boughs sweeping the ground on every side ensured them against discovery, unless in case of actual search.

These individuals continued to advance, directing their course to a portal of Gothic appearance which formed an egress from the now deserted garden.

Here they paused and looked from the grated entrance, as if to observe that it was unguarded.

Satisfied that no one was about, they passed through it hastily, and were soon lost in the shadow of the night.

As the reader may have anticipated, they were our hero and Violet Tremaine.

Thus the exploit of Jack Sheppard, which had ended in that worthy's escape, had also caused the preservation of the lovers.

For their persecutors had been so engrossed in the intended capture of the highwayman, that their other victims were able to elude pursuit and depart unwittingly without molestation.

CHAPTER CXXIII.

ROVING JACK'S WEDDING—AN UNINVITED GUEST.

THE reader must again suppose that a year has passed, and rushed by us like the wind.

The flight of time alters us and others without a sense of change, nor can we see whence it comes or whither it tends.

Yet its rapid march beguiles man of his strength as the wind robs the oak of its foliage.

In the pleasant village of Hackney (to which spot our story now relates) stood an old Gothic structure, inhabited by Sir Jocelyn Tremaine.

The mansion had originally been a hunting seat, and a considerable portion of its chase or wooded domain was still preserved to the owner.

It occupied a piece of flat ground planted with sycamores, and was approached by an avenue skirted by majestic chesnut-trees.

The present tenant of this ancient building was now a widower, and father of an only child, whose singular beauty had ever smiled encouragement to our hero.

The old baronet had seen much misfortune.

Being a Jacobite, he had unwisely mixed up with those political intrigues which ended in the disastrous overthrow of the Pretender and his adherents.

His apostacy, however, had reclaimed his confiscated estates, which, through the agency of Jonathan Wild, had been once more restored to him.

Early one morning two individuals were observed to be approaching his mansion.

The one was Ned Bush, the highwayman, the other no less a personage than Sir Ranulph Gayton.

He was no longer the Sir Ranulph Gayton of former days, but appeared as a man worn down by crime, poverty, and dissipation.

Those who had once known the sprightly gallant, would never have recognised him in the enfeebled spendthrift, Geoffrey Bradshaw, in which disguised name we must for the present speak of him.

To complete his metamorphosis he was attired in a garb assimilating to a priest, and wore a tall sugar-loaf hat.

His eyes, restless, darting, and black, contrasted forcibly with his complexion, which had become pale as death.

"You are certain we're in the right track," exclaimed Ned Bush, addressing his sleek companion.

"How could it be otherwise?" replied his companion, somewhat contemptuously. "The road from London is as straight as an arrow, and a fool might find his way."

"A fool, say you?"

"Yes, a fool; and, I take it, that that appellation neither applies to you or myself."

"Why, I don't know that: if making money be a proof of wisdom, Geoffrey Bradshaw, then are we foolish."

With the words Ned Bush exposed his receptacle for cash, which exhibited that condition facetiously known as "pockets to let."

"We are neither of us particularly young," he continued, "and yet we have scarcely a mag between us."

"Worse luck."

"But what is this plan of yours about Roving Jack? I don't see how we can force any money from him."

"That is because you are a blind dolt, Ned Bush," replied Geoffrey Bradshaw. "My experience of life has learnt me this lesson, 'the head robs better than the hand,' and that a man can pilfer with impunity, provided his reputation be unhurt. With this influence vice may sit down with an emperor, while virtue may starve. There is no difference between the highwayman, who filches a purse on the road, and the titled gambler, who beggars with cards, save that the latter conforms to the social law called honesty in trivial matters."

"But this is not the question; let us turn to our dupe, Roving Jack."

"For the present you must leave the matter in my hands, Ned Bush," returned his confederate, while a sudden idea seemed to fix itself on his hard features. "Yes," he continued, musing, "I must ascertain that information before——"

The speaker's deep thought was suddenly interrupted by the appearance of a third party, who had been also engaged in contemplation and humming unwittingly the following old song :—

> "Oh! Blarney Castle, my darlint,
> You're nothing at all but cowld stone;
> Och, it's you was once strong and ancient
> And you kept the Sassenach down;
> But one night the poor boys of the castle
> Look'd over the battlement wall,
> And found that owld Cromwell must take it,
> For they'd neither shot, powder nor ball."

The ballad, which was being sung with no unmusical voice by "Slashing Nat Wetherby," for he turned out to be the interloper, was here cut short by a mutual discovery that all parties present were known to each other.

"The top of the morning to you, gentlemen," said the gay spark, addressing Ned Bush and the other, "glad to fall in with pals in this outlandish place."

"Anything up?" he continued. "I'm good for a mount in Swell Street, the High Toby Spice, or simple Ken Cracking."

Of "Slashing Nat Wetherby," who has only figured lightly in the previous portion of our tale, it is necessary to speak, as he will play a somewhat important part in the next following chapters.

England may boast of her highwaymen and laud to the skies such knaves as Mulsack, Turpin, and Swiftneck; but Ireland, the birthplace of our present hero, has produced equally great rascals, and though little known, are nevertheless to be considered as luminaries (in their way) of the first water in the dominion of prigs.

"Slashing Nat Wetherby" was one of those worthies who had left his country for his country's good —or rather he had found the land of praties too hot to hold him, for his daring actions had surrounded him on every point with enemies in the shape of officers of police and plundered peasantry.

Redmond O'Hanlon, for that was the real name of this fugitive from Irish justice, was a renowned Rapparee.*

Over the broad province of Ulster he had rendered his name a terror, and levied black mail on each county to such an extent that its inhabitants had combined to exterminate the scourge that seemed likely, in the end, to involve them in one common ruin.

To avoid the determined purpose of this hostile league, who gave every indication of carrying it out with success, the runagate set sail for England.

---

* Rapparees, or Irish robbers.

where Redmond O'Hanlon, disguised as Slashing Nat Wetherby, managed to carry on his old trade of robbery with every success.

Having given this trifling history of the individual in question, we proceed to the point at which we broke off.

Sir Ranulph Gayton, *alias* Geoffrey Bradshaw, had no sooner encountered the new comer than he returned his salutation.

The meeting was *à propos ;* the Hibernian was just the person the wily baronet wanted, the very man to aid him in his design. He had a firm hand and a stout heart, and possessed all the distinguishing characteristics of a fine gentleman.

Added to these, were a perfect knowledge of the world, a captivating address, and perfect independence of the law of "meum et tuum," or, in other words, he paid no respect to the relative position of property.

"We are well met," said Geoffrey Bradshaw, grasping fervently the hand of Nat Wetherby. "I have been wishing for a friend, and fate has sent me one."

"You don't say so," replied the party addressed, winking at his insidious companion, as much as to say that he had only his word for the assertion.

"You are one of those illustrious heroes," continued the other, "of whom posterity will be proud.

"Who can finger a trigger, or handle a knife, like 'illigant' Redmond O'Hanlon?

"Who can produce such a dare-devil squadron as those who composed his band ?

"Show me, if you can, his equal in trotting a tit from its stable, or diving a fam into a cly."

"We've had enough, in all conscience, about the Irishman," interrupted Ned Bush, "hadn't we better turn our attention now to those sounds which strike like music on our ears ?"

This remark had been called forth by a merry peal of bells from the neighbouring church.

The presence of a spirit of noise, mirth, and caprice spoke from each brazen mouth, and at once seemed to keep up a perpetual rejoicing by their clamour.

"Pleasant bells those, very," observed Nat Wetherby ; "quite different to those of St. Sepulchre's, which I heard this morning from a cell in Newgate."

Bradshaw eyed his associate shrewdly, and, after a pause, remarked,

"Can you tell me, Nat, why those tinklers are ringing so gaily ?"

"Why, I believe," he replied, "that is, I've been told—mark me, I don't assert it as a fact, but, still, I hear—that there's a wedding taking place."

"A wedding ?"

"Yes."

"Do you know the name of the bridegroom?" hastily enquired Bradshaw."

"Well, if my information be correct," replied Nat Wetherby, drily, "the name of the wretched victim is no other than Roving Jack."

"That is right, quite right ; so you have received the intelligence on good authority."

"Sir John Warbold is a happy dog," continued the highwayman, "for the fortune of his wife will be paid down immediately after the marriage ceremony."

"Indeed ! this interests me. I was not aware of such a fact," said Geoffrey Bradshaw, on hearing the avowal, which at once changed the current of his thoughts, and troubled them anew. "The lady's name," he continued, "is Violet Tremaine, and the proud structure, with its rich domains, before which

we are standing, have been held by her family for centuries."

"So I believe," replied Nat Wetherby, whose further remarks were interrupted by the contemplation of the following scene.

It was the return of the wedding party to the ancestral home of the father of the bride, Sir Jocelyn Tremaine.

He headed the cavalcade, close behind him rode five or six gentlemen, and then came a carriage in which were seated the newly-married couple, Sir John and Lady Warbold.

The features of our hero were somewhat pale, as might naturally be expected from the anxiety he had suffered from that fatal passion, gambling, which had so nearly brought him to utter ruin.

But his determined manner and firm deportment, evinced to all who beheld him that he had become an altered and a wiser man.

Violet, the bride, appeared painfully agitated.

First becoming white as marble, anon suffused with blushes.

Murmurs of impassioned homage from the spectators greeted her as she pursued her way.

And there appeared not a man, of the many who gazed upon her, but would have given his life for a favouring regard.

The approach of the cortège had been watched by the inmates of the mansion destined to receive our hero and the guests.

Their best wishes are with him.

The flag ever used upon auspicious occasions is floating from the summit of its tower.

Its appearance is regarded as a favourable omen, and the neighbours for miles around flock to the given signal.

When the horsemen and carriage arrived at the avenue, all alighted.

Roving Jack and Violet leading the way, walked slowly along the broad gravel path towards the principal entrance.

The doors were thrown open.

And a crowd of servants rushed forth to bid welcome to the happy couple.

They passed on and entered the hall, followed by Sir Jocelyn Tremaine, and the company invited to the entertainment that was provided in the spacious room adjoining.

Here was exhibited to the view of the assemblage numerous tables, and glittering buffets, arrrayed with all the appliances concurrent with a feast.

Everywhere the walls of this apartment were festooned with flowers fragrant and blooming as the spring.

While mirrors wreathed with roses reflected the gleaming plate and sumptuous fare, beneath which the festive board seemed to groan.

We will now leave the scene of festivity, and those participating in it, and retire to an adjoining chamber.

It is evening, and sunset gilds the groves seen from the window.

While the grey mist which hangs over the afar off meadows proclaims that night is rapidly travelling on.

The apartment itself appeared lonely in the glimmery twilight.

It was ascended by a broad oaken staircase, supplied with curiously carved banisters and a richly-moulded ceiling.

Tapestry adorned its interior, and squares of black and white marble formed a flooring.

The room was large, antiquely furnished, and decorated by a single portrait painted upon a panel with the date—1588.

BLACK JACK BESS INTERCEPTS NAT WETHERBY.

Seated in the above chamber were two individuals.

These two personages were our hero and his beloved Violet.

Hark to their discourse.

"My bright and beautiful one," exclaimed the enraptured husband, " at last you are my own, and fate, which so long threatened to divide us, has given Violet to me, and vouchsafed sweet smiles where frowns were once paramount."

"Yes, dear husband," replied she, "when in our youth, we were poor, there was indeed little hope for us ; but when your rich and haughty uncle, the Admiral, died, and left you sole heir of his possessions, a welcome sprang from my father, whose forbidding looks had previously been rife, and his consent given without hesitation to our union."

"I remember, Violet," said our hero, "how my searching eye seemed ever bent upon the old man whenever he presented himself before me.

"My childish imagination was perturbed at a phenomenon for which, for the life of me, I could not account.

"With this," continued the speaker, " comes a thousand warmer and dearer recollections of my early attachment. How I assisted you at your lessons, dear Violet ; when I brought water to the flowers you had set with your own hand, or accompanied you in the wild songs of our native vale."

"Yes, and I also remember," interrupted Violet, " that once when my father looked at your exertions with a good-humoured and careless smile, he muttered to himself, 'If it should turn out so, why it might be best for both.'"

"The theories of happiness he has reared on these words, for——"

"The homeless outcast, Roving Jack, has become the representative of an illustrious and ancient family."

"And he would renounce all glory," exclaimed our hero, "unless his beloved Violet was a sharer in such good fortune."

He was waked out of this pleasing reverie by the approach of a servant, who had entered the room without the usual notice.

"How dare you, sirrah," thundered Roving Jack break in thus upon my privacy !"

"I beg your pardon, Sir John," replied the man, "that I have come upon you abruptly; but I have only obeyed orders."

"Indeed! by whom were such offensive instructions given?"

"A gentleman, Sir John, who would see you instantly."

"A guest?"

"No."

"Who can he be?"

"He refused to give his name. He is a man of singular appearance, and says his business is pressing, most important, and, above all things, secret."

"Business? Ridiculous!—this is a day to me of pleasure. I would not be disturbed to double my fortune. Tell him to call upon me on some other occasion."

"He will not leave the house, Sir John," added the servant, eyeing his master with a look of suspicion. "I was unwilling in the first instance to bring the message to you; but he besought me so, and said it was upon a most serious affair he wished to communicate."

"Serious?" exclaimed Violet, starting at the word. "What can this be?"

"Nothing, my life, nothing," replied Roving Jack. "But as this stranger is so importunate, I may as well see him. Go, sirrah, and bring the person to this room, where I will await his coming."

The servant bowed, and hurried to do the bidding, leaving our hero and Violet once more alone.

There was a pause.

The latter was the first to break silence, and seemed anxious to satisfy her curiosity as to the motive of the mysterious visitor, who was about to make his appearance.

"Sir John," she exclaimed, bursting into tears, "you should not hide, now, secrets from me. I have been told that a confirmed gambler can never be reclaimed. I did not believe it, for I entertained a better opinion of human nature than to suppose that the man, upon whose plighted word I had trusted, would allow a fatal passion to subvert resolution, principle, and honour."

"Violet, your suspicion that I am again plunging myself into the vortex of ruin from which I have been snatched is unjust," exclaimed our hero, who, for a moment, had remained dumbfounded at the unexpected accusation. "You cannot deem me so cruel," he continued, "and capable of such black ingratitude, after what I have suffered, to——"

"No, no," replied Violet, passionately, throwing herself into her husband's arms, "you do not understand me. I merely thought that your imprudence in admitting this stranger, might——"

"Lead to such a contingence," said Roving Jack, with a smile, and impressing a kiss upon his wife's lips; "but, there, dearest, dry your tears and once more return to our guests, who, doubtless, are surprised at our absence. I will dismiss this intruder, and be at your side again in a few minutes. Mark me," continued our hero, addressing Violet as she was quitting the room, "no more sighs, or I shall be angry. Remember, it is our wedding day, and offensive to lovers to pine at such a time."

As Violet passed through one door, another was opened.

In the recess stood Sir Ranulph Gayton, still assuming his character of Geoffry Bradshaw.

His features, though handsome, were malignant and fierce, and now lit up by the moon's beams which peered through the window, positively inspired aversion.

A peculiar sardonic grin settled on his curled lip, and his eye dazzled as some snake's upon a trembling bird under its influence.

Before Roving Jack was aware of this man's presence, his voice was heard to exclaim—

"Good evening, my worthy friend."

"Friend," echoed our hero; "you speak familiarly. Am I known to you?"

"Known to me; come, I like that," replied the other, with a sarcastic laugh. "Am I not known to you?"

"No."

"No?"

"I never saw you before to my knowledge," continued Roving Jack.

"Humph, I have often heard that the possession of wealth makes men forget their old acquaintances. Now I have proof positive of the melancholy fact."

"Sir," exclaimed our hero; "if this were not my own roof, and you my guest, although an unbidden one, I would say such words are most impertinent, and to me libellous; but suffice it now, that if you have any business to communicate, I will hear it, provided it be told without delay."

"And, otherwise——"

"I must leave you."

"Good; knowing that, I must take a chair."

With the words, this stolid individual took a seat, and drew a curiously-fashioned pipe from his pocket.

Loading the same with some Spanish tobacco, he lit it with a neighbouring lamp, and proceeded to stretch his legs upon one of the tables of the room, in which situation he puffed away at his leisure, and with the greatest nonchalance.

In a few minutes the whole region was redolent of the balmy weed, and filled with its vapour.

"I always smoke under emergency," remarked the disguised baronet, coolly; "therefore you will allow me such an indulgence upon such an understanding."

While he uttered these words, the speaker fixed a scrutinising look upon our hero, who appeared utterly amazed at his companion's deliberate assurance.

After a pause, he at length addressed him.

"Perhaps the gentleman who seems to make himself thoroughly at home in my house will have no objection to favour me with his name."

"None in the least. I am a public character, and generally known," exclaimed the party addressed. "I am called Geoffrey Bradshaw."

"Indeed!" replied our hero, staring in surprise at the announcement.

"I see you don't remember me."

"Your features are forgotten by me: but still I recollect that a person bearing the name you have mentioned was in the employ of my late uncle."

"Yes, you are right, Sir John. I was steward of his estates, and consequently know, by the death of the old admiral, that you have become a wealthy man."

"This is irrelevant."

"Perhaps not, Sir John," rejoined the steward, contemplating the fumes of his pipe. "Of course," he continued, with a wink, "you are aware that your relative, dying without a will, as heir at law you have succeeded to all his personal and landed property."

"And pray, sirrah, may I ask what in the name of goodness can this affair be to you?" asked Roving Jack, beginning to lose his patience with the imperturbable Bradshaw.

"What can the affair be to me?" enquired he. "More than you think for, Sir John. Had your uncle left a will you would have been very differently situated, seeing that he entertained no great affection for you, and a great deal for another person."

Treating our hero with a cunning leer, the supposed steward continued—

"Now comes the joke of my story. Admiral Warbold did make a will, and, what is more surprising, that will is now in my possession!"

This intelligence, as may be presumed, had a startling effect upon Roving Jack.

However, he essayed no remark, and, by a powerful effort, disguised his emotion from his companion, who continued—

"I'll tell you, Sir John, how it came about. Rummaging one day, while I was in your uncle's service, an old and secret compartment of an escritoire, I found the document of which I have spoken."

"And did you dare——" interrupted our hero.

"Dare? Bless you, Sir John, I dare do more than you imagine, which you will find out when you know me better," continued the other, with unblushing effrontery. "With the will, I found your uncle's sealed ring. I've brought it with me just to show that I am using no deception in the matter."

Here Bradshaw produced a ring, which he placed for Roving Jack's inspection.

"'Tis his own private signet," he muttered to himself. "How often have I searched amid his hoards for that memento, and without success? But let this matter pass for the present, Sir John, as we have to deal with a greater one," continued Bradshaw.

"The will——"

"Is still with me. I have not broken the seals of the envelope; I like to act honourably, and if ' you ' like to agree to conditions I shall deliver the will into your hands without knowing anything about its contents myself."

"But is it genuine? Is it dated?" asked our hero, almost unconsciously, for the mien and braggadocio of the man he confronted had caused a strange suspicion to arise in his mind.

"It is dated only four days before the admiral's death," replied Geoffrey Bradshaw; then speaking in a flippant manner, continued, "As to its being genuine, why the old man has written on the envelope what it comprises, and I suppose you can identify his writing?"

"I can," replied Roving Jack, somewhat eagerly; "that is a thing that no one can deceive me in."

"I am glad to hear you say so," returned the other, with a grim smile on his face; "you will be sooner satisfied about the fact."

Our hero, eyeing closely Geoffrey Bradshaw, next asked him his conditions, seeing that as he had spoken of money, most likely that was his incentive in this strange matter.

"Yes, Sir John, you will find me most compliant," replied the steward. "If you agree to the terms I shall dictate I will readily give up the will of your uncle which I now hold; if not, I make it public," continued the inexorable individual, stopping to light his pipe in the middle of the sentence, "and if," continued he, speaking at his leisure, "as is most likely, your defunct relative has not left you a shilling, why, of course, you have to return once more to degradation and poverty."

"What sum do you require for silence and secrecy?"

"Five thousand pounds."

"Five thousand pounds?"

"Yes, and don't hesitate about it," replied Bradshaw, significantly; "you've received your wife's dowry to-day, and that's twenty thousand pounds, or report's a liar."

"But if," said our hero, "when I have paid you this money, I open the will and discover the property is left elsewhere, I shall be a beggar."

"What the devil should you open it for?" added the unscrupulous baronet. "To find out you are ruined, eh? You let me have the rhino, and I'll give up the will."

"Once in my hands——"

"You can pop it on the fire," continued Bradshaw, "and who'll be the wiser? I hadn't curiosity enough to open the paper myself, why should you?"

"Where is the document?"

"At my lodgings, in Petty France."

"I will meet you there to-morrow."

"To-morrow will be too late; we must depart to-night."

At that moment a suppressed and stifled scream was heard.

It appeared to issue from some one apparently concealed in the chamber.

Bewildered by the strange event, its occupants proceeded to make a strict search of the apartment; but the eavesdropper, if there had been one, had stolen unperceived from it.

* * * * * *

It was early in the morning when Sir Jocylyn Tremaine arose from his couch and hastily bent his steps to the steward's chamber.

He looked grave and pre-occupied.

A silent suspicion of truth seemed, as it were, to have flashed upon him, and he soon reached his destination.

He rapped against the door of the faithful old man's room.

No answer was returned.

"I did not expect it," murmured one of the several attendants who had arrived.

"An entrance must be forced."

"Stay, let me try again," thought Sir Jocylyn, "before we have recourse to violence."

"Adam, Adam," he exclaimed, knocking sharply.

"Adam cannot answer," returned he who had first spoken; it was Wirth Wolfgang. With the words, he hurled his huge frame against the door.

It burst open.

The reason why no answer had been returned to the summons then became apparent to all.

The tenant of the room was a stiff and rigid corpse. (Vide illustration to Number 35.)

They entered the room with reverence, for the presence of the dead ever exacts a feeling of respect from even the wanton.

On each countenance awe was impressed.

There was a pause, and a voice heard uttering a prayer.

Presently that voice was hushed by a deep and heavy sigh.

Then followed a profound silence which reigned for some minutes amidst the gloom.

CHAPTER CXXIV.

PETTY FRANCE.

FEW of our readers are, perhaps, aware that a locality in the metropolis still bears the name which heads this chapter.

It is that portion of the Dacre estate which lies between the Broadway, at Westminster, and Castle Lane, near Pimlico. It is supposed originally to have derived its appellation from a numerous body of French Calvinists settling in this spot after the revocation of the edict of Nantes.

At the period of our story, Petty France was filled with squalid habitations and lawless occupants, and its foul recesses gave refuge to some of the most abandoned and ruffianly characters that ever disgraced community.

The coarsest ribaldry assailed the ear, and noisome odour afflicted the nose of the wayfarer who chanced to tread the terrible purlieus.

The kennels flowed with filth.

The roadway disclosed putrescent heaps of rubbish.

Still, there was something savagely picturesque in the aspect of the place, despite its loathsome and hideous features.

Its cluster of brown and old-fashioned houses built half of timber, with projecting casements, presented that superior effect which intricacy and intermixture ever produces over the tame uniformity of a modern street.

These dwellings were thickly inhabited; every chamber from cellar to garret were swarming with miserable inmates.

The rooms being almost destitute of furniture, and their tenants, in many cases, void of covering.

The main thoroughfare displayed here and there clothes-lines garnished with every description of garment, while the numerous alleys and passages leading from it gave greater signs of wretchedness and poverty.

In a word, the whole neighbourhood appeared like one of those hot-beds of squalor and vice, to escape from which and breathe again the purer atmosphere of the world without is a positive relief.

One night, in a narrow lane, guarded by posts and cross-bars that led into the notorious region that has been described, three men were seen.

They were severally known as Gregory, Harold, and Tony Wheeler, and have figured hitherto as members of Dick Turpin's gang.

The last-named had issued from a house, and down its steps upon which the moon had been clearly shining.

"Have they passed?" asked this worthy of his companions, who seemed to have been watching narrowly something that interested them.

"Yes," replied Harold, "and gone down Prince's Street."

"S'life! I'm glad to hear that," chimed in the individual rejoicing in the name of Gregory.

"So am I," continued the first speaker, Tony Wheeler, "for had the watch have come up here at this moment, they would have taken me as easily as a sucking babby."

"But you'd got your pistol?"

"No, I hadn't," was the reply of the roadster. "I lent them to Burley Bill, who's gone towards Hounslow to-night."

While these parties were yet speaking, a light had appeared at the casement above their heads.

This attracted the notice of Gregory, who exclaimed,

"Hilloa, comrades! who's that showing a glim yonder?"

"I reckon that it's Edgeworth Bess," said Harold, "waiting for the return of Slashing Nat Wetherby."

"She's a rum 'un!" chuckled Tony Wheeler.

An opinion in which Harold, otherwise Long Ned, perfectly coincided, if we may judge from the portentous nod of the head he gave after his companion's remark.

"She was a nice-looking girl at one time," continued Tony Wheeler.

"Yes," replied Long Ned. "That was afore she nosed upon Jack Sheppard, who turned her up for her pains."

"Well, I don't think she was so much to blame after all," interrupted Gregory. "Slashing Nat Wetherby won her affections, and you know how he can gammon the weak sex when he's a point to carry out."

"That's true," said Tony Wheeler; "but I'd have Nat beware that this Dalilah don't hand him over to the Philistines, as she has her former 'inamorato,' for they say she's jealous of him already."

There was now a shrill whistle given, and hasty steps resounding along the deserted thoroughfare followed the signal.

Presently a figure was observed approaching the late speakers.

As it advanced from the shade they recognised a pal.

It was he who had been the object of their conversation, namely, Slashing Nat Wetherby.

"Well, Nat, been to the heath to-night?" was the general greeting.

"'Fore George, no," he replied, with a smiling countenance, "I'd better game in view. To-night," continued the knight of the post, "I've been playing the gentleman, dancing with ladies from whom I have borrowed no end of necklaces, and a fabulous amount of money."

"You know, my dear boys, I was never known to doss the pross of the kae-keibosh, and the tidly wink fakement on the slomdrum; no, not for Joseph; or, in plain English, I always, on all occasions, practise cly-sneaking, vulgarly termed picking pockets."

After a general laugh at the adventure had subsided, enquiry was made as to its whereabouts.

Slashing Nat Wetherby was communicative, and enlightened his comrades on the vexed question.

He told them that he had but recently visited a delightful suburb, which had given a name to a useful vehicle called Hackney.

A particular friend of his resided in that vicinity.

Most likely many of the fraternity knew him as Roving Jack.

He had that morning immolated himself on the altar of domesticity.

He would not refuse the last sad office he could pay the wretched victim, therefore he accepted his kind invitation to the wedding feast.

Here he combined business with pleasure, and the rich booty which he presently presented to his accomplices clearly proved that these two occupations may at times be carried forward with considerable profit and some success.

Having delivered himself of this intelligence, Slashing Nat Wetherby next enquired after his chum, Ned Bush.

"He is waiting for you at your lodgings," was Tony Wheeler's answer.

"That's all regular," said Nat, dusting his boots with a whip he carried in his hand. "I've business with him," he continued. "Hark ye, lads, this night he and I hope to make a fortune."

"Indeed," replied one and all, surprised at this startling announcement.

"Aye, indeed," echoed the robber; "and I suppose if I require assistance you will afford it?"

"Of course we shall," formed the words of the general exclamation.

"I don't think it very likely that I shall require much help," continued Nat; "but if the beaks should hear of our doings before the 'queer cull' parts with his ochre, it will be necessary to strike a blow that——"

"Only give the word."

"That's all."

"To be sure."

Were sentences uttered in one breath by the community, and with such an emphasis, that they appeared as a guarantee for the fulfilment of the promised aid.

Satisfied with the friendly disposition of his confederates, Nat Wetherby requested each one in the first place to make himself scarce, and vanish from the place in which they were then stationed.

The victim would be here immediately.

He did not wish him to see strange faces lurking about.

He had only got the start of him by taking a nearer turn, and some fortuitous circumstance was alone delaying him.

With the word the whole party departed as some band of phantoms, but whither would have puzzled Mephistophiles to tell.

Suffice, Nat Wetherby was in an instant the sole person to be seen in the quarter.

After a pause he proceeded to the house at which it will be remembered the late visitants had observed a light.

Knocking at the entrance of the dwelling he shouted to one of its inmates.

"Hilloa, wench, open the door, and make haste about it."

Nat Wetherby had no sooner given the summons than a female looked out of a casement and demanded,

"Who's there?"

"One who owns a noble nag and a handsome mistress, and rides over Hounslow Heath by moonlight."

"Are you alone?" asked the same voice, which proved to be no other than that of Edgeworth Bess.

"Yes, girl," replied her paramour, "but I expect visitors, shortly."

"A man is sleeping here," continued Edgeworth Bess, "shall I wake him?"

"No; since that is the case, you must come down."

Obedient to his will, the woman closed the window, and in a few moments descended into the street to Nat Wetherby.

"I am here," she exclaimed bitterly.

"What, sulky again, Bess," cried the highwayman, jovially, "what the deuce, girl, ails you of late?"

"Ask your own heart the question," replied Edgeworth Bess, in a tone that showed her bosom was torn by some conflicting passions. "Even the down-trodden worm will turn and dart its harmless venom on its oppressor; but it must soon end," she continued, speaking to herself.

"How you are muttering," said Nat Wetherby; "but it doesn't matter; I suppose jealous women find consolation in a grumble."

Turning the conversation to one more agreeable, the highwayman inquired the names of the parties lodging above his apartment.

"Two men," replied Edgeworth Bess, as morose as ever; "one calls himself Bradshaw—he is a gambler; the other, Ned Bush, is now in your room, where he said he was to await you."

"Quite right; get some spirits, girl, from the tavern; see the mugs be clean and ready."

As he spoke, Nat Wetherby placed some money in Bess's hand, and observed, "The guests I have spoken of will soon arrive, and by one of them I mean to make a fortune; and see here, lass," he continued, producing a necklace from his pocket, "here's a shiner."

Avarice glistened in the eye of Edgeworth Bess while she exclaimed,

"Ha! diamonds! how they sparkle. Give me the trinkets, Nat; they shall be my care."

"Well, you shall have the jewels," said Nat Wetherby, delivering them to the keeping of his frail companion. "They appear to be without a flaw, and are rare specimens of the earth's greatest treasure."

"They could not be of any service to him in prison," she murmured to herself, as she placed the costly gift in her bosom. "And this," she continued, "is his last night out."

Seeming to depart for the drink Nat Wetherby had ordered, Edgeworth Bess left her lover.

She left him to accomplish in reality a vengeance for an injury she deemed she had suffered.

So hastened to dispatch a trusty messenger on her errand.

"Yes, yes," mused the unsuspecting robber, when he was left by himself, "the finding of this will must make me a gentleman. It was fortunate that Geoffrey Bradshaw thought my assistance necessary, or he might have plundered the victim without my knowledge.

"Though I have succeeded with this gambler," he continued, "yet would I rather transact business with a highwayman than a card sharper; but the old proverb tell us that beggars mustn't be choosers, so I suppose thieves must be so neither."

Two figures now appeared in the distance.

As they approached, Nat Wetherby discovered that they were those of our hero and Geoffrey Bradshaw.

He had no sooner recognised these parties than he glided softly into the house from whence Edgeworth Bess had issued, before which the new comers soon arrived.

"How much farther are we to go?" asked Roving Jack of his companion.

"Not another step," was the reply. "You see the casement above us in which a lamp is burning?"

"Yes."

"That lights the dwelling we must enter. In its uppermost attic," continued Geoffrey Bradshaw, "securely sealed, lies your uncle's will."

"Then let us at once proceed to the apartment," exclaimed our hero.

"We will do so when you have answered my question," said the other.

"A question?"

"Yes; have you brought the money with you?"

"You are very importunate on this point, I fancy," replied Roving Jack, testily. "On three occasions have you demanded this request, and on each I have said yes."

"Well, you must excuse my being particular, for I have reason for such apparent curiosity, at which you will not be surprised when you learn the cause."

As Geoffrey Bradshaw spoke, he felt for the moment desperately inclined; but on a sudden consideration his anger seemed to abate.

"But come," he continued, with a forced composure, "Wetherby and Bush will be waiting for us."

"How long am I likely to be detained?" enquired our hero, moodily.

"Oh! not long; half an hour or so, not more, certainly."

Roving Jack and his companion, on this assurance, entered the house.

As they did so, the light which had been placed in its casement disappeared.

CHAPTER CXXV.

A FRIEND IN NEED IS A FRIEND INDEED—THE TRUSTY MESSENGER.

WE must now shake hands with an old acquaintance, and once more make a friend of the reckless, jovial, and and merry Simon Smut.

So long as he had money he revelled in folly, and led a joyous life.

How fascinating is the practice of excess in front.

How deformed and unsightly behind.

At the present moment he was without a coin in his pocket.

He had sold his linen, and the proceeds had vanished in drink.

Every farthing he possessed soon galloped off in grog and toddled in toddy.

"Ah, Simon Smut, your bright taper is put out and replaced by a scurvy candle," he apostrophized, in drunken gravity, as he wended his way along one of the bye streets of Petty France. "People may well mock at you now since you will henceforth have nothing but water to drink."

Dunned by remorse and imaginary creditors, the intoxicated reprobate continued,

"I must turn from these evil ways, and come forth into the world with a heart full of contrition.

"Yes, I must reform, confess my faults, and be penitent.

"I'll cut prigging at once, and become a respectable member of society by going back to my old trade of chimney-sweeping."

The resolution of Simon Smut was somewhat damped at this moment by a pail of water.

The contents of the vessel having been inadvertently thrown out of a neighbouring window upon his luckless head.

"Well, they might have let me had a hint of the important arrival," thought Simon Smut, who unconcernedly took no notice of the affront further than shaking himself, poodle fashion, from the exuberant moisture. "I always heard that the locality I am traversing wasn't famous for politeness and manners, now I've a "gushing" specimen of the fact."

With these words, Simon Smut hurried to a neighbouring public-house.

He was dripping, damp and shivering.

A drop of something warm would keep out the cold.

It was while standing at the door of a tavern that the unlucky wight remembered he'd no cash to pay for the liquor.

But Providence, which guards its creatures, came to his rescue, in the shape of a woman, carrying in her hand a full-bellied bottle containing the required beverage.

Simon Smut no sooner descried this damsel than he gave the signal used by the knights of the road, who, he knew, infested the quarter.

His summons was answered, and himself greeted with the familiar words,

"Is that you?"

"Of course it's me," said Simon, resolutely, addressing the unknown, and taking the bottle she was holding in her hand.

"Don't ask any questions till I've wetted my whistle," he continued, satisfying himself by a copious draught from the vessel he had abstracted from his companion.

"I began to think you would never come," said she, after Simon had finished his libations.

"Oh, then, you did expect me?" answered the latter, artfully preserving the error the woman had fallen into, and which was materially aggravated by the darkness of the place.

"Of course; I relied upon you, since you gave me your word you would come."

"Yes, I'm always as good as my word," replied Simon Smut, conceitedly; "especially when there is anything to be got by it."

"But you must speed on your errand lest any suspicion should be aroused. Sir John Fielding, the justice, is now waiting for you," continued Edgeworth Bess.

"The devil he is!" muttered Simon Smut, and evidently astonished to find he had placed himself in something like a dilemma.

"Of course you remember that I have promised the magistrate to betray Nat Wetherby into his hands to-night, so you must conduct him and his men hither."

"Well, you see," said Simon Smut, addressing Edgeworth Bess obsequiously, and seeming to have hit upon a plan of withdrawing himself from a difficulty, "though I am at all times ready to oblige a lady, still, in the present instance, I think I can hardly do so."

"How? Do you refuse to——"

"No, I don't refuse, only I'd rather not."

"What reason can you possibly have for so suddenly altering your determination?"

"I'll be candid with you, mum," said Simon Smut; "you must know I've a strong aversion to appear in any matters in which the police authorities are interested. I once did so, and got more than I anticipated for my pains. A silver spoon got into my soot-bag; quite an accident, of course. But the big-wigs wouldn't have it."

"You forget that this is a very different case, and that a large sum is offered for the man we are giving up," said Edgeworth Bess; "and also that half of the reward will find its way into your pocket."

"True," said Simon Smut, clapping his forefinger to his nose, and assuming an attitude of meditation.

The voice of Nat Wetherby was now heard, and calling for the liquor he had ordered to be supplied.

Edgeworth Bess, who, as the reader may suppose, had been the companion of Simon Smut, hastily quitted his side at the summons, and entered the house from whence the sound proceeded.

Before doing so she requested her associate to remain within hail that she might again communicate with him.

Still wrapped in thought Simon Smut seated himself in a neighbouring nook to await the return of Edgeworth Bess, when his eyes fell upon a person who was rapidly advancing towards him.

It was a youth of about nineteen, with a slight figure, almost approaching to effeminacy.

But, in spite of his appearance, which also proclaimed timidity, there was a fire in the eye of this stripling which showed he possessed both spirit and resolution.

He was attired in a riding dress, fashioned according to the taste of the time, and in keeping with those habiliments highwaymen were wont to wear.

As this individual arrived at the spot upon which Simon Smut was standing, Edgeworth Bess again made her appearance, and in the dark, mistaking him for her confederate, whispered these words, in a low tone,

"You are still here, I find; so much the better;

had you departed my plan would have been foiled."

"Yes," replied the youth, answering at every risk, for he conceived by keeping up the deception he should succeed in the object for which he was visiting the place. "I suppose," he continued, assuming an air of confidence, "that you have not altered your mind with regard to our affair?"

"Well," said Edgeworth Bess, still deeming she was speaking to Simon Smut, "things have so fallen out that we must carry it out some other night."

"You don't say so."

"Nat Wetherby and his pals have brought a wealthy cull here to-night."

With the words Edgeworth Bess indicated the the house hard by, and the one from which she had issued.

"I suppose you've no idea who this party is?" said the youth, apparently without concern.

"Oh, yes; I know him well."

"His name is——"

"Roving Jack."

A feather's weight might have crushed the listener at this announcement.

For it was no other than Violet Tremaine, or rather Lady Warbold, in disguise.

But a few hours back she had been a happy bride, and gazed around a gay and brilliant ball-room; now she was a most unhappy woman, tracing in masquerade one of the most fearful neighbourhoods of London.

She had overheard the conversation between Geoffrey Bradshaw and his intended victim, and determined to track and defeat the ruffian in his deep-laid scheme.

Some good angel had watched over the devoted woman, and discovered to her as if by a miracle the path her husband trod.

"No," continued Edgeworth Bess, little suspecting the person she addressed; "Nat's time is not yet come. I'll wait till he has secured the rich man's gold and given it to me before I betray him; 'twill be the best for us both, don't you think so?"

"Yes, yes."

"Now, hasten on another errand," said Edgeworth Bess; "go to the rendezvous, where the justice and his men are expecting you, and say that nothing can be done to-night; but three days' hence the capture of Nat Wetherby may be accomplished."

"I'll do as you desire," said Violet, seeming impatient, but returning suddenly to her companion from whom she had departed.

"Let me see," she asked, "where did you say the officers are to be met with?"

"Where we appointed them to be, at the corner of Princess Street. Don't you recollect?"

"Oh, ah! yes, I recollect now," replied Violet, pretending to call to her mind the circumstances. "I'll get there with as much haste as my legs will allow me, and I warrant you will have no cause to complain of my speed."

No sooner had Edgeworth Bess withdrawn from Violet than she was startled by the voice of Simon Smut, who, from his hiding, had been a witness of the scene which had just passed.

"I say, my little cock sparrow," he cried, "I am rather curious to know why you have stepped into my shoes and undertaken a business that properly belongs to me?"

Violet was startled at first, but could not forbear a smile when she thought of the reasons which urged the inquiry.

"This must be the real messenger," she muttered, so consequently at once thought of some means to give a semblance to her assumed character. "You were past your time," she continued, "so, of course, as the work must be done, I accepted the office and——"

"Gammon!" replied Simon Smut, "that won't do for me; I have heard all, seen all, know all."

"There is sincerity in your tone and manner, and I will trust you."

"Don't, I trust nobody; ready money is my motto."

"Besides, your voice is not unknown to me."

"Well, I fancy yours is familiar to me," added the other.

"My name," he continued, "is Simon Smut, and I'm not ashamed to own it."

"Mine was Violet Tremaine; this morning I became the wife of your former friend, Roving Jack! If you would save him from great danger, nay, death itself, you will do as I direct you."

"Listen, madam," said her companion, "for so I must call you, though you have donned male habiliments, and for which I have no doubt you have good reason, seeing that newly-married women generally take the first opportunity of putting on the small clothes.

"Your husband," he continued, "I recollect upon one occasion did me an essential service. Now that act of kindness shan't be thrown away upon me, for I vowed then as I vow at the present moment, that if ever an opportunity offered I'd show my gratitude, and be as good as my word."

"I rejoice to hear you say so," replied Violet. "The time has now arrived for you to keep that promise.

"Go," said the speaker, "to the corner of Princes Street, it is not far from hence; you will there find waiting——"

"I know, the justice; I've heard all about it already."

Before Violet could answer, Simon Smut had taken to his heels.

CHAPTER CXXVI.

PLOT AND PLOTTERS—THE SECRETED WILL—NAT WETHERBY ATTEMPTS TO DRUG ROVING JACK —£5,000!—MURDER PREMEDITATED, AND ESCAPE ANTICIPATED—A STRANGER IN THE ROOM—WHAT INTELLIGENCE WAS BROUGHT TO THE ROBBERS' RENDEZVOUS.

WE will now retire to a chamber dignified as Nat Wetherby's lodgings.

It is in the house before which the proceedings described in the last chapter had taken place.

The abode was rather gloomy, and possessed a casement, near which stood two lamps, whose lurid glare fell upon the dingy red curtain adorning the same.

Two individuals occupied the room.

They were Geoffrey Bradshaw and Ned Bush.

"I tell you there is more money to be made of this young gallant," was the exclamation of Ned Bush.

"I know it," replied his companion, somewhat sullenly.

"Hear my plan."

"First listen to mine," continued Geoffrey Bradshaw; "'tis a simple and an easy one. This Roving Jack has——"

"Five thousand."

"Yes, all in notes, and placed in his pocket-book."

"This we must get from him."

"Undoubtedly," returned Geoffrey Bradshaw,

"and then refuse to give up the will unless ten thousand more be added."

"Don't you think that's letting him off too cheap?" put in Ned Bush, by way of remonstrance.

"We mustn't try for more," the other made answer, "lest in our avarice we overlook our main point."

"I see," said Ned Bush, "it's no use grasping at the shadow to lose the substance."

"A sudden fit of honesty may seize our dupe, and then the will——"

"Becomes worthless."

"You know we dare not make the matter public."

"Dare not!" exclaimed Ned Bush, in a fury; "and pray, why?"

"Merely because," resumed his confederate, "if we pursue such a course we must acknowledge how we came possessed of the precious document."

"Well," replied the robber, in his usual morose manner, "you can say I found it."

"But you didn't; you stole it."

"Ha!"

"Stealing wills, as you are aware, is a Tyburn job."

"Is it!" coolly remarked the individual addressed, who suddenly sobered down at the announcement, "then I shall with you object to its being made public."

"Where is Roving Jack now?" asked Geoffrey Bradshaw.

"In the room beneath us," replied Ned Bush; "Nat Wetherby is 'amusing' the gentleman with doses of strong waters."

"Is he drunk yet, think you?"

"No; but damned obstinate."

"He don't seem to take to the brandy at all kindly," continued the robber.

"He's thinking, most likely, of his uncle's will, and that ill disposes him to drink."

"I think I've discovered a way that will settle the affair out of hand in a jiffey."

"Hush! they are coming."

Geoffry Bradshaw had hardly uttered these words when the parties he had been speaking of made their appearance and entered the room.

Nat Wetherby, garnished with a bottle, seemed slightly inebriated.

Roving Jack, on the contrary, presented a sober aspect.

"I'll take no more," he said, addressing the highwayman, who was pressing the liquor on him.

"Another glass, my friend," cried the latter, still importuning our hero, "'tis right good Nantz."

"Not a drop."

While Roving Jack refused the spirit he encountered Geoffrey Bradshaw, whom he now addressed.

"Well met, sir; we will, if you please, settle our business without further delay. Where is my uncle's will?"

"In this house; and, since I have answered your question, be good enough to answer mine, Sir John," cried Geoffrey Bradshaw. "Where is your money?"

"Yes; where is your money?" echoed Ned Bush. "We must see that to know that we are on the right side."

"I dare say the gentleman means to act honourably," hiccuped Nat Wetherby.

Muttering to himself, he continued,

"I only wish I had the good fortune to meet him by moonlight alone on Hounslow Heath."

"When I see the will, the money will be yours," exclaimed Roving Jack, with hauteur.

"But you must give us some assurance," replied Geoffrey Bradshaw, "that you really have it."

"Will not my word content you?"

"No; I have given up taking men's words," continued the cunning tempter, "ever since I was seventeen; therefore, before I move a step further, I must ascertain whether the cash is to be forthcoming after I have performed my stipulation."

Roving Jack made no reply to this positive demand.

For a time he hesitated how he should act under the emergency.

At length he appeared to have decided.

There was a pause.

Suddenly but slowly he drew forth a large canvas bag.

This receptacle contained notes and gold, with a cheque signed.

The sum exposed amounting altogether to £5,000.

"You shall have the unsealed will for this amount, so I'll take the loose coin as an earnest."

Geoffrey Bradshaw, with these words, hastily snatched the bag; but his attempt to obtain it was frustrated by our hero, who, with an equally rapid action as his opponent, placed the money again in the pocket from which he had taken it.

"Not a penny will you touch!" he thundered, as he cast a defiant glance at his nefarious companions, "till I have the will you have promised me."

"Let's kill him outright," said Ned Bush, in an undertone to Geoffrey Bradshaw, to whom he had advanced, and producing a dagger as he uttered the words.

"No murder if it can be helped," rejoined Nat Wetherby, who had overheard the last remark.

"The gentleman acts fairly enough, I consider," he continued.

"Silence!" said Bradshaw, crossing to the speaker, "you don't know our game."

"Not exactly, perhaps," answered Nat Wetherby, smiling; "but I perceive you mean it to be a winning one."

Roving Jack having replaced his money, gazed with suspicion at his companions, and murmured,

"I am evidently among desperate characters; possibly, after all, only lured here to be murdered. I must endeavour to leave this terrible place at once."

Suiting the action to the words, our hero advanced to depart, when Bradshaw, anticipating his purpose, dashed forward, and restrained him.

"Hold, young man," he cried out, "we cannot suffer you to quit us."

"Ha!"

"Ned Bush," continued Bradshaw, "lock the door."

The order was obeyed; but too late to prevent the presence of a stranger.

Violet Tremaine, instructed by Simon Smut, had managed to enter the chamber stealthily during the preceding conference.

Unnoticed by any one present, she had glided into one of the corners where she was able to conceal herself by remaining behind the curtains that enclosed it.

From her hiding-place she could witness all that passed before her, and give notice to those whom she expected would soon arrive to her succour.

"Don't look so disturbed, Sir John," said Bradshaw, disdainfully, at Roving Jack, when he had intercepted him, "we mean to keep faith with you. You should have let us taken your cash, and you would have had your uncle's will before this. 'Tis secreted in the attic above this room, and there remains till you consent to our terms."

DENUNCIATION BY JACK SHEPPARD'S MOTHER.

There was a knock, a signal, and the door opened.

This gave Violet Tremaine an opportunity of escaping, while the new comer was conversing with his confederates.

She had learnt the secret of the will, and determined to profit by it.

It was Tony Wheeler who had arrived, and bringing intelligence that was by no means pleasing to some of the recipients of the news.

He had observed a party with apparently evil intentions waiting at the corner of one of the neighbouring streets.

"Ha! this is treachery."

With the words, Geoffrey Bradshaw eyed Roving Jack with distrust.

"Treachery, indeed," echoed the others.

"I knew not of this," said our hero, seeing that he was suspected.

"That I doubt," said Bradshaw, contemptuously; "if blood is to be spilled, yours will be the first."

"Tony Wheeler," he continued, "put these nabs off the scent for a few minutes."

"We must make this quiet."

"See that we are not disturbed."

"Trust to me; but hark, if you have any business to do here, douse the glims, for as the hour is late they may attract notice."

So saying, Tony Wheeler left the room and passed through the door; the door being again fastened by Ned Bush.

"I've hit upon a plan that will silence your scruples, Sir John Warbold," said Geoffrey Bradshaw, addressing our hero, who, by his manner and looks, seemed to think more than ever he was the victim of deception.

"It is evident," continued the disguised baronet, "by our proceedings that you fancy we have not your uncle's will, but you are mistaken, and you surmise without reason."

"I should certainly require some proofs of the fact," replied Roving Jack, "before I can remove my present doubt."

"You shall have those proofs," exclaimed Geoffrey Bradshaw, "you shall see the packet that contains disposition of the dying man's effects, and if you do not recognise your uncle's writing you shall pass free from hence."

This proposition was agreed to by our hero.

Nat Wetherby was then commissioned to fetch the document required from the room above.

While Roving Jack and his companions entered another chamber immediately beneath them.

The gust of wind occasioned by the sudden opening of the door of the latter apartment left all in darkness, save where the moonshine, which the side

row of two latticed windows dimmed, could imperfectly force its way in.

The doubtful and melancholy twilight was increased by a quantity of creeping plants on the outside walls, which, being neglected, they had completely overgrown.

In some places the vegetation had greatly diminished; in others, quite choked up the space of the trellis-work of the casements mentioned.

Altogether, the aspect was so desolate and the place appeared so well adapted for mischief, supposing those were enemies that were near him, that our hero could not help pausing at the entrance and recommending himself to the mercy of the omnipotent.

CHAPTER CXXVII.

THE STRONG BOX IN THE NEGLECTED GARRET—THE DISCOVERY OF THE WILL—NAT WETHERBY ARRIVES MOST INOPPORTUNELY—SOME LITTLE INSIGHT INTO THE GAME OF "HIGH TOBY"—HOW VIOLET SUCCEEDED IN LOCKING THE CONFEDERATES IN THE CUPBOARD, AND WHAT SHE GOT BY SO DOING.

VIOLET TREMAINE had no sooner quitted the apartment where she so fortunately had concealed herself than she hastened to the attic in which the coveted will proclaiming her husband a beggar was deposited.

This will, it was necessary for her to possess, but her endeavour to obtain it was beset with almost insurmountable difficulties.

In the first place, the chamber, almost devoid of furniture, was likewise totally dark.

The shutters being so firmly fastened that they refused to open to her exertions. After a time they yielded, but only afforded light enough to reveal the dilapidated condition of the neglected room.

This perplexity was followed by others equally adverse.

How was she to discover the hidden document, and, if found, how could she prevent its observation, seeing that into whosever hands it fell must lead to her husband's ruin?

Violet Tremaine, more uncertain in her purpose every moment as the necessity of its execution drew near, stole over the floor as the housebreaker treads in the chamber he is about to plunder.

In doing so, she came upon a box. It appeared to have something valuable in it, for the lock, though old, was a very strong one.

Intending to satisfy herself with regard to the contents of the newly-found chest, the resolute woman groped about the room for some implement with which she might force it open.

In this she succeeded.

She commenced her labour.

With it some good spirit hovered o'er her and directed her search.

There was a deeper glow than usual upon her cheek, and her fingers trembled as she raised them to complete the task.

At this moment footsteps were heard. Some one was ascending the stairs leading to the room she had entered.

The intruder, whoever he might be, was rapidly advancing.

No time was to be lost.

The box remained unopened, while its tough spring seemed to hold with the tenacity of a vice.

Finding her efforts useless, Violet, after a moment's deliberation, started back, and reclined as if sleeping on the floor.

She had scarcely assumed this position when Nat Wetherby made his appearance in the chamber.

He bore a lamp in his hand: its lurid glare disclosed his features, and gave a dusky outline of the various objects around him.

Staggering in semi-intoxication, the highwayman exclaimed,—

"Now for the will; it is in the strong box. Egad!" he continued, casting his eyes on the floor upon which it still remained, "I'd sooner be out half a dozen nights on Hounslow Heath than have such another job as this. There's a satisfaction in standing before a man and calling upon him to stand and deliver that's not to be found in a pettifogging robbery like this!

"No! 'Hurrah for the road!' says Nat Wetherby, where, mounted on a tit, snapper in hand, and a mask on the mug, you can prig like a 'gentleman.'"

It was at this moment that the highwayman's features were lighted up with a gaze of profound astonishment.

His eye had accidentally rested on the recumbent form of Violet, dressed in male habiliments.

Whether he had found any qualms in his heart, or that conscience had troubled his mind with ghostly apprehension, does not appear.

All that is known is, that at the sight of the sleeping youth, Nat Wetherby darted back as if a serpent was about to spring upon him.

He struck his hand forcibly against his forehead, as if to clear his brains of the fumes of the liquor which had muddled them.

Labouring under the same, and the superstition common to the age, he fancied that an apparition stood before him; for he knew the house was too well guarded to admit wandering mortals.

Appearing to be disturbed in slumber, Violet arose and confronted her scared companion.

She knew he must be one of the robbers—that nothing but deception could aid her—and, consequently, addressed the party in terms most familiar.

"Ha, my friend," she cried, "how do, how do?"

"Well, my friend," stammered out Nat Wetherby, "my friend whom I never saw before in all my life, how do you do?"

As he spoke he exercised his eyes as keenly as possible, to detect whether the individual before him was really flesh and blood, and not a ghost.

The highwayman was soon convinced that the previous supposition was erroneous. He was not dealing with, but drinking spirits, for his complaisant associate had almost immediately on introduction produced a brandy flask.

This action was proof positive, for Nat Wetherby had ever entertained the opinion "that the stiff uns always went in for the total abstinence principle." We quote Nat Wetherby's own words.

But dissertation apart, Violet, by a well-conceived plan, managed to put an end to the scruples or doubts of her companion, and the excellence of the "lush" she had handed him made them soon on the most excellent terms with each other.

"Have you been out to night?" said Violet, assuming the air of a highwayman, in which character she had appeared.

"What—on the heath?"

"Yes."

"Oh! you know me then?"

"I know you are a knight of the post, but forget your name."

"My name is Nat Wetherby. Slashing Nat Wetherby, as I am called; and my service to you," he continued, taking a lusty "pull" at the brandy that was now again offered to him by Violet.

"Nat Wetherby!" she murmured to herself; "why this is the very man Edgeworth Bess seeks to betray."

Resuming the conversation, she turned to the highwayman and said, in a tone which inferred doubt, "And do you mean to say that you have never heard of my exploits?"

"How the devil should I, seeing that your face is unknown to me?"

"True; I had forgot that," said Violet, boldly. "Of course you've heard of Fly-by-Night Dick?"

"What, 'the little' wonder that——"

"I am he," interrupted Violet, piqued; "but don't cast aspersions on my size. I shall grow bigger, never fear; my soul is too large to be confined in so small a body."

"Well, don't be offended," said Nat Wetherby, with a conciliatory smile; "I know you to be an ornament to the profession of prigging."

"But as yet I have been in an inferior grade to it," continued Violet. "To-morrow night, however, I commence on the 'High Spice Toby.'"

"The devil you do," replied Nat Wetherby, surprised at the announcement; "I've taken a particular liking to you—you are one of my own kidney—all pluck and——"

"No gammon," suggested the individual rejoicing in the name of Fly-by-Night Dick.

"I tell you what I'll do—I'll show you how to transact business on the road—we must work together."

The words had scarcely been uttered when Violet was startled by the presence of a third person.

It was Edgeworth Bess!

She had entered the room somewhat abruptly.

Seeing a stranger in it, she naturally recoiled, and was about to leave, when Nat Wetherby prevented the action and spoke as follows:—

"It's all right, Bess, this fine little bantam cock is one of my pals. He is going to make his first appearance on the mouching lay to-morrow night, and as I am anxious he should come off with credit——"

"He is giving me instructions how to proceed," interrupted Violet, suddenly struck with an idea. "Pray heaven it fail not!"

"What ought I to say?" continued she, addressing Nat Wetherby.

"Well, I'll tell you," replied the highwayman. "We will suppose you are mounted on a spanking prad."

"Scampering about the heath with a fine sky above me?"

"Yes; the moon shall be shining brightly."

"But, always hidden at the moment you wish her dark," added Violet, by way of parenthesis.

"Suddenly, you hear the sound of wheels in the distance: you curb your rein and draw out your weapons."

To give a perfect illustration of the preceding remark, Nat Wetherby, with the last words, brought out a brace of pistols.

He then started, pointed the fire-arms, and putting himself in what might be termed a graceful attitude, continued,

"Your money or your life!"

"Your watch—your diamonds—ah! I beg pardon I see a lady."

Nat Wetherby, then with a grace that might have done credit to Claude Duval himself, as he spoke took off his hat to Edgeworth Bess, whom he considered as the representative of a female traveller.

"Be not alarmed, madam," he continued, "I am Fly-by-Night Dick, who never yet hurt a woman."

"Nor ever will," rejoined the other.

"I'll trouble you for your earrings."

"The only reason I take them is because they hide your beautiful throat."

"Your necklace I take for the same reason.

"Then, of course," continued Nat Wetherby, with the coolest nonchalance imaginable; "you get your cash, jewels, et cetera, et cetera; you make a low bow to the damsel, a slight one to the gentleman, and bid them good night."

"Oh, I think I can do all that."

"Very good," continued Nat Wetherby; "but now let's see what notion you have of robbing a carriage."

"Oh, I've no notion whatever," replied Violet, diffidently.

"Then what is the use of your going to the heath to-morrow night?"

"To rob single travellers."

"My dear lad, it's a thousand times better to rob a carriage, because you get three or four times as much by it. Come; suppose we rehearse that now? Come here, Bess," continued Nat Wetherby, "you and I will be again the travellers."

Edgeworth Bess, who had witnessed the previous scene with something like contempt, refused to take a part in what she called the "mummery."

Sulkily, she reminded her paramour that his confederates were expecting him anxiously below, and that they were waiting for the will of Admiral Warbold he had been sent for.

Nat Wetherby assured her that it was quite secure; deposited safely in the strong-box which stood in the room; and that as she had the key he would instantly produce it, but first he was determined to finish the task he had commenced—that of instructing Fly-by-Night-Dick in his intended calling. The highwayman had taken quite an interest in the lad, and his welfare was certainly an object of consideration.

Disputation at an end, Nat Wetherby placed two chairs side by side. One of these was occupied by Edgeworth Bess the other by himself.

"Now, Fly-by-Night," he continued, addressing Violet, "we will suppose I and Bess are travellers in a carriage."

"Yes."

"Then stop us."

"Well," said Violet, naively, "what's the use of my stopping you when I have no pops?"

"Ah, that's true! here, take my barkers; but mind how you handle them, for they are loaded to the very muzzles."

Violet had no sooner received the pistols than she rushed to the door and doubly locked it.

Nat Wetherby and Edgeworth Bess for the moment could not account for this singular proceeding on the part of Fly-by-Night.

Suddenly, a conviction, swift as a lightning flash, darted across the highwayman.

He had been betrayed!

Before the door stood Violet.

The weapons with which she had been provided by Nat Wetherby were pointed at his head, while these words fell upon his ear—

"I mean neither of you mischief," Violet exclaimed; "therefore as you value life be wise and consent to my proposals."

"Name them!"

"Firstly; I see there is a key hanging from the waist of your mistress."

"'Tis the key of yonder box which contains a parchment of the greatest value."

"That must be mine."

"Go on," said Wetherby, smiling in rage.

"Having delivered the key, Nat Wetherby, you

will then enter with your companion into yonder cabinet which I see fastens firmly on the outer side."

Here Violet attracted the attention of the spectators to a curiously fashioned cupboard which stood in an angle of the room, and of dimensions sufficient for many modern chambers.

"In this recess you both must remain till morning," continued the lady, "when I promise to give you liberty."

"We have had enough of this," exclaimed Nat Wetherby, evincing impatience ; "how much longer do you mean to continue this child's play ?"

"Two minutes," replied Violet with the greatest calmness, "if in that time you refuse to accede to my conditions I must shoot those who are contumacious.

"Mark me," she continued, "during the moments of deliberation I shall watch you narrowly ; if I see the slightest sign of perfidy or attempt to give alarm, I fire ; remember I can but die, and you will die with me."

The words of Violet were so impressive, and her intent so positive, that in half the specified term Nat Wetherby and Edgeworth Bess found themselves under lock and key.

Violet had no sooner disposed of her prisoners, than she hurried to the chest that contained the Admiral's will.

The key with which Edgeworth Bess supplied her opened the box.

Gently and trembling she raised the lid, and brought from within a sealed packet.

She would now learn the fatal secret.

The secret that was to reinstate her husband, or brand his name with infamy.

Violet, so sweet, so gentle in thy loveliness, why does fate so chequer thy fortune?

You have attracted as many eyes as if an angel had descended.

As many blessings as if the benignant being had come fraught with good tidings.

No creature wert thou of an idle necromancer's imagination.

No woman bedizened with false or inconsistent perfections.

Thy merits made thy husband love thee well. Thy faults, amid thy good qualities, made him love thee better.

Trembling with excitement Violet broke open the packet, and found it contained the will she had so anxiously sought.

She fixed her eyes upon its written characters as under some hideous fascination.

As she perused them the tear which dimmed her vision faded away.

A smile played on her face as sunshine succeeds the summer shower.

"This indeed gladdens a grateful heart," she exclaimed in an ecstasy of joy. "My husband is here named sole heir of the estates and—"

Before Violet could read further she heard voices, and became conscious that some one was approaching her.

She could have no doubt that the voices were those of her enemies.

There was no time for hesitation or wavering doubt.

The moment had arrived to either save her or deliver her to darkness and death.

Hastily unfastening the door she had previously locked, she next concealed herself behind an old ponderous trunk that stood at the further end of the attic.

Ensconced in the hiding place Violet observed three individuals coming towards her.

They gazed about as if surprised.

After a pause one of the intruders, Geoffroy Bradshaw, exclaimed—

"Hang that fool, Nat Wetherby, what has become of him?"

"Can't you guess?" replied another of the trio, who turned out to be Ned Bush.

"Not I."

"He has got one of his drunken fits on him," said the highwayman in continuation, "and instead of searching for the will you requested is searching for more liquor."

"I plainly see," said our hero, who was the third speaker, "that this is some subterfuge. I find, when it is too late, that I have been only lured here for the purpose of murder and robbery.

"But mark me," he rejoined firmly, "I promise you that you will not effect your purpose without a desperate struggle, and that I shall dispute my life while blood flows in my veins."

"You are a bolder man than I took you for, Sir John Warbold," replied Geoffroy Bradshaw, "but your remarks are both unjust and unnecessary."

"They may appear so to you," replied our hero, "but still you must admit that there are some grounds for suspicion. I have demanded to see my uncle's will on several occasions ; on each it has not been forthcoming."

There was a heavy crash, and the bulky boarding of the neighbouring closet was broken into a hundred pieces.

From the shivered fragments emerged Nat Wetherby.

"Not a moment is to be lost," shouted the robber, as he issued forth.

"What do you mean, Nat?" asked the rest, surprised and stupefied at his strange appearance.

"Treachery !"

"Ha," cried Geoffroy Bradshaw, "this is your doing?"

With the words he darted a fierce glance, and was about to rush upon Roving Jack with a clasped knife.

"Hold ! no violence, Bradshaw," exclaimed Nat Wetherby, restraining the ruffian's arm, "I am not so sure he is the real spy."

"Whoever it may be, their punishment is a terrible one."

"Swear to it."

"We do."

"Entombed for life—passing a living death—let the carcass of the betrayer rot in the vaults of this house."

"Now for the will."

"It has been taken away by a youth."

"Unfortunate ! let us follow in pursuit," said our hero, rushing towards the door, from which he was flung backwards by Geoffroy Bradshaw.

"Fool !" he cried, "do you suppose I will suffer to escape the prey that I have snared ? The money that you have shall at least be my companions'. Your life or mine."

"Villain ! what injury have I ever done you," cried our hero, disdainfully, "that you should wish to murder me in cold blood?"

"Injury?" retorted the other, in scorn, "you have dared to love."

"A rival."

"And your bitterest enemy."

"Great Heaven ! I am in the power, then, of—"

"Sir Ranulph Gayton," cried Geoffroy Bradshaw, with the laugh of a fiend welcoming a condemned spirit to eternal flame.

His triumph was but that of a moment : the next, a bullet had pierced his arm, raised to stab Roving Jack to the heart.

The next moment our hero recognised his preserver.

And the voice of Violet sounded as celestial music in his ear.

Sir Ranulph Gayton, helpless, bleeding copiously, and writhing with pain, called on his confederates to avenge him.

They advanced to do his bidding as the second pistol of the intrepid woman, by a fatal mischance, hung fire.

Husband and wife were now at the mercy of their foes, when the words "No, you don't," resounded through the apartment, and the party who had uttered them entered the room.

Though this individual was in a dark attire it was evidently not that called evening dress.

And the hue of his habiliments seemed rather to have assumed it through the medium of soot than the process of dyeing.

"Who the devil are you ?" thundered the robbers, darting an intensely fierce glance at the intruder.

"No devil at all, only Simon Smut," that worthy personage answered drily.

"How did you get in ?"

"Down the chimley."

"The door was fastened."

"And the winder, also ; that's why I faked the flue."

"Why have you dared to gain admittance ?"

"Merely to introduce to your notice these here gentlemen."

While Simon Smut was yet speaking the room was filled with a posse of officers.

Before Geoffrey Bradshaw and his confederates could offer any resistance they were ironed and handcuffed.

While this was going forward Edgeworth Bess advanced from the cabinet which had concealed her and hastily left the room.

She had observed Nat Wetherby during the struggle pass secretly from the apartment, and make for the garden at the rear of the house.

He had gained the gate of the same when his mistress, following on his footsteps, intercepted him. (Vide illustration to No. 36.)

CHAPTER CXXVIII.

JACK SHEPPARD ONCE MORE IN THE BILBOES—STRANGE VISITORS AT THE MANSION —WHAT WIRTH WOLFGANG WILL ATTEMPT AT THE FOOT OF THE SCAFFOLD — THE HANGMAN VERSUS THE HEADSMAN.

WE now come to the most important epoch in the career of the housebreaker, highwayman, and cracksman par excellence, Jack Sheppard.

As we have hinted in a foregoing chapter, this renowned and notorious character had been handed over to justice by Edgeworth Bess.

The frail beauty having, in a fit of jealousy, transferred her affections to another illustrious satellite of the prigging community, Slashing Nat Wetherby.

The betrayal, capture and condemnation of Jack Sheppard we will omit, and at once bring the reader to a point of our story that requires more immediately the attention, namely, the night previous to the execution of the criminal.

At this period our hero and Violet had returned to their house at Hackney.

The latter was so much exhausted by the trials she had undergone that she was obliged to retire earlier than usual, leaving our hero in the library to his reading.

While occupied in this pursuit a domestic entered the apartment.

He stated there were two persons waiting without who wished to speak with him on most important business.

They were strange-looking individuals, muffled in cloaks, and would take no denial.

After a dispute, one of the parties named had found a means of silencing scruples.

Taking a ring from his finger, he requested that it might be shown to the owner of the mansion : and, at the sight of it his doors would fly open and welcome the possessor.

As soon as our hero saw the signet he recognized it as that one he had given to Jack Sheppard.

With this assurance the servant was requested at once to admit the strangers.

The two men the next moment were ushered into the presence of our hero.

The one was stout and tall, with large feet and hands ; and, evidently, by his bulky appearance, was endowed with great personal strength : his name was Wirth Wolfgang.

The other, was somewhat shorter ; but, being bow-legged, broad-shouldered, and long-armed, seemed equally powerful as the Dutchman.

This latter individual was no other than Joe Blake "alias" Blueskin.

The customary salutations having passed between the parties, who were known to each other, Wirth Wolfgang at once proceeded to unfold the nature of the visit of himself and companion.

The time was short.

The moments precious.

"Ja, Ja, Muntmeester," exclaimed the Dutchman, who had lighted his pipe to aid him in his deliberation, "I am afraid dat der jonker Jack Sheppard will chanse to hang to-morrow, if some one do not do him a shervice."

"Yes, Captain Sheppard," continued Blueskin, "will certainly die of the 'hempen fever' unless we take him from Tyburn for change of air."

"We will speak no further on this subject, Blueskin, if you please," answered our hero ; "it is to me a most painful one, since I can offer no assistance to the unfortunate young man."

"No ?"

"I have used my utmost interest to obtain a reprieve," continued the speaker, "but without effect. The Government, exasperated at the numerous robberies that have taken place within the last six months, are determined to make an example of the first highwayman taken ; and, consequently, your friend, Jack Sheppard, will become the victim."

"We must get him off," said Blueskin, "somehow or other, Sir John !"

"Impossible !" he replied.

"That's not a word in my dictionary," said Blueskin.

"I would make any sacrifice," continued our hero, "could I liberate the condemned man."

"If you mean what you say, Sir John, I think I can do the trick."

"But how ?"

"In the first place, I shall want a little ready rhino."

"How much ?"

"We'll say five hundred pounds."

"Which you shall have in welcome."

Almost as soon as Roving Jack had uttered these

words, Blueskin found himself in possession of the sum required.

"You will be faithful and guard your trust," said our hero.

If Blueskin had made no reply to the words addressed to him, the expression of his face would have given an answer.

"I shall not touch a farthing of the blunt, Sir John, though I were parching and I had not a mag in my cly," said the robber, "that which you have given me will be expended, to a fraction, in the service of Captain Sheppard."

"Your scheme then ?"

"You will shortly know."

"Should it fail ?"

"It won't—should it do so—why, hey for a rescue at the triple tree."*

Wirth Wolfgang, who had hitherto remained silent, now advanced.

He fixed his keen grey eyes upon the speakers, then turned to address them.

"Dat is right, dam right," exclaimed the phlegmatic Hollander, "vat you say is very proper and very goot, but vat I shall say is better nor goot."

"The devil it is," replied Blueskin, "then let's have it at once, Wirth."

"Donder un blixon," exclaimed the Dutchman, "how dat schnapps lapper of yours does run—away mit you."

"What scapper ?"

"I must have von vord mit mynheer in private."

"A secret, eh ?"

"Yaw, yaw."

"Can't I pal in ?"

"Nein ; not now, leave de affair in mein hands and it will be settled pravely."

"While I ——"

"Go back to de brandewine and hollandsche geneva dat we left in de room below."

"Is the parley genuine ?"

The Dutchman made no answer, but by way of assent, placed his hand upon his heart.

"Your token ?"

"Jack Sheppard."

As Wirth Wolfgang mentioned the well-loved name, Blueskin, without further hesitation, left our hero and his companion alone.

It should never be said of the faithful follower of the condemned robber that he stood in the way or offered any obstruction to the means that might effect his release.

"De crow Sheppard's kinchen is destined to de gibbet," remarked Wirth Wolfgang, with solemnity, after a slight pause.

"Alas, such was the fatal prophecy, which it appears now is likely to be fulfilled."

"Berhaps not," replied Wirth Wolfgang. "I may tell you something dat vill bring de colour in your cheeks, for I see dey are rader paler dan dey once was."

"They may well be so," replied our hero ; "the fate of my once firm friend afflicts me deeply."

"I have consulted, mynheer, dis lump of wood on de top of mein shoulders," continued the Dutchman, tapping his forehead, and indicating that by the latter remark he alluded to his head, "and I fancy dat de fate of dis poor lad may be averted."

"Averted !" echoed Roving Jack.

"Yaw," continued Wirth Wolfgang, "to hang 'Jack Sheppard' there must be what you call 'Jack Ketch ?'"

"A man of the name of Andrew Marvel at the present time fulfils that dreadful office."

"Dat is true—but he must be prevented in his vork.

"He must be made to drink—drugged—incapable of doing his dirty duty."

"But by what means can we——"

"Hush, hush, de lump of wood is busy," interrupted the stolid Dutchman, again repeating his peculiar action with regard to his head. "Vhen de Sheriff," continued the speaker, "shall find out dat de hangman is dronk, he will be on de horns of von dilemma. He will give a large sum to any one vat vill be his substitute. But," continued the Dutchman, "nobody vill ondertake de job."

"Then !"

"I shall offer mein services."

"You !"

"Yes ; I shall take de place. I, Wirth Wolfgang, once headsman of Amsterdam, and public executioner of the Seven United Provinces of Holland."

We shall not attempt to convey any idea of the magical effect the singular announcement had upon Roving Jack.

For some moments he remained silent, and seemed to loathe the presence of one who had hurried into eternity so many human beings.

At length, conquering the weakness, he remarked in a dry tone, "Suppose you succeed in obtaining your object, I can see no satisfactory result arising from it."

"Time will show—time will show," repeated the Dutchman.

"I do not see how I can assist you in this matter," said Roving Jack.

"You can do so, materially," replied Wirth Wolfgang. "You must give me your promise to do one thing"

"Name it !"

"To have an empty carriage waiting at the stables of the 'White Lion,' on the Edgware Road."*

"It shall be there as you desire ; so appoint the time."

"One hour before de execution is to take place.'

"Good !"

"Should I require furder assistance ?"

"You will have it."

"You must swear."

"I do most solemnly," said Roving Jack, in a firm voice.

"Dat will do," said Wirth Wolfgang, with a placid smile on his countenance, and hastily quitting the apartment, he rejoined once more his companion Blueskin.

CHAPTER CXXIX.

A HANGMAN'S HISTORY.

ON the morning appointed for the execution of Jack Sheppard, Andrew Marvel, the common hangman, was up betimes.

So early, forsooth, that an ordinary individual would have imagined that on those occasions when he was called upon to perform his terrible office he never went to bed at all.

Such an idea would have been fallacious, and have shown how little the individual was acquainted with the character of the party in question.

Yet Andrew Marvel, like other mortals, must take the customary repose due to nature, and take it

---

* The triple tree or gallows at Tyburn.

* The "White Lion," in the Edgware Road (now the Metropolitan Music Hall), was in Jack Sheppard's time a lonely roadside inn ; it was established in 1524, the year hops were first imported for the purpose of flavouring beer.

"well," though on arising he knows that he must hang his own father by his own hand.

He was cold-blooded, nervous and cruel, and would no more think of the blood (which by the sanction of the law) he was about to spill, than smoking a pipe, which he was then doing in his own little back parlour in Little Britain.

Andrew Marvel might be set down without injustice as one of the most repulsive and ill-looking mortals that had ever come upon earth.

He was fifty-eight years old, but a dry spare nature retained in him the vigour and activity of youth.

There was no expression in his countenance which indicated either conscience or mercy, while the same forbid every approach to that quality termed humanity.

He was sleek-haired, sleek-eyed and sleek-skinned; the latter, being of a pale and cadaverous hue, was enlivened by a mouldy suit of mourning, whose faded appearance seemed almost a mockery in respect of the departed.

This individual was not alone, but in the company of another who was engaged in a similar occupation to himself, namely, that of smoking.

He was a brother of the craft and a public executioner.

He was equally as stolid as his companion, but of certainly a less forbidding aspect.

"I suppose you have tucked up a good many in your time," said the last named party.

"Yes, some hundreds," replied Marvel.

With the words this speaker had finished his third glass and knocked out the ashes of his third pipe, preparatory to his loading a fourth.

"I suppose you find they take it pretty kindly, don't you?"

"Some does and some don't," was the curt rejoinder of Marvel, lighting his fresh supply of tobacco.

"I've done the office," he continued," for some of the most noted cracksmen and toby gloaks that have flourished for the last forty years. Mind, I began scragging at eighteen.

"For instance Jack Cottington.

"Mull'd Jack, as he was called, on account of his love of that liquor, suffered at my hands at Smithfields Rounds in 1695.

"He was a good un.

"Yes, he gave me this 'baccy box as a mark of esteem just as he was about to take the leap. I always uses it for my weed, in remembrance of the queer cull.

"Then there was Tom Waters.

"He was executed at Tyburn; he was only 26, but went off the stage in a most resolute manner.

"Old Mobb followed him, and came up to the crap like a hero.

"So did Swiftneck, Joyce, and Shorter.

"My toughest bout was with Colonel Jack, whom the great De Foe, author of Robinson Crusoe, has panegyrised."

"What of him," asked his companion of Marvel.

"Well, Colonel Jack, I never heard him called anything else, so I suppose he was christened in that name.

"Some say he was a native of this country, others that France was his birth-place.

"But that's neither here nor there.

"French or English there was never a better blood or a bolder blade that cried 'stand' to a traveller.

"He popped five guineas into my fist the night before he was to be turned off.

"He was the Admirable Crichton of the road.

"Could play the fiddle like an angel!

"And had broken, through his handsome looks, more hearts than there are minutes in an hour.

"On the morning of execution," continued Andrew Marvel, "this culprit was lead on a tumbril to the gibbet. He was attended by an armed escort, for the authorities had received notice of intended mischief. Arriving at Tyburn, and standing beneath the tree, the bonds which secured Colonel Jack were suddenly snapped like a piece of packthread while he himself dashed from his gaolers. He ascended, with the agility of a cat, the uprights which supported the gallows and stood upon the crossbeam at the top. From this point, while the thunder and lightning rolled and flashed—for a storm had set in—the wretch, flying from death, looked like some scared fiend to the sea of white faces who watched with breathless fear the startling catastrophe. From the eminence he leaped towards the surrounding multitude, who seemed prepared to receive the madly desperate man. In his effort he was frustrated by the upraised bayonets of the soldiery who guarded the scaffold. Bleeding and apparently paralyzed, the criminal was again brought to the rope. Before I could adjust the noose he, having no other weapon of offence, fixed his teeth firmly in the flesh of my right hand. The sudden and sharp thrill of pain that I experienced at that moment I shall never forget to the day of my death. As may be supposed, the grasp which held me soon relaxed, and I was freed from my foe. A blow from a musket had stunned and killed him. This last act made good the boast of the notorious Colonel Jack—'That the hemp was not spun that should hang him, and that he would never suffer at the hands of Jack Ketch.'"

Speaking, 'tis said, is dry work, an opinion in which Andrew Marvel coincided thoroughly, if we may judge of his frequent potations during the recital of the late narrative. If he was not what is usually termed "drunk" he had certainly reached the extreme limits of that state deemed as sobriety.

His companion, who was a foreigner, next expatiated on his calling.

Though it was of a similar nature to the hangman's, it differed widely in performance.

He took life with the axe not with the rope.

He recounted several remarkable events that had happened to him while fulfilling the office of public executioner.

These were listened to with something like wonder by Andrew Marvel, who, as they progressed, continued to ply at the bottle, which was ever and anon handed to him, and in the last instance prepared with a strong opiate.

"Dis sword," said Wirth Wolfgang, who turned out to be the associate of the hangman's, "has done some goot service in its day."

With the words the speaker pointed to a broad-bladed weapon that hung at his side.

"De guillotine," said he, "is de first model of dis instrument which I always carry about mit me; it was used only for criminals of high birth."

The Dutchman directed the attention of Andrew Marvel to a hollow dent near the hilt.

"You see dat?" Wirth continued. "You shall hear how dat came.

"When Delbitt, de grand pensioner of Holland, was decapitated my arm was diverted, and de steel come in contact with a tooth.

"Dat tooth," exclaimed the Dutchman, "turned de edge of mein sword and occasioned dis notch."

The speaker had scarcely concluded his remark when he noticed his companion dropped his head, then fall heavily on the floor of the apartment in which he had been sitting.

Yes, there lay Andrew Marvel, inert, enfeebled, senseless, and his enemy watching him.

It was something almost frightful to observe the silence that ensued between these two persons.

The one convulsed by the narcotic seemed to be experiencing the most horrible agonies.

The other scarcely breathing, and fixing his eyes in a wild and ghastly manner on the quivering body before him.

Satisfied, after a lengthened scrutiny, that he had succeeded in his object, the latter rose from a kneeling posture, and exclaimed—

"It is done! the opiate has taken effect, plunged in stupor and delirium, he will be incapable of——"

Wirth Wolfgang's sentence was cut short by a loud knocking that proceeded from the outer door.

It was shortly opened, when Amos Marrowfat, the sheriff "in esse" and alderman "in posse," made his appearance, followed by several officers of Newgate.

"Where is Marvel?" inquired the official, blandly.

The Dutchman shook his head, and seemed to "marvel" himself.

"We want the executioner."

"Yaw! yaw! I see," replied the apparently enlightened foreigner, "you mean Jean Ketch. I tink—dat is, I dare say he is taking von leetle nap."

The sheriff eyed the hangman and then the table, on which still remained several bottles.

On which discovery he apologetically observed:

"I am afraid he's been drinking?"

"Yaw."

"That's irregular."

"Very," was again the monosyllabic answer.

The sheriff proceeded to shake Andrew Marvel, but he would have been better employed in shaking the feather-bed with which the room was garnished, f r despite the agitation of the perturbed Amos Marrowfat, the prostrate man refused to stir.

"What in the name of patience am I to do?" exclaimed the sheriff. "This is, indeed, unfortunate. The presence of this drunken reprobate is absolutely indispensable, or I shall have to hang Jack Sheppard myself, and that is a duty I didn't calculate upon when I accepted my office."

No, Amos had brighter visions.

Civic honours.

Turtle soup. Green fat.

Calapash, Calapee, &c., &c., &c.

"Mynheer," said Worth Wolfgang, in assumed composure, "give yourself no furder trouble about dis matter."

"I haf hit upon von plan," he continued, "dat vill draw you from dis embarrassment."

"Indeed, I am very glad to hear that," said the sheriff, brightening up at the intelligence he received.

"What means," he resumed, "do you propose?"

"I know some von dat will ondertake your vork."

"You do not say so!"

"Yaw, and if you consent—"

"Willingly, if you think he is able to—"

"I will answer for dat."

"Has he performed the office before?"

"He has put away more dan you tink for."

"Quick, then, bring the substitute here."

"He is here already. 'Tis meinself dat shall hang dat teufel s imp, 'Jack Sheppard,'" replied Wirth Wolfgang, whose response more than ever shook the delicate nerves of the over-sensitive sheriff.

CHAPTER CXXX.

TYBURN.

JACK SHEPPARD was doomed to die on Monday, the 16th of November, 1724.

As early as nine o'clock in the forenoon, the sheriffs and their officers had arrived at the county goal of Middlesex.

As they did so, the bell of Newgate began to toll slowly, in company with the deep-toned bell of the church of Saint Sepulchre.

The morning was a dismal one, and well fitted to the melancholy occasion.

All was astir with despondency and gloom, and the general depression was heightened by the foggy atmosphere, which imperfectly disclosed the dense mass of human beings that had congregated around the prison which still confined the criminal.

At no previous execution within the memory of man, had there been so vast a concourse of persons as at that of Jack Sheppard. Their number seemed almost to be countless.

It was one cloud of heads as far as the eye could reach.

While in the vicinity of the doleful scene, house top, eminence, and projection was occupied by every description of human being, rich and poor—man, woman, and child.

In a short time a profound silence had assumed dominion over the anxious multitude—then a cry resounded through their ranks—

"He is coming."

The shout proclaimed that Jack Sheppard had left Newgate.

He was carried out in a cart containing his coffin.

The coffin serving for a seat to himself and the hangman, who, as the reader has been made aware, was Wirth Wolfgang.

This vehicle was protected by a strong force of constabulary and soldiers furnished with ball cartridge.

The mournful cavalcade slowly descended Snow-hill, and reached Holborn-bridge.

Here the mob, which had offered interruption, were dispersed, but not without bloodshed.

The train in a short time after this *contretemps*, came to the Crown public house, commonly called "St. Giles's Bowl."

Here a criminal taken to execution at Tyburn was allowed to halt, and take a draught of nut-brown ale for his finishing cup on earth.

The odd custom is thus described by an eminent writer—

On the site of the present church of St. Giles formerly stood a hospital for Lazars.

Chained to the gates of the edifice was a vessel of wood or broad-bottomed bowl. The prisoners conveyed from the City of London to Tyburn, and there to be executed for treasons, felonies, and other crimes were presented with this bowl. The same being filled to the brim with strong ale, of which they could drink as much as pleased them.

The ancient Lazar house falling to decay, still left its bowl which was removed to the "Crown" tavern, where the malefactor still continued to drown his fears in the tipple that deluded his ride to the "Nubbing Cheat" or Gallows.

When the cart which bore Jack Sheppard stopped before the "Crown," the landlord as usual issued from the house with the liquor destined to be given to the condemned criminal.

Jack raised it to his lips and quaffed.

"Your father, Jack, refused it," said the landlord with a malicious smile.

THE IRISH PRIEST WARNS THE CHILDREN OF THE OMADHAUN, OR MANIAC.

" I know it," replied the highwayman, " and so courted death and the gibbet. Had he drank like me he would have been saved from an ignomious end ; so 'tis sealed—so 'tis decreed by our mutual fate."

" What do you mean ?"

" My answer will be a simple one," replied the other, jocosely. " Mark me—Jack Sheppard will never die at the tree of Tyburn."

Once more the cavalcade proceeded on its journey, and were soon traversing the Oxford Road.*

The verdant fences that in summer season then lined the pathway, gay with the sweetbriar and the eglantine, were now nothing but bare and barren brushwood. Here and there might be seen the evergreen holly, with its ripening bunch of berries, seeming to say that Christmas time is not far distant.

But no Christmas pageant travels along the track, but one that must bring affliction to the contemplative mind. The leafless hedge-rows are hid from view by crowds of all stations and sexes, who glide quickly along the rugged thoroughfare to witness the last moments of a man about to be sacrificed by the law he has offended.

Though the crowd kept principally to the main route, the fields adjacent were covered with persons, thousands of whom were seen hurrying across these meadows to the place of execution, and breaking through every impediment that arrested their onward progress.

While the train came abreast of Marylebone Lane they suffered a second interruption. Near to the spot, but diverging from the lane, was an ancient Gothic ruin, called the cell of St. Mary the Good.*

The building, of small extent, and the only remains of a nunnery that once stood near it, possessed but one narrow-pointed unglazed window, defended by two cross bars of iron.

In this anticipated tomb, for some time a recluse had taken up her abode, subsisting solely upon the bread and water which the pity of the passers by induced them to deposit on her window sill.

Instances of this kind of seclusion, in former days, though they raised but little wonder, were yet, notwithstanding, frequent and customary.

Let us now look into the dark, damp, loathsome hole we have spoken of.

Upon the stone floor, in one corner, a female was crouched. Her chin rested upon her knees, while

---

* Oxford Road, now Oxford Street.

* Marylebone. A corruption of the name of a tutelar Saint, Mary the Good.

her arms and clasped hands encircled her knees. The faint likeness of the human form, under the garb of mourning she wore, was hardly discernible at first sight. But the ray entering at the window presently disclosed the tenant of this living tomb, and exhibited her as one of those spectres seen in dreams cowering upon a grave, or before the grating of a dungeon.

Without covering, in a habitation which admitted the winter's blast, but not the cheering sun, this poor creature seemed not to suffer—not even to feel.

At the sound occasioned by the rabble on the eventful morning of the criminal's execution, the apparently inanimate frame quitted its inert and lethargic nature.

The recluse shook all over, sprang upon her feet, and bounded to the opening of her cell.

Her eyes flashed fire. And her haggard face pressed against the iron framing of the window.

"Aha!" she cried, with a horrid laugh, as she beheld Jack Sheppard. "'Tis he! he calls me! I knew it would come to this, and for two years have tarried at this spot to meet him on the road to death."

Her brow wrinkled with horror. She stretched her skeleton arms out of her cell and beckoned to the cavalcade to stop.

At the earnest request of Jack Sheppard the summons was answered.

He was little prepared for the dreadful shock that positively froze the blood in his every vein.

In the appalling object that advanced from the noisome cell the highwayman beheld his own mother, whom report had given out had been numbered with the dead.

She was a complete wreck of what she once was. A shapeless figure, a sort of vision in which the real and fantastic were contrasted with light and shade. Scarcely could there be distinguished under her streaming hair the forbidding profile of an attenuated face. Her arms and feet entirely uncovered were semblant to those of a corpse. Her features ghastly white, and of the consistency of parchment, and stamped with that most fearful malady human flesh is heir to—insanity.

The poor maniac, tutored by an instinct peculiar to her affliction, had been seized of a dreamy idea that her wretched son would perish at Tyburn.

And for two years had incessantly watched the approach of the calamity from the window of her solitary abode almost night and day.

"Oh God!" exclaimed Jack Sheppard, "my crimes are fearfully punished, and it wanted but this to comple my misery."

His mother's scream of anguish seemed to petrify and turn him to the stone of the cell from which she had frantically issued.

His livid lips opened for the purpose of breathing, and quivered.

But he looked as dead, and as will-less as leaves driven by the wind.

The recluse, as she stood before her son, suddenly paused.

Her hands remained clasped. Her tongue mute. And her fixed glance awed each spectator into a death-like silence.

At length Jack Sheppard, having overcome his intense sorrow, addressed his mother in hopes of making her speak to him for the last time.

At the sound of his voice the recluse started.

Her long attenuated fingers drew back the hair from her brow.

And she darted her sad, astonished, distracted eyes upon her boy.

The gaze was transient as lightning.

"Oh, power of mercy!" she exclaimed, burying her face in her lap, and it appeared as if her hard voice was wrenched from her chest, "at least keep this one from my sight."

This shock, however, had, as it were, awakened the slumbering and distraught reason of the maniac.

A long shudder thrilled through her whole frame as she passed her hand across Jack Sheppard's forehead.

"I had once a son like you," she ejaculated, "but he is dead."

"Poor creature," said the highwayman, "it is better that she deem me so."

"No, no," she rejoined, in a whisper; "he was not hanged; they would have hanged him, but I poisoned him and Jonathan Wild. Shall I tell you how I did it? They said I was mad. Fools! they themselves were so. Ha! ha! ha! With my own hands I dug my boy's grave, and upon it planted wild flowers. I have daily visited the rude tomb, and held conversations with the sainted spirit.

"I feel pleasure in my loneliness when I am seated on the emerald turf that covers poor Jack's remains.

"Dreams, joyous dreams," continued the recluse, "throng round my heart when I visit the lost one, for the picture is real, and I live over years of bliss."

"Mother! mother!" interrupted Jack, agonised and unable to endure the scene longer. "Do you not recognise your son?

"He comes," he continued, "to take his last farewell on earth."

Like the sun bursting from an ebon rack, did a momentary beam of consciousness dart across the brain of the maniac.

Clasping Jack Sheppard in her fond embrace, she shouted in a voice of intense and celestial rapture—

"Yes, 'tis my boy; my brave boy!"

"Thank heaven she knows me," responded the highwayman.

The mother retained the son firm in her clutch.

She spoke not a word, but fastened her lip to his.

She stood absorbed in that kiss, and gave no sign of life, but a sigh which from time to time heaved her bosom.

Tears gushed from her eyes in silence like a midnight shower.

Suddenly the maniac raised her head, released her hold, and beckoned to Jack Sheppard to follow her into the cell.

"Come," she murmured, "let me drag thee from this abyss."

"My boy, my dear boy," once more she cried, "I have got thee; the gracious God has restored him.

"You all see, I have my son again; how beautiful and noble he is.

"Kiss me Jack. I do love thee.

"What care I whether other mother have children.

"I can laugh at them now.

"Ha! ha! ha!"

In such a strain the crazed woman ran on, while her son could repeat only in grief, at intervals, "My dear mother!"

"How I shall love you," continued the recluse, interrupting herself almost at every word with a kiss. "We will leave this place; I have some property belonging to the Trenchard family in France. You will go, Jack, with me, will you not?"

"O, mother!" said Jack Sheppard, at length

recovering power to speak through his emotion. "I cannot at present promise."

At that moment there was the clank of arms and tramp of horses, showing that orders had been given to the calvalcade to proceed.

"Mother! I must leave you now," cried Jack Sheppard.

The words seemed almost to choke him in their utterance.

The recluse turned pale.

"Oh, heavens! what say'st thou?" she exclaimed. "I had forgotten; they are searching for thee. What hast thou done?"

"I am condemned to die," uttered Jack Sheppard, in utter forgetfulness.

"Die!" shrieked the maniac mother, reeling as if stricken by a thunderbolt.

"Die!" she repeated, slowly fixing her glazed eye upon her son.

"Yes," he replied, "they mean to put me to death. The gibbet is waiting for me."

For some moments the recluse stood motionless as a statue.

She then shook her head doubtingly, and with sudden emotion burst into a loud laugh.

Her old terrific and appalling laugh.

"No, no! thou must be dreaming. It cannot be, it shall not be! Thy father died thus, but you must escape. One man hanged in a family is quite enough."

With these words, the mother, with that cunning peculiar to insanity, contrived to place a small packet in the hand of her son, without the action being seen or suspected.

"With those means at your disposal," whispered the maniac, "you may defy Jack Ketch and his accursed associates."

"But—"

"Not another word. You will see me again." Where?"

"I am forbid to tell, Jack. Rest satisfied that you have learnt thus much."

Before any were aware of her absence, the recluse had departed.

Whither she had vanished none could hear or tell.

*　　*　　*　　*　　*

Tyburn is now reached.

Discernable, and towering above the dense concourse surrounding the spot, is one sombre object.

It is a scaffold, whose massive timbers are hid by a sable covering of cloth, and crowned by a gibbet.

This gibbet had been known from the time of the fourth Henry as Tyburn gallows, or Tyburn tree (a deadly nevergreen).

> "I've heard sundry men oftimes dispute
> Of trees that in one year will twice bear fruit;
> But if a man note Tyburn 'twill appear
> That that's a tree that bears twelve times a yeare."

Taylor the Water Poet, "*The Praise and Virtue of a Jayle and Jaylers,* 1623."

On the platform stands a young man, Jack Sheppard, about to be launched into eternity.

At the terrible juncture he maintains his composure and wonted daring.

A smile imperceptibly plays upon his features as he witnesses the scene around him and its completed arrangements.

Beside the condemned culprit, his hangman, Wirth Wolfgang, is seen.

He wears a dress half gray and half brown, and leathern sleeves, being the habiliments used by executioners in the countries of the continent at this period.

His hair is lank, his figure burly, and he carries a coil of rope in his huge fist.

As he eyed Jack Sheppard, he murmured to himself,

"Prave boy. All hope is not at an end. Assistance vill not come too late."

In a musing attitude the eyes of the Dutchman became wild and fierce.

And they were seen to wander fearlessly over the soldiers who had taken up a position around the fatal beam.

His swarthy lineaments became ashy pale, as he drew a clasp knife from his thigh pocket, and seeming to bend as if in search of something, opened it with his teeth.

"My trusty knife," he said, in an underbreath, "must sever de rope, and cut down de body."

Jack Sheppard, who had been for some minutes engaged with the chaplain of Newgate, and further nerved by his pious exhortations, now bid the divine farewell as he advanced to the gibbet.

Wirth Wolfgang hastened to adjust the rope.

As he did so, the eager crowd pressed nearer and nearer to the centre of attraction.

The storm which had preceded the calm now burst forth in all its fury from the populace.

The groan which assailed the hangman seemed to him as some infernal imprecation.

The myriad of voices rent the air like a saw.

Maledictions thronged and echoed from every throat and mouth.

This outburst was but the event of a moment.

The next involved the executioner and his victim in a dense cloud of smoke.

There was a flash, a report of fire-arms, and a piercing scream.

As the mist cleared off, it was discovered that a bullet from a fire-arm had passed through Jack Sheppard's body.

By whose hand he had fallen, or from whom he had received his death-wound, seemed alike a matter of amazement and distrust to the vast multitude who beheld this mysterious occurrence.

CHAPTER CXXXI.

RESCUED FROM DEATH.

ONE tremendous shout of indignation followed the event related in the last lines of the previous chapter.

No sooner had Jack Sheppard fallen than a deadly fire was poured on the guards that surrounded him, and an attempt made by Blueskin and his followers to bear off the body of the renowned "captain."

The enterprise was successful, despite the furious opposition of the soldiery and constables, who, enraged by the sudden massacre of their comrades, fought like lions.

No person in the melée seemed so great an object of aversion as the hangman.

Bullet after bullet whizzed past him as he stood upon an elevated point, but he seemed, as by some miracle, to avoid each missile and to bear a charmed life.

Even when the crowd had pressed forward and taken possession of the scaffold, the executioner was spared from their fury, for he eluded their vigilance and contrived to escape by means which appeared to all mysterious.

The body of Jack Sheppard, as already stated, had been borne off by Blueskin and his trusty companions, and conveyed in secrecy to an old barn in the neighbourhood of Kilburn.

When night arrived it was left in the sole charge of the leader of this band, who undertook to guard the corpse till morning.

Left by himself Blueskin, for a short time, pondered as he gazed upon the remains of the gallant highwayman.

"Ah, Jack," he exclaimed, "I'm not a tame hound to be cowed by a look, but as your corpse lies before me I feel how fearful is the contemplation of death! Cold and inanimate clay bends a heart of iron, and teaches man his utter insignificance! But morality," continued the robber, "comes with ill grace from such lips as mine, and thought unnerves me for the work I have to do. It is almost the appointed time he promised to be here. I had better see that he doesn't mistake the road."

Blueskin here rose and re-placed the covering he had taken from the body of Jack Sheppard, whose repose in death he seemed to fancy he had violated.

Folding the grave-clothes decently, he for a while quitted the corpse.

Blueskin quietly pursued his way from the barn along a sweeping glade.

The trees of this path were so close that the branches made darkness over his head.

Traversing this he came upon the open road, upon which the moonbeams lay in silvery silence.

If Blueskin thought of anything saving the painful scene he had just witnessed, it was of the necessary guard to be observed in his night walk.

The time was dangerous and unsettled.

Scouts from the late execution were abroad.

In short, the danger of the place and period were such that the robber wore his loaded pistols in his belt and a cutlass, that he might be prepared for whatever peril should chance come across him.

He heard a distant bell proclaim seven of the evening, as he emerged from the wooded lane.

"'Tis the hour he named," cried Blueskin, "and he is true to his word."

For, with the last stroke of the clock, the speaker heard the sound of wheels.

As it became more distinct it was plain that the expected party was advancing nearer.

The next moment a carriage with men in liveries was seen approaching.

It suddenly stopped at the spot where Blueskin was standing.

On the door of the vehicle being opened, a young man alighted from it.

He was dressed in a rich garb, but carried a mask for the purpose apparently of disguise.

Despite of this, however, the attendant recognized our hero, Roving Jack.

He was followed by another person, who was also supplied with a visor and an ample cloak.

The cloak, with its adjunct, most effectually concealed the face and figure of their wearer.

He was no other than Wirth Wolfgang.

After a few words passing between the newcomers and Blueskin, the latter conducted his friends to the place where the body of Jack Sheppard was deposited.

Silently they carried the same through the sylvan grove, and, carefully hid from the view of the servants in waiting, placed it in the carriage.

These were enjoined to secrecy, and requested to return home by a different route.

These people had no sooner departed than Blueskin, attended by our hero and Wirth Wolfgang,

seized the reins, and hurriedly drove off from the scene of the late adventure.

Their destination will appear on further perusal of this chapter.

* * * * *

The scene now changes to a chamber of dungeon-like aspect.

It is a laboratory, and filled with all the lumber proper to the retreat of an alchymist, and an adept in the occult sciences.

At a quaint and grotesque table is seated such a worthy.

The dull flame of a lamp disclosing his person, dressed in an ample black velvet garb, and scull cap.

He appears apparently buried in a deep calculation, and occupied in deciphering the mystical characters written on a parchment before him.

At the feet of this student lay a dull and shapeless figure, screened by a cloth.

The white covering being stained here and there by spots of recently flowing blood.

Beside this stood another stately form.

It was that of our hero, Roving Jack.

Suddenly the latter was aroused from a reverie into which he had fallen by the voice of him who had been studiously engaged in his company.

"At length de work is accomplished," said Wirth Wolfgang, in whom the reader must recognise the hermetic philosopher we have lately alluded to, for the Dutchman was addicted to those pursuits which the age esteemed as little better than sorcery.

"De draught composed of de ingredients contained in dis manuscript," continued Wirth, pointing to the parchment before him, "will give life."

"To foil King Death when his jaws are opening to receive a victim is indeed a glorious triumph, Wirth," exclaimed Roving Jack.

"Yes," replied the other, "dat which at first was unintelligible, is now made clear as day to me."

"This elixir then——"

"Vill restore de dead to the living, vill renew youth, and give length of life to de possessor."

"How on earth, Wirth Wolfgang, have you obtained this extraordinary recipe?"

"Dat ish my secret, mynheer," cried he. "You are a goot man, and shall know it von day. De scroll is de labour of Chaldaic sages, who first fanned to a flame de Promethean spark. In a myriad of ages dat knowledge come to de doomed 'Vanderdecken'—'The Flying Dutchman.' Ja! whose representative on earth I now am."

"You fancy, then," continued our hero, "you will be able to re-animate and once again endow with life this perishing mass?"

With these words, the speaker pointed to the object lying at his feet, which being at length uncovered, disclosed the dead body of Jack Sheppard.

"Fancy? I can re-animate it!" echoed Wirth Wolfgang. "De matter is beyond all doubt. I hold de mystic preservative dat gives man immortality."

The Dutchman now pursued his apparently impious task with alacrity.

Consulting ever and anon the mystic parchment, as he proceeded in the confection of the "elixir vitæ," or "elixir of life."

In a short time, our hero beheld the alchemist pour the decoction he had prepared from variously coloured and peculiarly-labelled bottles, into a small phial.

It appeared a bright, transparent liquid, by the lurid glare of the charcoal fire, before which he was standing.

Wirth Wolfgang, holding the vessel still in his hand, advanced and leant over the prostrate body of the highwayman.

He first passed his hand, moistened by a portion of the fluid, over the dead man's temples, then forced the remainder down his throat.

The livid corpse in a moment quivered under the potency of the medicament as if it had received an electric shock.

This was followed by a violent trembling motion so powerful that the limbs of the sufferer moved to and fro as if they belonged to those of a vigorous being.

His brow, cold as marble, became presently warm with life, and beaded with sweat, as if in intense agony.

The effect of the elixir appeared to Roving Jack wonderful and instantaneous.

His hair stiffened where he stood, and he seemed for the time being transformed into some statue of stone.

He soon observed a blue flame issuing from the quickening clay.

The sightless orbs were lit up with the power of vision.

The discoloured and distorted features assumed their natural hue and expression, while the stiffened and rigid joints regained their wonted suppleness.

"You must swear," said the Dutchman, addressing our hero, "never to divulge what you are about to behold, and the charm will be complete."

"Most solemnly, I pledge myself," returned Roving Jack.

"Enough," exclaimed Wirth Wolfgang; "your oath accomplishes my purpose. Beware! lest you break it."

"I never will."

The Dutchman now flung some drugs upon the fire, and strong odour prevailed in the apartment.

On this the spell of death seemed entirely broken, and that one of the miracles of old had been wrought.

The apparently lifeless form of Jack Sheppard rose from his cerements with a convulsive start.

It resembled that of a sleeping man arising from a hideous dream.

He had thrown off his entranced thraldom, and had issued forth once more to the world of temporal creatures.

He gazed vacantly around the room as if he were the tenant of some supernatural abode; in fact the chamber, strewed with the implements used by its necromantic occupant, might have justified such a supposition in a mind far less excited than Jack Sheppard's under present circumstances.

As the highwayman gradually recovered consciousness his brain still reeled, and for some moments he had to press his hand before his eyes to exclude the terrible phantasma that pictured itself to his sense of sight.

Having at length overcome the failing, Jack Sheppard was at once amazed and delighted to hear the voice, and find himself in the presence of Wirth Wolfgang.

"Wirth Wolfgang, my scattered senses serve not to recount the incidents of the past hour. Tell me first, where am I?"

"In safety," was the Dutchman's curt reply.

"But what has happened is——"

"All for de best," continued Wirth Wolfgang, doggedly.

"After a fearful doom beneath the tree of Tyburn," exclaimed Jack Sheppard, "I ceased to think, feel, or suffer. Say," continued the highwayman, whose surprise seemed to increase every moment, "have I passed the realm of death? Do I awake to another being and a new life?"

"Ja, mein friend, you have been snatched from de grave dat vas yawning to receive your body."

"I do not dream, then; I still exist?"

"Yes; I am de instrument in de hands of heaven to, restore you once more to dis troublesome world."

"But how have you effected such a seeming impossibility? Armed with the weapon my distracted mother had placed in my hand, I fired into my own breast," rejoined Jack Sheppard.

"But you will not marvel when I tell you, mein friend," cried the Dutchman, "that the secret of prolonging life is within my reach, and I dare grasp it."

"You have leagued yourself with the powers of darkness."

"A man may be an adept in alchymy, and yet no sorcerer, mynheer," replied Wirth Wolfgang, dryly. "I possess the ingredients of a potion handed down by the fathers of ancient lore that confers to some great extent perpetual being to man."

"He who exists on such a condition," replied Jack Sheppard, "must be deemed the most wretched of his species."

"How so?"

"Is he not a stranger to the earth who outlives his race? The dearest tie which binds mortal to life, the love of progeny, is broken."

"There are other pleasures."

"But not to equal the one——"

"You talk like a boy, as you are," interrupted the Dutchman, with peevishness. "Say, is it nothing to be young again, to enjoy eternal youth, to bask for ever in the smiles of beauty?"

"He who loves truly loves but once."

"Think of the man who has lived a century only," continued Wirth Wolfgang, rapturously, "scarcely one soul of the thousands breathing is existent a hundred years after that. The being still lives on, though ten generations have gone to the grave."

"Sooner than suffer such a doom," replied the highwayman, "I would willingly again embrace the death from which you have snatched me."

"You will not regret your fate, Jack Sheppard, when you learn how it has been purchased," said a voice in close proximity.

It was that of Roving Jack.

He had retired from the chamber previously to the last conversation, deeming his presence at the moment of his friend's resuscitation might be prejudicial to its completion.

We will pass over the cordial greeting that took place between our hero and the highwayman, and go at once to the discourse that followed upon it.

When they were left alone, Roving Jack addressed his companion as follows—

"I can readily see that you are troubled at the means which have been used to revivicate, or recal you to life."

"Yes, Sir John," replied Jack Sheppard; "though I have been a bad and desperate man, I have ever respected the great truths that have been revealed to us. The divinity shapes our ends, and it is impious to endeavour to avert those laws which immutably govern the human race."

"Will you rest assured," said our hero, "if I tell you that your escape from death has been effected by no supernatural recourse?"

Jack Sheppard's breast dilated with rapture on hearing this avowal.

"Superstition has endowed untutored minds,"

continued the speaker, "with the idea that by par-
taking of a potion prepared by ancient sages——
"The elexir of life.
"Men could attain a length of days, outnumber-
ing those even enjoyed by the patriarchs of old.
"Illusion—error."
"The drugs used in the confection of that potent
draught were but the simple medicaments of the
earth, sent to raise to its office exhausted nature.
Hence ignorance has stamped as a miracle a common
human power. The restorative is used by the sons
of modern science in cases of suspended animation.
"A trance, it is sometimes called. Into such an
ecstacy you had fallen, and from which the pungent
properties of the chemicals fused by the Dutchman
have drawn you.
"Take my word for it, Jack Sheppard," continued
our hero, "there is no more magic than this in the
so called 'Elixir of Life.'"
We will now touch upon the concluding remarks
made in this curious confabulation.
"The world believes you dead," said our hero,
still addressing the highwayman. "It is better for
you and your welfare that they think so still."
"Ha! Wherefore?"
"You seem surprised, nevertheless I will repeat
the assertion."
"Your reason?"
"'Tis a simple one," said Roving Jack. "For the
few years I have known you, I have ever thought
you were intended for a different part to that which
you have played on the world's stage. You possess
a noble disposition, apt parts, and a daring spirit,"
continued our hero, "and should have written your
name in different characters on the scroll of fame."
"I see your drift, Sir John," replied Jack Sheppard.
"You can guess it."
"You would have me quit the road?"
"Yes."
"I cannot."
"Why?"
"The fearless and venturous life has charms for
one formed as myself, for which I am at a loss to
express."
During the conversation, Roving Jack had noticed
a peculiar restlessness and inquietude about his
companion.
On inquiry he found that the highwayman's left
arm had been injured by the shot he had intended
to take away his life.
Upon examination of the wound, it was discovered that unless attended to mortification would
set in almost immediately.
To prevent such a calamity, Roving Jack insisted that he must have a surgeon's aid.
The question now arose in his mind, how he
should obtain it without causing suspicion as to
whom or what the patient might be.
Wishing to preserve fully the incognito of Jack
Sheppard, our hero suddenly thought of a plan by
which he might accomplish his desired object.
Touching an alarum that stood on the table near
him, he summoned to his presence Wirth Wolfgang and Blueskin.
For what purpose, the incidents related in the
next chapter will clearly prove.

CHAPTER CXXXII.

HOW WIRTH WOLFGANG AND BLUESKIN ENTRAPPED
THE DOCTOR, AND HOW JACK SHEPPARD PRO-
FITED BY SUCH A PROCEEDING.

THE night was both stormy and dark as Wirth
Wolfgang and Blueskin traversed a lonely thoroughfare situate in the north-eastern district lying adjacent to the great metropolis.

They were muffled in cloaks which, while they
protected their wearers from the tempest that was
raging, also concealed their persons from the eye of
curiosity.

"It is a singular request, mein friend," said Wirth
Wolfgang, who had hitherto pursued his way in
silence, "but I suppose dere is goot reason for it."

"Yes, mounseer," replied Blueskin, who ever
favoured the Dutchman with a semi-French appellation. "It is Sir John's orders, and our duty to
obey them, seeing that he has always been a friend
to our brotherhood."

"Ja, what you say is true."

"Besides, it is to serve ——"

"Jack Sheppard?"

"Hush! no names; we are sworn to secrecy, and
blabbing might disclose the whereabouts of the
captain, who has so cleverly slipt out of the hangman's noose."

"I am dumb as Bumgarten churchyard in winter,"
rejoined Wirth Wolfgang, glancing up and down
the road as if to ascertain whether or not any one
had heard his indiscreet remark.

"I would not," he continued timorously, "hand
over the kinchen to Jean Ketch for all de vealth of
my native city, Amsterdam."

"I believe you," replied Blueskin, hastily, and
turning the conversation away from the subject
spoken of.

"But how," continued the robber, "do you think
we can most readily find out this doctor?"

"By a cautious inquiry," answered the other.
"Let us stand out of de rain for a few moments, beneath dis porch, vhere ve can consider how ve shall
proceed in dis affair."

As he spoke, the Dutchman indicated a rude out-
house which stood adjoining an old-fashioned
tavern on the road they were travelling.

Here Blueskin and his companion remained till
the rain, which appeared likely to cease, had abated.

They were leaving this temporary shelter when
they encountered a gentlemanly-looking man who
had issued from the tavern above named.

He was habited in a suit of dark cloth, and by
his demeanour was evidently a person of superior
position.

"There is no satisfying waiters," he muttered to
himself, as he was fastening the strings of the purse
he carried in his hand. "Five shillings, I thought,
was very handsome for the trifling accommodation
I have received, and, to exact more, would positively have been nothing less than an extortion, and
against such proceedings I will always set my face."

The speaker here looked upwards and seemed to
be contemplating the state of the weather.

"Yes," he continued, "I shall get home to my
wife, after all, with a dry skin, for the storm, which
threatened to be of some duration, is blowing off as
fast as it can."

Wirth Wolfgang, who had been silently watching the individual thus communicative to himself,
now jostled against him and greeted him with the
ominous monosyllable—

"Stop!"

At the word the accosted wayfarer started and
thrust the purse he still exposed into his most convenient pocket.

Recovering his composure, he eyed his oppo-
nents narrowly, and at once put them down on the
tablet of his imagination as robbers.

A species of fellowship most rigidly to be
avoided, especially when the novitiate is without
weapons.

He was armed in this case, however, with a gold-headed cane.

This he firmly clutched as he stood upon his guard, and resolutely demanded the reason of the late obstruction.

"Ve mean you no harm, mien friend," said the Dutchman, coolly.

"Nor much good, if I may judge from your looks," was echoed in silent response.

"Ve vant to ask you von question."

"What is it it?"

"Ve vould merely demand."

"Demand?"

"Ja, if you can tell us where to find de Doctor Cuticle."

"Oh, is that all?" replied the other, in a modulated voice, and dropping his cane from its menacing attitude. "Why, then, you are not far off the person you seek. I have the honour to bear the name you mention."

"Dat ish fortunate."

"Formerly of Lincoln."

"The noted physican, originally an expert surgeon."

"And who, within the last two years, has made a rising reputation in London," put in Blueskin, as an addendum.

"Gentlemen, I am that Doctor Cuticle, of whom you speak so graciously," cried the personage in question, making a slight bow in acknowledgment of their encomium.

"We have been to your residence, but not being so fortunate as to find you there, and being informed that you were probably walking in this direction," continued Blueskin, "we followed in the hope of overtaking you."

The doctor was all smiles and blandishments, when Wirth Wolfgang, with a glance askance, demanded—

"Muntmeester, vould you like to earn von large sum of gelt—vot you call monies?"

"Egad! I think I should," replied the now sprightly Cuticle. "Indeed, I should jump at it."

"Goot! Take dis purse as de earnest of liberality."

While he uttered the words the Dutchman realised their signification by placing a bag of golden coin in the hand of the astonished doctor.

"Well, now," he said, communing inwardly, "to look at these fellows I'd have sworn that they meant to have filched my purse instead of giving me theirs. But there—there's no judging by appearances in this vale of tears! What am I to do for this?" continued the recipient of the bounty, addressing aloud his singular companions.

"Save a life!"

"Save a life?" echoed the doctor, who, in meditation, silently added, "I thought they were going to take one."

"You must follow us, mynheer," said the Dutchman, mysteriously, pointing in the direction in which they were to proceed.

"Gentleman, you will pardon me," replied the addressed, evincing some hesitation in complying with Wirth Wolfgang's request, "but I usually inquire who does me the honour to seek my assistance. and what is the nature of the case to which I am summoned."

"Your clients are people of condition, as you may perceive."

Blueskin, as he spoke, alluded to the purse which the doctor had received, and which he still retained in his possession

"As to the nature of the case," continued the robber, "confidence in your skill is ample assurance

that you will ascertain it for yourself better than we can describe it."

"But to the purpose."

"Will you go with us?"

"What, now?" inquired the doctor, in a state of uncertainty.

"Instantly!"

"I really am quite unprepared," he continued. "I almost doubt if I have my case of instruments with me. Oh! yes, here they are; but I recollect," continued the son of the Esculapian art, "I have to call upon a dying patient, so if you will be good enough to give me your name and address, I will be wherever you please to appoint, as soon as possible."

"We have no time for that," said Blueskin. "Wirth, this trifling must be put a stop to."

At the given signal, the Dutchman flung his cloak over the head of the bewildered doctor, who, by the action, was entirely prevented seeing whither or in what direction he was going.

At first he was, though greatly alarmed and enervated, inclined to resist, but eventually succumbed on hearing one of his assailants exclaim,

"You'd better go quietly, doctor. If you obey you're not only safe but shall be handsomely rewarded for your trouble; continue to struggle, and you will repent your rashness."

The ominous click of a pistol near his ear told the captive that his persecutor would be as good as his word, and that discretion on his part would be the better part of valour, so, without further hesitation, submitted to his guidance.

We will now leave the trio we have just dealt with, who are pursuing their way in silence, and return once more to Jack Sheppard and our hero.

They are both still in the abode to which the former had been conveyed after his rescue from Tyburn.

The highwayman was reclining on a couch in the apartment, attended by his friend, Roving Jack.

The wound he had received had become excessively painful, and rendered a recumbent position absolutely necessary.

Our hero, while deeply deploring the sad condition of the prostrate Jack Sheppard, felt also acutely the terrible jeopardy in which he was placed.

Though the highwayman had contrived to elude the vigilance of the officers of the law, who believed that he had fallen by a shot in the affray at Tyburn, the slightest hint that he had escaped would bring again a host to his recapture.

Privacy was, therefore, to be observed, and the secret entrusted only to his firm friends, Wirth Wolfgang and Blueskin, which may account for their mysterious adventure with Doctor Cuticle.

"Well, Sir John, I shall soon be all right," said Jack Sheppard, as our hero was bending over him in solicitude. "As to the wound, it will soon heal under a surgeon's care."

"You heed it not, but——"

"The thought of how it came about will last to the end of my life."

"The wound, you say, was inflicted by your own hand?"

"Yes."

"Self-murder is a crime, Jack Sheppard, that receives not the pardon of heaven."

"I knew not what I did, and at the fatal moment I wished to die."

"How you came to be possessed of a weapon in the emergency is to me still a mystery," exclaimed our hero.

"The hand that armed me with the knife prompted me to do the deed. Darkness was upon my days, and the shadow of desolation flung over my heart; the bright flowers of my youth have been withered by the blast of guilt."

"On my road to the gallows," continued Jack Sheppard, "I encountered one of all others that had reason to curse me. Bereft of reason through my depravity, she breathed my name in harsh and discordant tones, and seemed to welcome me to the death I so justly merited.

"Frenzied beyond endurance at the sight, and standing before the face of heaven, with my soul stained with the misery and madness of the being who had addressed me, I took the weapon she secretly conveyed to me in the hopes of expiating my many crimes."

"The poor maniac, then——"

"Was my own mother."

As Jack Sheppard spoke these words, the sound of footsteps were heard approaching towards the apartment in which he was lying.

Presently three individuals passed through its door.

They were Wirth Wolfgang, Blueskin, and Doctor Cuticle.

The latter was blindfolded, and attended on either side by the former.

"Where am I now?" cried the doctor. "This is certainly the most unprofessional proceeding I have ever met with in the course of my practice; this handkerchief across my forehead blinds me. Am I never to see light again?"

"Remove his bandage," said Roving Jack; "then leave us with the doctor alone."

The order was obeyed in both instances, as Wirth Wolfgang and Blueskin quitted the apartment as soon as they had removed the covering from the eyes of their prisoner.

"Where am I?" he inquired, looking about the room, whose peculiar appearance we have described in the previous chapter.

"And who are you?" continued the doctor, eyeing Roving Jack from head to foot.

"Questions are idle."

"So I've been informed."

"Do what you are commanded."

"Yes."

"And you will not repent your obedience."

"That's as it may happen," replied the doctor, testily. "This is a very suspicious beginning."

"Fear nothing," said our hero. "Do as I require and you shall be safely conveyed back to the spot where you were found."

"Tell me, then, what I must do?"

"Your patient is there."

Our hero here indicated Jack Sheppard.

The doctor advanced to the couch, and, having examined the highwayman's wound, immediately applied himself to tend to and bandage the same.

This office he performed with great skill and patience.

"Well, sir. I trust you can give a favourable report of your patient," exclaimed our hero, when the doctor had completed his arduous work.

"Yes," he replied; "I think I may say he is now out of danger. Had surgical attention been delayed for a few hours longer mortification must have set in, and there would have been no hope for him."

"I rejoice to hear that you have succeeded so well in the case," ejaculated our hero, "and I regret that I have been compelled to use such unfair means to obtain your priceless assistance. But your apparent generous nature," continued the speaker, "will pardon me, I know, when I tell you that dire necessity dictated them."

"Well, sir," replied the doctor, "your candour

and frankness appear to me a sufficient guarantee for your assertion. I must confess, at first," he added, in good humour, "that I did not like the business. I tell you plainly that it has a bad look, and if anything is wrong you will answer for the consequence."

"Do not alarm yourself," cried our hero, "I will take all responsibility on myself. Do you honour me, doctor, with your confidence?"

"Sir," he replied, "in my profession the communications of patients are always received in such a quality."

"What you have seen here," continued our hero, "is a matter to be seen, not spoken of."

"You have my word."

"That is sufficient for a man of your reputation."

The next moment the doctor found himself in possession of a very heavily-laden purse.

He turned to thank the donor, but he had vanished like a shadow, while he himself was surrounded again by Blueskin and Wirth Wolfgang, who threw a handkerchief over his face, and led him blindfolded out of the apartment.

CHAPTER CXXXIII.

THE "CLEUGH A DHOIL," OR DEVIL'S GLEN—HAWKS-EYE, ALIAS JACK SHEPPARD—THE CURIOUS ADVENTURE OF OUR HERO AND THE HIGHWAYMAN WITH THE SOLITARY TENANT OF THE DISMANTLED LIGHT-HOUSE—SOME SLIGHT ACCOUNT OF THE "OMADHAUN,'" OR GUARDIAN OF THE BEACON.

WE must now, for a few pages, change again the scene of our story from merry London to the western and rugged coast of Ireland, which we need scarcely add is washed by the mighty waters of the vast Atlantic.

In one of the most remote districts of the province of Connaught, and lying adjacent to the ocean we have named, a young man known as Hawks-eye, a substantial farmer from the sister kingdom, was on his return from the chase.

In Hawks-eye, the hunter, the reader may recognise the redoubtable Jack Sheppard.

He had assumed the disguise for various purposes, which will be disclosed at a more fitting opportunity.

His more immediate reason being to keep up the supposition which existed in England that he had been killed in the struggle that took place on the morning intended for his execution.

For two years he had remained in seclusion, and but one person on earth knew of the existence, or lurking-place of the noted highwayman.

This individual, as may be guessed, was no other than Roving Jack, our hero.

Jack Sheppard, like most young men of the country he inhabited, was fond of the sport in which he had been occupied.

Its dangers and fatigue were congenial to the disposition he possessed, and his gun afforded him occupation and solace in the almost inaccessible recess of his newly-found and temporary home.

The wild ravine into which Jack Sheppard had followed the game through the past day was now behind him.

He was rapidly advancing to his farm when the night began to cast its shadows on him.

This would have been a matter of little consequence to the sportsman had he not imbibed the traditions common to the neighbouring peasantry.

THE CLEUGH A DHOIL, OR, DEVIL'S GLEN.

The spot he was traversing was in extremely bad fame, and each evening was asserted to be invested by supernatural beings.

As the moon became obscured by a black cloud, Jack Sheppard at once called to mind the terrific incidents of the region that surrounded him.

In fact, though naturally a brave man, they presented themselves with a readiness which he felt to be somewhat dismaying.

The dreary moor, upon which he stood, was called the "Cleugh à Dhoil," or Devil's Glen.

It was bordered on the west by the sea and rocks its principal headland being surmounted by a column of unhewn granite, which served for the purposes of a light-house.

This structure, for some period, had been inhabited by a solitary person, called " Omadhaun," a term, signifying in the Erse, or Irish tongue, " madman."

The only occupation of this individual, saving the cultivation of a piece of ground that surrounded his lonely abode, was supplying with oil the signal lamps, which, like the fire of the ancient's, was never extinguished.

Report gave out that this mysterious man was incited to his duty by being himself a sufferer by shipwreck.

It was said he had left the country of his birth with an only child to seek fortune in the Bermudas.

The vessel in which he had embarked was wrecked on the coast adjacent through the negligence of the keeper omitting to light the beacon at the usual hour.

Of the ill-fated ship which had foundered, he alone escaped death.

By a miracle the wretched father reached the shore, and discovered a cavern.

Here he lived for a time in misery, and cut off from all commerce with the world.

A single spring of water, and the bounties of the deep supported nature, and continued to give life to the exile, while remaining in his singular dwelling.

One day, while exploring the same, he came upon a fissure of the rock that disclosed a reticle of woodwork.

He passed through the aperture, and, removing some of the planks, found himself in a gloomy chamber.

Ascending a flight of stairs another chamber met his view.

The recluse instantly recognised it as the one occupied by the guardian of the light-house, whom

it was supposed was sleeping when the intruder entered.

That was a moment of agony.

As he gazed upon the slumbering man his feverish brain retraced the past in all its horrors.

Amidst the vivid lightning's flash he deemed he saw his drowned child call upon him to avenge her melancholy fate.

With a tiger's rage, the father, in a paroxysm of insanity darted on the man that had unwittingly been the cause of the daughter's death.

His hands grasped wildly the throat of his prey.

His glaring eyeballs held a terrible commune, and his lips breathed silently with curses the victim's name.

There was no hesitation, no mercy, no uncertainty.

Before the aroused dreamer could defend himself from the insidious attack his skull had been dashed against the rock, and his heart torn from his warm body.

Whether there was truth in these incidents, or that trumpet-tongued rumour spoke falsely, none could determine; but one thing was without denial, namely, that within the short space of eight months after the above related legend eight men had been employed in the service of the beacon, and had as strangely disappeared as their former colleague.

In fact, public mind yielded so to terror that, though the government had offered most liberal terms to any one who would take charge of the Pharos,* no one save the Omadhaun could be found to hold the office.

These particulars related impressed themselves strongly on Jack Sheppard as he passed along the Cleugh a Dhoil, or Devil's Glen.

He also remembered since the catastrophe had taken place the scene of it had been avoided, at least after nightfall, by all as being the battle ground of the fairies, or good people, and the kelpies, or evil spirits.

Jack Sheppard's courage, however, manfully combated and overcame these intrusive sensations of awe.

He summoned to his side the brace of greyhounds who had accompanied him in his sport, and looking to the priming of his piece, with a lighter step trudged homewards on his journey.

While thus proceeding, he was rather glad to distinguish a friendly voice shout in his rear, and at the same time make a proposition to become his fellow traveller on the unfrequented road.

He slackened his pace, and was quickly joined by a gentleman who had been at the chase like himself.

It was his friend and patron, Roving Jack, who resided with his father-in-law, Sir Jocylyn Tremaine, the baronet who, taking part again in the coming insurrection in favour of the Pretender, was settled on a small estate which he inherited in the neighbourhood.

"Now, Sir John," exclaimed Jack Sheppard, "I'm glad to meet you at any time, but more so than ever on such a desolate spot as the Cleugh a Dhoil."

Our hero smiled.

"Where have you been hunting?" continued the highwayman.

"Up the Curragh Bawn and the surrounding mountains," answered Roving Jack, returning the greeting.

"But will our dogs keep the peace, think you?" continued the speaker, indicating the animals playfully running by his side.

* Pharos, or ancient light-house.

"Never fear them, Sir John," replied Jack Sheppard; "they've scarcely a leg to stand on."

"How so?"

"I've led them such a rare dance since sunrise, but all to little purpose, for no birds have I seen to-day, and I begin to think that, with the troublesome times, they've taken wing and fled out of the country."

"Well," said our hero, "I have been more fortunate than you, Jack; I have shot a few brace this morning. You shall have half of the spoil," he added; "and then you will not disappoint——"

"Una."

"The handsome colleen that has ensnared your heart for the last six months."

"Many thanks, Sir John; I will accept the present for her sake."

"I will come with them to your farm to-morrow myself," returned our hero; "mayhap you will find me a plate at your table?"

"Willingly," exclaimed Jack Sheppard. "Una's foster-mother, Bridget, will be delighted, Sir John, for the good dame conceits herself that she's not distantly related to you, and your father, who was killed by——"

"Hush—hush, Jack," interrupted our hero; "not a word about that, it's a story better forgotten."

"I don't think so, Sir John; if it had been my case, I should have kept it in mind till the day I had got some amends for the injury received."

"I know my own affairs best," muttered Roving Jack, somewhat angrily.

"That may be, Sir John," answered Jack Sheppard, unabashed by the retort; "but still you must admit that you have heard that Sir Jocylyn's friend treacherously stabbed your sire after he had mastered his adversary's sword."

"It was a foolish brawl, I tell you," exclaimed our hero, still warm with excitement, "occasioned by wine and politics. You know among Prelatists and Jacobites rancour ever exists. Many weapons were drawn in the foolish dispute you have alluded to, and it is impossible to say who gave the blow that brought my father to an early and untimely grave."

"I can guess what bridles your tongue and spirit, Sir John," whispered Jack Sheppard. "All the world knows your courage but——"

"But what?"

"The two bright eyes of Lady Violet is the reason why her husband's steel is in its scabbard."

Our hero offered no reply to this apparently offensive remark, but rode moodily on with his companion, who paced with him on his side.

Suddenly, the horses on which the riders were seated swerved from the roadway, as if affrighted by the appearance of some extraordinary visitation.

"Ha!" exclaimed Jack Sheppard, with difficulty retaining his saddle, "what in the fiend's name can yon phantom be?"

The object which alarmed the speaker startled for the moment even his less prejudiced companion.

The moon, which had arisen during their conversation, was struggling with the clouds, and shed only a doubtful and occasional light.

By one of her beams, which streamed upon the column of the beacon light of which we have spoken, and which the horsemen had now approached, they discovered a form, apparently human, but of most singular aspect.

"Shall I give the fiend a shot?" exclaimed Jack Sheppard, who still persisted that it was an apparition that had come before them.

"For heaven's sake, no," returned his companion, holding down the weapon which he was about to raise to the aim. "For heaven's sake, no," he repeated, "'tis some deluded creature, and needs our pity rather than our anger."

"You must be mad yourself to think of going so near the kelpie," said the highwayman, holding Roving Jack in his turn, as he prepared to advance.

"I tell you it's a spectre," he continued. "I have seen the face a thousand times in life, but under far different conditions."

Our hero, however, in spite of the resistance offered, continued to advance on the path they had originally pursued, and soon confronted the mysterious being that had attracted observation, and saluted the same.

The addressed raised his eyes with a ghastly stare.

His head, which was large, was covered with a fell of shaggy locks, gray with age and sorrow.

His brows, prominent, overhung a pair of piercing eyes, set far back in their sockets.

The orbs rolled with a portentous wildness, indicating partial insanity.

The rest of his features were of the rugged, rough, heron stamp, while his body, thick and square, was supported by rather short legs, rendering the individual herculean in proportion, only the average height of man.

His arms were long and brawny, furnished with two muscular hands, and being unclothed, were at once noticed to be covered by nature's garb in the shape of a coating of coarse, wiry hair.

His dress was a sort of dark brown tunic, like a monk's frock, girt round with a belt of seal skin.

A cap of rough fur encased his head, which added considerably to the grotesque effect of his whole appearance.

And which appendage, at the same time shadowing his features, gave them more than ever their habitual expression—that of sullen, malignant, and morose misanthropy.

This remarkable personage was no other than the Omadhaun; or, the Solitary Guardian of the Beacon Light.

CHAPTER CXXXIV.

THE KEEPER OF THE LIGHTHOUSE WARNS OUR HERO AND JACK SHEPPARD OF THEIR DANGER —SOME INCIDENTS THAT OCCURRED AT A MIDNIGHT MEETING OF THE WILD RAPPAREES OF THE MOUNTAIN—A DISSERTATION UPON IRISH ROBBERS.

THE "Omadhaun" gazed for a few moments on our hero and his companion, Jack Sheppard, and appeared suddenly soothed into a better temper than usual at the visits of strangers to the lighthouse.

He, all at once, returned their greeting with cordiality, and burst into a wild and loud laugh.

The travellers were further surprised presently by hearing the old man pronounce distinctly their separate names.

"I could have sworn," exclaimed Jack Sheppard, "that I have met this strange being before, and since he knows me, it is plain that I have not declared falsely; but when and where the encounter took place," continued the highwayman, "I cannot, for the life of me, call to mind."

"Could you do so, Jack Sheppard," replied the Omadhaun, with a peevish gesture, "you would, I do not doubt, look upon me with greater loathing than you seem to do at present."

"Who can you be?"

"Once I was your enemy, now I am your firmest friend."

"The proof."

"Will soon be found in what I shall now tell you."

"Deeds are better than words."

"This night the lives of yourself and companion are threatened with a great danger—nay, death itself stares you both in the face."

"Who dares to harm us?" said our hero, startled at the assertion that had just been made.

"The Rapparees are abroad."

"The Wild Bandits of the Mountains may be conciliated."

"Thus think the children of clay in their ignorance," retorted the Omadhaun, with a malicious grin, "and thus they speak in their folly. Have you marked, good sir," he continued, "the young cub of the wild cat that has been tamed, how sportive and gentle it appears?"

"Truly."

"But trust the brute with your lambs," exclaimed Jack Sheppard, "his inbred ferocity breaks forth, and he tears, ravages, and devours."

"Such is instinct," replied our hero, to the remark.

"It is the emblem—the picture of the Rapparee or Irish robber," ejaculated the Omadhaun. "With money and freedom he is quiet, contented; but let superstition or poverty assail his hearth, he is as bloodthirsty and revengeful as the Indian of the American prairies."

"It is no wonder," answered Roving Jack, "that with sentiments so vicious and virulent, that these unfortunate outcasts of society should be regarded by the vulgar as in league with the arch enemy of mankind."

"Besides, they are rigid Catholics to a man; your creed differs from theirs," continued the Omadhaun, "and it is the oath of the community to exterminate by sword and fire, when opportunity offers, the hated race that embraces the reformed faith.

"The nobleman's castle and the helpless peasant's cabin are alike sacrificed by the ruthless brotherhood."

At this moment an armed man appeared on a steep eminence near to the spot upon which the speakers were standing.

He raised a horn which was attached to his waist, and sounded it.

He had no sooner done so than he vanished with the same stealth as he had appeared.

"You recoil," said the Omadhaun to our hero, who had started at the noise.

"Yes," he replied, "did you not hear?"

"I heard only," said Jack Sheppard, "the sound of a herdsman's horn, and, seeing they use such an instrument in their vocation, I presume it is one of them calling their flock together."

"No, friend, you are mistaken," remarked the Omadhaun, "'tis the signal of the Rapparees; they are about to hold a council, and that rallying sign denotes that they may hold it in safety, and that the Seider Derag or red coats (a name given to the military stationed in Ireland) are not in force in the neighbourhood."

"We shall be discovered," said our hero, "and doubtless fall by the hands of these bravoes."

"Had you proceeded on your journey, you would, in all probability, have been shot as spies," rejoined the Omadhaun, "but, by accepting my protection, you will pass safely to your homes."

"But——"

"Not a word. Follow me, and fear nothing."

Obeying the injunction, our hero and Jack Sheppard silently proceeded in the direction in which the Omadhaun was conducting them.

A hill was soon before the travellers, covered with an ancient forest of fir, flinging scathed branches across the roadway beneath.

This again led to the bridge of Brodynshame over the River Ayle and the Mulrea mountains, being the highest ground and one of the most romantic scenes in this part of hostile Ireland.

The bridge was formed merely of planks rudely and carelessly thrown over the intervening space between two immense rocks, and the least fall would have dashed a passer over to pieces, as the depth beneath was about two hundred feet.

It was in the gloomy valley among the mountains that a body of men had now collected, bound by the base yoke of fanaticism.

They were all armed with either pikes or muskets, while in most instances their tattered clothing was decorated with tarnished military accoutrements and cartridge boxes.

Each one wore a mask, and kept his features strictly from view.

At the moment the Omadhaun and his friends had reached the secret meeting place of these Rapparees, the former bid his companions conceal themselves beneath some overhanging brushwood.

From this point they observed the mysterious proceedings of these outlaws.

One of their number was striking a light and igniting a torch, whose lurid glare fell upon the wild associates and region around, imparting to them the appearance of some supernatural beings engaged in unholy rites.

The chief of the freebooters then advanced to the centre of a circle formed by his brotherhood.

He crossed himself, and seemed to mutter a prayer.

After a pause he exclaimed, with great vehemence,

"Comrades, the vengeance we are about to take shall be a terrible one. We will be as our foe! we will be without pity—without mercy for the victim! Blood for blood! Not his alone, but all who bear his detested and accursed name. We spare neither age, beauty, nor sex. All must die. He who hesitates to strike will die without the blessing of our faith, and his ashes will repose in an unconsecrated grave."

"Hold!" said one, in a voice of thunder.

It was that of the Omadhaun, who had sprung from his hiding-place.

"Hold, one and all," he continued; "I am your leader, and will not consent that you should butcher the innocent in cold blood."

"Indeed," replied the robber chief, coolly. "Has the Omadhaun forgotten his oath?"

The speaker was no other than Redmond O'Hanlon, once known as slashing Nat Wetherby, the flying highwayman.

"No oath," replied the addressed, "compels me to murder the guiltless."

"The terrible oath which binds the Rapparee, outlaw, and patriot, is this," cried Redmond, sternly. "If a heretic kills one of our creed, death is his! If more than one Roman fall, the entire family of the denounced, man, woman, or child are sacrificed. The law of retaliation. The edict is written, sealed and signed."

"I have neither read nor signed," said the Omadhaun, with sullen malignity.

"Since you admit this," replied Redmond, triumphantly, "you must here promise by a holy vow to conform to it."

The storm, which had hitherto been but partial, now broke forth with intense violence, as Redmond O'Hanlon addressed the Omadhaun.

"Swear, in the face of heaven!" exclaimed the chieftain, "whose dark canopy covers our heads—in the thunder's majestic peal, and lightning's dazzling and forked flash to accomplish to-night the work of extermination!"

As Redmond uttered the last word, the sentinel on the height gave the usual signal.

For a moment there was a profound silence, and each of the desperate band directed their gaze to one object.

It appeared to be an unfrequented tract upon which their attention was attracted.

Deserted indeed was the way, lined with tall poplars on either side, which had turned yellow in the autumn, and had shed their leaves in abundance across the road, which quite muffled the sounds of the footsteps of the horses which were seen heavily dragging a carriage in the distance.

The lights of the vehicle glimmered faintly in the widely extending flats, and seemed inconceivably lost in the melancholy region, which appeared so perfectly straight that one could see something like ten miles in front, diminishing in a point.

Presently could be heard the tinkling of the bells that adorned the animals' heads, and the rumbling sound of the carriage they were drawing, accompanied by the occasional words of encouragement of the individual driving.

This party in a few minutes became visible, and appeared as a man whose sturdy shoulders were covered by hood of a coat, with a broad black hat upon his head.

"There's a caleche upon the road, boys—plunder!" cried fifty voices, with the words poising their muskets.

"Lower your weapons," thundered Redmond, as he recognised the travellers, "and let them pass. These people of all others must be suffered to go free."

The men for the moment hesitated to submit.

"Do you hear me?" continued the outlaw, furiously, "put down your arms, or by the heaven above us, I'll cleave to the chine with my cutlass the first who offers opposition to my command."

Unwillingly the second mandate was obeyed, while all wondered why their leader for the first time in his life had refused to levy what was termed by the fraternity, "the Black Mail."

"Why have you let such a rich booty pass by us?" said the Omadhaun, addressing the outlaw as the travellers disappeared from their sight.

"I had good reason," replied the other, superciliously, then murmuring to himself, continued, "Una might be with them."

"Those reasons should be made known to the Brotherhood."

"Let them know that policy bridles my tongue."

"The Rapparee regards no secrets."

"What if I tell you these strangers are Romanists?"

"That matters little, since we rob alike the Papist and his antagonist."

"What I have done brings more red gold to the coffers of our band than twenty midnight raids."

"Sinse you say thus much, I say no more at present," replied the Omadhaun; "yet, mark me, Redmond O'Hanlon, I, in the name of our followers, hold you to the pledge you have given!"

"You will find me as true as the steel I carry," replied the outlaw. "But we have now other work to do than bandying words. Raise the cross of fire at once upon the mead and mountain-top, and none will dare to intercept us."

As Redmond O'Hanlon spoke, he seized a brand and plunged it into a peat fire at his side.

He then applied the burning torch to the combustible matter of which the beacon (which, in the meantime, had been set up) was composed.

The kindled signal in an instant, with its tall, pointed flame rising up from a thick cloud of smoke, is answered.

Look! a second blazes on the headland edge.

A third and fourth issue from the Nephin heights and Croagh Moyle mountains.

They light the enemies of the Rapparee's faith to perdition.

Ere another minute had elapsed, similar sheets of flames shot up right and left.

On the high lands, on the coasts, on the summits of the hills, or the eminences of the forests, so suddenly and strangely did these fires flash forth, that earth and air seemed, as it were, to have been tinged with a blood-red hue by the hand of enchantment.

The aspect of the Rapparees was more than ever dark and foreboding in the deep reflection.

Their savage features, fantastic garbs, and gaunt figures, made them look like beings of some infernal dominion.

Afar off, in the illumed scene, might be descried a considerable body of men advancing in another direction.

Their arms, accoutrements, and steady step proclaimed them as soldiers of the English army.

"Comrades," exclaimed Redmond O'Hanlon, as he beheld the Royalists, "our foe is near us—they rush upon their own destruction. Each to his post, and keep all in shade and silence. Without noise," continued the robber, "divide into little bands to avoid suspicion. Arrived within musket shot of the enemy, halt; there I will tell you on what I have resolved."

Redmond O'Hanlon raised his musket, and, as his companions were hastening to their rendezvous, firmly addressed in the following words:—

"Remember, I lodge a bullet in the brain of the man (were he my own father) who dares to move a step without my orders."

The whole band, either awed by the resolution of their leader, or admitting the necessity of the course he was pursuing, tacitly dispersed without offering the slightest opposition to his will.

They separated into companies and took every variety of route from the high road to the mountain, emulating in their march the wild inhabitants of the region.

The Rapparees had no sooner taken their departure than our hero and Jack Sheppard sprung from the place that afforded them the means of concealment.

"Well, Sir John," exclaimed Jack Sheppard, blithely, "I find that there are greater rogues here than on our side of the channel."

"They may appear so to you, Jack," replied our hero, "but you must bear in mind that superstition, and, I regret to say, that too often, oppression have exercised their baneful influence on poor old Ireland and rendered her sons, otherwise noble, vindictive and cruel beyond their nature."

"Oh, Sir John," added his companion, "you have always a good word for every one, but I cannot allow that these rascallians are for one moment to be compared to the Claude Duvals or Joe Hinds of merry England! Why, some of the finest gentlemen of the day are eminent on the road, and your true highwayman would consider he was disgraced if he did not conduct himself in a dignified manner."

"The Irish," said Roving Jack, "may, nevertheless, boast of some of her robbers. Power, the great Tory of Munster, was a savant and most accomplished scholar. Strong Jack Macpherson, the Leinster boy, was as noted for his strength of mind as his strength of body, which latter quality was so great that it was asserted he could break a horse-shoe with the grip of his hand. Delany, Carrick, and Cahir Na Cappul, were each men of cultivated minds, and equally generous and just."

"It is not for me, Sir John," replied Jack Sheppard, "to dispute with one that knows so much more than myself; therefore, I will confine my remarks to the Rapparees who have but now left us.

"They, I fear, are upon some dangerous errand. What their motive and where their destination may be I have failed to make out."

"How had we better act in this emergency?" asked the highwayman. "We dare not proceed on our journey. Every outlet is in the possession of the scouts, who guard the passers with the eye of the lynx."

"If we fall into the hands of these ruffians," said our hero, "we may not fare so well as we did on our late encounter with the Omadhaun."

"That name is well thought of, Sir John."

"How so?"

"We will bend our steps towards the lighthouse, its keeper will surely give us shelter till the morning."

To this proposal Roving Jack at once acceded, and prepared to accompany his associate.

The storm which had set in still continued to rage, but despite the fury of the elements the travellers journeyed onward with rapidity.

By the brilliant reflection of the distant beacons their dark forms were seen in a few minutes traversing the rugged roadway and pursuing the course over the rocky edges of the neighbouring mountains.

CHAPTER CXXXV.

THE FARM-HOUSE IN THE DERRY-CALGAICH OR OAK GROVE—THE MYSTERIOUS LETTER.

WE shall now turn to the chamber of a farm-house in the neighbourhood of the Rapparees' late rendezvous.

This room, which had all the peculiarities known to those acquainted with the dwellings of the Irish people, possessed in particular one above the rest, in the shape of a vast chimney stone-wrought mantle piece covered with many a cipher and now crackling with a fire of broom.

Its side, similarly adorned, formed a spacious cupboard, whose contents were hid by a broad curtain of green serge. This apartment, apparently built some two centuries since, had two entrances, namely, one at the back, and the other on the left of the chimney heretofore alluded to, while a winding staircase encircling the same led to the floor overhead.

On the night upon which the fiery cross had been raised by Redmond O'Hanlon, several persons had been engaged in the above homestead.

The nature of their occupation being household duties, Barney and Larry appearing conspicuous in laying a cloth for the "Misther and Misthress" who had been absent during the day and were momentarily expected home to supper.

Una, the adopted daughter of the owner of the farm, and who, as we have already acquainted the reader, had attracted by her beauty the notice of Jack Sheppard, was also a member of this party who appeared to be entirely under her control and guidance.

She was now standing at a window as if anxiously awaiting the return of her foster parents.

Flashes of lightning occasionally passed by the casement; but the storm which had raged was now ceasing, and the thunder afar off declined in the distance.

"What a fearful conflict of the elements," said Una, contemplating the lowering clouds in the heavens.

"Bedad! asthore, you may say that. May I niver see sich anither till I'm dead intirely; but be aisy in your mind, acushla, it's jist beginning to come to an end."

These words were spoken by one Patrick O'Shaughnessy, a tight Irish labouring lad, who, though he had a slight penchant for the colleen he was addressing, it by no means diminished his love for the potheen, Mountain Dew or Still Whisky."

"Murtagh and Bridget must have been overtaken by the tempest," continued Una.

"The misther won't pass Pat Killrooney's skibbeen without taking shelter from the drops, and a drop from the shelter," insinuated Patrick O'Shaughnessy.

These speakers were presently left alone, when Una addressed her companion,

"Patrick," she said, "have you observed the manner of your master to-day? I never saw him look so angry."

"Sure, he's not, I take it, in a vastly good humour about something," replied the simple-minded Irishman.

"And I have always thought Murtagh uncommonly cross," he continued, "when he's displaised."

"Usually," said Una, "a word from his wife or a smile from me will suffice to calm his naturally hasty temper. This afternoon he spoke with such harshness as almost to bring tears into my eyes, while his fixed glance riveted me to the spot upon which I was standing. Do you think, by accident, you have informed him of my love for the young Englishman, who has lately settled amongst us?"

"Whist! bad luck to me," whispered honest Patrick, "do I look like a dirty informer?"

"No, Patrick, I have wronged you by having such a suspicion."

"My maxim," the addressed retorted, "is niver to revail a secret especially when I don't know what it is."

"I have confidence in you," exclaimed Una, "and will trust you with mine."

"Sure, yez may do that same thing with parfect safety."

"Know, then," continued the maiden, "that I must quit the farm to-night by stealth for a short time."

"Then, musha macree," replied Patrick, with a cunning leer, "yez must take a journey through the key-hole, seeing that the Misther has got the key of the door in that great coat pocket he's got on."

"How unfortunate," muttered Una. "I promised to meet him at midnight, and I must be there."

At this moment the covered caleche which had passed the Rapparees on the mountains, stopped before the dwelling in which Patrick and his companion had been conversing.

Two persons descended from the vehicle and came into their presence.

They were Murtagh and Bridget Mackeen, the guardians of Una.

Murtagh Mackeen was a wealthy Protestant farmer, owner of many acres, and a determined enemy of the Papists and Rapparees, whose enmity, by his acts of oppression, he had excited.

He was a man of harsh and severe features, indicative of sagacity and revengement, while his wife, enriched by beauty and gentleness, was a most perfect semblance of humility itself.

"What a night," cried Murtagh, as he entered his house, shaking the moisture from his rain-soaked garments, which he then handed to his servant, Patrick, who retired with the garments. "I'm drenched to the skin," he continued, placing himself before the grate, which now emitted a bright glow.

"And you, my more than mother," said Una, advancing to Bridget, "how wet you are. Let me take off your mantle, and seat you before the fire."

With the words the damsel removed the cloak that covered the shivering farmer's wife, and led her to a stool standing in the chimney corner.

"Bridget has no one to blame for this but herself," returned her husband; "she should have remained at home, and not insisted in following me to the trial of this accursed Rapparee."

"I own my fault, dear Murtagh," cried the wife, meekly, "since you, who are so good in general, have treated me in this case as you have done."

"The actions of an enraged man," exclaimed the farmer, "are sometimes to be excused. I am violent, hot-headed, but I love thee, asthore, and for a thousand pounds would not have you reproach me with a tear."

"And yet, Murtagh," replied Bridget, "at the hall of justice you left me weeping, and desired me to quit your side."

"Why did I so? Because a man who has a woman leaning by his side must suffer that which he would not suffer otherwise."

Bridget offered no further reply, while her husband seated himself at the table to partake of supper.

The calm he now affected was a stranger to his heart.

The patient wife had observed when her husband left the tribunal, at which he had been a witness, that a pale and downcast air had settled on his face, and that a violent agitation had taken possession of him.

Again on the road the excited man had sang and laughed convulsively at the roar of the thunder that burst over their head.

These things considered by her in silence nerved her with some hidden feeling of energy, and proved that, though weak in body, her mind would be strong in a moment of peril.

Before falling to on the viands before him, Murtagh bid Una procure him a glass of Usquebaugh, the Irish word for whisky, or Water of Life.

There was a choice bottle of the spirit in the cupboard, the door of which being locked, the farmer presented a bunch of keys to the maiden to open it.

Una had no sooner received them, than she adroitly removed one of their number from the ring, murmuring to herself,

"This should be the key."

Having secured it, she quickly concealed the same in her bosom, then hastening to obey the farmer's order, placed the next moment the required beverage before him.

Murtagh drew the cork of the bottle, filled a glass, and swallowed the contents at a gulp.

"Excellent, by Jove!" he cried, smacking his lips after the draught.

"Come, wife," he exclaimed, to Bridget, who was still seated near the fire ; "won't you take supper ?"

"No. I am too fatigued," was her reply.

"As you will, acushla !" said Murtagh, with forced gaiety, then turning to Una, made a similar request.

"Thank you," she answered. "I cannot eat."

"How so ?" asked the farmer. "Girls at your age should not want an appetite. Now tell me—I have noticed for some time past that you are sad and anxious, and more than once I have surprised a tear in your eye. Are you not happy with us ?"

"How could I be otherwise," replied Una, "when you have been so kind to me ? Can I forget that you rescued me from the sinking vessel on your coast, in which my father perished, and have been my parents of adoption since that fatal day ?"

It was at this point of the conversation that Patrick O'Shaughnessy abruptly entered the room.

"Och, murther !" shouted the Irishman. "Here's somebody kilt !"

"Killed ?"

"Bedad, yes. He towld me so wid his own lips."

"Do you know the party ?"

"No, musha, but he calls himself a fri'nd."

"A friend, say you ?"

"Sure, and I did, bekase the gontleman speaks the truth, since he was introduced to the family circle by his horse pitching him clain over the garden hedge, where he now lies covered with mud and dirt from head to foot entirely."

"Did the traveller not give his name ?" demanded Murtagh.

"His name is Simon Smut, Esq.," replied the individual spoken of, who now appeared supported by two farm servants.

Despite the mire and besmeared appearance of this personage, the metamorphosis of the same was truly surprising.

He was no longer Simon Smut the chimney sweep, but Simon Smut the gentleman of independent means, travelling for pleasure and relaxation, and searching excitement in enterprise and adventure.

Being born with the silver spoon in place of the wooden ladle destiny, he had dropped into a fortune of which he was the only heir existent.

"My friends," continued he, "you behold before you a man whose daring spirit has led him into a most unpleasant difficulty of which you shall be made aware when I have recovered sufficient breath to make it known to you."

Murtagh could scarcely help smiling at the deplorable condition of his guest, who seemed as one dragged through a slimy pond.

"You are hurt," said the farmer.

"No, I hope not," interrupted Simon ; "it is in my head I suffer most."

"Quick ! bring a chair for the gentleman."

Murtagh's order was no sooner given than obeyed by the two attendants, who had brought in the sufferer.

He was further assisted by Una, who applied a vinaigrette to his nostrils.

This seemed to revive Simon Smut, who then enquired,

"Where is my horse? I recollect nothing. I only see the fire."

"A fire at this hour !" each one present echoed.

"Hush !" continued the traveller, in a whisper. "What you ask belongs to a terrible history. Before I tell it to you, tell me, if you have anyone on these premises I can charge with an important letter."

"Barney McFlin, here is the man for your errand, he has good legs, and will run eight miles in the hour."

With the words Murtagh pointed to one of the farm servants who stood in the chamber.

"Then Barney McFlin will answer my purpose," replied the guest, dryly.

"If the gentleman requires writing materials, they are here," said Bridget, who had busied herself in getting pen, ink, and paper.

"You will not regret your civility, my good woman," rejoined Simon Smut, taking the articles offered to him.

While the rest of the party stood aside he, in a mysterious manner, penned a letter, which ran as follows :—

"TO THE COMMANDANT OF THE ARMED FORCE IN CONNAUGHT.

"DEAR SIR,—As soon as you receive this epistle, delay not an instant, and put yourself at the head of a squadron and join me at the farm of the 'Mackeens' in the mountains where I attend you. Haste and speed! The matter is grave and pressing.

"SIMON SMUT."

CHAPTER CXXXVI.

SIMON SMUT'S ADVENTURE AT THE AMBUSCADE—THE HORSE AND THE RIDER—IRISH HOSPITALITY AND ENGLISH CANDOUR—EYES THAT SEE AND EARS THAT HEAR – THE KIND GOOD NIGHT—COMING EVENTS CAST THEIR SHADOWS BEFORE—THE FARMER'S DOG, AND HIS FAITHLESS SERVANTS—A FOOTFALL ON THE STAIRS.

SIMON SMUT having finished the letter signed and delivered it to the trusty messenger, who at once departed on his portentious errand.

Soon the writer found himself alone with the farmer, his wife, and Una.

"Now, my friends," said Simon Smut, "I can unravel to you the mystery of the epistle which I have just despatched. This evening," he continued, "I was travelling in the mountains from the town of Castlebar when I fell in with an ambuscade of the ferocious Rapparees."

"Robbers and insurgents ?"

"Just so," replied the guest. "I see you tremble. I must confess that I experienced some such fear in discovering myself in the midst of men known to be mortal enemies to those who unfortunately happen to have money in their pockets, or friends to ransom them, if the case is opposite, therefore I expected no mercy at their hands."

"And yet," interrupted Murtagh, "you appear to have received it, since I find you in my house safe and sound."

"Your pardon, farmer," apologised Simon Smut, "my horse, and not the intended assassins, saved me."

"Indeed !"

"Yes," added the speaker, "taking advantage of a momentary pause, I put spurs to my beast, and with the swiftness of lightning dashed through their scattered ranks."

"Fly before such miserable wretches," exclaimed Murtagh, with hauteur and malignity, "you did very wrong, stranger."

"Permit me to differ with you, farmer," again apologised Simon Smut. "Pray, tell me," he resumed, "how you would have acted in such an emergency ?"

"How would I have acted ?" repeated the farmer, vehemently and in a loud voice, "I would have sold my life with three-fold interest. I would have suffered my mutilated body," he added, in the same strain, "to have rested on the road-side, that our government might see the necessity of exterminating this hated incubus of our soil."

"Lower, a little lower, my friend," suggested Simon Smut.

"What do you fear?"

"Nothing; but it's as well to be prudent," continued the party interrupted, "raising your voice can do no good, and may do much harm."

Looking carefully round, he added, "There are eyes that see, and ears that hear, even through your walls."

"The gentleman is quite right," observed Bridget, the farmer's wife, "why expose yourself to the vengeance of the Rapparees, who never pardon? Remember our neighbour, murdered fifteen days since, for having denounced one of them."

"Let them kill me," shouted Murtagh, again, "no power on earth shall hinder me from saying aloud, and in all places, what I think."

"Husband!"

"You wonder," continued the enraged man, "why I wage war with these Catholics and robbers who twenty years ago inflicted an injury I must not forget."

"But you can forgive," answered Bridget, with celestial calmness.

"Never!"

With the word Murtagh Mackeen advanced to a large thick ring of iron. It was strongly embedded and fixed in the stone wall of the apartment.

He placed his hand upon the metal and exclaimed, addressing his wife. "Your puny hand would fail to move from its stubborn resting place this massive circlet; so with my hate," continued the farmer, "it is as firmly set in my heart, and nothing but death can snatch it from the stronghold."

At this moment the iron-tongued monitor of time proclaimed the twelfth hour.

And the abbey bell hard by tolled midnight.

"Midnight already," murmured Una, with emotion, suddenly recollecting her appointment with Jack Sheppard.

"Our guest," said Bridget, "has need of refreshment, and——"

"He is welcome to that which our scanty larder affords," continued her husband.

"Thank you kindly, good people. I will take neither bite nor sup," replied Simon Smut. "Anxiety has taken away my appetite, and I never drink when I'm labouring under excitement."

"But," the speaker continued, "if you will allow me to repose——"

"Patrick," interrupted the farmer, "conduct this gentleman to the chamber above, and see that he wants for nothing."

The man who had obeyed the summons, winked his eye in token of acquiescence, and bid the traveller follow after him.

The latter, thanking his host for his hospitality, and bidding the rest good night, did as Patrick had desired him.

We need not ascend the stairs with Simon Smut and his companion, nor mention the mishaps and blunders of the guide and guided, but leave the two stuck in a hole in the floor, that strangers had a mighty knack of putting their foot into, and return to Una and her adopted parents.

The damsel, on the departure of the guest, had lit two flambeaux, and opened the door of the corridor leading to the farmer's bed-chamber.

To this room his wife was about to retire, when an action on the part of her husband arrested her progress.

She had observed Murtagh draw a pipe from his pocket and fill it.

"Are you not coming to bed?" she asked, surprised at the unusual custom of her husband smoking at so late an hour.

"No," he replied. "I cannot sleep at present. Give yourself no uneasiness about me. When I am tired, I shall rest, not before."

Bridget, though affected by the rough remark, appeared to take no notice of it, and prepared to depart for the night.

Whether she concealed ineffetually or not her wounded feelings did not appear, but be it as it may, Murtagh, the following moment altered his demeanour, and took her hand, as if aware that he had been somewhat hasty with the woman he loved but too well.

"Bridget, mavourneen, you are disquieted by me," he cried.

"No."

"You know my impetuosity of old, but it is like the spark of a flint, vanishing as swiftly as it appears."

"A sentence spoken in anger by you, Murtagh," said his wife, "is no sooner uttered than neglected."

"Let me kiss thee, Bridget, for those words."

Murtagh then moved slowly towards his wife, and looking down with tenderness, fervently embraced her.

"You forgive me, too?" continued the farmer, addressing Una, who had also appeared piqued at his abrupt behaviour.

"I will answer for her," said the foster mother; "she is content with you. Look at her features, do they not smile approval?"

"They do, they do, asthore."

With the words Murtagh clasped the maiden in his arms, then bid her, with Bridget, leave him alone for a short space.

Thus exhorted, the two females withdrew, and proceeded to their chambers.

Both were moved to tears, Una sobbing audibly.

When they were gone Murtagh fell into a deep contemplation.

From this he was aroused by some one approaching him.

It was Patrick O'Shaughnessy.

Apparently disturbed by the new comer, he abruptly demanded—

"Who has gone the round of the farm to-night?"

"Patrick O'Shaughnessy did that same," was the Hibernian's reply.

"So much the better. You are a lad of precaution."

"Whist," continued the other, with his elegant brogue. "Show me the boy that would gainsay yez—och! and black's the white of his eye."

"Nevertheless, Patrick," said the farmer, "I have observed——"

"The divil doubt ye," muttered the addressed to himself.

"I have observed, I say," continued Murtagh, "that yesterday you omitted to unloose the house-dog, Cæsar; don't let it occur again."

There was now a second intrusion in the person of Larry Finch, another farm labourer, who entered the room hastily.

There was terror in the man's countenance as he uttered the following words:—

"Och! masther, masther, sure an' it's all over wid poor Cæsar."

"What has happened?"

"The poor dog has dropped down stark, stiff dead at the entrance of the farm, as natural as ony Christian."

JAEL, THE GIPSY GIRL, AND HER FOSTER MOTHER.

"The poor brute has been poisoned. Who has done it?"

Neither of the men could offer a reply to Murtagh's questions.

"I see," continued the farmer, malignantly, "he was too faithful a sentinel, and has died at his post."

After a pause, during which he sternly gazed at his companions, Murtagh at length addressed them, with bitter irony.

"I have six servants now upon my farm," he cried, "yet not one of them had the courage, though he had the power, to hinder this cowardly act. Such the effect of employing Catholics," continued the enraged yeoman. "Larry Finch, you leave my service."

"Faith, if you've no objection, I'd like to bear him company," said several voices in proximity.

These were those of the four remaining labourers on the farm, who, unobserved, had listened to the conversation that had taken place between their master and their fellow-servant, Larry Finch.

"What!" exclaimed Murtagh, gloomily, as if struck by a sudden conviction, "do you all desert me—on the same day—at the same hour? There is some plot, and——"

"Wait awhile ago, honey," said Patrick to the farmer, who had plunged into a deep reverie.

"Laive me," he added, "to spaike to the boys; I'll do it genteelly, an' they'll listen to me.

"Yer dirty bogtrotters," exclaimed the Irishman, turning, and speaking to the men, who opened their eyes in astonishment at the salutation. "What is it ye main?"

"We main to laive the masther," replied the perplexed peasants.

"Yez do, aye?" retorted Patrick, waxing warm with rising excitement. "Then let me jist have a word in private to iviry one before he goes; I'll begin wid Larry Finch."

"That's me," said the individual named, who appeared to entertain some doubts whether he was himself or somebody else.

"Larry Finch," continued Patrick, in a firm and by no means modulated voice, "do yez remimber last winter?"

"Bedad, an' I do; the snow was on the ground, the piercing winter's wind whistled through your mud cabin, there was no turf or faggots on the fire, no pratees in the basket, no bed on the flure."

"Who provided those same convainiences for the childer——"

"Murtagh Mackeen," interrupted Larry Finch, with feeling, "and Heaven bless him for that same."

"And yet," said the O'Shaughnessy, with a cutting smile of disdain, " ye ongrateful varmint, you'd be turning yer back on sich a good friend."

Larry got into a mighty bit of a fret about these words, and whispered something into Patrick's ear.

The communication made the listener jump higher than King Shamus ever did at Donnybrook Fair.

" By the holy poker! the cross of fire's on the mead, and it's all over wid the poor boy," he muttered to himself.

His limbs shook when he addressed Murtagh, and he trembled beneath the band which enslaved him as a member of the Roman faith.

" Masther," exclaimed Patrick O'Shaughnessy, and the word seemed to choke him as he spoke, " ye'll forgive a spalpeen, I know, when he tells you that he loves you and all your family,

" That he'd give his best heart blood at this moment to—but, there's a secret, and I'll have to discharge you till——"

Overcome with a profound emotion the speaker gave way to a flood of tears, and was totally unable to complete the sentence.

Uttering a cry of anguish and despair he eventually sprang towards his employer.

He flung himself upon his knees, and taking the outstretched hand of Murtagh, passionately implored him by signs not word to pardon his desertion.

His groans and remorseful ejaculations made those who listened shake with terror, but the grief of the poor peasant was too violent to last long.

By a powerful effort he overcame his emotion, and springing to his feet called upon his companions to follow him.

" Boys," said he, " this is no place for us. If we do wrong in leaving this worthy man, let those who compel us to such an act make atonement for the wrong."

With the words Patrick O'Shaughnessy precipitated himself from the apartment with a lighter step than he had entered it, for a means had now occurred to him by which he hoped to effect the salvation of the proscribed and his family.

Murtagh Mackeen, as may be supposed, after the exhortation, was soon left the sole occupant of the chamber.

It was then with a cold and distinct horror the farmer saw the terrible fate that menaced him.

His blood froze, and the formless phantom that appeared to his mind's eye, seared his brain and congealed the marrow of his bones.

The visionary dread was transient as lightning, for the next moment, he laughed his fears to scorn, but pondered on them still.

" So, Patrick," he mused, " he, whom I deemed the most faithful of my servants, has quitted me with the rest. In fact," he continued, " the fiend seemed to me the foremost in the plot, if plot there be. It is very strange, and were I subject to alarm I should.——Psha!" he exclaimed, again laughing down his terrors, " I have a heart. I shall not sleep to-night, and need fear no danger from a foe when—ah! well thought of—it is in the room above. Should any hostile arm or malice lurk about my dwelling, my friendly gun may offer me assistance."

Murtagh had no sooner ascended the staircase to obtain his weapon, than Una stole softly from the door of the corridor, and entered the apartment he had quitted.

She could hear nothing, see no one. Her foster mother had fallen asleep. Her husband fatigued, had doubtless, she thought, sought the chamber above which looked upon the garden.

This was unfortunate, as he might see her, as she was compelled to pass through it.

She must make the venture at all hazards

" For fate," she exclaimed, " which has made a poor girl guilty, will not destroy the means of repairing her fault."

CHAPTER CXXXVII.
ATONEMENT FOR THE PAST.

UNA had scarcely quitted her dwelling to keep her midnight appointment with Jack Sheppard, than Murtagh Mackeen descended the stairs, and returned to the room in which he had lately been standing.

He carried the gun he had spoken of in his hand, and proceeded to load it.

After he had done so he coolly remarked,

" Two good balls for those who may confront me."

Breaking suddenly the reverie into which he had fallen, the farmer advanced to the wall of the room upon which were hanging his hat and cloak.

He withdrew his arm with abruptness, which had been raised to reach them, and muttered to himself,

" No; the night is damp. I'll take another sup, and relight my pipe before I go round the house."

" I know not how it is," he continued, in a fit of abstraction. " I experience a strange feeling to-day. My heart seems pressed in a vice. In spite of myself I can't help thinking of the accursed assizes of this morning. I have never in my life once betrayed the truth—nay, in the very face of the judge—psha! I am getting childish. The fault is theirs, not mine."

In the profound silence that reigned after this soliloquy, a gentle tap was heard at the door on the outside.

Murtagh, unable to control the violent passions that rankled in his breast, listened with something akin to awe at the unexpected summons.

A minute elapsed, and the signal was repeated.

" Who's there?" shouted Murtagh, more than ever excited.

" One you should know," answered the man without.

" That voice!——"

" Open!"

" I will open!" cried Murtagh, now animated to the highest degree by rage.

" I never yet shut my door on a friend," he continued, " nor will I now close it though an enemy stand on the threshold."

Before Murtagh could advance to the door it flew furiously open.

In the recess stood the Irish Rapparee, Redmond O'Hanlon, once known to our readers as Slashing Nat Wetherby, the English highwayman.

The robber and the farmer pointed their guns at each other.

" Murtagh Mackeen," exclaimed the former, " I am armed as well as you. Lower your weapon and I will do the same. I have that to say which you should listen to."

Struck by the apparent candour and good faith of the Rapparee, the yeoman imitated the action of his companion, who, unmindful of the advantage he was giving, at once laid aside the piece with which he was armed.

Both adversaries then regarded his foe face to face, and after a pause, leaning on the barrels of their guns, communed with each other.

Murtagh was the first to break silence.

"What business," he cried, "leads the Rapparee to my premises?"

"I come here in peace and friendship," he cried; "a single word, and we may no longer bear enmity."

"You talk like a fool, Redmond O'Hanlon; "blood will not cool that has seethed in the veins for twenty years."

"Let the injuries of the past be effaced, and—"

"Never!" replied Murtagh, with anger and malignity. "I ask again," he continued, "what brings you hither?"

"Two things."

"The first?"

"To reveal to you a secret on which my happiness, your own, and that of your family depends."

"The second?"

"To save you from—"

"To save me!" echoed Murtagh, ironically. "I was not aware I am in any danger."

"You may be so," answered Redmond; "but, first, my secret; I love—"

"I know it."

"Indeed!"

"I know also that your passion is not returned."

"This is strange. I believed myself to be fortunate in my wooing."

"Simply through my contriving," smiled Murtagh, with sarcasm. "I have allowed your affection to grow, that it may augment the constraint. I wished," continued the farmer, "to implant such roots of bewitchment in thy being that they could be snatched only by tearing asunder thy heart."

"Hesitate before you act," replied Redmond, "or you may fall into the pitfall you have dug for others."

"Remember, Catholic," exclaimed Murtagh, "the night is advancing. At daybreak, in Castlebar, the prison doors will fly open. At the first sound of the bell a priest will enter the dungeon. The second will see the priest leave the gloomy cell, accompanied by a man. At the third stroke the miserable wretch will swing on the gibbet. The victim is thy comrade—thy brother; the executioner will be Murtagh Mackeen."

"Malignity maddens you," said Redmond O'Hanlon, as he gazed with a peculiar and sinister glance at his companion.

"You cannot reduce it to silence," the other returned; "your voice is less terrible than that of my own conscience. It was a terrible alternative."

"I fear to understand you."

"It was an intense struggle, and appeared to me endless," continued the farmer, after a wild gasp for breath. "The demon of malice nestled in my bosom, and pierced it with teeth of iron. Thee and thy comrades with one accord seemed to push me to the abyss of my cruel crime. As I ascended the steps of the tribunal, the rabble pursued me with cries and imprecations.

"Before the judges a thousand menacing eyes spoke for the innocent man I was about to condemn.

"I, who, in my life, have faced death oft-times without a nerve quivering, in the witness-box trembled like an aspen leaf."

Redmond O'Hanlon listened to the words of the vindictive farmer in silence.

His attitude was that of careless and assured composure.

But in his gathered brow and the boding glitter of his eye might be discerned some deadly purpose.

Measuring with his eye his associate from head to foot with appalling calmness, he addressed him—

"Murtagh Mackeen, thou hast avowed thy crime. My brother's blood calls for vengeance."

With these words the robber raised the gun which he had rested against, and, before Murtagh was aware, had pointed it at his breast.

He gave himself up for lost, when his enemy suddenly withdrew the weapon he had poised, and fired it through the window.

"No," exclaimed Redmond, "a vengeance more slow and terrible must await the betrayer."

The house of the farmer in a few moments was filled by a body of the wild Rapparees, who had been attracted thither by the signal their leader had given.

At the moment the men entered, a distant bell announced that a priest had entered the cell of their condemned comrade.

Each Rapparee was armed and masked.

Several, by their chief's order, seized Murtagh before he could offer the slightest resistance.

The prisoner remained silent and immovable as Redmond addressed his followers.

"There is not one of you," he cried, "but knows the fate of him for whom the bell has just tolled. He has been murdered by false testimony. The witness stands before you."

"The blood of the Mackeen for the blood of the O'Hanlon!" shouted twenty voices, while as many knives leapt from their scabbards.

"You will fail to intimidate me or make me tremble," said the resolute farmer, casting a look of defiance at those about to rush upon him. "I shall not seek even to defend myself, for defence against such long odds is madness.

"I shall not utter a cry," continued the speaker, "for my voice would alarm my wife, who, despite the clamour, still sleeps in yonder chamber. I ask but one thing—that you will lead me hence, not suffer blood to stain my threshold, hitherto free from guilt."

An imperceptible shudder passed through the frame of Murtagh Mackeen, as he heard, while uttering his last word, the second booming of the prison bell.

"Hark!" ejaculated Redmond, who had also caught the ominous sound; "your victim goes to die in the face of heaven, and in the face of heaven you shall make atonement. Forward, boys, lead the Mackeen to his doom."

"Adieu, Bridget, asthore," sighed the farmer, as he moved to depart with his executioners; "thy well-loved name will be the last that issues from my expiring lips."

"Thy wife will soon follow thee," sneered the Rapparee.

"Miscreant! her blood will not sink into the ground unavenged."

Suddenly impressed with an idea that he might save the unfortunate woman, Murtagh Mackeen called out her name aloud.

CHAPTER CXXXVIII.

"Last scene of all
That ends this strange eventful history."
Shakespeare

THE TOMB ON THE MOUNTAIN.

BRIDGET MACKEEN no sooner heard her husband's voice than she frantically rushed to his side.

Her surprise and anguish were truly painful when she discovered him a prisoner in the hands of his most bitter enemies.

She saw no more, for, overcome with terror at the sight, she fell without sense on the floor of the apartment amidst a loud and exulting roar of the wretches around her.

In the delirium she presently could observe a confused mass of threatening figures, black and shapeless, hurry her husband from her presence, while she was conveyed by others to her chamber, and there left to weep alone.

Redmond O'Hanlon was the last to quit the farmhouse, leaving his comrades to precede him with its owner to the place of execution.

He carefully secured all the doors save one.

This had escaped his notice, and the chamber contained no less a personage than Simon Smut.

This individual had seen and heard all that had passed during the previous half hour.

He watched Redmond O'Hanlon out of the house, and the robber had no sooner departed than his observer, pale and dismayed, threw himself from the top of the staircase, and at once attempted to escape.

In this he was frustrated, as he found every egress bolted and locked.

"There is no getting out!" exclaimed the dejected Simon Smut, on making the unpleasant discovery; "my life will pay the forfeit of my folly. Oh, that my proverbial penetration should have deserted me at such a moment."

The speaker was now more than ever alarmed by hearing one of the closed doors which stood near him burst open.

Was it a ghost or apparition stood before the awestricken traveller?

He felt so uneasy that he would fain have come to terms with his ghostly companion, had fear allowed him the power of utterance.

Suddenly he fancied he had discovered in the features of the mysterious being those of his hospitable hostess.

"Yes," he joyfully muttered to himself, "'tis the farmer's wife and no other."

Simon Smut was right, it was indeed Bridget who had broken from her chamber prison, and was standing before him.

"Oh, sir," cried the distracted woman, "if you are a man, you will prevent this butchery—you will aid me to rescue my husband."

"With pleasure," replied the addressed, blandly, "that is if you will show me how I can do so in safety with regard to myself."

"You must pursue the assassins," said Bridget, "and throw yourself between them and their victim."

"Impossible, my good woman," simpered Simon Smut, suddenly drawing in his horns at the rash proposal.

"Consider," he continued, "I am alone and without arms."

"Your presence will deter them in their dastardly act."

"I can't see it in that light, exactly," returned Simon Smut. "You may rely upon it, dame, that the moment I showed myself under the peculiar circumstances, I should find my body not dissimilar to a sieve that is drilled with holes."

Before Bridget could offer a reply, she was startled by a footstep that was approaching the door.

"Hark!" she cried, interrupting her companion, who began to show signs of terrible alarm, "did you not hear!"

"What?"

"Some one is coming to our succour."

"Most likely the dragoons I have sent for."

"No, by Jove; a woman!"

The latter remark was made by Simon Smut, as he suddenly observed a little door on one side of the chamber open without noise.

From the recess Una issued.

She appeared fatigued and distressed as if from travelling.

The moment she beheld Bridget, she threw herself weeping into her arms.

This gave Simon Smut the opportunity of ungallantly leaving the ladies.

Yielding to that great law of nature, self-preservation, he at once passed through the door which had given Una admittance, and was in a very short time out of all harm's way.

"Mavournen," said Bridget, addressing her foster child, "how have you escaped?"

"I will have no secret from you, my more than mother," replied the maiden; "you must know I promised to-night to meet my lover, and left the house by stealth, when—"

"Say no more," said Bridget, impatiently interrupting her, "I have neither the time nor inclination to listen. Answer me, as you value my love, has any body seen you return to the farm?"

"No one," replied Una, startled by the abrupt questioning of her companion. "You are pale, trembling," she continued, "why do you ask me this?"

"You are ignorant of what has passed," said Bridget, with her eyes suffused with tears.

"Your grief tells me something dreadful is going to happen, let me know the worst."

Bridget, though she trembled in every limb and joint, answered in a firm tone,

"Una, my husband is now being murdered."

"Merciful Providence!" she cried, turning aside in horror.

"His breast is now exposed to the deadly bullets of the Rapparees."

These words, spoken with difficulty, had the effect of arousing Una from her apparent insensibility.

"Why are we standing here," she exclaimed, "when we might save him?"

The maiden hastened to several doors but found them all locked.

Suddenly she remembered that by which she had entered still remained unclosed.

To her dismay she found this now fastened, for Simon Smut, in his hurry and trepidation, had touched the spring with which it was furnished.

There was a pause of terror.

Then a cry of joy.

"All hope is not yet lost," exclaimed the maiden. Heaven had inspired her.

By the window they could escape.

A strong cord, obtained from the nearer cupboard, was almost as quickly as the thought of it, fastened to the casement.

Una was the first to attempt to descend.

As she advanced to do so, two piercing eyes glistened in the shade of the garden at her foot, while the click of a gun fell upon her ear.

Slowly she withdrew and pushed back Bridget, who had advanced with her to the window.

"What can we do?" whispered the terrified girl, to her foster-mother.

"Since there is no one that can defend us," she replied, with forced calmness, "a plan, fearful and deadly, has crossed my mind."

"A plan?"

"Yes, let the one who is rescued live to avenge the other."

"This is a terrible alternative."

"Yet I am prepared to abide by it; my husband reproached me yesterday, accused me of weakness, want of fortitude—judge if he spoke correctly."

"Your words terrify me; what would you do, Bridget?"

"Listen, acushla, neither shudder nor tremble; you have told me that your presence here is a secret?"

"My entrance hither was unobserved."

"Good; you must still conceal yourself."

"Conceal myself?"

"Yes, behind the curtain that covers yonder cupboard. The robbers are returning and I have strength to meet my death when they arrive, for the ruffians are bound by their oath to destroy all who bear our name."

"Monsters!"

"Hear me out, Una. From your hiding-place, where none can suspect you, you must recognise my murderers. You will then denounce and bring them to justice."

"How?" exclaimed the maiden, becoming paler than death at the recital. "Remain silent, immovable, unaffected, while you are assassinated? I cannot."

"I exact it," replied the foster-mother, sternly.

"No. I will perish with thee, but can never consent to pass so direful an ordeal."

There was something terrible, at the same time awfully impressive, in the mien of Bridget as she spoke the following words,

"Obey me, girl, who am about to die, or the All Powerful will curse thee!"

Una fell on her knees, while at the same moment the third stroke of the prison bell was heard.

"'Tis my husband's death-knell!" shrieked Bridget.

There was a solemn silence.

Then the sharp rattle of fire-arms.

"He is dead!" slowly ejaculated the woman, in a voice that seemed to issue from a statue of stone.

By degrees her ghost-like face became as the living, and her glance flashed with livid and demoniac fire.

Imagination would fail to give to the aspect of the bereaved wife the shuddering nature which spoke in her eyes alone.

"I must be avenged!" she exclaimed. "Do you still hesitate?"

"No," replied Una, in a firm voice. "Your energy has become mine, and I live to hurl retribution on the heads of these assassins."

The measured tread of a body of men was soon heard approaching the farm.

"The ruffians return," cried Bridget. "Forget not the oath."

"I shall obey you implicitly."

"On your soul's salvation?"

"On my soul's salvation!" was the solemn reply of the maiden.

"Then God will sustain you."

"With these words, the foster-mother embraced Una convulsively, then led her to the green serge curtain hanging before the lofty cupboard of the chamber.

The latter had scarcely concealed herself behind the ample folds of the drapery, when Redmond O'Hanlon and his followers entered the apartment.

Each retained his mask, which effectually concealed his features.

"Woman," he exclaimed, furiously, "your husband is dead!"

The countenance of Bridget, on hearing this avowal, was the expression of perfect happiness, which ever dwells with perfect love.

"Since Heaven has prepared me for this cruel trial," she breathed aloud, "I can now meet death with a peaceful smile."

"You have pronounced your doom," retorted the leader of the banditti; "we now await to slay you."

"Cowards, then slay me here," cried Bridget Mackeen.

Noticing there was some hesitation in the action of the men who were ordered to advance, she continued,

"You stand back. Why so? Surely the boldest among you does not fear to complete his task of murder."

Suddenly struck with an idea, Redmond O'Hanlon addressed his followers,

"Since you object to make the sacrifice within the house I know a means by which I can compel this refractory woman to follow me out of it."

A suppressed scream at this moment startled the Rapparees.

"Unhappy Una! 'twas her voice," muttered the intended victim to herself. "She will fail to avenge me."

"Comrades," said Redmond, who had gazed round the room at the stifled cry, "I suspect treachery."

"Search the house."

As may be supposed Una fell into the hands of her persecutors the next moment.

Redmond O'Hanlon started as he gazed upon her features.

They were those of one he had met before.

Jael the gipsy girl and Una were one and the same.

"Welcome to Ireland, Jael," said Redmond, malignantly; "when last I saw you, you were a rose, the name of lily would now suit you better."

"Fearful man."

"I mean not to harm, Jael, but would befriend her. That look! Pshaw, girl, your face was made for better purposes than dying with thy foster-mother."

At the words Redmond pointed to Bridget Mackeen who had fainted on beholding Jael's capture, and whose form was now lying senseless on the floor.

"There is one way left to save you both," the Rapparee continued.

"Oh, speak! heaven will bless you for the act, and your name shall mingle with my prayers."

As the maiden spoke Redmond whispered in her ear.

Her cheek mantled with crimson as, with ineffable scorn, she uttered,

"Monster! I have no other term to characterize you. I only marvel that the fires of heaven do not on the instant hurl just and terrible retribution, and consume your body, as will the flames of hell most assuredly torment your black, pernicious soul."

"Be calm, colleen. Remember, I say I love you—resign yourself to me, if not for your own salvation for that of the one doomed to die."

Jael hesitated.

"Your answer," continued Redmond.

"Is this—death rather than dishonor!"

* * * *

Bridget Mackeen and Jael had scarcely been led out to execution when the Omadhaun entered the farm and confronted Redmond O'Hanlon and his followers, who still remained within it.

He eyed for a few moments with convulsive starts the group around him.

After a pause, he muttered sullenly,

"I did not think Redmond O'Hanlon would have ventured to disobey his chieftain's commands."

"For that matter," replied the Rapparee, "I can

answer to them that has better right to ask me than you have."

"This is mutiny."

"No; obedience to the bond which binds our secret brotherhood. It is a long leap and a short shrift with the Mackeen, who was our mortal enemy."

"He was no greater enemy than the rest of mankind," growled the Omadhaun, "all are of a piece—one mass of wickedness and corruption—wretches, who sin even in their devotions, and of such hardness of heart that they do not even thank the deity for the warm pure air they breath."

While yet speaking, the Omadhaun's attention was attracted by a glittering object lying on the floor of the apartment.

It was the portion of a golden cross.

He clasped it furiously, and burst forth into a terrific laugh.

"She is found," he shouted, "I felt that heaven could be so unjust. Tell me, Redmond, as you value life, from whence this bauble came."

"From the neck of the maiden we have but now condemned."

The Omadhaun gave a violent shriek like a wretch to whose flesh a red-hot iron is applied.

Gnashing his teeth, he flew to the door, when twenty knives barred his progress.

"Let him not pass," commanded the ringleader, Redmond O'Hanlon.

"Monster! Why do you stand before me? Know that in the woman you would sacrifice you behold my own child—my restored daughter."

"She must die—our oath compels it. Stand back, for we are desperate!"

The Omadhaun made no reply, but for a moment remained mute and irresolute as one stricken powerless and paralyzed.

Shortly, as if passion had restored him to the vigour of youth, he began to pace the floor with hasty strides.

He no longer laughed; he was terrible to behold as he paced to and fro.

The fox was turned into a hyæna.

Unobserved, he then unsheathed a long, sharp knife.

With this he dashed into the multitude that opposed him, and cut his way in safety from the farm, taking the precaution to barricade every entrance and outlet.

At this juncture, the trumpet of the advancing military was heard, while from the windows it was discovered that the house was environed on all sides by soldiers.

A pause of awful silence succeeded, broken only by the convulsive respiration of the Rapparees, who found the trap set for them complete.

A smart fusillade, or volley of musketry, was now commenced between those without and those within the farm.

The latter dispersing and scattering themselves over the building, and keeping up an incessant fire from the windows and every aperture of the same.

A few minutes only had elapsed, when it was discovered that the farm-house was on fire.

This event was succeeded by another equally terrible.

The flame, which had been partially smothered, now burst forth with a fierce glare, and a sound resembling an earthquake fell upon the ear.

It was the explosion of a mine, that had been sprung by the military.

It seemed to threaten, by its force, destruction to every object for miles around.

The air, for some minutes, was filled with a dense black volume of smoke, and total darkness reigned in heaven and on earth.

As the sombre cloud dissipated, the strife between the Rapparees and their assailants was clearly shown to be at end, their charred bones, and the blackened ruins of the fortress they were holding, being the only vestiges of the recent conflict.

* * * * *

Some two years had elapsed after the event just related, when some hunters by mere chance came upon a lonely cave in the Mintrea Mountain.

Their leader was no other than Jack Sheppard, who still retained his assumed name of Hawk-eye among them.

In the vaulted chamber that was at once entered were discovered two bodies in an advanced state of decomposition, and apparently clasped together with the firm embrace of death.

One of the wretched beings was a female, who, notwithstanding the hideous spectacle she now presented, gave evidence that in life she possessed beauty.

The other figure was that of a male, who, by his aspect, seemed to have perished in intense and convulsive agonies.

His black hair, blanched by sorrow in a single night, still fluttered in the current of air that forced a passage through the gloomy sepulchre.

His singular posture attracted the attention of those who looked upon his festering carcass.

He was leaning over the woman at his side, to whom he had crawled on his hands and knees, and holding her hand with a supernatural force, the bony fingers meeting round the wrist, as if they had been riveted to the fleshless arm.

There, never turning his eye from the only object for which he had ever existed, he was mute, immovable, and motionless as one thunderstruck.

Streams had flowed in silence from that eye, which till then had not shed a single tear.

Jack Sheppard, in the meanwhile, began to pant.

The perspiration trickled from his brow as he recognised in the fearful and livid mass before him the remains of those who were once known to him as Jael, the gipsy girl, and the mysterious Omadhaun. A letter found on the last-named revealed his real name and character.

The superscription ran as follows:—

"JONATHAN WILD,
　　　　　"Newgate,
　　　　　　　"London."

Thus had perished the once bitter foe of Jack Sheppard.

The highwayman carried on for many years his occupation of hunting in the wilds of Ireland and lived to be very old.

He was prosperous in his worldly dealings, and at length became a rich man, but after the discovery of the melancholy end of his betrothed, was never a happy one.

Our hero and Violet passed the remainder of their days at the mansion which the lady inherited by right at her father's death.

Here, in seclusion, retirement, and study, the former touched the verge of the present century, his wife having paid the debt of nature some few years previously.

The tourist in travelling in the vicinity of the west Irish coast may still see the ruins of the dwelling-house of ROVING JACK.

THE END.